WINDS OF DARKNESS

Of Darkness & Dragons, Book 1

Rebecca L. Snowe

WINDS OF DARKNESS
Copyright © **2019 Rebecca L. Snowe**
All rights reserved.
Published by **Rebecca West 2019**

Cover art by Maurice Mosqua

Printed in the United States of America.

ISBN: 978-1692663582
ISBN: 1692663585
First Edition

For Mom and Dad, who never stopped believing in me.

Darkness is coming,

Blood will follow,

War is here,

Death is upon us.

FROZEN SEA

ENNOTAR

• OSTGATE

IDUIRON

• ROTHBORN

WARULAN

SILVER SEA

DRIDUR

• CRYST

EROMOR

SYRWYTH

ORIDONN

SEA OF MONSTERS

B

WINDS OF DARKNESS

Of Darkness & Dragons, Book 1

PROLOGUE

The Unknown Voice

I find it fascinating how our children are symbols of life to us. Heirs that will carry on our legacies when we are dead and rotting in a grave. It has been said that they are a blessing from the gods, or from the Sisters, if one believes in the old religion. Blessings that eat our food, beg for our money, take our time. I never believed that my son was a blessing, not at first.

The sky was overcast, and darkness loomed the day my son was born, with heavy clouds of gray and black rolling over the castle and surrounding city. Wind came from the east. I remember listening to it snap the flags on the castle walls.

"Your Majesty," Knight Eyldrich said. His clipped footsteps stopped as he bowed behind me. "The queen has had her child; it's a boy. You're a father, Your Majesty." I heard the smile in Knight Eyldrich's voice. I did not smile.

A crow battled against the wind, trying to reach a window in the tower across the courtyard from me, where several of its companions sat, sheltered from the oncoming storm. I watched the bird, mentally willing the creature success in its fight for life. One missed wingbeat, one raise of its head, and the wind would catch it in its howling charges through the courtyard and dash it to pieces against the stone of the castle walls. The crow's fight for survival against the wind was like ours against the wiar and skinchangers, a never-ending struggle in a war that would not end.

"The boy has brown hair, Your Majesty," Knight Eyldrich said behind me, wind making his blue cloak snap with the flags. "But his eyes are blue, like the queen's."

Our fight against the wiar and skinchangers had been going on for over three hundred years now, a hundred and seventy-five years for the First Great War, and a hundred and fifteen for the Second. Now we were in the thirty-sixth year of the Third. Some said it would be the last war; others said that they would never end. But we were allies with the wiar now, something that would help us against the skinchangers.

The crow finally lost its fight against the wind, and I saw its beak open in a squawk as the wind threw it into the side of the tower, directly below the window that it had been trying to get to.

"Tell the other knights to have their horses readied," I said, watching the crow's body fall to the courtyard below, where a maid was hurrying toward the west wing of the palace with a basket of food. I looked up at the dark haze of rain coming down in the distance and the darker shapes of creatures swarming over the grasslands toward the city. A last desperate attempt of the skinchangers. "We go to battle."

I did not see my son for another four weeks. That last battle of the war would become known as the Last Great Battle, and it kept me busy. My wife hurried down the hall with him in her arms as I came into the castle one night, I hardly glanced at the red-faced, brown-haired, screaming child. I didn't look clearly at the boy until twenty years later. The day that he died. The day that I killed him.

My son came into the world when I was forty-one, eight years into my marriage and three into my kingship. He took after his mother. Plain. Big boned. I paid him as little attention as I did my wife. But when I turned sixty-one and realized that my days were not long numbered to be on Argdrion, I began to look at my son more closely.

My wife died seven years before the day I took my son's life. She was laid to rest in the cold, dank tomb under the castle, where royalty and knights from generations past lay entombed in stone. I was thankful for this, for the one person who would notice a change in him would be her, who had watched over him for most of his adolescence.

The day that my son died was in the beginning of winter, an abnormal, chilling winter that promised to freeze cattle and bury homes in drifts of snow in the upcoming months. Most of the city was hiding indoors, the dark streams of smoke rising up from chimneys the only sign that anyone lived in the snow-bound buildings at all. The castle was seemingly deserted as well. And quiet. Eerily quiet.

I had sent word by one of my knights for my son to come to the shadowed, chilly throne room, and as I sat waiting on the wooden throne at the far end of the lengthy room, I thought on the war and what it had taken from me. In my first battle, shortly after my father died, I lost the smallest finger of my left hand. When I was thirty-five, my horse fell on me in battle and broke my right leg in a way that still made me limp. On my sixty-first birthday, I caught pneumonia in the winter trenches, and four weeks later, I was told this was what would kill me.

The doors of the throne room opened, the moan of their pitted iron hinges emphasized by the cold quietness of the castle. My son came in, eyes glittering in light that streamed in beams through high, dust-streaked windows. He advanced slowly, face wary, suspicious. I had never shown my son anything more than acknowledgment, even on the battlefield, and my calling him was, I'm sure, strange to him.

"Your Majesty," my son said, his voice deep like his mother's, echoing through the dark rows of flaring stone pillars supporting the roof above our heads.

"I wish to show you something," I said, my voice joining the last echoes of his in the numbing air. "Something important." I pushed myself out of the wooden throne without another word and moved toward a door set in the wall behind two pillars. My son followed, his footsteps rasping on well-worn stone.

An abandoned cellar, half caved in from wiar and skinchanger attacks, supplied the spot for my son's last day on Argdrion—it was filled with cobwebs and mice droppings. A snowdrift filled in part of the ruined room, making a slanted wall that stretched toward the ceiling above, and broken pieces of barrel littered the floor, dark with long-dried wine and beer. I hobbled to the back of the freezing room, where a wooden door led to an ice house. There was no ice in the twelve-by-twelve stone room, only two old ice hooks lying on a table that was covered in a layer of fine gray dust.

My son glanced around the room of the ice house as I shut and bolted the door behind us and set the candle in my hand on the table. "I don't understand…" he began, looking at me.

"Clean the table off," I said, coughing as my lungs filled with stale, freezing air.

"Six months at the most, if you're lucky," my physician said, his stale voice echoing through my mind. "If you're not, two."

Two months to live. It was not enough for all that I had planned; it was not enough to get used to the idea of dying. My son did as I told him, using an old, brittle hand broom to sweep the table of its dust. Snow drifted in through holes where the chinking had fallen out of the stone walls of the ice house, settling in pointed piles all along the floor. I reached inside my fur-lined cloak with a gloved hand, heart beating rapidly.

My son finished clearing the table and turned toward me. "What is this about, Father?"

I slid a knife across his throat, the honed blade cutting through layers of skin, flesh, and veins. "The heart of one, the blood of both" whispered in my head as I, panting, lowered my son's body onto the table, back side down. I wished that the heart I would be getting was the one I had dreamed of for years, but it was not, and until I got that heart, this one would have to do.

There was sweat on my palms and a humming in my ears as I worked. I pulled a small steel cup from my cloak and set it under my son's gushing throat, filling it halfway with glistening red blood. His blue eyes closed as the cup slowly filled, and blood covered my hands and the table, dripping onto the floor. I put the knife to my forearm next, pulling back the black sleeve covering it and making a long, deep cut beside the other scarred-over marks. Symbols of past attempts, past failures. If I failed this time, the strain that came after would kill my sick body. I held the warm cup to my flesh, watching my blood trickle in and mingle with that of my son's in swirling red whirls.

The next part was the most difficult.

I used the ice hooks stuck into the table to pull back my son's ribs. The knife did the rest, cutting away the tissue from the glistening organ still throbbing beneath. Snowflakes, small and wispy, swirled around me as I worked, nesting in my whitening hair, gathering on the fur of my cloak. I inhaled the cold air, the iciness cutting into my weakened lungs like a knife. The war had taken many things from me. If I let it, it would take my life as well. I pulled the heart from my son's body, holding it up in front of me for a moment before setting it on the blood-soaked table beside the cup.

I slid the ice hooks, curving steel glistening red with blood, away from the heart.

Snowflakes that settled on the table turned a bright red before melting at the warmth of the blood.

It is said that the eyes are the window to one's soul. They are not a window; they are a door.

I lifted the cup of blood over the heart, the thought of the spell not working making my hands shake anew.

I reached inside my cloak with my four-fingered hand and pulled out the medium-sized black book that resided there. It fell open to the most well-worn page, the cracking leather binding rough against my fingers.

"The heart of one," I read, slowly, clearly, "the blood of both." I tilted the cup and poured the dark-red liquid over the still-warm heart. "Soul of the living, body of the dead." I knew the words by heart. I'd said them enough over the years.

The last of the blood dripped out onto the heart, the soft splash echoing through the ice house. "New life formed, life given to death," I said. "Repair that which is broken."

I set the empty cup down and picked the heart up. It was warm and sticky against my palm. "Bind the new." I set the heart into a black wooden box that I pulled from my robes.

"Body left behind," I murmured, snowflakes gathering on my lashes, "soul transferred." I let go of the heart, drawing my hand back to me. My own heart was racing, hope and dread surging within. I had gone over in my mind, many times before, each time that I had failed over the past years, rehashing what I said, how I had moved. To perform a spell was more than reading phrases out of a book and having the necessary components called for; it was breathing life into words, speaking them at the right cadence and exact tone that coincided with the action required for the spell. It was an art, one that took a lifetime to perfect.

I swallowed, my throat dry, cold. If I failed, I would die within a matter of hours. If I did nothing, the death in my lungs would take my life in months. I took in a slow breath, the icy air burning my lungs. "Release," I said.

My surroundings spun, the snow, the table with my son's body, and the rock walls of the ice house swirling around me in a whirlwind of white and gray and black.

What happened next I can only describe as a feeling of energy coursing through me, starting at my heart and pushing its way toward my eyes.

I fell to my knees, the knife slicing my hand as it tumbled to the floor. Snowflakes touched my face. I was aware of each one as it flattened against my skin and then melted. Pressure pushed against my eyes from the inside, making my temples throb. I felt like I was being pulled in two from the inside out. I pitched forward onto my hands, the cold, snow-dappled stones of the floor pressing into my palms as I screamed. I was afraid of failing more than anything as I crouched there in the ice house with every noise, every feeling of the things that touched my skin weighing me down. Afraid of failing and dying like any other man.

"Now," I sobbed, my head pounding. "Release!"

I slipped out of my eyes. My body fell to the floor as my soul poured into the icy air, dead, pale. I flew toward my new body, as light as a feather or a snowflake on the wind. I felt nothing of the coldness of the room.

I entered my son's body through his eyes, a feeling of unspeakable pain burning through the open throat and chest of my new body as they slowly mended back together. Pain and darkness but also power. The power of a younger, healthier body.

My blue eyes snapped open, staring up at the lichen-covered stones of the ceiling above me. I felt my broken ribs close completely, felt a fire burning through my throat. I screamed, gripping the table with my new hands. With all great victories comes pain, and life cannot be complete without victory.

My new body lurched as my throat closed, and I rolled off the table and onto the floor, tears streaming down my cheeks. Snow drifted down on everything, freezing where it landed in icy flakes. I grabbed the table with one hand and pulled myself up, staring breathlessly at the black box with my new heart in it. I heard the organ pump a single glorious beat, and then another, and another.

"I did it," I whispered. Then laughter. Another man's laughter. Nay, my own, rumbling up in my chest. I put a hand to the pale flesh of my chest and throat, feeling its smoothness. I laughed again, tears of joy leaking out of my blue eyes. I stood, spread my arms wide. After all the years, I had done it.

There is much I could say to speak of the work I underwent to move my old body outside into the snow. Of calling the palace guard and spinning a tale of how my "father" had died from an attack of pneumonia. Or how I inherited my own throne. But there is much that comes before that, and I am getting ahead of myself.

CHAPTER 1

Nathaira

Nathaira dreamed of her first kill.

Soft flakes of snow fell from the sky, landing gently on the backs of two gray wolves that crouched underneath a snow-laden pine. The wolves' eyes—one pair a dark, deep gold, the other a stormy sea green—intently followed the movements of a plump red doe that was stripping the bark off an ancient redwood in a clearing in front of them. Their bodies stayed motionless in the deep snow.

"Not yet, Nathaira," whispered the larger of the two wolves, a male with silver markings swirling around his eyes.

Nathaira blinked, the only sign that she had heard her father. "While hunting, one should never move unless absolutely necessary." That was one of the first things that Athrysion had taught her, and she did not want to mess this up. Not her first kill.

Nathaira blinked again, snowflakes catching on her fine black whiskers. Swirling brown marks ran down the top of her muzzle, joining together over her wet nose before running as one mark underneath. The wolf was one of Nathaira's favorite creatures to change into. Large enough to pose a threat to most creatures yet small enough to blend in and go unnoticed in the forest, the wolf was a thrilling animal that could run at swift speeds and smell the faintest of scents. It also often ran in packs, and this worked well for the clan when they were in animal form.

The snow turned from small delicate flakes to large wet ones, and Athrysion crept from the tree they were hiding under to get closer to the deer. Nathaira followed, the falling flakes hiding their movements and muffling any noise that they made.

The doe continued to ravage the redwood, the methodical ripping of bark off the tree's bleeding wood and crunch of molars as she chewed filling the air.

Athrysion paused again, and Nathaira stopped next to him and mimicked his movements as he crouched low in the snow. They were now twenty yards from the deer, and she fancied that she could smell its wild scent as the wind shifted toward them. A thrill ran through her. She concentrated on keeping her quivering muscles steady. Ever since she had been able to walk, she had prepared for this day, her twelfth year, when she would make her first kill alone and become a full-grown and a hunter among the clan. Becoming a full-grown was one of the greatest moments there was for skinchangers and the most anticipated time of a youngling's life.

"Now, Nathaira," Athrysion whispered next to her.

Nathaira let her straining muscles loose. She crept across the snow, striving to see the doe through the increasing snowfall. "Stay low to the ground, avoid fast movements, and step lightly." Athrysion's words drifted through her mind.

I'm too far off the ground. Nathaira crouched lower. Moirin had told her once of her own first kill. They had been sitting by the fire in the clan's tree home as a summer thunderstorm raged outside. Not able to sleep for the noise, Nathaira had slipped out to the fire to get warm and found Moirin by it, rocking Efamar.

"He's so little," Nathaira whispered, curling up on the dirt beside Moirin and peeking over her mother's tattooed arm at her little brother. He had dark-brown hair like Athrysion's, but his eyes were sharp blue like Zeythra's. "He has Zeythra's eyes," Nathaira said.

"Yes," Moirin said, smiling. "Sometimes, when I'm looking at him, I think I'm staring at your grandmother."

Nathaira smiled and rested her head against Moirin's slender, muscled body. "Will he ever be able to change?" she asked, watching her baby brother's chest rising and falling steadily under the racoon skin he was wrapped in.

"I hope so," Moirin whispered softly. Most skinchangers were able to change into creatures a few days after they were born. Not fully, but parts of their bodies would turn sporadically as they grew until they gained control over the power. Efamar had shown no signs of changing, and he was one month shy of a year old. The elders in the clan said he was defective. "But we will love him even if he cannot," Moirin murmured.

Nathaira glanced up at her and then back at Efamar. Thunder boomed overhead, shaking the tree around them.

Efamar woke up at the thunderclap, and his blue eyes darted around, looking for assurance. Nathaira put a hand out to him, and he took it, wrapping his fingers around her thumb, over her first tattoo.

"Tell me of your first kill," Nathaira whispered.

Moirin put an arm around her, and Nathaira leaned into her, welcoming the warmth of her body. "Your grandfather was dead by the time my twelfth year came," Moirin began. "Killed in the wars."

Nathaira watched Efamar as he began sucking on her finger with gummy baby lips. She hated the wars, hated what they had taken from skinchangers, what they had turned Argdrion into.

"My mother took me on my first hunt, though," Moirin whispered. "The rest of the clan said that she should be fighting in the wars with them, but as my only parent, she said it was her duty to take me. We went into the mountains. At that time, our clan was living at the foot of the Astarions."

Nathaira gently pulled her hand away from Efamar as he drifted back to sleep and wiped it of slobber on her knee-length tunic. The Astarion Mountains were in Warulan, the largest continent in Argdrion. She had learned that last week from Zeythra, who was teaching her Argdrion's geography.

"I wanted a bear for my first kill," Moirin said, "so Branwen took me to a cave where she knew bears often hibernated. We went as minotaurs, trudging through the snow up into the mountains."

Nathaira closed her eyes as Moirin continued to tell her story, of how she and Branwen had found an old bear and of her fight against it before she had finally killed it and become a member of her clan.

Nathaira paused several yards away from the deer, holding still as it glanced around. She missed Moirin more than anything. The deer swallowed its bite and turned back to the tree, ripping another shred of bark off.

Nathaira began moving again, her paws sinking into the snow. "Always get as close as you can before you make your attack," Athrysion's deep voice echoed through her mind again. "A wolf doesn't have the speed that a deer does, and the farther away you are when you make your presence known, the more chance there is of the deer getting away from you."

The deer, snowflakes sprinkling her deep-red coat, stood up on her back hooves again and ripped another long shred of bark off the tree.

Nathaira crept closer, praying to the Sisters to give her courage, speed, and strength. It was rare that a youngling failed to make their first kill, but Zeythra said it had happened. Outcasts, they were called, neither accepted by their clan or any other, forever destined to wander alone, clanless. Nathaira hoped that she would not be one of them. No, she wouldn't be one of them.

The doe fell back down on all fours and started chewing again, its large ears, which were rimmed with short black hair and centered with white, half-heartedly swiveling for sounds in the clearing and forest around her.

Now, a voice whispered in Nathaira's head. Nathaira moved. The deer glanced up at the crunch of snow and, seeing her, turned to run, but it was too late, and she was on the bleating creature before it could take three steps.

Dark-red blood splashed Nathaira's white muzzle as her fangs sank into the doe's neck. The doe let out a strangled cry as they stumbled to the ground. Hair, snow, and blood flew around them.

I will do this, I will do this… Nathaira bit harder on the thrashing deer's neck, and tendon, flesh, and muscle gave way beneath her elongated canine teeth. The deer's struggles to break free grew weaker.

Die… The doe convulsed under her paws once, twice, and with a last feeble bleat, fell still.

Nathaira let go of the deer. She slipped back into her natural form and knelt next to the lifeless body. "Your body, I bless," she whispered, her voice deep and rich for her age. "Your life, I grieve. Your soul goes to the Sisters. May it run free with your ancestors. In the names of Uatara, Rohiri, and Jophus, this I pray. Peace be yours."

"Well done, Nathaira," Athrysion said softly, slipping into his natural form as he walked toward her. "Clean, fast, merciful. We never take a life unless we have to, in defense or for food, for that is against what the Sisters have taught us, and we always take it as quickly and painlessly as possible."

Nathaira dipped her head at the praise, pride going through her. She had made her first kill.

"The clan will appreciate the food you have gotten them this day," Athrysion rumbled.

Nathaira stood, feet prickling from the iciness of the knee-deep snow. Yes, it had been a long, cold, and hard winter, and it was only halfway done. The doe was the first deer they had seen in over three weeks, since most had gone to the lower lands of Ennotar to graze where the snow didn't lie so deep, and the rest had been eaten by the packs of wolves that roamed the woods at night and scared Efamar with their howling.

"Nathaira," Athrysion said, interrupting her from her thoughts. Nathaira looked up at him, and he smiled warmly, white teeth showing beneath the wild brown beard covering his face. "You are a full-grown now."

Nathaira closed her eyes and let the words sink deep.

"I am proud of you, Nathaira," Athrysion murmured. "Very proud."

Nathaira's heart swelled. Athrysion did not often give praise, but when he did, she knew he meant it.

"Come," Athrysion said, reaching into a large bearskin bag he was carrying. "Zeythra will want to hear of your first kill." He handed her a leather jerkin, boots, and leather leggings, his tattooed arms turning white from the falling snow.

Nathaira took the clothing and slipped into them, her teeth beginning to chatter without the protection of the wolf's thick hair.

They knelt and picked the dead doe up, then started off through the forest with it swinging between them.

"We will eat well tonight," Athrysion said as they trudged through the snow. "We were lucky today."

"Lucky?" Nathaira asked, turning as she walked to look back at him over the carcass of the still-bleeding deer. His chest-length hair and beard were turning white from the snow. "How about skilled?"

Athrysion shrugged. "All right, but I didn't want to brag about myself."

"Athrysion," Nathaira growled.

He chuckled, a deep chuckle that made Nathaira laugh with him. It was rare that he laughed like that, she mused, turning back around. Very rare. It was because of the humans, she knew, and what they had taken from them.

Nathaira shifted the doe higher up on her shoulder. Moirin had once told her that she should love the humans as fellow creations of the Sisters, but she couldn't help agreeing with Athrysion that they were evil, dark creatures that were to be hated. After all, it was humans who had started the Great Wars and the Hunting, and the Hunting had taken Moirin from them.

"Come, Nathaira," Athrysion called softly, "I was teasing. You did well."

Nathaira smiled, pride warming her again. She stepped around a red-berried bush with a hat of snow and turned to ask Athrysion if they would go out hunting again after they left the deer with the clan.

The dream shifted.

A silver-tipped arrow whistled out of the trees and with a dull crunch, embedded itself into the middle of Athrysion's chest.

Time sped up as dark-red blood beaded out from the arrow, and Nathaira saw her surroundings whirl past and change as her body elongated and grew taller. More tattoos appeared on her right arm and shoulder and over half of her face. Her hair grew to past her hips. She was seventeen now, it was summer, and they were standing in the grass around the clan's tree home as fire raged through the clearing and slavers attacked the clan.

Nathaira screamed, her body slipping the rest of the way out of the shape of a bear and into her natural form. She ran through the grass toward Athrysion as he fell backward, the sharp, dry blades slicing at her bare legs.

She fell to her knees next to Athrysion, reaching for the arrow with frantic fingers.

"No," Athrysion gasped, blood gurgling at the corners of his mouth. Nathaira paused as he grabbed her hand. "Save... Efamar..." he whispered, eyes meeting hers. Blood bubbled out of the corners of his mouth and drained down the tattoos trailing over his face. Nathaira reached for the arrow again, and he pulled on her hand.

"You can't leave me," she whispered, tears flowing down her cheeks and cutting paths through the dirt covering them. She put her other hand over Athrysion's, her long fingers curling over his now bloodstained tattoos. "Not after Moirin."

"You. Will. Be. Fine," Athrysion pushed out. "You are strong, Nathaira, stronger than you know." He inhaled sharply, and Nathaira cried harder and reached for the arrow a third time.

"Let me pull it out, Zeythra can sew you up, and you'll be fine…" She pulled on the arrow, and Athrysion moaned.

"Nathaira. Stop." He gasped.

Nathaira, crying harder now, glanced up at him again.

"I love you," he whispered, tears leaking out of his eyes, "And so did your mother. Save… Efamar," Athrysion gasped, gripping her hand again. His grasp was so tight that Nathaira thought her bones would snap. "And run!" With a rattling gasp, he fell still, his green eyes staring unseeing up at the star-speckled sky above as a blood bubble burst in his open mouth and trickled down one cheek and into his beard.

"No," Nathaira whispered. She rubbed Athrysion's hand as it slowly slipped from hers. It fell with a thud to the matted and bloodstained grass. "No!" She grabbed his broad shoulders and shook him, willing him back to life.

A pine exploded in a burst of flames and sap behind them. Nathaira inhaled a sob, looking up sharply at the bright blaze of light and the dark figures silhouetted by it. Screams rang out over the smoky clearing, bodies of slavers and several of the clan lay scattered in the burning grass. Nathaira looked back at Athrysion, her long black hair falling around her face in a curtain as she frantically scanned his lips for sign of movement. There was none. She slapped at his chest again, sobbing as he continued to stare lifelessly at the sky above. He was gone, dead, like Moirin.

A scream rang through the clearing, Efamar's scream.

Nathaira wheeled, glancing around the clearing for her brother's small form. An elder fell to the grass several yards away, a silver spear protruding from her chest as her body slipped back into its natural, frail form. Fire lapped up the sides of the clan's tree home, devouring the ancient wood and turning it to black ash.

Efamar cried out again, and Nathaira lunged to her feet to see him at the edge of the clearing where the forest met the grass. There were five slavers around him, silver masks glinting as they threw a net of thick silver strands over him. She bolted forward.

Grass hissed past her legs, brushed against fur as her body changed midrun into a mountain lion. Nathaira hit the ground on all fours, sleek body flying across the distance toward Efamar.

Another cry filled the air over Efamar's screaming.

Nathaira skidded to a stop to see Zeythra fall to her knees in front of a slaver. Her grandmother glanced at her as her body wavered between that of the minotaur and her natural shape, before the slaver took her head off with one swipe of his sword. Nathaira screamed, body wavering back to her natural form.

Efamar screamed again.

Nathaira jerked backward away from Zeythra and darted toward him once more.

A spear whistled past her ear. Nathaira hissed and lunged sideways as two more followed. Three slavers ran toward her, a silver net held between them. Athrysion had told her before of the slavers, dark-skinned masked men from the continent of Araysann who captured creatures of all kinds and races to sell them to the highest bidders. He said that they only liked young specimens, ones that were not as strong and could not fight them as well as older creatures.

The first slaver drew abreast of her. Nathaira ripped his throat open with one swipe of her paw. She would make them pay for what they had done. The second slaver drew close, spear raised above his silver-masked head. Nathaira jumped to the side, paws sliding on the blood-soaked grass, and lunged for his throat with a snarl. She would kill them all. She hit the slaver in the chest, one paw knocking the sword from his hand. They tumbled backward to the ground, her fangs tearing the mask from the man's face as she pinned him underneath her.

The slaver's eyes were blue, like Zeythra's and Efamar's, but they were not filled with the hate and anger that Athrysion had always told her the humans' eyes were when they looked upon magical creatures. They were filled with fear. Scared, breathless fear. Nathaira paused.

The butt of a spear made contact with her ribs, and she roared and flew off the human and rolled away into the grass, pain searing through her side. The slaver jumped to his feet, and Nathaira rose with him, wheeling to face him and the third slaver as they warily circled her. They were trying to trap her, she realized. She hissed. Her eyes went to the slaver whose mask she had knocked off. He was shivering, and sweat drained down his dark face. He was terrified. It was a weak spot in the slavers' circle; Nathaira took it.

The slaver held his ground for three seconds as she raged toward him, before screaming and jumping to the side.

She flew past, legs stretched toward Efamar.

Fire burned through her shoulder. Nathaira screamed as a spear drove into her flesh, just below the bone of her right shoulder. She stumbled to the grass as yells rang out behind her, pain like nothing she had ever experienced filling her senses.

Efamar and the slavers circling him were a mere thirty feet away now. Nathaira could see her brother's blue eyes reflecting the light of the fire in the grass.

A glistening silver net was thrown over her, and Nathaira screamed again, a feeling like a thousand knives cutting into her flesh where the net touched overwhelming her. She changed back into her normal form as she fell onto her forearms, breaths coming like ragged gasps that filled her lungs with the smoke that billowed through the clearing.

Flashes of white and red filled her vision as boots appeared at the edge of the net. Nathaira gasped as fire exploded through her body. Her blood felt like it was made of lava, molten, red-hot lava that pushed through her body.

"We've got her," a voice with a strange, deep accent said in the general tongue. "Bring the other one and let's go."

Blackness hummed at the edges of Nathaira's vision. She saw Efamar scream again but did not hear the sound. The last thing she thought was that she and Efamar were the last of the clan, and then the dream faded to darkness.

CHAPTER 2

Hathus

Hathus Ryrgorion stared at the rusted iron bars of his cell door. Three years, five months, and twenty-one days. That was how long he had been in this cursed cell. Three years, five months, and twenty-one days—he knew from the marks he'd etched on the wall with a loose piece of stone—rotting in a dark, dank dungeon of Crystoln for the crime of stealing. Stealing! As if that was a crime for which you could lock a man away for the rest of his life…

Hathus blinked. The bars of his cell door still glared at him. He'd been staring at the bars for what seemed like an eternity now, and the only thing that changed about them was that they had grown rustier from the water that constantly dripped down from the slime-coated stone above his head. There were nine bars. The gods knew he'd counted them enough times, each exactly two inches in diameter and five feet tall. Not that it made a difference, but a thief's old habits die hard, and a good thief always noticed every detail of his escape route.

Of course, the rusty iron door was not his escape route, Hathus mused darkly. He'd found that out when he'd first been thrown into his cell and had beaten himself senseless for three weeks trying to break the door down. But it was the only possible escape route in the solid rock cubicle that was his home, and in case it ever became an option, he knew the exact measurements.

Hathus's stomach rumbled loudly, and he sighed as he held a bony hand up to it. *Gods, I'd like some food right now... A big juicy steak would be nice...* He licked his thin, cracked lips. *Or maybe a roll of steaming hot bread with thick brown crust and gobs and gobs of golden butter...*

His stomach growled even louder, and Hathus groaned, trying to think of something, anything, besides food.

A water drop splashed onto his forehead. Hathus glared up at the dark rock over his head. The only thing that there was plenty of in the dungeons of Crystoln was water. Constantly dripping from the ceiling, running down the walls in rivulets, and pooling in the low spots of the floor. He was so tired of the clear liquid that he vowed to never drink it again if he was ever set free.

A scratching noise in the moldy bed of hay across from him caught his ear, and Hathus softened his breathing to listen.

Something squeaked. Hathus grinned. A rat. The only other living things that came to his cell besides the jailer bringing food—when he felt like it. The scratching drew closer, and Hathus bunched what little muscles he had left, readying for the spring.

Closer, little fellow, that's it. He could see it now, all whiskers and fur and tail and beady glowing eyes.

Just a little closer, and you'll never know hunger or have to search for food in dungeon cells again.

The rat shuffled nearer. Hathus moved, snatching the unsuspecting animal from the floor with a bony hand before the rat knew what hit it.

The rat screeched loudly for a second, the sound echoing out the iron cell door and up the long stone corridor outside, before falling limp as Hathus broke its neck with one deft flick of his hand.

"There now, little friend," Hathus said, "I thank you kindly for giving me a meal. It seems like this might be my lucky day." He grinned and snatched the shard of rock that he used for counting the days—or what he thought were the days, he really couldn't tell in the darkness—and sawed at the rat's skin, slicing it from chin to tail with a dull shredding noise.

The smell of fresh blood and warm flesh drifted through the cell. Hathus closed his eyes with a sigh and let the scent fill his nostrils for a moment, imagining that he was in King's Tavern, getting ready to eat a meal of beef, potatoes, and sweet rolls.

A water drop splashed on his pointed nose, and Hathus's hazel eyes snapped back open. He wasn't at King's Tavern, and although he still detested rat after eating it for three and a half years, it was all the food he'd get until the jailer decided to bring him some.

Hathus ripped the skin off the rat's pink body with almost skeletal hands and after taking a deep breath, tore into the bloody meat.

He'd found out quickly when he'd come to the dungeons how the jailer exerted his power through hunger and that it could be weeks between meals. Apparently the crown saved money if most of their prisoners died within their first month's stay.

Hathus swallowed his mouthful half chewed and tore another chunk off the rat's body. Why the king didn't just order them executed, he didn't know, but he did know that he didn't like kings much. Rich, powerful, and dangerous, they reminded him of his father, and he hated to be reminded of him.

Hathus wiped a bloody hand across his heavily bearded mouth and threw the bones of the rat into a corner that was filled with white bones from hundreds of other rats. He picked at a piece of meat stuck between his teeth with his tongue. Once, he had eaten at the best establishments and slept in the finest beds. Now... Hathus sighed. Now he ate rat and slept on moldy hay. He shook his head, long brown hair tickling *his* thin neck and shoulders, and leaned back against the wall behind him. The hard rock pressed into his bones through the thin brown shirt he wore.

Gods, he wished he'd not gone to King's Tavern that night... He'd thought about it every day since the day they'd thrown him in his cell and regretted it more and more every time, cursing himself for his stupidity.

I had a good hand, too, Hathus thought mournfully. He gave up on trying to persuade the meat from between his teeth and sucked on it instead.

Of course, he could have fought—gods knew he'd wished he had enough times—but what good would that have done him? He'd be dead right now, and although sometimes he longed for death, the truth was that death scared him more than anything. More than even magic.

Something sharp bit at his neck. Hathus hissed and reached a hand up, pulling a flea off his skin. He held the squirming bug up in front of his eyes. It was fascinating, really, he mused absently, that he could see the small creature. After his many years of imprisonment in the darkness, he had developed a sort of night vision and was able to see most things in his cell from where he sat. The day markings on the wall, the rusty chains hanging from a partially dug-out iron rung, and a pile of broken white bones from the cell's last inhabitants that he'd long ago cracked open in a search for food.

The flea scrambled against his finger, struggling to get loose, and Hathus squished it and threw it in his mouth with one deft movement.

Dessert... He rubbed a hand across his bearded face again, skin crawling at the feeling of the sharp whiskers residing there. He wanted to shave, had wanted to ever since he'd grown a beard in this underworld hole. But there was little opportunity in the dungeons for personal cleaning, much less grooming. Hathus pulled his hand away from his face, letting it fall back to his side. He hated whiskers. If he ever got out of the dungeons, he'd shave every hour so that he would never have to feel whiskers on his face again.

Footsteps slapped on the wet stone tunnel outside, echoing into his cell.

Hathus glanced at his cell door at the noise. It was probably the jailer. The yellow-toothed weasel always came when he'd had food from a rat or two and never showed up at all in the long weeks when he didn't see a living thing and was forced to lick the walls to survive.

The footsteps drew closer, and Hathus could tell that there were more than one set as long, golden fingers of light flickered in the corridor outside, chasing away the shadows and penetrating the ancient darkness. He moaned at the brightness and threw a skinny arm up in front of his eyes.

Perhaps the jailer was picking up a dead body? Hathus peeked over the top of his dirt-covered arm as the footsteps drew closer. But no, he never did that; he just let them rot in their cells for the rest of the prisoners to smell and think about how it would be them before too long. Or perhaps he left them so that they would fantasize about getting some relief from their ravishing hunger by feasting on their fellows. Hathus had seen men beat themselves to death on the bars of their cage doors before, trying to get out and to the rotting body of their next-door neighbor.

The light glowed brighter, and a moment later it appeared, flickering and wavering outside the rusted bars of his cell door, blinding him.

Hathus covered his eyes with his bare arm again—he'd eaten his shirt long ago—and shrank against the slimy wall of his cell, pain searing through his head at the brightness.

Gods, why does it have to be so bright?

A key jangled on an iron ring. Hathus almost fainted as hope soared through him. Perhaps they were letting him go? But why would they do that after three and a half years of imprisonment?

They must be coming to execute me. Hathus paled, terrified.

They've gotten tired of my surviving all these years...

A loud click echoed in the dripping silence of his cell as a key slid into the rusty lock of the door. Hathus bunched up his limbs at the loud grinding and clanging of tumblers as they unlocked, followed by the squeaky groan of the door hinges.

"Come to kill me finally?" he croaked as boots slid over the stone floor of his cell and dark shadows moved in front of the glaring light. His visitors didn't reply, and Hathus struggled to stand as the footsteps drew closer.

Pain stabbed through his legs. Hathus cursed as he crumpled back to the floor again, his back scraping painfully against the wall beside him.

The gods be damned.

A hand grabbed his skinny arm. Hathus hissed at the sensation of it against his thin flesh and batted uselessly at it with a bony hand. He couldn't stand for more than a few seconds, much less fight off the knife he knew was headed for his ribcage. This was not how he'd pictured dying.

The gods be damned twice...

Another hand grabbed his other arm, painfully digging into the bones, and Hathus felt himself pulled roughly to his feet and dragged out of the cell, the blinding light filling his tearing eyes before he had time to register what was happening.

Hathus blinked. "If you're going to kill me," he said, eyes slowly coming into focus and the light morphing from a bright-golden blur into a torch, "why didn't you do it in my cell?"

The rusty door of his cell slammed shut with a loud clang, and Hathus jumped as the noise ricocheted off into the darkness.

He could make out the shapes of three men now—two holding him and one holding the sizzling light. The torchbearer turned and headed back up the tunnel the way he and his counterparts had come in, and Hathus winced as the two men holding onto his biceps followed. He glanced over his shoulder at the rusty door of his cell as it faded into the darkness of the hall, a grin tugging at his pale lips. He didn't know if he was going to his death or freedom—he hoped it was the latter—but he was free from his prison cell. After three and a half years, he was free.

Maybe this was his lucky day after all.

#

Hathus started catching glimpses of his rescuers—he began calling them that for lack of a better title—as his eyes gradually adjusted to the light of the sizzling torch. All were dressed in the same outfits—black leather gloves, black pants, knee-high black leather boots, black leather helmets, and black tunics—and all three carried long steel swords strapped to their hips.

Executioners, perhaps? The smile slid from Hathus's face as they turned down a side tunnel that gradually sloped upward. They turned down another tunnel, also sloping upward, and he eyed the swords hanging at his rescuers' belts, weighing the option of taking one and finding his own way out of the dungeons. He quickly dismissed the idea. The dungeons were far too vast to find a way out of them without a guide, and he was too weak to stand, let alone walk.

They continued their ascent through the dungeons, marching down tunnels, up stairwells, and past endless cell doors, until they reached a stone landing with an iron-barred and studded oaken door looming in the wall behind it. Two torches wavered in dragon-claw brackets embedded into the stone walls on either side of the door; water dripped from the ceiling above.

Finally. Hathus took a gulping breath of cold, dank air as they stepped up the last of the stairs—there had been one hundred and nineteen; he'd counted—and onto the landing.

The rescuer carrying the torch rapped two sharp knocks on the door with a gloved hand, the sound reverberating down the steep gray stairs behind them and off into the yawning darkness. A moment later, ancient levers turning on rusty pistons groaned loudly as the massive door swung slowly inward.

"You found him, then?" the stringy-haired, rotten-toothed jailer asked in a nasally voice. He peeked around the edge of the open door with beady yellow eyes that reminded Hathus of the rat that he had eaten.

The lead rescuer nodded, and the jailer grinned horribly, revealing dark, stained gums. He pulled the door open wide.

A stone room sat on the other side, round and dusty and embedded with several other wooden doors in its dark walls.

The room hadn't changed much since the last time he had come through, Hathus noted as the rescuers holding on to his arms dragged him through the door and into the room. The only difference was that now he was going through it headed for life instead of death. He hoped, anyway.

The jailer closed the door behind them with a heavy boom and, cackling, shuffled after them, the tails of his tattered brown coat dragging on the stone floor beneath him with soft rasping noises.

"Think yer going free, don't ya?" He chortled. His laugh sounded like a choking pig. "You'll see. Probably gonna feed ye to the lions in the arena. Be a fitting end for ye."

"How about you join me?" Hathus asked.

"Bah!" The jailer spat at him and shuffled over to a spindly legged table, the only piece of furniture in the room besides the rickety chair beside it. A melting tallow candle sat in the center of the table, and next to it, a key. The jailer pulled the key off with a loud scrape and hobbled across the well-worn stone floor to one of the oaken doors. He inserted the key into its ancient lock with a click.

The rescuer with the torch moved toward the door, and Hathus grimaced as the two dragging him followed, their fingers digging painfully into his arms.

"Do you think you could be any gentler?" he hissed as the jailer swung the door open and stepped aside to let them pass. The two men dragged him through the door without responding.

"I hope the lions tear you apart piece by piece," the jailer said, chortling again as they passed.

"I'll make sure to tell them you send your regards," Hathus replied sarcastically.

The jailer cursed and slammed the door shut behind them with a loud boom.

"Pleasant fellow, isn't he?" Hathus asked.

His rescuers didn't reply. He hadn't really expected them to. They started forward again, jerking him up another set of stone stairs that stretched onward into the darkness above.

They climbed for what felt like hours before another stone landing with an oaken door matching its counterparts below appeared in the flickering fingers of the torch carried by the lead rescuer.

Hathus sucked in a breath at the sight. Was he really going to be set free? He quivered at the thought. He longed to see Zen and Yar again, to feel the warmth of the brother suns' rays on his skin, to see his surroundings in light instead of darkness.

The lead rescuer produced a narrow iron key from his belt, and the same process was repeated with the door. They slipped him through and locked it behind them again.

A long, dark-wooded hallway greeted them on the other side, with aged tapestries covering its walls and dripping tallow candles in iron brackets staggered between.

The lead rescuer put his torch in an empty bracket with a click, and they moved off, the slapping of the rescuers' boots on the wooden floor muffled by the thick draperies on either side of them.

They were in the palace, Hathus surmised, shuffling along on bare feet. By why in the gods' and goddesses' names would they be in the palace? Unless, of course, the jailer was right, and he was going to be thrown to the lions in the arena...

No, they'd bring me out through another door if they were going to do that...

The candles along the walls threw wavering pools of light on the dusty tapestries between them, and Hathus let his eyes follow their glow. The tapestries were ancient, obvious by their frayed ends, but the pictures stitched into them were still visible, and although they were faded, they were easy to make out.

One tapestry, which clearly used to be dark red but had turned black with dust and age, had a depiction of centaurs playing in a moonlit field. It was from the early Third Age, Hathus noted from the flashy style.

Another, a royal blue, had an image of a griffin biting a man's head off in the simpler early Second Age style, and still another, in dark green, had stitchings of armies battling in the current detailed middle Seventh Age style.

They were histories, Hathus realized. Histories of Argdrion and what had happened since the beginning of time thousands of years ago. The centaur tapestry was of the time of peace before the Great Wars, when magical creatures had roamed free across the lands. The griffin biting the man's head off was an old tale about a man who had tried to steal a precious object from the griffins and paid for his greed with his life. And the other, of the armies battling, was of the Last Great Battle of the Third Great War, which had been fought on the Opherian Plains that surrounded the city of Crystoln outside and had claimed hundreds of thousands of lives in one day.

Hathus's fingers twitched.

Gods, but these pieces of dusty cloth are worth a lot of money...

The hallway ended at a narrow carved wooden door with a stone arch over it, and once more they stopped while the lead rescuer fumbled with an ancient lock, this one etched with twisting ivy.

Hathus swallowed. Was death waiting for him on the other side of the door? His knees weakened at the thought.

The man unlocked the door with a click and pushed it open on groaning hinges. A thick black curtain hung over the narrow opening like a shadow.

Hathus frowned. Usually when a door was concealed on one side by a curtain, it meant that one did not want others to know it was there.

Interesting...

The rescuers holding on to his arms stepped forward, and before he could think to step with them, he was flailing headfirst through the curtain and landing, sprawling, on the cold floor of a long, dim room.

Hathus groaned as the door shut again with a dull click and rolled over onto his back, every muscle throbbing. He stared up at the dark space above his head where the ceiling should have been. Not a sound besides his own labored breathing echoed through the still room. A shiver ran up his spine.

It's like a mausoleum...

He rubbed his thin arms against his bony body for some hope of warmth. Pushing himself up onto his elbows, he stared around the silent room. The walls were as black as night and dotted with a few sizzling tallow candles that did little to break the heavy darkness hanging like a cloak over the whole of the room. The floor was a very beautiful—and very expensive— type of silver-speckled black marble from Seyrwyth. It's small specks of silver glittered and sparkled like stars in the light of the candles. But it was the box, five feet tall and three feet wide and carved with strange, deep marks, at the far end of the room that caught Hathus's attention the most.

Hathus slowly pushed himself to his feet, testing his wobbly legs. They held, although just barely. It was like he was walking on piles of jelly. He took a tentative step forward. The leg he'd put his weight on gave out immediately, and he pitched forward and landed, very ungracefully and cursing all the way, flat on his face.

Son of a bitch...

"I fear that you are not as graceful as you once were, Hathus Ryrgorion," a soft but clear voice said.

Hathus scrambled backward, cursing and glancing wildly around him. "Who's there?" he gasped. No one replied. Maybe he'd imagined it... He had heard voices in his cell over the years, although usually not outside of one of the raging fevers he'd gotten every few months.

"As so often is the case when we are seeking something," the voice spoke again, "I am directly in front of you."

Hathus's gaze shot to the strangely carved black box.

"In answer to the question that I'm sure is going through your mind: Why you were brought here and not executed in your cell?" the voice went on. "It's because I have a proposition for you."

Proposition? Hathus eyed the box. He didn't think he was imagining the voice, so who was in the box? And why did they not want him to see them? "What kind of proposition, box man?" he said.

A hollow, rasping laugh rang through the long hall.

The hair on the back of Hathus' neck stood on end.

"Directly to the point. I like that, Hathus."

Hathus pulled his feet in, trying to stand again. He didn't like the man knowing his name. He didn't like any of this. "What do you want?" he asked. "And who are you?"

"To the first question," the voice replied, "the answer is a dangerous one that could gain you your freedom or your death. To the second, I'm afraid that that is a question I cannot answer, for my identity must remain a secret throughout the duration of our acquaintance."

Duration of our acquaintance? Hathus frowned, hands resting on the floor, ready to push himself up. "How do you know my name?" he asked, scanning the dark slits cut into the box.

"I know many things, Hathus Ryrgorion," the voice said. "I have eyes everywhere."

Hathus had a brief, unpleasant image of a multieyed creature sitting inside the ebony box, watching him.

"I would think," the voice went on, "that you would have a more"—it paused as if searching for the right word—"plausible question for me. Like 'What is your proposition that could gain me my freedom?' rather than asking something so mundane as to why I know your name."

Hathus glared at the box, struggling to push himself up. He gave up after a few tries and wrapped his arms around his shivering body instead. "All right, what is your proposition that could gain me my freedom?"

"Did you notice the tapestries in the hall?" the voice asked. "They're quite lovely, are they not?"

Hathus narrowed his eyes. The tapestries? What in the underworld did they have to do with anything? "I noticed them," he replied warily.

"My favorite has always been the one of the dragons from the Third Age. You know, 'The Seven Siblings of Rahys'?"

Hathus nodded. He'd seen it, and he knew the legend of the Seven Siblings of Rahys. Most people did; it was a popular fairy tale to tell misbehaving children. The legend was extensive, but the story was simple. Seven wiar siblings had risen up against their parents and tried to take over the world, and the Sisters, part of the old religion, had turned them into the monsters on the outside that they were on the inside. Then, they had cast them out of Argdrion and into an otherworld of darkness and fire.

"Dragons are so fascinating," the voice from the box said. "Creatures of legend, some say myth, living in a parallel universe to ours—an otherworld. It is said that hundreds have searched for dragons over the centuries, but as of yet, none have ever come back." A cough echoed from the box, and the voice was silent for a while.

"What does all this have to do with me?" Hathus asked after a moment.

"Oh, everything, Hathus," the man in the box replied.

The hair on the back of Hathus's neck stood up higher at the tone in his voice.

"You are a thief, are you not? Locked in the dungeons for stealing one too many times and being stupid enough to get caught?"

Hathus frowned but nodded.

"I have been told that you are one of the best thieves in Argdrion, is that true?"

Hathus glanced behind him, where he thought the door was at. Maybe he could try and make a run for it. "I am the best," he said, looking back at the box. He was good at his profession. Or he had been until he'd been caught and thrown into prison.

"Good," the voice said. "Then I do believe that you are the man I am looking for. You see, Hathus, I need a thief to get me something, a thief who is willing to go to a very dangerous place. A thief that is desperate and willing to do any job. Like you are, I think, Hathus."

"Who says I'm desperate?" Hathus asked, offended.

"Any man who has been in prison for nine months is desperate, Hathus."

Hathus blinked. "Nine months?" He shook his head. "I've been in prison for three and a half years…"

The voice didn't reply, and Hathus mentally tried to count back over the years. "What do you want me to steal?" he asked after a while, giving up on counting.

"Oh, first things first, Hathus," the man in the box said. "If you are to work for me, there a few things you must know."

The voice paused for a few moments, and Hathus raised his scraggly eyebrows. "For instance?"

"You are never to breathe a word to anyone about what we discuss or what you are to steal," the voice replied. "If you do, or if you try to cheat me or don't do what I pay you to do…" The man in the box paused. "Let us just say that it will be unpleasant for you."

Goosebumps sprouted on Hathus's arms. He didn't have to ask to know what he meant by that.

"If you succeed in what I ask, however," the man in the box went on, "you will be granted your freedom. If you refuse to do what I ask, you will be killed and your body thrown into the River Sar for the fish to eat."

Not much for choices, are we? "Well, then I guess I'm going to do what you ask, aren't I?" Hathus said sarcastically.

"You might regret that you said that, Hathus," the voice said.

Hathus watched the box, breathless. Steal something that they didn't want anyone to know about? It had to be a priceless jewel or some other rare artifact. He could handle that. And the gods knew he'd do anything to be free of the dungeons.

"I want you," the voice said after a moment, "to go to the Land of Dragons and bring me a dragon's heart."

Hathus laughed.

And laughed.

"You aren't serious," he said after a few minutes. "The Land of Dragons?" There were otherworlds, true, but a Land of Dragons?

"Oh, I am very serious, Hathus," the man in the box said. "I believe that dragons and their world are real."

Hathus stopped laughing.

He's crazy. And dangerous. Magic was outlawed in Argdrion. Unless the laws had changed since he'd been imprisoned. Anyone who used it or associated with it was asking for death.

"Will you do it, Hathus?"

Hathus pulled his legs closer to him. It was a death sentence.

He did not want anything to do with magic, even if it was just looking for an otherworld that didn't exist. He feared it, almost as much as he did death. He had seen what kind of pain magic caused, and he never wanted to see it again. But if he refused the offer of the man in the box, he was going to die…

Hathus stared at the box for a while. He really didn't want to die. "I'll do it," he said aloud. "But I have a condition."

"A condition?"

"Yes," Hathus said, warming up to the idea forming in his head. "I will look for your Land of Dragons and dragon's heart for six months. That should be enough time to find it. If it is as real as you think. And if I don't find it in that time, I get my freedom. No questions asked." He was rather proud of himself; it was a perfect plan. He wouldn't find the Land of Dragons, not in six months, or ever, and after the time was up, he would be free to go.

If he didn't get found out by the authorities and executed for associating with magic, that was. Hathus paled again.

The man in the box was silent for a while, and Hathus worried that he would say no and just kill him.

"You will have guards with you," the voice said after a few minutes. "To make sure that you do look for the Land of Dragons and my heart."

Hathus nodded. "Fair enough."

"Then yes, Hathus Ryrgorion," the man in the box said. "If you do not find the Land of Dragons in six months' time, you may have your freedom."

Hathus grinned, the reality that he was going to see the Brothers again outweighing his fear of magic and death for the moment.

"When do I leave?" he asked.

CHAPTER 3

Darkmoon

Darkmoon looked down the deserted hallway.

Shadows and dust mites swirled together in the moonlight shining into the wide, rug-laden hall. Lead-paned windows lined the outer stone wall.

He started down the hall, black suede boots making no noise on the thick and expensive but faded red rug covering the hall's stone floor. He was an assassin, the best in Argdrion, and tonight his job was to kill an heiress's son before the son could kill the heiress for her considerable fortune.

Darkmoon eyed a twisting golden candlestick atop a polished epharia table. The heiress was from an old and wealthy family in Warulan's east-coast kingdom of Dyridura. Well into her sixties, she had survived the last quarter of the Third Great War, the Hunting, seven husbands, five sons, and three daughters.

Darkmoon ran a slender, scarred finger over a white lace table runner with real threads of gold spun through it. The heiress's castle and surrounding lands sat twenty miles north of the Warulan coastal city of Ryrdion and was full of antiques and wealth from all of Argdrion. Some said that the heiress was a greedy old woman because she never came out of her castle except to shop for more antiques and because she never, ever gave money to anyone unless she dragged an equal amount of work out of them. Others said she was a hoarder for all the stuff held up in her castle.

Darkmoon stopped to admire a painting of an old woman and a sheepdog, the gray eyes of the dog and yellow of the woman's lifelike gaze piercing. The painting, half hidden by the shadows of the hall, was by the famous painter Jày Ahrnor, dead now for three hundred years. Darkmoon studied the brushstrokes on the sheepdog's shaggy hair, admiring the heiress's choice of decorations. Her collection of art, antiques, and treasures was almost equal to his own, though his was scattered between his mansions, which lay strewn throughout Argdrion's major cities.

Thunder rumbled outside, rattling the windows lining the hallway's outer wall and echoing through the shadowed and sleeping castle.

A door creaked in the distance. Darkmoon's sharp ears caught the whisper of hurried footsteps. When the heiress had hired him, she had arranged for a maid of her staff to be in the castle's third-story front hall at midnight to tell him which room the heiress's son was in. The son apparently had a habit of straying into odd rooms at strange hours of the night, and the heiress had wanted to make sure that Darkmoon found and killed him quickly without unnecessary time spent searching the massive, four-story, three-hundred-room castle.

Darkmoon reached a half-gloved hand into a pocket on the inside of his ankle-length black cloak and pulled out a cool, slender piece of chocolate. He popped the confection between his thin lips and started down the hallway again, his all-black clothing making him meld from shadow to shadow like he was one of them.

The hallway stretched the length of the front of the great castle and was met by multiple other stone hallways that led off into the bowels of the ancient fortress. The ceiling rose into a pointed trough and was supported by multitiered stone pillars that seemed to grow out of the walls.

Darkmoon walked past a dark, aged stone statue of a barking dog, the tip of its tongue and part of its muzzle missing and the lighter gray stone showing underneath. His steps were unhurried, smooth. He had been trained early on that quickness in a job resulted in poor work and that the methodical and thorough killer always reaped benefits.

A red-stained grandfather clock ticked out of the darkness ahead as he approached it. Darkmoon glanced at the silver hands. They pointed to 12:05 in the morning. The maid was late. He moved to the windows lining the outer wall. He didn't really need the maid to point him to his victim, but the heiress was paying him twenty thousand aray for killing her child, and he would do it the way she wanted.

The night outside was clear, with the three sister moons hovering full and heavy in the star-dotted sky. A soft wind blew from the east, rustling through the fir and redwood trees in the yard below, whistling through the pillars of a bell tower opposite.

Darkmoon scanned the stables and driveway of the castle before following the wall surrounding the ancient estate to the grassy slopes and thick fir forest beyond. It was said that the heiress's estate had been built before the beginning of the First Great War.

A movement disturbed the shadows hovering inside the bell tower, and Darkmoon's eyes darted back to the pinnacle of the building. A pigeon flapped out of the opening around the bell and flew to a nearby fir tree. Darkmoon went back to scanning the grounds around the castle. It was rare to find a building in Argdrion that had been built before the Great Wars, ended some thirteen years ago now.

Darkmoon found a spot in the wall around the castle that had obviously been rebuilt at some point in the last twenty years. He could see skinchangers and wiar running up the hill toward the castle if he looked hard enough, archers and knights hiding in the castle's tall upper stories.

Footsteps caught his ears again, and his eyes went from the wall to their own reflection in the lead-paned window in front of him. The left a deep emerald green and the right a piercing icy blue, his eyes were as unique as snow in the humid, jungle-covered BalBayr Islands. They were also symbols of death to Argdrion, for most who looked into them never saw anything else again.

Darkmoon stared at the reflection of his eyes and the white scar that cut his right eyebrow in half, listening to the footsteps hurry nearer. He hated his eyes sometimes. The left, the green, came from his father, and the right, the blue, was the same color that his mother's eyes had been. Every time he looked at his eyes, they were a reminder. A reminder of things that he had worked hard to forget.

The maid came around a corner of an adjoining hallway with a flushed face, her dark-brown hair in a slightly messy and loose updo.

"Are you here?" she whispered, voice terrified as she glanced up and down the wide hallway.

Darkmoon turned away from the window and approached her, his movements so quiet that she didn't know he was there until he had wrapped a hand over her mouth.

She screamed into his hand—he'd known she would—and he leaned forward. "Tell me where," Darkmoon whispered in her ear, his voice soft and even and with a deeper undertone that hinted at darkness.

"The study," the maid whispered as he slowly pulled his hand away from her lips. She was shaking against him, and Darkmoon could smell the fear coming off her. "He went in there over an hour ago, and when I left, he was writing some papers. I... I don't think he'll be leaving anytime soon. It... the study," the maid said, voice quivering, "is another story up. The only door with a set of armor beside it."

Darkmoon flicked his left wrist, and a cherry-sized iron ball rolled out of his black leather vambrace and into his half-gloved palm. The heiress had given explicit orders as to what was to be done with the maid to silence her. Darkmoon tapped the ball against the maid's temple, hard, and she fell limp in his arms, unconscious. The heiress's planning was almost as thorough as his.

The windows lining the outer hallway wall were latched together with small iron hooks. Pulling the hooks up on one set of double windows, Darkmoon lifted the maid's body up onto the thick, bird-dropping-streaked ledge, and after swinging her legs out over the edge, pushed her off.

The maid landed on the cobbles three stories below with a distant thump, face smashed into the stones and blood pooling around her head. Darkmoon slipped off up the hallway, cloak lifting behind him.

"Everything must look like accidents," the heiress's thick voice rang through his head. "My son's death, the maid's..."

A doorway with a set of steep stone stairs leading upward appeared out of the shadows twenty feet further down the hall. Remembering the maid's instructions, Darkmoon slipped up them.

Another hallway sat at the top of the stairs, dark, damp smelling, and filled with more antiques and statues.

Halfway down the hall, light spilled out from under a door. Darkmoon moved toward it. He stopped to listen at the heavy oaken door for a moment, glancing at an gilded suit of armor resting alertly beside him before reaching for the heavy iron handle and pushing the door open.

The son was in the middle of the candlelit room, fat body squished into a straight-backed chair as he leaned over a rich mahogany desk, scribbling on paper. Darkmoon slid into the study along one shadowed stone wall, the smell of old books, writing ink, manly perfume, and wine making his nostrils tingle.

The heiress, while in her son's rooms looking for a book, had found a letter in her son's handwriting three weeks before, describing his plans to have her committed to a mental institution seventy miles away so that he could gain her fortune early.

Darkmoon's fingers slipped into another pocket on the inside of his cloak and curled around the small vial residing there. He stepped across a rug of red and silver.

The son continued to write, the steady scratching of his quill and tinkling of the inkwell as he dipped his feather pen filling the study.

Thunder rumbled again, shaking the castle.

Darkmoon's eyes went to the yellowed paper the son was writing on, reading the freshly drying lines of black ink. The son was writing to a cousin, asking for help in proving to the courts that the heiress was losing her mind as she aged.

Darkmoon dug the fingers of his left hand into the son's graying hair and pulled his head back, pouring a drop of clear liquid from the vial into the man's left eye.

The heiress was a businesswoman as well as a survivor, and her first realization upon seeing the discovered letter had been that her son would have to die.

Darkmoon watched the son's pupils expand and then dilate as the poison pumped through his veins.

"I don't want any evidence on the body of foul play," the heiress had said two weeks before as they had sat at a small and out-of-the-way restaurant thirty miles away from her castle.

Darkmoon let go of the son's head. It hung in the position he had pulled it back into, brown eyes staring up at the cross-hatched mahogany ceiling above.

"Everyone must think that he died from a heart attack or some such other ailment common to men of his age and weight," the heiress had murmured, the black dress she wore in mourning of her seventh and recently dead husband giving her shrewd, aging face a sharp look.

The son's body convulsed several times, the heart attack induced by the poison rocking his body.

Darkmoon recorked and pocketed the vial.

"I want it to appear innocent," the heiress had said from the other side of the shadowed corner table. "Natural."

The son slumped sideways in his chair, mouth open in a last gasp for air, purple veins darkly prominent in his fat neck, eyes bulging out of his head. Darkmoon turned and moved back out of the study, his hand slipping into his cloak for another slice of chocolate.

The heiress was waiting for him in the hall downstairs, her dress a backless, low cut, rich blue and gold now instead of the black that it had been two weeks before.

"I'll wait until the morning to find him," the heiress said, her thick, aging voice giving no hint of emotion at the knowledge that her son had just been killed, and at her orders.

Darkmoon stopped beside her. The heiress was clever, one of the cleverest clients that he had ever had. "That would be best," he said calmly, tongue working on the chocolate.

The heiress looked down the hallway, slender hands folded in front of her hips where the rich blue of her dress made a V before turning into the gold skirt. "And the maid?"

"In the courtyard outside," Darkmoon replied.

She looked back at him.

"I'll take the rest of my payment," he said softly. He didn't remind her that the amount was ten thousand aray; she remembered what it was as well as he did, and he knew she was aware that if she shorted him, he'd kill her and take the money off her corpse.

The heiress turned to a spindle-legged table behind her and pulled open a drawer on the front, then took out two full black velvet bags.

Darkmoon took the bags from her, her fingers brushing against his as the bags traded hands.

"Stay," the heiress said, placing a slender, wrinkling hand on his muscled upper arm.

Darkmoon looked down at her as he cloaked the heavy bags. Her brown eyes were clear and sharp. She squeezed his arm firmly.

She wanted to sleep with him. He knew by the quick rising and falling of her breasts, the sultry undertone in her voice.

"I will not be easy on you because of your age," he said, watching her. He had known men over the years who would rape women to satisfy their urges, but he had never had to rape a woman in his life. Women begged him for his affections, threw themselves at him. His reputation as a lover was equal to that of being a killer, and sleeping with Argdrion's best assassin had become something of a status. Among the whores, anyway.

The heiress didn't blink. "I have heard that you can be... many types of lovers," she said, fingers still squeezing the thick muscles of his upper arm. "Rough, soothing, gentle, bold, depending on what woman you are with and what her preferences are."

Darkmoon looked down the hallway, the open window that he had thrown the maid's body out of letting in a cool spring breeze that stroked his thin face underneath his cowl.

"You've had seven husbands, heiress," he said, glancing back at her. "What is your preference?"

She slid her hand off his arm. Her eyes sparkled. "Bold," she said.

#

Later, slipping through the shadows of the city of Ryrdion, Darkmoon sensed that someone was following him. He slowed his walk as he moved down a sloping, deserted street, listening to the soft but perceptible rasp of shoe against cobbles. It had not been uncommon, when he'd first become an assassin, to have those who hired him to try and have him killed after he had done their dirty deeds.

Darkmoon walked lightly down a set of stone stairs running parallel to the street. After he had killed those sent after him—and then the ex-clients who had sent them—a few dozen times, people had realized it was best to leave him alone. That was when he had first made a name for himself as Argdrion's best assassin, back when he'd been young and killing had been conscious searing. Darkmoon slipped a slice of chocolate into his mouth, the familiar sweet soothing his tongue. Now killing came as easily to him as playing an instrument did for others.

The footsteps drew closer, and Darkmoon stopped as he reached the bottom of the stairs and turned to meet his stalker. A stooped figure in a frayed brown cloak that dragged on the ground around it appeared at the top of the stairs, outlined against the star-filled sky above.

The figure didn't speak as it slowly hobbled down the stairs toward him, and Darkmoon didn't try to fill in the silence as he watched it near him. He knew who she was, what she wanted. He'd known since he'd first heard the footsteps, maybe even before.

"There is darkness coming to Argdrion, Darkmoon," the seer said as she reached him. Her voice was old and frail and light, and she hung onto the iron railing running parallel to the stairs as if her life depended on it.

Darkmoon worked on the chocolate in his mouth, unfazed. A star streaked across the sky above, catching his quick eye for a moment.

"I have seen the signs in my dreams, in the smoke, in the wind. Signs of fire and death. So much death…"

"Have you, now?" Darkmoon said calmly, glancing at the seer. "Whose?"

"Everyone," the seer rasped. "And when the darkness comes, nothing will ever be the same again. But you can save her, Darkmoon," the seer whispered animatedly, grabbing his arm with a clawlike hand as she reached him. "You can save Argdrion."

Darkmoon snorted lightly. "I am an assassin, seer. A killer, and I am covered in as much blood as Argdrion."

"You will not be alone," the seer said. "Others will be called to save Argdrion—you are simply the first of many."

Darkmoon swallowed the last of the chocolate. "Well, it's flattering to know that I was asked first."

"You do not take me seriously," the seer said, watching him. "Argdrion has much to pay for, Darkmoon. Her lands cry out with the innocent blood that was shed on them, and the skies weep for the lives lost, for what happened during the wars and the Hunting."

"Then let Argdrion pay for her people's sins," Darkmoon said. His lips slid into a dark smile. "Let her fall." He would even help, if he cared that much.

"You do not mean that, Darkmoon—"

"Oh, but I do," Darkmoon replied, pulling the seer's hand off his arm. She hissed as his strong fingers bit into hers. "If Argdrion falls," he said, "I will watch from the sidelines and laugh."

"There will be no sidelines, Darkmoon." The seer quivered, voice urgent. "And you will not laugh when you see what is coming."

Darkmoon glanced up the street. Dawn was coming. He could see the streaks of red and gold starting in the east, above the gabled roofs of the city. He had to be going; he had another job to attend to, halfway across Argdrion, on the continent of Araysann.

"You will have dreams," the seer whispered. "And your past will haunt you."

"My past never haunts me," Darkmoon said.

"It should," the seer said sharply.

Darkmoon stared up the street as a dog barked, feeling uneasy for the first time since she'd approached. They weren't speaking of his years of killing but of something further back. Something that he had buried a long, long time ago.

"You will be reminded, Darkmoon," the seer said. "Of your past. Like you have never been reminded before. It will haunt your waking hours, plague your dreams, and perhaps it will make you remember what you were before you became this creature of darkness."

Darkmoon grabbed the seer around the throat and lifted her off the ground with one hand. "I told you," he murmured in her face, voice dark, soft, "I do not care what happens to Argdrion."

"Your past will burn you, Darkmoon," the seer hissed, gasping for air. "Like you should be burned." The seer's hood fell off her head, revealing thinning white hair and foggy gray eyes. "And perhaps through this, Darkmoon," she gasped, "you will find some spark of the goodness that I know is in you still, and you will rise up to defend Argdrion."

Darkmoon smiled, a dark smile with no humor in it. "There is no goodness in me, seer," he whispered. "There hasn't been for a very long time."

"You fear it, Darkmoon, your past," she panted, ignoring his words. "It is probably the only thing you do fear, but you fear it nonetheless, and you run from it, knowing that someday it will catch up with you, and then Argdrion will find out who you really are."

"No one knows who I am," Darkmoon said, voice growing cold.

"Just me," the seer whispered. Her lips began turning blue; her breaths weakened.

"Soon it will only be me," Darkmoon replied, watching her face lose its coloring.

"You can save her, Darkmoon," the seer whispered, eyes slowly closing. "And if you do not, Argdrion will fall."

Darkmoon opened his fingers, and the seer fell backward onto the steps with a dull thump and lay there, motionless, dead.

"NO!" a child's voice cried from up the street. "Please, no!"

Darkmoon staggered backwards, glancing up at a door up the street as it opened and a man with a tin pail exited. He had not heard that voice in years…

"Please…" A boy child flashed through his mind, hair black like his own, but eyes both green. There was fear in the boy's eyes, fear and horror.

The man started down the street. Darkmoon turned and slipped between two buildings.

"Please…" the child whispered.

Darkmoon leaned against the side of a building, breathing quickly. The seer was wrong. He glanced at the street he had left as the man found the seer's dead body and stopped to examine it. He would not save Argdrion. He pushed away from the wall and started down the lightening alley. He reached for another slice of chocolate, hand shaking. He wouldn't do it. Not if his past haunted him again, not for anything.

Darkmoon slipped the chocolate into his mouth, the dark sweet helping him to calm, to think. He had buried his past once before, many years ago, and he would do it again.

The boy cried out again, but Darkmoon ignored it. He slipped through two buildings and out into a market street just starting its day.

And Argdrion? Darkmoon sidestepped a wagon piled high with crates as its driver cracked a whip over two mules' heads.

Argdrion could burn in the underworld.

CHAPTER 4

The Unknown Voice

I was born on a night of ice and snow. I was told that it was the coldest and longest winter to ever hit the land, a winter of endless nights. That the night I was born was the coldest and longest night of them all. They say that Mother screamed and struggled for twenty-five hours to bring me forth—a sign, many said, that I was destined to struggle my whole life. I do not know if it was a sign.

My first memory was four years later, standing atop the tower with Father and the castle steward, watching the crows circle above us.

"Another battle lost," Father said behind me.

I found a broken piece of stone lying next to the short stone wall that ringed the top of the tower and threw it at the crows. They didn't miss a wingbeat, and the stone sailed harmlessly off in an arc through the cloudless blue sky.

"Our armies, fleeing again," Father murmured angrily. Father was a colonel under King Edomur, who lived in a massive white castle two hundred miles from us. Most of the time, Father was gone with the king and the other lords and their armies, fighting against the magical creatures that invaded our lands. Magic was bad, although I didn't know why, just that it must be, for we had spent hundreds of years fighting it.

"At this rate, we'll be finished before the year is up," Father said, voice edged with exhaustion.

He had been home for the last three days to heal from a wound in his side—it was the first time I had seen him for that long in over two years. I found another rock, cocked my arm back, and threw it at the crows. This time the stone found its mark, and a large black crow squawked angrily and shied sideways.

"Perhaps not, my lord," our castle steward said. He was a thin, aging man with a nose that jutted out at a curving angle and gave his thin face the appearance of a shrew. "News is circling that a new weapon has been discovered that may perhaps be able to defeat the enemy."

I searched for another loose rock, prying at the crumbling chinking between the tower's stones and kicking at tufts of grass that bravely struggled up from the cracks.

"Silver," Father rumbled. "I've heard the news too, Sar, but how can a metal be expected to defeat creatures that can change into animals or inanimate objects or the resemblance of our friends? Or the wiar, who have powers like gods?"

"It is said that it burns them, weakens their power," Sar said slowly.

I found a third chip of rock and readied to throw it at the crows. Sensing my intent, they finally flew off, their glossy black bodies glinting with shades of deep purple and blue in the warm midday light from the twin suns hovering above the tower.

"Yes," Father replied, "Lord Faynron from Eyld told me the other day that he witnessed this firsthand when a skinchanger he was battling touched the silver amulet he always wears. He said that the creature screamed like it had touched fire and partially slipped out of its animal form. Perhaps this new discovery is as powerful as he says, but even if it is, how are we to mine silver with the enemy pressing in on all sides and our cities being destroyed by the dozens?"

I knew that my father was shaking his head angrily; he did that a lot.

"I fear that soon there will not be anyone left to fight, much less work in the mines."

I ran to the edge of the tower to watch the crows fly away, a chip of gray rock clutched in the fingers of my left hand. The tower was the only one still standing at the ancient castle that my father had inherited from his father before him. The others had long ago fallen off the steep hill-side that the eastern side of the castle sat on.

Every year, the heavy rains came and washed away the dark-brown mud of the hill, taking more of our home down to the grass fields below. Last year the hill had crumbled beneath a section of the wall that ringed the whole of the hilltop castle. I had heard Sar say that this year he feared that the second dining hall would fall away.

"If the enemy breaks through our defenses at Western Barrow, I want you to evacuate the house," Father said softly, so soft that I barely heard him.

"Do you think they will?" Sar asked in an equally soft voice.

I knew that my father was frowning; he always frowned when he was worried. Mother said that there was need to worry right now, although I didn't quite understand why.

"Yes," Father said. "In a matter of weeks, if the battles continue to go like they have been. If only we could hold them through the fall…"

It was middle summer now. My nanny had been teaching me about the seasons and how one knew which was which. Winter was cold and snowy. Spring, a time of growing things. Summer, blazing and fierce. Fall, shadowy and cool.

"I will do as you wish if they break through Western Barrow," Sar said.

Something about the tone in his orderly voice made me listen closer to what he and Father were talking about. There was fear in his voice, the fear that had been haunting all the adults' voices lately. Father and Sar were quiet for a long time, and I started to search the tower top again for loose rocks to add to a pile I had started on the wall.

"I fear for him," Father said, making me pause as I deposited three jagged chips of rock onto my pile. He was talking of me, I knew. "I fear for what might happen to him, for what he will see and experience in the next few months."

"The young must grow up quickly in wars," Sar said quietly. "As we did."

"I know," Father murmured, "but I often wish that it wasn't that way. I'd like my boy to grow old, not die on some distant battlefield."

I arranged the rocks according to color, the different shades of gray spreading out in a line.

"He's strong, your son," Sar said, making me half think of liking the strict castle steward. "And I think, Lord Sythorn, that you needn't worry about him."

"He was born on a longest winter's night," Father said thoughtfully.

"Indeed, my lord," Sar replied. "And a child of the longest winter's night has long been said to hold a great destiny in his blood. Who knows, perhaps he will be the one to end these wars."

"Perhaps," Father said. "But I am beginning to doubt, Sar, whether they shall ever end…"

I did not hear the rest of their words. My young mind was stuck on what Sar had said of my birth. Was I destined for greatness? At four, I had never thought of such things before, but what if Sar was right, and I was to be a great man who would perhaps stop the wars? Or maybe my destiny was to be king. At four, the possibilities as to what I might become were endless.

But there was one thing that hung in the back of my mind as I rearranged the rocks by their size, something that I had worried over since I had first been able to form a thought: I did not want to die.

I had first realized this when I saw the bodies of several of my father's knights, sent back to the castle from the battlefields for burial. I was not supposed to see their bodies, mangled, burned, and so, so white. But Mother had been ill from a summer fever, and my nanny, a fat, stupid woman who lost me half the time and forgot about me the other, was on the other side of the castle.

I'd crept out of a covered walkway that ran parallel to the courtyard and was used by the servants to bring food from the kitchens to the castle. As the clatter of horse hooves echoed off the castle walls, the wooden doll I had been playing with hung by my hand. My young eyes caught what rode on the horses. I had never seen the bodies of the dead before that day, and as the page boy leading the five horses with the blanketed bodies hanging over their backs brought his solemn procession to a stop in the courtyard, I moved closer to get a better look.

Servant girls cried as men pulled the knights' bodies from the horses; a knight's dog howled as it realized its master was dead.

I'd wanted a better look at these still-covered objects. What made them ride horses like that, on their stomachs? Was it some kind of new game? And why did they not speak? Had they forgotten how? A blanket fell back as the last knight was carefully taken from a horse and lowered to the cobbles of the courtyard. His eyes, lifeless and glazed, met mine across the courtyard. I stopped my slow creep forward, a coldness washing over me. I did not know then that the knight's strange behavior was called death, but I did realize that although their bodies were here, they were gone inside.

A servant closed the dead knight's eyes with two fingers and covered him with the blanket once more, and the five bodies were lifted and carried inside. No one noticed me standing there, doll in hand, until the servants came back out to put the horses away, and when they did, it was too late. I had already seen what they did not want me to see, and what I had seen chilled me to my very bones.

My nanny told me later what death was, after much scolding and heavy hits of her hand on my backside for running away from her. How it was coming for us all someday, and that there was nothing we could do about it. It made me wonder. What was the point of life if one knew death was waiting at the end? Why did we work so hard to build ourselves homes and fight against the magical creatures to keep them from taking our lands if we would only join our ancestors and enemies in cold, dark graves someday? How could people be happy when they knew that the next day might be their last?

"Tomorrow," Father's deep voice drifted into my memories as I arranged my rock chips into a circle. "I leave tomorrow."

"But, my lord," Sar said, "are you sufficiently recovered?"

"I will have to be," Father replied grimly. "We need every man and woman we can get. With them, perhaps we shall be able to hold the wiar and skinchangers back until winter arrives, and then for a time we can regroup. Maybe put our efforts into mining silver in preparation for the spring battles," he added in a softer voice.

"Let us hope that we can hold them back, then," Sar said.

"No," Father replied, voice low. "Let us pray."

A last warm breeze of summer fluffed my brown hair as Father called for me. If I was destined for greatness, I thought, then perhaps I could find a way to not die as everyone else would. It was a foolish thought, Mother told me when I mentioned it to her the next day as we watched Father ride off for Western Barrow from atop the castle walls. But in the mind of a four-year-old, anything was possible.

Even the idea of conquering death.

CHAPTER 5

Nathaira

A cold drop of water fell onto Nathaira's sharp nose, and her golden eyes snapped open. Raining. It was always raining in Ennotar. She blinked as a raindrop fell in her eye and gasped as searing, cutting pain stabbed at her right shoulder.

Sisters, what happened? The dream of her first hunt and the slavers attacking the meadow floated through her mind. Then she remembered Athrysion's blood covering her hands and Efamar's screams and knew it hadn't been a dream at all. Nathaira closed her eyes. Dead. The clan was all dead. It felt like a giant's hand was crushing her heart in two.

A tear trickled down her cheek to mingle with the rain.

Athrysion, Zeythra, the elders… Efamar… Nathaira's eyes snapped open again. Efamar was not dead, or at least he hadn't been. She rolled over on her side and gasped as more pain seared through her shoulder. Where was she? Hard, wet wood met her palms as she strained to sit up. A whip cracked loudly as a slaver urged two mud-streaked horses to move faster.

Nathaira glanced up at the iron bars surrounding her. She was in a cage, on a wagon, in a slaver train. She was a slave. A human slave. The realization of that fact was almost as crippling as the knowledge that most of the clan was dead. Was Efamar a slave, too? Nathaira pushed herself to a half-sitting position and cried out as pain cut through her shoulder.

"I wouldn't keep using that arm if I was ya," a rough voice speaking

Argdrion's main language said behind her. "Yer liable to rip the wound open again, and ya can't afford to lose any more blood."

Nathaira looked up.

A dirty, lean-bodied woman, arms resting across raised knees, stared at her through the bars of another cage.

A human. Nathaira stared back.

"It's a clean wound," the woman said, scratching at a hairy leg. "I tended it myself when they threw ya in here, but ya move around too much and…" She made a cutting motion across her throat and a gravelly *ssslit* noise.

Nathaira narrowed her eyes. A human had helped her? She glanced down at her shoulder; it was wrapped in a dirty brown strip of cloth that looked to be from the woman's shirt sleeve. And someone had dressed her too, in a thin blue shirt pockmarked with holes and cut-off black trousers that flapped gently in a cool breeze.

"Where are we going?" Nathaira asked, also in the general tongue. Her voice came out a deep croak.

"Ostgate," the woman replied, "the biggest port in all o' Ennotar."

Oh, Sisters. "How long have I been out?" Nathaira whispered.

"About five days, I reckon. Was beginning to think ye'd never come to, I was, for 'ow long it was."

Five days. So much can happen in five days…

"Why are you in a slaver train?" Nathaira asked abruptly, eyeing the woman with a mixture of abhorrence and curiosity. She had never spoken with a human before, only seen them in the distance when the clan had run across the human hunting parties that occasionally came into the mountains. The woman's face was thin and pockmarked, her blonde hair scraggly and dirty.

"Slavers ain't too picky who they take," the woman said, hacking and then spitting a gob of dark-brown phlegm through the bars of her cage. "As long as there ain't no one around to speak out against 'em nabbing a bloke, they'll take 'em. Me? There ain't no one to speak up for me. I'm what ye might call a lawbreaker, and that's 'ow come I'm on this 'ere train."

Nathaira stared at the woman again. She didn't understand why the Sisters were letting this happen. And why, out of all the creatures captured, had she ended up next to a human? Hatred rose within her. The clan was dead because of humans. Moirin was dead because of humans. Everything wrong in Argdrion was because of humans and the wiar. At least the wiar had paid for their evilness with their extinction.

The woman hacked and spit again, the green and brown of her phlegm mixing as it sailed through the bars of the cage.

And yet she helped me... "Why did you help me?" Nathaira asked, curious.

The woman shrugged. "Ya would've died if I 'adn't, and although you may think that all 'umans are bad, we ain't." She picked at a tick on her face. "Most of you magic creatures think yer the only ones who suffered during the wars and 'unting, but yer not. There be many of us that never recovered from either of 'em."

Anger flooded through Nathaira. "What could you possibly know of what magical creatures have gone through?" she snarled. "Do you have magic? Were you hunted and driven from every corner of Argdrion until you had nowhere left to go? Did you feel the fire of the torturers, the silver of the hunters?"

The woman pulled the tick off with a pop, unperturbed by her ferocity.

"Well, my clan did," Nathaira said. "You know nothing of suffering." She turned away from the woman, inhaling as more pain ran through her shoulder and arm.

Sisters, why are you letting this happen? What is your reason?

"Ya got a family?" the woman asked after a moment, squishing the tick.

Nathaira didn't reply.

"What happened to 'em?"

"They died," Nathaira whispered, her heart tearing anew.

"Oh."

"All but my brother," Nathaira said softly, more to herself than the woman. A sudden thought occurred to her. She wheeled around. "A youngling of twelve years with eyes like a cloudless spring sky. Did you see him?"

The woman shook her head slowly and scratched at her leg again with long, scraggly nails. "Can't say that I did, but then, it's a long train, and 'e could be anywhere."

Nathaira turned her back on the woman again. It had been a foolish idea to ask her.

"But wait a moment," the woman said slowly. "I may 'ave seen a child a coupla days ago, but whether it was a boy or a girl, I can' say. Too far away like to tell. Curled up in the corner of its cage."

Nathaira sucked in a breath, hope rising within her. "Did you see its fingers?" she asked softly, staring at the team of horses pulling the wagon behind her. "Was there a black tattoo covering its right thumb?"

Every skinchanger received a tattoo on their right thumb on their eighth day of living to signify they were one of the people. If the child the woman had seen was Efamar, there would be a tattoo.

"Yah," the woman said unhurriedly. "It 'ad a tattoo on one thumb. It's 'ands was curled up over its 'ead, all protective like, so that's 'ow I know."

Nathaira was at the bars between them so fast the woman jumped. "What happened to the child? Did you see what happened to him?" She gripped the rain-slicked bars of iron until they groaned, barely feeling the pain in her shoulder.

"'e left," the woman said, eyeing her like she might change into a mountain lion and tear her to pieces. "The same day I saw 'im, 'alf of the wagons went down a crossroad, and the kid's wagon was one of 'em."

A raindrop landed on Nathaira's nose and hung there, quivering for a moment. She stared past the woman.

Gone. Efamar was gone, and she had done nothing to stop it. Athrysion's face flashed through her head. "Save Efamar, Nathaira…"

Nathaira slid down the bars of the cage to the bed of the wagon, numb to the pain in her shoulder or the rain drenching her clothes. Her last surviving clan member was gone, and she was alone.

#

The rain turned into a heavy downpour around midmorning, and by afternoon, the road was a muddy, miserable mess of puddles, streams, and potholes that slowed the wagon train to a crawl. By the time darkness came, they had only traveled a few miles, and the moods of the slavers were anything but friendly as they made camp in a large meadow.

Dirty white tents were set up and pits dug for campfires as the last of the wagons came to a stop in the wet, drooping grass, but Nathaira was oblivious to the slavers' ministrations as she sat in the far corner of her cage, staring into nothing.

Dead, dead, dead. The words were a constant, echoing chant in her head that couldn't be blocked out. Hadn't the clan suffered enough in years past without losing more? Weren't the humans happy with those of them they had slaughtered in the wars and the Hunting?

Nathaira looked up at a group of nearby slavers as they laughed at something, their silver masks wet with rain. She hated them. Hated their silver masks and their cages and their silver-tainted weapons. Athrysion had said that the reason the slavers wore masks was so that those they captured couldn't see their faces and, in case they escaped, couldn't come back to hurt them or their families. But what about the families that they hurt? Didn't they matter?

"Are ya just goin' to sit there feeling sorry fo' yerself all night?" the woman said loudly to be heard above the noise of the rain and slavers' work. "'Cause while that may make ya feel better, I don't see 'ow it's gonna 'elp ya."

Nathaira ignored her. The woman had helped her, saved her life, but she was a human, and humans were evil. She heard the woman shift, the chains on her wrists and ankles rattling, and felt the wet wagon bed move underneath her.

"At least ya don't have chains on ya like I do," the woman said. "Must be my 'istory of lock-picking and stealing. Bloody annoying, it is."

Efamar is not dead. Nathaira stared at a campfire wavering to life. Only where was he?

"Of course," the woman droned on, "at least I ain't being given tainted water like you are."

Nathaira turned slightly, glancing over her right arm to look at the woman. "What do you mean, 'tainted'?"

"With silver," the woman replied, rubbing at her crotch with one dirty hand. "The slavers give it to all you magic creatures to keep ya weak and powerless so's ya can't escape."

Nathaira glanced down at her legs, slick with rain where the trousers had been cut off. That would explain why her limbs felt like they were made of lead and why a constant, dull fire burned through her veins. The humans had been fond of silver ever since they had learned in the Second Great War that it could be used to control magical creatures like her people and the wiar.

"Real shame, really, that you ain't one for talking much," the woman said after a moment. "It's been damn boring since I was taken on this train. When I saw ya put in the cage next to mine, I was 'oping I'd 'ave some decent company."

"Why in Argdrion would I want to talk to you?" Nathaira said without really listening.

If I don't drink the water…

"Oh, I don't know," the woman said. "Maybe 'cause I know things that might be 'elpful to ya? Like where it is we's going?"

Nathaira glanced over her arm again, and the woman grinned. Her teeth were yellow.

"Ye ever 'eard of the arenas, skinchanger?"

"I've heard of them," Nathaira replied. Zeythra had taught her and Efamar many things about the humans and the history of Argdrion, including the massive arenas that King Athtiron, ruler of the kingdom of Eromor during the last half of the Second Great War and first part of the Third, had made to execute and torture prisoners of war in.

"Well, that's where we's going," the woman said. "An arena. The arena of Crystoln in Eromor, to be exact."

Nathaira watched several slavers in dirty ankle-length tunics struggling to erect a tent in the grass. The arena of Crystoln was renowned for its bloodbaths and brutality. It was said that rivers of blood flowed over Argdrion during the Great Wars but that the arena of Crystoln was covered in a lake of it. Thousands of her people had been slaughtered in the massive structure during the Third Great War, and hundreds more had been forced to "fight" for the humans while they watched, cheering as they died.

"How do you know this?" Nathaira asked the woman.

"I 'eard some of the slavers talking about it," the woman replied. "I would say yer brother is lucky to not be in our 'alf of the train."

Nathaira glanced away. Perhaps Efamar was lucky, or perhaps he was headed toward his death in a different arena. But then why would the humans send him to an arena when he couldn't change? They didn't know that, though…

I have to find him.

The solution to getting out was simple. She needed to stop drinking the water the slavers brought, and she would be able to change in a day or so, when the silver was completely out of her system. Nathaira glanced around the darkening field of wagons, campfires, slavers, horses, and guard dogs, wondering what creature was the best to change into.

"'ow old are ya, skinchanger?" the woman asked behind her.

Nathaira drew her legs closer to her chest as a chill shook her, hissing as fresh pain burned through her healing shoulder. She rested her chin on her knees. It was none of the human's business that her eighteenth nameday was nearing with the summer; it was none of the human's business about any of her life.

"I'm twenty-eight," the woman said, her chains rattling as she shifted. "Wouldna think so, would ya? I knows I look older, but I've 'ad me a 'ard life … You just gonna ignore me all night, skinchanger? 'Cause I'll keep talking til ya reply."

Nathaira pushed a wet strand of black hair out of her face and closed her eyes as the rain, which had misted for the last half hour, turned into a skin-pelting downpour. She stuck her tongue out to gather some of it, refreshing her parched throat.

The woman sighed loudly. "I thought I'd met me some quiet ones in me lifetime, but I do think that ya outdo 'em all. I know ya don't like me, but there's nothing else to do, and myself, I'm getting bored." She paused. "You still alive over there, or 'as that wound got to ya?"

A slaver's guard dog, an enormous creature with muscles rippling in lines beneath its black coat and a mangled scar stretching across its face, growled low in its throat. Nathaira's golden eyes snapped open to see it watching her through the bars of her cage. The dog's head was even with the wagon bed, its eyes peeking over. Nathaira met its gaze.

She wasn't afraid of it. She'd fought bears four times the dog's size.

They stared at each other for a moment before the dog finally broke eye contact and moved off.

"Those things give me the creeps," the woman said behind her.

Nathaira watched the dog walk away, its gait stiff and straight.

"They ain't natural." The woman shivered. "Those eyes, always watching ya; it's like they know that yer scared of 'em and are just waiting for ya to make one mistake so's they can tear ya apart. Yer braver than I am, that's for sure, skinchanger."

"Would you be quiet?" Nathaira yelled, louder than she meant to.

Several slavers at a campfire nearby glanced over at them, silver masks glistening with rain.

"Ya don't 'ave ta yell," the woman said. "I was just tryin' to get ya to talk, was all."

"Well, I don't want to talk, human," Nathaira spat, glancing over her shoulder at the woman. "Not now, not ever. So go away."

"Well, I would go away," the woman retorted, "but seeing's 'ow I'm locked up, that's kinda not an option."

Nathaira moved to the farthest corner of her cage. She curled up in a ball, trying to fall asleep.

Sleep eluded her, however, and as darkness fell over the meadow and the slavers disappeared into their tents for the nights, Nathaira found herself as wide awake as if she'd had a good night's rest. She rolled over onto her back, grimacing at the pain that jolted through her shoulder, and stared up at the sky.

The rain had stopped more than two hours before, and for a moment there was a break in the gray clouds looming over the meadow, revealing the dark sky and millions of twinkling stars beneath.

Somewhere up there was the clan, glittering stars watching over her. A tear, warm and salty, leaked out of Nathaira's eye and slid over her tattooed cheek. It was hard to believe that her clan was in the Sisters' Embrace, when just a few days ago she had sat with them around the fire they kept continually burning in the middle of their tree home. They were, though, and she was in Argdrion, never to see them again until she died hundreds of years from now.

And it was all the humans' fault. Nathaira's hands clenched into fists.

A star streaked in a trail of white fire across the sky and disappeared in the south, where the ocean and Warulan lay beyond.

Warulan. Nathaira shivered at the thought of the eastern continent and the arena of Crystoln on it. She had always longed to see more of Argdrion, but she hadn't dreamed of doing it as a slave going to fight in the arena.

One of the slaver's dogs, snoring in a pile with several others by the foot of a wagon, growled in its sleep and rolled over. Nathaira glanced over at it as clouds blew back over the stars. At least she could fight, though. Efamar could not.

"I don't know how, Athrysion," Nathaira whispered, looking back to the sky as the dogs continued to snore, "but I will save Efamar. I will not betray you. I will find him and save him."

A lone star winked through the clouds.

#

The slavers were up before the sky had finished growing light, taking down tents, stamping out fires, and hitching the horses back to the wagons.

The woman didn't talk as their wagon bumped and rattled after the others through a fir forest, down a steep and rocky hill with a waterfall crashing over it, and back into the forest again, and for that, Nathaira was thankful. She didn't relish listening to a human all day again.

At noon she was thrown a dry and moldy piece of rye bread, but fearing that it was tainted with silver, she tossed it to the black dog with a scar, who had taken to trotting along beside her wagon.

"'Ey!" the woman said, her first words of the day, as the dog sniffed the bread and trotted on. "Just cause ya ain't 'ungry don't mean all of us ain't!"

Nathaira ignored her. She could feel the silver fading from her veins, and in a few hours, she knew she would be able to change again and be free of her cage.

The axle of the wagon in front of hers broke not long after with a loud, grinding crack, and the wagon train came to a stop. It was an hour before it was repaired.

They were underway by afternoon, and as the rain began to pour again, they broke free of the forest and looked down on a large, sprawling wooden town that clung to the rocks like a barnacle and was covered by a cloud of dark smoke.

Beyond was the ocean.

Nathaira pushed herself onto her thighs as the wagon train slowly trailed down the hill toward the town. Ostgate. She moved to the edge of her cage to get a better glimpse of the raging gray sea beyond the town as it threw itself upon the rocky coast in foaming misty waves.

"Pretty, ain't it?" the woman asked, watching the sea too. "I was as awed as you when I first saw it, but after yer out on it for a week, you'll forget about its beauty and wish ye 'ad yer legs planted on good, solid ground again."

Nathaira breathed in the salty sea air as wind buffeted her face and drove rain into her eyes. The slate-gray ocean stretched for as far as her eyes could see in three directions away from the town and was broken only occasionally by black rocks jutting out of it like a giant's fingers pointing toward the dark sky. It was wild and powerful and the most beautiful thing she had ever seen.

Their wagon rumbled down the hill, and Nathaira turned her gaze to the town. Moirin had often told her stories of the humans and their dwellings. She had said that one could get anything they wanted in a human town.

"I wonder 'ow it is we'll die," the woman said, her gravelly voice breaking into her thoughts. "Do you think it'll be quick and merciful or long and slow?"

Nathaira glanced at her. She hadn't really thought about it at all. She wasn't planning on even going to the arena, much less dying in it.

"Me mum always said I'd die a 'orrible death," the woman went on. "'Cause of the way I live and all." She gave a bark of a laugh. "I guess she was right after all these years. Wonder if it makes her 'appy. Eh, Mother?" She glanced up at the gray sky. "You 'appy that I never did amount to nothin', after all?" She fell silent, and they rumbled past a large dirty pond and into the town.

It was filthy, that was the first thing Nathaira noticed. Everywhere her eyes rested there was mud and bird droppings and soot from the hundreds of smoking chimneys. It was also noisy.

"Bread!" a pale-faced man with a wild black beard yelled from a street corner.

"Fish!" another man with eyes tinged with yellow yelled from a smoke-stained shopfront.

"Rats!" a girl with a stick full of the stiff, swinging creatures called.

Nathaira watched two men with an ox-drawn cart struggle through the calf-high mud covering the streets, yelling for people to move out of the way as they went. How did the humans live like this?

A boy taunting a man whose head and hands were fastened in a wooden board ran up to the wagons, his filthy hands full of rotten vegetables and dirty eggs. "Loo'at the tattooed lady!" he yelled in a high-pitched, heavily accented voice. "She's got funny black markins over 'alf 'er body!"

A man drinking out of a bottle in the arch of a building with a worn sign reading "Tavern" hanging over the door glanced over at the boy's words and stepped out onto the street.

"It's a skinchanger!" he snarled in a hoarse, drink-worn voice. "I should know, I killed me enough of them in the Hunting!" The man took another swig out of his bottle and threw it against the side of the tavern with a crash. "Look what we've got here! A living, breathing skinchanger!"

Heads turned, and Nathaira moved away from the bars of her cage as a crowd gathered. A brown-splotched tomato whistled through the air toward her, and she ducked as it hit the bars of her cage with a splat and sprayed her with golden seeds.

The boy laughed.

"I lost my 'usband in the wars!" a bent and wrinkled old woman yelled. She waved a gnarled walking stick in the air. "To creatures like 'er and 'er kind!"

"I lost my brother and my right leg to one of those evil things!" another woman yelled.

Another tomato landed with a smack on the wagon bed, and Nathaira drew back with a hiss as seeds peppered her wounded arm.

"You!" a silver-haired man with one eye screamed, spittle flying from his mouth as he pointed a crooked finger at her. "It's creatures like you and the wiar that ruined Argdrion!"

He drew his arm back and threw an egg at her, and Nathaira reeled backward as it sailed through the spot she'd been a moment before and cracked open on the opposite side of the cage in an explosion of rotten yellow liquid and dirty shells. A smell like sulfur filled the air. Nathaira gagged as the crowd pressed around her wagon with hate-filled faces and outstretched hands.

"Kill 'er!" someone yelled. "Kill the skinchanger!"

Another took up the chant, and the rain-choked air rang with the cries as a hundred angry voices screamed for blood.

The wagon slowed to a crawl as several hands grabbed at the bridles of the horses pulling it. The slaver driving it started yelling along with the crowd as more rotten eggs, vegetables, and other sordid objects that Nathaira didn't care to think about pelted the wagon, driver, and horses and made the beasts add their screams of fright to the general racket.

A mud-streaked, blond-haired man reached through the bars of her cage, a savage expression on his face. Nathaira backed up, her heart racing as the man clawed at the wagon bed.

A whip crack echoed through the howling air, and a thin, braided cord of leather flew out of the back of the crowd and wrapped around the blond-haired man's neck. He screamed, and the crowd backed up as several slavers and their dogs pushed their way through the crowd.

"That is enough!" a tall slaver in a dirty white tunic yelled. He pulled on the whip in his hand, and the blond-haired man jerked backward and fell into the mud, a thin, bright-red welt circling his neck like a brand. "The skinchanger will pay for her crimes in the arena of Crystoln," the silver-masked, turbaned slaver yelled, voice thickly accented. "But I will not lose her to an angry mob of peasants seeking to get revenge!"

Crimes? What crimes? Nathaira glanced down at the blond-haired man as he coughed and pulled himself out of the mud. The only crimes committed had been by the humans in their murder of the clan and atrocities in the wars and the Hunting.

The blond-haired man spat a dark-brown glob of mucus at her as slavers circled the wagon, and it landed on the wagon bed next to her foot. Nathaira pulled her foot back.

"Now, unless you want to join the skinchanger," the tall slaver yelled, "I suggest that you move on and find better things to do with your time than hinder us!"

For a moment, Nathaira thought the crowd might attack the slavers, and she remained in her crouched position as angry glares and murmurs were thrown around. But then slowly the dirty boy moved away, and others soon began to follow until only a few—the blond man among them—remained watching as the slavers moved off. Her wagon began rolling again, lurching and rattling down the street at a crawl.

"Remind me not to get put next to ye again," the woman said in a slightly rattled voice.

Rain pounded on the wagon bed, washing away the objects thrown by the crowd. "If I 'ad known ye was so popular like, I would've asked for a different cage."

Nathaira ignored her, watching the blond-haired man stare at her until he disappeared from view.

They rolled past a large rundown building with smoke pouring out of seven chimneys and slowed to a stop by the sea, which crashed and raged like a living thing against the black rocks, marking the end of the land.

The slaver driving her wagon jumped down onto the road, mud squishing up around his ankles, and Nathaira wiped her black hair out of her face as he moved off among the wagons gathering around them and disappeared.

"I thought you said we were going to Warulan," she said, glancing over at the woman, who was picking corn out of her hair and popping it into her mouth with dirty fingers.

"We are," the woman murmured around a mouthful.

"Then where is the ship?" Nathaira asked, glancing out at the gray waves beating against the rocks below with a fury scarce matched.

"Oh, ya know about those, do ya?" the woman asked.

"My people are not ignorant," Nathaira replied coldly.

"Oh," the woman said, flicking a dark-brown blob off her arm. "Well, then in answer to yer question, the ship be out there." She pointed a hand toward the sea, and Nathaira followed it to see a dim shape far out on the water as the fog shifted in a cold, rain-driven wind.

"How in the Sisters' name do the slavers expect to get us out there?" she whispered.

"On rowboats," the woman replied, watching her. "I would'na throw around that name too much if I was ya."

Nathaira glanced over at her.

"The Sisters," the woman elaborated. "I've 'eard 'ow yer kind worship them and all, but those who worship the old religion ain't looked upon too kindly. Those words could get you killed, they could."

Better killed than to go to the Brothers' Fire. Nathaira glanced back out at the dark shape of the ship. They'd have to take her out of her cage to take her to it, and in the confusion of loading hundreds of creatures in the rain and fog, she would escape and find Efamar.

Footsteps squelched in the mud as if on cue, and Nathaira turned to see two slavers approaching the wagon, silver masks glistening with rain.

"Goodbye, then, skinchanger," the woman said as one slaver opened the door of her cage with a key from his belt and swung it open on creaky hinges. "Guess I'll see ya on the ship."

Not if the Sisters were on her side. Nathaira crouched in the corner of her cage as the other slaver, whip in hand, unlocked her cage and reached inside.

"On your feet, you," he barked, grabbing her by her wounded arm with a thick hand and pulling her toward him.

Nathaira snarled at the sudden pain and wrenched her arm out of the slaver's grasp. He yelled, and she kicked him in the chest before grabbing his head and slamming it into the floor of the wagon. The woman whooped as she jumped out of the cage and swung up on top, adrenaline rushing through her, and the slaver holding her backhanded her across the face and yelled something in his own language.

Two slavers unloading a pair of foxes from a nearby wagon glanced up and started forward. One of the foxes darted for freedom, and the men tripped over it and ended up sprawled in the mud.

Nathaira turned and ran, three dogs bowling through the mud below her with deep, bone-numbing barks as she jumped from bar to bar over her cage and across the woman's.

"Catch her!" a slaver yelled as thunder rumbled in the distance and rain began pouring harder.

A northerly breeze blew Nathaira's long hair out behind her as she reached the end of the cage. Leaping into the wind, she changed into a gray sparrow, flying out of her clothing as she was swept away with the breeze.

For a few joyful seconds, the dirty wooden buildings of the town drew nearer, and the shouts of the slavers and barking of their dogs faded into the distance, and Nathaira thought that she would be free.

A sharp whistling caught her ear, and a silver net shot out of a machine below and wrapped around her, pulling her toward the ground with a blinding pain.

Nathaira screamed and, changing into a peregrine falcon, tore at the braided strands with two-inch talons. One of her talons snapped in half, and she screamed again.

She hit the road with a thud, still tangled in the net. Mud filled her eyes and nose and mouth; Nathaira spat it out as she changed back into her natural form. Something warm and sticky drained down her right arm. Fresh, stabbing pain tore at her shoulder as well as her broken finger.

No! Nathaira rolled over onto her back as dogs and slavers ran toward her, tears of anger mixing with the mud in her eyes. She had been so close. She stared up at the gray sky above, gasping for air as silver burned at her skin.

So very, very close.

CHAPTER 6

Hathus

Hathus leaned over the rail of the *Eurosis* and let the sharp, salty sea breeze blow his lank brown hair out behind him. It felt good to be free again. And without his chest-length hair and beard. He ran a hand absentmindedly over his clean-shaven chin and smiled at the feeling of smooth skin again.

A lone seagull circled over the ship, its black and white body throwing a dark *m* on the deck as it loudly screeched past with the hope of a morsel of food.

Hathus glanced up at the bird, holding his wide-brimmed leather hat on with one hand and squinting against the Brothers' midday light. The *Eurosis* was a cargo ship, carrying goods from all corners of Argdrion to the continents and islands, and according to her captain was one of the fastest in the business. Hathus watched the seagull circle the vessel twice before it flew off toward the distant shoreline and their destination, the BalBayr Islands, pirate lair of Argdrion. He smiled at the sight of them.

It had been one month since he had been pulled out of the dungeons, talked to the Unknown Voice—the title he'd started calling his hirer after their first encounter in the dark marble room in the palace—and accepted the job of finding the Land of Dragons and bringing back a dragon's heart. That month had been the best of his life.

After being escorted out of the palace by the same men who had dragged him out of the dungeons, Hathus had received enough money to get cleaned up, buy new clothes, and pay for travel fare from Crystoln to the Land of Dragons. He'd also been set up in a comfy room in one of Crystoln's finest hotels. Eating a meal fit for five people was the first thing he'd done, followed by a rose-scented bath, which he'd soaked in for five hours. Then came a shave and haircut, and finally, a fourteen-hour nap in the king-sized bed.

Hathus watched sailors climbing through the rigging of the *Eurosis*, tying up sails and readying the ship for slowing down. He glanced down the deck at the three men that the Unknown Voice had sent with him to make sure he followed through on his part of the deal. He shifted, a quivering muscle in his leg giving him a cramp. The men were with him for another reason: to carry the two small chests of aray that the Unknown Voice had sent with him to pay for a ship to take him to the Land of Dragons.

Hathus glanced back up at the sailors in the rigging, the brim of his hat curling up in the wind. The whole thing was so ridiculous, but it was also terrifying. Terrifying because he was looking for a magical world, and if anyone who was on the side of the authorities found that out, he could be turned in and executed. Hathus shifted, uncomfortable at the thought. He'd had no choice, though, and as long as he was careful, in six months, he'd be free.

Free. The thought was like a cool glass of wine after being in the dungeons for three and a half years. Or nine months. He'd found out that his calculations had been wrong, and his time in the dungeon had been considerably shorter than he had thought. It had *felt* like three and a half years.

After his month of recovery in Crystoln, he had traveled from Eromor to the kingdom of Seyrwyth, where he'd found the *Eurosis* and set sail for the BalBayr Islands. From there he would look for a ship to take him to his final destination.

Hathus scratched at his sunburned nose and pulled the brim of his hat back down so that it shaded his face. He had bought the hat two days after he'd been set free from the dungeons, after he'd gone sightseeing in Crystoln and had his face and neck sunburned to a crisp. The hat was huge and looked stupid, but it kept his pale skin shaded, so he wore it.

Hathus picked at a peeling piece of skin on the tip of his nose. It would have to be a pirate ship that he hired, because only pirates would agree to be associated with magic by looking for an otherworld. Being on the shady side of the law, they didn't mind magic, and most of them had dealings in it themselves anyway. He didn't expect it would be too hard to find a ship willing to take him—the islands were teeming with pirates willing to go anywhere for the right amount of money. Even looking for a mythical otherworld. All he had to do was leave word around that he wanted a ship and was willing to pay big for it, and they would come swarming to him like sharks to prey.

Hathus pulled his brown leather coat open with a bony hand as the humid heat of the islands fanned the decks of the ship. He scanned the nearing coastline as the captain of the *Eurosis*, a rough-spoken but likeable man, yelled orders to the crew. He'd missed the islands in his imprisonment. The lush green of the jungle that dominated the parts of them not covered with buildings. The crystalline-blue water chock full of colorful fish enclosing them. And the hundreds of mismatched, brightly painted buildings crowding what land was not already covered by jungle.

A flock of green and gold parakeets winged past the ship in a colorful blur.

In the distance, the current pirate queen's palace roof gleamed atop the jungle-covered mountains dominating the islands' center. Hathus focused on the glinting, golden-doomed roof of the building.

Wonder what the queen's up to today? Though his legs were still weak from his long imprisonment, he found that he was able to walk now, albeit with numerous much-needed breaks, and he could stand like a normal man. His energy was coming back too, after nearly a month of mostly sleeping and eating, and he had gained ten pounds on his bony frame. He wasn't fully back to his former health by any means, but he was getting there.

Hathus grimaced as the ship hit a large swell that rocked him forward. He readjusted his grip on the railing. He hated traveling by sea. The constant swaying, the threat of a storm and sinking, the boring hours of nothing to do; he hated all of it. Still, it was better than being locked in the dungeons of Crystoln. Hathus leaned on the railing and watched Main Island loom closer. He wondered who the Unknown Voice was. Had wondered since he'd met him. Was he some rich noble looking for fame by hoping to find a mythical creature? Or was he just a crazy man? Whoever he was, he had to be a noble or a knight he'd concluded, because no one else could have used a room of the palace to talk to him.

Hundreds of ships choking the Main Island's massive half-moon harbor came into detail.

The golden sandstone fortress that guarded the largest island's harbor entrance from atop one of the towering cliffs glared down at them as the *Eurosis* sailed smoothly past and into the bay. A shiver ran up Hathus's spine as he glanced up at the massive structure, which shadowed the waters below like the fabled shadow of death.

The fortress had been built, it was said, by fifteen thousand ebony slaves from the indigenous tribes of humans inhabiting the northern deserts of Araysann. Captured by the Zarcayran slavers and shipped to all corners of Argdrion, the slaves were said to have erected the massive stronghold in just three years and afterward had been slain and tossed into the deepest part of the bay—directly below the fortress—where chasms ran for miles and bodies were never found.

Hathus watched the sandstone walls looming above them as they sailed past, imagining the spyglasses that were trained on them by pirates making sure they were a merchant ship and not a warship from one of the kingdoms, come to attack their haven.

There had been numerous battles fought on the islands since the first pirate queen had claimed them for piratekind, but somehow, even though many a powerful kingdom had stood against them, the pirates had always managed to win, and finally, after losing too many soldiers in the attempt to drive them from existence, the kingdoms of Argdrion had opted to leave the BalBayr Islands alone.

The *Eurosis* glided past the fortress, and Hathus breathed a sigh of relief. If the pirates had deemed them a threat, they'd have had twenty scorpion bolts through their decks and would be swimming with the dead slaves at the bottom of their watery grave. He tore his eyes away from the citadel as the *Eurosis* began to slow and turned his gaze to the noisy, crowded harbor ahead.

Hundreds of ships, pirate and merchant alike, covered the gently bobbing blue waters while sweating slaves and sailors unloaded their wares onto the curving docks that ringed the inner side of the bay.

The BalBayr Islands were a pirate haven, but they were also home to one of the biggest harbors in Argdrion and the busiest trading hub. Thousands of merchants slightly on the shady side of life flocked to the islands to sell their wares, buy items that couldn't be found on any of the continents, and spend their money on the hundreds of taverns, brothels, and other assorted pleasurable activities that the islands held. At the same time, these merchants pretended that they would never set foot on the barbarous islands for all the money in the world.

Hathus smiled. It was funny, really. Pirates mainly raided merchant ships for the treasures in their hulls, and yet the same merchants came to the islands to sell their wares to the pirates who raided them. It was a convoluted business.

Sailors jogged past, securing the last of the *Eurosis's* sails as the large ship neared the other ships crowding the harbor.

Hathus moved away from the rail and climbed the worn wooden steps to the forecastle deck, where the burly captain and his pock-faced first mate stood, their dark-green jackets flapping in a humid breeze that made shirts stick to skin and sweat appear in drops.

"Beautiful sight, isn't it, sir?" the captain rumbled, large feet planted shoulder width apart and hairy hands crossed behind his back.

Hathus nodded, resting a black-gloved hand on the hilt of the dagger at his hip as he stopped next to the captain. "Indeed it is, Captain," he said, "indeed it is." It was so good to see the islands again. It had been too long. Too very, very long.

"We'll be landing on Main Island in a moment," the captain said. He turned and murmured something to the first mate.

Hathus nodded in reply, putting a hand up to steady his hat against the breeze again. The BalBayr Islands were made up of over a hundred islands, several of which held the towns and cities that housed its population—the rest were too small for much more than a palm tree or an occasional loner's hut—but Main Island had always been the richest. And the one he loved the most.

"You'd better have more of a weapon than that to defend yourself if you're planning on roaming the streets of the islands," the captain said, jerking his head at the dagger at Hathus's hip before giving a quick command to his first mate, who nodded and jogged off to carry it out.

Hathus smiled inwardly. Some people didn't need big weapons to defend themselves as long as they had quick minds and even quicker feet. Besides, he'd never much liked carrying a larger weapon around. For one thing, it was too bulky and took up too much room. Harder to conceal too. And for another, it stated that you were not a person to mess with, and that invited many unwanted fights.

"I'll invest in one when I reach the shore," he told the hairy captain with a nod. The tangy sea air brushed his face and tickled his chest through the deep V in his white silk shirt.

The captain glanced sideways at him. "Is this your first time to the islands, son?"

Hathus told him yes. There was no need to tell the man he knew the islands like the back of his still-bony hand, and besides, it would be contradictory to what he'd told him when he'd boarded the *Eurosis*: that he was the inexperienced son of a wealthy businessman, coming to scope out a place for a new leg of his father's business.

"Well, take my advice, boy," the deep-voiced captain said, his dark-blue eyes taking on a fatherly shine. "Buy yourself a good weapon, don't stay in a tavern, and never drink anything that you don't see them make in front of you. Somebody's always trying to slip something into your drink on the islands so that they can sell you as a slave or rob you blind."

"I've got friends," Hathus said.

The captain glanced at the three men, who'd followed Hathus across the ship and were now standing several feet away, watching everything from under their concealing cloaks. "Yes, well, your father was smart to send them with you."

The *Eurosis's* massive iron anchor was thrown overboard with a splash, and they glided to a stop between two other merchant ships that were waiting for their turn to be unloaded onto the distant, noisy docks.

A rowboat was lowered into the pristine water of the harbor, and after bidding goodbye to the captain, who in turn bade him a safe journey and pleasant travels, Hathus grabbed his leather bag from his cabin below and, followed by the three men and their precious cargo, settled himself at the stern of the rowboat, one hand trailing in the blue water, the other still resting on the silver ball atop the leather-wrapped handle of his knife. Two sweating sailors in striped bandannas rowed him across the deep water of the harbor and toward the docks.

A balmy breeze rustled Hathus's hair, stroking his face with moist fingers as the sailors pulled back on their oars with bulging tanned muscles. Hathus breathed deeply of the wind as the two men brought the rowboat to a stop next to a rusty iron ladder climbing the side of a barnacled dock.

Bidding the rowers good sails, he snatched his bag off the damp bench next to him, threw it over his shoulder, and climbed up the creaky ladder two rungs at a time. The three men followed. Hathus barely noticed. After being trailed by them for almost a month, he was beginning to get used to their presence.

He swung a leg over the top rung of the ladder and onto the docks and smiled.

Hello, old friend. He closed his eyes and let the scent of the islands embrace and welcome him like a lover's perfume. Sweaty bodies, human and animal waste, rotten fruit and fish, alcohol, opirya and various other weeds, and last but not least, brothels.

Gods, but it feels good to be back.

Palm trees lining Wharf Street, the cobbled street that ran parallel to the docks, rustled in a warm breeze that blew in off the sea with a hint of salt, distant shores and excitement on it. Humans of all races and from all corners of Argdrion filled the air with an assortment of languages. Bejeweled and scantily clad men and women flaunted their bodies. Sellers bellowed their wares in the common tongue. And above it all was the noise of brawls, levity, and fun from the hundreds of taverns and houses of ill repute cramming the streets.

How I've missed this. Hathus motioned for a nearby dockworker, and the man, sweat glistening on his half-naked body, stepped over to him.

"Spread the word," Hathus said, handing the man three capus. "I need a ship, and I will pay well."

The man nodded, slipping the coins into his cut-off trousers, and Hathus moved off through the crowded docks. He headed toward a busy street that climbed up toward the island's center and was lined with noisy, crowded taverns. Two of the three men trailing him disappeared, off to put half of the money into a bank.

A wind-beaten wooden sign, half hidden behind purple-flowered bushes, read "Queen's Way," and Hathus stopped underneath it to watch the passersby's stream past for a moment. Slaves, thieves, prostitutes, pirates, sailors, rent boys, traders, gamblers, merchants, nobles. He grinned. The islands certainly held all kinds. It was part of the reason why he loved them so.

A two-story whitewashed tavern with weather-worn black trim and a matching black door caught his attention, and Hathus dove back into the crowd of pleasure seekers, sailors, pirates, and merchants and pushed his way toward it. While he waited for ship captains to come to him, he might as well have some fun.

A salt-corroded sign hanging above the tavern's door read "The Bloody Boar" in faded red letters sprawled beneath the crude depiction of a raging, blood-dripping boar. Uproarious laughter and cigar and opirya smoke spilled out of the open door and into the busy street.

Hathus peered inside.

Good, it's packed.

One of the first things he'd learned as a thief was to frequent the busier locations when stealing, for where there were more people, there were more distractions, and therefore less chance of being caught.

Hathus cracked his fingers and tucked his black leather gloves into his pockets. "Time to work again, old boy."

#

Six hours, three tankards of rum, and a gain of thirty yura later, Hathus scanned the smoke-choked tavern room for the five hundredth time before guzzling his fourth pewter mug of spiced rum and motioning to a passing barmaid for another. He pulled a tarnished gold pocket watch he'd stolen from a passing sea captain earlier from the pocket of his white silk shirt and checked the carved metal hands methodically. Three hours after the suns had set, still nothing.

"You going to move, fella, or do we just take your money and keep playing?"

Hathus looked up from the carved hands of the watch and smiled blandly at the scar-faced sailor glaring at him from across the pockmarked table. He had an assortment of coins in a pile in front of him. Golden aray, faced with the Sisters on one side and the sign of life—four triangles crossing—on the other. And silver yura, which were marked by the Brothers on one side and two intertwining staves on the other.

"Three aray and two yura," Hathus said, pushing the coins to the middle of the table.

Hathus eyed the coins. It was strange, really. The old religion was outlawed and all but gone from Argdrion, and yet the Sisters and Brothers were still on the two highest-value coins for all to see. He snapped the watch shut with a click as the sailor grunted and looked at his hand of cards.

They'd better be good, friend, because I do believe I've got the winning hand.

Hathus pocketed the watch and picked his own hand of cards up from the dirty tabletop in front of him. He smiled slowly.

Three Rowans and two Brys. What a coincidence. The chief god of Warulan and his lovely wife together.

He glanced around the table at the other players. The scar-faced, broken-nosed sailor; his pudgy friend; a dirty boy barely out of his teens with a nervous blinking twitch; and a muscled black man with brown and blond-dyed dreadlocks that were swept back from his head and hung well past the dark-blue, gold-buttoned vest he wore.

"Your turn, man," the scarred sailor growled to the dreadlocked man. He spat a wad of brown tobacco onto the already filthy wooden floor.

Hathus watched the dreadlocked man's strange amber eyes. He'd never seen eyes quite like them. They were kind of creepy, really.

The boy scanned his cards, his pile of money, and his cards again.

"I fold," the man with amber eyes said in a lilting accent. His lips broke into a wide smile as he placed his cards face down on the table and rested his long hands on top of them.

The scarred sailor snorted and pushed four aray out to join the growing pile. "I see your bet, fancy fellow, and raise it another two yura." He sneered at Hathus with a cocky, confident smile.

His friend shook his head with a sigh and laid his cards down on the table in front of him. "Too steep for me."

Now it was down to the dirty boy with the nervous twitch. Hathus eyed the youth over the top of his cards. The barmaid appeared at his elbow and, smiling widely, showed several missing teeth that somehow countered the effect of her low-cut ribboned blouse. She placed a fresh mug of rum in front of him. The dirty boy blinked several times and leaned out over the table to look at the pile of coins in the middle before looking back at his cards, his brow furrowing in thought.

"Are you going to go or not, boy?" the scarred sailor growled loudly.

The boy, blinking rapidly, started as if woken from a dream and quickly shoved five aray out into the pile, his hands shaking slightly. "See your bet and raise it one aray," he said quickly.

Hathus eyed him over his cards.

He must not do this much…

Where the boy had gotten that kind of money he would love to know, but right now he had more important things to do, like win. Hathus sipped the frothy bubbles off the top of his mug and let the fiery, spicy liquid drain down his throat.

He pushed five aray out into the growing pile of coins in the middle of the table and laid his hand face up on the table in front of him. "Full house, rowan high." It was all he could to do to not smile.

"Oh, that's a good one, honey!" the barmaid squealed. She leaned in front of him to look at his cards, and Hathus allowed himself a look at her copious cleavage before glancing around the table.

"No one else?"

The blinking boy shook his head.

Hathus leaned forward to collect his money.

"Wait, fancy fellow," the scar-faced man growled, slapping a hand with a tattoo of a naked woman on the back onto the pile of coins. "That's the fifth hand in a row you've won tonight. That seems pretty lucky to me. In fact, it seems like more than luck—it seems like cheating."

Hathus glanced up at the man. "Well, I've got another answer for you."

"Oh, and what's that?"

Hathus smiled. "Maybe you're just bad players."

"You…" The scar-faced man's chair ground loudly on the wooden floor as he pushed it back and reached for the dagger on his belt.

The smile faded from Hathus's face.

Someday I'll learn to keep my mouth shut…

The barmaid made some excuse about having to serve another table and disappeared into the smoke-filled room.

Traitor.

"I wouldn't do that if I was you, friend," the dreadlocked man said evenly.

"And why's that?" the scar-faced man growled, turning his wild gaze to him.

Hathus quietly began gathering his money. *Why does this always happen to me?*

"Well, for one thing," the dreadlocked man said calmly, "accusing a man of cheating when he is simply a good player is impolite. And for another, my scimitar is bigger than your knife." He flashed a humorless smile, and Hathus stopped counting his money and looked up.

The boy blinked rapidly.

The scar-faced man narrowed beady black eyes. "You're bluffing."

"Carry on with what you started and see if I am."

"Come on, Gyrd, let's just go," the scar-faced man's friend said quietly.

Hathus slipped coins into the leather purse on his belt.

Yes. Why don't you do that?

Gyrd stared at the dreadlocked man for a moment, and Hathus wondered if he shouldn't leave the rest of the money and go.

"Bastards!" Gyrd man spat finally. He threw his cards down on the table with a snarl and slapped his fleshy companion on the shoulder before kicking his chair over and stalking out of the smoky tavern, pulling his black knitted hat onto his head as he went.

Hathus let out a breath he hadn't realized he'd been holding as the door shut behind them. The three men the Unknown Voice had sent with him stood near the door. He scowled at them.

Thanks for the help, guys.

Hathus felt the black man's eyes on him. He glanced up at him. "Thank you for your help, friend," he said, smiling. "That was a good bluff, but I think I could have handled it myself."

"That I doubt," the dreadlocked man replied. "And it wasn't a bluff." He leaned his elbows on the tabletop, watching him intently.

Whatever. Hathus gave him another smile and went back to shoving his coins into the purse on his belt.

The blinking boy got up and wandered away, joining another table on the other side of the noisy, crowded tavern full of raucous pirates and scantily clad rent boys and whores. The barmaid came back and leaned on Hathus's chair again. It was funny how friendly people got when one had money.

The man continued to stare. Hathus could feel his strangely unsettling eyes on his face as the barmaid ran a finger with a painted nail over the square outline of his jaw and down the front of his shirt.

What is his problem, anyway? Does he expect a reward or something? Or does he want to steal my money?

Finally, annoyed, Hathus looked up from stashing his coins and raised his eyebrows. "Can I help you?"

"I noticed that you keep checking your watch and scanning the room like you are expecting someone," the dreadlocked man replied, his amber eyes still focused intently on him.

Hathus shrugged. "I like to keep track of my surroundings, make sure no one's sneaking up on me." He started counting again.

Thirty-five aray, seventeen yura...

"Could it be that you are seeking a ship?"

Hathus looked up from his counting again. "And why would I be seeking a ship?" He pursed the last of the coins and downed his rum.

"Perhaps you wish to go somewhere," the dreadlocked man replied, watching him.

Hathus eyed him over his empty mug. It was about time someone came.

"Or not." He smiled, shuffling the deck of cards and looking around the room again. It was best to not let him think that he was too desperate for a ship. There would be bargaining over the price of travel, and if he played it right, he might be able save some of the money that the Unknown Voice had given him for himself.

"I know a ship that can take you where you wish to go," the dreadlocked man said.

"Supposing I did wish to go somewhere, you don't know where that is," Hathus said, still not looking at him. He would have to be careful about what he said when he was hiring a ship. No one could know that the Unknown Voice had hired him to go to the Land of Dragons. He'd already thought up what he would say—that he had a theory that the Land of Dragons and the treasure rumored to be in it were real, but that the legend of dragons was made up to keep people away. Pirates loved the idea of looking for treasure.

"This ship does not care," the dreadlocked man replied. He told the barmaid to find another table. She made a rude gesture at them and stomped off across the room, her bright-red skirt swishing around her ample hips.

Hathus shuffled the cards again and glanced back at the dreadlocked man.

"This ship will take you anywhere that you wish to go in Argdrion," the man said. "For a price."

Hathus set the cards on the table in front of him, making a pretense of thinking about it. "That's just the thing, friend," he said after a while, looking back up at the dreadlocked man. "I don't want to go to anywhere *in* Argdrion."

CHAPTER 7

Darkmoon

Darkmoon ran a finger through the ash covering a broken, toppled cupboard. His fingertip came away black.

Death. The smell was overwhelming, and the signs, the signs were everywhere. Broken bodies beneath fallen wooden beams, burned skeletons buried in ash that still floated through the air and left a foul taste in his mouth, mangled chunks of flesh lying about like scraps thrown to the dogs.

Darkmoon glanced at a sign creaking in a plume of smoke that billowed up from a still-burning oil barrel. He knew this place. His eyes scanned the few letters on the sign that were not charred and black like the rest of the wood. He knew those words.

A raven cawed. Darkmoon's eyes darted to the bird, which was sitting on the upraised arm of a half-burned body. He was in a dream, he knew, but why here? He hadn't thought of this place in years. Years upon years.

"Darkness is coming," the raven squawked, blood draining out of its red eyes.

Darkmoon eyed it.

"Blood will follow…" the raven cawed.

Darkmoon turned and walked away. If this was a dream, then he could choose where it went and where it took him. And he did not want to be taken to this place.

His surroundings changed.

He was on a grass-covered hill, one of many overlooking a meadow of flowers. A warm wind made the grass around him sway and hiss against his black suede pants; the suns rested hazily, burning in the late summer sky.

The voice of the raven came on the wind, brushing against his ears, whispering in his mind, "Darkness is coming…"

Darkmoon ignored the bird, focusing instead on the two boys winding their way through the flowers below. He could hear what they were saying as if he were one of them, but then, at one time, he had been.

"Do you think Mother would like this one?" Darkmoon asked his brother, Cyron. They were twins, but Cyron had been born first, by three minutes. Sometimes those three minutes felt like three years to Darkmoon. Cyron was taller than him, stronger than him, braver than him, wiser than him, and he looked up to him like a brother that was years and years older.

Cyron took Darkmoon's delicate fingers and the fuzzy yellow dandelion held in them into his larger hands, already strong and muscled for a six-year-old. "I think that she would love it," Cyron said kindly. "You know how she always wears flowers, even at the castle."

Cyron smiled, his solid green eyes filled with warmth and kindness, as always. It was said that Cyron was the handsomer of the twins, and Darkmoon believed it. Whereas his own face was sharp and pale and his lips thin, Cyron's square face always had a rosy tint to it, and his lips were full and red.

Darkmoon's mouth broke into a smile at his brother's words. He added the dandelion to the bunch of assorted flowers in his other hand, his small fingers straining to wrap around the stems. Their mother loved flowers. There were always red or pink or yellow blossoms entwined in her long black hair or dangling in strands from her limbs. Vases of vibrant blooms were never wanting around her forest house.

Cyron moved off through the flower field, and Darkmoon followed, his smaller frame dwarfed by that of his brother. He trailed thin fingers over grape hyacinths and poppies as they walked, marveling at the velvety smoothness of the poppies' petals and the perfect roundness of the hyacinths' clustered heads. There was a hypnotizing power in flowers, something that made him want to curl up in a bed of them and sleep for hours with the suns warming his cheeks and the sweet, intoxicating scent of the flowers filling his nose.

Cyron knelt by a wild patch of black-bearded red irises, his black hair glistening in the Brothers' warming rays. "Some of these," he said, pulling the large flowers from their slender pale-green stalks with soft popping noises. "And then I think that'll be enough. What do you think, brother?"

Darkmoon slipped up next to Cyron, glancing down into his kneeling brother's eyes with his own mismatched blue and green ones. Some said that twins shared a mind, an unexplainable bond that could not be broken. But Cyron and he, they shared more than their minds—they shared a soul.

"And maybe some more yellow to accent the red?" Darkmoon questioned. He turned the sweet-smelling bouquet in the Brothers' warming noon rays to better assess the color. Bluebells, poppies, hyacinths, dandelions, bleeding hearts, and mustard seed. Mother was going to love them.

"You've always had an eye for the finer details, brother." Cyron smiled. "Yellow it is." He handed the red irises to Darkmoon and crawled to a nearby group of yellow daffodils bobbing in a warm summer breeze.

"Mother will be very happy with this bouquet," Cyron called as he pinched the daffodil stems to break them off. "I can't wait to see the smile on her face when we bring them to her. Which ones do you think she'll like the best? The bleeding hearts or the mustard seeds…"

A fluttering of wings caught Darkmoon's ear as he waited for Cyron to gather enough of the daffodils, and he looked up to see a raven, its glossy black wings glinting purple and blue in the sunlight, sitting on an iris stalk a few feet away. He frowned. How did such a large bird rest on such a small object without snapping it? He stepped toward the raven, flowers brushing around his legs as he walked toward it.

"Darkness is coming," the raven squawked, eyes burning like two bloody suns. "Blood will follow…"

Darkmoon stopped a few feet away from it, surprised. "Cyron…" he said as blood began draining out of the raven's eyes. "This raven can talk… and I think it's sick. There is blood coming out of its eyes."

Cyron didn't reply, and Darkmoon glanced over his shoulder to see why. The scenery changed again, going from the sun-warmed flower field to a cold hall of gray stone and towering pillars.

No roof sat over the middle of the hall, only a gaping and jagged hole that let in a mixture of falling ash and snow that covered everything in a fine gray film.

Darkmoon glanced down at the flowers in his hand. They wilted under his gaze and turned into a black ash that drifted away through his fingers and joined the snow and ash covering the floor.

"Darkness is coming," the raven's voice echoed through the rows and rows of pillars leading off on either side of him. Darkmoon looked up, his blue and green eyes going to the opposite end of the hall, where a stone dais and four wooden chairs sat.

"Blood will follow..." the raven cawed.

Wingbeats flapped by, and Darkmoon glanced sideways to see the raven flying between the pillars to his left. The bird disappeared into the shadows, the humming of its pumping wings fading into the distance.

He began walking, soft leather ankle boots crunching in the snow and ash coating the floor. It was cold in the hall, and not a sound other than his footsteps echoed through it. Darkmoon wrapped his arms around his thin body, scanning the hall as he walked.

Chunks of stone lay scattered over the floor, fallen from the roof above or blasted out of the fat pillars that held the remains of the roof up. Black tapestries with silver moons hung from several of the pillars or lay in heaps on the floor, ripped and smoldering.

A pile of stone and iron sat in the middle of the room where the roof had caved in. Broken iron candlesticks that would have stood taller than him if they had been upright lay thrown around the room.

Darkmoon moved around the heap of rubble that had been the roof. He glanced behind him, scanning the pillars and the darkness between them. There should be laughter in the hall, and candlelight and music and people in rich clothing and dark jewels. If he looked hard, he could see them in his mind and hear the music that played at the banquets that his father held.

His foot bumped into something hard, and Darkmoon looked back in front of him to see that he had reached the dais. Two straight-backed wooden chairs lay with their backs to him on the stone platform. Two others sat smashed on the floor on either side of the dais. One of those chairs was his, the one on the right side of the dais.

Long cobwebs, silver in color and heavy with ash and snow, hung from the arms of the chairs. Snow covered the chairs in a fine gray film.

Darkmoon's mismatched eyes caught on a leg that stuck out from under one of the chairs on the dais. It was naked of clothing and most of its skin, and maggots were crawling through the flesh. He paled and took a step backward. The chair belonged to his father.

A bare arm, obviously a woman's by the delicate hand attached to it—though it was bloodstained and burned—poked out from underneath the other chair, its flesh ripped off in strips, with black burn marks showing underneath. Darkmoon felt a scream bubble up in his throat. He backed up further, terror filling him. That chair was where Mother sat.

"Brother," Cyron said behind him.

Darkmoon wheeled.

Cyron knelt in the ash and snow in front of him, dressed in a simple blue tunic and black pants, his feet bare.

"Cyron," Darkmoon exclaimed, relieved. He stepped toward him. Cyron would tell him what was happening, why their father's castle was like this, if those corpses were their parents. Cyron would make it better. Cyron always made everything better.

Darkmoon met his brother's eyes. There was fear in them, and shock and sadness. Darkmoon stopped.

"Brother, why?" Cyron whispered. Tears glistened in his green eyes, wet streaks shone on his cheeks.

Darkmoon stared at him, sorrow and pain and fear filling him. He heard his voice, his adult voice, so soft and smooth, coming out of his child's mouth. "I'm so sorry, Cyron."

"Why?" Cyron whispered.

Darkmoon felt tears slipping out of his own eyes. "I'm sorry."

"Please," Cyron said. "Please, no..." He fell to his hands on the snow-and-ash-covered stones below, his head snapping back as he let out a scream that filled the ruined hall.

Darkmoon watched Cyron scream, heard himself saying sorry over and over again.

"Darkness is coming," the raven cawed, perched on a tipped-over candlestick nearby. "Blood will follow..."

Blood drained out of Cyron's nose and ears. He screamed again, and it spurted out of his mouth.

Darkmoon heard his six-year-old self crying.

"Darkness is coming…" the raven cried again. "Blood will follow…"

Darkmoon closed his eyes to Cyron's pained face, tried to close his ears to his screams.

"Brother!" Cyron screamed, terror in his voice.

Darkmoon put his hands to his ears, sobbing now. He heard Cyron fall to the floor, heard him twisting and writhing and screaming.

"Darkness is coming," the raven cawed, louder now. "Blood will follow!"

Darkmoon felt its wingbeats go by his face, saw it in his mind's eye as it flapped off down the hall.

"Darkness is coming," the raven cawed, voice fading as Cyron fell silent. "Blood will follow, war is here, death is upon us…"

"Good morning."

Darkmoon's green and blue eyes snapped open, and a dark-skinned, pretty-faced prostitute with red henna tattoos running over her face smiled shyly at him.

She blushed. "Did you sleep good?"

Her voice gave her away as still being in her teens, even though she tried to make it deeper, and seemed to be coming from a long ways away. Darkmoon blinked, confused for a moment.

Where am I?

The prostitute ran a small finger up his left bicep, and he closed his eyes, remembering. He'd come into Sussār early the day before, and having a day before the scheduled kill of his next victim, he'd found a brothel to occupy his time.

"I slept good," the prostitute whispered, fingering the black-iron-wrapped ebony claw that hung by a cord from his neck before tracing the three lengthy scars running down his left pectoral.

Darkmoon opened his eyes again, hearing Cyron's screams. Ever since the seer had approached him in Ryrdion, he had been hearing voices from his childhood. But this was the first dream that he had had, the first visual of his past.

A detailed silk covering with elephants stitched onto it hung over the bed, long ends sweeping down on either side and touching the sandstone floor. Darkmoon stared at the silk, seeing the hall.

She was a virgin, the prostitute, or had been, and he had payed highly for the privilege of bedding her.

"Darkness is coming…" Darkmoon saw the blood-eyed bird in his mind. The seer had said that his past would haunt him, burn him. But she had not spoken of the raven. Its warning was the same as hers, though, that darkness was coming to Argdrion, and death…

He heard Cyron's voice again, screaming his name. Darkmoon closed his eyes.

It had taken most of his money from the job of killing the heiress's son to get the prostitute. He wasn't sure that it was well spent. But he had to do something with the money he made, and since he already had more mansions and riches than most kings, blowing his earnings on one-night stands was all he had left. That and buying antiques and treasures. And chocolate. He always needed chocolate.

"How do you do it?" the prostitute asked.

Darkmoon opened his eyes again and glanced sideways at her, cocking his scar-cut right eyebrow in question.

"How do you stay so young and handsome?" she whispered. Her face was soft and youthful, and she blushed and looked down when he looked at her. "I've heard stories about you," she said. "Stories that you've been around for over fifty years." She glanced up from under dark lashes. "Are they true?"

Darkmoon looked back at the silk above them. "Don't believe everything that you hear," he said.

The seer had said darkness and fire was coming to Argdrion, and while he didn't really care if the world was destroyed, he did wonder what was coming. The wars and the Hunting had been horrible and devastating, and yet the seer had said that what was coming would be worse. What could possibly be worse than what had already happened?

"But how old are you?" the prostitute asked. She traced patterns across his chest with the fingers of one hand.

Older than you think…

Darkmoon continued to stare at the silk. And if this coming darkness was as horrible as the seer said, then how was he expected to save Argdrion?

He hadn't been able to save his family all those years ago. He hadn't been able to save himself.

"Brother…" Cyron whispered again. Darkmoon stiffened, the hall and its shadows and ash and bodies playing through his mind.

"Twenty-five?" the prostitute queried.

The hall disappeared again.

"Well, are you?" the prostitute pushed after a second. She was growing bolder; they all did after their first night.

"An assassin has many secrets," Darkmoon said tonelessly, hearing Cyron's screams. "If I told you mine, it wouldn't be a secret anymore."

The prostitute stuck her lip out in a pout and rested her cheek on his bare chest. Her skin was warm against his. Darkmoon didn't put his arm around her as she snuggled closer, didn't touch her. He never slept with the same woman twice. He didn't get attached, didn't stay, didn't fall in love. It wasn't that he was afraid of love; he just felt nothing toward the women he bedded. He stared at a stitching of a golden elephant in the silk above. He hadn't felt love in years, since before Cyron had knelt before him, begging him…

"How many people have you killed?" the prostitute asked, interrupting his thoughts once more.

Darkmoon saw the dais and the chairs again. "More than you've bedded," he said, pushing the memories from his head.

The prostitute giggled, breath brushing his chest. "Where did you get your scars?" she whispered, pushing herself up on her forearms and softly kissing the jagged white marks trailing down his chest.

Darkmoon glanced down at her. Her words echoed in his head, followed by a man's deep voice. "Scars are what make us, shape us into the monsters that we all become…"

The prostitute kissed his stomach, brown eyes playful, enticing. Darkmoon's mismatched eyes narrowed. He had not remembered that voice in years, had not remembered any of the voices of the past few weeks for a very, very long time.

"Your past will burn you," the seer's voice whispered in his head. "Like you should be burned. And perhaps through this, Darkmoon, you will find some spark of the goodness that I know is in you still, and you will rise up to defend Argdrion…"

Darkmoon dug his muscled fingers into the prostitute's long, thick brown hair. He would not let his past force him to do something that he did not want to do, would not let it control him. Nothing forced him to do anything, and he would never be controlled again.

He pulled sharply on the prostitute's hair, and she cried out as he flipped her over and pinned her to the bed underneath his crouching body. There was a time when he would have sliced her throat from ear to ear for asking about his scars. Indeed, part of him still thought about it. But she didn't know the memories it brought up, and besides, he didn't need the city alerted to his presence before he reached his victim that night. And a rich brothel lord screaming how the famous assassin Darkmoon had killed his freshly made prostitute would certainly attract attention.

"Don't ask me about things you couldn't possibly understand," Darkmoon whispered in the prostitute's ear, voice cold, deadly. She whimpered under him, and he pushed off her and rolled off the bed.

He moved to an ornately carved wooden cabinet with a ceramic pitcher and bowl atop it, the tan sandstone floor cold against his bare feet.

The prostitute sat up in the bed behind him, the silk sheets hissing around her. "I'm sorry," she whispered as he poured water from the pitcher into the bowl, "I did not mean to upset you." She was young and inexperienced. Last night it had interested him; this morning it did not.

Darkmoon lowered his head to the bowl of water and splashed his face, screams echoing around him.

"Did I do well last night?" the prostitute asked hesitantly. Her voice sounded far away through the water in his ears.

Darkmoon focused on the icy coldness of the water biting his face, pushing the voices away. He would scope out his victim's home today, learn the guards' shifts, the servants' patterns, its weaknesses. He pulled his head back, water dripping in rivulets from his loosely spiked hair and down his face, and grabbed a blue cotton cloth off the cabinet.

"Was I too hesitant?" the prostitute asked behind him as he breathed in the airy cotton scent of the cloth. "Too bold? I… I thought that maybe you weren't pleased with me. When we were done, you didn't say anything."

Darkmoon listened to his pulse beating in his wrist. It was funny, he didn't even remember what the prostitute's name was. But then, he didn't really care either. He threw the towel back onto the cabinet and leaned down to pick up his clothing from where he had left it.

"Brother..." Cyron whispered.

The prostitute slipped out of the bed, pulling one of the silk sheets with her to cover her nakedness. "Will you stay?" she whispered, stopping next to him. She hesitantly reached a hand toward him but didn't touch him.

Darkmoon pulled his black suede shirt over his head and tucked it into his dark pants. He reached for his many belts and began strapping them on. The girl had probably been sold to the brothel by her parents as a child and had been groomed her whole life to do one thing: serve other people. Many prostitutes and rent boys did so willingly for the money, but the majority were forced into it, and knowing no other way to live, stayed.

Darkmoon pulled a simple silver chain out of a pocket in his shirt, a necklace that he had removed from the body of a noble before he'd left Dyridura. The man had made the mistake of shoving himself in front of him as they boarded a ship bound for Araysann. Waiting until the crew were busy getting the ship ready to sail, Darkmoon had sliced the man's throat and dumped him overboard. He found that he was killing more since the seer had visited him and the voices had come—it helped drive them away, helped him ignore them.

Darkmoon motioned for the prostitute to hold out her hand, and she did, her soft brown skin warm against his fingers as he lowered the necklace into it. "For your first time," he murmured, reaching for his cloak, "you did well."

The prostitute blushed. Darkmoon wrapped his cloak around his shoulders and tied the strings that held it at his throat. His victim that night was the King of Kings of Zarcayra, residing in the summer palace not three miles away, in the heart of Sussār. Ruler over the provinces of Zarcayra and their lesser kings, the King of Kings was considered something of a god to the people of Zarcayra. His death would incite them greatly.

Darkmoon knelt and pulled on his boots before lacing his vambraces onto his muscular forearms. He stood again, glancing at the prostitute. She was watching him with love in her eyes, her hand still outstretched and grasping the chain. It was not uncommon for a new prostitute to fall in love with the first man who bedded her. Before she realized that they felt nothing for her, before the hundreds of others came and the days turned into months, and the months years. Darkmoon pulled the hood of his cloak over his hair. He shouldn't have given her the necklace. She would think that he cared for her.

He almost slit the prostitute's throat then, but Cyron, green eyes watching him, appeared in the shadows by the door where the rising suns' rays hadn't penetrated yet. Darkmoon stiffened.

He moved toward the door, and Cyron disappeared as quickly as he had come. He had lost the ability to feel and care and love years ago, but there were times when he found himself doing something almost kind, like giving the prostitute the necklace. It annoyed him. Annoyed him because kindness was weakness, and he had learned a long time ago that the weak never survived.

The prostitute spoke to him as he reached the door, but Darkmoon ignored her as his fingers found the intricately carved handle of the door. He had a job to do, and she was better off learning early that there was no one in life that truly cared for her, and there never would be.

Sandstone buildings lined the street outside. The city was just starting to wake up, with people hurrying toward shops or factories to work and early-morning shoppers out to find the freshest produce at the markets.

Darkmoon bought a loaf of fresh, warm bread from a bread stand and three dates from a maroon-turbaned fruit seller.

He made his way toward the palace, stopping when he found a spot on the suns-warmed tile roof of a two-story building that sat near the palace grounds. It offered him a view over the palace wall and into the courtyards and gardens inside.

The summer palace of Sussār was one of the largest in Argdrion, with several wings and seven towers making up its hexagonal pattern.

Darkmoon bit into a date, the sugary taste coating his tongue. His target slept in the eastern wing of the sprawling red sandstone palace, he knew that much, but his hirer had been lacking in the knowledge of the number of guards and security of the place.

"Brother..." Cyron said. Darkmoon ignored him, crooking one leg upright at the knee and laying the other sideways on the smooth red tile of the roof.

Juice drained down the back of his throat as he bit into the date again. He was expecting the palace to be well guarded, most were, and his predictions were not wrong. Six purple-cloaked lower guards stood at each of the four gates leading through the sandstone wall surrounding the palace grounds, and four gold-cloaked royal guards stood sentry at every door leading into the palace's buildings. There were guards in the tops of the seven towers circling the palace as well; he caught the flash of their gold cloaks in the Brothers' early-morning light.

Darkmoon finished the date. He ripped a chunk off the bread, rolled a smaller piece of the softer, whiter inside off, and raised it to his thin lips. He glanced at the Brothers, hovering in the cloud-dotted spring sky above the eastern city. The Sisters would be full tonight—he kept track of their cycles—but his clothing would enable him to blend in and be almost invisible.

Darkmoon looked back down at the palace. The guards would be limited as to what they could see at night, especially since they'd most likely have torches nearby to light the doorways. His main problem would be getting over the wall around the palace. Well over thirty feet high, the red sandstone was smooth and without bumps or ledges to latch on to. There was no way he could climb over it without a ladder or rope, and the guards patrolling it would certainly notice if he tried.

A group of purple-cloaked guards marched toward the gate directly in front of the building he sat on, dust kicked up by their sandals puffing into the air and flies buzzing around their turbaned heads. Darkmoon drew his hand away from the bread, watching the guards with interest.

A city patrol, returning from a night's duty. Darkmoon bit into another date, readjusting his seat on the cool tiles as the sharp, glossy slates dug into his rear. All he had to do was wait until the next patrol marched out for the day, take on a guard's uniform, and that night he would march through the wall as easily as easy could be.

Darkmoon swallowed his bite of date. It was perfect.

#

Darkmoon waited on the roof for another two hours before another group of guards marched out.

He heard the gates below opening on creaky hinges first. He sat up slowly from half dozing, crawled to the edge of the roof, and glanced over at the open gate. A patrol of ten guards marched under the ornately patterned sandstone arch covering the gates, purple cloaks fresh and untainted by dust and mud and manure.

Perfect.

Darkmoon followed the guards' movements from the rooftops, jumping from tile roof to tile roof as they marched down one street and then another. He had to wait until they were distracted to make his move, or he risked alerting the whole patrol.

He lunged over an alley between two buildings, booted feet thumping onto the tiles on the other side. He hunched over and ran across the roof, his shadow moving over the tile with him.

"Patrol, halt!" a deep voice called in the thick Zarcayran tongue.

The noise of many people talking, flies buzzing, dogs barking, and wagon wheels rattling over sandstone filled the warm air.

Darkmoon flattened his body to the tile of a rooftop and slowly crawled to the edge. The guards were stopped with their leader in the middle of a crowded street below. Their leader was marked by the red band encircling his purple turban, and he was talking to a sharp-nosed shayr.

They were discussing an offense that the shayr had against a patrol of guards that had looked too closely at his daughters the day before, their voices angrily matching each other as the guard leader tried to tell the shayr that he needed to take his complaints to the royal court and the shayr yelling at the guard leader that he wanted it handled now, in the form of aray being paid him for the offense against his daughters.

Darkmoon backed up on the roof and slipped over the back side of the building, then weaved through a side alley and came up behind the patrol of guards. They were all watching their leader and the shayr, so he grabbed the one closest to the alley and sliced a knife across his throat. He pulled the man back into the alley with him and quickly began easing him out of his clothing.

The shayr and guard leader argued for another ten minutes before the shayr, his face now a maroon color, finally screamed that he would take his issue to the royal court, since that was the only place he would apparently get satisfaction. The shayr stormed off, two ebony-skinned slaves hurrying after him.

The guard leader waved his men forward again, jaw tight, and the group of soldiers marched off down the street, pushing through a crowd that had stopped to watch the spectacle.

Darkmoon glanced at the men on either side of him as they walked, their dark faces pointing straight ahead as they marched along. He looked back in front of him, a small smile tugging at his thin lips. In a few hours' time, he would be inside the palace, and when he was, the King of Kings would die.

CHAPTER 8

Azkanysh

Azkanysh stared at the red sandstone wall at the back of the throne room. She was forty-one, mother of four, daughter of the late Shayr Haro, third wife to King of Kings Vosbarhan, and queen of Zarcayra. Yet here she sat, in a smaller golden chair behind the massive golden lyon throne that Vosbarhan sat in, her back to the throne room and her face to the wall a few feet away.

Voices hummed through the throne room. The first court session of the day was in progress—a shayr was accusing another shayr of stealing his prize mare.

Azkanysh watched a silver-backed scarab beetle clamber up the wall. She was used to sitting behind Vosbarhan, to being in the shadows, to being overlooked by the palace of Sussār. Women in Zarcayra were expected to be quiet, hidden, obedient.

The beetle made it halfway up the wall, its many small legs working furiously to find a grip on the smooth sandstone.

"You cannot come in here throwing such accusations against me!" Shayr Ehrkayn, the shayr accused of stealing, said loudly behind her.

Azkanysh focused on the voices, picking out each man by a raspy undertone or a nervous clearing of his throat or a sharp enunciation. She had never seen most of Vosbarhan's court, but she had learned whose voice went with whose name over the years, and now she could pick out most men after hearing them talk for only a few seconds.

"King of Kings," Shayr Shadarey, the accuser, said, "I requested this court session because I believe that Shayr Ehrkayn stole my mare, Heyrops, in anticipation of the upcoming Great Race in two days' time. I do not come before you without evidence of what I believe to be true, and at this time, I would ask the King of Kings for permission to bring forward a witness."

"How could you have a witness when what you accuse is a lie?" Shayr Ehrkayn said angrily. His voice was even but firm and reminded Azkanysh of her father.

Voices rang through the throne room, where the other shayrs and destūrs of all of the gods stood. The theft of a horse in Zarcayra was comparable to the murder of a human or even the use of magic, the greatest crime that there was in Argdrion. Horses were more than working animals or pets— they were family. From the time it was born, a colt was shown the highest care and love, often living in stables fancier than the house of its owner and having several slaves designated to its personal care.

If Shayr Ehrkayn had indeed stolen Shayr Shadarey's horse, it would mean his execution and the distribution of his lands and wealth among the other shayrs of Sussār. Azkanysh wondered if Shayr Ehrkayn's wives realized that they and their children would be sold into slavery if Shayr Ehrkayn was executed. She wondered if they cared.

"Permission for a witness granted," Vosbarhan said.

The golden double doors of the throne room boomed open, and Azkanysh turned her head. She sometimes wondered what it would be like to face the throne room, to see the faces of the Guardian Council and the nobility and holy men that filled its cavernous depths. Would she be scared to sit where Vosbarhan was sitting?

Whispers echoed through the throne room along with the steady slapping of sandals on the gold and white tiled floor.

"You bring slaves as witness against me?" Shayr Ehrkayn said with a laugh as the sandals stopped and the murmuring voices with them.

"I bring evidence of the truth," Shayr Shadarey replied. He was a man with a soft voice, a voice that hinted at intelligence.

"Three guards?" Vosbarhan spoke up.

"Yes, King of Kings," Shayr Shadarey murmured. "The men who guarded Heyrops."

"If they guarded your mare," said Tukayr, one of the twelve Guardian Council members, "then how is it that she was stolen?"

Shayr Ehrkayn and a few others laughed. Several murmurs ran through the throne room.

Azkanysh watched the beetle slip and slide down the wall a few inches before starting back up again. The Great Race was the largest and longest horse race in Argdrion. Today it was held by Zarcayra, but for more than four hundred years before that, it had been run by the thirteen kingdoms that had merged to form Zarcayra. The race was held every spring and covered over three thousand miles of Araysannian desert, mountains, and rivers. Millions flocked from all corners of Argdrion to watch it, and thousands of horses competed in it every year. Such a large race offered a large prize, a half a million aray, and such a large prize ensured that every year horses were stolen or lamed, riders murdered, and the race course susceptible to attempts at sabotage by dishonest contestants.

"They did not do their job properly," Shayr Shadarey said evenly, "and they will be punished for it, but before that they have words to say. Words that will prove that Shayr Ehrkayn stole Heyrops."

The throne room burst into chatter again, Shayr Ehrkayn's voice rising over them all. "It will prove nothing, Shayr Shadarey! Other than the fact that you are a lying, scheming snake who knows that your horse won't stand a chance against my stallion, Tetot, in the race, and you hope to, by this outrageous claim, eliminate me from the race!"

"Quiet!" the court crier yelled. "Quiet in the throne room!"

A slave rang a metal ringer against a bronze gong below the dais, and the throne room fell silent.

"Speak, slaves," Vosbarhan said.

Azkanysh heard the rustling of cloth on sandstone and in her mind's eye saw the slaves bowing low before Vosbarhan.

"Shayr Shadarey," a new voice said, "I beg you to pardon me in the loss of your horse. It is not I, Shayr, who is to blame, but my fellow guards, who were busy playing at cards and left me to guard the stables by myself."

"Liar!" another new voice spluttered. "We were all taking turns playing at cards and guarding the horse. You're as guilty as the rest of us!"

"You will all pay for your negligence," Shayr Shadarey said. "Just tell the king what you saw that ni—"

"Silence!" Vosbarhan roared.

Azkanysh shrank down in her chair, half expecting him to hit her.

"Shayr Shadarey," Vosbarhan went on in a calmer voice, "if you cannot control your slaves, then remove them from the throne room and let the court move on to other cases that have substantial evidence."

Hums of agreement filled the room.

Azkanysh adjusted her gold-threaded robes. She felt eyes on her, the crawling sensation that someone was staring at her. She glanced at the row of her personal slaves standing at the bottom of the back of the dais, and then at the gold-cloaked royal guards lining the walls of the throne room. One was staring at her, a young man with mud-colored skin and black eyes. Her skin prickled. In Zarcayra it was forbidden for a man to look upon a woman's face unless that woman was his wife or his concubine.

Azkanysh reached a slender hand up to the golden silk hanging over the lower half of her face, making sure it was in place. Ever since she was a child of three, she had worn a hijab, the customary head covering that women of Zarcayra wore. Hiding her face from the world, from the palace, from herself. If it had somehow come undone and the guard was looking at her mouth or nose or anything of her face except her eyes, then she would be branded a whore and thrown out of the palace, or worse, executed.

Her hijab's facepiece was in place. Azkanysh lowered her hand again and looked away from the still-staring guard. He was probably new to the palace, and judging by the shade of his skin, most likely from the far western lands of Zarcayra, where women were said to be freer with whom they showed their faces to. She glanced back at the guard again; he was still watching her. If Vosbarhan caught him staring, he would have him executed. Azkanysh looked away again.

"My apologies, King of Kings," Shayr Shadarey said. "My slaves will not cause trouble again."

Azkanysh heard several slaps of a hand against flesh as Shayr Shadarey hit his slaves. "Speak, you pigs," the shayr snarled.

"We ... we were attacked by men, Shayr Shadarey!" the first one who had spoken said hurriedly. Not allowed to address the King of Kings, he spoke to his master. "They knocked us out and took the horse Heyrops, shayr."

"Who?" Vosbarhan asked.

"Slaves of the house of Ehrkayn," the slave murmured.

The throne room began murmuring once more, and Azkanysh turned her head toward the throne again.

"And you three swear that these men who attacked you and took the horse Heyrops were slaves of the house of Ehrkayn?" Vosbarhan queried.

"They all agree, King of Kings, yes," Shayr Shadarey said.

"I was not asking you, Shayr Shadarey," Vosbarhan said in a voice edged with irritation, "I was asking your slaves. Slaves, you all agree that these men who attacked you were Shayr Ehrkayn's slaves?"

"Yes, Shayr Shadarey," the slaves voiced in unison.

"He told them to say that!" Shayr Ehrkayn shouted. "There's not a word of truth in their statements, King of Kings!"

"Quiet!" the court herald shouted again. "Quiet in the throne room!"

The bronze gong was rung again, and the throne room gradually fell silent.

Azkanysh heard Vosbarhan's fingers drumming on the armrest of his throne. He was annoyed, she could tell. He always tapped his fingers when he was annoyed. It was a habit he'd had since they'd first been married. She caught a movement to her left and turned her head partly to look at Vyzir Dsamihur, who stood on the dais a few feet away from Vosbarhan's throne, black-clad arms behind his back.

The only one of the court who she could ever see from her seat, Vyzir Dsamihur was the right-hand man to the King of Kings. He was a blank-faced man, someone who spoke in a soft voice, a man who was said by many to be guarded and more intelligent than people assumed. She supposed that he had to be to survive under Vosbarhan. He was the fifth vyzir who her husband had had since they'd been married. Before she had married Vosbarhan, he'd had two besides.

"King of Kings," Shayr Ehrkayn said, the rasp of his sandals telling Azkanysh that he had stepped closer to the dais, "Shayr Shadarey's accusations against me are false, and the fact that this court would even consider slaves' words against mine is highly insulting to me and my family." The shayr's voice drew further away, and Azkanysh guessed he had turned toward the throne room. "The house of Ehrkayn is an old and well-established house in Sussār. If we are to be treated with this type of disrespect and humiliation, then who is to say that your houses, my fellow shayrs, will not be treated the same?"

Voices hummed in agreement.

"When you lower yourself to the level of slaves or the poor by stealing another shayr's property, then how do you expect your house will be treated?" Shayr Shadarey spoke up.

"I ask that this court throw out this case on the grounds that Shayr Shadarey only has the word of slaves to back his accusations," Shayr Ehrkayn yelled above him. "And that my word against his slaves should be more than enough to prove my innocence!"

The scarab beetle fell off the wall and lay on its back on the mosaic floor as the throne room broke into a cacophony of voices.

Azkanysh glanced at the bug, watching its tiny legs kick in the air as it tried to turn itself back over.

The gong rang again. She looked back at the carved rumps of the golden lyons that surrounded Vosbarhan's throne, listening.

"What is the opinion of the Guardian Council?" Vosbarhan asked as the room fell silent once more.

Azkanysh heard the council begin murmuring amongst themselves.

The Guardian Council had been set up in Zarcayra after the thirteen kingdoms of Araysann had merged to become one, shortly after the start of the Third Great War. The council had been inaugurated for the purpose of representing, along with the king, each of the thirteen merged kingdoms. New members were elected, much like how a king came to a throne, with the eldest son of members taking on their father's robes when their fathers died. The Guardian Council's opinions in court sessions mattered almost as much as the king's ruling, and for a law or decree to pass, the King of Kings was required, by tradition, to ask and then act upon the majority of the council's opinion.

"King of Kings," Nupar Abayn'uni, one of the twelve council members, said after a few moments, "the Guardian Council has discussed and decided upon the matter of Shayr Shadarey's accusation of horse theft against Shayr Ehrkayn. We advise that Shayr Ehrkayn is innocent in that there is not enough significant evidence to his guilt."

"But I have one of his slave's markers, taken from the man by my own slave on the night of Heyrops's abduction!"

Azkanysh could feel the throne room glance at Shayr Shadarey.

"Impossible!" Shayr Ehrkayn spluttered.

"You did not say, Shayr Shadarey, that you had material evidence," Vosbarhan said.

Azkanysh heard his fingers stop tapping; he was becoming interested in the case.

"I had not thought, King of Kings," Shayr Shadarey said loudly, "that it would be needed. I had hoped my word, along with my slaves' testimony, would be enough to convince the court of Shayr Ehrkayn's guilt. But as it is not, I now produce this, a arm band from one of Shayr Ehrkayn's slaves, marking the man as his!"

The throne room inhaled as one, and Azkanysh assumed that Shayr Shadarey had held up the metal marker. She wished again that she could see what was going on.

"If you will look closely at the band, King of Kings," Shayr Shadarey said, "you will see the mark of the house of Ehrkayn on it, the prancing horse with full moons above it."

"You had it made!" Shayr Ehrkayn shouted. "Faked by one of the forgers in the Heart of Sussār!"

Azkanysh heard shouting and feet scrambling. The Heart of Sussār was the lowest part in the city, where the seven walls that cut Sussār into various sections of wealth or poverty met. It was a place where one could have anything imagined made, where brothels with slaves of all ages were found. Where, for a price, one could buy anything that their heart desired, where people who disappeared were never heard of or seen again.

"I would advise you, Shayr Ehrkayn," Vosbarhan said as the gong rang for the third time and the throne room grew quiet yet again, "to act like a shayr and refrain from throwing yourself at another shayr like some a commoner scrambling for food."

"He's lying, King of Kings!" Shayr Ehrkayn hissed, voice no longer calm and even. "I tell you, he's lying!"

"Bring the arm band here," Vosbarhan said.

Azkanysh heard the scuff of sandals on the dais, a tunic shuffling on the golden sandstone as a slave bowed low before the King of Kings.

The throne room was quiet for several minutes, waiting, expectant.

"A prancing horse with the moons in the background," Vosbarhan said finally. "Shayr Ehrkayn, due to the evidence given against you, and due to your behavior when said evidence was presented against you, I rule that you are guilty of stealing Shayr Shadarey's horse, Heyrops, and that for said crime you shall be executed, your properties and wealth distributed among the other shayrs of Sussār, and your family sold into slavery."

The slave rang the gong again, and Shayr Ehrkayn began shouting as the throne room exploded with voices. "It's a lie!" Shayr Ehrkayn screamed. "A lie! He just wants my Tetot out of the way in the Great Race. A lie, I say, a lie!"

Shayr Ehrkayn's voice faded as guards dragged him out of the throne room.

Azkanysh heard Vosbarhan stand.

"The King of Kings is now leaving the throne room!" the court crier yelled. "Praise the King of Kings, Commander of Armies, Chosen of the Gods!"

Azkanysh stood hastily, stepping away from her chair and going to her knees as Vosbarhan came around the back of the throne. He was followed by their eldest child and only son, Zarmeyr. The Guardian Council and Vyzir Dsamihur came after.

"King of Kings," Azkanysh murmured to the cold tiles of the floor. She could not have her head even with Vosbarhan's when she stood in front of him. If she did, it would mean losing it.

Vosbarhan didn't stop, his red robes brushing against her hands as he walked by and to a door in the back wall of the sandstone throne room.

Azkanysh stood again, waiting until the council and the rest of the party had passed before falling into place behind them. It was a rare occurrence for a King of Kings to rule opposite to what the Guardian Council had advised, but she did have to admit that she thought Vosbarhan's ruling had been right.

She wondered what Shayr Ehrkayn had done with Heyrops, if he had killed the horse or if he planned on reselling it in some distant part of the world. It didn't matter now. If the animal was still in his possession, it would be given back to Shayr Shadarey, and if it was not, then Shayr Shadarey would get Tetot.

Vosbarhan led them to the east patio, a sprawling sandstone appendage that jutted out from the third story of the eastern half of the palace and overshadowed the gardens below.

Canopies were set up on the patio, the purple and gold colors of Zarcayra warming in the Brothers' noon rays as they shaded the red sandstone.

Azkanysh chose a bench several feet away from the mosaiced table Vosbarhan sat down at, where she could sit by the fluted sandstone railing and look out on the pools and shaded pathways of the garden below.

Slaves brought food out, ceramic bowls of ripe fruits and cooked rices, plates of glistening cheese and strong-smelling salads, and pitchers of juices and wines.

Azkanysh took a slice of soft, sticky goat cheese, looking away from the patio and pulling back the cloth of her hijab to take bites from it. It had been twenty-eight years since she had come to live in the court of Zarcayra, at the palace in Sussār in the spring and summer and the palace in Tutayr in the fall and winter. Twenty-eight years, and nothing had changed in her life. She had bore Vosbarhan six children—two sons and four daughters, of which one daughter and one son had died of summer fever—submitted to his abuses, sat at the court sessions but not in them, watched her children grow under nannies and tutors, and eaten lunch and dinner with Vosbarhan every day of every year.

A slave in a gray tunic offered her a drink of mint, ice, salt, and sugar, and Azkanysh took it, turning back to the garden and sipping at the cool mixture. She had wished for death many times over those twenty-eight years, death and escape from Vosbarhan. Her mind strayed to the wives of Shayr Ehrkayn and his children, who would now be sold into slavery. Would his wives be upset? Or would they see it only as a changing of hands? Being a woman in Zarcayra was like being a slave, with little difference between the two other than the clothes they wore and the activities they took part in.

Azkanysh rested the drink on her lap, her gaze scanning the patio and its many occupants before coming to rest on three jeweled concubines standing around Vosbarhan. They were new to the palace harem; she could tell by their young and hopeful eyes. She had been like that once, before Vosbarhan had shown her what he was like, before hope had been beaten from her.

The concubines glanced at her, and Azkanysh noted the superiority in their khol-lined eyes. Her father had told her once, before she had married Vosbarhan, that not all men in Zarcayra had multiple wives and concubines. She had hoped that Vosbarhan would have only her when they had married, hoped that he would love her and cherish her so much that he would not need other women. But he had not, and now she was glad when new women came to the palace, for it meant that Vosbarhan spent his nights with someone else. That it was someone else who he beat.

Azkanysh turned her head to the railing again, taking another sip of her drink. "Mother."

Her two eldest daughters stood in front of her, one dressed in orange silk and the other yellow cotton, each strikingly accenting the other.

"Mother, we wish to talk to you," said Tamar, the oldest of her daughters. Although as different as the suns from the moons, her oldest daughters were both beautiful beyond compare. Paruhi, now thirteen, would be turning fourteen in a month's time, and Tamar was sixteen since last winter. Azkanysh was surprised that Vosbarhan had not found them husbands yet.

"Mother," Tamar said again, "Paruhi and I want to talk to you about our new mistress."

"If you have time," Paruhi added softly.

Azkanysh eyed her two daughters. Quiet and gentle, Paruhi had the curly, sunbrowned hair of her mother and the soft features and warm amber eyes of her father. Tamar was all Vosbarhan's side, with straight dark-brown hair, darker brown eyes, and sharp features. She was nothing like Vosbarhan, though. Headstrong and opinionated but loyal and generous. Azkanysh took another sip of her drink. She wished that she had seen more of her daughters as they had grown up, but being queen meant spending most of her time with Vosbarhan, and women other than the queen were not allowed in the throne room.

"She's an old bat," Tamar said, looking pointedly at Paruhi. "And we don't want her to teach us anymore. We want Mistress Ahani back, Mother," she added eagerly.

Azkanysh's heart skipped a beat. She quickly glanced at Vosbarhan, who was busy eating at the table across the patio.

"You know that you cannot," she said in a low, warning voice.

Mistress Ahani had been her daughters' teacher since they had been old enough to begin learning how to sew and raise children. But she had held ideas that had not agreed with the common beliefs and laws in Zarcayra. Ideas that involved freedom and equality for women, ideas that Vosbarhan had overheard, ideas that had gotten her exiled from Zarcayra. If Vosbarhan even heard Mistress Ahani's name mentioned, Azkanysh knew it would mean a beating for someone.

"But, Mother," Tamar whispered excitedly, "I have a plan of how we can get her back and how we can get Father to agree to it—"

"Tamar, stop!" Azkanysh hissed, glancing back at her daughters. "Do you want to get us all in trouble?" She looked at Vosbarhan again, her heartbeat quickening. She worried for Tamar. Her eldest daughter had a habit of saying what she thought without thinking about what it was that she was saying or who might be listening. Paruhi had more discretion, but she was easily led and usually followed whatever Tamar did.

"But, Mother," Tamar whispered, "Mistress Ahani didn't do anything to justify her exile, and it isn't fair that we should have to suffer under such a wicked woman as Mistress Lorrig—"

"Are you talking about that silly old woman who claimed to be a teacher?" Zarmeyr said, stepping up to join their conversation.

Azkanysh glanced up at her only son, her blood going cold. Seventeen since the winter, Zarmeyr took after his father in looks and personality. Dark haired and eyed and stern of face, he held himself like a King of Kings already and treated everyone but the current King of Kings like they were dirt under his feet. If he told Vosbarhan what they were talking about…

Tamar huffed through her nose, balling her hands into fists. "She wasn't a silly old woman. She was wise and kind and intelligent and—"

"Foolish and arrogant and insane," Zarmeyr finished, sneering. "Filling your heads with all those idiotic thoughts of women being equal to men. I feared for you, my dear sisters, feared for your sanity." Zarmeyr reached a sympathetic hand out to them, and Tamar slapped it away.

"Our sanity is fine," she hissed. "It is your insecurity that is threatened."

"Tamar…" Azkanysh warned. She glanced at Vosbarhan again. He wasn't looking at or listening to them.

"Insecurity?" Zarmeyr asked, face growing dark. "What do you mean insecurity?"

"I mean," Tamar snapped, "that all men are insecure." She stepped closer to Zarmeyr, glaring challengingly up at him. "And that you are afraid of women realizing that they're equal to you because it will threaten your power, and power is all that you care about."

"You are a stupid whore," Zarmeyr snarled.

"Zarmeyr!" Azkanysh scolded.

The patio fell silent.

Azkanysh's stomach dropped. Vosbarhan had begun listening.

Zarmeyr wheeled on her. "How dare you talk to me like that, woman! King of Kings, did you hear?" he said in a high-pitched call. "Your queen just reprimanded me!" His face was the color of a ripe plum, mottled purple and red.

Azkanysh met Tamar's gaze. Her daughter's eyes were filled with fear and regret.

"Azkanysh," Vosbarhan said.

Azkanysh stood slowly, the gaze of everyone on the patio on her. Her skin prickled in anticipation of the belt slicing into her, of Vosbarhan's hands turning her flesh purple and blue.

She moved slowly across the patio to where Vosbarhan sat, her eyes on her feet, her hands folded in front of her to keep them from shaking.

"Look at me," Vosbarhan said, voice dark.

Azkanysh glanced up, meeting his dark eyes. They were cold, as usual, and filled with annoyance.

Zarmeyr moved past her, stepping around behind Vosbarhan's chair with a sneer on his face.

"What reason do you have for speaking to our son in such a manner?" Vosbarhan asked evenly.

Azkanysh glanced at the concubines. There was smugness on their faces. They did not yet understand that someday they would feel Vosbarhan's wrath too. Her first beating had come on their wedding night, after Vosbarhan had made her a woman. They had been lying in bed, him sleeping and her still awake and overjoyed at what had happened. She had touched him then, wanting to feel him again, to have him hold her. She had awoken him from his sleep, and it had been her first lesson in how brutal Vosbarhan could be.

"I..." Azkanysh started, looking back at Vosbarhan. She could tell him of how Zarmeyr had spoken to Tamar, of what he had called her. But Vosbarhan would not care that Zarmeyr had insulted a woman, even if it was his daughter, and she did not want her daughters to feel the King of King's anger as well. "None, King of Kings," she said, bowing her head. "I am sorry."

"Do not speak to my son like that ever again," Vosbarhan said after a few heartbeats. His voice was cold, low.

Azkanysh could feel everyone watching them, waiting, listening. She did not think that Vosbarhan would beat her in front of them, but then, one never really knew what Vosbarhan was going to do.

"Leave," Vosbarhan said. He reached for a cluster of grapes in a wooden bowl on the table and pulled two off. "Leave our company."

Azkanysh bowed again. She backed away from him, turning as she reached the other side of the patio and slipping through the doors and into the palace. She did not look at Tamar and Paruhi. Vosbarhan would notice; Vosbarhan noticed everything.

Her steps carried her to the South Garden. Planted when the Sussār palace had belonged to a different kingdom and not remodeled, for whatever reason, like the rest of the palace and grounds had been, the South Garden was too far away from the palace for most to bother walking to and was therefore hardly ever occupied by anyone but the slaves who tended it. It was Azkanysh's favorite spot in the palace and surrounding lands, a place where she could feel distant from Vosbarhan, separated, safe.

A swarm of yellow-and-brown butterflies fluttered up from a fountain of the seven-headed sea god, Syrnyn, as she moved down a sandy path that stretched between blooming rose bushes. Azkanysh didn't look at them. She used to imagine when she was in the South Garden that she was not married to Vosbarhan, not queen of Zarcayra, not abused, unloved. She still did sometimes, but it was harder and harder to imagine as she grew older and her spirit faded. It was easier to just focus on surviving.

Azkanysh made for the center of the garden, where a small circular sandstone temple to Ehurayni, chief goddess of Araysann, sat among a grove of lilac trees. She wanted to pray, although why, she didn't know.

The lilac trees' overpowering scent filled her nostrils as she walked up the three sandstone steps to the temple. Small purple and white flowers littered the ground around the red building. Azkanysh slipped out of her sandals, handing them to one of the three slaves who trailed her, before moving into the temple.

It was cooler inside the compact sandstone building, and the air smelled dusty and unused.

Azkanysh knelt on the cool, dust-scattered floor, eyes going up to the cross-legged statue of Ehurayni. She had not come to the temple to pray for a long time now. Praying didn't matter to her as much anymore.

The six-armed statue of the mother goddess smiled at her, black diamond eyes glinting dully in the semidarkness of the temple.

"I do not know why I come to you," Azkanysh whispered, looking into those eyes. "You have never helped me before. Why do I think that now will be any different?"

A guard shifted outside, sandaled feet crunching in the sand.

Azkanysh glanced sideways at the noise, staring at the rough red sandstone of the wall several feet away. She could ask for Vosbarhan to beat her lightly, but it had never worked before, and she did not believe that it would work now. She glanced back at Ehurayni, eyes catching on a chip in the dark stone of the statue. She wanted to pray for something else, something that she had never dared ask for before out of fear of angering the family of the gods. She did not fear angering them now, though, only the pain that was coming.

"Ehurayni," Azkanysh whispered, "mother of gods and goddesses, wife of Drisahr Aruyn—the chief of gods…" She paused, listening to a bee buzz outside the shadowed temple. "I have come to you for many years," Azkanysh began again. "First to ask you for my husband to love me, then to show me mercy when I realized that love was not in him."

Azkanysh paused again, remembering the tears, the pain, the heartache, the numbness. "Today, though," she whispered softly, so that the guards and slaves waiting outside would not hear, "I have a different request of you."

Azkanysh stared into the small, dark eyes of the statue. "I want him dead," she murmured tonelessly. "Please, Ehurayni, I want him dead."

The goddess smiled at her.

CHAPTER 9

The Unknown Voice

I killed my first creature when I was ten.

My father's prayers and Sar's hopes that our armies would hold the skinchangers and wiar back until the winter of my fourth year proved fruitful, and as the long months of winter in Argdrion raged, humans mined silver and prepared for the spring. The tide of war turned the spring of my fifth year. It was due to the silver, Father said.

"Without it," I often heard him say after that year, "we would have surely lost, and the wiar and skinchangers would be living in our home right now."

The Third Great War started in the fifth year of my life, a new era of hope for humans, a new century for Argdrion.

"I hate him," I said softly as Mother ran a wooden-toothed comb through my straight brown hair.

"You don't hate him," she replied kindly. The rhythmic scraping of the comb against my scalp filled the stillness of her room along with the rustle of her velvet sleeves.

"Yes," I said, staring out a slit of a window in front of me, "I hate him."

We were speaking of my only cousin, my mother's elder sister's son. A year younger than me, my cousin was a short, plump boy with an angelic face and the nature of Setaron, god of the underworld. Or rather, only when the adults were not around did he hold the underworld god's likeness. When around our parents, Ciril's behavior matched his face. I didn't complain of this to Mother, though. I never complained. There was too much on my mind for complaints.

"Well, I'm sure that you will feel cheerier when you're out in the sunshine, playing with Ciril," Mother said, setting the comb down on a wooden stool beside her. "It's a beautiful summer day out, and this will be the last summer you'll have to play."

I saw her lips purse in her reflection in the tarnished silver standing mirror beside the window. I didn't tell her that I didn't want to "play" like other children my age did; her mind was already worried over the announcement that Father had given two nights before at the dinner table. He was home for leave. With the war going better, he was home more often, and it had been the three of us at the long, dark table in the dining room instead of the usual two.

"In four days, I go back to the battlefields, son," Father had said as the few elderly servants left at the castle set plates of venison, boiled eggs, and wild berries on the table. "You'll be coming with me."

Mother dropped her partially raised wineglass, spilling bright-red currant wine over her faded blue dress and the stone cobbles of the floor. "He's too young, Rubayn," she whispered, voice trembling.

"Nonsense," Father replied, sipping at his own wine as a stick-thin, white-haired servant hobbled out and cleaned up Mother's mess. Her face was white, like it always got when she was scared. "My sister and I, the gods rest her soul, were ten when we started going to the battlefield with our parents," Father said.

"Times were different back then, Rubayn," Mother replied, voice strained.

Father glanced up at her. "How?" he asked.

"The situation was more desperate."

"The situation is still desperate," Father said, setting his wineglass back down and reaching for the silverware beside his plate. "We may have silver on our side, but the skinchangers and wiar are far from being beaten." His face grew dark. "United as they are, they may never be beaten."

"I won't allow it," Mother said.

I looked up at her from my venison. Mother rarely made stands on anything; she was usually sick in her bed from whatever flu was going around, but when she did, she held her ground. She had the day Father had wanted to stop my education in favor of my learning the art of weapons, and due to her influence, I had learned both, gaining a love for higher learning as well as skill in swords and other instruments of killing.

"There is nothing you can do about it," Father said, slicing into his venison with a growing vigor. "All able-bodied humans must help in this fight if we are to win against the other races. Being as sickly as you are, you wouldn't understand this."

It was a harsh blow, one that I saw Mother recoil at.

"You know I would be out fighting if I could," she said tightly.

"But you can't," Father said angrily, throwing his silverware down. Mother flinched at the noise. "And our son will not stay at home to be pampered by you while there are men out there who are fighting and dying!" He stood, his chair scraping loudly against the flagstones, and stalked out of the room.

I knew Mother was thinking of that night as she smoothed down my cowlick. I could see it in the darkness in her brown eyes. "There," she said, smiling at me in the mirror. "Now let us go meet our guests."

The Brothers sat directly in the sky above the castle as Mother and I waited in the courtyard for the carriage and riders to draw closer. Beads of sweat trickled down between my shoulder blades beneath the brown tunic I wore. I waited for my cousin with a certain dread, the dread one gets when a headache or stomach flu are coming on.

The usual greetings were given as my aunt and Ciril stepped out of their dust-coated carriage. Mother hugged her sister and admired the bump in her belly that kept her from fighting. Ciril and I stared at each other. Although my cousin was a stupid child, I think that he knew that I loathed him with a ferocity scarcely matched.

"When are you due?" Mother asked as servants appeared from the cooler shadows of the castle and began unloading the wooden trunks on my aunt's carriage.

"October," my aunt replied, all blushing smiles. "Jon is hoping for another son, but I'd like a girl."

Mother turned to me and Ciril, still staring at each other. "Why don't you boys go and play. Son, you could show Ciril the stream. It's hot today—maybe you could go swimming." The tone in Mother's voice told me that I had better not "lose" my cousin in the fields again, like the last time he had come.

"Yes, Mother," I said without emotion. I turned and moved off toward the castle, my cousin trailing me.

"I thought Aunt Dussa told you to take me swimming," Ciril said as I walked down a long, dark stone hallway. His curly chestnut hair bounced as he skipped along next to me.

"The stream is down in the forest at the edge of the fields," I replied, not looking at him. "Find your own way."

"I'll tell our mothers that you're trying to get rid of me again if you don't come with me and show me," Ciril trilled.

I stopped, staring at him. He smiled annoyingly, round face dimpling. "I have to get a book first," I said, turning. I started walking again.

"A book?" Ciril mimed. "Why do you need a book to go swimming?"

"Because I'm going to read while you swim," I said, stopping in front of the age-stained oaken door to the library.

"My parents said that you're more interested in reading than fighting," Ciril taunted as we slipped inside the library, and I browsed the shelves for a book to read, "but I didn't realize that you were weak enough to want to read when you could be swimming."

I had an idea of what he meant by that, but I didn't respond. Father was not the only one who didn't like my aspiration for higher learning, but he was the loudest voicing it. "In times of peace, higher education is all right," he'd often tell me, "but this is war, son. And in wartime, one must make sacrifices."

I did not want to make sacrifices, and I saw no reason why I could not give myself a higher education by reading, and fight too. I pulled a red leather book off a shelf and inspected it. It had gold lettering with the title *The Saddle and Its Development* on the front. I moved back out of the library, carefully shutting the heavy door behind us with a soft click.

"I could tell our mothers that you're ignoring me," Ciril said, skipping along next to me again as I walked back up the hallway. "Reading a book instead of playing with me."

"You wanted to swim, Ciril," I replied. "Fine, but let me alone, or I'll lose you in the fields again."

He shut up after that.

#

I found a moss-covered rock in the shade that had a perfect divot on top for me to sit on. While Ciril stripped his pudgy form of leggings and tunic and jumped, whooping, into a deep pool in the slow-moving stream winding through the oak forest bordering Father's fields, I delved into my book with a keen interest.

I had been reading for over an hour before Ciril got bored with his swimming and came out to bother me.

"What are you reading?" my cousin asked, leaning on my rock. Water dripped onto my book, and I angrily dried it up with my sleeve and pulled the book away from him.

"I doubt you would understand it," I replied evenly. "Even if you could read well."

My cousin had started his schooling at four, the same age I had, but although I had learned to read by the time I was five, he still could not read more than the simple grammar books children two years younger than him read.

"I can fight, though," Ciril said in his taunting voice. "And I hear you can't."

"I can fight fine," I said, turning the page in my book and trying very hard to block out his voice and concentrate on the words. The chapter I was reading was going over the advancement of the saddle and how the Kingdom of Heyrostis in Araysann had added stirrups to the simpler design first invented by the nomadic tribes in Oridonn over three thousand years before.

Ciril snatched the book out of my hands. "Then fight me!" he cried, jumping back as I lunged off my rock at him. "Fight me for your precious book."

"Give it back, Ciril," I warned, following him.

"Nah!" Ciril laughed, his pudgy legs glowing pink as he backed through a beam of sunlight streaming through the leafy foliage above us. "Fight me for it, unless you're too weak!"

He bounced around a thin, curving oak tree and stuck his tongue out at me. I was not going to chase him; I knew that if I did it would only encourage him. I hoped that ignoring him would make him lose interest in taunting me and drop the book, so I knelt in the grass, spreading myself under the trees, and studied a lone bluebell.

There were lessons to be learned in everything, even such small, delicate things as flowers. I stroked the velvety petals of the bluebell, the sweet scent the flower released brushing my nostrils. Alone in a sea of grass and trees, the little flower still reached for the suns above and gave the world the glory of its beauty. I wanted to be like the lone bluebell, always growing, always pushing upward and onward. I heard a splash as I studied the finer, darker lines of blue in the bluebell. I glanced up and saw my book floating in the stream.

"Ciril!" I screamed, lunging to my feet and running to the water. I dove in, pushing through the water to the slowly sinking book.

My cousin laughed, kicking at July mushrooms.

I snatched the book out of the water and swam back to shore, my clothes pulling me down.

"It's just an old book, anyway," Ciril said, continuing to kick at the mushrooms with his bare feet. They fell over in chopped-up piles of white and red, the darker undersides of the domes glistening softly. "There were thousands more in that room we went in. What's so special about this one?"

I opened the book as I climbed out of the stream. It was ruined. A section of pages tore away from the spine as I held it up, waterlogged paper falling away from the thicker paper of the inside of the spine.

"Maybe now you'll play with me," Ciril said, his back to me. "It's boring to swim alone. We could play dunk the diver and see who can hold their breath the longest."

I set the book down on the rock I'd been sitting on.

"Or maybe we could play blind man's bluff. I played that in the water with my friends last time Mother took me to town to see them. It won't be as much fun with just two people, but it's better than watching you read."

I picked up a rock lying by the stream and brought it down on my cousin's head. It wasn't a very big rock, no larger than both my fists put together, but the force of the blow behind it was more than enough to make it a dangerous weapon.

Ciril crumpled to the grass.

I stared at him for a moment, lying in the destroyed mushrooms with a slowly building trickle of blood seeping out under his head. I knew that I had killed him, but I did not feel anything. Not remorse, not happiness, not regret. He deserved death.

I rolled Ciril's body into the stream and ground the pool of blood in the mushrooms into the grass with my heel. I knew what I would tell our mothers. An accident while swimming. Ciril and I had been diving into the water, and Ciril had hit the large rock sitting a few feet out in the pool. I threw the rock I had used to kill Ciril into the pool and stripped my shirt and shoes off to make it look like I had just had time to put my pants on before running back to the castle. The book I buried under a nearby log.

The run through the fields took my breath away, and when I got back to the castle, I appeared panicked and out of breath from fear. Father was the first person I ran into, and when I told him my made-up story of Ciril's accident, he gripped my shoulder and told me to show him where.

Ciril had floated downstream by the time Father and I and Sar returned to the forest, and his naked, pudgy body lay lodged between two rocks a hundred yards from where I had killed him.

"Too bad," was all Father said before he and Sar pulled my cousin's body out of the stream. I gathered my clothes and Ciril's and followed them back through the yellowing fields around the castle. Cows watched our slow procession, their lazy brown eyes following our movements as they chewed mouthfuls of long, drying grass.

My aunt screamed when she saw Ciril's body and fainted on the flagstones of the courtyard. Mother and two of Father's knights carried her inside.

No one questioned my story of Ciril's mishap, and his death was forever remembered as a horrible, horrible accident. My aunt went into labor that night and lost her child.

The next day, I went to the battlefields with Father.

CHAPTER 10

Nathaira

"I'm beginning to think this is a 'abit with ya."

Nathaira groaned and squinted up at the woman, who was leaning through the flat, horizontal iron bars in between them with a strip of brown cloth in one hand. The smell of urine, sweat, salt, tar, and puke assaulted her nose. Nathaira gagged.

"What happened?" she croaked as the woman pulled her long black hair apart with dirty fingers and dabbed the rag at her head. Nathaira hissed as pain tore through her skull. She slapped the woman's hand away and pushed herself to a sitting position, only to moan again as more pain shot through her throbbing head.

"Well, let's see," the woman replied, putting a dirty finger up. "Ya tried to escape, but the slavers stopped ya before ya could, and after a nice, well-placed blow to yer 'ead, loaded ya on the ship with the rest of us slaves, cold as a snowflake and with a bump the size of an egg on yer 'ead. That was yesterday noon; we've been at sea for almost a day now. I 'eard 'em say they expect we'll land in the kingdom of Dyridura on Warulan's coast in about two weeks." The woman eyed her. "You 'ave a liking for getting knocked out or something?"

Nathaira ignored her and gingerly felt around the swollen, painful lump on her head. She glanced down at the shackles adorning her hands, feet, and neck—all were burning like rings of fire against her skin and glinting dully in the semidarkness.

They're making sure I don't escape this time. Nathaira groaned and put her head in her hands, hissing as fresh pain shot through her arm, head, and finger.

"Yer arm wound opened back up like that when ye took that fall," the woman said, scratching her leg through a hole in her brown woolen leggings. "I patched ya up again, but ya better be more careful with it or yer like not to 'ave any blood left at all."

It doesn't matter. Nathaira stared at the blackness of her hands. She had failed to escape, and in that failure, failed Efamar, and only the Sisters knew where he was right now.

"That was cool like, 'ow ya changed into a bird and all," the woman said as the loud, creaking groan of wet wood echoed through the cell.

Nathaira glanced up at her over her hands.

The bleeding strip of cloth dangling from the woman's hand swayed with the motion of the ship. "I never seen a skinchanger in action before. Pretty impressive, really. Do ya 'ave to practice a lot to be able to do that, or does it just come naturally?"

Nathaira stared at the woman. That was twice now that she'd helped her. Why? She was a human, and humans hated her people.

"It comes naturally," Nathaira said after a moment, not really knowing why she was telling the woman this. "But younglings have to practice it like any other magic to get good at it."

"So, it's kind of like walking? All babes can walk, but they 'as to learn and practice like?"

"Yes," Nathaira said, looking away, "it's a lot like walking."

"Isn't it kind of embarrassing to lose your clothes like that in front of everyone, though?" the woman asked.

Nathaira glanced down at the new clothing the slavers had dressed her in, another pair of black trousers and a pockmarked shirt, though this one was brown. "No, it is a normal part of changing," she said softly.

"Huh." The woman pulled her hand back through the bars between them, the chains attached to her wrists clanking against the metal.

"Oh, who cares about 'ow the monsters change? She'll probably turn into a bear the first chance she gets and eat us all before we reach the arena."

Nathaira started at the new voice and peered into the darkness behind the woman. Two sets of eyeballs stared back.

"These be my cell mates," the woman said. She jabbed a thumb over one shoulder at the two men sitting against the side of the ship that made up the back wall of their cells. "The slavers was running out of cages to put us all in, so's they shoved us less-dangerous creatures into cells together." The woman scratched at her stringy blonde hair, the noise echoing through the dimness. "Yer lucky that they don't trust ya so's ye don't 'ave to share with the likes of these two."

Nathaira turned away.

Lucky? Wearing chains and trapped in a slaver ship, lucky?

"Shut yer mouth, ya stupid whore," the man who had spoken before growled. "It'd be a lot more fun in 'ere if you'd loosen up."

"By loosen up, they mean spread me legs so theys can 'ave their way," the woman said softly.

Nathaira glanced back over at her.

"But though I may be a thief, I ain't no slut to sleep with any man that comes along like." The woman grinned. "Besides, they don't 'ave any money to pay me with."

Nathaira eyed her. Moirin had told her once how some humans sold their bodies to other humans for money. When she'd first heard, she'd been abhorred. Her people only slept with one other in their life, their true mate, and the thought that one would lay with others for money was beyond appalling.

An animal whimpered nearby, and Nathaira glanced down the dark hallway at the rows of other iron-barred cells scattered between the arching wooden beams that held up the deck above. How many creatures were trapped in the darkness, waiting to be slaughtered in the arena?

"I'm sorry about yer brother, by the way," the woman said.

Nathaira glanced back at her.

"I know that's why ya was tryin' to escape, to find 'im and all."

Nathaira looked at her manacled hands folded in her lap. Yes, she had been trying to escape to find Efamar. Only she had failed, and now he was farther away from her than before.

"We can talk about it, if ya want," the woman said again after a moment.

Nathaira looked up at her. "I don't," she said shortly. She turned her back on the woman and curling up in a ball, chains rattling on the floor as she moved, closed her eyes, and slept.

#

The days passed. Nathaira knew by the water—tainted with silver and stale, brown, and rancid tasting—brought down to those crammed in the hull by a slaver each day.

She avoided drinking it for the first few days, but after five days without water, her body couldn't handle not drinking anymore, and she was forced to drink or die. With all the silver attached to her now, it didn't really make a difference if she drank it or not, Nathaira mused darkly as the slaver walked away on the seventh day. She would never escape from the ship. Her only hope was when they reached land again and had to travel from Dyridura to the kingdom of Eromor and the arena there.

The smell in the ship's hull only increased as the long, dark, and miserable days dragged by. The scent of death added to it on the eighth day when a deer and badger passed on to the next life. Nathaira whispered the Prayer of Death for them as slavers dragged their bodies past.

A storm assaulted the ship on the ninth day, tossing the massive vessel around like a piece of driftwood on the waves it made, and for two days Nathaira listened to the sea raging against the ship's sides and thunder crashing in the sky. Would they make it to Warulan or become another wreck at the bottom of the Silver Sea?

The woman didn't try to talk to her after their first conversation, but Nathaira could feel her eyes on her each day as she lay dozing in the back of her cage.

"Come on, sweetie," said one of the men to the woman on the tenth day at sea. "Quit being such a 'igh and mighty lady, and let's 'ave some fun."

Nathaira heard scuffling on the floor behind her, and a moment later the scratching of nails on skin echoed through the dim light.

"That'll teach ya to keep yer dirty 'ands to yerself!" the woman said.

A crack sounded from the other cell.

Nathaira glanced over her shoulder. The woman was pinned to the floor by the quiet man while the other sat on top of her, ripping at her clothing.

There was a moment when she thought to turn away, to ignore what was happening. The woman was human… but forcing a fellow creature to mate was wrong no matter who it was done to. Nathaira moved to the bars. "Get off her," she warned.

"What are ya going to do about it, skinchanger?" asked the man on top of the woman. He didn't look up. The woman was kicking at him and calling him multiple different things. "Ya can't change with all that silver on, and there are iron bars between us." He ripped the woman's shirt open with one hand, and she cursed even louder as he grinned at her nakedness.

"HELP!" Nathaira called, her chains dragging on the floor behind her with a loud grating noise as she moved to the front of her cell. "Help, down here!"

The man who had spoken cursed loudly, and Nathaira turned as the woman ripped her hands free from the other man's hold and threw the chain around her hands into the face of the man on top of her.

The man yelled as blood gushed from his cheek, and pulling the woman's head upward, he slammed it into the floor with a loud crack. The woman fell limp, and they all stared at her quietly for a few moments.

"You've killed her," Nathaira said softly.

The man on top of the woman stood and wiped a hand across his cheek. "Served her right," he spat, fastening the latches on his trousers with one dirty hand. "She should 'ave cooperated like I wanted."

"What is going on?" an accented voice yelled.

Nathaira turned, and the men slunk into the shadows at the back of their cell as the hatch at the end of the hull opened and several slavers climbed down.

"She 'it her 'ead!" said the man who had spoken before as the turbaned and masked men moved down the hall between the cages. "Must have gone mad from the darkness, 'cause she just started yelling and pulling at 'er clothes, and then…" The man moved into the light of the slaver's torch and shrugged. "She tripped and 'it 'er 'ead. Seems to've killed 'er."

One of the slavers glanced at her, and Nathaira stared back. They wouldn't believe her account over one of their own kind, and what good would it do anyway? They wouldn't kill the men; they were valuable.

The door of the other cell groaned loudly as the slavers opened it and dragged the woman's body out into the hall.

Nathaira watched as they pulled her past, the woman's head bumping along the floor and leaving a dark trail of blood behind them.

I should say the Prayer of Death…

Nathaira glanced at the men. The talkative one sneered at her.

The Prayer of Death was a blessing, an honoring of the deceased. Could she say it over a human?

We should love the humans as fellow creations of the Sisters. Moirin's voice murmured in her head. Nathaira turned her back on the men.

"I won't love them," she whispered. She remembered the help the woman had given her.

A deer bleated from up the hall, crying for its homeland and herd.

Nathaira stared into the darkness. "Your body, I bless. Your life, I grieve…" she whispered.

#

The rest of the journey at sea passed quickly.

Slavers brought silver-tainted water and stale food each day, but it wasn't enough to thrive on, and Nathaira spent most of her time curled up in the back of her cell trying to ignore her growling stomach and the constant, dull pain from the silver in her veins.

Fifteen days after the ship had left Ennotar, she sensed that their journey was ending, as a noticeable lull occurred in their speed.

Feet pounded on the deck above. The deep groaning of metal on wood echoed through the darkness. Nathaira lifted her head.

A heavily accented voice drifted down from above. "Let's get these creatures unloaded!"

Animals rustled as the ship grew still. Nathaira pushed herself into a sitting position as the hatch at the end of the hallway opened and a blinding, golden stream of sunlight glared into the hull.

Nathaira climbed to her feet and moved to the front bars of her cage, chains dragging loudly behind her. Was Efamar in the same position as her right now, or was he still in Ennotar? Or worse, lying at the bottom of the ocean like so many others who couldn't stand the long sea voyage? No, she would not believe that. He was alive, and she would escape and find him.

A wooden platform slowly lowered through the hatch on creaky pulleys. A cougar snarled fiercely as two dozen slavers began unlocking cages and dragging creatures out.

"Yer turn to die, skinchanger," the man who had killed the woman said as the slavers drew closer. Nathaira heard the methodic click of locks unlocking, the creak of cage doors opening, and the crack of whips as animals were dragged by chains to the platform.

Nathaira glanced over at the man. He sneered widely, his mouth full of black and broken teeth. "I'll bet yer the first one they kill in the arena. Give ya a taste of 'ow short lives feel, since all of us ain't prone to living for 'undreds of years like yer kind. 'Ow do you think they'll do it? Burn ya at the stake? Or maybe whip ya to death with silver; I 'eard that was a favorite during the wars."

Nathaira ignored the man. He laughed loudly, a grating, cackling laugh that made her hair stand on end. Whatever lay ahead for her, she hoped he met a worse fate.

Three slavers dragged a pair of screaming mercats out of the cell next to hers. Nathaira stepped back as they disappeared up through the hatch, the elongated striped forest cats snarling and hissing ferociously. She would be next.

Cold and salty sea air fanned her sharp face as the slavers dragged her out of the hull and over to a wooden ramp attached to the deck of the ship. Nathaira breathed in the wild smell like she'd never breathed air before.

Warulan. Nathaira glanced at the massive half-moon bay around her, cut off from the sea by a curving row of salt-eroded statues in the likeness of human gods and goddesses. With the vanquishing of magic from Argdrion had come the decline of the old religion, as the humans now called it, for they, along with asserting magic was evil, had come to believe that the Sisters were just moons and that gods and goddesses had made the worlds.

Nathaira stared at the statues ringing the harbor. All their wealth and all their power, and yet still the humans had nothing.

Dozens of wagons loaded with iron cages, many of them already full, waited in rows on the docks below.

Nathaira winced as the slavers threw her into a cage on a wagon at the back of the rows. She tried to find a comfortable position where the manacles on her wrists and ankles didn't dig in and the collar around her neck didn't chafe. She eyed the milling crowd of onlookers at the edge of the docks and the towering, mortar-washed buildings beyond. The buildings, unlike those in Ostgate, were clean and well-sized, and the people were dressed in richer outfits of fur, leather, and silks that hugged their bodies in a slimming manner. Since the wars and the gain of new lands from the skinchangers and the wiar, Warulan had quickly become the richest continent in Argdrion.

Rich by my people's blood.

"How much aray do you figure she'll bring?"

"At least two hundred thousand, maybe more."

Nathaira glanced over her shoulder at two fur-clad men standing nearby, watching her like she was an animal that couldn't understand them.

One was as plump as a boar, the other slender and pale.

The plump one, looking like an overstuffed brown bear in his fur coat, whistled, the beard covering his pudgy face ruffling in a sea breeze. "I'd love to see that kind of money," he said. "Imagine what a man could do with it."

The pale man snorted. "Yes, but I'd want an easier way of getting it than capturing the likes of her."

His companion grunted in agreement.

Slavers with a growling wolf approached a wagon beside the men, and they moved off through the gathering crowd.

Nathaira looked back out at the crowded harbor, the ships' masts a forest of trees covered in ropes and sails. So, she was valuable to the humans. Two hundred thousand aray... If her buyers were willing to pay that kind of money for her, then they probably wouldn't want to kill her off immediately in the arena... Not that she intended to reach the arena.

Boots thudded loudly on wood. Nathaira glanced sideways as three slavers hauled the two men who had killed the woman toward her wagon.

"Looks like we're going to be cell mates again, skinchanger," the talkative one said, sneering as the slavers tossed them into the wagon's other cage and slammed the door shut with a clang. "Too bad there's bars between us," he leered. "Or we'd 'ave the same fun with ya what we 'ad with that woman bitch."

"If you did, you would lose more than some skin from your face," Nathaira replied calmly. The man glared at her. She turned away from them and leaned against the opposite side of her cage.

A slaver climbed into the seat of the wagon and cracked a whip over the heads of the sorrels pulling it. The horses lurched forward, and the wagon rumbled across the dock after the others, forming a slowly crawling line down a crowded street of the town.

Nathaira watched mortar-washed buildings of pale white and dark stone go past, the towering buildings looking like glaring sentries.

A large crowd cheered loudly as her wagon rattled past. Nathaira turned her gaze to several men and women in strange costumes—one man covered in moss and leaves from head to foot and another with antlers on his head—hopping around on a raised platform in front of the group of humans.

Actors. Moirin had told her about such people. She had said they were wonderful to watch.

"…Going to the arena in Crystoln for King Uranius's birthday," a middle-aged man with graying sideburns said as Nathaira's wagon slowly came even with him. "He's turning ninety-four this year, you know, and his chief advisor, Torin Ravynston, is throwing him a week-long birthday celebration with all the arena sport you can get."

Nathaira glanced at the man.

"Yes, I heard that," said a woman in a slender red dress. She held a small groomed dog on a gold chain. "And I also heard the king hasn't picked a successor yet. I wonder if that's part of the advisor's plan, to get on his good side." Her dog sniffed the air as the wagon passed and started yapping shrilly. The woman swatted it with an ivory-handled fan she was using to cool herself.

"Maybe," the man said. "But if he hasn't picked one yet, I doubt he will now. The council will just have to vote in the next ruler when he dies."

Nathaira watched more buildings roll past as her wagon rumbled on down the street and the man and woman drew out of earshot. King Uranius, the only son of King Athtiron and Queen Alvyna. They said that he was crueler than even his father had been, and that in the Hunting, he had been at the front of every major slaughter, covered in skinchanger and wiar blood.

The wagon train journeyed through the city at a slow but steady pace. At noon it passed the last building and rumbled across a stone bridge spanning a dark-green river and out onto a dusty road marked as the West Road by a faded sign next to the bridge.

The days blurred together.

Nathaira watched the passing scenery with interest, at first sprawling oak forests, then steep and craggy mountains. She thought of the clan often as the wagons rumbled along, thought of their deaths and the fact that she would never change with them again in this life. But mostly she thought of Efamar and wondered where he was, and if he was alive.

She tried to change for the first few days, even though she knew that it was useless with so much silver adorning her. After five failed attempts, she gave up. She would have to wait until the arena, when the humans removed her silver bindings so that she could fight.

The men from the ship mostly ignored her, and Nathaira did the same to them, but occasionally the talkative one would get bored and taunt her with gruesome tales he'd heard of the arena and what was going to happen to her when she got there. Impaling, beheading, whipping. It didn't bother Nathaira; she had heard the tales too.

The third day on the road, the wagon train entered the Astarion Mountain Range.

On the fourth, it wound down a dark and twisting pass leading through towering cliffs that echoed every footstep, wagon creak, and whip crack the train made.

Nathaira stared up at the cliffs, jagged faces of granite streaked with gray scars.

"Eysran Pass," the talkative man said. "I 'eard thousands of skinchangers died 'ere when they ran from the 'umans."

"Actually, only three hundred died," Nathaira replied without looking at him. "And my people ran from yours on purpose to draw them into a trap that later cost your people ten thousand lives." She could feel the man's scowl. Her lip twitched upward softly.

"Ya think you're so damn smart, skinchanger," the man growled, "but it doesn't change the fact that yer just an animal, like the ones ya change into." He snorted. "Why, I bet ya even sleep with ani—"

Nathaira was at the bars between their cages before he could finish, her hand wrapping around the man's throat and cutting him off. "You talk too much, human," she hissed, golden eyes burning.

The man gasped and clawed uselessly at her fingers. Nathaira squeezed harder, letting all her hatred, all her anger at what the humans had done to the clan go into the squeeze. "You think your kind so much better than mine," she snarled. "You think that there is so much more honor among humans than among skinchangers." She gripped harder, and the man's hands fell to his side.

Moirin's face, soft and caring, flashed through her mind, followed by Athrysion's as he taught her how to kill mercifully and swiftly, but only for a reason. She could kill the man, Nathaira knew. Her fingers curled tighter at the thought. The man gagged, his tongue turning blue.

But choking to death would be too quick, too merciful. It would be better to let him go to the arena and die one of the deaths he'd taunted her with.

"You know nothing of honor," Nathaira said finally, shoving the man backward into his friend, who had not moved from his position by the back of the wagon. She turned away from them.

The man never spoke to her again.

On the fifth day of their journey, the wagons rumbled out of the last of the Astarion Mountains and into a vast, waving plain of grass that stretched as far as the eye could see in all directions.

The Opherian Plains. Nathaira looked at the rippling grass from the bars of her cage as her wagon inched down a rocky hill and out onto the sprawling land. She'd heard the elders talk of the plains. They'd said that one could travel for five days across them and never see anything but grass, grass, and more grass.

The days dragged by as before, the only thing to be seen the waving grass and an occasional bird in the endless sky.

Wind blew constantly through the axle-high grass on either side of the road. At night the temperature dropped so low that Nathaira would wake with frost on her skin.

On the third day of traveling, yelling echoed back from the front of the train, and Nathaira turned to see white walls looming out of the grass. Her heart grew as cold as the frost that melted off her skin each morning.

Crystoln. Nathaira pushed herself to her feet, chains rattling as she took in the vastness of the stretching walls and city-covered hills inside. Covering over two hundred thousand acres and surrounded by a one-hundred-foot-high white marble wall, Crystoln was the prize jewel and capitol of Eromor and the largest city in Argdrion. It was also impregnable. And the last large-scale battlefield site of the Third Great War.

The wagons rumbled closer to Crystoln, and Nathaira craned her neck back to peer up at the white walls as the wagons rolled over the River Sar on a three-wagon-wide bridge of white marble blocks.

The front of the long and dusty line of wagons moved past two massive oaken gates thrown open wide and through a thick arch cut out of the white marble of the wall. Dark spots on the wall slowly came into view. Nathaira squinted to make out what they were as her wagon drew closer. They were bodies, she realized with a sinking feeling. Decapitated, whole, mangled, burnt—all with long streaks of dark, sun-dried blood marring the white wall beneath them. Her stomach roiled.

The smell hit her a second later, like bear fat left too long in the suns or maggot-infested entrails.

Nathaira put a hand over her nose as details came into view: a bloated stomach, flesh-picked fingers, empty eye sockets, a twisted hand blackened from flames, hair hanging from heads between stark white spots of bone. Magic users. She did not have to ask to know what crimes had warranted such horrific displays.

Her wagon rumbled past the gates and through the arch, and Nathaira tore her gaze away from the bodies on the wall to look at the jostling and pointing humans crowding the wide street on the other side.

"Move, skinchanger!" yelled a man with an immaculately trimmed yellow beard from the watching crowd.

"Yes!" a woman called, golden earrings in the shape of the suns dangling from the cuffs of her ears. "If we're to pay to see you, show us that our money will be well spent!"

"Show us that you are as fierce as they say your kind are!" an ebony-skinned man with silver rings on all his fingers yelled.

Nathaira didn't move.

The slaver driving her wagon twisted in his seat and tapped the top of her cage with his whip. "Do something, animal," he said haltingly in the general tongue, "or they'll not want to see you in the arena." His voice sounded contorted behind his silver mask.

Nathaira glanced up at him, his figure ringed by the Brothers' glaring midday rays. She snarled. She could feel the man's eyes narrowing. Calculating, weighing. He turned back around after a second and yelled in his own tongue at the horses pulling the wagon.

The wagon train wound through the massive city on a maze of twisting, turning, and confusing cobbled streets, climbing ever upward toward the distant black roofs of the palace.

Nathaira watched the dark roofs draw closer, remembering what Moirin had taught her about the Great White City. Crystoln had originally started out as a simple farming village, but due to its strategic location by the River Sar, it had grown by leaps and bounds throughout the ages until it had become Eromor's capitol and the largest and wealthiest city in Argdrion. Its arena had helped bring thousands to its many gates during the Third Great War, and mining from the silver mines under the city's eastern area had brought the rest. It had been Crystoln where it was first discovered by the humans that silver was the skinchangers' and wiar's weakness, and during the long and bloody years of war, Crystoln's silver mines had been the largest producers of silver in Argdrion.

How many lives would have been spared if the city had stayed a farm village, Nathaira wondered. And how different would Argdrion now be? Better, for sure, whatever the difference.

The wagon train turned down a wide street lined with tall stone walls and ambled toward a stone arch with depictions of skinchangers, wiar, and animals carved into it.

The arena was suddenly before her. Nathaira moved to the front bars of her cage, peering through the men's cage in front of her at the massive structure. Her blood grew cold. The arena's tall, dark stone walls towered threateningly above her.

Sisters, let this not be where I die.

Her wagon rumbled closer to the arch, and Nathaira squinted up at the etchings on the water-streaked rock as she passed underneath. The impression of a wiar, flames sprouting from her hands, and a skinchanger standing atop a grassy knoll in front of hundreds of charging humans caught her eye.

A depiction next to it showed the same wiar shaking hands with a human king.

A third carving showed the wiar and humans united to fight the skinchangers.

Nathaira narrowed her golden eyes. The wiar had betrayed her people in the wars when they had joined the humans against them. Every skinchanger knew the story, and every skinchanger hated the long-dead race more than anything in Argdrion, more even than the humans.

The wagon train passed underneath another stone arch, and several blood-red flags with Eromor's crest of a roaring black dragon snapped in the wind atop the thick rock. A flock of night-black crows squawked loudly from the wall next to the arch.

They are waiting for the next creature to die. Nathaira watched the birds as her wagon rumbled through the arch and came to a stop in the massive courtyard on the other side. Her driver jumped off and disappeared into the throng of wagons, horses, and slavers.

The loudly cawing crows hopped sideways on the wall, their feathers glinting purple and blue in the Brothers' midday rays.

Two dozen men appeared out of the darkness of a third arch that was set into the wall around the arena, black leather masks and an assorted array of deadly weapons on their belts speaking of power and fear. They moved as one toward a group of slavers.

Nathaira watched the masked men and the slaver as they animatedly argued for a few minutes until one of the black-masked men nodded and the slavers moved toward a door in the opposite side of the courtyard.

The quiet man began crying softly as the black-masked men spread out along the wagons. The talkative one cursed and told him to shut his gob as the masked men approached their wagon.

"Welcome, friends!" a large hairy man with a fat, bouncing gut hanging out from under his black leather jerkin said loudly.

Nathaira watched him silently.

"I heard you're a lively one, skinchanger," the man said, stopping in front of her cage. "I hope you aren't planning on giving us too much trouble."

Nathaira didn't reply.

The man grinned too amiably and pulled a key from a pocket.

"It's open, sweetie," he said, swinging the gate of her cage open, "open wide." His smile grew wider, and Nathaira noticed that his teeth were a dirty brown and his gums black.

"Not going to give it a try?" the fat man cooed. "Come on. I heard you have more fire than that!" He laughed loudly, belly jiggling. "Look what we've got here!" he yelled. "A skinchanger who's tame!"

He reached through the gate, and Nathaira hissed as he pulled her out of the wagon by the chain between her hands. She landed on her side on the stones of the courtyard, swallowing a cry as pain snaked through her body.

"Just be sure you stay tamed, skinchanger," the fat man said, leaning down. His breath smelled like rancid garlic, and his stomach touched his knees. "The slavers may not be willing to kill you for trying to escape, but here?" He stopped smiling, "You think about escaping, and you'll pray that your mother and father never spawned you."

Nathaira glared at the man, and he laughed and jerked her roughly to her feet. He flung her at two other black-masked men. "Take her below and give her some decent food. I want her ready for the arena in two days."

The men nodded, and Nathaira hissed again as they dragged her across the courtyard toward the third arch. Her heartbeat quickened as they neared the wall of the arena. She willed her legs to move, to run, but they were like lead from the silver in her veins.

The arch yawned above her, darkness in the middle stretching out toward her.

Nathaira fancied she saw blood running from the carvings of dying creatures that were cut into the gray stone. She tried to move her legs again as the men pulled her up the well-worn steps leading toward the arch, but they were like stones hanging from her body. The men stopped at the top of the stairs, one inserting a key into the lock of a black epharia door.

Nathaira struggled to pull her arm out of the grip of the man fumbling with the door. He didn't look at her.

Sisters, don't let me enter the arena, please!

The door swung open silently, and cold air brushed Nathaira's skin. She stopped moving.

Steep stone stairs led downward into darkness, and a low pounding echoed up from below.

"Welcome," the darkness seemed to whisper.

The hair on Nathaira's arms slowly rose on end. She tried to move again, but the men stepped forward, pulling her with them as they started down the stairs into the blackness.

"Welcome to the arena."

CHAPTER 11

Hathus

I thought you said you were taking me to your captain's ship." Hathus glanced at Sidion, the dreadlocked man from the tavern, and then back at the jungle in front of them, which stank like the pits of the underworld, its trees swaying in a warm night breeze.

After leaving behind the warmth and noise of the Bloody Boar, his "guide" had led him through a maze of the Main Island's back streets and slums and down a series of dark, deserted alleys and to the edge of the city, where the dense jungle grew in tangled, crowded miles of green vines, trees, and creeping undergrowth.

"I am," Sidion replied, a grin spreading across his face.

Hathus raised an eyebrow. "I don't see any ship."

Maybe he's a slave trader. His skin prickled at the thought.

Another grin. "You will." Sidion pulled a curved sword from a sheath at his right hip and started down a barely discernable path into the jungle.

Hathus watched him fade into the darkness. There was always a possibility that Sidion and his crew were going to murder him and the three men the Unknown Voice had sent with him and take their money. He waved a hand in front of his face as a large mosquito looked for food on his nose.

Maybe I should go back to the tavern. Hathus glanced over his shoulder at the stucco buildings of the city and then at the three shadows close behind him. He had to at least make it look like he was trying to find the Land of Dragons in the six months allotted him, though, and if he just kept waiting for the "right ship" to come along at the tavern, the men would get suspicious.

Hathus nervously glanced back at the jungle and started off down the path after the distant sound of Sidion hacking at plants with his scimitar.

The noise of the jungle closed in around them as they walked— barking monkeys, screeching parrots, trilling frogs, buzzing insects, and the occasional distant roar of a jaguar, all filling the humid night air in a chorus of tunes.

Hathus cursed as a fat jewel beetle landed on his arm, and slapped a glossy palm leaf out of his face as they skidded down a hill and through a murky stream.

I hate the jungle. The pirates wouldn't have to kill them; the jungle would do it for them, and all they'd have to do was take the money off their dead bodies.

Hathus wiped a hand across his sweat-drenched forehead as Sidion chopped through a tangle of sweet-smelling vines with fat pink flowers hanging from them.

Not that I want to die, but there are easier ways to kill a man besides having mosquitos eat him alive.

He slapped at another mosquito biting at the back of his neck. The palm of his hand came away dotted with flat black splotches.

They climbed up a steep hill before Sidion stopped shortly, holding up a hand. "See?" He smiled widely. "The ship."

Hathus looked up from leaning on his knees and trying to catch his breath and saw the golden lights of half a dozen ships' lanterns bobbing in a shimmering lagoon below. "Which one?" he breathed, trying to gulp in as much of the humid, foul-smelling jungle air as possible before his lungs burst.

Gods, I need to get my stamina back. He brushed a hand over his chin to clear it of mosquitos.

"That one," Sidion said, pointing at the closest ship as the three men from the Unknown Voice came up the hill and stopped next to them. Their cloaks were covered in bugs.

Hathus sucked in a breath and straightened, holding a thick dead vine out of his way so he could see better. It was not uncommon for the more famous and wealthier pirate captains to have fleets of ships. But he really only needed one, not seven. "So, who's your captain, and why doesn't he come into town himself?" Hathus asked.

"Doesn't like the jungle," Sidion replied.

"Huh?"

Sidion stepped closer, nodding toward Hathus's hand.

Now that he thought about it, something cold and slimy was wrapping around his arm. Hathus looked up sharply as the vine he'd moved out of the way twisted. A large black-and-tan boa constrictor wound its way up his arm, tongue flicking out of its mouth. Hathus screamed.

"Get it off!" he yelled, jumping backward and trying unsuccessfully to shake the snake off his arm.

Sidion laughed, a deep, throaty chuckle, and whipping his scimitar around, chopped the snake's head off with one swipe. "Makes a good stew." He grinned.

Sidion pulled the snake's body off Hathus's arm, its cold, scaly flesh sliding against his skin. Hathus shivered. "Gods above, why are there creatures like that on Argdrion?"

Sidion wound the dead reptile over his shoulders and, grinning again, started down the hill toward the lagoon.

Hathus shook himself and cursed, then leaned over and retrieved his hat from where it had fallen on the ground. He stood, cramming the hat on his head and glancing around the dark jungle for more snakes, and quickly followed Sidion down the hill.

A small rowboat bobbed in the gentle movement of the dark water of the lagoon. Dumping the snake's body in the bottom, Sidion motioned for Hathus to climb in before taking the oars. Hathus obeyed; the three men followed as usual.

The oars dipped methodically into the water beneath them with soft splashes as they glided across the lagoon. Hathus watched them for a moment, mesmerized by the pattern, before turning his eyes to the dark hulls of the ships filling the harbor. There were seven of them—six larger ones and one slender, smaller one. All were made of epharia wood.

They sailed toward the smaller ship.

Golden squares of light bobbed on the surface of the water around the vessel, reflecting from the creaking lanterns atop the deck. The soft, gentle creak of ropes and pulleys filled the air above the splash of Sidion's oars.

Scorpion bolts poked through weapon ports in two rows along the side of the ship, polished steel glinting in the semidarkness. In fact, all the ships had scorpion bolts protruding from portcullises, Hathus noted. He raised an eyebrow. Whoever this pirate captain was, he was well-armed. He noticed a name sprawled across the back of the smallest ship and peered through the gloom to try and make it out as Sidion pulled the rowboat alongside the towering hull. A curling *D* and *R* was all he could read.

"Up you go," Sidion said, smiling again.

Hathus looked over at him as Sidion stashed the oars in their holders on the rowboat's sides with soft thuds. He glanced up at a gently swinging rope ladder that hung over the dark side of the ship.

I really hope he isn't a slave trader. Hathus swung his bag over his shoulder and grabbed ahold of the coarse ladder; it smelled of tar and salt.

A tattooed hand with a depiction of a sea serpent on the back grabbed his as Hathus touched the epharia railing, and strong arms pulled him over the side and set him upright on the main deck before he could think about climbing over himself.

"Thanks..." Hathus began. He trailed off as he noticed the woman, tattooed hands on her curving hips, standing in front of him. Curly brown hair peeked in wisps from underneath a red bandanna wrapped around her head. Eyes like a storm-tossed sea surveyed him openly and without timidity. A curving body that would compete with the fabled goddesses of Veryala swayed easily with the ship's gentle movement, and a blue star tattoo stuck out on her left cheekbone, accenting her bronzed skin and playful smile.

"And who might you be?" the woman asked in a deep, strongly accented voice that marked her as a native of the BalBayr Islands.

Hathus bowed low, sweeping his leather coat out behind him. "My name is Ha—"

"A customer who wishes to see the captain," Sidion interrupted. He hopped easily over the black railing of the ship and landed gracefully next to the woman, the snake's body wrapped across his broad shoulders again.

Hathus glanced at Sidion, annoyed at the interruption. It had been a long three years…nine months, whatever, in the dungeons, and he relished talking to a beautiful woman again.

The woman smiled, dark lips pulling back from slightly crooked white teeth. She stepped sideways and motioned at a lantern-lit hallway leading under the poop deck. "Well, then, second mate," she said to Sidion, making Hathus look back at her, "let's take him to see the captain."

#

A lone lantern swung from a chain in the middle of the cabin, illuminating a heavy wooden table covered with maps, sextants, compasses, and various other sailing instruments. Shadows played around the edges of the lantern's circle of light, concealing the features of a who man sat behind a massive carved mahogany desk by the back wall.

Hathus ducked his head to avoid hitting the softly creaking lantern as the woman led him into the captain's cabin. The three men came next, with Sidion following. Sidion shut the door behind them with a click that echoed through the crowded room.

The first thing Hathus noticed about the epharia-wood cabin was the smell—mainly opirya, fine wine, and perfume. The second was the elaborate, somewhat gaudy decorations scattered throughout. A tiger skin lay sprawled underneath the table; a thick, gold-stitched tapestry sectioned off sleeping quarters; diamond-covered candlesticks adorned a dresser with carved lyon-paw feet beneath an oil painting of a naked Araysannian woman. Ornate rugs of all dimensions and designs lay scattered around the floor where the tiger skin was not, and on a slightly squeaking chain perched above the shadowed figure of the man behind the desk sat a diamond-collared monkey as white as snow and with eyes like emeralds.

Someone was doing well as a pirate, Hathus mused. He scanned the room greedily, fingers twitching as he imagined how much money he would make cleaning the place out.

"A customer to see you, Captain," the woman said. She perched on the edge of a small table sitting against one wall with several jade, opaque, and obsidian statues of gods and goddesses scattered atop it. She pulled a thin-bladed dagger from her belt and began flipping it up in the air and catching it as it came back down.

Hathus stepped toward the mahogany desk, noting a golden lyon-shaped hookah sitting half in the light of the lantern and beside a glass inkwell of purple ink.

The shadows behind the desk moved, and a slender right hand missing its three main fingers slid out into the lamp light. Rings on the two remaining fingers glinted dully, one ring an opulent blue diamond gilded with gold, the other a simple silver band.

"A customer, you say," a soft, feminine voice asked. "How may my fleet be of service to you?"

A cloud of white opirya smoke drifted out of the darkness. Hathus stifled a cough at the sickly-sweet smell. "Your man Sidion," he said, "stated that your ship was for hire?" He saw that the three men who followed him were standing in the shadows by the door, listening.

No need to worry, men, I'm not going to go back on our bargain. He'd never seen any weapons on them, or even seen their faces, but there was an aura of doom around the men that made his skin shiver and told him that they would kill him in a most unpleasant way if he didn't fulfill his bargain with the Unknown Voice.

An extravagant gold-gilded pendulum clock on one wall of the cabin chimed midnight in musical notes. The monkey blinked.

"That is correct," the man in the shadows replied softly, another cloud of smoke drifting toward the epharia ceiling. "Sidion tells me that you wish to go somewhere 'not in Argdrion.' I wonder, where could a man possibly want to go that is not in Argdrion?"

Hathus looked up, unease spreading through him. How could Sidion have told him that when Sidion hadn't left his side since the Bloody Boar? It smelled too much like he was being watched, and he didn't like to be watched.

"Yes," Hathus said slowly, warning bells beginning to chime in his head. "I want to go to the Land of Dragons." He shifted, nervous about speaking of magical otherworlds out loud, nonexistent or not.

The room fell silent, the soft hissing noise of the woman twirling the knife stopping suddenly as the clock chimed its last strike of twelve.

Hathus could feel the woman's gray eyes boring into his back. A bead of sweat slipped down his neck. What if they turned him in? He doubted it, but what if?

"Interesting," the voice in the shadows said, as calmly as if he'd just been told it was raining.

Hathus shifted on his feet again. His shirt was starting to stick to his back from the perspiration dripping down his spine, and it was annoying.

"And you believe that the Land of Dragons is real?" the man in the shadows asked.

Another cloud of smoke drifted out and tickled Hathus's nose.

If I breathe in much more of this stuff, I'm liable to start having hallucinations. "Yes, but not dragons," Hathus said gradually, reciting the words he'd gone over in his mind. "I believe that there can be truth in all stories, and in the story "The Seven Siblings of Rahys," I think the truth is the treasure. We know that there are otherworlds, so it's possible that the Land of Dragons is real and that the treasure said to be there is real as well. The dragons are probably just a made-up myth to keep people away from such wealth."

"Interesting," the pirate captain said again. "And a good theory. There can be truth in all stories and legends. As a pirate captain who searches for treasure, I've learned this. Sometimes the most common of stories have held a kernel of truth that no one noticed until someone did, and then that someone found a vast treasure."

Another puff of smoke came out of the shadows. "I knew a man," the pirate captain went on, "who believed a story about a mermaid and a rich pirate. The story was long, but the general idea was that the rich pirate was hypnotized by the mermaid and jumped into the water to be with her. She ate him, of course, but the story told of a medallion of gold and ruby that the pirate wore, and that medallion lay at the bottom of the ocean. This man I knew went looking for that medallion, and, surprising all of us, he found it."

"It's true," Sidion said.

Hathus glanced at Sidion, eyes meeting the woman pirate's for a moment. She raised one side of her mouth at him and went back to twirling her knife, the blade flashing in the lantern's soft glow.

"So you'll go?" Hathus asked, looking back at the shadows where the pirate captain hid.

"It depends on the price," the pirate captain said.

Hathus smiled, gradually growing less edgy.

And here's where we get down to business. "I'll pay you twenty thousand aray," he said, purposely lowballing. The Unknown Voice had given him fifty-five thousand aray to fund this trip, but it was never wise to let the opposite party know how much money one actually had or was willing to pay.

A puff of smoke drifted out of the shadows behind the desk. "Eighty."

Hathus snorted. "Twenty-five."

"Seventy."

"Thirty-five," Hathus said.

"Sixty-five."

"Forty-five."

"Sixty."

"Fifty," Hathus shot back.

And five thousand left over for me...

"And half of everything we find, if the Land of Dragons is not just a story," the pirate captain said.

"Deal," Hathus replied. He motioned for the men to step forward. One did, carrying one of the two trunks with him. "Here is twenty-five thousand aray," Hathus said, waving a hand at the trunk as the man set it on the desk beside the hookah. "You'll get the rest of your money when we return to the islands."

The pirate captain sucked on the hookah, the clicking of the pipe ringing through the room. "Open it."

Hathus nodded at the man, and he obeyed, the glare of gold filling their eyes as the lid fell back.

The man moved back to the shadows by the door. Hathus ran a hand over the coins. "Beautiful, are they not?"

"Ooo, I do love the clink of coins!" the monkey exclaimed.

Hathus lurched backward as the creature, its razor-sharp teeth glinting in the lantern's light, hopped down onto the desk and jumped into the chest. "What in the underworld is that?" he yelled, pointing at the monkey.

Sidion, the snake still dangling across his shoulders, grinned. "A monkey."

"I can see that," Hathus hissed. "But why is it talking?"

"He's a very clever monkey," Sidion said.

"But monkeys don't talk!" Hathus exclaimed, eyeing the laughing creature as it dug its small pink paws into the aray. It had to be magicked. His nervousness came back.

"That's what you think, stupid," the monkey replied. "How else do you think Sidion told the captain about your destination?"

Hathus took another step backward. He didn't like this. He was already too involved with magic as it was, looking for an otherworld. The more magic he was around, the more chance there was that someone would turn him in, and he'd be executed. He remembered the first time he had seen someone executed for using magic, and he shivered violently at the memory.

He'd been ten, walking home from school with his mother. It was during the Hunting, and everyone was nervous. Nervous that they would be accused of using magic, nervous that someone they knew was using it, nervous that their turn to walk to the block would be next.

"How was it today?" Hathus's mother asked. She was a soft-eyed woman with brown hair held back in a long braid. Hathus didn't look at her. School was like it always was—hard lessons, crueler teachers, and vicious classmates.

"I hate it," he'd said, watching a troop of dragon-crested soldiers jog past. Everyone avoided eye contact with the soldiers, but that day he didn't. His father abused him and his mother at home. He feared for his life on the streets, and at school his classmates picked on him and beat him up because his family was wealthy.

"I can find you another school…" his mother started.

"Don't bother," Hathus had said tonelessly. "You know that it will just be like the others." It was true, and they both knew it. For the last five years, he had been moved from one school to the next, and at every school it was the same. The children hated him because their families were poor from the wars, and his was rich.

"It's not my fault that Father is in mining," Hathus whispered, sudden tears pricking at his hazel eyes.

His mother put an arm around him, pulling him close. "I know," she whispered.

The only thing that made up for his classmates' cruelty were the things he stole from them. It had started as a way to make himself feel like he was getting back at them, lifting a pen from their desks, an apple from their lunch bags, but now it was an art that he had gotten good at, an art that he enjoyed.

Drums began beating a solemn tune, making Hathus look up.

"My gods," his mother whispered, "they've found another one."

Hathus went cold. He had never seen what happened in the execution squares scattered throughout the city when the drums rolled, but he knew what it meant for the people of Crystoln: death. Father had said that people were so panicked about magic, and rightfully so, that they would turn anyone in. Mother said that their race had run out of magical creatures to hunt, so they found magic among themselves to satisfy the authorities' lust for blood.

The crowd around them began milling toward the executioner's square ahead, and Hathus felt his mother pull him with them. "I don't want to watch," he whispered, digging his heels into the cobbles.

"I know," his mother said quietly, gripping his arm with an ashen face. "But you should. Your father wanted you to."

Hathus stopped resisting. Whenever his father "wanted" anything from them, it meant getting beatings until they complied. It was easier and less painful to just do as he said.

Three people were lined up in the middle of the executioner's square, kneeling in front of blocks with their hands tied behind their backs. One was a little girl, Hathus saw with growing fear. She was not much older than him.

"Magic is evil," a priest standing on a raised platform yelled, "and those who use it are the spawn of Setaron!"

Hathus watched spit fly out of the gold-robed man's mouth. It landed on the black dragon helmets of the soldiers below him.

The crowd screamed their agreement; rotten fruit and eggs sailed toward the kneeling people.

The little girl began crying.

"Let this be a lesson to all who might hold the notion of using magic!" the priest cried. The crowd screamed again.

Hathus moved closer to his mother. He could feel the hatred in the air, could see it on the enraged faces around him. Three executioners in black clothing and masks stepped forward, wide-bladed axes raised above their heads. Hathus watched, grotesquely transfixed.

"If you use magic," the priest said, sounding bored. The axes fell as one, and three heads popped off in spurts of bright-red blood. "You die." Hathus buried his head in his mother's dress as the heads plopped into baskets.

"If you know of anyone who uses magic or you suspect of using magic," the priest called, "turn them in. Or you are as guilty as they are!" He turned and marched out of the square, the soldiers trailing him. The executioners began to clean up the heads and bodies.

"Azaria is a rare monkey," the pirate captain said, snapping Hathus back to the present, "and quite helpful at times."

Hathus shook his head to clear it of the vision of the little girl's decapitated body, head lying a few feet away. "Just keep him away from me," he hissed, glancing at the monkey.

"Azaria will not bother you," the captain said.

The monkey picked a coin out of the chest and returned to its perch, eyes glinting as it studied the gold.

"Well, then," the pirate captain said after a moment. "It seems that we are at an agreement, yes?"

Hathus nodded stiffly.

"My first mate, Bathia, will take you to your room."

Hathus glanced at the woman.

"I hope you will find it agreeable," the pirate captain said.

Bathia moved toward the door, and feeling dismissed, Hathus made to follow.

The pirate captain's voice stopped him. "Since we are to be in the same company for some time now, I feel we should introduce ourselves."

Hathus turned back partway.

The shadows behind the desk moved, and a body appeared. "My name is Langor," the dark-haired man said, blowing a puff of smoke out of his slender mouth and making the dagger earring in his left ear sway. "Langor Blackwell. What is yours?"

Hathus eyed the man for a moment. He didn't look like a pirate captain, he looked like a pimp or a pampered noble. "Hathus Ryrgorion," he replied after a few heartbeats.

"Well, Hathus Ryrgorion," Langor Blackwell said, blowing another puff of smoke out, "welcome to the *Daemon's Cry.*"

CHAPTER 12

Darkmoon

There were people in the garden, a woman and a man. The woman was one of the King of Kings's harem, judging by her rich red tunic and hijab, but the man was a lower guard of the palace with a purple cloak and turban.

Darkmoon, hands splayed out on the tiled roof of the red sandstone building he perched on, glanced over the edge and through the swaying green branches of a young willow.

The King of Kings's concubine moaned loudly as the guard kissed her neck. The willow continued to sway in a chilly night breeze.

Darkmoon felt the breeze sneak under his cloak and run along his legs, tickling the flesh through the black suede pants he wore. The city guard patrol had marched back to the palace shortly before sundown, and after going with them toward their barracks, he had ducked into a garden when the opportunity had risen, and there he had hidden until darkness had come over the palace and most everyone had gone to bed.

Except for these two, apparently. Darkmoon reached a half-gloved hand into a pocket on the inside of his cloak and pulled out one of the pieces of chocolate residing there. He slipped the sweet into his mouth. His victim, the King of Kings, lay in bed in the tall sandstone building three hundred yards in front of him, in the eastern wing of the Zarcayran winter palace. To reach said building, he had to go through the garden below and past the

King of Kings's concubine and her guard.

Or through them.

Voices came on the wind, a woman asking for mercy, children crying. Darkmoon concentrated on the guard and concubine. He did not have time to listen to the voices—he had a job to do. He raised himself up on his forearms, black cloak pooling beneath him as the breeze died away. He slipped over the edge of the building he crouched on, a temple to the Araysannian goddess Anihita, and hung by his fingertips on the incised sandstone bordering the tile rooftop before dropping and latching on to a vine-covered sandstone lattice that climbed up the side of the building.

The concubine moaned again as Darkmoon quietly climbed down the lattice. He pulled two thin-bladed daggers from the black leather belts snaking around his middle and over his shoulders and dropped softly onto the glossy lily plants covering the ground behind the willow.

"Oh, Barsayn!" the woman gasped, throwing her head back as the guard lifted her dress with an animalistic growl.

Darkmoon stepped from the shadows behind the willow. "I hate to break up this affair," he said calmly in Zarcayran, "but you're in my way."

The concubine and guard jumped at his voice, and with a yelp, the guard let go of the half-naked woman and sprinted off down the gravel path.

"Brother…" Cyron whispered.

Darkmoon threw a knife at the concubine.

She hit the gravel beneath her, a dagger embedded up to its handle in her throat. Blood gurgled out of her swollen mouth. He sprinted after the guard.

He caught up to him thirty yards away, cutting ahead of the man by a side path and appearing in the gravel in front of him as the guard ran around a corner.

The guard skidded to a halt, face going through a thousand different expressions as he realized that he had not been found out by his superior and then spotted the glinting dagger in Darkmoon's hand.

"You know, Barsayn," Darkmoon murmured in the general tongue, "it's not polite to leave a woman before you satisfy her."

The guard hissed and drew a curved sword from his hip with a shing of metal against metal. "Who are you?" he said in a haltingly accented voice.

"Brother..." Cyron whispered again.

Darkmoon raised his head so that the guard could see his eyes shining out from underneath his cowl.

The guard's sword fell to the gravel, his dark face turning white beneath his turban. "Did he send you?" He gasped. "The King of Kings?"

"No," Darkmoon said. He let the other dagger in his palm fly, and the guard hit the path in a shower of gravel.

Darkmoon rolled the dead man over with one black boot. One of the first things that he had learned about killing was to always make sure that his victims were dead. There was nothing worse than failing to kill a target and having the person tell the world about it. It was bad for an assassin's name, messing up a kill.

The guard's eyes were open, and his mouth was slowly working up and down as blood gushed out of his throat and bubbled out between his flushed lips.

Darkmoon knelt next to the man, watching him spasm as he choked to death on his own blood.

"Brother, why?"

He stiffened. The guard fell still, eyes staring up at the star-filled sky above.

Darkmoon pulled his dagger out of the man's bloodied throat. The weapon made a dull sucking sound coming out. "You should have stayed at your post," he whispered, running a hand over the guard's body and finding a small bag of coin. He wiped his dagger off on the dead man's tunic.

A woman's sobbing whispered in his ear. Darkmoon stood, a lean shadow in the moonlight, and moved back to the concubine's body.

Her round brown eyes stared lifelessly up at the swaying branches of the willow above, her mouth hanging open in a shocked O. Darkmoon unclasped a delicate silver bracelet from her dark wrist and ran a tanned hand over her breasts and down to her hips for hidden pockets. A pearl-handled fan met his searching fingers. He pulled it out and set it on the gravel beside the woman's head.

Cyron flashed through his head again, kneeling in front of him with horror in his eyes.

Darkmoon paused as he pulled his dagger from the concubine's throat and quickly wiped it off on her gold-stitched tunic. He stood, slipping the small knife back up under his vambrace with a practiced bend of his hand. The fan and bracelet he deposited into a pocket inside his cloak.

"Brother…" Cyron whispered.

Darkmoon hissed. "Leave me alone."

The voices stopped.

He glanced around the garden, bushes swaying in a soft breeze making the only noise now. He turned as somewhere in the distance a dog barked and stepping over the concubine's body, moved toward the eastern wing of the palace.

#

The rest of the gardens leading to the eastern wing of the palace were deserted, and Darkmoon passed fishponds full of lotus, sandstone gazebos, and luscious flower beds without seeing anyone. He stopped by a flower bed full of lilies as he neared the dark-red wall of the eastern palace wing, the voice of Cyron back again, whispering in his ear. The voices were getting worse every day, and at night he kept dreaming of the ash-filled hall and the blood-eyed raven's warning.

Darkmoon picked a large white lily from a tall stalk and lifted the sweet-scented flower to his pointed nose. For years he had mastered burying the past and ignoring the voices that haunted him, until finally they went away. And yet in one night, and by one conversation with a seer, all the memories and whispers and pain were back. He crumpled the lily in one hand, the white petals moistening the black leather of his glove. He was stronger than this, and he could, and would, bury the past again.

He moved to the towering wall of the eastern palace wing and jumped into the air, latching on to the sandstone. He began climbing.

Ledges stuck out from the wall, and carvings and drawings in the red stone made niches and holes that Darkmoon's searching fingers found and used to pull himself up with.

Three stories up, he glanced back down at the garden below, which was bathed in the soft white light of the Sisters. The breeze had picked up again, carrying with it the cool smell of the desert outside the city walls and beyond, the snow-capped Eastern Mountains. The flowers and trees filling the garden swayed softly to its whispers. Darkmoon hung his body by one arm and, swinging back and forth to gain momentum, arced up and onto a wide sandstone windowsill.

The thing he liked about Araysann above Warulan was the architecture. Whereas Warulan's buildings had glass windows and locked shutters, Araysann's windows were merely beautifully carved openings with the occasional sheer silk hanging in front of them to keep bugs from making the building their new home. It made for an airier atmosphere and left the building feeling less cramped and enclosed.

Darkmoon slipped through the wide opening of the window, pushing through a sheer gold curtain, and landed softly on the multicolored haft-rangī floor of a lengthy hallway with several carved doors staggered along its inner arabesque sandstone wall.

The royal wing. Darkmoon glided down the airy hallway, scanning the semidarkness ahead for signs of movement.

"Brother, why?"

Darkmoon stiffened, gliding past door after door. His footsteps were soft, quiet.

He slid around a corner and stopped at the sight of two very bored-looking, gold-cloaked royal guards before quickly stepping back into the shadows of a geometric carved arch.

"Tell me why, and we can do this together… Together, like we always have been."

Darkmoon closed his eyes as Cyron kneeling before him flashed through his mind again. His breathing quickened.

"Together," Cyron whispered. "Stronger together, like always."

One of the guards coughed lightly, and Darkmoon's mismatched eyes snapped open. He stared at the wall of the hall opposite, seeing Cyron's green eyes in the red sandstone. They hadn't been stronger together; that was why he had done what he had.

Darkmoon turned and peeked back around the corner at the two guards. They stood on either side of double golden doors, wooden spears in their right hands, curved swords on their left hips. Wavering torches sat in gold brackets on either side of the guards, throwing red and orange fingers onto their dark faces and golden turbans.

Darkmoon eyed the golden lyon engraved in the middle of the golden doors between the guards. The King of Kings's bedchambers lay through the doors, and his target. His hand went to the belts crisscrossed over his well-muscled chest and the weapons hidden there. Two throwing stars slid out of the supple black leather at his urging, the thin beaten steel almost weightless in his palms.

"Brother," Cyron whispered.

Darkmoon threw the stars at the guards, and Cyron's voice stopped.

The guards slid to the haft-rangī floor, blood bubbling out of their mouths, throwing stars in their throats.

Darkmoon moved out from behind the arch, collecting his weapons from the guards' throats and wiping the blood off on the men's cloaks. He tested the handle of one door. It was unlocked. He listened at the cool gold for a moment before softly pushing the door open and slipping inside.

Quiet snoring filled the cavernous bedchamber, visible through an arabesque-patterned arch that led from the antechamber to it.

Darkmoon carefully shut the door behind him again, the latch sliding into place with a soft click. He moved through the antechamber and into the bedchamber, glancing at the carved ivory bed dominating the center of the room.

Impressive.

Two dark shapes rose and fell in perfect unison on the bed, the gentle whisper of wind at the window moving through the bedchamber.

A yellow lyon-skin rug with five-inch tusks glowing softly in the darkness watched Darkmoon with cold glass cat eyes as he crept onto it, its thick fur muffling what little noise his boots made as he moved across it and toward the bed.

Ten feet high and covered in carvings that were intricately designed to depict the different animals and plants of Araysann, the bed was curtained off with gold and purple silk so sheer it seemed almost nonexistent. Darkmoon eyed it. He would like a bed like it in one of his mansions.

He slid aside the silk curtaining with one hand and scanned the two sleeping figures inside. The queen was as beautiful as he had heard she was, with chest-length curly brown hair and a sharp face. The King of Kings had the look about him of a man who had been handsome in his younger years but had lately begun to show his age in the lines in his face and silver dominating his black mustache and full head of hair. He looked like a man who usually got his way, and from the bruise covering the queen's left eye, mostly from violent actions.

Darkmoon pulled a long, slender knife from a sheath at his hip and leaned over the bare-chested King of Kings. "If I had a wife as beautiful as you do," he whispered, voice soft, "I think I'd be a bit more careful how I handled her." He raised the knife.

His mother's face replaced the King of Kings's, blue eyes filled with so much sadness. Darkmoon inhaled and drew back, voices washing over him like a flood.

"Together, brother," Cyron whispered.

"Mercy, please, for my children," his mother's voice cried.

"Brother, why?"

Darkmoon gasped, knife falling from his hands as he reached out for a nearby chair to steady himself.

A woman's screams filled his head, followed by people sobbing and Cyron again. "Brother, why…"

The queen moaned and rolled over. Darkmoon sucked in a deep breath and glanced at the bed. His mother was gone, replaced by the sleeping King of Kings and his queen again. He moved away from the chair and to his knife, crouching down to pick it up from an intricate rug before moving back to the edge of the bed.

The queen lay with her back to the king now, dark-red welts crisscrossing her flesh in angry marks.

Darkmoon leaned over the King of Kings again, concentrating on pushing the voices away. He put his forearm back on the king's chest and raising the knife again, drove it deep into the sleeping man's throat. The voices stopped immediately.

Warm droplets of blood rained over the sleeping King of Kings and the queen, staining the gold silk bedsheets beneath them red like wine.

The King of Kings's eyes opened, wide and filled with fear—the kind of fear that men felt when they realized they were dying.

The King of Kings jolted sharply several times, Darkmoon held his arm against him firmly for a few moments, the smell of blood filling his nostrils, enlivening him, driving the voices into silence. He withdrew the knife from the King of Kings's throat as the man's movements grew weaker. Blood pooled in the divots of the sheets.

"Hello, King Vosbarhan," Darkmoon whispered. He leaned on the king's chest, making him moan. The sound came out as a gurgling vibration. "I would say that many will mourn upon your death," Darkmoon murmured, "but judging from the looks of your queen, I doubt that is true." He smiled, but there was no humor in it.

The king attempted to swallow, but for the hole in his throat couldn't, and more blood bubbled out of the wound as he gasped and spit out a mouthful of the dark-red liquid.

"It's a sad thing when a man goes on to the next life friendless," Darkmoon whispered as the king's brown eyes began to lose their color and his breathing slowed.

The king coughed once and let out a long, heavy sigh.

Darkmoon straightened and wiped his knife off on a clean part of the sheets. A moan escaped the queen's lips as he finished cleaning the weapon, and he glanced up as she slowly woke. He was surprised that she hadn't awoken earlier.

"Vosbarhan," the queen murmured. She sat up and turned, dark hair pooling over her breasts. "Vosbarhan, did you call for me, husband?"

"He won't be calling anyone anymore," Darkmoon said quietly.

The queen gasped as she noticed him. She cried out as she saw her husband's blood-covered body. "Who are you?" she whispered, eyes filling with fear.

"Me?" Darkmoon asked, sheathing his knife with a soft hiss of leather on steel. "I'm nobody, just a messenger. From Eromor to your husband." He glanced down at the dead King of Kings. "Ex-husband."

The queen opened her mouth to scream, but Darkmoon cut her off. "I wouldn't do that if I were you," he said, a deadly edge to his voice. He moved around the golden couch at the foot of the bed and stopped in front of the trembling woman. "Someone might hear you, and we wouldn't want that, would we?"

The queen pulled back from him like he was a snake. "If you're going to kill me," she whispered, "then get it over with."

Darkmoon hummed in acknowledgment, running three fingers down an ivory bedpost.

"Mercy," his mother whispered in his head again.

His fingers curled around the bedpost. "Why would I want to do that, Your Highness?" he asked, glancing over at the queen after a moment. "The whole point of giving a message is so others can hear it, and if I kill you..." Darkmoon let the sentence hang. There was no need to finish it.

"But why?" the queen whispered. "Why kill my husband? He was loved by all his people..."

Darkmoon gripped the bedpost harder as his mother's screaming echoed through his mind again. "Let's not lie to each other, Your Highness," he said, voice strained. "Your husband may be loved by a few of the shayr of Zarcayra, but judging from that bruise on your eye and the old ones on your breasts and marks on your back, I would say you want to thank me about now."

The queen didn't reply, just watched him silently.

Darkmoon glanced at her, suddenly wanting a cold shower and a good night's sleep. No, what he really wanted was to kill more people. Killing shut the voices up, killing blocked out the memories. He had only been paid to kill the King of Kings of Zarcayra, though, and as he'd told the queen, he had a message to give her.

"My message is simple and not hard to remember," Darkmoon said softly. He backed up from the bed, heading toward a window in a row lining the back of the bedchamber. "Eromor."

The queen inhaled. "Eromor? What does it mean?" Her face went white. "Did they send you? But why would they want my husband dead?"

"That," Darkmoon replied, turning and jumping up onto the sandstone sill of a window, "is something that you will have to take up with them." He pushed aside the see-through curtain hanging over the window.

"Who are you?" the queen asked behind him.

Darkmoon stared down at a torch-lit courtyard below and the city beyond the wall encircling it.

"Together, Brother..."

He turned, raising his head so that the queen could see his eyes. Her reaction was like that of the guard in the gardens, a sharp gasp followed by the paling of her skin.

Darkmoon left her there screaming. After jumping from the palace window to the wall below, he ran along it and slipped into the city as the palace awoke and bells rang the news that an intruder was among them.

A door opened as Darkmoon slipped down a narrow alley. A shadowed face peeked out of a doorway, trying to see what was going on and why the bells were ringing. He drew a knife out of his waist belt. Cyron watched him from across the street. He had been hired to kill the King of Kings of Zarcayra…

Darkmoon moved closer to the open door, watching the face behind it. He would kill many more this night, as many as it took to drive the voices away. As many as it took to give him peace. The door opened wider as the bells grew louder.

Darkmoon ran toward it.

CHAPTER 13

Azkanysh

Vosbarhan was dead.

Azkanysh stared at the thousands of silent faces looking up at her, a warm breeze filled with the glassy scent of sand pulling at her black tunic, robes, and hijab. She could not believe it. She almost wanted to lean down to the body lying on the elevated stand in front of her, Vosbarhan's body, and feel for a heartbeat. Was it truly possible that her master was dead? The man who had tortured her, beaten her, raped her, abused her, kept her secluded…

Vyzir Dsamihur cleared his throat behind her, and Azkanysh blinked and realized that they were waiting for her to move. Every face in the crowd below, every Guardian Council member and shayr and destūr and destūry and her children on the wall behind her, all were waiting for her to start the ceremony that would begin Vosbarhan's funeral. She leaned forward, stretching her black-painted hands out and over Vosbarhan's silent form. Vosbarhan was dead, and they were on the West Wall of the palace, the wall that overlooked the city, where royal announcements, weddings, inaugurations, namings, and funerals were held.

Azkanysh balanced her body over Vosbarhan's, bowing over him, paying reverence to him. She had done so for twenty-eight years. After today, she would no more. She wanted to scream, to dance, to run, to jump. But mostly she wanted to sit somewhere where there were not thousands of people watching her so that she could think about what this change of events meant.

The six destūrs and seven destūries, one man for each of the six gods and one woman for each of the seven goddesses of the Family of the gods, begin murmuring behind her, their joined high and deep voices floating through the silent air around her.

Azkanysh straightened, blood rushing to her head as she rose back up to a standing position. She scanned the watching crowd filling the massive square sixty feet below the wide expanse of the West Wall. She had never stood facing so many people before; it almost made her want to shrink away. But she was finding that she enjoyed standing before them, relished the feeling of being seen, of being noticed. She bowed over Vosbarhan again. She would bow over him thirteen times, one for each member of the Family of the gods.

The destūrs and destūries continued to chant, their voices rising and falling in unison. "The King of Kings is dead, the land lies in mourning…"

Azkanysh straightened again, blood rushing back into her head in pounding waves. She did not mourn Vosbarhan's death.

It had been three days since she had awoken to find Vosbarhan dead in the bed next to her and an assassin in their room, and in those three days, she had felt no sadness, no remorse, no sorrow. She did not expect that she ever would.

Azkanysh bent forward again, placing her arms over Vosbarhan's body. She felt gratitude toward the man they called Darkmoon, love, even. She had been in a prison when the assassin had driven his knife into Vosbarhan's throat. When he took Vosbarhan's life, that prison had suddenly faded away like the mist that hung over the Akhuran River in the mornings. She could still smell the scent of Vosbarhan's blood, feel its warmth splattered over her. Nothing had ever felt so good.

Azkanysh rose for the third time, growing used to the blood rising to her temple.

Vosbarhan was dead, his body cleaned and dressed in a black tunic, turban, and robes. She glanced at him. He looked like he was sleeping, so peaceful, rested. It angered her that he should be peaceful. He deserved nothing but torment in death. Torment and pain and fire and torture.

The golden lyon crown atop Vosbarhan's head glittered sharply in the Brothers' noonday rays. Azkanysh blinked against the brightness and bent back over.

After her part to begin the funeral, the destūrs and destūries would anoint Vosbarhan with the Water of Life and the Water of Death from the two massive bronze bowls that resided in Drisahr Aruyn's main temple outside the third wall of the city. The water was to signify beginning and end, the road that all must walk.

After the anointing, the royal children would each place a gift to their dead father upon Vosbarhan's body, gifts that would help him in the next life.

Next, the royal guards would move the body to a carriage that would be pulled through the streets of Sussār by lyons, slowly moving through the seven levels of the city so that all could see and say goodbye to the King of Kings.

From there the body would go to the tombs of the Kings of Kings on the east bank of the Akhuran River, which wound through the fields around Sussār before stretching off into the desert. It was believed that a King of Kings should not be buried inside the city. It was considered disrespectful to the new King of Kings and degrading to the old to be in the shadow of his successor.

Finally, to end the ceremony, Vosbarhan's name would be etched into the Arch of Kings that stretched over the main road leading into Sussār so that all would remember him for generations to come.

Azkanysh bowed over Vosbarhan for the fifth time, although for which god she had lost track. Vosbarhan had beaten her the night of his death, slashed her back with a short whip for reprimanding Zarmeyr.

"Bless his body in death," a destūr murmured behind her. "Make even the path for his soul to the Aboveworld..."

Azkanysh straightened again, her back beginning to ache from bending over and straightening so many times. She did not know if Vosbarhan's soul would go to the Aboveworld and be with Drisahr Aruyn and Ehurayni, but she hoped that it would not. Vosbarhan should be with Setaron in the underworld, should burn for all eternity in the god of the underworld's caldrons of fire. Azkanysh bowed again, fingertips brushing against the soft black cotton of Vosbarhan's tunic. She had loved Vosbarhan when she had first met him. Loved him until they had become man and wife, and he had made it plain that he wanted only one thing from her: an heir to the throne.

Azkanysh stood again. She remembered the first time that she had met Vosbarhan, remembered the feelings of joy and happiness and excitement that had coursed through her. She had been twelve upon that first meeting, twelve and just starting her first bleed.

"It is a good sign," her mother had whispered as they waited in the cool sandstone hallway of the house while Azkanysh's father met the King of Kings and his party in the courtyard outside. "A sign that the gods and goddesses approve of this marriage."

Azkanysh had glanced at the door at the end of the hallway as a horse whinnied. She hoped that her mother was right, but what if she wasn't? This marriage had been arranged by her father and the King of Kings, a political move that would help both their families. But what if the King of Kings did not like her when he saw her? What if he thought her too young or too ugly or too wild? Her father said that her tendencies to do things that other young women did not do made her special, things like climbing trees and racing horses and swimming with the maids in the hidden pool in the apple orchard. What if the King of Kings did not think that? What if he did not want a wife who longed for adventure and freedom?

The door at the end of the long hallway ground open, and Azkanysh squinted as afternoon sunlight streamed in, playing on the red and gold tiles checkering the floor and on the golden sandstone of the walls. She made out her father's short, plump form in the doorway, his light blue turban and robe making him look like a piece of the sky.

"Azkanysh," he said, waving the fingers of one hand, beckoning her forward. "Come, daughter."

Azkanysh glanced at her mother.

"Just breathe," her mother whispered, squeezing her arm as they started toward the open door. "Be welcoming and kind, and breathe."

Someone cleared their throat softly, bringing Azkanysh back to the present. She bowed over Vosbarhan's body again, glancing at his still face as she leaned over him. The palace slaves had done a marvelous job of covering the gaping wound in his throat with plaster and makeup, and if she did not know better by the pale pallor to his skin and the lack of breath in his chest, she would think that he was merely sleeping. But Ehurayni had answered her prayer in the garden three days before, and Vosbarhan was indeed dead.

Her mother's words had been lost in her head when she had first seen Vosbarhan all those years before, and she had forgotten how to breathe for a moment. He had been twenty-seven when they had first met, twenty-seven and widowed two times. Both wives had died in childbirth, along with their children.

Her mother had gently pushed against her back as they moved out into the courtyard with her father, and Azkanysh raised her head and stepped forward, alone, toward Vosbarhan. Her step faltered as he swung down off his horse and turned to face her, her breath failing again, heart hammering. He was taller than her five three by a good foot, with broad shoulders and narrow hips. His face was sharp and lined but alluringly handsome, and his skin was a smooth dark brown that accented his dark, almost black, brown hair and eyes. He was the most beautiful man that she had ever seen.

"Shayra Azkanysh," Vosbarhan said. His voice was not deep, but it was not high-pitched either. It was perfectly controlled.

Azkanysh had stared at him, too dazed to remember to bow.

Azkanysh straightened for the ninth time, the destūrs and destūries still murmuring behind her. She should have known by the cold, uncaring look in Vosbarhan's eyes that he was a cruel man that first day that she had met him.

"The river to the Aboveworld is golden." The destūry's higher-toned, feminine voices rang out over the destūrs. "But peace waits in the fields of the Family, peace and eternal life…"

Azkanysh bowed for the twelfth time, her cloth-covered nose brushing against Vosbarhan's stomach. He smelled like sweet pomegranates, the perfume that the palace slaves had bathed him in to rid his body of the smell of blood and steel, steel from the assassin's blade. One could say that it did not matter what Vosbarhan had been; he was dead now, and she was free. But she still felt hatred toward him, hatred and vengeance. A vengeance that made her want to push his body off the wall, to throw it to the cobbles below for the city dogs to eat and the poor to rob.

Azkanysh stood for the thirteenth time, bowed for the last time.

The destūrs and destūries stopped murmuring.

She stood again and lowered her arms, muscles burning, and stepped backward as a destūr of Drisahr Aruyn and a destūry of Ehurayni stepped forward.

The destūr's robes were the deep red of Drisahr Aruyn's color, the destūry the dark bronze of Ehurayni. Both carried flat carved wooden bowls in their black-painted hands.

The rest of the destūrs and destūries started murmuring again. "There is a light at the edge of the world, I see it through the darkness," they chanted. "It is the River of Life, leading to the world above."

The destūr and destūry with the bowls stopped by Vosbarhan, one at his head and one at his feet. The destūry at his head reached into her bowl with long fingers and gathered water on them. She splattered it over Vosbarhan's face and chest.

"There is a fire beneath the world," the other destūrs and destūries chanted. "I feel its threat against my flesh. It is the River of Death, leading to the world underneath."

The destūr at Vosbarhan's feet reached into his bowl, throwing water on Vosbarhan's black-slippered feet in a sprinkling motion.

Azkanysh felt a bead of sweat draining down her back beneath her black tunic. The heat of the Brothers was murderous on the West Wall. It was a wonder no one had fainted yet. She'd had little time to think in the last three days about what would happen now that Vosbarhan was dead. But in the few moments that she had, one thought had stood out over the rest: She would become ruler of Zarcayra.

She had overheard one of the Guardian Council members whisper it to another the night of Vosbarhan's death, when guards and slaves and council members and Vyzir Dsamihur had come running into the royal bedchamber at her screams. Azkanysh had not been able to focus on anything else as guards searched the palace grounds for the assassin, and Zarmeyr wept and slaves hauled her, dripping with blood, out of the bedchamber and escorted her to a different room to rest and be cleaned. The law of Zarcayra stated that a ruler must be eighteen years of age or older to take the golden lyon crown of Zarcayra, and as Zarmeyr would not be eighteen for another nine months, and Vosbarhan had no brothers or legal heirs by his other wives, the crown fell to the queen.

"To enter the world above," the destūrs and destūries chanted, "a soul must be filled with deeds of goodness and light, as the Family are made of goodness and light. To go to the world below, one is filled with evil and darkness, like Setaron, god of death and darkness. For the world above, we strive in this life, but when the shadow of Death has come and separates our bodies from our souls, the gods will look into our souls and see to which world we will travel. Only they can see the true spirit within a man, only they can tell if he was good or evil."

Azkanysh stared at a hawk sitting on the roof of a building at the edge of the crowd below, its feathers ruffling slightly in the warm breeze. She was not a god or a goddess, but she knew what was in Vosbarhan's soul.

She watched the hawk spread its wings and fly away on the wind, presumably after some mouse it had spotted in the grass by a building. She did not care where she went in the next life. After what she had gone through in this one, she didn't expect it could be any worse. But this life was changing now, or it would when she took the golden lyon crown.

The destūrs and destūries fell silent once more, and the two who had anointed Vosbarhan moved back to join their fellows in a long line behind Azkanysh. She glanced sideways at Vyzir Dsamihur, his standard black attire matching everyone's today. As right hand to the King of Kings, the vyzir was in charge of Vosbarhan's funeral and the order of actions that took place.

Vyzir Dsamihur nodded at the royal children, signaling for them to come forward.

Azkanysh looked ahead of her. At first she had been terrified at the thought of becoming ruler of Zarcayra. She had lived her life being ruled, not ruling, and the idea of running a kingdom was almost horrifying. But why shouldn't she be able to run a kingdom? She did not know what she was capable of yet, but she was eager to find out, eager to learn.

Zarmeyr came forward first at Vyzir Dsamihur's nod, his face, so much like Vosbarhan's, set and tight.

Azkanysh watched him walk past. There were tear stains on her son's cheeks, still glistening in the blazing brightness of the Brothers' morning rays. Zarmeyr reminded her of herself when she was young, his adoration for Vosbarhan and the belief that the King of Kings had loved him matching her own, of a time. Only, she had come to realize that Vosbarhan loved no one but himself, and Zarmeyr never would.

Tamar and Paruhi came after Zarmeyr, followed by Kayani, the youngest of her children. There were tears in Paruhi's amber eyes, but Tamar's lips were arched slightly, almost as if she was trying not to smile. Azkanysh met her eldest daughter's dark eyes. There was a twinkle in them.

"For my father, King of Kings Vosbarhan," Zarmeyr shouted to the watching crowd, "Fourth King of Kings of Zarcayra, Ruler of Kings, Commander of Armies, Chosen of the Gods, I give this, my sword, that he may have a weapon to defend himself in the next life." Zarmeyr placed a sword in a red velvet scabbard on Vosbarhan's chest and after bowing, stepped backward.

The crowd bowed in return.

Tamar stepped up to Vosbarhan as Zarmeyr backed up, her black robes brushing against Azkanysh's as she walked past. Azkanysh watched her daughter, watched the strong strides she took, the confidence in her stature. She had been confident like that once, confident and strong and fierce. When had she lost it? That first year of marriage to Vosbarhan? Or had it drained away slowly over the long hard years that had followed?

"For my father, King of Kings Vosbarhan," Tamar shouted to the watching crowd, holding up a single white candle high in the air, "Fourth King of Kings of Zarcayra, Ruler of Kings, Commander of Armies, Chosen of the Gods, I give this, my candle, that he may have light in his next life." She placed the candle on Vosbarhan's chest, next to the sword, and after bowing, backed up.

The crowd bowed again, a sea of bending bodies.

Tamar moved back next to Zarmeyr, and Azkanysh watched Paruhi step forward. She did not understand the tears in her middle daughter's eyes. Vosbarhan had never paid his daughters any more attention than he had his son. Paruhi was gentle, though, given to crying at the death of birds that ran into pillars in the palace or of fish in the garden ponds. Paruhi would make a good wife. Subservient, obedient, quiet. But was that what a woman was supposed to be? There had been a time when Azkanysh had not thought so.

"For my father, King of Kings Vosbarhan," Paruhi shouted to the crowd, voice lighter and softer than Tamar's, "Fourth King of Kings of Zarcayra, Ruler of Kings, Commander of…"

Azkanysh let her daughter's words fade. After Vosbarhan's death, the palace slaves had urged her to move to another room besides the one that she had shared with Vosbarhan. They said that it would not be good for her health to sleep and wake up in the room where her husband had been murdered.

But she had insisted on staying in the room, and the room remained hers. She wanted to be reminded of Vosbarhan's death. Azkanysh had even made the slaves leave the ivory bed with its unremovable bloodstains. She enjoyed smelling Vosbarhan's blood as she slept, relished waking up to the sight of it on the stark white of the bedposts.

Paruhi placed a loaf of bread on Vosbarhan's chest, beside the sword and candle.

Azkanysh felt another drop of sweat drain down her back to join the first. When she became Queen of Queens, she would have more power than any man in Zarcayra. More power than the shayrs, more power than the Guardian Council, more power than her son.

Paruhi stepped back from Vosbarhan, and Kayani moved forward. Azkanysh glanced at her youngest daughter. At eight, Kayani was already becoming a beautiful girl with long, curling brown hair, greenish-brown eyes and a face that was neither sharp nor soft but somewhere in between. She had the personality of a spoiled monkey, though, a personality that matched the monkey that Tamar had gifted her on her sixth birthday and that she now carried everywhere with her. The monkey was being held by a slave today, Azkanysh noted, and Kayani walked to Vosbarhan alone.

"For my father, King of Kings Vosbarhan," Kayani yelled over the watching crowd, voice bored, annoyed, "Fourth King of Kings…" Kayani's gift to Vosbarhan was a gold-and-white-painted ceramic flagon of wine, to go with the bread that would feed him in the next life.

Her youngest daughter stepped back to join her siblings, and Azkanysh saw Vyzir Dsamihur step forward out of the corner of her eye. Her heart beat faster. He would pray over Vosbarhan's body, as right hand to the King of Kings, and then… Then he would ask for the gods' and goddesses' blessing before placing the golden lyon crown on her head. She felt its weight already, smelled its metallic scent.

Vyzir Dsamihur moved to Vosbarhan's body, bowing his head and folding his long hands together over him.

The crowd bowed their heads with him; those on the wall did the same.

Azkanysh stared straight ahead. She would not bow for Vyzir Dsamihur's prayer. His prayer was a prayer of thanks to the gods and goddesses for the life that Vosbarhan had been given. A request for their blessings on him in the next life. She saw Zarmeyr watching her from where he stood, head down, a few feet away. The darkness in his brown eyes was murderous.

Azkanysh glanced away, her heartbeat quickening.

Vyzir Dsamihur straightened after several moments, sunlight catching in a wide beam on his slender body. "King of Kings Vosbarhan has been taken to the next life," he called out over the watching crowd.

The crowd murmured blessings and made the sign of peace, palms raised up and outward, heads bowed.

"His son and heir, Prince Zarmeyr," Vyzir Dsamihur went on, "is not yet old enough to take on the golden lyon crown of Zarcayra as the next ruler."

The hawk returned to its perch in the building's window. Azkanysh glanced at it, her breathing quick.

"Until Prince Zarmeyr comes of age to take the golden lyon crown next year," Vyzir Dsamihur called over the crowd in a slow, even voice, "another ruler will be appointed in the King of Kings's place." The vyzir reached for the golden lyon crown atop Vosbarhan's head, lifting it from his graying hair with long fingers.

Azkanysh watched the crown rise from Vosbarhan's head, watched it glint and gleam in a thousand different colors as the Brothers' rays hit it full on.

"Queen Azkanysh," Vyzir Dsamihur called, "step forward."

Azkanysh obeyed, her gaze going over her children as she moved past them. Tamar's eyes were full of pride and joy and excitement. Paruhi looked sad but also proud, and Kayani simply looked annoyed—probably at being made to stand in the hot suns for so long. Zarmeyr's eyes were full of hatred. Pure, unhidden hatred.

Azkanysh stopped in front of Vyzir Dsamihur as the vyzir turned sideways. Vosbarhan was to her left, and beyond, the edge of the wall and the crowd below.

"Kneel," Vyzir Dsamihur called.

Azkanysh obeyed again, going to her knees on the warm sandstone of the wall in front of the vyzir. She forced her breathing to slow, to be calm. The Guardian Council member's tone had not been happy when she had overheard him tell the other council members that she would take on the golden lyon crown. She'd no doubt that few would be happy of her succeeding Vosbarhan. A woman had never ruled Zarcayra before, had never sat on the golden throne, had never worn the golden lyon crown.

"Queen Azkanysh," Vyzir Dsamihur called as the breeze died down, "First Wife to the late King of Kings Vosbarhan, daughter of Shayr Haro…"

Azkanysh met Vyzir Dsamihur's brown eyes. They showed nothing of what he was thinking. As Queen of Queens, she could pick a new vyzir, if she so desired. She could grant the title of shayr and shayra to a commoner, she could rule at court sessions, order arrangements in the palace, visit the lower kings of the twelve provinces and demand more taxes. As Queen of Queens, she could do whatever she wanted.

"As vyzir of Zarcayra," Vyzir Dsamihur called, "I appoint you, Queen Azkanysh, to be ruler of Zarcayra, Queen of Queens, until such time as Prince Zarmeyr, heir to the throne, is old enough to take on the golden lyon crown of Zarcayra."

Vyzir Dsamihur lowered the golden lyon crown onto her head. Azkanysh felt its weight push down around her hijab. She met Vyzir Dsamihur's eyes again as the crowd broke into applause. They were still unreadable.

Vyzir Dsamihur offered her a hand. Azkanysh took it, her legs almost buckling under the added weight of the crown as she stood. She turned toward the crowd, scanning the cheering faces. They were cheering for her. But was it genuine or forced? Azkanysh heard Tamar's voice above the voices of those on the wall, yelling her name.

Vyzir Dsamihur stepped up behind her. "It would be good, Queen of Queens," he whispered in her ear, "to show them that you hear their cheers by raising your hand."

Azkanysh turned her head toward him. She did not know what went on in Vyzir Dsamihur's mind, whether he was for her or against her. She did not know if anyone other than Tamar was for her wearing the golden lyon crown.

The crowd cheered louder, bowing and saying her name over and over and over.

Azkanysh looked back at them. Whether anyone was for her or not, Vosbarhan was dead, and she was free. Her lips arched into a smile beneath the black cloth hanging over the bottom half of her face. Vosbarhan was dead, and she was Queen of Queens of Zarcayra.

Azkanysh raised her hand.

CHAPTER 14

The Unknown Voice

Mother died in my fifteenth winter. That winter was a light one, and the battles between us and the skinchanger and wiar continued to rage throughout it. Father and I, while fighting in the north, glanced up one day to see Bran, one of our castle servants, riding into the rainy, muddy army camp, face long. He bore bad news: Mother was near death. He said that Sar thought that we should return home if we could.

We rode for three days straight, only stopping for a few hours each night to rest our horses. Everywhere we rode, there were signs of the war, in the gaunt faces watching us race by, in the cattle-bare fields, the burnt forests and destroyed towns.

It is said that something good always comes of something bad, and I suppose this is true, for if Mother had never died when she did, I might never have found the book that changed my life. Or at least it would have been many years before I did.

Mother was asleep when we arrived, her auburn hair spread out on the white pillow around her, and her eyes closed. She looked already dead—the fever that had taken hold of her this time had done its worst and ravaged her body. I had never seen her so pale or so thin.

There was a physician by her bed, an ancient man with white hair and spectacles. Where Sar had managed to find him, I didn't know. Most of the country and city physicians were on the battlefields, tending to the wounded.

"Pneumonia," the physician told Father and me as we walked, dripping, into Mother's room. "I told her to stay indoors, what with the fever she had picked up, but she insisted on going to the wall of the castle every day to see if you were coming home yet. It seems she got her wish finally, although not in pleasant circumstances, to be sure."

I stopped by Mother's left side, winding my leather-gloved fingers through her pale soft ones. Mud caked the floor from our boots, and water dripped off our cloaks and onto the wolfskin rug underneath the bed.

"Will she wake?" I asked, staring at her slowly rising chest. I knew that to ask if she would live was foolish.

"Who knows," the physician said, voice tired. He laced the belts on his leather bag. "I gave her poppy to ease the pain; it could be what helps her to pass on to the next life." He lifted his bag off the overstuffed green velvet chair it had been sitting on and glanced at Mother. "Sometimes, though, they do wake, right before the end. I will pray for her sake that she does. I know that she wanted to see you again before she departed this world."

A servant offered to give the physician a cup of warm ale and a plate of food, and he gratefully accepted and left the sickroom.

Mother did not wake before she died, and I never had the chance to speak with her.

I was in the library when a servant brought me word of her passing. After sitting with her for four hours, I couldn't stand the waiting for every jagged breath to be the last and had escaped to the secluded, peaceful room. It was raining again after an hour break when the knock sounded on the library door, and at first I did not register it as a knock for how loud the heavy drops pounded against the lone lead-paned window of the library.

"Come in," I said as the second knock echoed through the rows and rows of bookcases and stacked books in the library. I knew in my heart what the news of the person on the other side would be.

Sar entered the library, his white hair whiter now, if that was possible, glowing in the faint light of the tallow candle I had lit to read by. "She's gone, my lord," he said softly, aging voice tired, pained.

I looked up from the book I was reading, an old tome on siege engines. "My father?" I asked.

"With her now," Sar replied, a glistening tear running down his lined cheek.

"I'll be there in a minute," I said softly.

Sar nodded and retreated as quietly as he had come, shutting the door softly behind him. I stared out the window at the rain. All around me was death. Every day I saw it—human, wiar, and skinchanger alike, falling in the battles that we fought. They said that trillions had perished in the First and Second Great Wars combined, and that millions more would fall before the Third was done. There was an opinion held by many that the wars would never end, and Argdrion would forever remain in a perpetual state of combat.

I closed my book with a soft thump, the rain beating against the windowpane matching my mood. I hated death, hated it more than anything. But mainly I feared it, for I knew that it was coming for me someday. Every day Father and I rode out to battle the enemy, and every day I wondered if I would live to see another as I watched knights who I had grown up with die.

So far, I had been lucky as thousands fell around me, only losing a finger on my left hand, but for how long would I remain so? I had thought of running once, away from the battles, but really, there was nowhere in Argdrion where one could run and be away from war, and what good would it do anyway? The shadow of death still hung over us all, waiting for our time to run out by old age or sickness or some freak accident. I threw the book in my lap across the room, and it hit a dusty bookshelf full of books and knocked several to the floor. I stared at the mess for a while, pondering our dreary existence.

The rain stopped as I stood and made for the door of the library a half hour later, and in the distance, the throaty rumble of thunder echoed toward the castle. I reached a gloved hand for the library door handle. My eyes caught on something among the books that had fallen on the floor.

I moved to the pile, squatting and pushing aside books to get to the one that had caught my attention. It read "Spells" on the front in long silver letters and was bound in smooth black leather. I turned the book over, scanning the cracked leather of its back. What was a book of magic doing in Castle Sythorn? And how had I never seen it before? I had scoured all the libraries, shelves, and books before I left the castle for the battlefields with Father. How had I missed this book?

My first reaction was to throw the book into the fire in the dining hall of the castle, but my curiosity got the better of me, and instead I opened it up.

Spells met my eyes. Spells to heal wounds, start fires without tinder and flint, make creatures sick, turn liquid into poison.

I had been trained from a very young age to hate magic. Magic was what had started the Great Wars, magic was what had killed millions of our race, magic was what tore families apart, magic was what would ruin Argdrion.

I grew angry as I read, angry at who had written the book, angry at whoever had put the book in the library. It could have been left over from before the Great Wars; Castle Sythorn had been around for well over 450 years, but why hadn't it been destroyed? Or had it been forgotten?

"The Heart Spell," I read as I flipped through the book. I turned two pages back to look at the words again, my eyes catching on what I read underneath. *A spell to give longer life...*

I didn't go to Mother's room for another hour. The heart spell captured my attention like nothing ever had, started a fire in me that I could not put out. When I did go to her room, my aunt was there, talking to Father about burial arrangements.

"I think that she should be buried with our parents," she said, crying softly.

"I'm not hauling her seventy-five miles to be buried with long-dead relatives," Father replied as I slipped into the bedroom. It smelled of death and medicine.

Mother lay like she had when I first arrived at the castle, with her hair still spread out on the pillow around her. Her hands were folded on her breast now, and her lips were pinched in a look of pain and sadness.

"And I suppose you'll want her buried here?" my aunt snapped.

"Yes," Father said, voice boding no argument. "Where I will be buried when I die, and my son beside me."

My aunt glanced at me for the first time, a look of distaste coming onto her face. She had hated me since the day that Ciril died. I think she knew somehow that it had been me who had killed him, although she had never said anything about it. I ignored her and moved to Mother's bedside. They said that there was peace in death, but she did not look peaceful. She looked scared.

I felt the weight of the book *Spells* tucked in my tunic. The heart spell had spoken of changing one's soul into the body of another, and thereby enabling one to live in other bodies forever. It scared me, this idea of magic, but it also enthralled me with the power that it could give. I stared at Mother's fearful expression. I did not have to die like she had. The knowledge gave me a thrill of hope.

Mother was buried at Castle Sythorn the next morning, so that Father and I could return to the battlefront as soon as possible. Father had wanted the burial to be the day before—hours after she died, but a priest had to be fetched from the closest church, and my aunt had insisted on waiting at least one day for Mother's soul to leave her body. It was an old tradition, and one that usually took three to four days. But time was pressing in war, something Father often said, and I stood in my travel clothes the next morning by a freshly dug grave as the priest of Drago, god of the dead, said words over Mother's open casket.

"The shadow of Death must come for us all," the priest said as rain splattered loudly against the wooden lid of the box Mother lay in. "And though we may flee from it, he will always find us in the end. This is the natural way of the world; this is how it has always been and always will be. Blessed are the dead, for they no longer feel the pain of the living but rejoice in the pleasures of the Aboveworld." The priest turned to look at Father and I, standing with Sar and my aunt and the castle servants at the head of the grave. "If you wish to say your goodbyes," he said sympathetically, "now is the time."

My aunt stepped forward, crying quietly as she knelt by Mother's casket and placed a single gray winter rose on top of her still form. "Goodbye, sister," she sobbed, backing up as Father stepped forward and told my mother's body goodbye.

I wanted to say that Mother's soul was not there as Sar stepped forward for his goodbye, that it was just a body they were talking to, a lifeless shell, and that it was pointless to pay reverence to it. Somehow I knew that it wouldn't matter to them. They believed that this was what waited for us all, the inevitable end of all things.

My turn came to step forward. I didn't say anything as I stared down at Mother's graying face, glistening wet with raindrops. What was there to say?

"May Drago escort Lady Sythorn to the Aboveworld in blessed peace," the priest said as two servants stepped forward and lifted the lid of Mother's coffin. My aunt flinched as they nailed it over the box, barring Mother from our view. "May she spend countless hours with those gone on before her in the peaceful bliss that belongs to the righteous. It is the gods and goddesses who give us life," the priest said as the servants lifted the coffin and lowered it by ropes into the deep, dark hole beside it. "And it is the gods and goddesses who take it away at their own choosing. Bless the gods and goddesses." The priest bowed his head and prayed. I stared down into the grave.

Later, as Father and I rode back toward the battlefields, I heard my father sniff. Just once. When I glanced at him, there was a tear mingling with the rain on his bearded cheeks.

I put a hand to my saddlebags as we rode back past the same burnt forests and empty fields we had passed the day before, my fingers finding the smooth binding of *Spells*. I had learned something on this sad trip.

I had learned that even in the darkest hours, there were small slivers of light, and I had learned that a man may not die.

CHAPTER 15

Nathaira

A deep, echoing thrum vibrated down through the dark catacombs, bouncing off the stone walls and filling the air with its tune.

Nathaira inhaled sharply, her nostrils filling with cold, damp air, and jolted awake. She listened to the noise. She could hardly sleep because of it.

She moved to a sitting position and stared around at the dark stone walls of her cell. Her new home. Until the humans decided they wanted to see her blood shed in the arena.

Nathaira stretched her neck, the muscles strained and tight from holding up the weight of the silver collar around it. She ran a finger over the raw flesh underneath and hissed at the tenderness of it. The pounding increased, vibrating through the stones around her and shaking her body.

A piece of stone broke loose from the ceiling above and landed with a loud clap on the floor next to her leg. Nathaira picked it up and rolled it between thumb and forefinger. Efamar had always loved stones. He used to beg her to take him to the rivers so that he could look for unique ones. She tossed the shard away angrily, and it clattered dully against the wall a few feet away and fell to the floor. If she ever found Efamar, she would take him to a river every day so he could collect as many rocks as his heart desired.

Nathaira pushed herself to her feet and hobbled to the rusty door of her cell. She gripped the cold bars, glancing at her broken finger, which had healed slightly crooked, and then peering at the hallway outside.

A shaft of filtered light streamed down through an iron grate bearing off a tunnel in the rock above, playing across the uneven stone floor, glimmering dully off the bars of dozens of other cells.

Nathaira stared up the dim hallway, waiting for the masked guards to come back. It had been three days since they'd brought her to her cell. Three days of waiting and thinking and pacing, and then more waiting.

The pounding grew more intense, shaking the bars underneath her hands.

Nathaira cocked her head and listened.

"The crowd cheering," a voice said from across the hall.

Nathaira started, glancing at the bars across from her and the darkness behind.

"They cheer like that every time something gets killed," the voice said, hoarse and grating. "I was afraid it would bring the arena down on me when I first got here. You'll get used to it after a while."

Nathaira peered across the hall, catching a glimpse of white in the cell. "Who are you?"

Chains rattled loudly on stone, and an old, skeletal man with wispy white hair dangling around his gaunt face appeared behind the rusted gate. He grasped the bars with bony hands, his eyes like bulbous blue orbs. "A murderer awaiting execution." He cackled, revealing several missing teeth and rotten gums.

Nathaira gagged as the smell of urine, infection, and waste drifted across the hallway to her.

"Killed a woman in a bar fight, I did," the old man wheezed, foggy blue eyes popping out of his stretched face. "She tried to take my ale, and no one takes my ale and gets away with it." He grinned again, and Nathaira saw that he only had three teeth, two of them turning black. The man made a throat-slicing motion. "I slit her throat, I did, with a butter knife. It was a messy affair." He giggled. "They say she gurgled blood for three hours before she died." The old man's face grew solemn. "Served the bitch right. She didn't pay her coins for that ale, I did."

"You would kill a woman over a drink?" Nathaira said, abhorred.

The old man sniffed loudly as snot dribbled out of his beaklike nose. He wiped the back of a dirty hand across his face. "So?"

"You're vile."

"Eh, and where do you get off being so high and mighty, sweetie?" the old man called, voice echoing off up the tunnel. "Think you're better than me, do you? Hah! I bet you're in here for something terrible yourself, now ain't ya?"

Nathaira ignored him. She didn't have time to listen to a human; she had to get out. She turned her back on her cell door and paced to the back of the cell, chains dragging.

"So, what are ya in for, sweetie?" the old man asked. "Let me guess: being a prostitute without a license? Yer sure pretty enough."

Nathaira paced back to the door, glancing up the hall again.

I'll have to wait until they take me to the arena and remove my shackles to make my escape... Her chains groaned loudly as she turned and walked back the other way.

"No?" the old man cooed, screwing up his face in concentration. "Okay, then, stealing? Although they'd only throw you in prison to rot for that."

He was quiet, and for a moment Nathaira hoped that he had tired of her.

"Ooo!" the old man squealed loudly. "I know! You're a murderer like me!" He cackled like they were suddenly long-lost friends. "That's what ya are, a murderer!"

"I am no murder or thief or prostitute," Nathaira growled, growing annoyed with his ramblings. "I am here simply because I am not a human like you." She turned and stalked back to the door of her cell. "Because your kind are dark, evil creatures who hunt and kill whatever they consider 'evil' and 'beneath them.' Because," she shouted, hitting her palms against the bars of her cell door as anger flooded through her, "your kind killed my clan and enslaved me and brought me here to die in their arena for their amusement!"

The old man slid down the bars of his cell door. "No need to get riled, sweetie," he said with another cackle. "I was just trying to make conversation."

Nathaira stared at him, surprised that he wasn't alarmed that she was not human.

She turned back around. Sisters, but she hated this. The waiting, the not knowing, the planning, only to have it fall short. It had been weeks now since her and Efamar's capture, and he'd been far apart from her then—where was he now?

Footsteps echoed down the hall.

Nathaira's head snapped up. There was more than one set, so it couldn't be the broken-nosed keeper who brought her food every morning and night; it must be men coming to collect the next victim to go up top. But who? She turned toward her cell door, anticipation building within her.

A torch, flame light flickering and bouncing off the walls of the tunnel, threw fingers of gold and orange into her cell. Nathaira squinted against the glare as three masked guards dressed in black appeared in front of her cell door.

"Time to go, skinchanger," one said. "The crowd's been screaming for you for the past three days."

The door swung open with a heavy groan, and a mountain of a man with greasy black hair hanging out from under his leather skull cap stepped inside. "If you know what's good for you, you'll give them a good show," he said, reaching for her.

Nathaira growled as meaty, hairy hands ran down her arms before grabbing her chains.

"What, no fight, skinchanger?" the guard mocked. "I hope you'll amend that spirit when you get up top."

Nathaira spat at him.

The guard laughed and jerked on her chains, pulling her out of the cell and into the tunnel.

One of the other guards slammed the door shut with a resonating clang.

"I'll see ya, sweetie!" the old man called as the guards started off up the tunnel. Nathaira glanced over her shoulder at him.

"In the next life!" the old man yelled, cackling hysterically.

They marched silently, passing rusty cell door after rusty cell door rooted deep into the walls of the tunnel.

Several times Nathaira caught a glimpse of creatures through the bars, a mercat's black-striped coat, a human foot, a brown bear's beady yellow eyes, but most of the inhabitants of the cells shied away from the light of the guard's torch, and the cells they passed appeared as if deserted.

The pounding grew louder as they marched, vibrating the tunnel floor under their feet and knocking small pieces of rock down from the ceiling with a steady chorus of clatters.

Natural light appeared at the top of the third flight of stairs they marched up. Nathaira sucked in a breath as it caught her eye.

Almost there. She felt goosebumps rise on her arms.

The guard holding the torch snuffed it out in the sand under their feet as they stepped into a tunnel of darkest stone, and Nathaira blinked at the blinding white light streaming through a massive iron gate at the other end of the tunnel. This was it. This was the day she'd been waiting for. This was the day that would decide if she escaped to save Efamar or died.

The roaring of the crowd was deafening now, pulsing through the air in deep, bone-numbing waves.

A black-masked female guard, wavy blonde hair stretching to her waist from underneath the black leather skull cap on her head, straightened as they approached, and with a nod from the guard with the blackened torch, she pulled, muscles bulging, on a massive wooden wheel wrapped in chains.

The gate creaked open at the pace of a snail, groaning loudly on ancient hinges as it disappeared into a dark slit in the stone above.

Nathaira watched the sand in the arena outside bounce and jump to the roars of the crowd through the gate's studded iron slats.

Sisters, help me to escape and find Efamar. The thick iron spikes lining the bottom of the gate banged against the stone above with a resonating clang, and the guards dragged her forward and out onto the hot sand.

The crowd roared.

Nathaira glanced up at them as the guards pulled her. There were thousands of humans sitting in staggered rows for hundreds of feet into the sky around the sandy pit of the arena. All of them were staring at her.

Nathaira glanced around.

The fighting pit was more a field than a pit, easily covering over three acres, and was surrounded by a towering wall of white marble scarred and stained with splatters of long-dried blood. Another iron gate stood in the wall on the opposite side of the arena. Eleven stone towers with black roofs and the red flags of Eromor flapping on top dotted the wall that ringed the top of the arena. It was the net that caught Nathaira's eye the most, though.

Made of silver and with cords as thick as a human arm, it stretched over the whole of the arena, creaking metallically, as an impassable ceiling.

Nathaira's eyes ran the length of the massive structure. It was too much silver to allow a magical creature to retain their magic when they neared it, and attempting to fly out would mean a fall to the death. She narrowed her eyes against the net's gleam. Zeythra had told her of the net that covered Crystoln's arena, but she had hoped that after all the years since the wars, it would be old and weak or maybe even gone. She had been foolish. Escaping would be harder than she had thought.

The guards stopped suddenly, and Nathaira glanced back down to them as they pulled her to a stop with them in front of a four-pillared booth of raised marble that jutted several feet out over the wall and was shaded with a red silk cloth.

Trumpeters ringing one side of the arena on top of the wall blew on long flaring brass horns, and the crowd gradually quieted as the harsh notes rang through the air.

A blood-red, dragon-crested flag cracked in a warm breeze atop one of the towers. Nathaira glanced up at it, the glint of an iron bolt from a portcullis in a tower's marble wall catching her eye.

Scorpions. Nathaira narrowed her eyes. Giant crossbows of black iron that had been first invented during the Second Great War to kill skinchangers and wiar at long range, it was said that one bolt from the elongated machines could impale four creatures at once.

A man in red attire with the dragon crest emblazoned across the front of his tunic and a pinched face stood in the marble booth and raised his thin arms high above his head. "My good people of Eromor!" the man shouted, his voice shrill and off key, "today we gather in celebration of King Uranius's ninety-fourth birthday!"

The man moved an arm to those seated behind him, and Nathaira followed where he pointed as the crowd went wild. An aged figure in a black wooden chair stared back at her with foggy eyes. A black iron crown of dragon talons adorned the sparse white hair of his head and a robe of red with black bear fur lining it hung over his frail body.

King Uranius. Nathaira's hand's curled into fists. So old and feeble, and yet the cause of so much death. Why had the Sisters not taken his life instead of the clan's?

The guards fell to their knees next to her, and one tugged on her chains for her to do the same. Nathaira ignored them.

"Bow, you damn animal!" the hairy-handed guard hissed, kicking at the back of her legs with one foot.

Nathaira snarled at him as pain ran up her sore limbs. He pulled a short whip from his belt with a look of pure hatred on his face. The crowd sucked in its breath in anticipation.

A tightly toned voice stopped the guard midswing. "Let her be, guard. Her defiance will be quelled soon enough."

Nathaira glanced up at the canopied booth and noted the speaker—a slender, black-haired man with a finely pointed beard and mustache and dark, brooding eyes. He sat in a high-backed black chair next to the king's.

The king motioned with a speckled skeletal hand, and the man leaned over to him. "The king says that her spirit is admirable and her fierceness commendable," the black-haired man said, his face leaving no hint as to what was going on in his mind.

The guard growled, "Yes, chief advisor."

Nathaira glanced at Uranius again, finding very little sign of life in his whitening eyes.

The herald started again. "We have a special treat for this week's celebration festivities!" he yelled as the crowd shifted in their seats. "A skinchanger!" He waved a hand at her. Nathaira raised her head higher as all eyes turned to her again.

"Brought from the far reaches of Ennotar and brought at great expense to His Royal Majesty, for your entertainment and pleasure!"

The crowd cheered.

"His Majesty hopes that you will enjoy this rare creature," the herald yelled.

The crowd yelled louder and clapped their hands together.

"Now, without further ado, let the fight begin!"

The following roar was so loud that Nathaira thought she might never hear again.

The two guards holding her drew long swords, the brushed steel hissing against their leather sheaths, and backed up to a safe distance and leveled them at her. The sweaty-palmed guard pulled a key from his belt and began unlocking the manacles binding her sore and chafed wrists.

Nathaira watched the guard from half-lidded eyes, her mind racing for a way to escape as he pulled the shackles off her wrists and knelt to undo the ones on her ankles. She would never be able to get over the wall before a bolt found her heart, and flying out was not an option. What was left? Digging? There was rock underneath the sand, and below that, the catacombs.

The manacles around her ankles snapped open with a click, barely audible over the yelling of the crowd, and cool air stroked Nathaira's raw skin. She glanced around her. Moirin had told her once that there was no way out of the arena of Crystoln. Was she right?

The guard stood again, key in hand, and Nathaira looked back at him as he unlocked the collar around her neck and pulled it off harshly. "Prepare to die a ghastly death, skinchanger." He sneered, stepping back to his companions.

Nathaira watched them walk back the way they had come. The gate slammed down behind them with a heavy thud.

Trumpets blared again, the crowd quieted, and the second gate groaned open.

Nathaira pivoted on one heel, watching the dark tunnel entrance as the gate disappeared into the rock above. For now, she would bide her time. Learn the arena's weaknesses and strengths before she made her escape.

A black hoof slid into the sunlight, followed by a curly-haired leg.

Nathaira crouched, power surging.

Sisters, help me to defeat whatever comes out. For Efamar, help me.

The shadows rippled in the tunnel, and a tail with a knotted black mass of hair on the end flicked out next to the leg.

Nathaira heard the wind shifting the grains of sand around her. A human coughed high up in the stands.

The shadows broke completely, and her opponent stepped into the arena.

A minotaur.

The arena breathed inward as one.

Not the smartest of creatures in Argdrion, minotaurs had poor eyesight but excellent hearing and a sense of smell that more than made up for their lack of sight. The one in front of her, a male from the size of it, had beady black eyes blinking in the glare of the two suns and wet black nostrils flaring for a scent. It was one of the largest that Nathaira had ever seen. Well over eight feet tall, he carried a double-bladed battleaxe that was as tall as he was.

Nathaira shifted onto the balls of her feet. What distant regions of Argdrion had the slavers scoured for such a creature?

The minotaur raised its head, thick, curling black horns stretching out for three feet on either side of it. It sniffed at the air, testing it for the scent of its opponent. It seemed confused for a moment, turning its head first one way, then the other, and it gripped its axe tightly in front of its chest with leathery black hands.

It was disoriented, Nathaira realized. She glanced up at the watching crowd that was waiting tensely for her or the minotaur to move. There were too many smells and sounds—the breathing of the humans, the flags atop the wall, flapping in the wind. She looked back down at the minotaur.

It gave her an advantage, and an advantage could very well win her the fight.

Always attack first, Nathaira, when the odds are in your favor. The usual stab of pain came with Athrysion's words, the realization that he was gone striking deep once more.

Nathaira slid out of her clothing. Hoots and whistles echoed down from the watching crowd as the Brothers' rays warmed her naked skin. She ignored the jeers, curling her toes into the sand and letting the feeling of the wind on her cheeks fill her senses. She felt freer without her clothing, ready for changing.

"For Efamar," Nathaira whispered as the breeze blew to the minotaur, and its head turned toward her. She lunged into the air, her body shrinking into an eagle.

The crowd oohed in amazement.

The minotaur growled as she sped toward it, small ears swiveling and nostrils flaring. Nathaira stayed above its line of sight, letting the breeze carry her along to save energy. She veered to the left as she neared the half-bull man. Minotaurs' skins were too thick for most creatures to pierce without getting severely mangled by the animal's fury in the process, but like all animals, they did have weak spots. Diving, Nathaira went for one.

The minotaur turned as she neared it, catching her movement now. It let out a bellow and raised its axe.

Nathaira drove her beak deep into its left eye.

Blood squirted over her head and filled her nostrils.

The crowd cheered.

The minotaur roared.

Nathaira pulled her beak out of the minotaur's eye with a sucking sound, fluttering in place for a moment as the creature screamed.

The minotaur screamed again, a low, rattling noise, and Nathaira flapped to the side as a hairy black hand came toward her.

The minotaur roared, spittle mixing with the blood draining down one hairy cheek, and staggered in a circle with a gnarled hand over its wounded eye.

Nathaira circled behind it, pity surging through her. She held no ill will against the creature. The only reason they fought was for the humans' amusement. Minotaurs were ill-tempered and would attack on sight, yes, but if left alone they were quiet animals that kept to themselves and bothered no one. It wasn't right that it should die for the humans' amusement, or that she should have to kill it. Nathaira glanced up at the screaming crowd, now chanting, "Kill, kill, kill!" She dropped to the sand behind the minotaur and changed back into her natural form, breathing quick but lightly.

The massive half-man, half-bull turned slowly, blood glistening on the hair covering its chest.

The crowd gradually quieted. Somewhere in the distance, Nathaira heard a crow caw.

The minotaur pulled its hand down from its hurt eye, eyelid closed over the bleeding wound.

Nathaira took a step backward, sand crunching beneath her feet.

With a roar, the minotaur charged.

"Change, you stupid creature!" someone yelled in the crowd.

Nathaira held her ground, kneeling on all fours in the hot sand and calming her breathing as the minotaur neared. The ground shook under her palms.

Nathaira closed her eyes, thinking of Efamar and the night the slavers attacked. She pictured the fear in her brother's blue eyes, Zeythra's decapitated head, Athrysion's lifeless body.

A skinchanger can only change into that which they have seen, Nathaira, Athrysion's voice murmured in her mind. *And that is why I will show you every creature that I have ever seen so that you may copy me and know many options in case of a fight.*

The minotaur drew closer, ground thumping with its pounding hoofbeats.

Nathaira waited until she felt grains of sand pelting her, waited until she could smell the minotaur's rancid breath.

Breathing deeply, she let her power flow through her. Her muscles screamed as her hands rounded into hard, three-toed hooves and her back widened and grew thick gray armor. Her skin felt like it would break as it stretched over her growing face. Three massive horns sprouted on her nose.

The crowd inhaled sharply.

The minotaur skidded to a halt ten feet away, sniffing the air to assess its new opponent.

Nathaira's eyes snapped back open, small and beady in the rhyno's rough gray face. She dug her back hooves into the sand, and with a bellow that shook the ground, charged.

The minotaur remained still for only a moment before giving an answering roar and raising its axe high above its head, charging too.

Time slowed for Nathaira as she thundered across the arena. She was aware of each miniscule grain of sand ricocheting off her thick armor, of every bone-numbing step she took, of the crowd, hyped to a frenzy now, screaming for death, of the spittle from the minotaur's mouth and blood from its wounded eye flying around its head, of the last step she took before they reached each other.

They met with a crack like thunder.

The sound of bones snapping filled Nathaira's ears, and she sensed more than saw the minotaur's dark body sail over her head as a dull, numbing pain ran through her body.

Time sped up again, and she dug her hooves into the ground beneath her, sand spraying into the air in a sheet. She wheeled, grinding to a stop as the crowd's roar threatened to bring the creaking silver net down on all their heads.

The minotaur lay some thirty feet away, its legs twisted oddly to the side, broadaxe still held firmly in its hands.

Nathaira snorted sand out of her nose, watching the creature. If it was dead, she'd be surprised. She remembered Moirin telling her stories of minotaurs receiving a hundred wounds in a fight and still living.

As if reading her thoughts, the minotaur stirred and grunted. It climbed to its feet, broadaxe glinting in the Brothers' rays as it used the weapon to push itself up.

The crowd fell silent again as the creature lifted the axe up to chest level.

A bone, gleaming white against leathery black skin, stuck out at a jagged angle from the minotaur's left hip, but otherwise it appeared unhurt.

Nathaira dug her hooves into the sand and charged again.

The minotaur held its ground this time, waiting until she got within three feet of it before jumping into the air and landing on her back.

Nathaira roared and skidded to a halt, trying to throw the creature off. Rhynos weren't easy to kill, but they did have one weak spot in their five-inch-thick armor—the crack where their neck and back armor met. The spot where the minotaur was sitting.

Nathaira bucked wildly, lunging into the air and hitting the ground in explosions of sand. The minotaur hung on, the sharp black claws of its right hand digging lines into her back armor as it raised its axe with its left hand.

Nathaira dropped, the ground shaking as she hit. She rolled over and over with the minotaur underneath her. She felt its claws let go on the fourth roll. She changed into her natural form on the fifth and, lunging to her feet, wheeled, whipping her black hair out of her face as she went.

The minotaur favored its left arm as it scrambled to its feet, spitting blood and sand out of its mouth like teeth.

Nathaira took a step backward.

"Death, death, death!" the crowd chanted, shaking their fists in the air in time to their screaming as they pounded the stones beneath them with their feet.

Nathaira glanced up at them. They acted like this was a game. But then, for them it was game, a game of other's deaths.

The minotaur raised its axe in its right hand, still favoring its left arm. It threw its horned head back and let out a roar that could be heard above the noise of the crowd.

Nathaira glanced back at it. Its gaze leveled on her. She turned and ran, long black hair streaming behind her as she tore across the arena.

The minotaur started after her.

The crowd booed.

The minotaur was fast, even with its leg broken.

Nathaira could hear its footsteps drawing closer as she neared the marble booth where the king and his party sat. She pumped her arms as she got closer. Sand kicked up by her bare feet stung her cheeks; her breath was burning fire in her lungs.

The wall loomed in front of her, dark stains of blood marring its mottled white color in streaks. Nathaira met the eyes of the black-haired man sitting beside the king, the man who had told the guard to not whip her. There was nothing in his eyes, no feeling, no emotion. It was what all the humans' eyes looked like.

Now! Athrysion's voice screamed in her head as the minotaur's axe whistled through the air behind her. Nathaira lunged into the air and ran up the wall beneath the king's booth.

The minotaur's axe embedded deep into the stone beneath her left heel, and a shower of sparks and dust sprayed her legs.

The crowd cheered.

Nathaira flipped over backward and sailed over the minotaur's head as it tried to pull its axe out of the wall.

She landed in a crouch in the sand behind it, her magic coursing wildly through her veins again.

Time slowed once more as her body elongated and darkened and changed into a black viper. Nathaira heard the crowd yelling as if from a distance as her eyes traveled over the raging minotaur's body. She zeroed in on a large cut on its arm, a flap of loose, hairy skin revealing bloody flesh underneath. Time sped up again, and Nathaira moved, whipping through the sand toward the minotaur.

The minotaur bellowed as its efforts to pull its axe from the wall proved fruitless. Using the moment of distraction, Nathaira lunged into the air and sunk her fangs deep into the creature's wound.

The crowd went deathly silent.

The minotaur stopped roaring and went rigid.

Nathaira let go of the hairy creature's arm and fell to the ground. She slithered a few feet away, changed back into her natural form, and crouched, watching. If her bite didn't kill it, she didn't know what would. The black viper was the deadliest of all snakes in Argdrion, so deadly that one bite would kill a full-grown skinchanger in one minute.

The minotaur let go of its broadaxe as if in a trance and turned slowly, blood from its arm and chest wounds turning the sand at its feet bright red.

It blinked several times. Nathaira looked for the telltale signs of death and prayed that it would be a painless and swift one—it deserved that much.

Not a sound came from the watching crowd.

The minotaur took a step forward, black eyes clouding. It let out a rattling gasp.

Please be swift. Nathaira met its gaze as its head swiveled her way, and for a moment she felt a connection with the creature, almost as if it was thanking her for taking it away from the arena.

The minotaur groaned loudly, and with another rasping gasp, fell face down in the sand with a ground-shaking thud.

Nathaira pulled her clothing back on and silently moved forward, kneeling by the body of the minotaur and placing a hand on its hairy back.

The crowd watched, breathless.

"Your body, I bless," Nathaira whispered softly, curling her long fingers into the minotaur's thick, coiled black hair. "Your life, grieve. Your soul goes to the Sisters. May it run free with your ancestors. In the names of Uatara, Rohiri, and Jophus, this I pray. Peace be yours."

A tear slipped out of Nathaira's eye, running down her cheek and falling onto her knees. She hated the humans. But she also feared them. Feared that she would never leave the arena of Crystoln, feared that the minotaur's fate would one day be hers.

The groan of a gate opening echoed across the arena, and the crowd's silence was broken, the ground shaking once more with their cheers.

Footsteps crunched in the sand behind her. Nathaira stood and turned, waiting as the same three guards came toward her with weapons drawn. She glanced over her shoulder at the minotaur as a guard clicked the manacles onto her wrists. Another tear slid down her cheek.

CHAPTER 16

Hathus

The next few days blew past.

Hathus spent most of his time at the rail of the *Daemon's Cry*, watching Langor Blackwell's fleet of black ships cut a path through the Sea of Monsters and trying very hard not to get seasick. They were sailing to the Eastern Sea and the city of Alahvar on the southern tip of Araysann.

Hathus watched sunbrowned pirates hurrying over the decks of the ship keeping pace to the left of the *Daemon's Cry*. He'd overheard a conversation during his month's rest in Crystoln, a rumor of a worldwalker in Alahvar, one of the last. Humans who dabbled in the magic of world hopping, worldwalkers were an almost extinct breed who excelled at traveling from one world to another and made their money by taking others with them. Before the wars, anyway.

Hathus ran a hand over his freshly shaved chin. The job of finding the Land of Dragons was one of the easiest jobs he had ever had, but it was beginning to grow more and more dangerous. For pretense, he would look for the worldwalker to make the Unknown Voice's men think that he was searching for the Land of Dragons, but to do so would put him at even more risk than he was already in. More than being on a pirate's ship with a magical monkey, more than looking for an otherworld.

Hathus let his hand rest on the railing again, the smooth, polished black wood slightly damp against his palm. He was used to being in dangerous situations, but this newness of being around magic was making him jumpy.

A sail unrolled on the ship opposite the *Daemon's Cry* and began flapping in the warm breeze, fanning its fellows.

Hathus glanced at the massive piece of black cloth, his hat brim flapping with it. All of Langor Blackwell's ships had the same black silk sails, but the *Daemon's Cry* stood out from the rest of the ships she sailed with by having screaming white daemon faces imprinted in the middle of her sails.

Hathus craned his head back to look up at the sails above him and the horrific faces stitched into them. Blackwell said that no kingdom fleets would dare attack his ships when they saw that face. But then, didn't all pirate captains say that?

And if they were attacked, and if the kingdom's fleet won… Hathus heard the drumrolls again, saw the girl's head fall from her body.

"Nice day, is it not?"

He jumped, startled.

Bathia leaned on the railing next to him, crossing one wrist over the other.

Hathus nodded. "Yes," he murmured, eyeing the Brothers and the clear-blue sky, "a very nice day." He glanced back at Bathia. She was a beautiful woman, the first mate, and her authority and power over the crew was impressive. He fancied the idea of trying to kiss her but quickly threw it away. There were too many pirates around, and if she refused him, it would make him look stupid.

They were silent for a while, watching the glistening, greenish-blue water roll past.

"Those men that are with you," Bathia said after a few minutes. "They're rather different, aren't they?"

Hathus glanced at her again. If by different she meant that he never saw them eat, drink, sleep, or go to the bathroom and that they spent most of the day lurking in the shadows, watching him, then yes. He'd half wondered if they were human several times but had given up worrying about it after the first few weeks. They never spoke to him or bothered him, and most of the time he forgot they were even there.

"Are they friends of yours?" Bathia asked.

Hathus snorted, glancing back at the ship opposite. "I wouldn't call them friends," he said, coat flapping in the air blowing by the speeding ship. "Acquaintances, maybe, but not friends."

Try guards.

"Are they partners in this escapade of yours?" Bathia queried, looking at him.

"You could call them that," he said.

Hathus eyed her, noticing a pendant of the three moons hanging from a braided leather cord around her neck. A spike of fear rose in him. Old religion worship was one of the greatest crimes there was, greater even than a magic monkey or looking for an otherworld.

"What's that?" Hathus asked, nodding at the pendant.

"It was a gift from my mother," Bathia said, following his gaze to the necklace.

"Did your mother believe in the Sisters?" Hathus asked, growing more nervous.

Bathia looked up at him, "No. Only fools believe in the Sisters." She watched a pirate whistling a catchy tune walk by. "No," she repeated, "she simply loved beautiful things."

Hathus nodded, relaxing. "Does she live on the islands?" he asked, gripping the rail with one hand and his hat with the other as the ship lurched over a rising wave. His fingers brushed against Bathia's hand as he moved his hand down the railing, and he shivered at the contact. During his month's rest in Crystoln, he had spent numerous days at the brothels, catching up on the sex he'd missed, but that had been weeks ago, and Bathia was so filled out and…

"She did," Bathia said softly, making Hathus look up from eyeing her breasts, "but she's dead now." There was sadness in her voice, and bitterness.

"My mother died in the Hunting," Hathus said, not really knowing why he told her. He didn't like to think about his childhood or his mother; it cut too deep.

"I'm sorry," Bathia said, looking at him again. "We all lost someone we loved during that time."

Hathus nodded, a pirate on the ship opposite catching his eye. The man reminded him of someone that he had thought about every day during his stay in Crystoln's dungeons. Short and slender, the pirate had a brown pointed beard that gave his face a satyrlike look and ears that could be mistaken for a faun's. It wasn't the Fox, though, his old thieving partner, because from what he'd learned about him during his resting month in Crystoln, he'd been killed in a bar fight.

Hathus gripped the railing of the *Daemon's Cry* as she jumped over another wave. His blood burned every time he thought of the Fox, dead or not. He still remembered the night that he had betrayed him as well as if it had happened yesterday.

There had been a large crowd at the King's Tavern that night, larger than usual. Having just pulled off one of the largest heists that they had ever done, he and the Fox had decided to celebrate at Crystoln's biggest and most popular drinking establishment. Hathus stared at the ship opposite. He remembered every face that had been at the underworld tavern that night: Byn Jarral, the half-breed Araysannian smuggler; Drago Flayngor and his thick-bodied thugs; Bordain, the always-smiling gambler who had a penchant for backstabbing.

The ship lurched over another small wave, and Hathus felt his stomach rise with it. No matter how much time he spent at sea, he never got used to the rocking and pitching motions of ship riding. He spread his legs farther apart, mimicking Bathia's stance.

He should have known that the Fox would betray him… The Fox always had been a greedy one. That was part of the reason they had paired up in the first place.

"You and I would make a great team," the tiny man had said with a grin when they'd picked the same night to rob the same mansion. "Imagine all the houses we could clean working together!"

At the time, it had seemed like a good idea, Hathus recalled sourly, even though he usually preferred to work alone. And for the next year, they had been partners in crime. It had been a good year. Maybe too good.

He still didn't know how the Fox had done it. They'd been sitting at the same dark corner table for most of the night, watching whores and rent boys make their rounds of the King's Tavern's many rooms in the hope of coins as the occasional bar fight broke out, but when the soldiers had come in, poof, the Fox had vanished, and Hathus had been too full of wine to do much more than watch as the place was ransacked.

It was said later that magic had been reported at the underworld tavern, and he supposed that he was lucky he hadn't been one of those accused of it and thrown into the arena—if rotting in prison could be deemed lucky.

"We should reach Alahvar tomorrow, midday," Bathia said, breaking Hathus out of his memories.

He took in a deep breath and glanced at her again. "Good, we'll find our worldwalker and be on our way."

She looked at him, squinting against the Brothers' light. The two suns hung directly above them now, golden rays filtering through the flapping black sails of the *Daemon's Cry*. "I may be wrong, and call me on it if I am," Bathia said, "but I have a feeling, Hathus Ryrgorion, that you don't really believe there is a Land of Dragons."

Hathus looked away.

Why does she think that? I was good about not mentioning the Unknown Voice. Did she suspect he was lying because of the men who were following him? He knew it wasn't a good idea to have them trailing him everywhere. One maybe wouldn't be that bad, but not three—they were too suspicious.

Hathus suddenly felt cold, despite the warmth of the day. That was the other danger to this job he'd taken: that someone would find out the real reason that he was looking for the Land of Dragons. He paled, remembering the Unknown Voice's threat that "something unpleasant" would happen to him if anyone found out what he was doing.

He looked back at Bathia, putting a smile on his face. "I told you that I think it's real, didn't I?" he asked, keeping his voice steady.

"Yes," Bathia said, "but people lie."

Hathus stared at her for a moment before she smiled and pushed off from the railing. "There are many vast treasures to look for in this world, Hathus Ryrgorion," Bathia said. "I simply wonder why a man would go to an otherworld that most believe doesn't exist and is said to be home to monsters just to look for a legendary treasure." She walked off, calling out orders to a group of pirates who were lounging and playing cards by a mast.

Hathus watched her, the smile fading from his face.

#

True to Bathia's predictions, the Araysannian coast was spotted the next morning, and by noonday the *Daemon's Cry* was sailing under a massive arch of pale red sandstone and into Alahvar's harbor.

Hathus glanced up at the towering cliffs surrounding the harbor and the red-roofed city perched atop them.

"Impressive, isn't it?" Bathia asked, appearing at his elbow.

Hathus nodded absently as the *Daemon's Cry* slowed to a stop among the hundreds of sailing ships and exotic, brightly painted boats crowding the dark-green waters around them.

And imagine all the aray its people must have.

"I stared at it myself when I first came here," Bathia said. "Wait till you see the inside. I'm sure you'll love it."

Hathus smiled widely, envisioning how much coin he would pick up.

Blackwell appeared on the main deck, and pirates began disappearing over the sides of the *Daemon's Cry* and into the lowered rowboats below in a cacophony of shouts and hoots.

They glided across the harbor toward the city in a sprawling manner, pirates yelling across the water at each other about how many tankards of beer they'd drink, games they'd win, and whores and rent boys they'd bed as the rowboats wound between the maze of ships and fishing boats.

Hathus glanced up at a towering ship sporting a blood-red flag with a pierced silver heart in its middle as they sped underneath the ship's shadow. Another pirate ship. He felt like he was back at the BalBayr Islands.

Instead of wooden docks, wide sandy beaches ran along the bottom of the cliff faces and made up the landing point for cargo and rowboats. Above, in dark holes scattered over the red sandstone of the cliffs, thousands of red-billed gray-and-black seabirds filled the air with their cries as they swarmed over the pale rocks and fed their young.

Sand appeared suddenly under the teal water of the harbor, and pirates jumped nimbly over the sides of the rowboats as the boats ground to a stop on the white beaches.

Hathus climbed out of his boat as pirates pulled it up onto the beach. He glanced around at the fishermen lining the waterfront as they unloaded glistening nets full of silver tuna and emerald blackfish and yelled to one another in the general tongue and an assortment of others. None of them paid the pirates any attention. Alahvar was known for being a city open to people on all sides of the law, just as long as no one caused any trouble inside her walls.

The pirates began moving toward a series of narrow, well-worn steps that were carved out of the cliff face and led to the city above. Hathus followed as a ship's bell signaled half past noon. He groaned as he reached the base of the stairs, glancing up. His strength and stamina were slowly and surely coming back, but seven hundred feet of stairs was not going to agree with him.

"Afraid of a little exercise?" Sidion asked, his bulging arms glistening with sweat from the humid air. He flashed a grin as he brushed past.

"No, just too much," Hathus muttered.

He was the last to reach the top of the cliff, panting and cursing the whole way, and for a moment he leaned against the side of the sandstone gateway leading into Alahvar and gasped for air as the last of the pirates disappeared into a wide, crowded street full of brightly colored canopies, milling people, and bored-looking camels.

"You okay?"

Hathus rolled his head sideways to look at Bathia as she came up next to him. The three men hovered in the shadows of a wall nearby. "Fine," he panted. "Just winded."

Bathia smiled and leaned a hand against the rough sandstone next to his head. "Blackwell is looking for this worldwalker you say is here," she said, watching the town through the arch. "You're closer to getting to the Land of Dragons and your treasure."

Hathus rolled his head back to look ahead of him and at the harbor and sea beyond. Was she testing him? Trying him for his reaction?

But why would she do that? Gods, I'm getting nervous... "Good," he said aloud. "Another couple weeks, and we'll see if I'm right." He looked back at Bathia. "Or you."

She glanced at him, squinting, and smiled. "I can't believe that you've never been to Alahvar before."

Hathus shrugged.

Bathia grinned. "You don't know what you've missed, Hathus Ryrgorion. Come, let me show you." She slapped his arm and started into the city.

Hathus groaned and watched her for a moment before pushing away from the gate arch and slowly following.

"Come on!" Bathia yelled.

Hathus sighed and picked up his pace.

#

A half hour later, Hathus glanced up at Bathia, who was throwing her head back in raucous laughter with a group of pirates, and grinned. She certainly liked her liquor. For the last hour, they'd scrounged through Alahvar's busy streets, trying one loud, pirate-filled tavern after another. Personally, Hathus didn't taste the difference in beer at the different places, but Bathia seemed to be having fun, and it was fun to watch her.

The pirates roared even louder at some crude joke that Hathus only caught part of, and he smiled again as his eyes caught Bathia leaning on the bar countertop and laughing loudly. Hathus sipped at the strong gold liquor in the ceramic mug in front of him. She was even more beautiful drunk.

A dark-skinned woman in a golden silk top, split skirt, and strands and strands of clicking, swinging wooden beads, glided by his table to the exotic tune of an Araysannian horn player behind a shade in one corner. Hathus rested his chin on one hand, watching her. He knew that they weren't going to stay in Alahvar for the night, but perhaps he had time to try some of her women before they found the worldwalker and left.

He frowned at the thought of the worldwalker. If he was lucky, they wouldn't find him, and the job would be over before it had started.

Hathus watched the dancer sway, eyeing the tight muscles of her stomach. If they found a portal to the Land of Dragons—which they wouldn't—they wouldn't be able to get through without a worldwalker.

"Are you always this boring? Or just on special occasions?" Bathia turned a dinged-up wooden chair around and straddled it, setting her ceramic mug down on the tabletop with a loud thunk. Her tanned face was tinged red from laughter and drink.

"Oh, special occasions only," Hathus replied, leaning back and looking at her.

Bathia laughed and crossed her bronzed arms on the back of the chair.

Hathus smiled. He liked the way Bathia laughed, her whole body going into the motion as she threw her head back.

"So," Bathia said, "you've been with us for two weeks now, and I don't know anything about you other than you believe in fairy-tale worlds. Where are you from? You got any family?"

Hathus swallowed a mouthful of beer. What could he tell her about himself? Nothing about his early years, that was for sure, and definitely nothing of his imprisonment or being a thief—that was something he didn't want anyone knowing. The thief part so people wouldn't be wary of him and watch their treasures more closely and the imprisonment part because... well, he really didn't know why. Maybe because he was ashamed for having let himself get caught.

"No family," he said. "Not anymore, and I'm from Crystoln, originally. Although I don't really call any one place home."

"A drifter," Bathia said, reaching for her mug.

Hathus shrugged. "Sort of. How about you?" he said, diverting the subject away from himself. "You're from the islands, but were you born there?"

Bathia took a long drink out of her mug, shaking her head. "No, I was actually born in Warulan, but I moved to the islands when I was three." She set the mug down. "You go to school? You strike me as being educated."

Hathus smiled, noting how she'd quickly changed the subject back to him. "I'm glad. My mother would be happy to know that all those years she sent me to school paid off."

Bathia laughed. She rested her head on her crossed arms, half-empty beer mug dangling from one hand. "I went to a school on the Main Island, although I'm sure it wasn't as fancy as the ones you went to."

"Why do you say that?" Hathus asked, smile fading. "You have no idea of the kind of schools I went to."

"You're paying us fifty thousand aray to look for a mythical otherworld," Bathia said, watching him. "I think that your parents must have had money, or maybe someone is helping you out."

Hathus narrowed his eyes at her. She was drunk and didn't know half of what she was saying, but she wasn't that drunk, and he got the feeling again that she was testing him and trying to find out the truth behind his story.

But then, maybe he was just growing paranoid.

He shrugged. "My parents were a little wealthy, yes." The old feeling of unfairness rose in him again, the unfairness of others picking on him for having rich parents.

A shaft of sunlight fell into the dark room, and they both glanced up as Sidion appeared in the doorway of the tavern.

Bathia raised a tattooed hand in greeting.

The dreadlocked man wound through the maze of crowded tables, dancing women, and laughing pirates to their table, his chest gleaming in the light of wavering candles scattered throughout the room.

"Captain wants to see you, Hathus Ryrgorion," Sidion said.

Hathus took a drink of beer, glancing up at the second mate over the rim of the mug.

"He's found your worldwalker," Sidion elaborated.

Shit.

#

Hathus scanned the dim tavern. The place looked like where one would find an assassin. Or be assassinated. Dark stained sandstone walls, dinged wooden tables with scowling customers crowded around them, and a bartender with double swords crossed on his back and a black turban shadowing his scarred, mustached face. It was exactly where he'd pictured a worldwalker living.

Sidion made a path through the tables toward an alcove in a corner. Bathia followed him. Hathus followed her. The bartender and a bat-eared Araysannian desert fox sitting on the counter next to him watched their every move like hawks watching their prey.

Hathus slipped a hand toward his dagger. The place was like an underworld lair, which normally he wouldn't mind—gods knew he'd spent enough time in them over the years—but there were underworld lairs and then there were underworld lairs, and he'd learned a long time ago which ones were wise to visit and which were not. This one definitely wasn't one of the former.

They reached the back wall and the alcove nestled in it, and Sidion pushed aside a dusty dark-purple curtain and slipped inside.

Bathia disappeared after him.

Hathus eyed the curtain. He wanted to run. Get away from all this magic while he still could. He heard the footsteps of the three men who followed him, trailing him through the tavern.

Gods, I appreciate you getting me out of the dungeons, but did you have to do it the way you did? Hathus slipped his hands into his pockets and moved through the curtain. His step faltered as his gaze fell on a man sitting behind a bottle-covered table dominating the alcove.

"Is this the man you spoke of, Blackwell?" the man asked, his voice low and strangled. His face was covered in scars and held only one eye, and it was so icy blue as to be almost white. The other was permanently sealed shut by a jagged white scar that ran from his hairline to the high collar of his dark-blue shirt.

Hathus felt his insides turn. The first word that came to his mind to describe the worldwalker was grotesque. Lank hair the color of freshly fallen snow fell to the man's bony shoulders. His lips were twisted and burned and held the shade of freshly healed skin, and his nose looked as if it had been broken numerous times and healed crooked. Where eyebrows should have been there was only pale white flesh, and everywhere that his long-sleeved shirt and black pants didn't cover, his skin was burned and scarred to the point of mutilation.

Bathia moved to one of the chairs around the table.

Hathus, realizing he was staring, stepped after her as the curtain fell into place behind him with a soft swoosh.

Blackwell appeared out of the shadows behind the table, blowing out a puff of smoke from a slender whale-tusk pipe. He nodded, the silver dagger in his left ear bouncing up and down.

"Hathus," the pirate captain said in his soft, unassuming way. He waved his two-fingered hand at the worldwalker. "Wylam Caine. Caine, Hathus Ryrgorion."

Hathus stared at Caine. The worldwalker was the most horrifying man he had ever seen.

Caine's eerie blue eye met his, and he looked away.

"You're wondering where I got these scars," Caine said.

Who wouldn't? Hathus glanced back at him.

Caine smiled a slow, twisting sneer as his burned lips pulled away from teeth that were broken and stained yellow.

Hathus resisted the urge to shudder.

"Humans," the worldwalker rasped, his voice reminding Hathus of someone who'd had their throat cut and was trying to wheeze through the opening in it. "Humans gave me these marks. Our brethren." The worldwalker held his hands up in display, burned and scarred like the rest of his body, with several fingers that had obviously been broken at one time and grown back twisted and bent at grotesque angles. He smiled wider.

The hair on the back of Hathus's neck stood on end.

"They tortured me because I have magic," Caine wheezed. "But I, unlike so many, was lucky enough to escape before they could tire with me and throw me in the pits with the rest of the bodies."

Hathus shifted on his chair, a sudden image of deep holes full of mangled, twisted bodies filling his mind.

"Enough about me, though," Caine said, reaching for a small black bottle of whiskey next to his elbow. "I was told you wish to go the Land of Dragons." The worldwalker took a swig out of the bottle, eye peering over the top.

Hathus nodded. "That's..." His voice cracked, so he coughed and cleared his throat. "That's right."

Caine set the bottle down with a clink and folded his mangled hands in front of him. "Why?"

Hathus blinked. "Why do you want to know?" he countered.

"Because if I'm going to risk my ass getting you there, and presumably back in one piece, I'd like to know why," Caine replied, staring at him.

Hathus eyed the worldwalker. "I believe that the legends of treasure there are real," he said after a moment.

Caine stared at him for a second before taking another long drink out of the bottle. The noise of the liquid glugging out of the glass container filled the small room.

Azaria shifted in the shadows on Blackwell's shoulder. Hathus glared at the monkey as it scratched behind its ear with one paw.

"Believe there's treasure there, eh?" Caine said, his sudden raspy voice making Hathus jump and look back at him. "That's funny."

Hathus raised in eyebrow. "Funny?"

"Yes," Caine rasped. "Funny because there were others who believed that too."

Hathus was suddenly interested. "Really?"

"Mmm," Caine said, drinking out of the bottle again. "Before the wars, there were treasure seekers who thought the Land of Dragons and its treasure was real but that the dragons part was made up to keep people away."

Hathus shifted on his chair. Maybe his idea wasn't so unique after all. "What happened to them, these people who went looking for the Land of Dragons?" he asked. He had a feeling he wouldn't like the answer.

Caine smiled slowly, mangled lips pulling back from ruined teeth. "They never came back."

They could have just gotten lost. What am I saying? Of course they got lost. The Land of Dragons isn't real. "Well," Hathus said, "I plan on coming back."

"I'm sure they all did, too," Caine said.

The alcove was quiet for a minute, the only sound Blackwell's steady inhaling and exhaling through his pipe and Azaria's scratching.

"You know," Caine said after a moment, "in the old days, before the wars ravaged the lands, I would travel from one world to the next like you'd travel from one continent to the other." The worldwalker snorted, a rasping wheeze of a noise. "Now?" he said, his voice growing dark. "Now I hole up in this shithole of a tavern, waiting for the day someone will turn me in to the authorities and the job the torturers started will be finished."

"So…do you know of a portal to the Land of Dragons?" Hathus asked after a minute.

"Yes," Caine replied.

Hathus frowned, annoyed. He hadn't thought that the gossip he'd heard of the worldwalker being alive was true, much less that the man would agree to "look" for the Land of Dragons. But then, most people would do anything for money. Even pretend to look for a world that didn't exist. "And will you take me there?"

Caine glanced up. "Yes," he wheezed, draining the last of the liquid from the bottle and setting it down on the table by the others. "I'll take you."

"Well, then I guess that's all settled," Hathus said. "Blackwell can show you to the ships. We'll leave at sundown." He stood, ready to be away from the worldwalker and his magic.

"I must ask you something, Hathus Ryrgorion," Caine rasped.

Hathus glanced back up at him.

"Do you really believe that the Land of Dragons is real?"

Hathus stared at him for a minute. Why was everyone asking him that? Had he really become that bad at lying after such a long time without practice?

"Yes," he said after a few heartbeats, "or I wouldn't be here asking you to show me where it is."

Caine nodded. "Then you must understand, Hathus Ryrgorion, that going to the Land of Dragons is not like sailing to Warulan and back. It is a dangerous path, and I cannot guarantee you that we will return from it."

"I…" Hathus started, suddenly realizing that the worldwalker wasn't pretending.

He really does believe there is a Land of Dragons…

"I'll take my chances," Hathus said.

Caine nodded, watching him with his ghostly blue eye. "Well, then," he said with a dark smile, "let us go to the Land of Dragons."

Hathus smiled back.

He's a fucking nut.

CHAPTER 17

Darkmoon

Darkmoon slipped past a faded road sign that read "Northport, thirty miles."

The sign creaked dully on rusty chains in the cold, fog-shrouded night.

A salty wind from the nearby ocean rustled through the ancient spruces and pines looming along the sides of the road, parting the thick fog just enough to show him a glimpse of the path ahead and a small clearing cut out of the ancient forest to one side. The dark steeple of an old stone church covered in thick moss and creeping vines loomed like a dagger out of the mist swirling through the clearing.

Gliding toward the ancient building, Darkmoon stepped off the road and onto the dew-soaked grass around the church and disappeared into the shadows next to the weathered building like he was one of them. His fingers found the iron latch on the door of the old building and the ancient, iron-barred oak boards creaked open in front of him.

His oddly mismatched eyes quickly scanned the shadowed pews and dusty curtains as the door moaned shut behind him.

Empty. Almost. Darkmoon's gaze caught on the round stone altar dominating the center of the room. Fat dripping tallow candles flickered in a circle on the floor around it, and a statue of the goddess Aemora, Protector of the Innocent, sat cross-legged on top.

Darkmoon glided down the main aisle of the church, the worn stone cool under his suede boots. He kept his head down as he walked, pretending to be deep in worship even as his eyes roamed the shadows around him from underneath his dark cowl.

Ancient oiled wooden pews, hewed from rich black epharia wood imported from the far northwestern continent of Ennotar, glistened red and gold in the light from the candles atop the altar. The candles were kept burning all hours of the day and night by a servant of the goddess, as was custom, so that any who might see them could come and seek shelter at her feet.

Darkmoon pulled a piece of chocolate from his cloak and popped it in his mouth. The ebony ring on his right hand glinted dully in the light of the candles. He wasn't coming for protection; he was coming for the money owed him for the job he had completed in Zarcayra. He stopped in front of the altar.

The naked deity on top stared at him from under finely varnished brows, her long, curling bronze hair hanging between her fat breasts and down to her crossed ankles.

Darkmoon eyed the statue. He'd often wondered how anyone could expect protection from a goddess who couldn't even protect herself from the elements by putting on some clothes. But then, he supposed that many liked the idea of a naked goddess. More exciting that way.

Rain began tinkling against the glass panes of the church's windows.

Darkmoon glanced at a nearby window, curtained off with thick red drapes, and saw Cyron standing by it, watching him. He looked back at the deity, ears cocked for noise of his money-bearer's presence. There were rumors circling through Warulan… rumors that Zarcayra was planning to attack Eromor for killing their king.

Darkmoon let his eyes travel to the dusty beams supporting the ceiling of the church. Two men sat partially hidden in the shadows crowding the rafters, crossbows in their laps. Maybe the coming war was the darkness that the seer had spoken of, the darkness that would make Argdrion fall. But he doubted it. War was horrible and dark and terrifying, but this one couldn't be any worse than the last.

"Help me, please…" a woman's voice from the past begged.

The sound of several sets of footsteps splashing through puddles outside drove the voice away. A few seconds later the door at the back of the church creaked open.

"I didn't know you were a worshipper of the goddess Aemora, Darkmoon," a low-pitched raspy voice said.

Darkmoon turned. "Oh, I'm not," he said softly. "I simply enjoy looking at a naked woman, be it a statue or otherwise."

Three figures in muddy indigo cloaks stepped from the shadows by the door, their leather boots scuffing softly on the stones beneath them.

"You're fast, assassin," the hooded figure who had spoken before said. "Only three weeks since you were hired, and you've already managed to travel across half of Argdrion, kill the king of Zarcayra, and be back in Warulan at our designated spot on time." The figure shook his head. "That's impressive."

"I like the sound of coins clinking together," Darkmoon replied, hearing one of the men in the rafters shift.

The raspy-voiced man snorted. "I've heard. Your love of money is second to none but your love of killing."

Darkmoon gave a humorless smile, eyeing the three figures. "I wonder," he said after a heartbeat, "which of you will attack first?"

They shifted, cloaks rustling softly around them. "What do you mean?" the same speaker as before asked. "We simply came to pay you your money due."

Darkmoon motioned at the figures. "It only takes one to pay me my money; there are three of you."

Five, actually…

"We are cautious," the raspy-voiced man said artfully. "You are a dangerous killer."

Darkmoon ran his tongue over his teeth to clean them of chocolate. He was enjoying their banter; it was amusing, and it kept the voices away.

Almost.

"Brother…" a breeze creeping under the church's door whispered.

"You're also each carrying a new bag of money," Darkmoon said, nodding his head at the three figures. "Probably advance payment for killing me." He smiled again, a little humor in it this time, and shrugged. "Well, for attempting to kill me."

The three figures were quiet for several moments.

"Well," the speaker, obviously their leader, finally said, "you are clever, aren't you, assassin?"

Darkmoon bowed his head in assent, whispers murmuring in his ears.

A tense silence fell over the room, the smell of urine drifting through the musty air from the figures.

Darkmoon watched them; they were afraid. As they should be. "Any last words before you die?" he asked softly.

Those in the rafters were the first to move.

Darkmoon's ear caught the sound of the triggers of their crowsbows clicking a split second before two bolts whizzed through the empty air where his heart would have been had he not rolled to the side.

The bolts echoed off the stone floor with loud pings, sending sparks flying into the cold air inside the church.

Darkmoon slid into the darkness, hearing the barbed weapons skidding off under the pews as the three figures by the door threw the hoods of their cloaks off.

A middle-aged man with graying hair and a burned face and two brown-haired women scanned the shadows as they drew their weapons, a sword for the man and one woman and a battle-axe for the other woman.

Interesting. Darkmoon pulled two throwing stars from a belt at his waist and jumped nimbly to his feet, sent the fine-edged weapons toward the three people.

One woman caught a star in her throat with a sharp crunching sound; the man dodged the star aimed for him and caught it in his arm instead of his neck.

He's fast. Darkmoon rolled behind a pew at the front of the church. He peeked around the edge and eyed the man, keen ears listening to the men in the rafters reload their weapons. The woman he'd hit dropped her sword with a loud clatter and slumped to the floor, gagging on her own blood.

"Where'd he go?" the raspy-voiced man hissed. He slapped away the remaining woman as she tried to help him pull the star out of his arm.

"You missed me. Did you see, assassin?" the raspy-voiced man called. The star clattered to the floor, the noise echoing sharply off the high stone ceiling above their heads. "You can't hide forever, you know. You'll have to

come out and face us sometime if you want to leave this church alive…
unless, of course, you are *scared?*"

Darkmoon pivoted on his crouched haunches and leaned against the
pew behind him, pulling two daggers out of their sheaths and holding them
up in front of his face. If the man was trying to unnerve him, he was playing
a losing game. He turned one dagger so he could see the raspy-voiced man,
who was holding a hand over his bleeding sword arm as he motioned at the
remaining woman. She nodded and padded softly off into the shadows, a
limp in her walk.

"Come, Darkmoon," the raspy-voiced man called. "We know you're
there, and we all know how this has to end. Why don't you quit hiding and
come out and play?"

Darkmoon grinned, white teeth flashing in the shadow of his cowl. He
watched in the reflection of the knife as the woman's darker shadow glided
through the black shadows lining the wall. It had been some time since he'd
been hunted; it would make the killing that much more fun.

The crossbowmen shifted in the rafters above him. Darkmoon glanced
up as dust trickled down around him, glittering golden in the candles'
flickering light.

"Brother…" the wind whispered again.

Cyron appeared among the pews several rows in front of him.

"It is as I feared," the raspy-voiced man went on. "The great assassin
Darkmoon is nothing more than a scared little boy."

Cyron vanished.

Darkmoon looked at the remaining woman, who was sneaking down
the row of pews directly in front of him now, her head turning from side to
side as she scanned the darkness. He leaned down and glanced under the
pew and, lying on his back, rolled underneath.

"Just a scared, weak little boy," the raspy-voiced man went on, "trying
to be something that he is not."

The woman's footsteps drew closer, leather boots hissing softly on the
stone floor.

Darkmoon softened his breathing as she drew near, listening, judging,
waiting. Her first leather boot came into view, followed closely by the second,
and he threw a muscled arm out and swept her legs out from underneath

her. He slit her throat as she collapsed to the floor.

The noise of the woman's axe hitting the stones next to her echoed loudly through the church.

"Elwysa?"

Darkmoon wiped the woman's blood off his hand and knife as the raspy-voiced man called out for her. The blood was warm and sticky on his fingers.

"Elwysa, where are you?"

Darkmoon sheathed his knife and slid over the woman's body, black cloak trailing behind him as he merged with the darker shadows lining the wall. Rain pattered dully on a window beside him.

Darkmoon's mismatched eyes moved from the raspy-voiced man, who was still listening, head cocked, for any sound from the woman, to the two shifting crossbowmen in the rafters, peering at the opposite side of the church with their weapons at the ready.

Fools. After one shot, a wise bowman moved to a different location to keep the enemy from knowing where they were. Darkmoon pulled a knife from his belt and aimed for the crossbowman closest to him.

Cyron appeared again several feet away, green eyes watching him. "Please…" he whispered.

Darkmoon let his knife loose with a quick fling of his wrist. His brother melted away.

The bowman gasped as the knife drove deep into his throat, and his crossbow fell out of his hands and clattered to the stone floor below with a crash. He joined his weapon a second later with a heavy thud, body bending over a pew.

The raspy-voiced man cursed and ducked behind a pew. The other crossbowman wheeled around and shot into the shadows where the knife had come from.

Darkmoon slid off as the bolt stuck harmlessly into the maroon curtain next to him in a puff of gray dust, keeping to the edge of the room as he moved toward the raspy-voiced man's position.

"You're down to just two now, friend," he called softly as the remaining man in the rafters hastily rewound his weapon with a whirring sound. "I wonder, who will go next?"

Another bolt whistled out of the rafters. Darkmoon heard it hit a pew behind him. He glanced up at the remaining bowman, frantically and clumsily winding his weapon again. He pulled a star out of the black leather vambrace on his lower arm.

The bowman spat blood as the star cut the vein in the side of his throat. He flipped over backward and fell toward one of the circular iron chandeliers that hung from the church's rafters. There was a snap of bones as the man's foot caught in the chandelier, and he hung there upside down as his weapon smashed into a pew below.

Darkmoon slipped off into the shadows again. A boot scraped on stone. His oddly colored eyes darted to the noise as he crept between a set of pews. "There's just you now," he said, just loud enough to be heard over the now pouring rain. "Why don't you come out and play? Don't tell me you're *scared*?" He spotted a trail of glistening blood drops on the age-worn stones in front of him.

"Mercy, please..." his mother's voice whispered.

Darkmoon tried to ignore it, gliding around the edge of a pew and melding with the shadows in another row as his eyes scanned the church for the raspy-voiced man.

Where are you? Ahh... A movement in the shadows across the room caught his eyes.

There you are...

"You know," Darkmoon called, "I really doubt you're getting paid enough for this."

The raspy-voiced man wheeled about and scanned the shadows around the edges of the church.

"Is it really worth it?" Darkmoon said, moving toward him.

The other man hissed and turned, swinging his sword wildly from side to side as he slowly backed down the main aisle of the church.

"And did you think that a mere five could take down the best assassin in Argdrion?" Darkmoon said softly.

The man turned sharply, slicing at thin air as Darkmoon swished past.

"That's cutting." Darkmoon stooped next to the dead woman among the pews and quietly lifted her axe from the floor next to her. "It would wound a sensitive man's pride." He crept up behind the raspy-voiced man who now stood in the middle of the church, frantically searching the shadows on either side of him.

"Where are you?" the man hissed, turning from side to side with his sword held out in front of him. "Show yourself, coward. Or are you afraid to face me?" Silence echoed through the church as his words faded away into the rafters.

"I am afraid of no man," Darkmoon whispered in the man's ear.

The man cried out and flailed wildly, swinging his sword at nothing. "Where are you?" he snarled. "Where?"

Darkmoon moved up behind the man again, the axe raised. "Behind you," he said softly.

The raspy-voiced man swung around again, and with a sickening crunch, Darkmoon put the axe into his skull.

They stared at each other for a moment, the dying man's eyes wide with shock as they met Darkmoon's unfeeling blue and green ones, before blood gurgled out of his open mouth, mingling with the flow gushing from his head, and he fell backward with a heavy thud onto the stone floor of the church.

"You really should have just paid me my money," Darkmoon said tonelessly. He knelt beside the dead man and rifled through his pockets.

A piece of paper met his searching fingers first. Darkmoon scanned it and tucked it into his waist belt before his hand closed around something hard and coins chinked merrily. He pulled a silk purse out of the man's shirt pocket, tucking it into his cloak.

Cyron screamed, the noise echoing faintly through the church.

Darkmoon stood, then stepped over the raspy-voiced man's prostrate form and moved to the other bodies littering the floor, kneeling by each one in turn and pulling a bag of coins of equal weight from their pockets before methodically removing his weapons from their throats and wiping them clean them on their clothes. He replaced them in their designated spots.

Thunder rumbled ominously, shaking the floor of the church with its fury.

Darkmoon glanced up, eyes catching on Cyron, who stood a few yards away.

"Your past will haunt you," the seer's quivering voice whispered in his ear. "Burn you, like it should, until you remember the man that you were before you became this creature of darkness…"

Darkmoon stood again, slipping toward the back of the church and gathering his last remaining star from the cold floor and the bag of coins that had fallen out of the pocket of the man hanging from the chandelier.

Blood dripped from the man, landing on the floor of the church like rain. *Plop, plop, plop.*

"Only you can save Argdrion, Darkmoon," the seer's wavering voice moaned through the church. "Only you…"

Lightning flashed as Darkmoon pulled the ancient door of the old church open, illuminating his dark frame for a moment as rain bounced off the muddy grass outside. He pulled his cloak tighter around himself, more voices echoing through the falling rain. Voices of pain, despair, sorrow.

He stepped out into the rain and moved past the fading roadside again, disappearing into the night.

#

A few hours later, Darkmoon shifted from one buttock to the other on a hard, unforgiving tavern chair, continuing to ignore the pewter mug of stale beer that the tavern maid had brought as it separated into two disgusting shades of brown instead of one. He did not drink spirits. It made one weak and vulnerable, and he would never be that again.

The roaring fire in the tavern's great stone hearth let out a crackle across the room, and his mismatched eyes darted to it as a party of drunks at a table by the door yelled loudly. He'd been sitting here for almost three hours now, watching the crowd of strumming bards, carousing drunks, and a sweating, bald-headed tavern owner who had the face of a boar and the build to match, and nothing had changed in the noisy, crowded room.

Darkmoon glanced at the mug of ale, the last frothy bubble popping on its surface, and back up at the room as a woman the size of a house threw her head back in laughter at a song about a king and a goat that the group of traveling bards strummed out on rebecs and lutes.

The woman laughed even louder as the bards came to the part in the song where the king met a female goat herder, slamming a meaty fist down on the top of the table she sat at. A timid-looking man sitting across from her jumped, his iron-rimmed spectacles and a dusty bag of books giving him away as a teacher.

Darkmoon went back to scanning the room. It was an old song and one that everyone had heard so much it wasn't even funny anymore. Not that it had been that funny to begin with. He drummed the fingers of his left hand in a steady, rhythmic beat on the tabletop in front of him. He didn't know how long he'd have to wait—the piece of paper in the raspy-voiced man's pocket had only said the name of the tavern he now sat in and today's date, but he couldn't really blame anyone but himself for that since he'd killed all his would-be killers before he'd found the note and had the need to ask them what time.

Darkmoon watched a red-faced man brush past the dark corner he sat in.

The hours dragged on.

The bards packed their instruments into dusty traveling cases and moved on, and a dirty group of travelers with dark expressions pushed through the tavern door and noisily called for drinks, but still the man Darkmoon waited for remained absent.

A pretty brown-haired serving girl cast him a curious glance as the clock on the wall struck one, and the tavern slowly started growing empty, but Darkmoon ignored her. He had other things on his mind tonight, like money.

The rickety door across the room creaked open loudly around two in the morning, and a dark-hooded figure slipped inside and surveyed the now-empty tavern.

Darkmoon watched the newcomer from underneath the shadow of his black cowl, fingers still drumming a steady groove in the tabletop.

The newcomer's gaze turned his way.

If his employer was surprised at seeing him instead of the "killers" he'd hired, he didn't show it. Instead he picked his way through the maze of empty chairs and dirty tables and pulled out a chair opposite him with a dull scrape. He sat down stiffly.

"I half expected to find you here," the man said after a moment. His voice had a tense edge to it, like he had a lot on his mind.

Darkmoon watched him silently. He could tell his employer was annoyed. People sat more erectly when they were annoyed. He shrugged nonchalantly after a moment. "You should have sent more killers," he said. His employer glared at him.

"I assume you took the money off them?"

Darkmoon nodded.

"And I also assume you want yours paid you."

"That would be nice," Darkmoon said softly. "Unless you'd like to end up like your killers."

The other man stared at him for a minute, and for half a heartbeat Darkmoon thought he might be foolish enough to try something. He quickly dismissed the idea. His employer wasn't a stupid man and wouldn't risk a scene in such an open place. It might reveal his identity, and that was something he had gone through great pains to keep secret throughout the duration of their acquaintance.

"Fine," his employer said after a moment, reaching into the dark folds of his cloak and pulling four medium-sized black leather bags out. "thirty-four thousand aray, as agreed." He placed the bags on the stained table in between them with a clink and drew his hands back into the folds of his cloak.

They were noble hands, Darkmoon noted. Smooth and clean.

The red-faced tavern owner wiped a meaty hand across his sweating brow and stifled a yawn across the room.

"Forty thousand," Darkmoon replied softly, not touching the bags before him as he drew his eyes away from the room.

His employer looked up sharply. "You already got the six thousand from those you slew, money that I gave them, if you add that to the fourteen thousand in front of you, that makes forty thousand."

"I took money off dead bodies. It matters not to me who paid it to them," Darkmoon said. "You owe me six thousand aray still."

"And if I refuse to pay it?" his employer asked.

Darkmoon stared into the darkness of his employer's hood. "Then you are more foolish than I thought you were."

They stared at each other for a moment.

If it is a waiting game you want, you will not win.

"So sure of yourself," the other man hissed finally, reaching into his cloak again and pulling out another leather bag and throwing it on the table with the others. "You know, one of these days, someone's going to kill you."

"I doubt it," Darkmoon said. "And if they do, at least I'll die a rich man." He reached over the table with long arms and pulled the bags to him.

"Where will you go after this?" his employer, ex-employer, asked, watching him.

Darkmoon didn't look at the man as his slender fingers quickly ran through the coins in the dark leather bags. Voices whispered around his head; he ignored them.

"Why?" he asked. "Want to send more killers after me?" He could sense the man's eyes narrowing.

"I simply thought that perhaps you were going to Crystoln for the king's ninety-fourth birthday celebration," the man said. "I heard that they managed to procure a skinchanger for the arena, a rare treat indeed."

Darkmoon leaned his chair back on two legs, the old wood protesting loudly, and watched the other man for a minute. He'd heard about the skinchanger, and he was planning on going to Crystoln to see her, but the fact that his ex-employer was interested in his travels bespoke more of deception than friendly conversation. The King's Highway to Crystoln was long, and there were many places for killers to hide.

"You really don't want it known that you hired me, do you?" Darkmoon said after a moment, tearing his eyes away from Cyron as he appeared behind his ex-employer. "Afraid someone will find out that you had the king of Zarcayra killed?"

The man didn't move. "How could they?" he asked evenly. "As far as Zarcayra is concerned, Eromor hired you, and you don't know who I am."

Darkmoon watched a bead of perspiration drip out of the darkness of the man's cowl. "Yet you hired killers anyway," he said softly.

"I don't like loose ends."

"Neither do I," Darkmoon replied.

They stared at each other for a moment again before he dropped his chair to all four legs and stood. He threw an oyrcu on the table with a chink for the untouched beer.

His ex-employer followed his movement as he slowly walked around the table.

Darkmoon leaned down next to him, placing a hand on his shoulder. "Two things," he whispered. "First, if anyone tries to kill me again, I'll find you and make you rue the day that you contacted me."

"What if I didn't send them?" the other man asked, voice even but tight.

Darkmoon ran a slender fingertip along the edge of his cowl. "Well, then I'll apologize when I see you in the next life."

His ex-employer snorted. "The only afterlife you'll see is the darkest corner of the underworld."

Darkmoon smiled humorlessly. "Might be kind of nice. I've always enjoyed the heat. Second," he went on. "Don't bother telling yourself I don't know who you are. I've known that since you first hired me." He leaned closer, tightening his grip on the man's shoulder. "Lord Ravynston."

The nobleman went rigid.

Darkmoon stood. He made it his business to know who he was working for, although many tried to keep their identities a secret from him for fear of blackmail, and three hours after the King of Eromor's chief advisor had approached him in a tavern in Crystoln, he had, after some sniffing around, found out the man's identity.

Darkmoon slid his hand off the stiff advisor's shoulder and reached into his cloak for a piece of chocolate.

The bartender blew out a lantern behind the bar. Darkmoon picked up his bags of money. "Goodbye, Torin," he said. He turned, voices whispering in the crackling fire. He knew what Torin's plan was: to get the dragon throne of Eromor.

He wound through the maze of tavern tables and chairs and to the front door. The old laws of Eromor stated that if the king or queen died naturally and with no heirs, then the eleven lower advisors and the chief advisor would vote in a new king from the standing nobility. If the king died unnaturally, however, and with no heirs, then the chief advisor would take on the position of ruler. Torin simply had to have Uranius murdered, and in a way that didn't point to him, and the throne was his. Darkmoon pushed out into the night.

A forest crowded around the tavern, broken only by the straight line of the King's Highway running through it. Darkmoon started off up the road, keeping to the shadows pooling at its edges. He had killed Zarcayra's king for Torin, and now Torin would hire an assassin who would kill Uranius and claim that Zarcayra had hired them to do it in reciprocation of the King of Kings being killed. Uranius would be dead unnaturally, and Torin would get the throne.

It was a good plan, he had to give Torin that. But there were flaws in it, flaws that, if it were his plot, he would never have overlooked.

A wolf howled in the distance, the eerie notes echoing through the forest.

Cyron appeared in the road ahead, silent, watching.

Darkmoon slowed.

"Brother..." Cyron's voice, separate from his body, whispered through the trees.

Darkmoon saw the hall again, felt the old pain. He sped up his walking and pushed through his brother's image, making it disappear into the mist.

A light appeared out of the darkness ahead, a farmhouse nestled among the trees.

Darkmoon made his way toward it, the voices hissing through the trees, screaming in his ears. Killing was what quieted the past.

Darkmoon moved around the back of the farmhouse, away from the lantern on the front porch and to a half-open window in the back. He glanced through the window, eyes scanning the shadowed room and the sleeping shapes inside.

Two beds sat in the room, one against the back wall with the parents in it and the other directly below the window with two small sleeping children in it, a boy and a girl. Darkmoon's gaze rested on the children. Killing was what helped him, but how many would it take to quiet the voices completely? His hand went to the belt wrapped around his waist and the knives hidden there.

A dozen, seventy, a hundred... Darkmoon slid the window open the rest of the way. Maybe it would take a thousand, or two. It had taken that many the first time... He pushed aside a lacy yellow curtain.

He wondered if Torin's movement was the darkness coming to Argdrion. If he was supposed to stand against him to save the world.

He watched the children's chests rise in fall.

"Brother…" Cyron whispered.

If Torin was who he was supposed to stand against, then the seer would be disappointed. He didn't care what Torin did, he didn't care what anyone did. Darkmoon slid a knife from a sheath on the belt around his middle and climbed through the window.

CHAPTER 18

Azkanysh

A warm breeze thick with the scent of lotuses and lilies blew through the arched throne room and fanned Azkanysh's cheeks through the black cloth covering her face. It was her first day on the lyon throne, the fourth day after Vosbarhan's death, and her first time facing the throne room.

Vyzir Dsamihur had advised her the day before, after Vosbarhan's funeral had ended, telling her that she should call a court session to discuss what Zarcayra should do about Eromor's blatant act of war against them in having Vosbarhan murdered. Personally, she did not care that the Warulanian kingdom had killed Vosbarhan, but the move was a strike against Zarcayra's honor, and if they did not retaliate, it would make them look weak, bendable.

Azkanysh scanned the throne room. There were over three hundred people in it this morning, all men. There should be women in it too, members of her own sex.

"The first court of Queen of Queens Azkanysh," the court crier yelled out over the watching throne room, "Fifth King of K— Er, Queen of Qu…" The herald glanced at her before starting over. "Fifth Ruler of Zarcayra, Commander of Armies, Ruler of Kings, Chosen of the Gods, is now in session."

A slave in a black tunic rang the heavy bronze gong beside the dais that the throne sat on, and Azkanysh shifted. For years she had wondered what it would be like to face the court and throne room, to sit on the throne and wear the golden lyon crown. She smiled slightly beneath her hijab. She felt powerful, commanding, untouchable.

Vyzir Dsamihur, standing a few feet away to her left, raised a hand to his mouth and coughed lightly.

Azkanysh glanced at him, but he was looking straight ahead. She looked back at the packed throne room, at the faces watching her. They expected her to say something, she realized, to start the court session. But what was she supposed to say? What had Vosbarhan said to start court sessions?

"Today's court ..." she started.

Vyzir Dsamihur coughed again.

Azkanysh glanced at him again.

Vyzir Dsamihur took a step toward her, leaning over to whisper in her ear. "Louder, Queen of Queens," Vyzir Dsamihur whispered. "The throne room is large, and those in the back will not hear you."

Azkanysh nodded, and Vyzir Dsamihur backed up again. "Today's court," she began again, forcing her voice to rise in volume, "is being held to discuss how we, Zarcayra, will react to Eromor's killing of our King of Kings, Vosbarhan."

Her blood burned at the taste of Vosbarhan's name on her tongue, making her want to puke, to spit, to cleanse her body of his name and memory. But then, why should she? He was dead and rotting in a tomb outside the city, and she was sitting on his throne and wearing his crown. How it must anger him. The thought made Azkanysh smile wider.

Heads nodded in the throne room.

Azkanysh shifted again, the worn gold of the throne digging into her body in numerous places. She relished sitting on the throne, seeing the throne room and having the court look up to her, but she was nervous about holding her first court session. They said that a King of Kings's first court session, or in her case, Queen of Queens, decided how they would rule the kingdom. What if she did something wrong and gave the men of Zarcayra reason to laugh at and mock her? But then, would they not laugh and mock her anyway? She had overheard several of the Guardian Council members whispering among themselves that morning as they walked behind her to the throne room. They had been talking about her, about what a fool she would make of herself on her first day of ruling.

"A woman cannot rule a kingdom," Tukayr had whispered to Nupar Abayn'uni. "A woman cannot even rule herself safely. How does anyone expect her to rule others?"

"I am sure that her first court session will prove to Queen of Queens Azkanysh just how incapable she is of running the kingdom," Nupar had replied evenly. "She will step out from under from the golden lyon crown by the end of the week."

Azkanysh's tapped her fingers against the gold of the throne's armrests. She had no intention of stepping out from under the golden lyon crown. And if she did, who did the Guardian Council expect would take it up? The law still remained the same, and whether they liked it or not, she was, at the moment, the only legal heir to the crown.

"If I may insert something, Queen of Queens," Nupar Abayn'uni said, stepping forward from the rest of the Guardian Council, who were spread out in a half circle before the dais, "I think that this court session's first order of business should be to decide if the kingdom will go on with the Great Race, which has been suspended these last two days, or if this traditional event should be canceled this year in lieu of certain devastating events."

Azkanysh glanced around the throne room as murmuring broke out. She had forgotten about the race being suspended and waiting to start at a word from her. It made her look stupid. The look in the throne room's occupants' eyes said that they knew it. It was a bad start. She frowned.

"Yes," she said, raising her voice again as several men at the back of the throne room put hands to their ears. "Thank you, Shayr Abayn'uni, for reminding the court."

Nupar dipped his head.

Azkanysh glanced at Vyzir Dsamihur. How did she start the discussion off? The shayrs with horses in the race did not want the race to be canceled, but most of the city agreed that holding the race after Vosbarhan's murder would be disrespectful. She would like to disrespect Vosbarhan's memory, but angering the kingdom so soon after putting on the golden lyon crown would be unwise.

Azkanysh looked back at the Guardian Council. They were watching her expectantly, waiting for her to ask them their opinion. She eyed them.

She did not wish to ask for their opinion on this or any matter. But tradition was tradition, and again, she did not want to anger the kingdom so soon after putting on the crown.

"What does the council think?" she asked.

Nupar stepped back to the other Guardian Council members, moving into a circle with them to discuss the matter.

Azkanysh watched them. She did not like Nupar Abayn'uni. The eldest son of a wealthy shayr of Sussār, he was a man who had been in politics his whole life and a man who had been one of the rare few close to Vosbarhan. She had heard rumors about him over the years, rumors that he had killed a prostitute for not giving him enough pleasure, rumors that he had helped Vosbarhan dispose of several disobedient lower kings of the provinces...

"We think it best, Queen of Queens," Nupar said after a few moments, stepping away from the rest of the council and toward the throne again, "that the race be should be canceled this year. Our kingdom has been dealt an overwhelming blow with the death of our beloved King of Kings Vosbarhan, and going on with such a boisterous and joyful event after his death would be dishonoring him."

Azkanysh nodded, remembering almost too late that she was wearing a crown now. She reached a hand up to steady it from falling off, and noticed several men laugh softly among themselves. Her face heated.

"If I may, Queen of Queens," Vyzir Dsamihur spoke up.

Azkanysh glanced at him.

"I must say that I agree with the Guardian Council's opinion." Vyzir Dsamihur said. "Not only would holding the race be disrespectful so close to King of Kings Vosbarhan's death, but as we all know, the Great Race is a costly affair. I think it would be unwise to spend the royal funds on it when they may be needed for other more important things."

Azkanysh glanced at the crowd. Heads nodded throughout the throne room. She had a feeling that everyone but her knew what Vyzir Dsamihur was talking about. Zarcayra was not wanting for money, and although the Great Race was expensive, the royal reserve could easily afford it. Was he talking about going to war?

"Then, after thinking over the Guardian Council's and your advice,

Vyzir Dsamihur," she called loudly, "I rule that the Great Race will not be held this year."

The slave by the gong rang it again, and Vyzir Dsamihur moved back to his former position a few feet away.

Azkanysh waited as the murmuring died down in the throne room. They needed to discuss what Zarcayra would do about Eromor's act of war now, but first she had another ruling to announce. She felt a old desire rising in her, the desire of a twelve year old girl who had longed for freedom for the women of Zarcayra.

"It has come to my attention," she called, "that our throne room is lacking in members of my gender. I..." She paused as several men glanced at each other. "I wish to change this. As Queen of Queens, I do not want any to be unwelcome in the throne room of Sussār. Therefore, I rule that from this day forward, women shall be allowed into the throne room during court sessions."

The crowd in the throne room stared at her.

Azkanysh felt the mounting fear that always came when she spoke up about something. Vosbarhan had usually hit her for it, and she had learned to keep her opinion to herself early in their marriage. But she was Queen of Queens now, and no one would dare hit her anymore.

"Queen of Queens," Tukayr said after a few heartbeats, "it is customary to ask the Guardian Council for their opinion on matters before making rulings. Perhaps, Queen of Queens, you have forgotten this tradition..."

"I have not forgotten anything." Azkanysh cut him off, "I simply do not feel that the Guardian Council's opinion is needed on this matter. I wish for women to be in the throne room during court sessions, and now they shall be, according to my ruling."

The throne room continued to stare at her.

"The next order of business, I believe," Azkanysh said, heart pounding, "is of what Zarcayra shall do in response to Eromor's act of war upon us."

The throne room exploded into a chorus of voices, forgetting, for the moment, her startling ruling.

"Call in the armies!" a man yelled.

Azkanysh glanced in the direction the voice had come from, eyes catching on Zarmeyr, who was standing at the head of the gathered shayrs and destūrs. Her son's face was dark and angry, like it always was now.

"Yes!" another man called. "Let us go to war with Eromor and avenge Zarcayra's honor!"

Azkanysh glanced in the direction of the new voice. There was no standing army in Zarcayra. Zarcayra was made up of twelve provinces with kings who paid subservience to the King of Kings, and now the Queen of Queens. Each province made yearly payments from the wealth of their lands, such as food, horses, metals, and when the King of Kings called for it, they sent their men from ages fourteen to sixty to war. The men of Zarcayra had not been called to war in over thirteen years, since the ending of the Third Great War.

The slave rang the gong again for order in the throne room, and the court fell silent, watching her.

Azkanysh realized they were waiting for her to stay something again. What should she tell them? She was thankful that Eromor had killed Vosbarhan, but she could not tell them that. She had no idea if the armies should be called out, she had no idea of how armies worked at all. She resisted the urge to look at Vyzir Dsamihur again. She would figure this problem out on her own, without the help of any man. She opened her mouth to speak, remembering hearing Vosbarhan say something once about Eromor having the largest army in Argdrion.

"I agree that Zarcayra's honor must be avenged!" Azkanysh called over the watching court.

Heads nodded, encouraged, she went on. "But while I want as much as any of you to make Eromor pay for their act of war against us, it has long been that they hold the largest army in Argdrion. If we go to war with them, I wonder, will we win? And if we do not win, what will become of our honor then?"

The throne room broke into clusters of men murmuring together.

Azkanysh brushed a buzzing fly away, motioning for the fan slave. What she had said was good, she could feel it. She would make her first court session grand yet. And the people of Zarcayra would respect her, revere her.

The Guardian Council, murmuring together for the last few minutes, broke apart.

"What our Queen of Queens says is true," Tukayr called, black mourning robes swaying as he turned partway toward the crowded throne room. "Eromor does hold the largest army in Argdrion, and if we go up against them in open combat, it is not guaranteed that we will win."

"But we cannot let Eromor get away with murdering our King of Kings!" yelled the same man who had shouted for the armies to be called in.

Shouts of agreement rang through the throne room, and it was several minutes before order was restored again, even with the slave ringing the gong.

"How much larger is Eromor's army than ours?" Azkanysh asked.

All eyes turned to her.

"At least half again, Queen of Queens," Nupar said, eyeing her.

Voices broke out again.

"What if we allowed women to join?" Azkanysh called. "Then would our army be as large as Eromor's?"

The throne room fell silent, this time without the slave having to ring the gong.

Azkanysh heard several horses whinny in the distance. More than a dozen flies buzzed through the warm, stuffy air of the throne room. The desire rising in her was growing, turning into a firestorm of ideas that raced through her mind.

"That... that would make our army larger than theirs by far, Queen of Queens," Nupar said slowly. "But it is impossible for women to be in the army."

Azkanysh felt a neckache coming on from holding up the crown. Allowing women to fight in the army would be a step toward a liberty that the women of Zarcayra had never known. A liberty that the other women of the world knew and had, a liberty that the men of Zarcayra kept from them. If she was to bring the women of Zarcayra freedom, would it keep husbands from beating their wives? Keep women from being raped with no repercussions?

Her skin prickled. When she had been young, she had dreamed of freedom for the women of Zarcayra, dreamed of them being allowed to work, of owning land, of divorcing their abusive husbands. As Queen of Queens, she could give that freedom to them. But could women be in the army? The men of Zarcayra said that they could not, that they were weak, frail, fragile. But then, who was to say that they were right? After all, Eromor had women in their army, and they were one of the most powerful kingdoms in Argdrion.

Azkanysh remembered seeing an Eromorian woman once, a trader who had come to the palace with fine diamonds for Vosbarhan to look at. She had peeked through the back door of the throne room as the woman trader had shown Vosbarhan an array of glittering diamonds, watching to see how it was that Eromorian women acted. The woman had had blonde hair that was cut short and tousled on her head, and she had been dressed in slender leather pants and a sleeveless shirt of dark-blue cotton. She had also had many rings on her slender fingers and long necklaces draped over her breasts. The men of the court had been outraged at the woman's dress and self-assured attitude, but Azkanysh had thought that she had looked powerful, free.

"Why can women not be in the army?" she asked aloud.

The throne room, filled with hushed voices again, glanced at her once more.

"Because, Queen of Queens," Nupar said, "women are weak, and in a fight, they would only be in the way of the men." The shayr's voice was even and slow, like he was explaining something simple to a child.

"Eromor has women in their army," Azkanysh said, the ides in her mind blossoming and sprouting into a million other different ideas. "And during the Great Wars, they won many battles with the weaker sex among them."

She must tread carefully, she thought. For if she was to bring freedom to the women of Zarcayra, she would have to do it slowly. The men of Zarcayra would not like their women getting freedom, and if she made too many changes too quickly, it could mean an uprising in the kingdom and inner strife. But if she could start the changes off with one that could be deemed necessary, like women joining the army to make it large enough to stand against Eromor's, then perhaps it would soften the hearts of Zarcayra's men and pave the way for more changes later on, greater changes.

"Women cannot be in our army," Zarmeyr abruptly said, stepping forward.

"So, are you saying, Prince Zarmeyr," one of the council spoke up, "that we should not go to war with Eromor?"

"Of course not," Zarmeyr spat. "My father, King of Kings Vosbarhan, was slaughtered in his own bed by those animals. I say yes, we should go to war with them, but not with women among us. Eromor has women in their ranks, do they not? And with the weaker sex in their ranks, although their army is larger than ours, we will be able to defeat them easily!"

The throne room erupted into cheering and yells of agreement. Zarmeyr turned toward Azkanysh. She met her son's eyes; they were wild and angry. She felt fear again for speaking up.

"If I was seated on the lyon throne," Zarmeyr said forcefully, malice and scorn in his voice, "I would have gathered my armies already and have them sailing this very moment for Eromor!"

"These sentiments are good and well," Shayr Jahayan, an older Guardian Council member, spoke up, "but may I remind you, Prince Zarmeyr, that the women of Eromor are trained in combat since birth and that they have more than proved themselves capable of holding their own in battle during the Great Wars. Without women in their army during the wars, Eromor would never have held back the armies of the skinchangers and wiar at the Fallows, and then who knows where we would all be now? Maybe slaves to those magical creatures, or worse, dead, like them."

A few murmurs of agreement ran through the throne room but less than those that had agreed with Zarmeyr, Azkanysh noted. She resisted the urge to sink down in the throne. She did not have to fear men's reactions, she reminded herself, she was Queen of Queens now and held more power than any of them.

"Are you agreeing that we should allow women into our army, Shayr Jahayan?" Zarmeyr hissed, turning on the older man.

"I am saying," Shayr Jahayan replied calmly, wrinkled hands folded in front of him, "that we should at least consider the possibility. I, for one, would feel more comfortable in going to war with Eromor if we at least held an army that was equal to theirs in numbers."

"What do you think, Vyzir Dsamihur?" Nupar asked abruptly.

Azkanysh glanced at the vyzir, as did the court. He had been silent up until now, watching the court proceedings with his usual blank face. She looked back at Nupar. While a vyzir's opinion was also valued in court sessions, it was not tradition for the King of Kings to heed to it like it was for him to heed to the Guardian Council's opinions. So why had Nupar asked Vyzir Dsamihur his opinion? Azkanysh scanned the council. Did he know that the vyzir would agree with him and hoped it would persuade her to rule how the council wanted? Was Vyzir Dsamihur working with them against her?

"I believe," Vyzir Dsamihur said slowly, "that Zarcayra's honor should be avenged and that we should go to war with Eromor."

"And do you think, Vyzir Dsamihur," Tukayr spoke up, "that women should be allowed to join Zarcayra's army so that our army may stand in equal size against Eromor's?"

Vyzir Dsamihur was silent for a long moment. Azkanysh glanced at him again. He dipped his head finally. "Yes."

The throne room erupted into a hundred animated voices.

Azkanysh looked back at the Guardian Council, trying to read their faces to see if they had expected Vyzir Dsamihur's answer. Several of them looked annoyed, so she surmised that they had not. Did that mean that the vyzir was on her side? She looked at Vyzir Dsamihur again, standing with his hands behind his back and watching the throne room.

If she was to bring freedom to the women of Zarcayra, then she would need supporters, allies who agreed with her and her visions. Was Vyzir Dsamihur one of those allies? And how did she find out if he was? That he thought women should join the army so that they could go to war with an army equal in size to Eromor didn't mean that he wanted freedom for Zarcayra's women. It could simply mean that he wanted to avenge Zarcayra's honor, as many did.

"The Guardian Council would like to give their opinion, if the Queen of Queens has time for it," Nupar said.

Azkanysh glanced at him, narrowing her eyes. He was daring her to make another ruling without asking their permission. She would not, though, not yet anyway. She knew, with growing animation, how they would advise. With Vyzir Dsamihur counseling for women in the army and the kingdom calling for Eromor's blood, they would have to advise for the ruling to keep the peace. And they wanted revenge as much as anyone else, the chance to avenge Zarcayra's honor.

"What does the council say on this matter?" she asked.

Nupar dipped his head. "We advise, Queen of Queens, on allowing women in the army so that we may have an army equal to Eromor's in the upcoming war." His voice was tight, annoyed.

The throne room burst into voices, most angry, some exuberant.

"Then as Queen of Queens of Zarcayra," Azkanysh shouted, quieting the voices, "I rule that Zarcayra shall go to war with Eromor, and shall allow women to fight in her army so that we may win this war and avenge Zarcayra's honor!"

The throne room exploded with a roar.

Azkanysh stood, keeping her demeanor calm. Excitement coursed through her. She had ideas to think over, plans to form if she was to bring freedom to Zarcayra's women.

"Her Royal Highness, Queen of Queens Azkanysh," the crier yelled, "Fifth Ruler of Zarcayra, Commander of Armies, Ruler of Rulers, Chosen of the Gods, will now leave the throne room."

Azkanysh stepped away from the throne as the room murmured "Praise the Queen of Queens." She descended the sandstone stairs from the dais, feeling triumphant, powerful, but still slightly scared. Scared at her own boldness. Allowing women in the army was a first move among many, a move that would lead to the women of Zarcayra gaining new freedom. Along with allowing women in the throne room, it was a very good start to her rule. She turned as she reached the bottom of the stairs, making for the door behind the throne.

Zarmeyr stepped toward her, his albino bodyguard trailing after him. "This plan of yours is foolish, woman," her son snarled.

Azkanysh paused as the golden doors of the throne room boomed open and the court began streaming out. She glanced at Zarmeyr, the animosity in his voice making her recoil subconsciously in anticipation of a blow.

"You may be ruler of Zarcayra now, but you won't be for long," Zarmeyr hissed, stepping closer and jabbing a finger at her. "I will be eighteen in a year's time, and when I become King of Kings, I will have you put away where you belong, in the harem, with the rest of my father's whores."

Azkanysh slapped Zarmeyr so hard across the face that her hand stung. She stared, shocked, as her son reeled backward. She had never hit a man before. Fear filled her, but she had to follow through.

"I am the Queen of Queens," she said, voice shaking, "and your mother, and as such you will treat me with the respect and honor due."

Zarmeyr moved a hand to his reddening face, eyes equally filled with shock. They grew dark quickly, the shock replaced with hatred and animosity. "You will never be Queen of Queens over me," he spat, stepping forward again so that he was inches away from her. "And as soon as I am king, you will no longer be my mother, either."

Azkanysh took a step backward. She heard Vyzir Dsamihur and her entourage of royal guards step forward, their sandals rasping on the mosaic tiles of the throne room floor.

Zarmeyr's eyes moved away from her face and to the guards.

He would not dare hit her now that she was Queen of Queens, Azkanysh realized, and if he did, she could legally have him whipped. She raised her head. She did not need to fear her son. She did not need to fear anyone anymore. "I think it would be best if you left, Zarmeyr," she said in a cold, even voice.

Zarmeyr stared at her for a moment, eyes spitting fire. He turned finally and jerked his arm for his bodyguard to follow, stalking off down the throne room, his sandals slapping loudly on the floor underneath him.

Azkanysh watched them go, her breathing quick. She had slapped a man. Her breathing slowly calmed. If she had done such a thing when Vosbarhan was alive, it probably would have cost her her hand. But Vosbarhan was not alive, and as Queen of Queens, she held the power to do whatever she wanted.

"Queen of Queens."

She turned at the voice. Shayr Jahayan bowed in front of her. "Queen of Queens," the aging Guardian Council member said, "I wanted to let you know that I am grateful for your suggestion in court today, of having women join Zarcayra's army."

"Grateful?" Azkanysh asked, surprised and wary. "Why?"

Shayr Jahayan looked around them at the rest of the council filing out of the throne room after the court. "Not all of us, Queen of Queens," he murmured, stepping closer, "agree that women are of the weaker sex or that they should be controlled by men."

Azkanysh stared at the shayr. His breath smelled like garlic and onions, and his face was covered with age spots. His eyes were still young and sharp, though, and right now they were filled with sincerity.

"You think that women are equal to men?" she asked, aware that Vyzir Dsamihur was listening intently.

"That is a question, Queen of Queens," Shayr Jahayan whispered in a voice so low that Azkanysh had to lean closer to hear him, "that I think you know the answer to. Here." The shayr put a wrinkled finger up to his chest, over his heart. He bowed again, and turning, moved away.

Azkanysh stared after him. She had a possible ally in Shayr Jahayan. But could she trust him? Vosbarhan had trusted no one during his rule, not even his vyzirs. Was that the answer to a successful reign?

She turned, meeting Vyzir Dsamihur's gaze. His eyes were unreadable, as usual. She started toward the door again. She needed to pray.

She headed to the South Garden and the small temple among the lilac trees.

The statue of Ehurayni watched her as she knelt among the dried flowers and dust, diamond eyes glittering.

"Ehurayni," Azkanysh whispered, folding her hands in front of her black robes, "thank you, for taking Vosbarhan." She had not had time to come to the temple since Vosbarhan's death, had not had time to thank the goddess properly. "You have freed me from my prison, shown me light in the darkness."

A green and black backed beetle skittered across the floor of the temple, legs scratching lightly against the sandstone beneath it. Azkanysh closed her eyes. "There are many who want me to fail, Ehurayni," she whispered, thinking of the court session and the snickers of the men in the throne room. "Many who do not believe that a woman can rule a kingdom. At one time, I would have agreed with them. But I do not agree with them anymore, and no matter what they may think of me, what they may say, I will not give up the golden lyon crown."

She opened her eyes again, staring up at the statue. "I will rule this kingdom, and I will bring freedom to the women of Zarcayra."

CHAPTER 19

The Unknown Voice

The war was finally going in our favor. I was seventeen, and in the two years' time since Mother's death, much had happened. The witches and warlocks, magical creatures, had allied with us after lengthy treaty discussions, and with their help, along with the silver, we were finally managing to push the wiar and skinchangers back.

It was a hard thing, to ally with the enemy, but in times like these, it was necessary to defeat the greater enemy. As King Edomur said, "If we beat the skinchangers and wiar, we'll destroy the witches and warlocks next. Let them think we are at peace with them for now, when they're helping us, but in the end, they are evil magical creatures like any of the rest, and we will wipe them from Argdrion, the gods willing."

There was hope in Argdrion as the second winter after Mother's death ran into the long middle months, hope that we would win the Great Wars.

I grew more and more fascinated with magic during these two years, secretly studying the book of spells that I had found from cover to cover, and watching, when time allowed, the few prisoners of war that were brought into camp. It was rare that we captured the enemy, as the skinchangers were notorious for being hard to take prisoner. It wasn't that they killed themselves for fear of what would happen to them. It was more that us humans were forced to kill them most of the time, as they would not stop fighting. Only when one was knocked unconscious could a skinchanger be taken prisoner, and when this happened, it was a great occurrence in camp.

If the skinchangers were feared by us in battle for their fierceness, the wiar were held in a far worse view, something bordering on an insane, terrified paranoia that kept all of us on constant edge and made lords and ladies execute cowards in droves in order to keep their soldiers on the battlefield. The wiar were never captured during the wars, and as they always took the bodies of their dead with them, we never had a chance to see them up close. They preferred to fight from afar, usually, weaving their magic of fire and ice and wind and a thousand other powers that wreaked chaos in our ranks, and when the rare one did come among our ranks, hundreds fell.

The witches and warlocks changed this, though, and as the twelfth year of the Third Great War dawned, the wiar appeared less and less on the battlefields, and the skinchangers were left to fight us alone. Many said that the wiar were scared. It wasn't until later that we would learn that they were just waiting as the tides of war turned, waiting to see who would emerge the victor so they could ally accordingly.

Father's estates became mine during the second winter after Mother's death. His death came about by hand, although the action wasn't predetermined.

Father had advanced through the ranks of our kingdom as the years of war progressed, and by the time of his death, he was second to King Edomur in position on the battlefield.

Father was wounded badly one day, and since he was the right-hand man to the king, I was allowed to take him home for healing at our castle. It was a long trip, that journey, and I filled the spare hours waiting for Father to rest from the bumpy roads by reading the book of spells. It was this action that made me have to kill him.

It was snowing as the morning of our fifth day of travel dawned, and as the roads were fast becoming invisible in the heavy downpour, our train of knights, Father's wagon, and the servants and I waited for the storm to let up in a small copse of trees. I sat beside Father as the knights nervously paced the perimeters of our small camp, the book of spells nestled in my fur-robed lap.

I felt Father wake before I saw him staring at me, and when I did, it was too late—he had seen what I was reading, and the look in his gaze as our eyes locked made my blood go cold. He fell into another feverish sleep a few minutes later, but as we rode the rest of the way to Castle Sythorn, I thought over what I had to do.

I knew that I had to kill him. If he healed, he would have me executed for using magic, and I could not die. Not now, not ever.

Sar was waiting for us in the courtyard of Castle Sythorn, and as servants carried Father to his room, I told Sar of how Father had been wounded by a skinchanger in the form of a mountain lion that had torn open his stomach and loosed his intestines.

Servants with hot water and towels were busy running up and down the halls of Castle Sythorn as I entered it. A rider had been sent to fetch a physician.

I was not allowed to see Father as Sar directed the servants on how to stop the bleeding from his stomach and give him poppy for his pain. The old steward said I looked dead tired and should rest. I did not rest, pacing the floor of my old upstairs room instead, worrying that Father would wake and tell someone what he had seen. I doubted that anyone would believe him in his feverish state, but if he said it enough, they might start to wonder. Everyone feared magic users in their households—that was why daughter turned on mother, neighbor on friend.

The same physician who had tended Mother arrived three hours later, and as he saw to Father's wounds, I crept down the stairs of the castle and into the long hallway that led to Father's room. The physician was in there for over two hours. When he came out, I cornered him.

"How is he?" I asked, my voice filled with worry, although of a different kind than the elderly man thought.

"Fine," the physician replied reassuringly. He laid a thick hand on my arm, face tired. "His wounds are bad, but your father is strong, and I've no doubt that with an extended rest and good food, he will make a full recovery." The words were like a knife in my gut.

"Our victory at Fallows," the physician said, "it cheered all our spirits."

I glanced up at him. Fallows was a farming town turned forest after its destruction in the First Great War. It had been the site of a large battle the year before, a battle where we had had a rare victory over the enemy.

I thanked the physician, watching him walk away. I turned slowly toward Father's door.

He was awake when I went in, the feverish state gone from his dark eyes and a wide white bandage wrapped around his middle. He did not speak as I went to the bed, although he was looking at me.

"How could you?" Father said after a long while.

I chewed at my lip, expecting a troop of knights to come in any moment and arrest me. I could lie to him, I knew, tell him that it wasn't what he thought, that I was studying magic in order to understand how the enemy worked and thereby gain an advantage over them. It wouldn't work, that lie, so I told him the truth.

"I don't want to die," I said simply, meeting Father's steely eyes. They were filled with confusion for a moment, but it was quickly replaced with the cold, hard hatred that I had seen earlier.

"But you will die," Father said, voice cutting. "And I will be shamed for having a son that was a magic user."

I pulled the book of spells from inside my tunic.

Father hissed. "The evil is still on you. Curse you!" he snarled, reaching for a bell that had been left by his bedside. I snatched the bell away from him and moved to the tall, nail-studded door of his room, sliding the bolt into place.

"Do you have any idea what is in here?" I asked, moving back to Father's bed.

He glared at me, bushy eyebrows meeting where his forehead cinched. "I don't care," he snarled.

"Eternal life," I said, my voice growing animated. "Or close to it, anyway. I found this book, Father, on the day that Mother died."

"You'd desecrate your mother's death day with magic?" Father hissed.

I ignored him. "In it," I said, holding *Spells* up like a priest's book of religion, "is a spell that enables one to move one's soul into the body of another creature. Think about it, Father, you could change into the body of a younger man and have more years!"

"I don't want more years," Father said, "I want a son that I can trust, a son that will carry on my family's good name!" He grunted as he tried to reach for his sword, which was lying on a chair next to the bed. He failed, and I moved to the sword and kicked the chair out of his reach.

I repocketed *Spells* and lifted a pillow off the bed. "Well, I do want more years," I told Father, "and I will not be executed for that." I put a knee on his chest and crammed the pillow over his face.

Father had always been a large, strong man, but although I was slender, I had gained muscle in the last seven years of fighting, and he was wounded and weak from loss of blood.

We struggled for over ten minutes while I desperately tried to smother him, and he thrashed around to break free. How no one heard us, I do not know, but none did, and as fresh blood seeped through the bandage around Father's reopening wound, his struggles gradually lessened until he lay still. I kept the pillow over his face for another two minutes after he had stopped moving.

When I took it away, there was blood on it. Our struggling had not only reopened his stitched-up wounds but damaged something internally so that he was bleeding from his mouth. I set the pillow beside Father and turned his head so that it looked like he had bled on it that way, and unbolting the door, yelled for Sar and the physician.

"Strange," the physician said as he examined Father's body Sar stood next to me, his old frame stooping. "I was sure that he would live." The physician pulled a sheet up and over Father's head and turned to me. "I'm sorry, Lord Sythorn, it appears that he had internal bleeding that I did not see." He shook his head sadly, and I told him that he could not have known and that it was no one but the cursed enemy's fault.

Father was buried beside Mother in the family cemetery outside the castle walls three days later.

King Edomur came to Father's funeral, along with a procession of one hundred knights, a great honor for my family and a long and daring ride for the king. Some of the servants said he was foolish for leaving the battlefields, others that he must have loved Father greatly.

"I cannot begin to tell you how much this grieves me," King Edomur told me as the funeral procession wound back to Castle Sythorn for the customary dinner. "Your father was more than my right-hand man, he was my friend."

I nodded quietly. I did not feel remorse for what I had done. It had been necessary, but after a dream the night before of Sar finding out the truth and my head being cut off before the whole army, I was on edge that someone would find out what had really happened.

King Edomur placed a chainmail-gloved hand on my shoulder and looked me in the eye. His eyes were the sharpest blue that I had ever seen, piercing to my soul. "I know that there is a war on, Lord Sythorn, but I can give you one week to grieve your father's death. He would want that for you, I'm sure."

"Without disrespect, Your Majesty," I replied, "I rather think that my father would want me back by your side, fighting against the enemy. As he often said, war waits for no one."

I could not stay at Castle Sythorn. There were no young bodies for me to practice the heart spell on, and I would feel restless so far away from the battles and news of what was happening. Besides, I had plans to get a skinchanger body for my soul—the creatures lived to a thousand years, well more than a human's short ninety.

King Edomur nodded sharply and moved off with his knights. I watched the funeral procession disappear up the hill toward Castle Sythorn, the wind pulling at my dark-green cloak. A flag had been placed over Father's grave, the dark-green field with a white stag on it that marked our family crest.

Father's freshly filled grave contrasted starkly against the snow-covered bump that was Mother's grave. Sar had likely put the flag there, I mused as I stared down at my parents' graves. The old steward had been close to my parents, closer than I ever had been. But how could one be close to those they knew would pass on to another life while they stayed behind, forever living on?

I glanced up as the sound of snow coming over the woods caught my ears, small, hard snow that hissed as it hit the bare branches of the forest and bounced when it landed on the ground. I was to be eighteen at the end of the year, but I felt older already. If I was lucky and managed to survive the war, I would maybe live to be eighty-five, ninety at the most. That gave me only sixty-some-odd years left to walk Argdrion. It was not enough.

My hair ruffled in the wind, making my scalp tingle. I needed to try the heart spell soon. The longer I waited, the older I would get, and the closer to death I would come.

I looked back at my parents' graves, Mother's adorned with several frozen and wilting gray winter roses. I would not lie next to my parents in Castle Sythorn cemetery. I turned and started back toward Sythorn, snow pelting my fur-lined cloak and dark hair.

No matter what I had to do, I would not end like them.

CHAPTER 20

Nathaira

For nine days, Nathaira was brought out of her cell and the dark catacombs to fight in the arena. Mostly she fought against one or two animals, but more often than not, she was paired against groups, such as a pack of wolves one day and a group of hyenas the next. She was the star attraction in the arena, she was told. A novelty, a wonder.

For nine days she fought and won, only earning several none-too-serious wounds that were tended to by the physicians in the catacomb hospital. The murderer across the hall was her third victim, the two men who had murdered the woman her fourth and fifth. Nathaira said the Prayer of Death over each body but those of the murderers.

For nine days, the crowd cheered for her, yelling as she took lives and shed blood. For nine days, she watched every move that the humans made until every minute detail was ingrained in her memory like the images of the clan's death.

For nine nights, Nathaira sat on the floor of her cell and thought over the things she had observed during the day, and on the tenth day of her imprisonment in the arena, she knew how she was going to escape. She'd learned that humans, like all creatures, were creatures of habit, and in habits there were patterns that could be relied upon to be repeated.

Every day the iron gate leading into the arena opened on aged hinges and stayed open while an escort of three guards led her into the fighting pit and removed her shackles. Whether the humans didn't think she would be able to get past the guards and make it to the gate before the scorpions in the circling towers shot her dead, or whether they didn't think she'd be able to find her way out of the tunnels, Nathaira didn't know. Whatever the reason, it was a flaw in the humans' system, and it was her only hope of escaping.

Blood pounded in Nathaira's ears as the guards pulled her up the familiar route to the arena above. The roar of the crowd hummed through the tunnel walls on either side of them.

Sisters, she prayed, *help me to be swift and cunning...*

The iron gate leading to the arena ground open.

Help me to escape, please, that I may find Efamar.

They marched out onto the hot sand, and Nathaira glanced upward at the towers holding the scorpions. The marble structures threw long gray shadows over the crowd-filled benches beneath them.

She looked over her shoulder at the yawning black mouth of the tunnel and the still-open gate.

Sisters, make this work.

Her ankle manacles fell away with a crunch in the sand. Nathaira took a slow, deep breath as the hairy-handed guard moved to those on her wrists. A few more seconds and she would be free. Her throat felt suddenly dry, and she swallowed with difficulty as the handcuffs fell away from her wrists. Cold air brushed her raw skin, and the guard moved to her neck collar. Only one more restraint. Nathaira closed her eyes and listened to the key turning in the lock as energy slowly spiked through her veins.

Boots crunched in the sand.

Nathaira's golden eyes snapped open. Seven guards, silver weapons gleaming in the Brothers' light, jogged into the arena and spread out around her.

Had they guessed what she was planning? But how could they? Her collar slipped off with a click, barely audible above the chanting of the crowd, and the hairy-handed guard backed up to his fellows, silver chains and manacles banging against his leg.

Nathaira's full power surged through her, enlivening her body, filling her veins. She glanced at the extra guards, anger and despair filling her. She could fight them, she knew, but there were too many to win, and she would never make it to the gate, much less through the catacombs and outside.

"Move," a guard behind her said, jabbing a silver spear into her back.

Nathaira snarled at him. His companions lowered their weapons. She stepped forward, the gate opposite slowly grinding upward and disappearing into the stone above.

Five figures stepped out from the shadows of the tunnel—four guards and a red-haired woman in black and red leather and iron shackles.

The crowd cheered.

The woman and her guards moved across the arena, Nathaira watched them as they stopped several feet in front of her. The woman was tall and slender but with muscles that defined her arms and legs under her leather suite.

The woman caught Nathaira's eye, smiling slowly.

"Good people of Crystoln!" the herald yelled loudly from the king's red-canopied booth. "Today, on this eighth day of King Uranius's birthday celebrations, we bring you a rare and exciting treat!" The herald waved a hand at the red-haired woman. "This assassin was caught two days ago as she attempted to kill our dear and beloved king, Uranius!"

Nathaira watched the woman as the crowd hissed and booed. She was all that was standing between her and freedom.

"Praise the gods!" the herald yelled. He brought a hand to his mouth and kissed it and put it to his chest in a sign of thanks. "She was apprehended before she could."

There were several laughs from the crowd at this obvious statement.

"In punishment for her attempted crime," the herald yelled shrilly, ignoring the jeers, "the assassin will fight the skinchanger… to the death!"

When were the fights not to the death? Nathaira glanced up at the eleven towers surrounding the arena again, scorpions nested within glinting in the Brothers' rays, and back down at the guards surrounding her and the iron gate behind her. Fresh despair swarmed over her.

Sisters, why do you not help me?

"Let your bets be placed," the herald yelled, raising his storklike arms high in the air. "And without further ado, let the fight begin!"

The ground shook with the crowd's cheers. The woman's guards unlatched her shackles and handed her a curved short sword.

Nathaira watched them as they backed out of the arena with her own guards, the two iron gates falling into place behind them with deep clangs. She took in a slow breath. She had no doubt that she could defeat the human woman and live to escape tomorrow, but the thought of waiting any longer to be free and look for Efamar, even if it was only for one more day, was maddening.

"I've never killed a skinchanger before," the woman said.

Nathaira glanced back at her. The herald had called her an assassin, a professional killer. Moirin had told her of them, had wondered at how one could kill others for money.

"I suppose it's not that different from killing an animal," the woman killer said lightly.

Nathaira curled her toes into the hot sand under her feet, concentrating on the energy coursing through her veins.

The woman whipped her sword through the air with a high-pitched hiss. "Isn't that what you are, skinchanger? A magical creature that looks like a human but changes into an animal?"

Nathaira heard a child crying up in the benches encircling the arena. Felt a soft wind stroke the fine hairs on her arms.

"I think it's rather fascinating, really," the woman said, moving ever so slightly to the left.

Nathaira moved with her. Judging by the crowd's reaction to the woman, she must be dangerous. She wouldn't attack first. There was a lethality about the woman that stated she was deadly. She wanted to learn her moves, gauge her skill.

When you do not have the advantage over your opponent, Athrysion's deep voice came to her in her mind, *learn as much as you can about them. Their muscle twitches, eye shifts, finger movements. All these can tell you something of how they will act in the fight.*

"I think I'd rather like being able to change into any animal I had the fancy to," the woman said.

"If you wanted to be hunted like a criminal and sentenced to death simply for being born," Nathaira replied, stepping with the woman again as she slid to the left again.

The woman shrugged. "I'm already a criminal," she said. "And as you heard, I have been sentenced to death. Or one of us has. That's the sad thing about these games—only one can come out the victor, no matter how good both opponents may be."

Nathaira saw the woman's muscles tense beneath her leather suit. She was getting ready to attack.

"I was trained in eastern Oridonn," the woman said, voice as casual as if she were discussing the weather. "At the Ijiyn School of Assassins. Who trained you? Or is your power natural?"

She was trying to distract her, Nathaira knew. It wasn't working. She saw the slight shift of the woman's hands on her sword, the curling of her fingers as she adjusted her grip.

"There is a school for killing?" she said, not wanting to talk about her life. If she kept the woman talking, maybe she could turn her own game back on her.

"Multiple," the woman replied, moving slightly again. "Killing is a very sought-after art. That's why there are so many assassins in Argdrion. That and the fact that many of us want the fame that comes with being a hired killer."

"Fame?" Nathaira queried, moving with the woman again. She was trying to get behind her; Nathaira would not let her.

"Yes, ever since Darkmoon turned killing into a famous title of employment, hundreds have tried to achieve the same thing."

"Who is Darkmoon?" Nathaira asked, the name odd on her tongue.

The woman killer looked surprised for a moment. "I guess you wouldn't know about him, would you?" she said, reverence coming into her voice. "Darkmoon is the best and most famous assassin in Argdrion. No one knows the exact number of kills he has made in his lifetime, but it is believed to be well over a thousand. He's never been caught, never failed at a job."

"If he is so famous," Nathaira said, hearing the crowd shifting with impatience, "then why doesn't someone kill him? Surely he is easy to find."

The woman laughed at her. "Darkmoon is never 'easy to find,' and no one dares try and kill him. To do so would be a death wish. There have been a few who have tried," the woman said, voice growing slightly fearful. "They were never seen again. Even the authorities do not bother him—he's that lethal."

Someone in the crowd screamed, "Fight!" Several others took up the chant.

"They're growing restless," the woman killer said, glancing at the crowd. "It appears we will have to appease them." She looked back at Nathaira.

Nathaira stared into her eyes for a moment. They were a rich golden brown.

The woman lunged first, moving so quickly that Nathaira was almost caught off guard. She reeled backward as the woman sliced her sword at her. She changed into a fox and darted a few feet away.

The woman turned, red hair flying behind her as she raised her sword again. The crowd was chanting louder now, making the net above the arena groan. The woman charged again.

Nathaira changed into a nighthawk as she neared her, and flying over her head, she dove with talons outstretched, reaching for her neck. If she could cut the major artery running down the side, she could end this fight before it had begun.

The woman wheeled, sword raised, and Nathaira screamed as the weapon sliced into her right wing. The sound came out as a squawk.

She fell to the sand with a thud, blood flowing out of a long, neat cut in her shoulder and down her right arm as she changed into her natural form.

The crowd roared its approval, making the net rock.

"I heard that you were taken in Ennotar after your clan was killed," the woman said, standing above her. "That must be hard for you, losing your people."

Nathaira grabbed a handful of hot sand and threw it in her face.

The woman dodged to the left and lunged toward her again.

Nathaira rolled out of the way as the woman's sword hit the ground next to her and scrambling to her feet, took off at a run.

The crowd grew silent, waiting to see who would die first.

The form of a griffin would be able to take the woman down. Nathaira glanced at the gate she had been brought through. But once she killed her, then what? Another kill, another night in her cell, and tomorrow another day in the arena. She looked up at the scorpions and the creaking net, the screaming crowd and sleeping King Uranius. A plan formed in her mind.

Nathaira looked back at the woman, red hair streaming behind her like fire, and back to the gate. She stopped.

The woman skidded to a halt.

Nathaira turned to face her, sand pelting her in the face as the woman's boots dug into the ground.

The crowd inhaled sharply.

If she was worth so much money, then the humans wouldn't want her dead just yet. And if she refused to fight the woman killer, then the guards would have to come out to save her, and the gate would open.

Nathaira glanced back at the gate that she had come through. At least, that's what she hoped.

"I refuse to fight you," she said, warm blood trailing down her arm and dripping onto her foot. She looked back at the woman. "I've had enough of fighting."

The woman watched her for a moment, calculating, judging. "You don't strike me as the kind that gives up," she said.

Nathaira watched her silently.

Sisters, for Athrysion's sake and Moirin's, help me escape.

"You're playing at something," the woman said, sword held in front of her, eyes narrowing, "but what is it?"

"I am not playing at anything," Nathaira replied, her breathing slowly evening out again. "I simply have had enough of death and pain and humiliation, and as you said, my clan is dead. There is nothing left for me in this world."

The woman stared at her for a moment, and Nathaira prayed again to the Sisters to help her escape. Blood still trickled down her arm, mingling with the sand on her skin and forming it into thick gobs.

"I will try and make your death swift," the woman said. She lunged.

Nathaira waited until the woman was almost upon her before jumping to the side so that the sword strike aimed for her leg did not cut it off as intended but merely sliced open the skin above the knee. She screamed as pain tore through her thigh.

The crowd shouted their disapproval.

Fresh blood dribbled down her calf and mingled with that from her arm. Nathaira stumbled backward.

Sisters, let this work, please!

The woman turned, boots crunching in the sand. "It will be easier if you hold still," she said, twirling her bloody sword in one hand.

Nathaira blinked as the Brothers' midafternoon rays glinted sharply off the polished weapon.

The woman lunged forward again, feigning a throat blow but really going for her side.

Nathaira jumped away again so that the sword just grazed her back.

Most of the crowd was standing by now, screaming their disapproval and throwing whatever loose objects that they could find down into the arena.

Nathaira ducked as a brown glass bottle sailed by her head. She glanced over her shoulder at the guards behind the gate. They were murmuring among themselves and pointing at her and the woman.

She glanced down at the blood trailing over her naked body. She prayed they came out soon; she didn't know how many more wounds she could take before she would pass out from loss of blood.

"You know," the woman said, moving toward her slowly, "I think that if you weren't a skinchanger, or if magic was not outlawed, you might make a good assassin." She lunged again.

Nathaira ducked, screaming as the woman's sword found the wound on her arm and made it deeper. She fell to her knees in the sand, white-hot pain searing through her body as spots danced at the edges of her vision.

Oh, Sisters, please let the guards come!

Chains rattled.

Nathaira breathed a prayer of thanks as a dozen guards jogged out into the arena.

"So fierce," the woman said behind her. "I could train you how to kill."

Nathaira watched the guards jog toward her, heard the woman's boots crunching in the sand as she stepped up behind her.

The woman's sword hissed through the air as she raised it high. "It's too bad that it has to end like this," she said. "I rather liked you."

Nathaira listened to the woman's sword whistle toward her. Ducking sideways, she wheeled on her knees. She drove three eagle talons into the woman's heart.

The crowd went deathly silent.

The guards jogging toward them slowed to a stop.

Nathaira stared into the woman's eyes—they were wide and shocked. "I do not give up," she said fiercely. "And I will never be like you." She pulled her talons out of the woman and wheeled around as she fell sideways to the sand. She lunged toward the tunnel entrance, body rippling into a silver wolf.

Screams echoed down from the crowd as she broke through the middle of the surprised guards, teeth slicing into the throat of the hairy-handed one as he jumped in her way. Somewhere high in the benches, trumpets blared as her silver legs flew over the ground. Nathaira barely heard them. The gate was open.

She glanced up at the towers and the creaking net and back at the guards running through the sand behind her. She pushed herself faster. Tears leaked out of her eyes with every step she took. A dark trail of blood glistened behind her.

An iron bolt, four feet long and lined in deadly pointed barbs, whistled through the air above her and landed with an explosion of sand by her left shoulder. Nathaira howled as hot sand pelted her wounds.

"Close the gate!" someone yelled above the screams of the crowd and the yells of the guards behind her.

No!

Chains rattled; the gate began grinding shut.

Nathaira ran faster, her muscles on fire and her wounds feeling like they were ripping open wider. They couldn't close the gate, she had to get out, had to get free, had to save Efamar.

She was five feet away.

The gate moved closer to the ground, closing the gap inch by inch.

Nathaira heard the whistle of another bolt as it screamed through the air toward her, heard boots hitting the sand behind her.

Four feet, three feet, two feet, one…

She changed into a red fox and slipped underneath the gate and into the tunnel with five inches to spare, running into the darkness.

The bolt hit the iron slats of the gate behind her with a resonating clang.

CHAPTER 21

Hathus

"Lovely day, isn't it?"

Hathus slowed his third trip around the main deck of the *Daemon's Cry* at the raspy voice and glanced over at Caine, who was leaning against the black railing of the ship and staring out at the passing sea with his one disturbing blue eye.

"Yes," Hathus replied, slowly moving to stand by the white-haired worldwalker. He followed Caine's gaze to the water gliding past. "Yes, it is."

It had been three days since they'd set sail from Alahvar, and although he still thought Caine was a grotesque nut, he was beginning to get bored with walking the ship decks for hours on end. Bored enough to talk to a magic user. It didn't really matter if he talked to him anyway, Hathus mused, just being on the same ship was enough to convict him if a kingdom fleet happened to spot them.

"Reminds me of the first time I sailed the seas," Caine wheezed, not seeming to notice Hathus's remark. "I was only seventeen when I set sail on the Sea of Monsters, seventeen and green as a willow branch with great dreams of adventure and excitement." The worldwalker snorted, an unpleasant noise that sounded like a camel hacking out a hairball. "It ended in excitement well enough, although with adventure I can't say. Depends on your point of view, I suppose."

Feeling expected to ask, Hathus offered the question of why as they watched a pod of blue whales keeping time with the pirate ships blow tall, glistening streams of water into the cloudless late-spring sky.

"The ship sank," Caine said, still not looking at him. "Caught in a sea battle between two of the biggest sea monsters I have ever seen."

Hathus paled. "Sea monsters?" he asked, glancing sideways at Caine.

"Aye," Caine replied, finally looking at him.

Hathus shivered as the worldwalker's ghostly blue eye met his and quickly looked away. "That must have been terrifying," he said, leaning on the railing and watching the ship opposite. He had only heard stories of monsters in the Sea of Monsters, but thankfully he had never seen any.

Caine shrugged, the suns sitting directly over their heads, making his pale skin appear even paler. "A little, I suppose," he wheezed, "but mostly it was exciting. One doesn't get to see sea monsters every day, you know." He was quiet for some time.

"So," Hathus said after a while, "how did you manage to escape if the ship sank?"

"Even at seventeen, I knew a little magic," Caine said quietly, gazing back out at the sea now.

Okay, whatever that means… The worldwalker fell quiet again. Feeling their conversation was over, Hathus pushed away from the railing and made to move off across the ship.

Perhaps there was a game of cards going on in the crew's quarters. For the last several days, some of the crew had been holding rowdy games of Gods and Goddesses, and after being invited in, he had managed to win a few oyrcu off them. It wasn't much money, but it was better than nothing, and with no real games to play in, no nobles to thieve from and no whorehouses to visit, it was the most exciting thing to do on the *Daemon's Cry*.

"How long were you in the dungeons, Hathus Ryrgorion?" Caine rasped.

Hathus stopped, cold fear gripping him.

How in the underworld does he know about that? He pivoted on the heel of one brown boot and glanced back at Caine, who was still staring out at the passing sea with his one blue eye. "I'm afraid I don't know what you are talking about."

"Oh, I think you do," Caine said, pulling a tarnished copper flask out of his shirt and pulling the lid off by his teeth with a click. He threw his head back and poured dark-brown liquid into his mouth and wiped the back of one hand across his mangled lips, turning.

Hathus glanced at a passing pirate to avoid the worldwalker's eye. It gave him the creeps, that eye.

"I can always tell a fellow prisoner by looking at them," Caine rasped. "I don't know which dungeon you were in or why you were in it, but the white pallor to your skin, the fact that you can never seem to get enough to eat, and your frail frame give you away."

Hathus stepped closer, glancing around to make sure no one else was listening. Caine had been watching him? Why?

"I could just be sick," he said, trying not to prove the worldwalker right by showing any reaction to his words.

Caine smiled, his breath smelling like alcohol. "I don't think so," he rasped.

Hathus stared at Caine, growing panicky.

"Oh, don't worry, Hathus Ryrgorion," Caine said reassuringly, "I'll keep your secret. I understand how a man who's been in the dungeons doesn't want the world to know." He took another drink out of his bottle.

"As I said before," Hathus said forcefully, "you're wrong." He turned to go.

"Am I?" Caine croaked behind him, making him pause. "Well, then I'm sorry for bothering you."

Hathus glanced over his shoulder at the worldwalker again, his pulse racing. Caine smiled slowly at him, a gruesome grimace that made Hathus's hair stand on end. "Have a nice day, Hathus Ryrgorion."

Hathus turned and hurried off across the deck.

He spent the rest of the afternoon in his cabin, lying on his back on the queen-sized bed that dominated the room's center as he went over and over Caine's words in his mind. The worldwalker had pegged him right, that was for sure, but why had he bothered saying anything at all if he was going to keep his secret?

And why was he so damn nervous and jumpy? Every little noise of the ship—a sail cracking, a rope creaking, the crew laughing—was making him start like he was robbing an armory.

What is wrong with me?

Hathus picked at a string on the bed's quilt. It wasn't like being in the dungeons was a crime. He just preferred that others didn't know about it, a matter of pride, really.

So why did Caine bringing it up make him nervous?

Perhaps it was because the man made his skin crawl every time he looked at him. Hathus stared up at the box-beamed ceiling above him, listening to the noise of the water rushing by outside as a shaft of afternoon sunlight streamed in from his cabin's open porthole and warmed his stomach. And then there was the fact that Caine was a magic user. He hated being around so much magic—it was making him sick with worry.

Hathus scratched at an itch on his leg. But what other choice did he have? He had to at least make it look like he was trying to get to the Land of Dragons for the sake of the Unknown Voice's men, and according to legend the only way to get to an otherworld was through a portal, and the only way to get through a portal was by collaborating with someone who knew where they were and how to get through them.

Hathus scrunched his eyes up and ground his fists into them.

Gods, but my life has gotten complicated… and stupid. He pulled his hands away from his eyes, knuckles bright red, and rolled over onto his stomach.

His chamber pot slid out from under the bed partway with the ship's movement, catching Hathus's eye. The laughing satyrs adorning it seemed to be mocking him.

His father had always said that he would amount to nothing in life. "You don't know what you want is what's wrong with you," he'd told Hathus once. "You need to have a clear goal in your mind that you strive toward day by day until you reach it."

Hathus rested his chin on his hands, staring at the chamber pot. He had a clear goal in life, had since he was a young boy. He wanted personal peace. Peace from fear, from pain, from hurt. But he had learned early on that there was no such thing as peace in life, so he had set his sights on something else: wealth. Wealth was the only thing that could make up for everything wrong in the world, the only thing that could give him joye from its pains and sorrows.

Hathus rolled over on his back again, watching the sunlight dance over the epharia ceiling. His mother had wanted peace too, but she never got it, not even in death.

Unexpected tears pricked at the backs of his eyes. Hathus blinked hard to stop more from coming and pushed off the bed, one foot numb. He moved to the door of his cabin, shaking his foot to get circulation back in it.

I'll just have to keep an eye on Caine… Eye… The man's only got one eye. He allowed himself a grin as he slipped out of the cabin and into the narrow wooden hallway outside.

"Good afternoon, sir," Godet trilled merrily from across the hall.

Hathus glanced up at the cabin boy of the *Daemon's Cry*, who was standing a few feet away, opening the door to Blackwell's cabin.

The glistening black wood, carved with snarling daemons, shone gold in the suns' rays, which streamed down the hall.

"Afternoon, Godet. You know, I told you to just call me Hathus. None of that sir business." Hathus grimaced. "I'm afraid it's a little too fine for me."

Godet smiled, the freckles dotting his cheeks blending together, and switched a heavy silver platter of fruit from one hand to the other.

A purple macar rolled off the edge and bounced down the hall.

Hathus leaned down and snatched the fruit up as it rolled past.

"All right, sir," Godet panted. "I'll remember that in the future, sir."

Hathus bit into the macar, the sour, tangy taste filling his senses. He rolled his eyes as the cabin boy disappeared through the door. He'd not been able to get him to call him by his name since he'd boarded the *Daemon's Cry*.

"Oh, and by the way, sir," Godet said, peeking his head back around the door.

Hathus glanced over his shoulder at the dark-haired boy. "Captain says you're invited to a fine dinner tonight. With Mr. Caine and the first and second mate."

Crap.

"Seven o'clock sharp, sir. You're having lobster!" Godet disappeared through the door again, shutting it behind him with a click.

Great, a whole dinner with that creepy bastard. Hathus stared at the daemons on Blackwell's cabin door. They seemed to be laughing at him. He stuck his tongue out at them and moved off up the hall, finishing the macar as he went.

"We sailed into the Eastern Sea's southern current three hours ago," Bathia said as he climbed up onto the poop deck and moved to stand next to her by the wheel.

"Good?" Hathus ventured.

Bathia glanced at him, carved golden hoop earrings dangling and glittering in the setting suns' light. "Caine says that the portal he's taking us to is in the southern current. We should be there in two to three days."

Hathus nodded, resisting the urge to roll his eyes. Caine still insisted that there was a Land of Dragons. It worried him that they were setting their course according to the worldwalker's direction. What if he was leading them to their deaths in unknown waters?

Hathus glanced over at Bathia, a salty sea breeze stroking his cheeks and ruffling his hat brim. "Do first mates always steer the ship?"

"Hmm?" Bathia looked up. "Oh, no. My father used to let me steer his, from time to time, and I developed a love for it that I can't shake." Bathia smiled softly. "The feeling of directing her where you want to go, the power you hold over it, the world at your fingertips. It's wonderful." She turned the wheel to the right, the breeze pulling at her curly brown hair that wasn't hidden beneath her bandanna.

Hathus watched her for a moment, thinking again how he wouldn't mind sleeping with her. "Your father," he ventured, pulling his hat off as the shadows of the sails blocked the setting suns' light from hitting him. "Was he a pirate captain too?"

Bathia's face hardened suddenly. "Yes," she said shortly, voice clear there'd be no more discussion.

They were silent for a while, watching the sky as it turned from red to pink to gold while the Brothers met the green-tinted sea.

"Caine," Hathus said after a while, glancing over at Bathia again. "What do you think of him?"

Bathia turned the wheel to the left slightly and glanced at him. "What do you mean?" A golden ray of sunlight fell on her bronzed skin and the dark-brown wood of the wheel, making the blue tattoos of various sailing instruments on her knuckles glow.

"Does he seem…" Hathus squinted against the setting sunlight, "slightly strange to you?"

Like the fact that he actually believes the Land of Dragons is real…

Bathia lifted her hand slightly and let the wheel turn under it. "Yes, but then I accredit that to his being tortured in the Hunting."

Hathus grunted, a chill running up his spine at the name. He saw the square again, heard the little girl's head hit the cobbles. "I'm worried," he said slowly. "That he might be leading us on a wild goose chase."

Bathia glanced at him. "You think he's crazy?"

"A little."

He's a magic user. Of course he's crazy.

"Well, I suppose we all are, a little."

Hathus cocked an eyebrow in agreement. He was beginning to think that he was crazy for accepting this job. But then, he hadn't had much choice. The Unknown Voice's words came back to him. *If you do not accept the job I offer you, then you will be killed and your body thrown into the River Sar…*

"Are you afraid that he won't find the Land of Dragons?" Bathia asked.

Hathus watched a shoeless pirate creep out onto the screaming daemon figurehead on the opposite end of the ship. "Yes," he lied.

"You really do believe that it is real, don't you?" Bathia said.

Hathus looked at her, watching a stray curl blowing over her cheek. "You know I do. What about you? Do you believe?"

Bathia grinned. "If I did, I wouldn't tell you. That would make people think that I believed the old religion."

Hathus eyed her for a moment, trying to decide if she was serious, and then laughed as he realized she was joking. He liked Bathia. Liked her open frankness, her confidence, her sense of humor. "Kiss me," he murmured.

Bathia looked up at him. "Or what?"

"Or I'll kiss you," Hathus replied.

She took a step closer to him, one hand still on the wheel. "And what makes you think, Hathus Ryrgorion, that I would let you?"

Hathus moved closer to her, so that they were inches apart. "Shall I try, and we can see?" he whispered, hand sliding onto her hip as he imagined where this might go.

"Mr. Ryrgorion, sir, First Mate, Blackwell sent me to tell you dinner's ready," Godet called up, appearing at the foot of the stairs.

Hathus cursed the cabin boy inwardly as Bathia stepped back to the wheel.

"We'll be there in a few minutes!" she called back to Godet. She turned the wheel to the left again, keeping the *Daemon's Cry* evenly spaced between the two ships behind her.

"How about magic, Hathus, what do you think of it?" Bathia said, glancing at him. "You've obviously not too much against it since you're willing to look for an otherworld and be in the company of a magic user. And Azaria," she added with a small smile. Everyone knew how he hated the creature, how he purposely went below decks to be away from the monkey when it was up on the main deck.

Hathus squinted into the sunset. Why did everyone have to talk about magic? "I think that it's harmless enough..." he began slowly, searching for something to say that made it look like he was okay with magic. He had to be, if they were to believe his lie of believing in a magical land. "...if used by the right people."

"And who are these 'right people'?" Bathia queried, glancing at him again.

"Those that use it for good?" Hathus asked.

She laughed. "Ah, but see, Hathus, that's where disputes start. Some people believe that magic can be used for good or evil, depending on who's using it, while others believe that it is simply evil, no matter who uses it or what they are using it for."

"And what do you believe?" Hathus asked, glancing at her.

"I believe," Bathia said, waving over a nearby pirate and handing the wheel to him, "that we should go eat dinner."

She moved off to the stairs that led to the main deck and the cabins.

Hathus smiled softly. He turned back toward the water, watching the Brothers sink the rest of the way into the Eastern Sea. His mother had believed that magic was only as evil as the person who used it. She had paid for that belief with her life. His smile faded, and he turned toward the stairs. He had asked his mother about magic once, why it was considered evil. His father had overheard her telling him that not all magic was evil, that it could be used for good in some cases. The next morning a patrol of soldiers had come to their door to collect her. She had been beheaded that same day in an executioner's square.

Hathus stepped down onto the main deck and ducked into the hallway leading to the cabins. He didn't really know or care if magic was as good or as evil as the person who used it. All he knew was that he feared it, and when this was all over, and he got his freedom, he was never going to be around it again.

CHAPTER 22

Darkmoon

He was a boy of six again, standing in the great hall. But it was before it had been destroyed, before the fire had consumed it.

There was no one in the hall besides himself, nothing but darkness and shadows and moonlight.

Darkmoon took a tentative step forward, the wide gray flagstones of the hall floor cold against his bare feet. He wanted to call out, to see if anyone was there. But he was afraid to, afraid of what the shadows might hold.

A low wind drifted through the hall, whistling softly as it wound between the pillars.

"My child," his mother whispered, appearing out of the shadows between two pillars to his left. Her slender white hands were folded in front of her, and her long black hair flowed loosely down her back. There was a crown of flowers on her head, the one she always wore in place of the silver crown his father had given her.

Darkmoon stopped, relief flooding over him. He hated to be alone. When he was alone, he was scared—of the shadows, of the war, of darkness. That was why he always followed Cyron. Only Cyron was not here… He turned toward his mother, opening his mouth to say hello.

"My son," she whispered, voice pained, "I forgive you." Her blue eyes met Darkmoon's, stopping him from speaking with the look of sorrow in them. A tear slipped out of her left eye, following the path of the others draining down her alabaster cheeks. There was a stoop to her frame, a stoop that made her look old.

Darkmoon's mouth closed slowly. He remembered suddenly why Cyron was not there, why he was alone. The pain came to his heart. He began crying quietly.

"My child," his mother said, floating toward him.

Darkmoon stepped backward. She was an illusion, and if he reached out to touch her, she would not be there.

"I forgive you," his mother whispered.

Darkmoon backed up further, shaking his head. He did not want her forgiveness. Tears slipped out of his eyes. He did not deserve it. Not for what he had done.

His mother swooped toward him, her light-blue dress making her hair look even blacker than it was. "I forgive you," she murmured, flying through a tall eight-pronged iron candlestick as if it was not there.

Darkmoon stumbled over a flagstone, terrified now. They hated him for what he had done. He hated himself. Hated that he was still alive and that they were not.

"I forgive you," his mother whispered again, gaining on him. She opened her arms wide, eyes boring into his. "For MURDERING US ALL!" she screamed. She threw her head back and screamed again, a scream of pain and agony that echoed through the long, dark hall.

The skin on her body melted away in patches to the floor then, the smell of burning flesh filling the hall as fire lapped at her arms and hair and legs.

Darkmoon turned and ran, sobs wracking his frame. Pillars sped by him, massive cylinders of dark stone that made him feel like an ant in comparison. He glanced over his shoulder as he reached the middle of the hall. His mother was gone, replaced by dappled shadows and moonlight. He slowed, breaths burning in his lungs. He was alone again.

He wandered between two stone pillars, tears draining down his cheeks, goosebumps trailing along his skin as the hall grew steadily colder. He had the vague feeling again that there should be music, and hundreds of people and candlelight and his father sitting on the dais with a crown on his head.

A raven cawed in the distance.

Darkmoon looked sideways to see it sitting on a nearby candlestick, watching him. Its eyes were red like blood. "Darkness is coming..." the bird squawked, blood oozing out of its open beak. Darkmoon turned away from it.

His father stood before him, face hidden by shadows but hands outstretched toward him. They were long hands, his father's, muscled and narrow.

"Son," his father said softly. His smooth voice was strained.

"Father..." Darkmoon whimpered, crying softly again.

"Son, help me," his father whispered. His voice was filled with pain.

Darkmoon saw two silver tears fall out of the shadows where his father's head was. They fell to the cold floor below, landing on the gray stone in dark splashes.

He was a man again, a man in black clothing and with a white scar cutting his left eyebrow in half.

His father faded, replaced by his mother once more. She said nothing, simply stared at him with her tear-filled blue eyes.

Darkmoon met her stare. He had no words for her. There were no words that could be said.

His mother put a hand out to him, straight in front of her with her palm facing toward him. He met it, matching his larger hand to her own.

The hall changed, turning into ruin.

Darkmoon felt ash and snow settling on his shoulders and head, smelled smoke and burning flesh.

His mother's hand changed against his, the skin on her hand shredding and blackening and blood dripping down her arm. "My son," she whispered, eyes sad and pained, "I forgive you." She faded away into ash, trickling to the floor.

The hall faded around him, replaced by another hall of tan sandstone and a red-and-brown mosaic floor.

Darkmoon glanced around him. He remembered this place, remembered this day. He started down the hall, peacocks on perches and monkeys in cages, watching him from between fluted sandstone pillars. He was twelve now, and already his kill record was longer than both his arms combined.

"My greatest pupil," a calm, even voice said from a sandstone dais ahead of him. "And yet I hear that you've failed me."

Darkmoon stopped in front of the dais, going to one knee and looking up at a wooden chair and the man seated within.

Straight silver hair stretched to the man's broad shoulders. An Araysannian tunic of red silk with golden peacocks strutting across it covered his thick, muscular body. Eyes so hazel they were almost golden stared out from a strong, scarred face.

"I was ready to reward you for last night's work," Arayn J'altayr said quietly, "with a woman." He reached a hand out and pulled one of three scantily clad women standing beside his chair to him.

The woman, brown hair short against her head, cried out at the grip on her bare arm.

Darkmoon met the woman's eyes. He judged her to be seven years his elder, and yet she showed more fear than he did. Fear was a weakness, a flaw.

"They're virgins," Arayn J'altayr said, eyeing the women. "The three of them." He waved his free hand at the women collectively. "Borgayn bought them off a slaver train yesterday. Quite tempting, are they not?"

Arayn J'altayr looked at him, and Darkmoon stared back. Arayn J'altayr had introduced him to women very soon after he had come to him. The first one had been thirty-six, he seven.

"I saved you from death," Arayn J'altayr murmured, watching him. "I gave you a home and a name, trained you so that you would never be weak again." He let go of the woman, and she backed up to her fellows, body shaking. "And yet," Arayn J'altayr said, plucking a grape off a bunch in a bowl on the table beside him with scar-covered fingers, "Borgayn tells me that you did not complete your mission last night as instructed."

Darkmoon glanced at Borgayn, who was standing a few feet away from him, reaching a finger through the bars of a monkey cage. His blood roiled. He hated Arayn J'altayr's right-hand man, hated him almost as much as Arayn J'altayr.

Borgayn turned from pestering a delicate golden spider monkey, his chestnut eyes meeting Darkmoon's.

Darkmoon let the venom and hate swirling within him seep into his eyes. Borgayn smiled slowly.

"You were told," Arayn J'altayr said, bringing Darkmoon's gaze back to him, "to kill Shayr Kaamar and his lovely wife and two daughters, but instead you killed only Shayr Kaamar."

Borgayn stepped toward him. Darkmoon turned slightly toward the muscled, blond-haired man, his hand curling up softly toward a knife in his left vambrace.

Arayn J'altayr held a hand up, sun-tanned skin contrasting sharply with his silver hair. No one knew where the middle-aged assassin was from, or what his true name was. Birth names were as closely hidden as emotions at Arayn J'altayr's home, and Arayn J'altayr was the best at hiding his.

"Wait, Borgayn," Arayn said softly. "I wish to hear first why he disobeyed me. Go on, Darkmoon." He rested an elbow on one of his chair's armrests and leaned his chin on his knuckles. "Tell me why you did not kill Shayr Kaamar's wife and daughters."

Darkmoon held Arayn J'altayr's gaze, not replying. What was there to say? That he still saw visions of his mother? That he heard voices from his past and that they made him freeze? Arayn J'altayr had worked hard to drive the memories out of him, but they still came occasionally, and when they did, he was helpless.

"Please don't tell me," Arayn J'altayr said quietly, "that you are gaining a conscious and do not want to kill women and children?"

Darkmoon felt the cool steel handle of his knife against his fingertips. He wanted to throw the weapon at Arayn J'altayr's throat, wanted to throw a thousand knives at the assassin lord. But he was not good enough yet to kill Arayn J'altayr, and he would not try until he was.

Arayn J'altayr motioned for one of the women to step forward, glancing at them when they hesitated. The blonde-haired one took a tentative step toward him, the gray silk cloth wrapped around her body quivering with her tremoring. Arayn J'altayr directed her to stand in front of him, her face toward Darkmoon.

"Show me, Darkmoon, that you are not gaining a conscious," the assassin lord said quietly.

Darkmoon pushed himself up from his kneeling position. Arayn J'altayr was testing him. Arayn J'altayr was always testing him. He walked up the four steps of the dais to the woman, stopping in front of her and glancing up into her green eyes. There was fear in her eyes, but she had not yet realized what Arayn J'altayr wanted him to do to her. He wished that she would. He wanted to see the terror of death in her eyes. The terror that he saw in all his victims' eyes, the terror that kept him alive. His fingers slid the knife in his vambrace into his palm.

The woman saw the movement. Her eyes widened, realization of what was happening flashing in them. She cried out and made to jump away, but Darkmoon was too fast for her. He grabbed her bare arm with the fingers of one hand as she scrambled backward and brought the knife up and drove it deep into her stomach, above her belly button, where her ribs made an arch.

Warm red blood splashed over him, and all three women screamed.

Darkmoon pulled another dagger from a belt at his hip and brought it up in a slashing motion, cutting the blonde-haired woman's throat open from collarbone to chin. She stopped screaming and fell sideways onto the dais. He met Arayn J'altayr's eyes.

"You know that I must punish you," Arayn J'altayr said calmly.

Darkmoon saw Borgayn moving toward him out of the corner of his eye, felt the slice of the hooks in his flesh, the heat of iron against his skin. Someday he would kill Arayn J'altayr, and Borgayn too.

Borgayn grabbed his arm with fingers of iron, dragging him backward down the hall as the remaining women sobbed uncontrollably and servants came to take away the dead body.

Darkmoon met Arayn J'altayr's eyes as Borgayn pulled him through the oaken doors of the hall. He didn't blink. Someday, he would kill them.

Darkmoon's mismatched green and blue eyes snapped open. A dark box-beamed ceiling looked back at him. Thunder rumbled across the city outside.

Arayn J'altayr...

He sat up and glanced out a window across the room from his bed. He had not thought of his trainer in years. Not since he had killed him.

Lightning flashed outside, reflecting off the white stone of the building opposite and sending light into his dark hotel room. Darkmoon looked down at his weapons, which sat on a chair with his dark clothes beside the ornately carved bed he lay in.

He had been fifteen when he had finally felt strong enough to kill Arayn J'altayr. It had been in the winter, on a dark and stormy night much like now.

"Darkmoon," Arayn J'altayr said, coming in from a long journey. The white-haired assassin slowed, rain dripping off his cloak and onto the sandstone floor beneath him.

Darkmoon stepped out the rest of the way from the shadows he stood in, the sound of rain pounding against the tile roof of Arayn J'altayr's home echoing through the long hallway they stood in. The hallway was bordered by short pillars on the left and glass-paned windows on the right. The entry doors to the house stood behind Arayn J'altayr, heavy wood dark with age and staining.

"What are you doing up at such an ungodly hour?" Arayn J'altayr asked, moving to a wooden table between two pillars and throwing his muddy riding gloves on it. He pulled the stopper out of a crystal flagon of red wine and poured the liquid into a matching crystal glass.

Darkmoon drew a knife out of his vambrace.

Arayn J'altayr set the wine flagon back down, pausing at the slight hiss of steel against leather. "I always knew it would come to this," he said softly, scarred fingers wrapping around the wineglass.

Darkmoon moved forward.

"From the day I first found you in that smoking ruin of a palace," Arayn J'altayr murmured, "I knew that someday you would kill me." He raised the wineglass to his mouth and downed it in one swallow.

"How?" Darkmoon asked, his voice, still young and light, had a deeper undertone to it now.

Arayn J'altayr turned around, hazel eyes calm. "You're too powerful for this world, Darkmoon," he said softly. His hair had turned white in the last three years, and there were age lines mixing with the scars peppering his face now. "You always were."

Darkmoon stopped two feet away from Arayn J'altayr, the knife raised in his hand. He could hear footsteps approaching outside. Borgayn coming in from making sure that the slaves put the horses away.

"I'm not going to kill you quickly," he said softly. "Borgayn, yes, but not you. I'm going to torture you, like you tortured me. And when I'm done, and you're begging me to slit your throat, then I will smile and burn you alive."

Arayn J'altayr stared into his eyes. The front doors opened behind them.

Darkmoon wheeled, letting the knife in his hand fly. The weapon flashed, end over end, through the shadows of the hallway before embedding itself deep into Borgayn's throat with a crunch. Darkmoon turned back around, picking up the crystal flagon with one hand and bringing it up to meet Arayn J'altayr's head.

He left Borgayn in the hall, choking to death on his own blood as he dragged Arayn J'altayr's unconscious body through the quiet shadowed halls of the assassin's home. He burnt Arayn J'altayr's home to the ground that night, and while it burned he took his old trainer to the sewers that ran under the house, and there he tortured him for three weeks.

Darkmoon pushed off the bed as thunder boomed directly above the hotel, making his room rattle. He pulled his clothes off the chair and slipped into them, his mother's voice whispering in his ear. He needed to kill.

He slipped out of his room and into the street outside, thunder booming overhead again as he closed the back door of the hotel after him. It had been four days since he had met with Torin Ravynston in the tavern near Northport. He had come into Crystoln the day before and spent the day watching the games held in the arena in honor of King Uranius's ninety-fourth birthday.

Darkmoon scanned the dark street ahead of him, looking for a body to kill. A drunk or homeless person would be enough, just something to drive away the voices.

"I forgive you…" his mother's voice whispered in his head.

Darkmoon ignored it and kept walking, scanning the doorways and side alleys for signs of life. The games from the day before had been interesting. It had been some time since he had seen a skinchanger, and the one that Crystoln had bought from the slavers was a beautiful specimen. Now he'd heard she was loose in Crystoln, running through the city streets as citizens panicked and soldiers examined everyone to see if they were the skinchanger.

Darkmoon heard a drunk singing an off-key shanty. He headed toward the noise, his mother's voice whispering on a breeze heavy with the scent of rain. Arayn J'altayr had indeed begged him for mercy at the end of the three weeks, when his ears and nose and lips were gone and his skin was red and shredded.

Darkmoon found the drunk behind a stack of broken crates outside of a closed tavern door. He put a hand behind the man's head and slowly sliced a knife across his throat, relishing the sound of his breath leaving him, the warmth of his blood on his skin. He had let Arayn J'altayr beg him for two days, and true to his word, he had smiled.

Then he had erected a stake on the mountaintop where Arayn J'altayr's house had stood, tied his old trainer to it, and burned him alive. That was the first time that people began fearing the name of Darkmoon, the first time that he rose to something more than just another hired killer.

A dog barked in the distance. Darkmoon lowered the drunk's body backward onto the cobbles. He wiped his knife off on a clean part of the man's puke-stained clothes and moved off up the alley.

"Son…" his father's voice called from the darkness of an alley.

Darkmoon paused, listening to the sound of crying on the breeze.

"The past will always be there," Arayn J'altayr's voice said in his ear. "We can't deny it, and we can't forget it, not completely. But we can learn to live with it, and if you want to survive, Darkmoon, you must learn to live with your past."

Darkmoon's fingers twitched as a dog walked across the street in front of him. Through Arayn J'altayr's help, he had learned to live with his past as a child, and he had survived. But killing was not helping this time. He didn't want to admit it, but it was not, not like it should be.

A woman's scream echoed through the dark alleys around him, real and not from his memories or past.

Darkmoon glanced in the direction that the noise had come from. A woman—or man, for that matter—getting raped and murdered in Crystoln's backstreets was not uncommon. But where there was a murder going on, there was a murderer and a body to kill. He moved in the direction the voice had come from, fingers twitching. He didn't know why killing was not helping, but the time that the voices and past did not haunt him was growing shorter and shorter after every throat he sliced, and he was beginning to fear that it would disappear completely.

The scene of the crime was not hard to find—the woman being raped made enough noise to wake the dead.

Darkmoon stopped in a dark alley, surveying the small courtyard and the three people within it.

Only the woman was not a woman, but the skinchanger, and she was not being raped—she was being captured for the reward posted on her head for her return to the arena.

Darkmoon listened to rain coming toward the upper part of the city from the lower part.

"Hold still, skinchanger," the man holding the skinchanger said roughly. He was a massive man with scars covering his body and dark hair that fell past his waist. "Just one blow, and you won't feel a thing."

The skinchanger struggled in the man's grip, the other man, a youth with pimples dotting his face, giggled.

Darkmoon pulled two knives out of his waist belt. He would keep killing as long as it did help, and when it did not, then he would figure out something else to drive the past away.

"You can save her," Darkmoon, the seer's voice whispered in his mind. "You can save Argdrion."

"My son," his mother said, appearing in the mist swirling in an alley opposite, "I forgive you."

Darkmoon aimed the first knife for the larger man's throat and let it fly.

CHAPTER 23

Azkanysh

Azkanysh glanced over the railing of the balcony and at the massive training yard far below. It had been five days since she had ruled that women were to be allowed into the army with men, and already thousands had been conscripted.

They had been pouring into Sussār for days on end, receiving weapons and clothing and training as the ships that would carry the army to Warulan readied in the harbor directly below the front of the palace.

A slave held up a brass platter with a ceramic pitcher and cup on it.

Azkanysh nodded at the man, and he poured red wine into the cup and held it out to her. She took it, pulling back a corner of her black hijab and raising the cool vessel to her lips.

The army was to sail for Warulan in three days. Hardly enough time, many said, for them to train properly for the upcoming war, but as Vyzir Dsamihur had mentioned, they would have time on the ride over to train, and once they reached Warulan, they could practice as they marched.

A stocky trainer bellowed out an order in the yard below, and the hundreds of men and women marching to the right stopped and wheeled around.

Azkanysh took another sip of the wine. Tension was high in the city right now. Two days before, a diplomat from Eromor had arrived at the palace, asking for audience with the court. The man had brought a letter from King Uranius of Eromor, a letter claiming that Eromor had not hired the assassin that had killed Vosbarhan and asking that terms of peace be drawn up between their two kingdoms.

She had sent the man away in rags, an old custom that told Eromor they refused their offer. Most felt that the offer was another attempt to humiliate their honor. Personally, she wanted the war to continue. If it ended before it began, women would never fight alongside men, and the chance to prove to the men of Zarcayra that women could help them win a war would pass.

The soldiers below moved to the left at the trainer's yell. Azkanysh rested her half-empty cup on the railing, fingers tapping against it. She had been restless the last few days, restless with wanting to make more changes in Zarcayra. There were numerous things that she had in mind to change, such as the law that stated women could not inherit, the unspoken tradition that allowed men to beat and abuse their wives, the laws that kept women from working and earning their own wages.

The last was the most prominent in her mind this morning, for if women were allowed to work and earn their own wages, then there would be no need for them to rely on men, and it would open up new possibilities, new avenues of freedom. Azkanysh raised the cup to her lips again, the sweet wine inside cooling her throat. She had been told by Vyzir Dsamihur that the women of Zarcayra were as unhappy about the ruling that they were to be conscripted into the army as the men were. They felt, the vyzir had informed her, that their place was at home raising children, not fighting on distant battlefields where they would only get in the way of and hinder the men.

Azkanysh lowered her cup again and pulled her hijab back over her face. It angered her that the women of Zarcayra did not realize that she was trying to gain them freedom. But Zarcayra had done a good job of brainwashing its women into thinking they were the lesser beings that men believed them to be. She had been like the women of Zarcayra once, simple, compliant, weak. Vosbarhan's death had opened her eyes, reminding her of what she had believed when she was younger, that women were as equal as their male counterparts and should be treated as such.

Azkanysh tapped her fingers against the cup. She would make Zarcayrans see how they needed their freedom, make them love her and appreciate what she was doing for them.

"Right!" The thick voice of the trainer below echoed up to the balcony. The soldiers in the training yard moved back to the right, the spears in their right hands glinting in the Brothers' midmorning rays.

Azkanysh glanced out at the city beyond the training yard and at the heavy plumes of smoke drifting up from the factories lining the Akhuran River outside. All over the kingdom, factories had been running nonstop for the last few days, making clothing and saddles and weapons and tents for the army as the day that they would set sail drew closer.

The slave stepped forward again with the pitcher as she lowered her cup for the third time, but Azkanysh waved him away. If she ruled that women could work, then not only would it be a step toward the freedom of Zarcayra's women, but it would speed up production in the factories and increase output in the kingdom. She rested her cup on the rail of the balcony again. She had decided that this reason was how she would pitch her proposition to the Guardian Council, urging them to approve in favor of women working so that the kingdom could increase production, double manufacturing.

She had thought, a few days before, to simply bypass the council again and rule for women to be allowed to work. But although her young reign was going well so far, too many rulings opposite to what the council advised could tip it upside down. Azkanysh did not want that right now—she had too many plans, too many dreams.

The soldiers in the yard below turned again, marching toward the distant wall surrounding the palace in perfect unison. Azkanysh watched them, remembering other armies marching away from the palace during the Third Great War. Her father had been in one of those armies. And he, like thousands of others, he had not come home.

She waved a fly away. The council would not easily agree with her idea of allowing women to work, she knew. She would need to convince them, persuade them, encourage them with sound logic and good reasons. That was why she had called Shayr Jahayan here this morning, to see if the elderly councilmember was on her side as he had led her to believe in the throne room five days before, and to see if he would help her persuade the council to advise her way.

"Queen of Queens?"

Azkanysh turned partway at the voice.

A slave bowed from the red-and-brown painted arch of the doorway, sweat glistening on his neck in the early-morning heat. "Shayr Jahayan is here, Queen of Queens," the slave said, bowing lower.

"Show him in," Azkanysh said, turning away from the railing and handing her cup to the slave with the platter.

The slave at the door bowed again and backed out through the door.

Shayr Jahayan stepped onto the balcony, black tunic spread tight around his pot-bellied stomach.

"Queen of Queens," the elderly shayr said, bowing at the waist.

Azkanysh moved to a nearby table adorned with several platters of fruit and cheese, motioning for the shayr to sit. She settled into the wooden chair opposite him, waving over the slave with the pitcher again. "Wine, Shayr Jahayan?"

Shayr Jahayan dipped his head. "Yes, thank you, Queen of Queens."

Azkanysh waited as the slave poured a red stream of glistening wine into Shayr Jahayan's cup. What she would ask of Shayr Jahayan would be no small matter. But if there was one thing that she had learned from Vosbarhan, it was to ask favors of allies to prove their loyalty, test their sincerity. She had heard him a thousand times in the throne room ask some lower king of one of the outer provinces to give him slaves, spy on another of the lower kings for him, to quell the desert tribes.

And while she knew that the lower kings of Zarcayra had not loved her husband, they had feared and respected him, and respect was what she wanted from the council and the people of Zarcayra. The slave finished pouring and bowed, backing up to his former position by a sandstone pillar a few feet away.

"I called you here today, Shayr Jahayan," Azkanysh started, "to discuss a matter of great importance to me."

Shayr Jahayan sipped at his wine, looking up at her over the rim of the cup. "I am humbled, Queen of Queens. Any way that I may be of service to you, I will gladly comply."

Azkanysh glanced around the wide balcony. Vyzir Dsamihur was not with her this morning, as he had affairs to attend to with arranging housing for the gathering army in the city. She was glad that he was not with her. Although she found herself relying heavily upon his knowledge of the court and its workings, she didn't trust him yet, not enough to confide her plans in him. But then, she really didn't trust anyone enough to do that. Not all her plans, anyway…

"I have an idea that I would like the Guardian Council's approval on," Azkanysh said, looking back at Shayr Jahayan. She waved another fly away and snapped her fingers at a slave with a fan a few feet away. The girl jumped forward, waving her ostrich plume over the table.

"But I fear that this idea will not bode well with the council," Azkanysh went on, "and that they will not offer me their approval." She rested a hand on the cool mosaic pattern of the table. "I could rule over the council's head, I know, but I wish to encourage harmony in the kingdom and would greatly appreciate it if I could somehow convince the Guardian Council to see the matter my way."

Shayr Jahayan set his cup down and reached for a silver-stitched napkin with a gnarled hand. "How do I come into this matter, Queen of Queens?" he asked, wiping at his white mustache.

"You are, forgive me," Azkanysh replied, "one of the eldest members of the Guardian Council, Shayr Jahayan, and your opinion and advice, I am sure, is greatly valued among the younger members of the council. If you were to…" She paused, looking for the right word. "Present to the council my idea, advise them that it is a good move in Zarcayra's favor, then I am sure that it would soften the council's hearts when I approach them with the matter."

"And what is this matter that you speak of, Queen of Queens?" Shayr Jahayan asked, watching her.

Azkanysh held up her hand for the slave to stop fanning. "I wish for women to be allowed to work," she said, watching Shayr Jahayan closely for his reaction.

He eyed her for a moment, small eyes thoughtful. "There is fire in you, Queen of Queens," he said after a few heartbeats. "A fire that has been hidden, I think, for many years." He reached for his cup again.

Azkanysh raised her head. "And do you not approve of this fire, Shayr Jahayan?" she asked defensively.

Shayr Jahayan smiled softly. "No, Queen of Queens, I am thrilled by it." He leaned forward, face growing animated. "This kingdom has long been in the darkness, and your fire, Queen of Queens, is the light I believe that it needs."

Azkanysh relaxed. "You led me to believe in the throne room, Shayr Jahayan, that you would support me in my endeavors as Queen of Queens," she said. "I hope that I did not misjudge you."

"You did not, Queen of Queens," Shayr Jahayan said, meeting her eyes. He leaned backward, sipping at his wine. "I never married, did you know that, Queen of Queens?" he asked abruptly, changing the subject.

Azkanysh eyed him. She did know it—most of the court did. But what did that have to do with their conversation?

"Many said it was because I wanted to live a life of religious piety," Shayr Jahayan said. "Serving the gods. Others that I simply enjoyed being alone. But the truth is, Queen of Queens, that I did not marry because I saw what marriage did to my mother, and I feared being the same kind of man that my father was to a wife, should I take one."

Azkanysh stared into Shayr Jahayan's eyes. They were filled with sadness and memories but also anger.

"I have long seen the wrongness of how the women of Zarcayra are treated," Shayr Jahayan said in a hushed voice. "And I have long prayed for a ruler who would see it too. Who would make it like it was when the thirteen kingdoms ruled in Araysann." He looked up from his cup. "When you took the golden lyon crown, Queen of Queens, I had hope that my prayers had finally been answered." He motioned for the slave with the pitcher forward.

Azkanysh watched Shayr Jahayan as the slave refilled his cup, her heart beating rapidly. Was Shayr Jahayan being truthful? Or was he simply filling her head with pretty lies and flatteries? But then, why would he? To gain her trust, maybe, but what could he hope to gain by it? The council had no lawful power, only traditional, and anytime that she wanted to go over their heads, she could.

Azkanysh reached for her cup, taking a quick drink of wine. Maybe it was stupid, but she was going to believe that Shayr Jahayan was telling her the truth. It would mean a great ally, an ally that, hopefully, would be the beginning of many. She would need allies if she was to bring freedom to the women of Zarcayra. Allies who would back her, support her, help her.

The slave bowed and backed up again. Azkanysh leaned forward in her chair, setting her wine cup back down on the table. "Our task will not be easy, Shayr Jahayan," she said quietly, watching the Shayr. "Zarcayra will not change its old ways and beliefs willingly."

Shayr Jahayan leaned forward as well, meeting her dark eyes with his own. "Then we will make them, Queen of Queens," he said eagerly. "And with the gods and goddesses on our side, as I believe they are, we will bring freedom to the women of Zarcayra."

CHAPTER 24

Tamar

Tamar glanced out the arching windows lining the back wall of her bedchamber at the harbor below, which spread away from the orange sandstone cliffs that Sussār perched on. Dozens of golden-trimmed warships with purple sails crowded the deep-blue water. She grinned.

The ships were leaving today.

She ran across the blue-and-gold peacock-patterned rug covering the red sandstone floor of her room to the five-legged dressing table Grandfather Heyros had given her for her twelfth nameday.

Yelling voices drifted in through the many windows dotting her room. Tamar's heartbeat sped up. After almost two weeks of gathering, the army was finally sailing for Warulan and the kingdom of Eromor. She yanked on the handle of the top drawer of a white uylian wood table checkered with gold and blue-painted squares and cursed as the drawer came out and crashed to the floor in a shower of hijab pins, hairclips, and assorted jewelry.

"Sorry, Ehurayni!" Tamar groaned, kneeling among the mess and praying that the chief goddess would understand the reason for her cursing as she quickly grabbed an ivory comb painted with brightly robed men and women.

She had watched for days with the rest of the palace as conscripted men and women had poured into Sussār and joined the thousands already there in training for the upcoming war. She had never seen so many in Sussār, not even at Father's funeral or Zarmeyr's annual birthday feast.

Tamar tugged the comb's fine teeth through her hip-length hair, dark brown and straight as a board, and uttered another curse as one of the teeth broke off in a nasty knot. "Sorry again, Ehurayni!" she exclaimed.

She threw the broken comb on the floor with the rest of the drawer's contents and jumped over the sprawling clutter, running to her four-poster bed.

She had known as soon as the guards had awoken the palace the night of Father's murder with their shouts and torchlight that things would be different for her and the rest of the palace, not to mention Zarcayra. And when Mother had taken the golden lyon crown as Queen of Queens, Tamar had felt in her soul that a new dawn was coming to Zarcayra, a dawning of freedom and equality and adventure.

She scanned the clothing lying haphazardly on the bed: a pair of night-black slippers, an ankle-length black tunic, a hijab, and two black long-sleeved robes. She was so sick of seeing black and wearing it that she could scream. If her idea went as planned, she wouldn't be wearing the black for very much longer—she'd be wearing purple.

A horn, one of seven that sat in the seven towers that circled the main dome of the palace, blew loudly and deeply, and a thrill ran up Tamar's spine again as the sound filled the air.

Whoooh, whoooh, whoooh.

It shook the floor underneath her bare feet. Named the Horns of Ryr for their forging at the brother smith god's hands, legend said the solid gold horns were the ones that King Amysos had taken into battle with him in the First Age when he had fought against the armies of the Furies created by Setaron, god of the underworld, as they tried to overrun the lands of men.

The horns were only blown on special occasions. Seven had been blown on the day that Father died but only one was sounded for smaller occasions such as the one now, which reminded Tamar again that the ships were leaving today.

Her idea had come to her when Mother had ruled that women were to be allowed into the army with men in order for Zarcayra's army to match Eromor's in size and strength. At first, it had been nothing more than a breathtaking notion that seemed too fantastic to be plausible.

But as the days passed and she watched women marching with men in the training yards and women wearing the purple of the army's colors and women walking through the city wearing swords on their hips, Tamar's idea had turned into a plan that was too good to not be conceivable.

Tamar pulled her tunic on over her cotton undershirt, yanking at the bottom seam as it bunched up around her hips. The only thing that stood in the way of her idea becoming a reality was getting Mother's permission. She was sure that she would give it, though, for if the last few weeks of her new rule had proved anything, it was that Mother would help the women of Zarcayra get the freedom they deserved.

Tamar snatched a silver pin off the table beside her bed and wound her hair up in a messy bun atop her head, then pinned it in place. She reached for her hijab, quickly fashioning it over her head with experienced hands. The robes were next, and to finish off the costume, a silver necklace of a moon that matched the ones Paruhi and Kayani had.

Tamar tucked the necklace down inside her tunic. Jewelry was forbidden as part of the mourning process, but the necklace was a gift from Mistress Ahani, and the only thing she had to remember her mistress by besides memories.

Tamar glanced at herself in the polished mirror above the dressing table. It wasn't her neatest outfit, and she grimaced when she noticed that her hajib was crooked, but then her outfits never were, and who cared anyway? It wasn't like anyone special would be in the palace, and even if they were, she'd much rather wear the purple tunics that the soldiers did.

If Mother says yes, I will, she thought with a thrill.

The door of her room, made from a light wood with golden strapwork crisscrossed over it, opened as Tamar turned away from the bed. For a moment, her younger sister's cry of astonishment rang out over the constant sounding of the horn.

"Tamar! Grandmama's ivory comb!"

Tamar snatched another silver pin off the table by her bed and pulled up a side of her hijab, stabbing at her falling hair. "Oh, don't be so uptight, Paruhi," she yelled above the noise of the horn. "Neither one of us ever liked the ugly old thing anyway." She glanced in the mirror above the uylian wood table at the reflection of the broken comb and wrinkled up her nose in disgust. "Why anyone would want such a thing is beyond me, much less gift it to their granddaughter."

"Tamar!" Paruhi scolded, lifting her black tunic and robe and gingerly stepping around the pile of objects littering the floor. "It was extremely kind of Grandmama to give that to you."

Tamar rolled her eyes. They didn't see Father's mother very often, just once a year when they traveled to the Temple of the Gods and Goddesses in the Eastern Mountains for the Day of Offering, but the few times that she had seen the peevish old woman, they hadn't gotten along very well.

"Too strong willed and adventurous," the hawk-nosed crone said, pinching Tamar's face with a clawlike hand. "Just like her mother. You'll have a hard time with her, Vosbarhan. Best marry her off to a good, controlling husband to keep her in check before she does something wild that will shame the family."

The old donkey, Tamar thought darkly, struggling to get the second pin to stick in her hair in a position that held her hair up and kept it from falling out from under her hijab.

"Here," Paruhi said gently, clothes rustling around her as she moved behind her.

Tamar let her hands fall to her sides as her younger sister gently lifted her hijab and rearranged her hair. She hated Father's mother, hated visiting her, hated listening to her, hated looking at her fat body. Not everyone agreed that women should be controlled like Grandmama and the masses of Zarcayra did. People like Mistress Ahani had not believed it, and Mistress Ahani was the wisest person that she had ever known.

"You really shouldn't speak poorly of Grandmama, Tamar," Paruhi said softly behind her, pulling Tamar's hijab back around her shoulders and straightening it. "It's not proper."

Tamar rolled her eyes again and turned. She took her younger sister's hands in hers. "Hang proper," she said forcefully. "The woman is a toad, and don't tell me you don't think so too." Tamar let go of Paruhi's hands and wheeled, heart still racing as the sound of the horn drummed through the room.

"I know," Paruhi said quietly, looking at the floor. "But she is our grandmother, and you really should be more respectful. We are princesses, and as such, we should act the part."

Tamar contained a snort. Paruhi had gotten those words straight from Mistress Lorrig, a spider of an old woman who taught her and her sisters how to behave like shayras. Mistress Lorrig had replaced Mistress Ahani after Father had banished Mistress Ahani from the palace for voicing opinions that were not true about women. Tamar still hated Father for it, even if it was disrespectful to hate the dead.

The horn sounded again. *Whoooh.*

Tamar grinned. The army was marching onto ships in the harbor.

She ran toward the door of her room, leaping over a low ivory couch as the red sandstone beneath her feet shook and a white bottle-necked vase quivered atop a mosaic display table across the room.

"Where are you going in such a hurry?" Paruhi called, starting after her.

Tamar stopped with her hand on the door, her cheeks pink with excitement. "The army is sailing for Eromor today!" she shouted above the noise of the horn. She glanced at Paruhi, grinning. "And I mean to be with them!"

#

"You know that as royalty we can't fight, Tamar," Paruhi said softly six hours later.

Tamar watched the roaring, lyon-crested purple sails of Zarcayra's war ships unfurl with sharp snaps in the harbor below. She and Paruhi stood on a narrow balcony that overlooked the harbor, the Brothers' setting fire lighting the sandstone around them in hues of red and orange and gold as the twin suns sank toward the distant tan line of the mountains of Khayn in the west.

I should be on them.

The ships glided out of the harbor in a long double line, their sails' sigils gleaming gold and orange as the sky blazed five different shades of pink.

The thought to turn away crossed Tamar's mind, but it would have been admitting defeat in a way, and she would never admit that. Mother may have refused her request to go with the soldiers to Eromor, but she would still watch the ships sail.

The distant noise of the crowd gathered by the harbor below rang up to the balcony, echoing in Tamar's ears as the ships' horns bellowed again.

"You shouldn't be fighting anyway, order of the queen or not," Master Maigar, Zarmeyr's teacher, had said when she had stormed out of the throne room. "You're just a woman, and a girl of sixteen, at that." She probably shouldn't have hit Master Maigar in the nose then, but he had made her so furious!

A girl of sixteen, hah! She knew that, given the chance, she could fight as well as any boy her age, and women were more than capable of standing up against men in open combat.

Tamar caught a glint of gold on the docks below—Mother's golden lyon crown. She had opted to watch the ships sail from the palace instead of with Mother and the rest of the court and city at the harbor. After Mother's refusal to allow her to join the army, she didn't feel like being around her or the court.

"It's not like you know how to fight, either," Paruhi said quietly, breaking their silence.

Tamar didn't look at her. "I would be trained, and all one needs to fight is quick hands and feet, strong arms and a sharp mind."

Paruhi didn't say anything.

The wrongness of it all was that other women were being allowed to fight. Girls the same age as her were on the ships right now, sailing for Warulan and Eromor, sailing for victory and heroism and adventure and freedom, everything that Tamar had ever wanted.

Mistress Ahani had told them stories when she had been at the palace, stories of women heroines all over Argdrion who went on great adventures and fought and explored and were something. Something besides subservient wives who bore children and hid in their husband's shadows their whole lives. That was what Tamar wanted to be, not a slave under a master but a heroine who made a name for herself. Someone to be remembered, to be told about in stories.

Paruhi placed a tentative hand on her arm. "I know that you are upset about not going, Tamar, but I would miss you horribly if you had gone with the army... Besides, I don't want to face the crowd at my nameday party tonight alone."

Tamar didn't look at her sister as a cooler breeze promising the coming night fanned their hijabs and brought the faint ding of ships' bells to their ears.

I should be on those ships... She had waited two hours to see Mother, who'd been in a meeting with the Erāyn Khan and the Guardian Council discussing the details of Zarcayra's attack on Eromor. Two hours for what she had been sure was going to be a yes. But Mother had not even looked at her when she had finally gotten a chance to speak, had not even looked at her to say no.

"But you decreed that women can fight in the army!" Tamar said, trying to keep her tone even.

"Yes," Mother replied, still not looking at her as she gave instructions to Vyzir Dsamihur. "But that is for ordinary women, slaves, commoners. You are a princess, and your place is here."

No, it isn't, Tamar thought darkly as the last of the ships glided out of the harbor and the crowd slowly started moving back into the city.

My place is on the ships, with the rest of the soldiers.

"I don't really understand why you want to go so much anyway," Paruhi said, trying again. "Fighting and getting wounded, not to mention the chance of dying far from home and family. What is so desirable about that?"

At least I won't have people telling me what I can and can't do constantly...

"And besides," Paruhi said, "Mother might need us now that she is Queen of Queens."

"Mother will never need us, Paruhi," Tamar replied stonily. It was mean to say it and would hurt Paruhi's feelings, she knew, but it was true. Mother had shown them little more attention than Father had growing up, and now that she was Queen of Queens, she showed them even less. Zarmeyr was the only royal child who had ever gotten attention from either of their parents.

Paruhi didn't say anything for a while, and Tamar began to feel bad when her sister spoke again. "Do you miss him, Tamar? Father? I feel like I should. I did cry at his funeral, but I don't miss him now, not like I thought I would... Do you think I'm evil because I don't?"

Tamar watched the royal party that had seen the ships off as they started back toward the palace. "No," she said quietly. Father was the one who was evil, and if Paruhi was evil for not missing him, then she must be Setaron, for there was not a day went by that she did not smile because he was gone.

Paruhi was silent again. "Zarmeyr misses him," she said after a while.

Tamar frowned darkly. Yes, Zarmeyr would miss Father. He had always been his favorite, if Father could have had favorites, and every day of every year growing up, he had made sure to remind them of that. At first it had bothered her, when they were children, but then she had come to not care, just as she had come to realize that Father didn't love her and that she didn't care that he didn't.

She wished that Zarmeyr had died with their father. It wasn't nice, but she was mad at the moment, and she did.

"Tamar?" Paruhi asked, touching her arm again.

"I should be on them," Tamar said as a horn blew from one of the ships below. "I should be on the ships."

"But…"

"I should be on them," Tamar said forcefully.

Paruhi sighed and pushed away from the railing they leaned on.

Tamar listened to her footsteps fade away into the palace.

She stood on the balcony until the Brothers sank to seemingly rest on the rooftops of Sussār, watching the last of the ship lights fade into the distance until the Eastern Sea swallowed the vessels up into its vastness.

"I should have been on those ships," Tamar whispered darkly as lanterns and torches began popping into life over the city. The noise of musicians warming up in the palace behind her for Paruhi's party caught her ear.

But if not on those, then why not another?

Tamar glanced at the docks far below and the bobbing vessels in the harbor in front of them. A slow smile crept across her face beneath her black hijab.

Yes, why not another ship?

#

Laughter echoed out over the garden, along with the slow, gentle strums of ouds and sitars.

A guard shifted in the shadows by the sandstone wall surrounding the palace grounds, and Tamar crouched down next to a statue of Drisahr Aruyn, holding her breath. She watched the man for a moment before pushing away from the statue and hurrying to a cherry tree that sat closer to the wall.

It had taken her over three hours to get away from Paruhi's party, first because she had to at least make an appearance at her sister's nameday celebration, then because an old shayra had caught her ear and had not stopped talking about her son and how rich he was for over an hour.

Tamar had gotten away finally, though, with the excuse of a headache. She'd hurried to her rooms, sending her slaves away with the reason that she wanted to rest, and then had begun hastily filling a leather shoulder bag she had snatched from the kitchens earlier. Then she had made her way into the South Garden where she stood now, waiting for the guards patrolling the walls to look away so that she could climb over the wall and get out into the city.

More laughter drifted through the garden, and Tamar leaned against the trunk of the cherry tree, the rough bark pressing into her bare palms. She felt bad about leaving Paruhi on her nameday, but she couldn't stay at the palace the rest of her life, twiddling her thumbs while she waited for a husband to come along. She wanted freedom and excitement, and tonight she was going to get it.

The guard shifted again and looked toward the palace as the music changed to a sharp, high-pitched melody. Tamar darted for the wall and a lanky wild pear tree beside it. She didn't know why the South Garden had not been trimmed and cleaned so that its trees did not offer visitors ways to get over the wall, especially after the assassin had killed Father, but she was thankful that it was not, for getting over the thirty-foot-high structure was the main obstacle in her plan.

The guard was still looking toward the palace. Tamar secured her bag over one shoulder and reached for a low-hanging branch on the pear tree and pulled herself up and into its foliage.

It would be easy to get to the docks once she got out of the palace, and once there all she had to do was find a ship bound for Warulan and sneak on board.

A thorn on a branch stabbed into her finger. Tamar hissed and held her breath as the guard glanced in her direction.

The guard eyed the tree for a moment before turning and looking back toward the lights of the palace again.

Tamar stuck her bleeding finger in her mouth and started climbing once more. Once she was in Warulan, she would find out where the army had landed and make her way to them to join their ranks as a commoner. It was a beautiful plan, one that made her heart beat faster.

She came even with the wall, the rough stone rising out of the semidarkness like a sentinel. The city lay beyond, glittering with thousands of torches and lanterns and candles as the Sisters made their slow nightly journey across the sky.

Tamar stretched a foot out for the wall. The branch she was holding on to gave a loud crack, and she sucked in a scream as the other branch she was standing on bent under her weight.

The guard drew his sword with a shing of metal against leather. "Who's there?" he called, starting toward the pear tree.

Tamar jumped toward the wall, latching onto the top with her fingers and hanging there as the guard's footsteps drew closer.

The guard stopped in front of the pear tree, sand crunching under his feet as he scanned the dark branches.

Tamar pressed her face against the roughness of the wall, concentrating on not making any noise.

The guard stood there listening for a few moments before sheathing his sword again and muttering to himself, moving off.

Tamar pulled herself up and on top of the wall. She had chosen the South Garden because it had trees growing close to the wall, but also because she had seen from a palace window earlier a hay cart with a broken wheel parked close to the outside of the wall.

The cart was still there, yellow hay glowing softly in the silvery light of the Sisters.

Tamar stood on top of the wall, tensing her muscles for the jump. The cart was a good four feet away from the wall, wooden tongue resting on the cobbles of the street.

Footsteps crunched in sand in the garden behind her, and she glanced over her shoulder and through the branches of the pear tree.

Another guard approached the one by the wall—a replacement. Neither one had noticed her yet. Tamar looked back at the wagon. It was now or never. She jumped, flailing her arms out as she neared the wagon. She hit it in the middle, hay puffing up around her as she sank down into the cart's middle.

A dog barked in a walled yard on the opposite side of the street as Tamar climbed out of the cart. She grinned. Jumping to the cobbles below, she hurried off for the docks.

She stopped at an intersection of three streets several hundred yards from the palace, scratching at hay inside her tunic as she peeked around the dirty stucco wall of a shop closed for the night.

No one was in any of the streets, so Tamar darted down the one to her left. She kept to the shadows as she ran, glancing over her shoulder every few minutes to make sure she wasn't being followed. She half expected palace guards to come running down the street any minute, shouting, ready to take her back to the palace and a life of boredom. But no guards came, and she made it the two miles to the docks without seeing anyone.

Dark water lapped at the sunbaked pillars of the creaking docks as she crept onto them, filling the air with gentle clapping noises as it licked at the aged wood and released its sweet, rich smells to the night.

Tamar glanced behind her again as she moved farther out onto the docks, pulling her bag higher up on her shoulder. She stole into the maze of barrels, cotton bales, and boxes of assorted sweet and tangy-smelling spices that littered the ancient wood.

Hundreds of ships and boats rested, creaking in the dark water of the stretching harbor, some the size of houses and some so small that they would fit only three men.

Tamar scanned the harbor. She hadn't really planned how she would find a ship that was sailing to Warulan, just that she would.

Ehurayni, there are so many of them. And how do I get out to them? Tamar spotted a few tethered rowboats bobbing in the water directly in front of the docks. Maybe she could take one and go out among the ships, looking for ones with foreign markings that indicated them as traders.

Footsteps tapped on the wood of the docks. Tamar glanced up quickly and, judging they were heading her way, hurried toward a rowboat. She slipped over the side of the dock and dropped into the boat, pulling a canvas tarp over herself as the footsteps clicked closer and closer.

The steps stopped in front of the rowboat. Tamar held her breath, the rough weave of the canvas scratching her nose.

A man grunted, and a moment later the rowboat rocked as he dropped down into it.

Tamar gripped the leather strap of her bag.

Ehurayni, help him to not see me, please!

The boat rocked again, and oars dipping into the water a moment later caught Tamar's ear. She felt the boat moving forward, the heavy breathing of the man as he pulled at the oars sounding from a few feet away.

The rowboat stopped its steady movement ten minutes later.

Tamar waited as the man secured the oars in their holders and tied the boat to the side of a ship. She heard him move up a ladder a few moments later, the rough creaking of the rope mingling with his grunts and heavy breathing. When his footsteps faded above her, she threw back the tarp.

A medium-sized ship sat in front of her, dark sides rising up into the star-filled night sky in splendid glory.

Tamar disentangled herself from the tarp and moved to the front of the rowboat, grabbing ahold of the rope ladder.

The main deck of the ship was deserted when she climbed over the railing, but lantern light shone from the captain's cabin at the front of the ship, and voices drifted up from the crew below decks. She crept to the window of the captain's cabin, peeking in at the heavyset man pouring himself a glass of wine. He was the man who had rowed her to the ship. Tamar could tell by his quick breathing and the sweat on his brow.

A door in the cabin opened, and Tamar ducked back out of the window as a ebony skinned slave came into the room with a platter of food. "Your dinner, sir," the slave said, setting the platter on the heavy desk in the cabin.

The captain grunted. "Tell the men to quit playing at cards and get to sleep," he said in a rough, croaking voice. "I want them up before five tomorrow, readying the ship for sailing."

"Yes, sir," the slave replied, glasses clinking as he cleaned up the desk.

Tamar chanced another peek through the window.

"We'll set sail before first light," the captain said, refilling his glass with wine. "I want to make Kaymaar by nightfall tomorrow. We've got a small shipment to pick up, and then we'll be off for Eromor."

Eromor! Tamar's heart leapt into her throat.

"Eromor?" the slave said, voice troubled. "I thought that trading had stopped with them since King of Kings Vosbarhan's death."

"Maybe for everyone else," the captain replied, grinning and showing several missing teeth, "but that's where we'll make double the profit that those fools who are running goods to Warulan's other kingdoms are."

The slave nodded and moved out of the room, and the captain turned toward the window.

Tamar gasped and ducked back away from it again, plastering herself against the wood of the cabin as the captain came to the glass and peered out at his ship. Kaymaar, located west of Sussār, would be a slight delay... but Eromor! It would save her time to be set down directly in the kingdom, and from there it would be easy to find the Zarcayran army and join up with them.

The captain moved away from the window. Tamar hurried off across the main deck of the ship.

She climbed through an open hatch and down into the hull of the ship, slowly moving among barrels and boxes and bags of goods as her eyes adjusted to the darkness.

The first place she found to hide was covered in rat droppings, but the second was clean, although small, and concealed just enough from view so that she could see who was walking by without being seen in the process.

She was headed to Eromor. Tamar bit back a laugh as she squeezed between two ceiling-high stacks of crates and into the small, dark hole between. She set her leather satchel on the damp wood next to her and pulled her knees to her chest, tunic stretching over them. She was headed to Eromor to join the army. The thought sent a thrill through her veins like nothing else ever had. She grinned into the darkness and rested her head on her knees.

Mistress Lorrig be hanged, she wasn't going to be a boring old shayra. She was going to be a war hero.

CHAPTER 25

The Unknown Voice

Four years after Father died, I had my chance to change into a skinchanger body.

"We expect they'll come from the north." Lord Acknor, King Edomur's new right-hand man, looked up at those of us around the rough-hewn table, his bearded face thin, tired. We were all tired during those days; the war had sucked the life from us, taken our years. I was twenty-one since the winter, and already I felt thirty.

"We should never 'expect' that they will come from anywhere," I said. I had advanced since Father's death, earning myself a name that, although I was young, made the older lords and ladies listen to me. "Remember in the Battle of Eysran, we thought they'd come from one direction too."

I did not have to finish. Everyone remembered Eysran. A pass through the Astarion Mountains in the west of Warulan, Eysran had cost us over thirty thousand in one day and had been a battle that we were still feeling the effects from years later.

"Lord Sythorn is right."

Everyone in the ragged army tent bowed as King Edomur pushed through the tent flap. Two knights followed him, a woman and a man. "We should never underestimate the enemy." King Edomur looked at me, sky-blue eyes as piercing as ever. "I fear that this action has been your fault of late, my lords and ladies," he said, his gaze moving on from me.

"Your Majesty?" Lady Loriyl said. An old family from the eastern forests, the Loriyls were a straight-faced, serious group that looked at war like they did their business of alemaking. There was always a profit to be made—one just had to look close enough to find it.

"Let me speak plainly," King Edomur said, advancing to the table and glancing down at the spotted map that lay on it. "We've been losing too many battles lately, my lords and ladies." He glanced up at those around the table, silver brows accentuating his eyes. "Cawforn, West Marsh, Whitegate. The wiar may have seemingly deserted their allies, but the skinchangers, although less crafty, are still beating us like they did in the First and Second War." He didn't have to raise his voice. Those around the table felt his words in the stinging way they were meant.

"Well, in part, Your Majesty, it's due to the witches and warlocks," Lord Acknor said softly. "Ever since they demanded more money two months ago and refused to help till they got it…"

"I thought we paid them already," King Edomur said.

Lord Acknor was quiet for a moment, and I felt the uneasiness in the tent. "You instructed me to bargain with them, Your Majesty," Acknor said, wiping a hand across his bloodshot eyes. "We did. For three days straight, but an agreement of funds could not be reached. They kept asking for more aray than we could afford, and I thought it best to let them wait without it for a while in the hopes that they would agree to our sum."

"And did they?" King Edomur asked.

I heard the displeasure in his voice, barely perceptible, and felt a twinge of pity for Lord Acknor. Lord Acknor was growing old, though, and perhaps it was time a new right-hand man to the king was chosen. I hoped that it would be me. As right-hand man, I would have access to prisoners of war and the chance that I had been waiting for: to change into a skinchanger body.

"No, Your Majesty," Lord Acknor replied, "they have not."

King Edomur nodded. "I want whatever amount of funds they ask given to them," he said quietly. "We cannot afford it, I know," he went on as Lord Fray opened his mouth to object. "But we also cannot afford to lose the support of the witches and warlocks. Not yet, anyway. This war is far from over, lords and ladies, and until it is, we will have to continue to make uncomfortable and painful decisions."

Lord Acknor nodded and turned to a servant with whispered instructions.

"Tomorrow I leave for the kingdom of Seyrwyth to meet with the rulers of Seyrwyth, Dyridura, and Visguroth," King Edomur said. "We will discuss a plan to help end this war. I pray to the gods that we will be successful."

"I will pack my bags, Your Majesty," Lord Acknor said as the servant he'd been talking to left the war tent.

"No," King Edomur said softly. "I'm afraid, old friend, that it is time for you to retire."

A small spark of interest ignited in me as the lords and ladies broke out in murmurs. King Edomur was going to pick a new right-hand man.

King Edomur raised a gloved hand for silence. He moved to Lord Acknor, the other lords and ladies parting for him. "Your service has been invaluable, Willym," Edomur said, "but you are not the young man that you once were, and I am afraid that this war has taken its toll on you."

There was a stiffness in Lord Acknor's posture, but his face looked almost relieved.

"Go home, my lord," King Edomur said, placing a hand on Acknor's shoulder. "And rest. If all goes well, you will not have to come back to this pit of the underworld again. Lord Sythorn." King Edomur turned to me, and I felt the eyes of all turn. "Pack your bags. You will travel with me to Seyrwyth in the morning."

I bowed my head and said, "Thank you, Your Majesty."

The king moved back out of the tent, and my heart beat steadily quicker. I did not care for the influence and money that being right-hand man to the king brought, as I knew many did, but this was perfect.

The lords and ladies began filing out of the war tent, and I followed, pulling my chainmail gloves on as I stepped out into the Brothers' afternoon rays. I looked up at the dusty camp, filled with glinting weapons and crying wounded. I was one step closer to my skinchanger body.

One step closer to defeating death.

#

We reached the kingdom of Seyrwyth five days later, trotting into its half-ruined capital just after sundown.

I followed King Edomur up a long flight of gray stone stairs, the swarming city spread out below us. Seyrwyth had been hit hard at the beginning of the Third Great War, but although its lands had been nearly devastated, thousands still clung to its main city, waiting for victory or death.

A middle-aged man greeted us at the top of the stairs. He wore a glinting gold crown wrapped around his head and was missing his left arm at the shoulder.

"Tylon," Edomur said as we moved past flickering torches set in brackets in the stone on either side of a rounded doorway. "It is good to see you alive."

Tylon sounded familiar, and I placed him as the King of Dyridura as we followed a servant with a torch down a deserted hallway.

Two queens waited for us in a circular stone meeting room of the palace, Queen Alistar and Queen Dussa of the kingdoms of Visguroth and Seyrwyth respectively.

"King Edomur," one of the queens said, stepping forward as we entered the room and offering Edomur a black-gloved hand. She had long red hair and a burn mark that marred half of her aging face.

"Queen Alistar," Edomur replied, taking the offered hand and shaking it briefly.

I followed Edomur to the makeshift table sitting in the center of the room, a half-broken door balanced atop crates.

The meeting went on for hours. Maps were unfolded on the door, and papers with reports of news from over all of Argdrion were read. Everywhere, we were losing battles. Ennotar, Oridonn, Warulan, Araysann… the list of battles we had lost on each continent was endless.

"If we could gather enough troops to make one large assault here," King Edomur said, placing a finger on the map by Lake Grayl, "where they gather in force, it could change the tide of the war on Warulan."

"Yes, against us," said Queen Dussa, a hawk-faced woman with black hair and blacker eyes.

"Or for us," King Edomur said, glancing up at her. "Our reports of the skinchangers' numbers are that they are weakening, and with our armies combined, and the silver that King Tylon has been pulling from his new mine, I believe that we can slaughter them."

"And if we don't?" Queen Alistar asked. "We cannot afford a blow that great without victory, King Edomur."

I grew restless as the fourth hour of the meeting ticked by on the brass pocket watch I had inherited from Father, and a decision was still not agreed upon. As the fifth hour began, I excused myself to attend to my pressing bladder.

"Third door on the left," Queen Alistar told me as conversation paused. "Careful that you don't go in the second—that's where we're keeping our skinchanger."

I promptly forgot about the restroom. "You have a skinchanger here, Your Majesty?" I asked, my heart beating faster.

"Yes," Alistar replied, leaning over the current map spread out on the door. "A younger male. We're hoping with the right persuasion he will give us information of his people's plans."

I nodded and bowed, then left the meeting room. A skinchanger, not one hundred feet from me. I pulled *Spells* from underneath my chainmail tunic and glanced around the dark, deserted hallway. If I put much stock in the gods and goddesses, I would have believed that they were helping me.

I tried the second door of the hallway, but it was locked. I had expected it to be, but after a few moments with my knife jiggling around in the keyhole, I got it open.

The room on the other side was dark, eerily so. I had the nagging thought that maybe the creature was waiting for me, but knowing that Queen Alistar would not leave it unchained, I pushed the thought away and shut the door behind me.

I felt on either side of the door and found a torch, striking a flint from my pocket. The torch popped to life, and the room became clear.

I took a step backward as a skinchanger appeared in the semigloom, chained to an iron ring in the middle of the room. The creature stared at me, its eyes green like moss. I had never seen a skinchanger in its natural form alive before, only as whatever animal the ones I fought in the battles chose to change into. The one before me looked like the dead bodies that we collected and burned: naked, muscled, and covered in swirling black tattoos.

The skinchanger had long, straight brown hair that reached past his wide shoulders, and his arms were covered with red burn marks and scars over the tattoos.

I stepped closer, eyeing the silver chains stretching from his ankles, wrists, and neck to the iron ring in the floor. I doubted that he spoke my language, and no one could learn the complicated languages of the skinchanger, but I didn't need to talk to him, just figure out how to place my soul into his body.

I put *Spells* on a wooden stool that sat several feet away from the skinchanger and held the torch up, circling him. He didn't turn with me as I walked around him, but he was listening to my footsteps, and I saw that his muscles were straining. He had to be in considerable pain, for any small amount of silver that touched the creatures was said to feel like having molten lead poured on you. With all the silver he had chained to him, I was surprised that the skinchanger was still awake. I would need to remove it after I killed him, as well as put my clothes on his body. His face was young, like Queen Alistar had said he was, but it was not covered in tattoos, so it would make it easy to get out of the city if I kept my head down and my cloak up.

I had thought of the fact that after I changed into a skinchanger body I would be a hunted creature, but I was confident that I could live in the deep forests behind Castle Sythorn and not be discovered. The temptation of the longer life of a skinchanger was too great to worry about anything else. Satisfied with my plan, I pulled my knife from my belt and went for the skinchanger's throat.

What went wrong with that first attempt to transfer my soul into the body of another creature, I do not know. But as I said the last of the heart spell and fell to the floor, writhing in pain, it was obvious that I had not performed the spell correctly. I lay there for I know not how long, the smell of my and the skinchanger's blood stinging my nose, the coldness of the stone floor chilling my body.

The kings and queens were still deep in discussion when I, after having cleaned myself of blood with water from the pump in the bathroom, returned to the meeting room. I saw by my watch that I had been gone for almost an hour. I must have looked as horrid as I felt, for King Edomur stopped talking and glanced at me.

"Are you all right, Lord Sythorn?" he asked, blue eyes showing concern in the light of two tallow candles they had lit on the door.

"Yes," I said, feeling like I was looking at the world through a haze.

I fainted then. The last thing I saw was King Edomur rushing toward me.

I was told when I awoke three days later that King Edomur's coup had been successful, and that the skinchangers had been deeply wounded. I felt little joy at the news. My attempt to change into another body had failed, and I was still headed toward death.

CHAPTER 26

Nathaira

A cat howled loudly, and Nathaira's head shot out of a barrel of garbage by the noisy tavern's back door as the sound echoed up the dark deserted alley. Soldiers coming? She glanced around with feverish eyes, but the shadows crowding the narrow street were quiet as a cloud concealing the Sisters drifted away and the three moons' silver glow sparkled on the damp cobbles.

Nathaira went back to digging through the reeking barrel. It had been nine hours since she escaped from the arena, six hours of hiding and waiting until darkness had fallen over Crystoln and three of wandering the massive city's backstreets, trying to find her way out.

Nathaira's fingers closed around a stiff rind of bread, and she pulled her hand out of the assortment of fish heads and bloody bones crowding the barrel and shoved the food into her mouth. The rind tasted like rotten plants and dirt, and her stomach immediately jumped toward her throat as she chewed it, but it was food, and she forced herself to swallow. She had lost too much blood in the last nine hours, her body needed some kind of nourishment.

After sliding under the gate and into the tunnels beneath the arena, she had changed into a nighthawk and following her memory and senses, made for the top. She knew the Sisters had been helping her, for she had only seen one patrol of guards, and ten minutes after delving into the maze of stairwells, doors, and tunnels underneath the arena, she had reached the courtyard above.

A soldier had been at the gate as hundreds of screaming, panicked arenagoers shoved and pushed each other out of the courtyard outside and into waiting carriages, but he had been so busy trying not to get trampled underfoot that he had not even noticed her.

Footsteps echoed from the other side of the tavern door, and Nathaira glanced up quickly as a bolt unlocked with a heavy click.

The scarred tavern door swung inward.

She ducked into the darkness, the dirty shirt and trousers she had taken off the body of a dead drunk to hide some of her tattoos flapping around her.

A boy wearing a stained white apron stepped out into the narrow alley, murmuring under his breath as he dumped a fresh bucket of table scraps into the barrel. Golden light and loud laughter from the tavern room behind him spilled out into the alley as he slapped at the bucket.

Nathaira watched the boy from her hiding spot behind a stack of broken crates, her eyes hurting at the light.

The boy slapped the bottom of the bucket one last time, muttering the whole time. He turned and stepped back inside the tavern.

Nathaira slipped out of her hiding place as the sound of the bolt locking echoed through the shadows. She turned and hurried off up the alley.

Her feet stumbled over an uneven stone in the road, and she winced as pain shot through her back, arm, and leg. Warm blood seeped down her pants and onto her foot, she put a hand to her leg.

A dog howled nearby.

Nathaira glanced over her shoulder at the shifting darkness. Nine hours of freedom and still she was no closer to Efamar than she'd been that morning. She had thought it would be easier to find her way out of Crystoln.

Tears of anger pricked at the backs of her eyes, exhaustion pulling at her with whispering hands. The Sisters may have helped her escape the arena, but it certainly didn't seem like they were helping her now.

Nathaira looked up at the cloud-dotted sky as another wispy cloud drifted over the three moons. She would have to trust that they were, though, and that she just couldn't see it yet.

Laughter echoed ahead of her, and Nathaira veered down a side alley as drunken feet scraped on cobbles.

She had used the humans' panic at the arena to her advantage, joining a flock of passing sparrows and flying unnoticed to the lower city. From there she had hidden as one of the stray dogs frequenting the city's cobbled streets and alleys. As time had worn on, though, and she lost more blood from her wounds, her power had begun to weaken, and her body had shifted permanently back into her normal shape. She had been left creeping through the alleys powerless, tired, and fading.

Nathaira scanned the dark stone buildings on either side of her. Now she had no more power than if she were a human. She also had no idea of where she was. Everything looked the same: tall stone buildings, narrow streets, deserted doorways.

Her stomach rolled as she stumbled underneath a vine-wound stone arch stretched between two rock buildings, and Nathaira gasped as sudden pain tore through her, like a knife sliding into her flesh. Bile built in her throat. She leaned over and hurled the bread up, crying out as the retching motion caused her wounds to hurt again and fresh blood to seep out of them.

A door creaked on rusty hinges.

Nathaira staggered onward, throat burning with the acrid taste of bile.

The alley turned abruptly and sloped downward in a series of narrow, uneven stairs, and Nathaira moved closer to the wall to steady herself as she slowly climbed down them. If she could just find an abandoned building or empty barrel to hide in… The soldiers were everywhere, though, and if she stopped, even for a moment, they would find her and drag her back to the arena for beheading or burning or something far worse.

One of her legs wobbled underneath her, and Nathaira leaned against the warm stone wall of a tall building shadowing the alley. She stared up at the stars.

Can you hear me, Athrysion? Moirin? I know that you are watching over me, but I feel so alone. I worry that I cannot do this, that I will not find him…

The cloud covering the moons drifted north in a cool night breeze. Nathaira glanced at the Sisters. They pleaded with her to not to give up, to keep moving. Or were they calling her to them?

The distant slap of footsteps on cobbles caught her ear. Nathaira pushed away from the wall and stumbled down the last few steps of the stairwell.

She passed a doorway, and for a moment she thought she saw Moirin standing in it, beckoning to her with slender, tattooed hands. When she blinked, the vision was gone and only swirling mist remained.

Nathaira stumbled onward, the fever making her head throb.

One of the elders stood by the side of a building, her wrinkled, tattooed face following her movements. Nathaira stared at her.

It's my imagination. You're not real...

Another footstep echoed through the darkness.

Nathaira stopped.

It came again, the rasp of a leathered boot on rock.

She stumbled into the blacker shadows by the edge of the alley, peering into the darkness behind her. Nothing. Had she imagined it?

Nathaira watched the shifting shadows of the alley for a few minutes before taking a cautious step back out into it.

A man appeared in the swirling mist. Over six feet tall, he had a long black beard that reached to his waist and an empty socket where his right eye should have been.

"Hello," the man said, voice sounding like the slow, deep growl of a minotaur.

Nathaira took a step backward, fear pushing the fog of the fever away.

The man reached over his shoulder, biceps bulging, and pulled a long and dented sword from out of a sheath on his back.

Nathaira wheeled to run.

Another man, a skinny youth with oozing pimples spotting his face like the plague, blocked her path with a wide, crooked grin. He drew a short, twisting steel dagger of obviously low quality from the wide leather belt around his waist. "She don't look like no skinchanger to me, Greyr," the youth said nasally. He twisted his thin mouth into a red pucker and spat a dark, glistening gob of phlegm onto the cobbles of the alley.

Nathaira stepped back from him, turning so that she could see both men. Panic raced through her. She couldn't change right now, and she couldn't fight in her weakened state. Her only option was running, but could she run fast enough?

"She's it," the one-eyed man growled. He pointed his sword at her, and Nathaira took another step backward, swiveling to keep both men in her vision as they moved toward her.

"The posters said she's got three wounds," the one-eyed man said. "Like she does, and no human I have ever seen has tattoos like that."

The pimpled youth grinned, showing brown teeth, and held his dagger up in front of him with a gleam in his yellow-tinged eyes. "Well, then, let's finish her off and collect this reward you talked about."

"Careful," the one-eyed man rumbled. "She may be wounded, but she's still a skinchanger, and dangerous."

Nathaira glanced at the darkness of a joint alley and the fast-closing gap around her. If she was to run, she thought desperately, it would have to be now. She bolted.

A hairy hand grabbed her by the arm before she took three steps, and she screamed as her shoulder wound pulled further open.

"Hold still, skinchanger," the one-eyed man growled, face so scarred and twisted that Nathaira could barely make out the shape of it. "Just one blow and you won't feel a thing."

The pimpled youth giggled hysterically behind them. Nathaira twisted in the one-eyed man's grasp as he raised her up in the air and brought his sword even with her neck.

Sisters, help me, please!

Shing. A high-pitched hiss echoed through the alley, followed by a sharp crunch.

Nathaira stopped twisting, staring at the steel dagger point protruding from the one-eyed man's throat as dark-red blood bubbled out of his open mouth and out from the hole the dagger made and drained down his beard. The dagger melded into two as she stared at it, before going back to one as her head cleared for a moment.

The pimpled youth cursed foully.

The Sisters had heard her. Nathaira wrenched her arm out of the one-eyed man's grasp as his eye grew large. She fell to the cobbles, fresh blood from her wound running down her arm in rivulets.

The youth cursed again.

Nathaira crawled away from the one-eyed man as he crumpled to the cobbles with a gurgling grunt.

"Who's there?" the youth shouted, dagger held in front of him.

A black figure sped out of the shadows, and the youth screamed and arched backward, his dagger clattering to the cobbles.

Nathaira lurched to her feet and fled.

Doors flashed by her as she reached an intersection and dove down the alley to the right, her breath coming in burning gasps that pierced her lungs and made her head sway. She raced through a fog of silver mist, heading down a flight of stairs lined with shadows.

Her right leg connected with an unseen board. Nathaira cried out at the fresh pain and put her hands out as she pitched forward into the shadows.

She hit the stairs on her chest, rolling over and over down the hard surface until she landed on the street below.

White dots swam in front of her eyes. Her chest felt like it had caved in.

Nathaira felt the cold stone of the street pressing into her face, felt her nose stuck in a crack between two cobbles.

It was the footsteps that finally roused her, so soft that she thought she'd imagined them.

"There're not many who hear me coming," a smooth male voice said.

Nathaira raised her head—a pair of black suede boots stood a few feet away. She sucked in a breath, gasping as pain threatened to blind her. Another human. A soldier, perhaps, or maybe just a citizen wanting the reward on her.

The boots bent, and a lean, black-clad man with a dark cloak that shadowed his face and pooled on the cobbles around him came into view. "I would give you a hand up," he said, "but I doubt you could stand at the moment."

Nathaira moved one hand under her, every muscle screaming at her to run.

"I'm actually surprised you were able to make it this far," the man continued as casually as if he were discussing the weather, "considering the amount of blood you've lost." He loosely pointed a slender finger at her shoulder wound, which was flowing openly, before resting his forearm on one knee.

"If you're going to kill me," Nathaira whispered, her head feeling like a forest fire was raging through it, "do it." She saw Zeythra standing a few feet away, silver hair flowing past her hips as she stared up at the stars.

"That seems pointless," the man said, a black ring on his right middle finger glinting dully in the moonlight streaming through the mist around them. "Considering you'll be dead from blood loss in under an hour."

Nathaira glanced up the man, a cool night breeze fanning his cloak out around him. He wore all black—pants under suede boots, leather vambraces over a shirt. For a moment she wondered if he was real or if he, too, was part of her hallucinations.

"I can heal you," the man said, voice soft, even.

Nathaira slid her other hand underneath her. He was lying. He was probably going to kill her and collect the reward on her head. She wiggled her legs slowly, testing to see if she could run on them. But if the man was going to kill her, then why hadn't he already done it? And why would he bother telling her he'd help her?

"Why?" she asked, her voice a hoarse whisper. "Why would you help me?"

The man looked up at the Sisters, then glanced back down at her, the darkness of his cowl still concealing his face. "Because you interest me."

Nathaira swallowed, her throat parched. If the man was telling the truth, it could be her only chance to get out of the city and find Efamar.

But he's human, and humans killed the clan and took Efamar. Sisters, what do I do?

Another cloud drifted over the three moons, throwing the alley into darkness again.

Zeythra disappeared, only to be replaced by Athrysion bending over a fire as he gutted a fish.

Nathaira felt blood trickling down her back and leg, between her fingers. The man was right. If she did not get help, she would bleed to death. And she could not die, not yet, anyway. She had to save Efamar.

"I will accept your help, human," Nathaira rasped after a moment. The words tasted like poison on her tongue. "But if you betray me," she whispered, glancing up at the man through blurry eyes, "I will kill you."

The man held a half-gloved hand out to her.

CHAPTER 27

Hathus

The slender tallow candles adorning the center of the elegantly arrayed table sizzled loudly as the *Daemon's Cry* leapt over a wave and hot wax fell in white drops onto the silver platter of broiled lobster underneath.

Hathus, chin in one hand, stared at the burning lights intently as the flames rocked from side to side with the rolling of the ship, then steadied and burned straight again. He didn't want to be here; his stomach felt like it would come up his throat at any minute. And if he kept listening to the bullshit that Wylam Caine was feeding the rest of the dinner party, it would.

Hathus leaned back in his wooden chair, which was carved with mermaids, as Caine's voice grew low to match the mood of his story. "I knew that I wasn't going to get out of that world alive if I stayed and listened to their song much longer…"

Hathus resisted the urge to snort.

He's making it up off the top of his white head. There were otherworlds, yes, history spoke of them, but they were just empty worlds with no life in them, and Caine's stories of worlds with flying horses or half-human, half-octopus creatures that lured in travelers with singing was ridiculous.

Hathus put a hand to his stomach as it lurched uncomfortably again and reached for the glass of wine by his plate. As promised, there was roast lobster, but that wasn't all. The cook had served up a luxurious dinner of white cream soup, roast lamb, chocolate pudding, sweet rolls, and spiced green beans. Hathus sipped at the wine, focusing on the dark-red liquid and nothing else as his stomach rolled again.

I shouldn't have eaten so much. But when they had started their dinner several hours before, the sea had been calm, only becoming rough and rocking in the last half hour.

"Then what did you do?" Sidion asked in his lilting accent. He was seated to Hathus's left in a red-velvet cushioned chair, dreadlocks streaming over his shoulders. Sidion leaned forward, the chair creaking.

Caine's voice grew low. "There wasn't much I could do with seven of them around me."

Hathus rolled his eyes and glanced out the dark windows behind Blackwell's head. The moons had risen over an hour ago, and the jumping water outside glowed silver and white in their white light. Hathus watched an especially large wave bow before the prow of the ship following them.

He hoped that they were not in for a storm.

The *Daemon's Cry* had been through two earlier in their voyage, and both times he'd spent the day with his head over the saytr chamber pot in his room. He knew the wickedly smiling creatures on the pot so well now that he could remember the number of hairs on their heads.

Azaria, perched as usual on Blackwell's shoulder, caught his eye, and Hathus resisted the urge to throw a sweet roll at the monkey as it crossed its emerald eyes at him and stuck out its narrow pink tongue. The creature knew that he hated it and took every opportunity to rub it in his face.

Hathus glanced around the table at the others. Sidion, sitting to his left and Caine's right, smiling at a joke the worldwalker was telling. Bathia listening intently to Caine from his other side. Blackwell silently stroking Azaria's head at the opposite end of the table. Even Godet, hovering in the shadows by the door with a silver platter of crystal glasses and expensive wine, was listening to Caine's stories.

Hathus picked at the boiled green beans on the gold-rimmed plate in front of him with a detailed silver fork and wrinkled up his bony nose in disgust. He'd always hated vegetables. Even his imprisonment and near starvation could not make him like the mushy pieces of foul-tasting food.

Who wanted vegetables when one could have bread or meat? It was like asking for water when you could have wine. Hathus shoved the long beans under his half-eaten mashed potatoes, the sight of them making him sicker.

"Still eating, Mr. Ryrgorion?"

He glanced up at the worldwalker's voice. "No," Hathus said shortly. "Just playing."

"Watching you throughout dinner," Caine rasped, "I would say that you hadn't eaten in months."

Hathus narrowed his eyes at the worldwalker.

"Hathus has a healthy appetite," Sidion said, teeth flashing.

Caine smiled blandly. "Yes, of course."

"What about the winged horses?" Bathia asked. She was dressed in a black leather corset over a red silk shirt and looked more beautiful than Hathus had ever seen her. "Did you keep the men on the ship from killing one and bringing it back to Argdrion?"

Hathus reached for his crystal wineglass again as Caine went back into his story.

Why does he care so much that I was in the dungeons? The creepy son of a... Hathus took a vicious sip of the wine. It went down the wrong pipe, and he started coughing furiously.

Everyone looked at him.

"Are you all right, Hathus?" Sidion asked in his lilting accent.

Oh, yes, I just like choking to death, it's so much fun.

"Try taking a sip of wine," Bathia offered, her kohl-painted eyes etched with concern as Godet hurried over with a glass of water and a towel to wipe up the mess.

Hathus shook his head and pointed at the wine to signal that it was what he'd choked on.

"Try some water, then," Bathia said.

Godet offered a sparkling glass of water.

Hathus waved the freckled cabin boy away and pushed his chair back from the table with a scrape. "I'll be fine," he choked out, coughing. "I just need some fresh air." He turned and stumbled from the room, the cool night air stroking his face as he shut the door softly behind him.

The main deck was empty except for two pirates taking their turns on watch and another turning the wheel on the poop deck. Hathus crossed the deck and climbed the well-worn stairs, coughing all the way to the forecastle deck without being hailed by anyone. He wiped at tears with a white silk handkerchief.

A soft wind blew his lank hair and dark leather coat out behind him and filled the daemon-faced sails of the *Daemon's Cry*.

Hathus breathed deeply of the salty smell of the breeze as a sail cracked sharply above him. At least now he didn't have to listen to Caine anymore. He didn't know why he was letting the worldwalker get to him so much. It wasn't like it really mattered if Caine knew he'd been in prison.

Hathus leaned on the railing, coughing a little. The clouds covering the Sisters drifted apart, and the three moons' white light glittered like diamonds on the dark water around the ship.

He wondered what it would be like to be a moon, sitting up in the sky watching everything happen below like a god. If the moons could think, were they wondering what he was doing right now? Hathus sighed. He did. He'd wondered ever since he'd begun pretending to look for a mythical land.

He glanced up at the three sister moons—Uatara, Rohiri, and Jophus—and leaned his chin on one hand. He'd always felt sorry for Jophus, the smallest and farthest away of the moons. She seemed so lonely and sad sitting off by herself to the right of her two larger sisters.

Did she feel like he did? That she was just a pawn being dragged around by the will of others? Or was she content in her position? Hathus sighed again and looked back down at the swiftly moving black water beneath him, curling away from the bow of the *Daemon's Cry* in thick sparkling waves.

Laughter echoed up from the back of the ship.

He glanced behind him and at the light spilling out from the hallway leading to Blackwell's cabin.

I hope Caine chokes on a lobster claw...

The *Daemon's Cry* slowed noticeably, the rocking waves smoothing out into flat black water.

Hathus looked back at the darkness in front of them.

A soft light flickered off to one side of the *Daemon's Cry*. Hathus frowned. Another of the pirate ships? But no, they were all behind the *Daemon's Cry*, and who had green lights anyway?

Hathus paled.

It can't be a kingdom fleet, not this far out.

The light flickered again, and he frowned. It looked like… fog, only green fog. A light, gold-tinged green.

Hathus moved to one side of the deck to get a better look, his hand trailing over the polished epharia-wood railing. Yes, it certainly was fog, rolling toward the pirate fleet out of the moon-dappled darkness in swirling, wispy waves.

Hathus grabbed a rope hanging down from the rigging above, the coarse material scratchy against his palm, and stepped up onto the railing to get a better look.

"What is it?"

He almost fell overboard. "Don't do that!" he hissed as one of the watchers, a scar-faced woman with long blonde hair, moved to the railing next to him.

"Sorry," she said. "But what is it?"

Hathus glanced back out at the approaching green mist, arm curled around the rope. "I don't know. But I've never seen anything like it," he murmured. It made him uneasy.

The woman pirate moved closer to the rail, hand on a massive curved sword at her left hip. "Neither have I, but it feels evil."

Hathus glanced down at the woman, prickles running up his spine. A breeze, cooler than the ones that had brushed the decks of the *Daemon's Cry* earlier, fanned their faces and blew the pirate's long hair against his boot. He looked back at the approaching fog.

"Did you hear that?" the female pirate asked, straining over the railing as the other watcher—a young man with a face pockmarked from fever—climbed the stairs behind them.

"What?" Hathus asked, listening for a sound above the water hissing by the *Daemon's Cry*'s hull and the rigging creaking above their heads.

I don't hear a damn thing.

"It sounded like a child," the woman pirate whispered.

Hathus glanced down at her again, the hair on the back of his neck slowly standing on end.

What if it was the Land of Dragons, he wondered worriedly. But why would there be a child in the Land of Dragons?

What am I thinking? The Land of Dragons isn't real…

The wind blew harder, whistling past his ears, and he suddenly caught the faint but distinct wail of a cry.

"There!" the pockmarked younger pirate said, coming up next to them.

"I heard it," Hathus whispered, contemplating going below decks.

"Go warn the lookout in the crow's nest, Wyon," the woman whispered to the younger pirate. "There may be another ship ahead. We don't want to run into them."

Wyon nodded and hurried off, and the wind grew stronger, snapping the sails and moaning through the rigging like a living thing.

Hathus pressed closer to the rope as it blew his coat out behind him, soaking through his clothing like icy water. A sail above his head cracked loudly, and he looked up at it.

"Do you smell that?" the woman pirate asked, sniffing the air.

Hathus looked back out at the approaching fog. A strange, sickly smell tickled his nose, a smell like death. He swallowed, unease turning into fear.

What in the gods' name have we gotten into?

A tendril of fog blew past, and Hathus followed its movements as the soft green mist wound through the railing and snaked across the decks. More fog followed, blowing over the sails of the *Daemon's Cry* and blocking out the Sisters' light.

"I don't like this," the woman pirate said softly, pulling her sword out of its sheath. "It isn't natural."

Hathus held a hand up as a strand of fog floated by. He gasped as it sailed through his fingers, leaving his flesh feeling like it had been burned by ice. His body grew suddenly deathly cold. "Perhaps we should turn back," he whispered, sticking his hand inside his coat to try and get warmth back in it.

The other pirate ships were not visible anymore, and the fog was growing thicker.

"Shh!" the woman pirate hissed. "There it is again." She moved around him and cocked an ear to the wind, and Hathus quickly jumped to the deck beside her and did the same, pulling his coat tighter around him as the fog crept across the deck and passed through his thin cotton shirt and gripped his bones with icy hands.

A child's cry, closer this time, drifted to them on the wind again, and a tickling chill ran up Hathus's spine. There was something about the voice that didn't sound right. Perhaps it was the fog or his keyed-up imagination, but it didn't sound human. It didn't sound alive.

"Hello!" the woman pirate called out next to him.

Hathus grabbed her arm. "Are you insane?" he hissed.

The pirate glanced at him. "There's a child out there!"

"We don't know that!"

The pirate pulled her arm away from him. "We've heard its cry. There's a child out there and it needs help." She stepped away from Hathus. "Hello!"

"Don't."

Hathus jumped at the raspy voice and turned as Caine, Bathia, Sidion, and Blackwell moved up to the railing next to him.

"But there's a child out there that needs help!" the woman pirate exclaimed, turning toward them.

"A *child*?" Bathia said, glancing into the fog around them. "Are you sure, Droisis?"

"The only thing that needs help out here is us," Caine said quietly, peering into the fog with his one blue eye.

Hathus glanced at Caine. What did he mean, they needed help? He took a sideways step away from the worldwalker.

Sidion spoke up. "We should hail the other ships so that we don't run into each oth—"

A man's scream, hair-raising and otherworldly, echoed from the other side of the ship, and everyone but Caine jumped and wheeled as wind whistled through the rigging above them with a scream of its own.

"What was that?" Bathia whispered, pulling two straight daggers from her belt.

"Souls," Caine rasped, his ghostly blue eye darting around the ship at a rapid pace. "Trapped in a portal between this world and the next, never allowed to leave either to go on to the afterlife."

Hathus's face whitened, panic spreading through him as he realized suddenly how very high up and out in the open they were on the forecastle deck. "How is that possible?" he whispered.

No one heard him.

"How did the souls get in the portal?" Bathia asked, gripping her knives as she peered around them into the swirling green mist.

"Shipwrecked trying to world hop," Caine said. "And when you die in a portal, you can never leave it."

"There's a portal near here, then?" Sidion asked in his lilting accent. He pulled his scimitar from the sheath on his hip with a dull hissing noise.

Caine nodded. "There used to be," he wheezed. "It was destroyed in the Hunting. All that's left now is the remains and the souls."

"Will they bother us?" Blackwell asked softly.

Caine glanced at him. "Only if we bother them. Don't hail them," the worldwalker said, looking around the ship decks again. "And don't touch them. They don't like to be reminded of the fact that they're trapped and others are not. If they are, they will try to take you with them. And believe me, you don't want that."

Hathus pulled his coat tighter around him, feeling sick. He'd heard stories of ghosts before, souls of the dead that were attached to this life in some way that wouldn't let them leave for the next. His mother had told him that she saw the ghosts of those executed hovering near the executioner squares on rainy days. He had always prayed he wouldn't see them.

The fog grew thicker around them, making visibility off the decks impossible, and more and more voices echoed through the mist as the *Daemon's Cry* drifted deeper into the fog.

Hathus thought he heard a man yell "Turn back!" and another "There's death ahead!" but he couldn't be sure because of the wind moaning through the rigging. A cold, damp wind that oddly didn't fill the black sails of the *Daemon's Cry* with its breath.

"Mommy," a child's voice, faint but distinct, called from the fog to their left. "Mommy, I'm scared!"

Droisis stepped toward the noise.

"What are you doing?" Hathus hissed in a panicked whisper. He grabbed the woman pirate by the arm as she passed. "You want to bring them all down on us?"

"I have a child," Droisis hissed, turning toward him. "And I would hope that someone would help her if she needed it."

"It's not real," Caine rasped. "That child has been dead for hundreds of years."

"But what if it is not?" Droisis asked, glancing at the worldwalker. "What if you're wrong, and there is a ship out there with living people on it who need our help?"

"I'm not wrong," Caine said.

"Listen to what he says, Droisis," Sidion said in a low voice. "He knows what he is talking about."

Does he? Hathus wondered. Caine was the one who had brought them this way, right into the soul's arms.

"Mommy!" the voice called again, quivering and filled with fear.

A chill ran through Hathus at the note of desperation in it. He'd heard that desperation before, when families had been ripped apart during the wars and the Hunting and children had roamed the streets as orphans.

"Mommy, why am I so cold?"

Droisis pulled away from Hathus roughly and stepped over to Caine. "What if you are wrong?" she hissed.

The worldwalker's eerie blue eye turned toward her. "There are no ships of the living out here but us," he rasped.

"Mommy, I can't swim," the voice cried, louder this time.

Hathus glanced at Bathia. Her dark lips were drawn and thin. "Maybe we should turn the ship around," he whispered to no one in particular. He thought about going belowdecks, but the cabins were on the opposite side of the ship and he would have to walk to them alone. It was probably safer with the pirates and Caine.

"Mommy, help me! Please help me!"

"Oh, I don't care what you say!" Droisis moaned. "I can't let a child call for help and not answer! Over here!" she yelled, running toward the side of the ship. "Over here, little boy. Swim toward us and we will help you!"

"NO!" Caine yelled. "Stop her!"

Hathus lunged after Droisis as she ran for the railing. He caught a glimpse of Sidion beside him as the female pirate leaned over the side of the ship and yelled "Over here!" into the swirling green fog.

A boy, white as the moons, with rivulets of water running down his clothes and face, appeared out of the mist in front of the pirate.

Hathus skidded to a halt, heart hammering.

What in the gods' names…

Droisis stood transfixed, staring at the boy.

"Don't let it touch her!" Caine yelled behind them. "It will use its power of fear to draw her away!"

For a moment, nothing happened. The child stared at Droisis, water dripping off it, and Hathus wondered if perhaps the worldwalker's fears were unnecessary. But then Droisis stepped toward it, hand outstretched, and the soul grabbed her arm. She gave a bloodcurdling scream, and the soul pulled her over the railing and into the fog.

"NO!" Sidion yelled.

Hathus started after Sidion as he ran to the rail, not wanting to be alone. Water glistened on the black wood where the boy's feet had touched it.

"Drisahr Aruyn, where is she?" Sidion cried.

They peered into the fog as the other's ran to the deck behind them, but there was nothing but swirling green mist and wind.

Hathus took a step backward, fresh fear rising in him. He wanted to be back in the dungeons. The dungeons had been safe, if horrible, and at least the only death he would receive in them was from starvation, not from otherworldly monsters cursed for eternity.

"We have to help her!" Bathia cried frantically as she reached the rail. "Sidion, order a boat!" Bathia wheeled toward the second mate, and he turned to go, dreadlocks swaying.

Caine, looking up at the fog above them with an expectant expression, put a hand up to stop him.

Wind screamed through the sails, and the creaking iron lantern hanging by the top of the stairs went dark as the gust tore through the ship.

Caine looked over his shoulder at the darkened lantern. "She is beyond our help," he whispered.

Hathus met Caine's eye.

"They will come now," the worldwalker said quietly.

#

A soul, mouth open in a piercing cry, lunged out of the fog.

Hathus screamed and dropped to the deck as the otherworldly creature flew over his head, an ice-cold sensation prickling his skin as the soul sailed through the spot where he'd been standing a second before.

A thousand more screams filled the fog-shrouded air. Souls darted out of the fog on all sides of them.

"Get fire!" Caine yelled above the high-pitched wails. "They are afraid of fire!"

Hathus threw his arms over his ears to block out the screams as another soul, a young girl, flew through Wyon's body.

Wyon staggered sideways like he'd been stabbed, his skin slowly turning the color of snow as the soul whisked away. He fell backward to the deck with a thud, mouth open, eyes staring unseeing into nothing.

Hathus screamed again and shoved the dead man's cold arm off him.

Caine raised his hands into the air, and with a string of unintelligible words, balanced a ball of blue fire between them.

If Hathus had not been so terrified of the souls, he might have been terrified of the magic. Bathia and Sidion pulled flint and steel from their clothes. Hathus started crawling across the forecastle deck toward the stairs.

A soul hissed past him. He ducked and crawled faster, the yells of the crew coming up on the main deck to see what the noise was all about mingling with the cries of the darting souls.

Oh, gods, we are all going to die. Hathus rolled sideways as another soul flew by, white dress dragging on the deck beneath it as it hissed along. He glanced over his shoulder as Caine's fire burst into a raging inferno.

A soul heading toward the worldwalker screamed and darted over the side of the ship at the light, and more cried out as if they'd been burned as the fire reflected off the swirling fog and lit the night-black sails above with a ghostly glow.

Hathus started crawling again, the rough, wet planks of the deck digging painfully into his hands and knees. A splinter stuck in his hand, and he cursed, pulling it out. He continued crawling, more screams from all the ships ringing through the air.

Wylam Caine had known this was coming.

Hathus glanced back at Caine again. The worldwalker's scarred face was lit with a bluish glow as he held the fire in his hands out toward the attacking souls.

He had talked as if he had known about the destroyed portal with its souls caught in it and yet failed to mention that they were sailing towards it. Why? Did he want them to all die?

A group of pirates, eyes filled with determination and fight, charged up the stairs in front of him. Hathus crawled toward the railing as they tore by, waving swords above their heads and yelling battle cries at the top of their lungs.

A screaming soul, the same boy who had dragged Droisis away, tore toward the oncoming pirates, and with an ear-piercing scream, flew through three of them before they knew what hit them. Hathus blanched as the pirates hit the deck with respective thuds and stared lifelessly into nothing. He scrambled to his feet and dove down the stairs two at a time, the remaining pirates following him with terrified screams. He took off across the deck.

"You can't kill them!" an aging pirate with wispy yellow hair yelled from his position by one of the masts. "Weapons have no effect on them!" The man waved his sword wildly around his head, blue eyes wide and crazed. "Nothing can stop 'em! We're all dead men, you mark my wor—"

A soul, water dripping off her hip-length black hair and thin muslin dress, dove out of the green fog shrouding the sails overhead and tore through the man before he could finish his sentence.

Hathus lunged toward the hallway under the stairs, Caine's words of "Get fire, fire scares them!" ringing in his ears.

Blue fire lit up the sky from the upper deck as his hand closed around a flickering lantern swinging from a nail in the hallway, and he and several pirates nearby glanced upward as flames caught in the sails of the *Daemon's Cry*.

"They're standing against them on the forecastle deck!" a female pirate with one eye yelled. "Captain, the first and second mate, and that worldwalker. Let's go up there and help them!" She tore off up the stairs two at a time, three pirates trailing after her as the sails crackled and burned.

Hathus made to follow.

Wait, what in the underworld am I doing? he thought wildly. He stopped, glancing around at the pirates falling to the deck.

A pirate with a yellow bandanna tied around his dark curls fell down the stairs from the poop deck with a thud, eyes staring unseeing up at him. Hathus took a step backward. He wasn't going to risk his life for a bunch of pirates, or anyone, for that matter.

A soul darted down from the forecastle deck and raced across the main deck, screaming.

Hathus turned and ducked into the hallway, swinging the lantern in front of him like a sword.

Wood creaked behind him.

He wheeled as footsteps thudded overhead. The cabins. He needed to get to the cabins. He turned and hurried down the hall, scanning the doors on either side of him as he went.

Blackwell's cabin had too many portholes. His had one, and according to the layout, so should Bathia's. But Sidion's, situated between Bathia's and the stairwell, should have none.

Hathus stopped in front of the dark epharia door, testing the L-shaped handle, then pushed inside.

The second mate's cabin was smaller than his and had no furniture to hide behind besides a simple bed draped with a dark-blue quilt and a heavy, iron-braced trunk with a jade statue of the head Araysannian god Drisahr Aruyn atop it, but there were no portholes for souls to come through and a heavy bolt on the door. It was perfect.

Hathus shut the door behind him, blocking the bulk of the screams out. He slammed the bolt into place and moved over to the bed, the lantern throwing eerie circles of light on the room's black walls.

"Cowardly, aren't we?"

Hathus jumped at the voice and swore as Azaria appeared from behind the trunk and hopped up onto the bed. "How in the underworld did you get in here?" he hissed.

Azaria grinned, needlelike teeth flashing in the lantern's flickering gold flame, and settled on the well-worn quilt next to him. "Blackwell left me here to keep me safe."

Hathus shifted over so that the monkey's long white tail didn't touch his hand and balanced the lantern on one knee.

"Couldn't take trying to be brave anymore?" Azaria asked, glancing sideways at him with shining emerald eyes.

A scream rang down from the deck above, and Hathus pulled the lantern closer to him with a shiver, his hands shaking slightly. "I have no idea what you're talking about, monkey," he murmured, glancing up as a thud echoed through the cabin.

Gods, don't let me die, please. I'll do anything you ask...

"Oh, I've seen you strutting around like you're a brave man, trying to impress Bathia," Azaria said, digging intently through the hair on his foot with his hands.

Hathus glanced sideways at the monkey, opening his mouth to tell it to fuck off. He stopped as another moaning cry, followed by a thud, echoed down from the deck above. Would there be any pirates left when the souls got done with them? *If* they got done with them...

"The plain fact of the matter is, Hathus Ryrgorion," Azaria went on, seemingly unaffected by the screams and thuds of the dying ringing down from above, "that you are a selfish, uncaring coward. I saw it in you the first night you boarded the *Daemon's Cry*. I can tell traits in people, you know, it's one of my many talents."

Hathus glanced at the monkey. "Leave me alone, magic rat," he spat.

Azaria grinned. "So, you don't deny it. That means I was right."

"No, you're not right," Hathus hissed. "I just find my time more valuable than talking to a monkey."

"But you're talking to me right now," Azaria said, looking back at his foot.

Hathus grimaced as an especially heavy thud resonated down through the ceiling. "Fuck off."

Azaria grinned again and pulled a squirming black flea off his foot, threw it into his mouth, and smashed it between his teeth with a loud crunch.

Hathus felt his stomach turn. He didn't miss the days of eating those.

"You probably had a bad home life," the monkey said while chewing the flea. "Maybe your father was abusive? Or perhaps gone a lot?"

Hathus didn't look at the creature. "My father was an asshole who beat me half the time and was gone the rest."

"Sad," the monkey said, shaking his head.

Hathus glanced up as running footsteps pounded over their heads.

A heavy object hit the deck with a loud thud a moment later, and he jumped as a long, low wail rang through the air.

Gods, how had he gotten into this mess? He pulled the lantern closer to himself as more muffled yells and wails rang through the cabin.

"You won't get very far with Bathia, you know," Azaria said. "Being a coward, I mean."

Hathus glanced at the monkey out of the corner of his eye. "Who says I want to 'get very far' with her?"

"Oh, I've been watching you," Azaria said. "Believe me, she won't have anything to do with a coward. Her father was a coward, you know, left her and her mother in Eromor when the king's men came looking for him. Her mother spent three years in prison for her husband's crimes and only got out when Bathia raised enough money by being a pirate to bribe for her freedom."

So that's why she didn't want to talk about her father. Hathus stiffened as another wail echoed down from above. "She know you're telling everyone her life secrets?" he asked.

Azaria grinned, white cheeks pulling back from his pointed teeth. "I know everyone's secrets on the ship—it's a favorite pastime of mine."

Hathus glanced at the monkey. "That's weird."

Azaria shrugged. "It's something to do. Life can get boring around here, as I'm sure you've found out."

Well, that was one thing they had in common. Hathus glanced up as another thud shook the ceiling above. At the moment, though, he'd give anything for those long, boring days at sea again.

The soul was in the room so fast he barely had time to register it was there.

A high-pitched wail pierced the air as it sailed through the door like the wood wasn't a solid barrier. It raised a hand in front of its face and shied away from the glare of the lantern.

"Holy shit!" Hathus yelled, the springs of the bed groaning in protest as he jumped up on it and backed toward one wall of the cabin. Azaria dove behind his leg in a blur of white.

The soul, a young woman with short, water-soaked blonde hair and lifeless green eyes, darted back and forth in front of the circle of light the lantern gave off, screaming at a piercingly high pitch.

Hathus held the lantern out in front of him like a sword. He backed up further toward the wall.

The soul continued to dart forward and shy away, still screaming.

"Oh gods, what do we do now?"

"Don't ask me," Azaria whimpered. "I'm just an animal."

Hathus could have kicked the monkey, but it would have required him to take his eyes off the soul, which was watching him like a cat its prey, and he thought that probably wasn't a very good idea.

Oh, my gods I'm going to die.

The soul screamed louder.

Hathus blanched, and something warm and sour smelling trickled down his left leg.

Azaria cursed and jumped away from him. "I'm the one who should be pissing!" the monkey yelled. "I don't have the light!"

"Well, what in the underworld do you expect me to do?" Hathus yelled back, holding the lantern out again as the soul made another dart for them. "You said it yourself, I'm a coward!"

"Well, I didn't think you were a pissing coward!" Azaria screeched.

"I'm scared, okay?" Hathus yelled.

"So am I!" the monkey yelled back.

The soul flew closer, and Hathus held the lantern out further. He was going to die. They both were going to die. He fleetingly wondered if he could give Azaria as an offering when the lantern sputtered and flickered.

The blood drained from Hathus's face. "No," he whispered, shaking the light as it wavered and steadily grew dimmer. "Gods, no!"

The soul, sensing that his defense was dying, hissed and rushed closer.

"Do something!" Azaria yelled frantically, grabbing Hathus's arm and shaking it roughly as the light grew dimmer and shadows began closing in. "Make it burn again!"

"I'm trying!" Hathus screamed, shaking the lantern harder and praying to every god and goddess he could think of for divine help. The light sputtered and grew brighter, and for a blissful moment he thought some benevolent being had heard his prayer. But then the lantern popped like a hot nut, and the room went as dark as ink as it blew out.

Oh shit.

The soul tore forward.

Hathus sensed more than saw its dim shape flying through the air toward him, and with a yell, he blindly threw the useless lantern at it.

Azaria squealed, white fur flashing as he leapt off the bed.

Hathus dove to the floor. He landed on his left shoulder, but he barely noticed the pain that raked through him as he rolled toward the door.

The soul screamed in the darkness behind him.

Hathus reached a hand up for the bronze handle of the door.

Gods damn it, it's locked! He felt for the bolt above it. It was locked as well.

The soul screamed and tore toward him again, and Hathus hissed and rolled to the side, icy fingers of air brushing against his skin as the soul swept past. He felt for the door again as the soul whirled away from him.

The jade statue shattered on the floor with a crash as the soul darted around the room. Hathus lunged to his feet and scrambled for the door as it let out another scream. His fingers reached for the bolt to push it back, latched onto the cold iron.

Blinding, icy pain shot through his left hand.

Hathus gasped and staggered backward as the soul flew away from him.

He glanced down at his hand slowly, a freezing wave of ice creeping out from it and through his body. White, his hand was turning white. Even in the darkness, he could see it.

Hathus blinked, shocked, as the snowy color crept up from his fingers and danced along his palm. It looked like frost creeping over glass.

The soul screamed at him again.

Hathus turned as it wheeled, frost creeping through his veins and turning his blood to ice. The room was spinning.

Why was the room spinning?

The soul started forward, translucent white arms outstretched, mouth open in a scream.

Hathus fell to his knees, ice dancing in the edges of his vision.

He was vaguely aware of a faint clicking noise as the screeching soul sped toward him before fire lit up the cabin in a blinding flash of yellow and he plunged into an ice-cold oblivion.

CHAPTER 28

Darkmoon

Darkmoon's balled knuckles made contact with the fighter's jaw, and stained teeth went sailing as the sweaty, shirtless man flew backward and landed on his back in the sand.

The crowd gathered around the fighting pit—a mixture of thieves, middle-class nobility, whores, rent boys, and lowlifes—went wild, filling the air with roars of approval.

Coins flashed in the light of several cast-iron candelabras as bets were made. The candelabras, seven feet across and holding over three -hundred fat yellow candles each, creaked as they swung gently back and forth from the wooden beams overhead.

Darkmoon wiped sweat out of his eyes with the back of one hand. The only thing besides killing that kept the voices and memories of his past away was the fighting pits in the underworld districts of most of Argdrion's major cities. That and the skinchanger.

Darkmoon narrowed his eyes as his opponent, a massive, bald-headed man with scars covering every inch of his muscle-lined body, slowly climbed to his feet. After he had killed the two men trying to kill the skinchanger, he had followed her with the aim to kill her too. But when he had reached her, he had found out something extraordinary and puzzling. When he was with the skinchanger, the voices stopped. And the visions and memories.

He felt a bead of sweat drain down between his bare shoulder blades.

Every instinct had told him to kill the skinchanger, but he had wanted to know why the voices stopped around her and had offered to help her instead.

The fighter growled and slammed his fists against his chest in a threatening motion. "You'll pay for that, Darkmoon," he snarled. "You may be the best assassin in Argdrion, but here in the pits?" The fighter grinned cockily. "Boyrs rules, and Boyrs isn't afraid of anyone. Do you know what my name is, assassin?" The fighter leered.

Darkmoon glanced at the chanting crowd. "Boyrs, Boyrs, Boyrs."

"Let me guess," he asked sardonically. "Boyrs?"

The fighter spat a mouthful of blood to the side as more ran down his hairy chest, not noticing the sarcasm. "You're learning, Darkmoon," he said. "Maybe you'll even walk out of here alive."

Boyrs was annoying, and it would be fun to kill him. Darkmoon spread his arms wide and bowed mockingly low to the fighter, the night-black claw on the black cord around his neck dangling down in front of his chest. "I'm sure that I will," he said. "And I'll be wiping the streets with your hideous face."

"No one wipes the streets with my face," Boyrs snarled savagely. His black eyes glinted in the hanging candelabras' light as grains of sand fell off his tight-fitting brown trousers.

Darkmoon straightened, the claw bouncing back against his left pectoral. He shrugged. "Well, then, your ass. It makes no difference to me."

"Bastard!" Boyrs roared, foam flying from his mouth as he surged forward.

Darkmoon waited until the fighter was three feet away from him and he could see the stitch lines on the man's thick head before rotating slightly on one bare heel and stepping out of the way.

Boyrs sped by in a flurry of spit, blood, and sweat, eyes widening as he found he had no object to stop his mad run with. Cursing, he stumbled and fell facedown in the sand.

The crowd cheered again, more coins flashed.

Darkmoon turned. He had taken the skinchanger to a brothel that he often frequented and whose owner he knew quite well. There he had healed the skinchanger's extensive wounds and left her to rest, going back out in the streets to think. The voices had started again almost as soon as he'd left the skinchanger's side, whispering in the shadows, calling on the wind.

A brown-haired woman by the edge of the arena yelled out his name. Darkmoon glanced at her, narrowing his eyes against the light. She waved frantically at him. "I love you!"

He glanced back at Boyrs. Being the best assassin in Argdrion caused him to have many admirers, fans who followed his work and sent letters of adoration to his mansions. He'd bedded a few of them before and killed numerous others. Tonight, he was not in the mood for the former activity.

Boyrs growled, climbing to his feet again. "Is this how you kill so many, by running away and refusing to fight them?"

"I am not running away from you," Darkmoon said softly. "Nor do I refuse to fight you. I am right here. Come get me."

Boyrs roared and lunged forward again. Darkmoon stepped to the side as he ran past again, and the man barreled by in a flurry of sand and sweat.

His time spent thinking in the streets had yielded no answer as to why the skinchanger stopped the voices, so he had come to the pits to fight. It annoyed Darkmoon that the voices stopped around the magical creature. Annoyed him because his own efforts to quell them were failing. Until her. How could a creature make his past fall silent when he could not? Was he growing weak?

Boyrs charged at him again, and Darkmoon brought a forearm up and smashed it into the man's mouth. Blood and more teeth spurted everywhere; the crowd roared their approval and took up a new chant. "Darkmoon, Darkmoon, Darkmoon."

"Take me!" the brown-haired woman screamed. "I'm yours, Darkmoon!"

Darkmoon didn't look at her.

Boyrs wiped a scarred arm across his bleeding mouth and spat a tooth into the sand at his own feet.

"Boyrs will beat your face into the sand!" Boyrs snarled, spit and blood flying out of his mouth.

"Or Boyrs will die screaming in agony," Darkmoon replied.

Boyrs snarled, spittle flying from his mouth, and lunged forward again.

Feigning a left punch, Darkmoon slid to the right as the man blocked to the left and jumped into the air, delivering a roundhouse kick to the scarred fighter's head with a crack that echoed through the domed cavern of the fighting pit.

Boyrs reeled backward, and the crowd fairly fell out of the stands as they screamed with a savage fury.

"Brother…" Cyron said.

Darkmoon sprinted forward again before Boyrs could recover. Running up the fighter's thick back, he flipped over the man's head and delivered another kick to the muscled man's left ribcage before landing lightly in the sand in front of him.

The crowd cheered as one at the crack that resonated through the air. Darkmoon caught the sound of bones snapping in half as Boyrs shrieked.

He smiled softly.

"Brother…" Cyron said again.

Darkmoon glanced at the dark shadows above the rising stands around the pit. His brother and mother watched him. The smile faded from his face at the tears streaming down their cheeks.

"You're a bastard!" Boyrs coughed, blood seeping out of his mouth and trailing down his cheek in a bright-red stream.

His family disappeared. Darkmoon glanced back at the fighter. The rib he'd broken had damaged something internally; he could tell by the color of blood draining out of Boyrs's mouth. The man would be dead in a couple hours. It wasn't good enough, though—he needed to kill him now, needed to drive away the memories.

The crowd still chanted his name, the pulsing sound shaking the blood-splattered sand and unloading more dust from the wooden beams that supported the tavern floor above.

Darkmoon moved toward Boyrs, sand scratching against his bare feet.

The fighter looked up at him when he drew near.

"Bastard," Boyrs spat again, grimacing as another cough shook his body.

His vocabulary is sorely lacking, Darkmoon mused. He glanced up at the chanting crowd, sweat trickling down his chest and back. He didn't know what he would do with the skinchanger, now that he had saved her and healed her. But he did know that it had a been a foolish mistake to help her. Skinchangers were a race bound up in and revolving around honor, and when someone saved their life, they stayed with that person until the debt was repaid. He didn't want the skinchanger with him. He didn't want anyone with him.

But she had stop the voices...

"You know what I think?" Boyrs coughed.

Darkmoon glanced back down at him, the chanting of the crowd almost deafening.

"I think that you're a coward," Boyrs said, squinting up at him with a leer. Most of his front teeth were gone. "Did you hear me, Darkmoon? You're a coward." Blood bubbled out of the fighter's mouth, draining down his chin and dripping onto the sand.

Darkmoon looked at the crowd again.

"A damn fucking coward," Boyrs spat, coughing again. "Always running away when I get close to you and dodging in when my back is turned... You're a damned coward, and you don't fight like a man."

Darkmoon knelt on one knee in the sand in front of Boyrs. "Few people are brave enough to say something that like to me," he said quietly.

Boyrs sneered and grimaced as more blood drained out of his mouth. "Well, I am. What have you got to say to that, Darkmoon?"

Darkmoon glanced at the roaring crowd again, one arm resting on his knee. "I'd tell you you're right."

Boyrs frowned. He'd clearly been expecting a different reaction.

"I don't fight fair." Darkmoon looked back him. "Because if I did, you would have been dead three seconds after I walked into this arena."

The sneer faded from Boyrs's face, replaced by the realization that he was going to die. His eyes met Darkmoon's. Darkmoon grabbed the fighter's jaw and the back of his head with both hands, and in a lightning-fast move, snapped the man's neck in half.

The crowd went deathly silent.

Darkmoon stood, brushing sand off his pants.

"Brother, please..."

Boyrs, eyes still open in shock, fell forward into the sand with a thud.

The crowd erupted into an ear-shattering roar.

Arena workers jogged out to collect Boyrs's body.

Darkmoon turned his back to the crowd and, pivoting on one heel, walked to the stone wall surrounding the pit. He pulled himself up and over, the crowd's cheers filling the air behind him in a pulsing, vibrating tune.

"You fought beautifully, darling," a brown-haired prostitute purred. She wore a tight-fitting sleeveless gold dress with openings that ran down the sides and showed her ribcage every time she moved. She sidled up next to him as he moved to the bench where he'd left his weapons and clothes.

Darkmoon picked up a stained white cotton towel from off the bench and began rubbing the sweat off his chest as behind him another set of fighters entered the arena.

"I don't think I've ever seen something so… mesmerizing," the prostitute purred, watching his movements hungrily.

Darkmoon threw the towel on the bench and grabbed his shirt. "I don't want your services tonight," he said coldly.

The prostitute raised an eyebrow. "Who says that's what I want?"

"It's your business," Darkmoon said, pulling the shirt over his head and tucking it into the waist of his suede pants. He reached for his half gloves and vambraces. "Just like mine is killing."

"Help, me, son, help me…"

Darkmoon whipped his cloak around his shoulders and picked up his many belts from the bench.

The prostitute shrugged and made to move off.

He grabbed her arm and stepped up behind her. "I'm missing a knife," Darkmoon whispered in her ear. "If you don't want another one in your stomach, I'd give it back."

The prostitute stiffened against him, inhaling sharply. "I just wanted it for a souvenir," she whispered, voice fearful. "A keepsake of the great assassin Darkmoon."

Darkmoon almost drove a knife into her back, but a rent boy and woman moved past him and stopped a few feet away, kissing in the shadows of a pillar. If he killed the prostitute, he would have to kill them too, and then the guards lining the outer walls of the pit, and then the arena attendants removing Boyr's body… A killing spree would drive the voices away, he knew, but he had business to attend to upstairs.

He buried his sharp nose into the prostitute's neck. "Give it back," he whispered.

She jumped and reached a shaky hand into her dress. "Here." She held the knife up over one shoulder.

He took it and stepped back, shoving her away.

The prostitute fled.

"Brother..."

"I forgive you, my son..."

Darkmoon wound his weapon belts around his torso and hips and pulled the hood of his cloak over his head.

The crowd grew louder as the fighters in the pit started their dance. He moved past the rent boy and woman and to a set of aged stone stairs.

#

The fighting pits of Crystoln were run by the underworld lords of the city, with each one having several pits in his or her possession, and each one fiercely trying to rival the other.

Darkmoon walked along the stone deck ringing the upper half of the cavern the fighting pit lay in, the cheers of the crowd below him shaking the stones beneath his feet. He wasn't picky about which fighting pit he went to, but tonight his selection had been more than just a passing whim.

He glanced over the ledge at the new fight going on below. The underworld lord who owned this particular pit, N'san Hor'ayn, was an old acquaintance of his and owed him money for a job he had completed two nights before of killing a rival underworld lord.

Darkmoon paused at a curtained alcove in the wall of the cavern and pushed aside the red curtain and slipped inside.

The thick, dusty cloth muffled the sound of the fight outside as it slid back into place behind him.

It was said that N'san Hor'ayn was the richest man in Eromor after the king, and indeed, dressed in a floor-length tunic of gold-stitched red silk, golden slippers, and enough jewels to supply the financial needs of three kingdoms, the underworld lord looked it.

"Darkmoon, my friend!" the dark-skinned, overweight underworld lord boomed as Darkmoon moved to a round wooden table the lord sat at and slid onto the bench opposite. "So good to see you again!"

N'san grinned widely, and Darkmoon saw a small sliver of his reflection in the silver teeth filling the underworld lord's mouth. He put one foot up on the dark wood of the bench and rested his forearm on his knee, long fingers dangling loosely.

"Never could get over that addiction could you, N'san?" Darkmoon nodded at the golden bowl of puffy white creatures in front of the bearded underworld lord.

"Living octopus." N'san smiled. "Developed a love for them working by the ocean as a boy and haven't been able to quench the addiction yet." He reached into the bowl with a fat manicured hand and pulled one of the jiggling creatures out. A dull sucking noise filled the room as the creature's cups pulled off the sides of the bowl. N'san tossed the writhing sea creature into his mouth.

"But I am being rude, my friend!" N'san snapped two thick ringed fingers, and a silent manservant with a wide scar cutting his ebony face in half diagonally brushed through the curtain with a silver platter in his hands. "Have some chocolate, Darkmoon. We shall both satisfy our addictions together!"

The servant bowed in front of him with the platter. Darkmoon eyed the stack of dark, slightly foggy sweets in its center. "You wouldn't be foolish enough to try and poison me, would you, N'san?" he said quietly, glancing up from the chocolate to N'san.

N'san beamed. "Darkmoon, I would never poison a friend! Go on, take a piece."

Darkmoon pulled a slice of the dark substance off the platter, voices whispering in his head.

The servant bowed again and backed out of the room as silently as he had come.

"Brother…" Cyron whispered.

"So, my friend," N'san said, cutting him off. He raised thick eyebrows toward the golden turban wrapped around his head, "how can I help you?"

"You know why I'm here, N'san," Darkmoon said quietly, his insides churning as the other man loudly chewed the octopus into mush.

"Ahhh." N'san sighed. "So delicious. You really should try one, my friend." He dabbed at his short, curling black mustache with a white napkin.

"I think I'm good, thanks," Darkmoon said blandly, swinging the hand with the chocolate piece gently. His ring dully reflected the light of a lone tallow candle sitting in the center of the table.

N'san smiled widely and pulled another octopus out of the bowl. Its small, bulbous eyes seemed to stare pleadingly at Darkmoon.

"Have I ever told you that there's more to life than money?" N'san asked.

Darkmoon smiled slightly. "Yes, like employers who pay their debts off."

N'san threw his head back and let out a loud laugh, the golden rings in his ears bouncing up and down with his ample stomach as the octopus wrapped its tentacles around his hand as if trying to hang on to life for one minute longer.

Darkmoon's skin prickled. He hated N'san's laugh—it reminded him of the laugh Arayn J'altayr would give after making him kill someone.

"Ah, my friend," N'san roared, slapping the table with one hand and throwing the octopus into his mouth, "you are so right!" He bit down on the creature, and several tentacles still attached to his hand fell onto the table with soft plopping noises. "But as it is, I'm afraid that I do not have all the money that I owe you yet." N'san spread his ringed hands wide apologetically. "Times have been very hard around here lately, you see." He shrugged, his pointed beard scraping over his red silks. "I'm afraid that I just can't pay you at this time." N'san chuckled loudly like it was all a joke.

Darkmoon smiled slowly, flipping the chocolate piece along the back of his slender fingers so that it wouldn't melt. "They say that a man's life is worth more to him than all the aray in Argdrion," he said softly, glancing up at N'san. "I wonder, is that true?"

N'san chuckled, expression never changing. "I know your point, my friend." He held his hands up in front of him peacefully. "And that is why"—the underworld lord reached a fat hand into his red robes and drew out a small bag of darkest purple—"I brought this." N'san shook the bag, and the merry chink of coins ricocheted off the alcove's stone walls. "It's half of the money due. Tomorrow I expect to get money from a deal, and I'll pay you the rest then, okay?"

Darkmoon eyed the bulging bag of coins. He could kill N'san, burn down his establishment, and slaughter everyone in it. He flipped the chocolate end over end along his knuckles, Cyron's voice echoing in his mind. But there was another idea forming in the back of his mind, an idea that was strange and wrong and utterly stupid.

N'san held the bag out farther.

Darkmoon took it and deposited it into his cloak. "Keep the rest of your money, N'san," he said. "But there is something that you can do for me tonight to make up for it."

The smile faded slightly from N'san face. "That was not our deal, my friend."

Darkmoon shrugged too. "Neither was waiting for my payment, but…" He shrugged, looking at the chocolate. "Times are hard, as you said."

N'san stared at him. "What kind of something?"

"There is a woman," Darkmoon said slowly. "She needs to quietly get out of the city. I do not wish to leave Crystoln at this moment, but you know this city's secret ways out as I do and could guide this woman."

N'san continued to stare at him for a moment, before smiling widely. "Anything for you, my friend!" he boomed. "I will help this woman out of the city, and you will be paid in full."

Darkmoon dipped his head. "I will bring her to the sewers in the west factory district in three hours' time. Meet me there, and come alone."

He slid off the bench and stood. He didn't know why he was doing this. Maybe it was because the skinchanger reminded him of himself, of a long time ago, and she needed help as badly now as he had then. Or maybe it was because he wanted to be with her again, to quell the voices, and if he turned her in or just sent her back out into the streets, he had no excuse to be by her side.

N'san struggled to his feet, folding his ringed hands in front of his large stomach. "I will be there," he said.

Darkmoon moved out onto the balcony, the underworld lord following. A fighter fell to the sand below them, the crowd roared its approval.

"I heard you killed another one of my fighters, Darkmoon," N'san said.

Darkmoon felt the underworld lord look at him. He glanced up at him. "I told you: Invest in better people."

N'san smiled widely, but it was edged with annoyance. "I'll remember that, friend."

Darkmoon turned, keeping to the wall so that N'san had to walk along the edge of the balcony. Whispers followed him, murmuring in his ears.

"It was good to see you again, my friend," N'san said as they reached the top of the stairs that led to the pit below. "One always wants to know that they have friends in such times of trouble."

Darkmoon stopped, cloak hissing against the stones. "Are we friends?" he asked, glancing up at N'san. "I never thought of us as such."

N'san smiled, silver teeth flashing. "In a manner of speaking."

"Mm." Darkmoon looked down the stairs at the rent boy and woman, who were still kissing, although more passionately now.

"Help me, son..."

"I hear that Zarcayra is going to attack Eromor," N'san said in a fake hushed tone. "And that they have made their women soldiers, and now their army outnumbers Eromor's by half. Dark tidings... I wonder if the king will start a conscription."

Darkmoon glanced up at N'san. "I wouldn't worry too much about it, N'san," he murmured. "Untrained soldiers will fall under trained ones nine times out of ten, and even if Uranius starts a petition, there will always be enough lowlifes and their coin left to keep your businesses running."

N'san bowed his head. "I was thinking only of the poor families that will be torn apart, believe me."

Darkmoon snorted and started down the stairs. Torin Ravynston's plan wasn't exactly going as he wanted it to, but then, plans often didn't. He wondered how Torin was taking it.

"Watch those octopuses," he said over one shoulder. "You eat too much and you'll start to look like them."

N'san let out another booming laugh. "Ah, Darkmoon," the underworld lord called as the crowd roared loudly again. "You make me laugh, my friend!"

Darkmoon's fingers twitched as he reached the bottom of the stairs. He walked past the rent boy and the woman and tossed the chocolate into a dark corner.

CHAPTER 29

Azkanysh

"Here, Queen of Queens," the black-turbaned factory owner said.

Azkanysh glanced at the royal party around her: Shayr Khait, who owned the massive sandstone factory around and above them, Vyzir Dsamihur, Shayr Jahayan, several other shayrs who owned factories along the Akhuran River, and of course, the usual entourage of guards and slaves.

She looked back at the factory owner who stood at the top of a set of stairs, motioning for them to follow him. She started toward the man. Her first move toward encouraging the Guardian Council to vote in favor of women working in the factories was to visit the factories themselves and see how they worked.

"It would be wise to acquaint yourself with the shayrs who own the factories, as well as their managers," Shayr Jahayan had advised her during their meeting on the balcony two mornings before. "Let them see you, Queen of Queens. Listen to them tell you about their factories and learn how they are run. We want the council's approval in our favor on this matter, yes, but it would also be good to at least be on friendly terms with the factory owners so that if the council does advise in our favor, they will not feel like we came at them from behind."

Azkanysh watched a man sitting cross-legged on a pillow sew the seam of a purple tunic as the royal party moved down the stairs after the factory owner. Hundreds of men hunched over articles of clothing held in their laps on this level of the factory, their work illuminated by torches in brackets on the sandstone pillars that held the domed roof of the building up over their heads.

Azkanysh stopped, watching another man pull a needle the length of her smallest finger through a large square of black cloth that was slowly forming into a long-sleeved robe. Why was it that women were trained in the art of sewing? They were not allowed to use it by working in shops or factories. Slaves performed the tasks of mending in most households throughout the kingdom, and clothing was bought from shops. The only time women sewed was to make patterned handkerchiefs or other such trivial decorations. Busywork, Azkanysh believed it was called.

She continued down the stairs to the next level, the royal party following. She could use the fact that women were trained in sewing as an argument for allowing them to work in the factories. Maybe it would persuade the council to advise her way. She doubted it, but maybe.

Shayr Jahayan had been helping to influence the Guardian Council in the last few days, pointing out to them that women working in the factories would speed production up, increasing the building of more factories as more money was made.

Azkanysh stopped on the second level of the factory, where yards and yards of freshly dyed cloth hung drying on wooden racks. This particular factory was a clothing factory, consigned a few days before to make tunics, cloaks, and turbans for the army. Now they made clothing for the common people again, and yards and yards of coral pink and blood-red silk, honey-colored linen, and a thousand other colored cloths filled the tables stretching between pillars.

The royal party stopped behind her, and Azkanysh glanced back at them, addressing Shayr Khait. "How many articles of clothing do you produce each day, Shayr Khait?"

The lean-faced shayr stepped forward, dipping his head. "On average, eight hundred, Queen of Queens," he said, glancing around them at the milling workers. "But of course, with the shortage in laborers, we are producing much less."

Azkanysh watched as several men moved yards of dried cloth from the racks before handing them up to the men on the next level, where the sewers sat. She glanced at Shayr Jahayan, standing a few feet away with the other shayrs.

"So I have heard," Azkanysh said, starting down the stairs again. "Shayr Jahayan tells me that there are not enough eligible workers with all the men from fourteen to sixty gathering for the army."

Shayr Khait grunted in agreement behind her. "It is true, Queen of Queens. We are beginning to think of hiring the elderly, even though they will not be able to work as hard or fast."

Azkanysh stepped onto the bottom level of the factory. So, the factory owners were desperate enough to hire elderly. And if they were desperate enough to do that, perhaps they would be willing to allow women to work.

"Over here is something that might interest you, Queen of Queens," Shayr Khait said as the last of the party moved off the stairs and onto the floor of the factory. The shayr moved over to a massive iron pot suspended by iron beams over a glowing hole in the floor. "This is where the cloth is dyed, see?"

Azkanysh moved to the pot, a slave with an ostrich-plume fan following.

"We spin the cloth over there," Shayr Khait said, waving a hand at rows and rows of looms across the room. "And then we put it in here, where the dyers make it whatever color is wanted. In this one, black as you can see, for the mourning."

Shayr Khait motioned for her to look into the pot, and Azkanysh glanced over the edge at the bubbling liquid inside. Yards of cloth floated, half submerged in the roiling dye, slowly turning dark purple as sweating workers stirred the liquid with stained wooden paddles.

A large glistening black bubble burst with a dull pop in the middle of the pot. Azkanysh took a step backward. "How many workers do you have here right now?" she asked, glancing up at Shayr Khait.

"Five hundred," he replied, looking around them, "but we used to have over two thousand." There was annoyance in his voice. And stress.

Azkanysh looked around the factory again. It was one of the smaller ones on the river, she was told, and she could see that it was wanting for workers by the gaps among the men and the hurried steps and exhausted faces of the overseers. How were the larger factories faring? And how desperate were their shayrs becoming? Her eye caught Shayr Jahayan's, and the elderly Guardian Council member dipped his head slightly.

"Tell me, Shayr Khait," Azkanysh said, turning back toward the tall shayr, "would you be opposed to letting those whom you normally would not allow to work in your factories work, if it would help speed up production?"

The shayr's face grew annoyed. "I would take anyone at the moment, Queen of Queens," he said, voice tight.

Azkanysh glanced at Shayr Jahayan again. "Even women?" she asked.

Shayr Khait looked at her sharply. "Women cannot work as long or as fast as men. They would only cost me money."

Azkanysh narrowed her eyes at the shayr. "And yet you would hire the elderly, who also 'cost you money.'"

Shayr Khait's dark eyes narrowed in turn. "The elderly will not distract my other workers, Queen of Queens, will not keep them occupied with something besides their work."

Azkanysh held Shayr Khait's gaze. It was an argument that she had heard often from men in the city after she had first ruled that women were to be allowed in the army. They said that women working alongside men would distract them, encourage them to look at them and not focus on fighting.

"Women working alongside men will only cause trouble," a shayr had loudly proclaimed during a court session the day before. "We all know what enticers they are, enchantresses who lure men away from the right path and lead them into sin. It is our duty to correct them, to lead them, to guide them away from this natural-born wickedness. Allowing them to work among us as our equals will only encourage them to further practice their sinful ways. We should pray! That the gods will forgive us for shirking in our duty!"

When he would not stop yelling that Zarcayra's army was going to be massacred because of the women among it, Azkanysh had ordered the guards to remove the man from the throne room. The Guardian Council had whispered among themselves.

"I intend to rule for women to be allowed to work, Shayr Khait," Azkanysh said evenly, still holding the hawk-nosed shayr's gaze, "whether the men of Zarcayra agree with it or not."

"And I will not hire them, Queen of Queens," Shayr Khait said, voice even but tight. "Even if you do."

Azkanysh stared at him, blood burning. Ruling for women to be allowed to work would only fix part of the problem of the discrimination against them. It wouldn't fix the factory owners' prejudices, wouldn't make them see women as anything other than lesser beings who couldn't work alongside men. "And if I rule that you have to hire women," she hissed, "then you will hire them, Shayr Khait."

Vyzir Dsamihur stepped closer. Azkanysh ignored him. "I intend to bring freedom to the women of this kingdom," she hised, moving closer to Shayr Khait so that he could see the rage in her brown eyes, "and whether you and the other factory owners approve of this or not, I will do it, and you will do as I say."

Shayr Khait stared at her for a moment before bowing stiffly. His face was dark, livid.

Azkanysh swept past him, moving back up the stairs with the fan slave hurrying beside her. She had lost her temper, had not been diplomatic. Vyzir Dsamihur would be angry with her. But how could one fight against prejudices with kindness? Against discriminations with diplomacy? Vosbarhan had been diplomatic, but he had also been cruel and forceful. Maybe that was what she had to be too. Maybe that was what Zarcayra needed.

#

Two days later, Azkanysh focused on the line of neatly written black words in the book in her lap, mouth slowly forming the letters and sounds. "The white stallion runs swiftly across the desert," she read slowly. "Proud and free."

"Good, Queen of Queens," her tutor said in an uninterested voice. "Now read the next line, and try and work on enunciating each syllable more clearly."

Azkanysh glanced up at the slender bald man in his black robes. He sat, looking at a book on the table across from her, one hand resting on the pages and the other twirling a pen. A sought-after tutor of the noble families of Sussār, Master Ishkhan had a reputation for seemingly not paying attention during his lessons. He did pay attention, though, so much so that she had found that she couldn't move a finger without him knowing about it.

Azkanysh adjusted the heavy book in her lap, the musty smell of old pages and fading hints of ink assaulting her nose. She felt like a child again, trying to learn the art of needlepoint from her mother. But she was determined to learn to read and write, to become educated like the men of Zarcayra.

In Zarcayra, it was not believed that women needed to be educated—some even thought it would be dangerous for their safety, like giving freedom to sheep. It was a common saying in the kingdom that women had no more need of letters and numbers than pigs of gold and silk. Azkanysh smoothed the page of the book out, scanning ahead. She believed that women needed education as much as men, believed that the only reason men did not want them to have it was fear of their realizing that they were their equals.

"In the east we see the suns rise," she read aloud, "ready to meet the day."

Three slaves in black tunics fanned her and Master Ishkhan, keeping away the heat of the day as well as the flies and bees that buzzed constantly through the palace. Summer was still a few days off for Argdrion, but already it was blazing hot in Zarcayra, even in the heart of the palace.

The sandstone of the palace walls and the rooms around and above them kept them somewhat cooler than out in the warmth of the courtyards and gardens, but Azkanysh still felt the heat in the sweat dripping down her back and in the flushing of her skin. She wished that she did not have to wear black anymore for the extra heat it brought. But Vosbarhan had only been dead for two weeks, and there were still ten weeks to go before the court would be able to put away the colors of mourning. For a moment, she wondered if she could opt out of the mourning period and go back to cooler, lighter-colored clothing.

"Queen of Queens," Master Ishkhan said without looking up, "you are focusing too much again on each letter sound by itself and not the sound that all of them make together to form a word."

Azkanysh glanced up at him again, motioning for a slave to refill the ceramic pitcher that sat on the table between her and the teacher.

The woman stepped forward and took the pitcher, disappearing into the shadows of the palace.

Azkanysh started reading again. "An ancient race, the horse is the spirit of Araysann. Without them, our ancestors would never have been able to cross the blazing deserts, the mighty mountains, the raging rivers." She stumbled over several of the larger words and reread them again. Master Ishkhan made no comment.

It angered her the more she thought about it, that she had not been allowed to learn reading and writing. The feeling that mastering the art of words gave her was something that no one should be deprived of—a feeling of intelligence, power, equality. It was a feeling that she planned on giving to all the women of Zarcayra. But first she still had to rule for women to work.

The slave returned with the pitcher, and Azkanysh leaned back as the woman poured lemonade into the ceramic cups in front of her and Master Ishkhan. She had called a court session today for the purpose of bringing up the idea of women working. Shayr Jahayan had said that he felt hopeful about several of the council members approving of the idea, that many of them seemed open to his reasoning.

The slave bowed and backed up, and Azkanysh looked back at her book. Vyzir Dsamihur had approached her in the evening of the same day they had visited the factories. He had been unhappy with how she had acted to Shayr Khait, with how she had spoken to the shayr.

"A King of Kings or Queen of Queens," Vyzir Dsamihur had said tightly, "should never lose their composure in public. It makes them look rash, uncontrolled."

Azkanysh stared at the next line in the book. Vyzir Dsamihur had as much as called her a child, a fool… Maybe she had been, but she was sick of biased views, sick of conceited shayrs, of being thought weak just because she was a woman.

"What do you think, Master Ishkhan?" Azkanysh asked glancing up at the teacher. "Of our chances of winning the war against Eromor." She reached for her cup, the lemonade cooling her flushed face. Many held doubts that they would win because of the women among them. She was praying for victory. If the army did win against Eromor, it would mean more than just redeeming Zarcayra's honor; it would prove to the men of Zarcayra that women in the army was a benefit, that they could be more than just childbearers.

Master Ishkhan looked up from the notebook in his lap. "I think, Queen of Queens," he said slowly, dark eyes careful, "that is something best asked of a more political or military-minded man. I, personally, am just a teacher, and I try as much as possible to stay out of such matters. Now, the next line, please." He pointed a hand at her book and went back to his own.

Azkanysh started reading again. "The first horse was given to Araysann by the Family, before humans were born, when darkness covered the world. It was to be a light to humankind, a light to show them the way and help them walk it…" she read slowly, clearly.

"Again," Master Ishkhan said, tapping the table with a long finger. "And remember what I said, put your letters together into words, not just sounds."

Azkanysh started over again. "The first horse was given to Araysann by the Fam…"

Footsteps sounded in the hall outside. She looked up.

"Queen of Queens," Vyzir Dsamihur said with a bow, appearing in the doorway of the airy room, "there is a matter which demands your attention."

There was an urgent edge to the vyzir's voice, a worried gleam in his eye.

Azkanysh closed the book in her lap with a heavy thump. "It appears, Master Ishkhan," she said, addressing the bland-faced tutor, "that we will have to take this up again later." She stood.

Master Ishkhan stood with her, bowing and gathering his books.

Azkanysh waited as he backed out of the room before turning to Vyzir Dsamihur. She had not spoken to him since he had reprimanded her, had not acknowledged his existence. The man was too bold with his opinions sometimes. It was something that made her consider finding another vyzir. But who would she find who did not think like all the other men in Zarcayra, that women were inferior? If possible, she would have elected Shayr Jahayan to the position of vyzir, but one could not be on the Guardian Council and a vyzir.

"What is it, Vyzir Dsamihur?" Azkanysh asked coldly.

"Princess Tamar, Queen of Queens," Vyzir Dsamihur said with a bow. "She is missing."

#

"How long?" Azkanysh asked Vyzir Dsamihur as they hurried down the long arabesque-patterned hallway.

"It is uncertain, Queen of Queens. Mistress Lorrig noticed her absence this morning when Princess Tamar did not show up for her lessons, and when she went to look for her, found that she was not in the palace."

Azkanysh glanced at the fat, heavy-jowled woman panting along next to her. She did not like Mistress Lorrig. The spindly legged woman reminded her of a great bloated spider. She had planned on replacing the mistress with her daughter's former mistress, Ahani, exiled from the kingdom six years now, but now it appeared that would have to wait until they found Tamar.

"Could she perhaps be in one of the outlying gardens?" Azkanysh asked as they turned down a side hallway.

Their footsteps echoed softly on the mosaic flooring of the hallway, like whispers in the great domed scroll room in the center of the palace.

"I assure you, Queen of Queens," Mistress Lorrig wheezed, "I looked everywhere for the princess. She has a habit of skipping on her sewing lessons and hiding from me, so I know where to look for her. If you ask my opinion," Mistress Lorrig gasped as they started up a wide set of sandstone stairs, "Princess Tamar has probably gone into the city. I had trouble with her twice last week trying to sneak out of the palace to do that. When I asked her why, she said that she wanted to see something besides shayrs and shayras." Mistress Lorrig added a snort at the end of her last words that sounded like something between a growl and clearing of her throat.

Azkanysh glanced back at the squat woman again. Tamar, sneaking into the city? She had never heard anything about it. But then, Vosbarhan wasn't the only one who had not paid attention to their children. Her reasons were valid, though, she had not wanted to spend too much time with her daughters when Vosbarhan had been alive for fear that he would think they were conspiring against him, and when Vosbarhan died... well, she had to rule, and being Queen of Queens was time-consuming.

"Do you think it's possible that she went into the city?" Azkanysh asked Vyzir Dsamihur, glancing at him.

The vyzir dipped his head. "Anything is possible, Queen of Queens, but I think that you should hear what Princess Paruhi has to say before we search the city for Princess Tamar."

They reached the top of the stairs and started down a third corridor with a haft-rangī floor and a domed and polygonal roof of red sandstone.

Azkanysh stopped at a wooden door decorated with golden strapwork, waiting for one of the gold-cloaked guards on either side to open it.

The bedchamber on the other side looked unnaturally clean for being her eldest daughter's.

Azkanysh glanced around the sprawling chamber. Three female slaves, faces filled with fear, bowed low to the floor as her gaze traveled over them. Paruhi stood by the arching windows lining the back of the room, her eyes large with fear above her black hijab.

Azkanysh looked at Tamar's four-poster bed. Its gold silk sheets were unwrinkled.

"Queen of Queens," Paruhi said softly, bowing.

Azkanysh stepped toward her. "Vyzir Dsamihur says that you have something to tell me about Tamar."

Paruhi glanced at the vyzir. "Yes, Queen of Queens," she said, looking back at Azkanysh. "Just that, I think that maybe she went to the docks to look for a ship."

Azkanysh narrowed her eyes. "Why would she need a ship?"

Paruhi looked at her feet. "She wanted to go with the army, Queen of Queens, and when you said no..." Paruhi let the words hang, still looking at her feet.

Azkanysh narrowed her eyes. Tamar had approached her a few days before, asking permission to sail with the army for Warulan, and she had refused to let her go. Royalty was not expected to fight alongside the commoners, and if they did, it was considered disgraceful. Would Tamar have disobeyed her command and gone after the army? Azkanysh glanced at Tamar's body slaves. Yes, her daughter would.

Damn it.

"Do you have anything to say on this matter?" she asked sharply, turning toward the slaves. "Did you see anything?"

They bowed as one, faces ashen, bodies shaking beneath their black tunics. "Princess Tamar sent us away early last night after coming back from the banquet, Queen of Queens," the braver looking of the slaves said. "She told us that she had a headache and wished to be alone. When we came in this morning, she was not in her bed..."

"And you did not tell anyone?" Azkanysh snapped, feeling a headache coming on.

"She often dresses herself and leaves her rooms early, Queen of Queens," the same slave replied, voice trembling. She bowed lower to the floor.

Azkanysh stared at them. If the kingdom found out that Tamar had disobeyed her and run away, it would make people angry. They would say that she was weak and incompetent, that she couldn't control her own daughter, let alone run a kingdom.

"I want guards searching the docks for her," Azkanysh said aloud, still watching the slaves. "Have them ask around and see if they can find out if she did indeed get on a ship." She looked pointedly at Vyzir Dsamihur. "Discreetly."

The vyzir bowed. "Yes, Queen of Queens."

Azkanysh looked out the windows lining the back of the bedchamber, a ship's bell ringing in the harbor outside. Tamar's slaves could be threatened to keep silent, and Paruhi and Mistress Lorrig wouldn't tell anyone. She did not think Vyzir Dsamihur would tell anyone—a vyzir did not blab the secrets of their ruler to the kingdom, even if he was against said ruler. That left the problem of what to tell the kingdom about Tamar's absence. "Mistress Lorrig?"

The wrinkled mistress waddled closer.

"Didn't you have a sickness last week?" Azkanysh asked, looking sideways at the old woman.

"Yes, Queen of Queens," Mistress Lorrig wheezed, dipping her head. "But it did not last long."

It was perfect. "Princess Tamar caught it," Azkanysh said, "and it turned into a complicated case of summer fever. She is direly sick and will not be allowed to see visitors for an indefinite amount of time."

Mistress Lorrig's eyes glinted, like she liked the idea of giving Tamar a severe illness. "Yes, Queen of Queens," the old woman croaked. She bowed low to the floor, her black tunic pooling around her.

"I will need a physician paid to 'treat' the princess," Azkanysh said, looking back at Vyzir Dsamihur.

He dipped his head, eyes unreadable.

Azkanysh glanced at the slaves again. "If you speak of any of this," she said in a low, dangerous voice, "I will personally see that you are executed. Do you understand?"

They bowed as one, bodies trembling.

Azkanysh looked at Paruhi. Her daughter blanched.

"Not a word, Paruhi."

Paruhi bowed.

Had she missed anything?

A knock, sharp and loud, rang through the quiet room.

Azkanysh glanced up at Vyzir Dsamihur, heartbeat quickening. Had someone found out about Tamar's disappearance already?

"Who?" the vyzir called.

"A message for the Queen of Queens," a male voice called.

"Close the curtains on the bed," Azkanysh said quickly, pointing at the bed.

The slaves hurried to obey, the double layer of gold and lilac silk swaying in a breeze as they pulled them shut.

Azkanysh glanced at Vyzir Dsamihur, nodding sharply. He stepped across the room and opened the door of the bedchamber.

A purple-cloaked guard stepped inside, bowing stiffly at the waist. "Pardon the interruption, Queen of Queens," the heavily breathing man said, "but there has been a murder."

Azkanysh paled. "A murder?" Had Tamar gone into the city and been assassinated?

Oh, Ehurayni, let it not be Tamar...

"Yes, Queen of Queens," the guard said, sweat trailing down his face. "Shayr Jahayan was found stabbed in his home this morning, dead."

Azkanysh felt her breath knocked out of her.

CHAPTER 30

Tamar

Tamar peeked around the edge of a water barrel. Dozens of crewmembers moved over the main deck of the ship, sweating and cursing as they unloaded boxes and barrels from the hull to the stone dock below. The ship she had snuck onto in Zarcayra had gone to Kaymaar, like the captain had said, before docking in Northport, a major coastal city on Warulan's western coast.

Tamar waited for an opening in the crew working on the ship's deck. Two men ran into each other as one tripped, and they started cursing and fighting, drawing the attention of everyone else on the deck. She jumped to her feet and made for the railing of the ship, climbing down the rough rope ladder hanging over the side. She heard the captain's voice yelling for order as her foot touched the worn granite of the dock, and a moment later crewmen started climbing over the side of the ship again with barrels and boxes. Tamar was already twenty feet away by that time, just another person milling in the crowd.

Strange smells drifted on the warm, salty air of the harbor, smooth, savory smells that made her stomach growl and her mouth water. Tamar craned her head back to look up at the towering gray stone buildings lining the docks, red and green ivy climbing up their sides in spreading vines.

"Get out of the way!" a man rolling a barrel yelled.

She jumped to the side as he went past, noticing several men and women workers watching her. She did stand out in her black clothing, she realized, and nowhere that she looked did she see women wearing tunics or hijabs. They were all dressed in shirts with the sleeves rolled up and trousers and boots.

Tamar glanced around her. Two towering stacks of crates a few feet away caught her eye, and she slipped between them, pulling at her hijab. If she was to fit in while in Eromor, then she should look like one of them.

A ship's bell rang out in the harbor as Tamar finished unwinding her hijab. She pulled the black cloth off completely and stuffed it between two boxes, salty air stroking at her bare cheeks. It felt strange, feeling the wind on her face and pulling at her hair, strange but good. She pulled her robe off as well and rolled the sleeves of her tunic up, then moved back out into the crowd.

She went with the flow of the crowd, moving away from the docks and up a cobbled street into the town.

Women were everywhere, sitting on wooden scaffolding and working on constructing buildings, selling food and clothes and tools and a thousand other goods in shops, driving teams of horses pulling wagons, talking in groups. Tamar had never seen so many women doing so many different tasks in her life.

She stopped at a stone shop lined with lead-paned glass windows, breathing deeply of the enticing smells issuing from it. It had been a day since she had last eaten, since the food that she had stolen from the palace had run out sooner than she'd expected. She stared at a steaming loaf of bread. She didn't have any money to buy food with, though, because women in Zarcayra weren't thought wise enough to handle money. All that they wanted was bought for them by their men.

Tamar started walking again. She had to find the army, they would have all the food that a soldier could ever want to eat.

"I heard there are over a hundred thousand of them," a male voice to her left said. "They landed twenty-five miles up the coast, in Eromor, and are heading inland."

"And Eromor's army," another male voice said, "are they going to stop them?"

Tamar slowed to listen, pretending to look in a shop window at the slender dresses displayed on wooden mannequins.

"They are," the first man said, "but they are not coming all the way to the coast. I heard that they are going to make their stand at Whitegate."

"But what about the cities and towns in between?" the second queried. "Who will defend them?"

"No one, I suspect," the first man replied. "But then, I don't think Zarcayra is too interested in a few small towns and farming villages. I heard they're aiming to meet Eromor's army head on."

Tamar slipped behind the men and moved off up the street. Whitegate! The battle that had raged there during the Second Great War was legendary. And now she was going to be a part of another battle at the same location that could potentially become just as famous. It was all so exciting!

But first she had to find the army. She glanced in a passing shop door, at the long counter inside and the sweating shopkeeper behind it. She knew where the army was now, or where they were headed, anyway. All she needed to do now was ask somebody how to get to Whitegate.

She stopped beside a man tacking up a news poster on the side of a tavern. "Excuse me," she asked, "can you tell me how to get to Whitegate?"

#

Eight hours later, Tamar scanned the road ahead of her as a late-night wind blew the dust covering it into spinning brown clouds that whistled off among the rocks looming on either side. Following the directions of the man tacking up the poster, she had started out earlier on the King's Highway from Northport with a wagon train that she had been lucky enough to run into. After five hours of bumping along with them, she had set off on foot when they had taken a side road that lead up the coast of Warulan.

Tamar pulled her leather bag higher up on her shoulder. The man with the poster had said that the King's Highway led directly to and through Whitegate. He'd also said that it was lined with cutthroats and thieves that waited in packs for travelers.

A nighthawk gave a piercing scream somewhere to her left, and Tamar's gaze shot in that direction. Darkness had fallen over two hours before, and she hadn't seen any cutthroats or thieves. But it didn't mean that they weren't out there, watching her. The thought made her arm hair stand on end.

The nighthawk flew low over the road, swooping down to snatch a foraging mouse from the ground, and the mouse's scream echoed through the rocks as the hawk's talons dug into it.

Tamar shivered. Mistress Ahani had told her a story once, of the nighthawks and the shields they had graced as sigils. "Only found in Warulan and Ennotar, the large silver-and-black birds are creatures of darkness and night," her silvery-haired mistress had begun. "Disliked by many for the bad luck it is thought they bring, it wasn't until the Third Age in Argdrion that the nighthawk became a sigil of death to all who saw them. For it was in the Third Age that the Knights of Gorth arose, daemons who called themselves men and slayed the innocent for an unholy cause they said was justice. No one knows where the Knights of Gorth came from…"

Mistress Ahani's voice grew soft and low. "They just appeared one night, six figures in black on horses of darkest night. For nights on end, they rode over Warulan and Ennotar, appearing out of the mist and leaving no trace behind but those who they had killed and these words written in blood: 'For justice, the innocent are slain.' And then one night, they didn't come, and they were never seen again. The nighthawks remained, though, and it is believed when one is seen that death is coming, and the Knights of Gorth are near."

Another screech echoed through the cool night air, and Tamar sped her pace up. She didn't think that the Knights of Gorth could still be alive after thousands of years, but the thought that they might be was terrifying.

Her stomach grumbled, too loudly for the quiet darkness surrounding the road. It had now been almost two days since she had last eaten. She didn't know how much longer she could go without food. But the army couldn't be that much farther away. They had only landed in Eromor two days before her, and she'd seen signs on the road in front of her that they had come this way. Thousands of footprints, piles upon piles and piles of fairly fresh horse manure. And over there on a wild rosebush, a piece of purple cloth from a soldier's tunic that flapped in the night wind.

Her stomach rumbled again. Tamar grimaced. There was food at the palace, she thought morosely. More food than she could eat in a lifetime. And if she didn't like what the servants brought her, all she had to do was ask, and she could get whatever she wanted. A split peppered chicken with sautéed watercress would be good right about now, she mused, and maybe a slice of chocolate cardamom cake with whipped goat's milk and sugared strawberries to finish it off...

Her stomach gurgled loudly again, and Tamar put a hand to it to try and quiet it. She was not at the palace, and while those things sounded good, she was on the adventure of a lifetime, and that was better than food any old day.

A jagged chip of black rock bounced down from the towering rocks ahead and landed on the road with a dull thud.

Tamar slowed her steps.

Robbers... Her heartbeat sped up. Or maybe something worse. She scanned the serrated rocks on either side of the highway, thinking of the Knights of Gorth.

The nighthawk screamed again.

Tamar frowned. Something about the call wasn't like the other calls—it was too deep in pitch.

Another rock bounced down onto the road, dust puffing up around it.

She took a step backward, her skin prickling. Sudden movement would probably draw in whatever was lurking in the rocks, but if she did nothing it would come for her where she stood.

Was that breathing? A footfall caught her ear. Tamar swallowed. They had surrounded her, whoever they were, which meant that she wouldn't be able to run.

She turned her head slightly, listening for any other noise that would alert her as to where her attackers were. Her only chance of escape now would be to catch them off guard, to surprise them. She swallowed, breathing quickly. She took a breath and turned, screaming and punching.

"Calm down, girl," a deep, husky voice said from the darkness in front of her. "Or you'll hurt yourself." A muscular man in a purple cloak with the fanged golden lyon sigil of Zarcayra stepped out of the darkness and glared at Tamar with eyes that could cut steel.

She blinked as the shadows shifted and ten more dark-skinned men in purple cloaks and turbans appeared out of it. "You're soldiers of Zarcayra," she cried, relief and joy spreading through her.

"Yes," the first soldier replied stonily. He was a Gond Salāyr, judging by the red band around his turban. "So quit kicking and punching before you make me mad, and I kill you." His face had the look of one who was unaccustomed to smiling, and his brown eyes held no warmth.

Tamar stopped swinging her arms in front of her, face flushing with embarrassment.

"She's not wearing a hijab, Gond Salāyr!" a stocky soldier with a fat nose said angrily, moving up behind the Salāyr.

"It would appear that way," the Gond Salāyr replied.

"It's against the law!" the stocky soldier hissed.

"I had to take it off," Tamar said, fear skittering through her as she remembered the execution of a woman in Sussār once who had not been wearing a hijab. "To fit in with the Warulanians."

The Gond Salāyr stared at her a moment. "See that you get another as soon as possible," he said. He swept past and started up the middle of the road.

Tamar let out a breath she hadn't realized she'd been holding. She'd found the army of Zarcayra! Or part of them, anyway. They were probably scouts making sure that no one was sneaking up on the main body of the army.

"Don't mind Paramiz," said a soldier with a slightly bent nose. He had a five-day-old mustache and a dot of a beard and the bluest eyes that Tamar had ever seen. The rest of the soldiers moved past her. "He's always like that."

"Yeah," another baby-faced soldier cut in with a grin as he walked past. He had a curling beard that made him look only a little older than her. "Ornery as a jackass with a bee on its nuts."

The blue-eyed soldier winked at Tamar, his face mischievous but likeable.

Tamar's heart skipped a beat.

The soldier moved off after the rest of the soldiers, and she followed him, skipping to keep up.

"What think you, Gond Salāyr?" asked a thirtysomething soldier with a thick build and heavy eyebrows as Tamar caught up to the group. The Gond Salāyr stood in the middle of the road, one scarred hand resting on the handle of his curved sword.

"I think this was a wasted trip," the Salāyr replied, scanning the road on either side of them. "There's no troop of Eromor soldiers out here, and there's no threat. A damn wasted trip."

"Well, not entirely, Gond Salāyr," the blue-eyed soldier replied in a cheerful voice. "We found a girl and probably saved her from being killed by robbers."

"And a shitload of good that does us, Aghasi," the Salāyr retorted, turning and glaring at Tamar with his piercing brown eyes. He was a handsome man, middle-aged, with silvering hair and a short silver-shot black beard that was separated into three slender beaded braids.

Tamar offered him a smile, but he ignored her.

"She's too young to bed, and we don't need some damn stray tagging along with us. Why are you out here anyway, girl? Did you lose your gond, or are you one of the camp slaves trying to run away again?"

Tamar's face flushed red, and she opened her mouth to tell the Salāyr to mind his tongue when he talked to a princess, but then she remembered that she wasn't a princess, not here, anyway. "Please, sir," she said instead, moving after the bearded Salāyr as the soldiers began moving again. "I am neither a soldier nor a slave, but I want to be a soldier. That is why I'm out here, to find our army and join them."

The Salāyr snorted, his leather ankle boots kicking up puffs of dust that danced in the moonlight. "What makes you think, girl, that we need you?"

Tamar blinked. She hadn't thought of them *not* needing her. Mother had said in the throne room that Zarcayra would need as many women to join the army as possible if they wanted to win the war with Eromor.

"Why wouldn't you need me?" she asked, running to keep up with the Salāyr's long strides. "If we want to win this war against Eromor, we will need every able-bodied man and woman that Zarcayra has to offer."

"I've got another question for you, girl," the Salāyr said. "Why do you want to join Zarcayra's army?"

That was easy. "To help win back our honor," Tamar said fiercely.

"Aww, come on, Paramiz, look at her," Aghasi said, moving up beside them. "She's obviously Zarcayran."

"That's Gond Salāyr, Aghasi, not Paramiz," the Salāyr replied huskily.

"And why didn't you join the army in Zarcayra?" he asked, glancing at Tamar.

Tamar swallowed. That wasn't so easy to answer. "I... I was in Eromor, Gond Salāyr," she said, mind racing. "Apprenticed to a dressmaker in... Northport since I was ten, and when I heard of our kingdom going to war with Eromor and that we were allowing women to fight, I decided to join up," she finished lamely, using the name of the port town since it was the only other Warulan city she could remember besides Crystoln.

The Salāyr's dark eyes narrowed at her, and for a moment Tamar thought that he had seen through her lie.

"It might come in handy having someone who's been in Eromor for a while," he said after a few heartbeats. "What's your name, girl?"

"Yeva," Tamar replied quickly, using the name of a slave girl she had had once.

"And do you speak the general tongue fluently, girl?"

Tamar nodded. It was one thing that Father had insisted they all learn, so that the royal family of Zarcayra was not thought backward and stupid like most of the royal families of Nilfinhèim's kingdoms were because they only knew their own native dialogues.

"Good." The Salāyr stopped again, eyeing her for a moment. "Welcome to the thirty-fourth gond of horsemen," he said finally. "I'm Gond Salāyr Paramiz, and you will address me as Gond Salāyr and Gond Salāyr only. You'll be taking Yurrig's place."

"But, Gond Salāyr," the soldier with the fat nose said, "she's a woman!"

Tamar's blood heated at the implication in his voice, like she would slow them down because she was not a man. Her hands balled into fists.

"Yes," the Salāyr replied tonelessly, "but we will all have to get used to them among us in the battlefield since our Queen of Queens forced us to let them in the army."

Tamar opened her mouth to snap at him that the Guardian Council, a group of men, had approved of the ruling, but he kept talking.

"Aghasi, since you were so helpful in voicing your opinion, the girl is your responsibility. Get her ready for fighting by the time we reach Whitegate. And keep her out of my way until you've trained her. I can't stand green soldiers."

The Salāyr eyed her. "And find her a hijab." He moved off again, the rest of the gond following.

Tamar fell into place with Aghasi and the baby-faced soldier, her heart beating rapidly in her chest.

I'm a soldier!

"My name is Maigar," the baby-faced soldier said, craning his head to look around Aghasi with another grin. He was always grinning, Tamar noticed.

"Hi," she said, grinning back.

"And I'm Aghasi, as you heard," Aghasi said, smiling at her.

Tamar felt her stomach do a small leap, but she quickly pushed it down. "Hello, Aghasi," she said, nodding. "I'm Yeva."

"Welcome to the army, Yeva," they said together.

#

"Paramiz is a harsh on the outside," Aghasi told Tamar over a crackling fire an hour later, "but underneath he's really not bad. And he's got good reason for being the way he is."

Tamar glanced up at the blue-eyed soldier over the wooden bowl of stew and slice of thick brown bread balanced on her knees. They had walked for over an hour after she had run into the gond, until they had reached a sprawling valley where the Zarcayran army had encamped for the night. She had never seen so many people in all her life—thousands upon thousands of them crowded into the long valley in a mass of smoke, tents, horses, fires, and trampled grass.

Her wooden spoon scraped dully over the bottom of her bowl.

"More?" Aghasi asked.

"Yes, please!" Tamar said eagerly, holding her bowl out.

Aghasi reached around the wavering fire and took it from her.

"Why does the Gond Salāyr have good reason for being harsh?" Tamar asked, pulling the hijab that Aghasi had found her, along with standard military boots and tunic, back over her face as the blue-eyed soldier filled the bowl from an iron cauldron over the flames. "What happened to him?" She didn't like wearing a hijab again after going without one for over a day.

It felt like prison after freedom, but she couldn't be around Zarcayran men without a hijab, and if she wanted to be in the army, she had to be around Zarcayran men.

"He sat on a stick," one of the other soldiers of the gond said, "and it went right up his backside, like this." He made a graphic gesture with his hand and then burst into laughter with the rest of the gond.

Tamar took her bowl back from Aghasi, fingertips brushing against his as he handed it to her. Her stomach fluttered at the contact.

"He had a wife and daughter many years ago," Aghasi said, smiling and shaking his head at the other soldier's joke. "When he was a young man not much older than me. It's said that his wife was the most beautiful woman in their town, a small farming village just west of the Red Mountains."

Tamar traded the bowl from one hand to the other, the wood hot, and blew on the stew inside to cool it. The thick soup was grainy, and the meat tasted strangely like how camels smelled, but after two days without food, she didn't care if it was dog flesh and mud that she was eating, just as long as it filled her aching stomach.

"Paramiz was just a farmer at that time," Aghasi went on, stirring the fire with a long stick and sending orange sparks up into the star-filled night sky. "And a blacksmith like his father before him. In those days the desert tribes were especially active, raiding along the Isāyr River and disappearing back into the dunes and mountains before the soldiers of Zarcayra could apprehend them."

Goosebumps rose along Tamar's arms. Fierce nomadic tribes of men that resided in the wild regions of Araysann, the desert tribes mutilated their own bodies to make scars and were said to be masters of torture. They also kidnapped women and forced them to bear children for them before murdering them and the female children that they bore and leaving their bodies in the sand for the jackals to eat, keeping only the male children to carry on their tribe. Tamar looked up at the gond, now sitting quietly and somber-faced around the crackling bonfire. From what she'd seen of the "civilized" men of Zarcayra, they did not treat their women much better than the desert tribesmen did. But at least they didn't murder their wives and daughters.

"What happened?" she asked in a hushed voice.

Aghasi jabbed at the fire again, tanned face grim. "The tribes attacked Paramiz's town in the night, when they were sleeping. He tried to fight them, but he was not trained in the art of war back then, and he was struck down with a sword before he could take five steps out of his house."

Tamar could imagine the slicing sound of the wide shortswords that the desert tribes used as Aghasi spoke, smell the sharp, metallic scent of blood.

"The barbarians thought Paramiz dead, and by some luck or blessing of the Family, he was left among the slain with only a deep wound in his head that knocked him unconscious while the tribes ransacked the town. His wife and child, though…" Aghasi shook his head, the fire making a long, distorted shadow of him on the ground behind the rock he crouched on. "It is said that the desert tribes leave no man or child alive when they raid. Paramiz found his child like all the rest, hanging, burning, from the blood-splattered doorpost of their home. His wife was carried off with the rest of the women."

Tamar felt a stab of pity for the graying Salāyr. It had been hard losing Akabi and Isày to the summer fever when she was twelve. How would it be to lose loved ones to the desert tribes? To find their mangled and tortured bodies or to know that they had been hauled away to be raped and then murdered?

"Paramiz became a soldier so that he would never be helpless to save those he loved again," Aghasi said, making her look at him again. "They say that he didn't sleep for four months straight, learning how to use the sword and that he still spends six hours a day practicing with it."

"Aghasi."

All in the gond jumped, startled at the husky voice of the Gond Salāyr. "I thought I told you to get the girl ready for battle."

Aghasi pushed himself to his feet as Paramiz stepped into the fire's light. The rest of the gond did the same. "She was hungry, Gond Salāyr."

"Yes, well, now she has eaten," Paramiz said, "so ready her for battle."

Tamar stood.

Aghasi nodded.

Paramiz disappeared again.

"Is he mad at us?" Tamar whispered as the rest of the gond sat back down again and began murmuring over their food.

Aghasi motioned for her to follow him, and they headed away from the fire.

They moved past another roaring fire with another gond seated around it on the mangled grass and to a shadowed weapons rack beyond.

Aghasi pulled a iron-tipped wooden spear off the rack.

Tamar caught it as he tossed it to her.

"Paramiz won't be mad," Aghasi said. "Everyone knows about his past, but he refuses to acknowledge it or speak of it."

"But why?" Tamar asked, frowning as Aghasi grabbed another spear and took a fighting stance in front of her.

"He blames himself for what happened."

"But that's silly!" Tamar said, the wood of the spear smooth against her fingers. She turned the spear in the light of the nearby fires, admiring its symmetrical shape. "He wasn't to blame for what happened."

Aghasi shrugged. "Paramiz feels he was. If he had been a soldier, then he could have saved his wife and child."

"We can't help what status we are born into in life," Tamar said, glancing up at him.

Aghasi looked at her, blue eyes puzzled. "No, but we can change that status. Me, I was born the son of a disgraced shayr, but instead of bemoaning my station in life, I became a soldier and found honor for my family's name. Now, defend yourself."

He moved so fast that Tamar barely had time to raise her spear before his cracked into it.

"Good," Aghasi said, blue eyes sparkling, "You've got a quick eye and fast hands. But how are you for footwork?" He moved to the left and brought the dark wooden staff of his spear toward her head.

Tamar ducked and brought her own spear up to touch Aghasi's stomach. His purple tunic wrinkled under the wood.

His brows went up. "Good. Have you had training before?"

Tamar took a step backward. "No, but I'm a fast learner."

Aghasi laughed. "Fair enough." He lunged.

Tamar hissed as he hit her in the right arm and then lower stomach before lunging backward out of her reach. She gasped for air.

"Never let your enemy distract you," Aghasi instructed, pointing the tip of his spear at her. "Always be on guard, even when you are with someone you trust, or you'll not live to see your grandchildren."

Tamar nodded, gritting her teeth and raising her spear. She knew that from the stories of heroes and battles that Mistress Ahani had told her, but she had let his sparkling blue eyes distract her. She wouldn't make that mistake again.

Aghasi lunged again.

This time, Tamar was ready for him. Jumping to the right to avoid his jab, she twirled behind him, purple hijab and cloak billowing, and lifted her spear over her head. She brought the shaft down onto Aghasi's back with a resounding crack.

The rest of the gond slowly gathered to watch them, laughing.

Aghasi winced and hopped around to face her again. "Good," he said, firelight from a dozen campfires playing across his brown face. "But you should have taken the advantage while you had it and finished me off—"

Tamar lunged before he could finish speaking and feigned a left, then right-hand blow, both of which he parried with speed and grace like she'd never seen before. She brought her spear down toward his head.

Aghasi easily parried the blow with his own weapon and knocked the spear out of her hand, grabbing it as it flew away. "You should have aimed for my legs," he instructed. "They were left unguard—"

Tamar dropped to the ground and slid between the blue-eyed soldier's outstretched legs, grabbed his left ankle, and yanked him off his feet.

The rest of the gond laughed louder and made catcalls as both spears flew from Aghasi's hands.

He hit the ground with a grunt. Tamar rolled sideways and grabbed her spear from where it had fallen on the trampled grass. "Don't let your enemy distract you, remember?" she said, panting, as she put one knee on Aghasi's chest and held the tip of the spear up to his throat.

Aghasi's blue eyes widened. "You *are* a fast learner."

Tamar grinned. "The best."

The ring of gathered soldiers grew silent, and she looked up to see Paramiz watching them.

"You fight well, girl," the Salāyr said.

Tamar pushed away from Aghasi, cheeks turning red as she realized how close they were. She hastily climbed to her feet as Paramiz walked toward them.

"What did you say you were again?" he inquired, eyes boring into hers.

"A dressmaker's apprentice, Gond Salāyr," Tamar said quietly, her breath slowing as the excitement of the fight wore off.

Paramiz's eyes searched hers for a moment before he turned and addressed the gathered soldiers. "In four hours' time, we march for Whitegate and the army of Eromor awaiting us there!"

The gond grinned, several of them bumping each other.

"I want everyone ready in two!" Paramiz said in a voice used to giving commands.

Now there were scowls.

"And these tents and weapons taken down and packed!"

Someone cursed, but Tamar couldn't tell who.

Paramiz glanced over his shoulder at her as the gond began filing away, grumbling. "You are very bold for a dressmaker's apprentice. But I wonder"—the Salāyr stepped closer, so close that Tamar could see there were specks of gold in his brown eyes—"is that all you are? The girl I saw attacking Aghasi, she had the confidence of a noble, not a servant."

Tamar swallowed. "I don't know what you mean, Gond Salāyr," she said, keeping her voice even as her heartbeat sped up.

Paramiz stared at her for a moment before turning and following his grumbling men.

Tamar watched him go, breathing quickly again. He couldn't possibly know who she was. Unless he'd seen her at a public event before, but it was doubtful that he could prove it, and even if he could, what could he do about it? He didn't know that Mother had said she couldn't come to fight. No one did but her and Paruhi, and Paruhi wasn't here.

"Come on," Aghasi said from behind her, sticking his spear back in the rack. "You can help me saddle the horses."

CHAPTER 31

The Unknown Voice

Her name was Alvyna, daughter of King Edomur, and I detested the very idea of her with all my being.

"My lord," Sar said as two aged menservants greased and combed my dark-brown hair back and dressed me in the green and white colors of Castle Sythorn. "I realize that an arranged marriage is a…" The old steward paused, looking for a word. "Difficult thing. But I am told the princess is a wonderful woman, and this alliance is a great honor for Castle Sythorn. And, my lord, you are thirty-three now." He paused again. "Forgive me, but it was time that you found a wife, carried on your family name."

I stared at my reflection in the full-length mirror in front of me. Medium height, muscled but slender, brown hair, brown eyes… Sar said that I looked more and more like Father every day, but I thought I saw more of Mother in my reflection. It didn't really matter how I looked, though— bodies were temporal.

"And why is that, Sar?" I asked, holding my arms upward and away from my body as one of the menservants slipped my quilted green overcoat with the white stag sigil on it over my tunic and light chainmail.

"Sir?" Sar asked, confused. The steward had always been old, but of late I had noticed that he was showing his age more and more. In the increasing slowness of his walk, the stooping of his back, and the quivering in his voice. I hated old creatures around me; it reminded me of what would happen to me someday if I failed at changing into a new body.

"Why is it time that I found a wife?" I repeated, turning to look at Sar as a manservant strapped my oiled leather belt and heavy broadsword on.

"Well, my lord…" Sar began.

I raised a hand, stopping him. The menservants paused their work. "Don't ever pretend to know what is best for me, Sar," I said softly. I reached for the brown leather gloves lying on a tall rounded table and slipped my hands into them. "I may not be as hard a man as my father was, but I assure you that I am a much more dangerous one, and I do not appreciate being told what to do."

"Forgive me, my lord," Sar stammered out. "I did not mean to tell you what to d—"

"Good," I interrupted. "Don't." I pulled the gloves tighter over my fingers. Four times after the skinchanger, I had tried to move my soul into different younger bodies. Four times, four failures. There was a fast-growing line of thick white scars on my forearms. I wore long sleeves constantly.

The menservants took a step back from me, my outfit completed, their work done. I tugged at the strings of my cloak, tied together in a knot at my throat. I was angry after my last failure and subsequent recovery three months before. Angry at the spell for not working. Angry at the castle servants for worrying over my health after so many bouts of "sickness" as I recovered from my failures. Angry with myself for being scared to try the spell again.

I had realized after my last failure to change into a new body that it would be wise to focus my attentions on more than just longer life. Castle Sythorn was slowly falling into ruin as the last of Father's funds were depleted in furnishing my knights and myself for the war, and if something was not done soon, I would join the hundreds of other homeless lords and ladies that lived on the battlefield and scrambled with the common soldiers for food.

Sar bowed slightly, a stiff bending of his waist. "My lord," he said, motioning for me to go to the horses and meet my future bride. I swept past him and into the stone hallway outside, chainmail clinking.

Marrying Princess Alvyna, while not a welcoming prospect, would make me son-in-law to the king and give me new power and wealth. King

Edomur was by no means rich—not many were after three hundred years of war—but joining his family would ensure me a place to live when Castle Sythorn had collapsed completely, and I was told that being son-in-law to the king would mean a small pension.

Horses and knights stood in the castle courtyard, breaths coming out in white puffs in the icy winter morning air. It was six minutes past five, I knew, because I had glanced at the ancient pendulum clock in the entrance hall.

The ride to King Edomur's city and castle was a long one, and it was well past dark when we finally reached the towering structure four days later. Servants greeted us at the massive front doors and took our horses.

The double oaken entry doors, twenty feet high and studded with iron nails, groaned shut behind us as we stepped inside the castle, cutting off the howling wind that had picked up minutes after we had ridden into the courtyard.

"This way, Lord Sythorn," an ancient-looking female servant said. She held a candle in a pewter plate in one hand and hobbled off down a long, wide black marble hall. I followed, my knights coming after me.

Our footsteps resounded loudly off the shadowed walls of the hallway, filling our ears before echoing off into the quiet darkness of the castle. I felt like I was walking in a mausoleum for how still the castle was, a mausoleum of aged servants waiting for the war to end or the enemy to invade.

King Edomur was in his throne room, a massive chamber made from black marble and lit by a few flickering candles scattered in multipronged stands throughout rows of marble pillars. I saw Alvyna first, seated next to her father in a smaller cushioned wooden chair. I disliked her immediately.

Her hair was chestnut in color and hung straight and lifeless over her wide shoulders. Her body was long and ungainly, her face straight and plain, and her eyes were the dullest shade of summer blue I had ever seen.

"King Edomur," I said, my voice echoing through the throne room as I bowed to the tall gray-haired man. My knights went to one knee behind me, bowing their heads in turn.

"Lord Sythorn," King Edomur said. His voice had taken on a wheeze in the past few years. He was growing old. "Thank you for coming in such harsh weather."

The wind moaned past the cobwebbed windows high up in the walls of the throne room, as if to affirm his statement.

"I would not have asked you due to such weather, but as you know, the winter is the only time where we may be at peace in our homes."

I straightened and nodded. King Edomur had spoken to me three months before, during the fall battles, telling me that there was something important that he wanted to discuss with me.

"I have but one child, as you know, Lord Sythorn," he had begun when I arrived at his tent one evening after a battle. "A daughter, Alvyna."

I dipped my head, dried blood from skinchangers I had slain that day crumbling off my face and falling to the dirt below. Everyone knew of Princess Alvyna and how her father would not let her join the battles after he had lost his four sons at the beginning of the Third Great War. Some complained about the princess's absence from the war, but I understood that a king must have an heir.

"You also know," King Edomur went on, "that I am growing old, Lord Sythorn, and my time on Argdrion will soon be finished."

I said nothing. There was nothing I could say. He had told me once that he liked this about me, that I never flattered him with lies of "No, my king, you will live for many more years" or other such things like the other lords and ladies did. Perhaps this was why he had chosen me for his right-hand man.

"I can feel it in my bones," King Edomur murmured. "The shadow of Death is coming for me." He paused, and I heard the distant shouts of the night battle going on.

We had learned in the beginning of the wars to have two separate halves of the army—the day fighters and the night fighters. When the skinchangers and wiar fought, they were stronger than us and could see better in the dark, and they often attacked throughout the night as well as the day.

"My daughter needs a husband," King Edomur said. He looked up at me, blue eyes glinting in the light of a candle on the table beside him. "Someone to help her rule, to help her carry on the kingdom line."

I knew before he spoke his next words that he wanted me to marry his daughter. The same sinking feeling that had filled me then filled me now.

"Lord Sythorn," Princess Alvyna spoke up, bringing me back to the present and the chilliness of the throne room. "Do you remember me? We've met before."

I stared at her for a moment, trying to remember a meeting between the two of us. "I do not recall us meeting before, Your Highness," I said.

"We were children," she said, watching me. "And it was at your cousin's birthday party. What was his name? Oh yes, Ciril." She smiled at the memory, and my insides curled. I knew the birthday party that she spoke of, the only one that I had ever attended for Ciril.

I had been six, and I had not wanted to go any more than I wanted Ciril coming to Castle Sythorn. But Mother had insisted as usual, and I had spent the day watching the other children bob for apples, eat iced cake, and race each other around my aunt and uncle's wood-shingled house. There had been a royal there that day, a small girl with dull blue eyes and flat chestnut hair. She had asked me to play with her and the others, and when I had refused, she sat with me under an apple tree, in the grass, with the bees.

"The apple tree," I said aloud. "Yes, I remember now."

"I thought that you were handsome then," Alvyna said, "and it would appear that your good looks have not forsaken you."

She was bold, something that made up for her lack of looks. I still did not want a wife. But when King Edomur had beseeched me to marry his daughter in his tent three months ago, I had known that I could not refuse. Being king would give me power, something that I was learning was as important as longer life.

"Thank you, Your Highness," I said, dipping my head. I did not return the compliment.

"The wedding will take place the day after tomorrow," King Edomur said, coughing lightly. "I realize that you would like more time to get to know each other, but although the war is going in our favor, we cannot afford to put your union off. The snow is already melting in the lower city, and the battles will start soon."

I felt Alvyna's blue eyes on me, but I did not look at her. The gods willing, I would never have to look at her more than on our wedding day and night.

"In times of war, we must all make sacrifices, Father," she said.

King Edomur nodded. "There are rooms prepared for you and your knights, Lord Sythorn, in the eastern wing of the palace," he said, addressing me. "My servants will show you to them."

I nodded and turned, my knights following.

"And Lord Sythorn," King Edomur called.

I pivoted to look back at him. In the dimness of the throne room, he looked weary.

"Sleep well."

I dipped my head.

Footsteps sounded in the hall after us as the same ancient female servant led me and my knights to the eastern wing, and I turned to see Princess Alvyna hurrying after us, skirt whispering around her long legs. I did not want to talk to her but stopped all the same, waiting as my knights moved on.

"Lord Sythorn," she said, slowing as she reached me, "I realize that you don't know me, and I'm sure that this is hard for you, marrying a strange princess." She paused, catching her breath. Her cheeks held a reddish glow from running that only heightened her plainness. "So I wanted to say," she went on, "that if you don't want to follow through with this marriage, you needn't feel like you must due to loyalty or love for my father."

I watched the ancient servant and my knights disappear around a corner, wondering how I would find my rooms.

"My lord?" Princess Alvyna said.

I looked back at her, noticing that she was taller than me by a good three inches. If I said that I did want to go through with the marriage and not because I felt loyalty or love toward her father—which I did not—then she would think that I held an attraction for her. If I didn't follow through with the marriage, however... Well, I knew what would happen to me then—poverty and the poorhouse. I decided to be bluntly honest.

"I am not marrying you because of your father," I said, the distant howl of wind around the castle echoing through the long, deserted hallway. "To put it plainly, Your Highness, my lands have been hit hard by the wars, and I need money and a place to live, the money that comes with being son-in-law to the king."

I expected her to be hurt or offended with me, but she just smiled slowly. "If honest is what we are being," Alvyna said, voice amused, "then the only reason I agreed to this marriage was the prospect of a younger man around. My whole life has been spent with the ancients that tend this castle while everyone else is off fighting, and I would like to see what it is like to have a young, vigorous husband."

If my heart had not been focused on longer life, I might have liked her.

"Now that we understand each other, would you like me to show you to your rooms?" she asked me after a moment.

I glanced down the hall where my knights had disappeared to. "I think that I can find my own way," I said, not wanting to be in her company for longer than I had to. I bowed shortly. "Your Highness."

She curtsied, slender white dress brushing on the dark stone beneath her.

We parted with a mutual understanding that night, an understanding that would remain with us throughout our marriage. We did not marry for love, and we would never pretend that we did. It was a business deal, our marriage, and as we wed in the chapel of King Edomur's castle two days later, neither of us expected differently.

"I do," Alvyna said, kneeling beside me in a plain white dress and lacy veil, her voice clear and deep. There was a small crowd gathered in the candlelit marble room behind us, those who had been able to get through the snow encasing the city and surrounding countryside. I heard myself echo Alvyna's words, watched the gold-robed priest anoint her with water from a bowl of Brys, goddess of fertility.

That night after the wedding feast, we consummated our marriage in a large stone bedroom given to us by King Edomur. There was no joy in it for me. I could think only of the heart spell and the new power I would have as son-in-law to the king.

CHAPTER 32

Nathaira

Nathaira dreamed she was flying. Her arms had changed into long, sinewy wings, and her body was covered in gold and white feathers that ruffled in the wind as she raced through the sky.

Athrysion was next to her, a massive red-and-bronze griffin with a snow-white ruff and glistening black talons.

At first Nathaira was surprised, because she remembered him dying. But when Athrysion smiled at her, green eyes lighting up like she remembered, she knew that his death and the last month must have been a horrible, dreadful nightmare, and she was finally awake again and everything was all right.

"Wonderful, Nathaira, is it not?" Athrysion asked, his deep voice caught by the wind and blown away behind them as they soared over a thick forest of green pines and golden oaks and toward a distant snow-capped mountain range.

Nathaira nodded and pumped her wings faster, gaining three feet on him as the wind whistled in her lyon ears like a living thing. She glanced back at Athrysion. "But let us see who can reach the mountains first, shall we?"

Athrysion screeched an ear-piercing cry from his curved golden beak, and Nathaira laughed and flew faster as he strained to catch up to her. It felt good to laugh again. It had been so long since she had. But no, it hadn't been long. That was all a dream, wasn't it?

The scenery changed so fast that her head spun. She was no longer in the form of a griffin but in her natural body and falling toward burning trees.

She flailed her arms as the trees loomed larger and a meadow appeared beneath them. She hit the grass on her side, pain ricocheting through her body as she rolled over and came to rest by a decapitated body. The head lay a few feet away, eyes staring lifelessly at the fire-filled sky above.

Nathaira screamed and jumped backward. The body and head belonged to Zeythra.

An answering scream, her scream, echoed back.

Nathaira wheeled.

It's all a dream, it's all a dream, it's all a dream, she chanted over and over in her mind. She saw herself across the meadow, weeping over Athrysion's blood-bathed body.

No. Nathaira stumbled backward, her foot catching on Zeythra's body. She sprawled onto the burning ground again.

The grass shifted into sifting golden sand underneath her, and the sky grew light as thousands of angry yelling voices filled her ears.

"Kill the skinchanger! Kill the skinchanger! KILL THE SKINCHANGER!"

Nathaira glanced wildly around her as the chant shook the sand underneath her.

"You're nothing but an animal," the woman killer from the arena hissed, red hair framing her face like a halo. "A filthy, useless animal."

"Save Efamar, Nathaira." Athrysion appeared next to the woman, a silver arrow protruding from his chest as drops of blood fell to the sand below. "Save him, Nathaira."

"Athrysion!" Nathaira cried, reaching a hand out for him with tear-filled eyes.

"Nathaira!"

She started at the voice and tore her eyes away from her father to see Efamar being dragged toward an execution block by three burly black-masked arena guards.

"They'll behead ya, probably," the man who had murdered the woman on the ship said, sneering in her face, his rancid breath making her gag. "Or burn ya alive at the stake." He laughed a cold, echoing laugh, and Nathaira cried out as she was suddenly tied to a pole with leaping golden flames roiling around her.

"More fire!" yelled the man who had saved her from the men in the alley, his eerie eyes glowing with a fire of their own as flames billowed around his head. "We need more fire!"

A massive log landed on the flames in front of her, and Nathaira screamed in pain as cinders shot up in her face and flames lapped at first her back, then her leg and arm, melting the skin and gnawing at the flesh.

"More fire!" the two-color-eyed man yelled, throwing his hands up in the air on either side of him as dark-gray smoke billowed over his black-haired head. "We need more fire!"

Nathaira started and cried out, but strong hands held her down.

"Let me go!" She thrashed against her captor. "Don't burn me. LET ME GO!"

"Gods, she's strong, isn't she?" a woman's scared voice said.

Nathaira sucked in a ragged breath. She'd heard that voice before—the woman friend of the man who'd rescued her. Her eyes snapped open, and she saw the man with the different-colored eyes leaning over her. Darkmoon, his woman friend had called him. Wasn't that the name of the famous killer the woman killer in the arena had spoken of?

"It was a dream," the man said firmly, his voice soft and smooth and somehow soothing. "Just a dream."

Nathaira inhaled sharply. Cold air filled her lungs, and the man slowly let go of her chest and moved to her right arm, where the woman in the arena had wounded her. His scent, a mixture of leather, steel, and something unfamiliar that Nathaira could not identify, wafted off him to her nostrils as his cool, scarred skin brushed against hers.

Oh, Sisters, it was just a dream. Nathaira blinked, a last tear trailing down her cheek. For a moment... for a moment she had let herself believe that Athrysion wasn't dead and they were together again, flying as they had once done.

"Where have you taken me?" she asked, remembering the man saving her, traveling through dark alleys and then going into a gaudy human house with several painted women in it. She must have fainted then, for she did not remember coming to a bed.

Nathaira glanced down at the man.

His face was thin but attractive and had a white scar that ran up from his right eye and cut his eyebrow in half. "A bedroom," he replied. "To heal." He murmured something unintelligible, and she hissed as a sharp, stabbing pain snaked up her arm.

Soft golden light trailed along her flesh in whorls, away from where the man's slender hands touched it. Nathaira gasped, watching as her torn arm slowly mended itself back together beneath the light. "You have magic," she whispered in awe.

The man glanced up at her, his eyes unreadable. She had never seen such beautiful yet eerie eyes, one an ice blue and the other emerald green. "Yes."

"I'll dump the water," the woman said abruptly from behind the man.

Nathaira watched her as she picked up a white bowl off a small table by the bed and quickly left the room. There was fear in the woman's eyes; she had noticed it when she had first come to the human dwelling. Fear of the man Darkmoon. Nathaira glanced back at him. Was it because of his magic?

She eyed him. She knew that humans could learn magic from spells and incantations and such, but since the Hunting, there weren't many who dared to. What made this human so reckless? And how did he know magic as advanced as healing and yet did not look a day older than twenty-five? Such magic took years upon years to learn. More importantly, why had he offered his help, and so far, followed through on it?

"What do you want?" Nathaira asked, feeling like a thousand tiny, delicate needles were prickling her flesh where the man's hands touched her. The woman on the slaver train had helped her too. Why did some humans help?

The man glanced up at her. "Want?" He raised his right eyebrow, scar wrinkling. His hair was the color of darkest night and was slightly messy from his hood.

"Why did you save me?" Nathaira asked. She still felt light-headed, but the heat from the fever that had raged through her body was gone.

The man looked back at her arm. "I told you, you interest me." His right hand trailed up her skin, a smooth black ring circling the middle finger etched with barely discernable runes. Nathaira inhaled sharply as mended skin followed the man's hand.

She held her arm up, examining her healed flesh with fascination. Athrysion had spoken of such healing spells in the wars. He had said that they could be beautiful or terrifying.

The man stood from a straight-backed wooden chair he'd been straddling by the edge of the bed. He wiped his hands off on a bloody white towel on the table.

Nathaira looked back up at him, remembering the alley. She had never seen someone move as quickly and lethally as he had. Who was he? There was something about him... something that told her that he wasn't quite what he seemed to be, although what it was, she could not say.

The man stood by the bed, dark-gray buckles and fastenings connecting the straps and belts crisscrossing his black shirt, glinting dully in the light of a roaring fire across the room. "You should rest," he said, watching her.

Nathaira stared back.

"You've had a long day, and your body needs reviving." He pulled a dark-brown square of food from his shirt pocket and slipped it into his mouth, turning as if to go.

Nathaira grabbed his wrist with the hand of her newly mended arm, the strong, supple leather of the man's vambrace digging into her palm. "Give me one good reason I should trust you, human," she said softly.

The man's eyes, like two pieces of cold stone, met hers. "You shouldn't," he said. "But you really have no choice, do you?"

He was right. Nathaira let go of him, anger seeping through her. Anger that a human had saved her life again. Anger that she had been forced to take his help to survive. Now she owed him a debt, and skinchanger honor demanded that she could not leave him until it was repaid.

Oh, Sisters, what is your purpose in this? Moirin had told her once that there was a purpose in everything that the Sisters did. It had been after she had lost a child, before Efamar was born, when Nathaira had been three.

"How can the Sisters let such horrible things happen?" she had asked Moirin, finding her by the baby's grave. Moirin slipped an arm around her, a cold rain drizzling down on them.

"Maybe it's not horrible," Moirin said quietly.

Nathaira glanced up at her, a question on her lips.

"Maybe," Moirin went on, "there is something that the Sisters want us to learn, and there was no other way that we could learn it but through this experience."

Nathaira looked back down at the grave, so small beside the larger one of an elder who had died years before. "But how?" she whispered, tears pricking at her eyes for her lost sibling.

"That, I do not know," Moirin said, hugging her closer to her side as the rain wet their raven hair, and cloaks. "But we must always trust in the Sisters, Nathaira, and know that they always have a purpose in everything that they do."

"Now, as I was saying," the man said, bringing Nathaira back to the present, "I suggest you rest." He turned again, black cloak swishing around him, and slipped silently over to the door, his movements graceful, fluid, lethal.

"You're an assassin," Nathaira said, assuming he was the man the woman killer in the arena had spoken of. She said the words with disgust. Creatures that killed without cause went against what the Sisters taught.

The man paused, one hand on the curling iron handle of the door. He glanced over his shoulder at her. "Yes." His eyes met hers, and Nathaira's fingers slipped into eagle talons. There was death in his eyes and a coldness that she had never seen in any other creature. It alarmed her. And made her wonder again why he had saved her.

"Now rest," the man said. He opened the door and disappeared through it, shutting it softly behind him.

Nathaira stared at the spot where he had been, eagle talons slowly slipping back into fingers. Part of her wanted to leave right now. She glanced at a window beside the bed. But the other part knew that she did not have the strength. And there was the debt. Coldness gripped at her heart at the thought. Skinchanger honor demanded that she repay the killer for saving her life, that she stay with him until her debt was paid. But how could the Sisters expect her to stay with a human? Much less one who went against everything they taught?

Nathaira glanced down at her mended arm. She felt at her back and leg and face. Her skin was as smooth as glass. She looked at the door again, remembering the woman on the wagon train and the help she'd given her. Was Moirin right? Were not all humans evil? Sometimes it certainly seemed so.

She rested her head on the lavender-scented pillows behind her, sleep haunting her senses. But how could some be evil and some not? Wasn't a race characterized by its people? How could it be both good and bad?

Nathaira closed her eyes, exhaustion pulling at her. She didn't know anymore. And no matter what Moirin had said, she didn't see how the Sisters could possibly have a purpose for indebting her to a human.

#

When Nathaira awoke later, it was night.

Soft, silver moonlight streamed through the window by the bed, playing across the large boxy room and the dying fire.

She owed a human a debt. Nathaira closed her eyes at the fresh realization. A dog barked outside, and her eyes snapped back open. Athrysion would say that she did not owe humans anything, that what they had done in the wars and during the Hunting canceled out any debts. But then, Athrysion probably never would have taken a human's help in the first place.

Nathaira swallowed, throat dry, and slowly moved to a sitting position, grimacing at her still-sore body, which ached from a night spent running through the alleys. She glanced out the window at the star-dappled night sky.

Sisters, I slept a long time. Her stomach growled loudly, reminding her that it had now been two days since she had last eaten.

A thick black blanket that had not been there before fell to the floor as she slowly slipped out of the bed. Nathaira stepped over it and padded to the window, goosebumps trailing over her naked flesh. She put her hands on the cold bubbled glass of the window, eyes straying to the tattoo on her right thumb. It was the first that had been inked onto her skin, when she was a babe of eight days. All skinchangers received a tattoo there at eight days of age to show that they were one of the people, and every time something significant happened after that, they received another.

Nathaira glanced at the marks trailing up her arm. Each one stood for an important event in her past: Moirin's death, the clan moving to Ennotar's mountains not long after, the last male elder dying at nine hundred and three.

Nathaira looked up at the Sisters, hanging low in the night sky and surrounded by a million winking stars. She would have a tattoo inked for each clan member dead, one for her capture and escape, and one when she found Efamar.

A star streaked across the sky in a white blur of light and disappeared behind the dark rooftops of the looming stone buildings across the street. Nathaira followed its trail with her eyes. She hated the massive dark buildings the humans called homes. They looked like cages with their locked doors and paned windows. She longed for the soft feel of pine needles and ferns under her feet again and the sight of tall, thick trees.

She glanced back up at the stars, wondering which one was Athrysion and Zeythra and Moirin. "I miss you," she whispered, a tear trailing out of her eye and down her cheek.

Footsteps sounded from the hall outside. The door of the bedroom opened, and a golden shaft of light fell into the room and glittered on the windowpane.

Nathaira turned sharply, shielding her eyes against the brightness.

The blonde-haired woman friend of the killer stepped through the doorway, diamond earrings swaying. "Are you awake..." She trailed off, seeing the empty bed.

Nathaira slid toward the curtains hanging on one side of the window. Had the killer betrayed her? Healed her only to turn her in? But why would he do that?

The woman's eyes moved to her. "Oh, there you are." Her voice was soft and nervous. She shut the door behind her and clicked across the room to the table by the bed, setting the candle in her hand on its dark top. The flame sputtered dully and threw a faint circle of gold on the blue-painted ceiling.

Nathaira eyed the woman, noting the tight-fitting silk gown she wore and the smell of musk hanging over her. "You're a whore." It was rude and blunt, but she didn't care. Whoring was against what the Sisters taught.

The woman glanced over at her. "I am," she said quietly.

"You sell your body to men for money," Nathaira said.

The older woman shrugged, eyeing her tensely. "It's a living, and not as bad as you may think."

It was evil. They stared at each other for a moment.

"I know who you are," the whore said after a while.

Nathaira stiffened.

"But you needn't fear. As long as you are here, you are safe," she added hastily.

Nathaira stared at the woman. Another human helping her. Why?

Running feet echoed off the cobbles outside.

Nathaira glanced out the window and quickly moved behind the heavy blue drape, shadowing it as a squad of soldiers jogged by in the alley below. Burning torches in their hands threw ghostly shadows on the tall buildings on either side.

"They've been combing the city all day," the woman said softly, her slender dress rustling around her as she moved around the bed and to the window and glanced over Nathaira's shoulder. Nathaira looked up at her, and the whore stepped back, a warm, sultry smell of flowers, spices, and herbs emanating off her beneath the smell of musk.

"Do not worry," the whore said quickly, voice afraid again. "I will not turn you in to that man."

"The king?" Nathaira asked, watching the soldiers as they disappeared round a bend in the alley. It grew dark once more.

"The chief advisor," the whore said, tapping her foot in a quick, jolty rhythm. "Uranius is so old and frail that he can hardly run his kingdom anymore. Torin Ravynston, his chief advisor, has almost completely taken over running the affairs of the kingdom now."

She turned abruptly and moved back around the bed, picking up the heavy black blanket from the floor. "But enough of that. Right now I would guess what you're wanting is a bath and some food." The words were meant to be kind, but there was no warmth in the whore's voice.

She is terrified of me, Nathaira realized. *But more terrified of him.* "Where is the killer?" she asked, watching the whore shakily fold the blanket.

The whore glanced up at her, looking slightly startled. "Darkmoon? He had business to attend to." She refolded the blanket again as a corner slipped out of her fingers. "He didn't say if he'd be back," she said, avoiding Nathaira's gaze.

Maybe she wouldn't have to repay his debt. Surely if he didn't come back, the Sisters would not make her find him and repay him.

Two younger girls that she remembered seeing earlier in the hallway downstairs appeared at the door, their hands full of bottles, towels, and bars of strange-looking stuff. Their eyes were full of the same fear that haunted the older whore's gaze.

"What is that for?" Nathaira asked, glancing from the younger whores to the older one.

"Your bath," the older whore replied, still messing with the blanket.

Nathaira glanced down at her bloody, dirt-stained body. It had been over a month since she'd had a bath. The thought of clean skin was tempting. She looked back up at the three whores.

"You have a stream?"

#

Nathaira had always bathed in the rivers and lakes in the forest, so she had never had anything like what the humans called a bath.

For one, her bath water was collected in a large oblong object that was made of polished bronze, something the humans called a "tub." For another, the water was warm. And not the warm water in shallow forest pools from the Brothers' rays, but real hot water. Hot enough to boil the dirt off her body and out of her hair and soothe her aching muscles. Nathaira had never experienced something so wonderful before in all her life.

The older whore appeared in the doorway of the small bathroom adjoining the bedroom and moved to a fluted wooden table with bottles on it. She selected a glass vial full of dark red liquid, pulled the cork out with a pop, and poured it into the bath water.

Nathaira pulled her legs away from the liquid as it swirled into the cloudy bathwater. She grabbed at the whore's hand. "What is that?" she hissed.

The whore jumped. "It's bath oil," she stammered. "It will make your skin smell good. See?" She held the bottle up for Nathaira to smell.

Nathaira sniffed it cautiously. It smelled like roses and morning dew and made her think of picking wildflowers with Efamar for Zeythra. She nodded at the whore and released her hand. There were so many things about the humans that she did not know or understand. So many things that both fascinated and disgusted her.

She scooted down further in the tub, her skin prickling as the pink oil spread throughout the water and soothed her aching joints. The smell of the liquid filled her nostrils. She almost felt like a traitor for enjoying something so much that was human-originated.

Nathaira sat up again, rivulets of water streaming off her, and began washing the dirt and dried blood off her skin with a rag the older whore had given her. She did need a bath, and as Moirin had told her once, "When among the enemy, use everything to your advantage."

"What do your tattoos mean?" one of the younger whores, the one with red hair, asked cautiously. She was standing in the corner and watching her with the younger blonde-haired whore. Nathaira glanced up at them. They had not said a word to her since she'd come to the brothel.

"Nothing that you would understand," she said, turning back to scrubbing at her skin.

The three whores left a few minutes later, slipping out of the bathroom and clicking down the hall outside.

A soft knock sounded at the door a half hour later.

Nathaira looked up from rinsing her hair as the three human women came back in.

"Is this to your liking?" the older whore asked apprehensively, holding up a long-sleeved sky-blue tunic, black cotton pants, black laced boots, and a two-piece black leather vest that was open in a deep U in the front and held together by leather ties.

Nathaira stared at her.

"I realize that they're not what you're used to," the whore said, her voice faltering, "but I'm afraid they're the best and most usable clothing we have. Our other clothes… well, they're not for traveling… and not very practical."

"Oh, I don't know about that," a male voice said softly from the doorway leading to the bedroom. "I think they're very practical. Easy to get off."

The killer stepped into the room from the adjoining bedroom, and the three whores glanced up at him. Nathaira noted the look of terror on their faces.

"What happened while I was away?" he asked.

The older whore began stammering out an answer. Nathaira wiped at her leg with the rag, annoyed.

Why had he come back? To turn her in? She had a feeling that he would have done it already if he was going to. She stood as the older whore finished telling the killer of what had transpired while he had been away and pulled a towel off a chair by the tub. She wrapped it around herself before stepping out onto a tightly woven red-and-brown rug. The conversation lulled. Nathaira glanced up to find the killer eyeing her.

He grabbed the chair, flipping it around and straddling it. "Have a nice bath?"

Nathaira reached for another towel to dry her hair with.

"Myself," the killer said, "I usually find they're more enjoyable with company."

The two younger whores giggled nervously. Nathaira glanced at them.

"Are you hungry?" the older whore asked, pushing the younger ones toward the door. "I think we'll go get some food for you. What do you like to eat?"

Nathaira wrung her long hair out over the tub and looked at the woman. "Meat," she said. "And fruit."

"Bread?"

"No!" Nathaira said, harder than she'd meant to. "No bread," she added in a softer voice. She'd had enough moldy, worm-riddled bread during her stay at the arena to last her a lifetime.

The older whore nodded and pushed the younger whores ahead of her, then slipped out of the room again.

Nathaira listened to the sound of their heels fading into the distance, envisioning a fat, juicy venison steak and a bowl of tart berries. Her stomach growled loudly at the thought, and she put a hand to it consolingly. She could eat a whole deer for how hungry she was.

Her hair dripped on her feet in cold, wet drops. Nathaira finished wringing it out over the tub and threw it over her shoulder. She laid the towel she'd used to dry it with on the edge of the tub, then moved to the clothes the older whore had left lying on a chair.

Human clothes. Nathaira fingered the shirt.

Athrysion would be abhorred.

She picked up the black cotton trousers and let the second towel, which she'd wrapped around her body, drop to the floor, and began pulling them on.

"You know," the killer said behind her, "if you strip like that in front of people too often, they'll get suspicious of you or think you're a whore too."

"I do not care what your kind think," Nathaira replied tonelessly. She tied the laces on the trousers and reached for the shirt, the soft blue material cool against her skin. She heard the killer shift in the chair, the worn wood creaking.

"I did some inquiring today," he said as she opened the shirt up.

A clink rang through the room, and Nathaira glanced over her shoulder to see him smelling a jar of bath oil.

"I may have found you a way out of the city."

Nathaira, holding the shirt above her head, froze, hopeful, suspicious, and wary all at once.

She turned to look at the killer, meeting his mismatched eyes as he glanced up over the jar of bath oil at her. "Why would you help me out of the city?"

He twirled the jar with the fingers of one hand, eyeing her half-naked form. "Do you need a reason? I would think that you would be happy to get out of Crystoln no matter who was helping you."

Nathaira turned around again, pulling the shirt down over her head. She pulled her hair out from underneath the cloth and threw it over one shoulder. True, she didn't need a reason, but she did want to know why he was continually helping her. It didn't make sense, and she didn't like things that didn't make sense.

She pulled the small chest-length black leather vest off the chair and wrinkled her nose up at it, then tossed it aside. "How?" she asked, picking up one of the calf-length black boots from beside the chair and sitting down to slip it on.

"Through the sewers," the killer said.

Nathaira glanced up him.

"It's the safest way," he said with a shrug.

"I'm not complaining," she replied, lacing the ties on the front of the boot up and reaching for the other. "When do I leave?"

"Tonight," the killer replied, still watching her. "I have an... acquaintance that will meet us there. He will show you the way out of Crystoln."

Nathaira pulled the second boot on and tied the laces. Another human helping her? She was growing more and more nervous with how many humans were getting involved with her. What if one of them turned her in? And was the killer telling the truth? Would he truly help her out of the city?

The three whores pushed back into the room with a platter of steaming slices of turkey and glistening fruit held in their pasty white hands.

"You can eat," the killer said, looking up at them. "And then we'll leave." He picked a fat purple grape off the tray as the older whore set it down by the tub.

Nathaira nodded, scarcely hearing his words as the aroma of the meat filled her nose. Her stomach growled loudly again.

Sisters, but I'm hungry.

CHAPTER 33

Hathus

He was warm, so warm. It had to be the underworld. The soul had killed him, and now he was in the underworld, paying for all the things that he had stolen.

Gods, not the underworld. I'm too young!

A pain stabbed at Hathus's left arm, like needles jabbing into his flesh.

I've been consumed by the flames… Only isn't it that you burn forever and ever but never get destroyed?

Something cool and soft touched his forehead, and Hathus screamed and opened his eyes. The first thing he saw was Godet, bending over him with a wet rag in one hand.

The cabin boy's freckled face broke into a smile. "He's awake!" he yelled.

Hathus grimaced at the noise, his head feeling like someone had kicked it, let him rest, and then kicked it again. He squinted against the Brothers glaring down at him through gaps in the flapping black sails and creaking rigging above him. So, he wasn't dead and burning in the flames of the underworld. That was a relief… But what had happened? And why did his arm still feel like it was on fire? He tried to sit up so he could look at it, but Godet was back, dabbing at his forehead with the wet rag.

"I'm glad you're awake, sir," Godet said sincerely. The cabin boy grinned widely, his freckles joining into one giant freckle as his cheeks dimpled. "Alton—he's the physician of the *Daemon's Cry*—said you might not come to after being touched by that soul, but I prayed and prayed to Edeva that you'd get better, and she answered my prayers!"

The souls... Hathus remembered now. The green fog, the souls attacking the pirate fleet and being trapped in Sidion's cabin with one, the soul touching him and his hand turning white.

How am I not dead like the others? He opened his mouth to reply, to tell Godet that the Warulan goddess Edeva, goddess of health, healing, and life, probably wasn't all that fond of him since he'd slept with several of her priestesses once, but Godet was already talking again.

"You've been out for over a week, and everyone else was sure that you were a goner for how pale you were. That's why Alton had you brought up to the main deck—he thought the sunshine would be good for you."

Hathus frowned.

"And the sunshine does seem to be doing you good!" Godet beamed. "You look better already, although you're still a little pale. But not as pale as the others!" The cabin boy submerged his rag in a wooden bucket of water beside him and shuddered. "The fleet lost thirty-five crew in that green fog, including one of those men of yours, and every one of them was as white as this rag in my hand!" Godet held the rag up.

Hathus paled.

Thirty-five dead. Gods, that's a lot... At least I lost one of my guards, though... He opened his mouth to ask if Bathia, Sidion, and Blackwell were still alive, but Godet cut him off again.

"Captain says that he lost more crewmembers in that fog than he's ever lost in any battle before, and besides you, there's five others what was just wounded."

Wounded? How wounded? Hathus tried to sit up again, but Godet blocked his path.

"We lost two sails too, from the fire of that worldwalker fellow. He says that we were lucky any of us got out alive. He says that he's seen whole ships taken down by those soul thingies."

Droplets of water sprinkled the dark wood of the deck as the cabin boy dunked his rag into the bucket again with a splash.

The hair on the back of Hathus's neck stood on end. Caine had led them into the souls, had led them to death. But why? What could the worldwalker possibly gain from killing pirates? Unless he wanted revenge for what had happened to him in the Hunting.

Godet wrung the rag out over the bucket and put it back on his head, as gentle as a mother tending her babe.

"Does Caine still think he can find the Land of Dragons?" Hathus asked, jumping at the chance to get a word in.

The cabin boy nodded, his oversized white shirt making him look five times thinner. "I think so. He says that we got off course in the fog, and it'll take him a while to refigure where the portal is, or something like that, but that he can still get us there."

Or he'll lead us into another trap that kills the rest of us...

Footsteps sounded on the deck. Hathus turned his head slightly to see Bathia coming toward them. He smiled, relieved to see her alive.

She didn't smile back. "You're awake, then," she said, straddling a dark-brown wooden barrel next to Godet as the cabin boy rinsed the rag again.

Hathus nodded and grimaced as pain shot through his head.

"I suppose you don't remember much of what happened?" Bathia said.

Hathus frowned at the frostiness in her voice. "Uh, yes, I remember."

Why is my left arm hurting?

Bathia grunted and pulled a knife from a sheath on the back of her belt. "Alton said you might not." The weapon's etched steel blade flashed in the Brothers' rays as she tossed it up into the salt-tinged air and caught it again with deft fingers.

"Is Sidion all right?" Hathus asked, suddenly worried that perhaps the second mate not making it out of the fog was the reason for Bathia's attitude.

Bathia didn't look at him as she tossed the knife into the air again. Flash, flash, flash. "Yes, he's fine. He's on the poop deck."

"And Blackwell?" Hathus questioned.

"He's fine too."

Okay, then, so what gives? Hathus eyed her.

Is it her time of the month or something?

A stab of pain, like a knife shearing through bone, jolted through his left arm, and he cried out as white spots swam before his eyes.

"I'd better give you some more medicine for that," Godet said, voice worried. The cabin boy dropped his rag into the bucket with a splash and reached for his right arm. He tried to pull him up and failed, only causing Hathus's right arm to hurt almost as much as his left.

"You're heavy, sir," Godet panted.

"It's Hathus," Hathus said weakly, feeling like he might pass out again. Tears pricked at his eyes.

"Can you help me, ma'am?" Godet asked.

Hathus glanced up at Bathia with the cabin boy. Her gray eyes were dark and filled with anger.

What in the underworld has gotten into her?

"Thank you, ma'am," Godet murmured as she leaned down.

Hathus cried out again as the two pirates pulled him to a sitting position, more stabbing pain running through his left arm in waves.

Gods, he felt like shit. And all because a soul had touched him. What was it like to have one fly through you?

"Here you go, sir," Godet said, concern in his young voice. He held a wooden spoon full of jiggling black liquid up in the sunlight.

"Whoa!" Hathus jerked his head back from the spoon, a smell like burning sulfur filling his nostrils. "What in the five seas is that?" he croaked, the pain in his arm a throbbing inferno now that made his head pound.

"It's medicine, sir," Godet said anxiously, pushing the spoon toward him again. "For your hand."

"My hand?" Hathus frowned.

The cabin boy's freckle-spotted face paled. "Oh, sir! I wasn't supposed to tell you like that! I didn't mean to, sir. It's just that you have to take your medicine or the pain will be worse..." Godet trailed off.

Hathus glanced down at his left arm, the frown fading from his face. His hand was gone. He felt like he was standing on top of a cliff and then suddenly the cliff collapsed out from underneath him, and he was standing on nothing but air.

"The soul, sir," Godet said in a very small voice that Hathus barely heard. "It touched your hand, and Alton said it had to come off before the cold spread to the rest of your body, or you'd die. I'm sorry, sir."

Hathus closed his eyes, praying that it was just a horrible nightmare and he was going to wake up, and everything would be the way it was, and... He opened his eyes again. His hand was still gone, with nothing but a bandaged-wrapped stub in its place.

"Please, sir," Godet said quietly, the suns' golden rays warming the black decks around them. "You've got to take your medicine, sir, or the pain will become unbearable."

Hathus opened his mouth slowly as the cabin boy brought the wooden spoon up to it, his eyes plastered to the ugly white cotton-wrapped stub where his hand had once been.

Gone. The medicine tasted like tar and dung, but he hardly noticed as the thick liquid drained down the back of his throat.

Gone, gone, gone.

"Well, sir," Godet said, standing and looking down at him sorrowfully, "I've got duties to attend to, sir, but I'll be back later to give you more medicine and help you if you need it."

Hathus was vaguely aware of the cabin boy trotting off across the busy deck, the wooden bucket bumping against his leg and splashing water over the sides onto his dirty bare feet as he went.

Gone, gone, gone. His eyes moved to Bathia, sitting on the barrel and watching him with an unreadable expression. "What did Alton do with my hand?" he asked softly, not really knowing why it was suddenly important to him to know what had happened to his missing piece of flesh.

"Threw it overboard with the rest of the soul-touched crew," Bathia replied tonelessly.

Hathus shivered as an image of his limb floating down through deep, dark waters with snow-white corpses flashed through his mind.

"Only they were sung and prayed over before they went," Bathia said.

Hathus squinted up at her, noting the harsh tone in her deep voice. "Is it just me, or did somebody wake up with a stick up their ass?"

Bathia looked up, eyes narrowing.

"Ever since I woke up, you've been harping and bitching at me with a nasty little voice," Hathus said, anger at her lack of pity filling him, "and I'd like to know what in the underworld for!"

"Okay, Hathus Ryrgorion," Bathia replied in an ice-cold voice that sent shivers up his spine. "I'll tell you what for." She leaned down from the barrel and pointed the knife at him. It flashed in the Brothers' rays.

"You hid in a cabin like the coward you are while others fought and died so this fleet could take you to your destination."

"I paid you to take me there," Hathus snapped, leaning back from the knife. He remembered what Azaria had told him of Bathia hating cowards.

So that's why she's mad, because I didn't fight. Gods, and I'd thought it was something serious.

"That's not the point," Bathia hissed.

"Well, what is?" Hathus asked. "And what was I supposed to do?"

"Fight!" Bathia barked, making him jump. "Like a man."

He drew back farther as she stuck the dagger closer to him, the blade so keen he was sure one could cut their eye just looking at it. "Well, I'm no fighter," he said, glancing down at his stub with another jolt of sickness as he realized anew that it was gone. "And I knew that if I went back up there, I'd just get in your way. I was thinking of you guys, really."

Bathia laughed, a short, brittle laugh with no humor in it. "No, you were thinking only about yourself, not anyone else. I see now that you never think of anyone else, Hathus Ryrgorion."

Hathus glared up at her, the pain shivering up his arm and through his stub fading as the gods-awful medicine worked its magic. "I think of others plenty of times," he said. "And besides, I did fight down there! I lost my gods-damned hand fighting!"

He raised his stump into the air in front of her, and Bathia drew back. There, that would show her. What in the underworld did she expect from him anyway? One of the damn heroes in the bedtime stories his old nanny has used to tell him? And when had he become Hathus Ryrgorion again instead of Hathus?

Bathia stared at him for a minute, her expression unreadable. "Even Godet was helping us fight," she said finally, her voice low, quiet. "A cabin boy not even twelve years of age. A child."

Hathus looked away, guilt rising.

"A child fought in your place while you simpered and whined like a coward. If you expect me to feel sorrow for you, Hathus Ryrgorion, you are sadly mistaken. I feel no sympathy for you. You deserve exactly what you got: a coward's portion." Bathia hopped off the barrel and turned to go.

"I never claimed to be a great hero," Hathus said, glancing up at her again.

Bathia stopped, looking over her shoulder at him. "No, you did not. But I didn't think you the kind of man who would leave your friends behind to die."

Hathus blinked, taken aback. "You consider me your friend?" he asked, surprised. No one had ever been his friend before.

Bathia eyed him, her face tired. "I did," she said finally. She turned and walked away, bandanna flapping in a breeze.

Hathus stared at her as she disappeared across the main deck, her words echoing in his mind. She had thought him her friend. The idea was like a snowstorm in the BalBayr Islands. Sure, he liked Bathia and had wanted to sleep with her, but he had never considered her more than an acquaintance that would one day be gone like all the rest. That was the way his life had always been, would always be.

Hathus absentmindedly reached his left hand up to feel the stubble across his cheeks and dropped it back to his side as he remembered his hand wasn't there anymore.

Cowardly but alive, that had always been his motto.

A salty sea breeze fanned his face and pulled his lank hair to the side. Hathus glanced over the railing behind him. He was not brave, and if he ever had been, his father had beaten it from him. Bravery only caused pain, he'd learned that at age four, when he'd tried to stand up for his mother against his father. He'd been so black and blue that he couldn't go to school for three months.

He had stayed alive being a coward, though, he mused, watching the glistening greenish-blue water speed past. And that was enough.

Hathus glanced down at his left hand and paled as he saw the stump where it had been. Caine had cost him his hand, had killed thirty-five pirates. He stared at the white cloth wrapped around his stump, shock rising in him again. Most of his kind hated magic, but he did not hate it, he only feared it. Feared it as an evil that destroyed lives and took loved ones. Magic had ripped his city apart, haunted his world, destroyed his family.

Hathus turned his handless arm over, tears pricking at his eyes as he looked at it.

Magic had wrecked his childhood, and it was for magic that he had been brought out of the dungeons. No matter what he did, he could not seem to get away from it.

Voices drifted across the deck. He looked up to see Caine down the deck, talking to several pirates. He felt the cold fear from earlier creeping through him again.

If he was not careful, magic would kill him.

#

Hathus stared at his cotton-wrapped stub. It had been four days since he'd awoken to find his hand gone and still he could not get used to seeing it missing.

Water gushed by the hull of the *Daemon's Cry*, churning up into angry white foam that sprayed the sides of the ship and left the black wood glistening.

Hathus let his gaze wander from his stub to the waves. Bathia had not said one word to him since their fight four days ago, but he had caught her watching him several times, a mixed look of anger and pity on her face.

He picked at a loose string on the sleeve of his coat. He could handle her anger, but he hated the pity. He didn't need pity, didn't want it. He pulled the string out and let it catch on the wind and zip away. Maybe he should have fought that night with the souls.

A pirate in knee-high boots walked by, whistling. Hathus ground his teeth together as the tune caught his ear. The second day after he had awoken from being attacked by the soul, he had found out that the reason the soul had not finished him off was because Azaria, after lighting the lantern in Sidion's cabin with a flint and steel he'd found in Sidion's chest, had chased the soul away. He could deal with the monkey saving him if that was all that had happened, but then the crew, catching wind of the incident, had started hailing the magic creature as a hero, even making up a song about it that they sang and whistled constantly.

Hathus started pulling at another loose string sprouted by the ripping out the first. The song was growing in length by the day, but the general idea was that Hathus Ryrgorion was a coward, saved by a monkey that he hated.

He yanked viciously at the string, but it didn't come out. He hated

Azaria, hated the pirates for mocking him, hated Bathia for pitying him, hated Caine for costing him his hand, hated the Unknown Voice for bringing him out of the dungeons.

A boot scuffed on wood.

Hathus glanced up to see Wylam Caine standing a few feet away, watching him with his ghostly blue eye. He felt suddenly cold despite the warm air stroking the decks of the *Daemon's Cry*. The worldwalker had made no more signs of wanting to kill them since the incident with the souls, but he had known about the creatures and had led them into them. Hathus couldn't forget that. Every time he looked at his hand, he was reminded about it.

"What do you want?" he said. He looked back at the waves hissing past, heart racing. He'd been thinking of going to talk to Blackwell about his suspicions of Caine, but just like with Azaria, the worldwalker was being hailed a hero for helping drive the souls away long enough for the *Daemon's Cry* and the other ships of the pirate fleet to sail out of the fog. Who would believe the fleet coward against the fleet hero?

Caine stepped up to the railing beside him and leaned against it, his blue shirt flapping in a warm, salty sea breeze that made the sails above their heads snap and crack. "Bad luck about the hand," he wheezed, staring out at the waves speeding past.

Hathus didn't look at the worldwalker. He hated looking at him; the man's scarred and pitted face made his skin crawl. "Some seem to think I deserved it for being such a coward," he said quietly.

Gods, please don't let him kill me...

"Namely Bathia," Caine rasped.

Yes. "Namely Bathia."

"I have found in my travels that women are fickle things," Caine said, glancing sideways at him. "I'm sure she'll get over it soon enough. All of us have our moments of cowardice."

Hathus didn't reply but moved a very small amount to the left to get farther away from the worldwalker.

What did he want? To shove him overboard? He could just imagine Caine going on a killing rampage and shoving pirates overboard. His hand strayed toward his knife.

"There are fine metal smiths in the north of Warulan," Caine said, nodding at his stump. "I'm sure that you could get yourself a new hand crafted for you there and hardly notice that you'd lost one at all."

As if a metal hand can replace my real one. "Thanks," Hathus replied, putting his hand back on the railing. He noticed out of the corner of his eye that Caine was watching him going for his knife. "I'll remember that."

If they ever got back to civilization. The last week he had been beginning to doubt it. Along with Caine out to kill them all, he'd overheard Blackwell say the day before that they were farther out in the Eastern Sea now than he'd ever been before. Even if Caine didn't kill them, they might get lost at sea and starve to death. Or get caught in a storm. The number of ways that they could die seemed to be rising by the day.

A group of dolphins appeared in the water below them. Hathus watched the glistening gray creatures jump through the waves, keeping pace with the ships. The only good thing that had come out of the souls was that one of the men who followed him had been killed and thrown overboard. If he could just get rid of the other two, perhaps he could forget this whole "finding a dragon's heart" thing and go back to his old life before he lost more than his hand.

"You know, I still think that we are alike, you and I," Caine said, folding his burned hands in front of him on the black railing.

Hathus glanced sideways at the worldwalker and then looked back at the jumping dolphins as the coldness creeping through him sped up. "How so?" he asked, moving ever so slightly farther away again.

"We both have been in prison, we both understand the meaning of surviving, and we both know what it is like to make hard decisions that may affect others in order to stay alive ourselves."

He's talking about the souls... but why? Is he admitting that he tried to kill us? Hathus swallowed. "Meaning?" he asked, hand slipping toward his knife again.

"Meaning," Caine replied, not looking at him, "that you are a man who understands the meaning of sacrifice."

The dolphins began chattering merrily.

Hathus looked sideways at the worldwalker. "You knew that we would run into the souls," he said after a moment, heart racing. It was a dangerous thing to see, but he wanted to see what Caine's reaction would be.

"And if I did?" Caine rasped, turning and staring at him.

Hathus shrugged like he didn't care and glanced back out at the sea. "It doesn't matter much to me if a few pirates die," he said, the coldness gripping at his heart. "I simply want to go to the Land of Dragons."

It matters if I die, though… And you tried to kill us, me… Oh gods, what kind of psycho am I with?

Caine smiled, the action making the scar that cut his lips in half widen and turn whiter. He squinted against the Brothers' midday rays. "And you shall, my friend," he wheezed. "You shall."

"Something up ahead!" a voice called down from above.

Hathus glanced away from Caine and up at the crow's nest and the pirate within, on top of the mast behind them. The pirate leaned over the side of the half barrel, hands cupped at his mouth for extra volume. "Dead ahead. Something in the water!"

Hathus whitened.

Don't tell me there're more souls?

He saw Blackwell and Bathia turn up on the forecastle deck and look out ahead of the *Daemon's Cry*. He glanced at the horizon with them.

A massive dark circle rose from the surface of the ocean ahead, towering into the cloud-dotted sky for over a hundred feet.

Hathus sucked in a breath. "What is it?" he whispered, hand tingling.

Caine glanced at him, face animated. "That," the worldwalker rasped, eye flashing, "is the portal to the Land of Dragons."

Hathus glanced sideways at Caine.

He still believes that the Land of Dragons is real. Hathus looked back at the portal in front of them, growing darker and darker as the pirate ships cut through the ocean toward it. What if it was?

Hathus studied the portal, a gaping, swirling hole of blackness. Or what if Caine was leading them into another trap that would kill them all? After almost getting killed by souls, he could believe just about anything, but the idea of dragons was still ridiculous, even in otherworlds. Which left the notion that Caine was leading them into a trap that would kill them all. Hathus paled at the thought.

"Having second thoughts?" Caine asked, still watching him.

How do we even know that it is a portal? Hathus thought. He looked back at the worldwalker, spray stinging his face and moistening his wide-brimmed hat. He had never seen a portal to an otherworld before, but his mother had told him what she'd heard they looked like. He'd been plagued by nightmares as a child, and oftentimes she'd come to him when he awoke the house with his screaming, telling him stories to soothe him back to sleep.

"They can come in all different sizes," she whispered as she rocked him to sleep one especially bad night. "Some of them are as big as mountains while others can fit inside a book. The wiar, I've heard, call them gaps. Gaps in the energy that separates Argdrion from the other worlds. Most of the time you can see the portals, but occasionally they are invisible. They look like circles of pulsing energy and are some of the most powerful and beautiful things there are."

"I want to go through one and get away from Father," Hathus whispered into the darkness of his bedroom. He felt his mother draw in a breath, her smell of clean skin cocooning him.

"Me too, Hathus," she'd whispered after a few long moments. "Me too."

"You could call them that," Hathus said, gripping the railing. "Doubts."

Gods, please don't let me die. "Do we have to go so fast?" he asked, glancing up at the pirates scurrying like monkeys through the rigging above them.

"A portal is not like a port," Caine rasped as a slowly rising wind ripped at the sails and their clothes. "If we want to get through it without being torn apart by the force of the magic's pull, we have to be going as fast as the energy inside the portal."

Hathus whitened. "So there's a chance that the ship could be pulled apart?"

"Always is," Caine replied as several crewmembers tied barrels and other loose objects down around them. "Make sure everything's secure!" the worldwalker yelled. "Or the wind will pull it off the decks and into the portal! Portals are a dangerous business," Caine wheezed in a quieter voice, "and not for any idiot to fall through randomly. Although it has happened before..."

Hathus glanced back at the portal, noticing rippling lines around its edges where the darkness met the blue of the sky around it.

The worldwalker was going to kill them all. He thought about hitting Caine over the head and screaming for the pirates to turn the ships around, but Caine was already moving down the main deck.

"Speed!" Caine yelled up at Blackwell, who stood on the upper deck with Bathia and Sidion. "We need more speed, or the ships will be torn apart!"

Blackwell nodded, dagger earring bobbing, and Bathia's deep voice rang out over the *Daemon's Cry*. "Lower more sail!" she yelled as Sidion signaled for the other ships to do the same. "Get lively now, we haven't got all day!"

Pirates scrambled up the rigging, and a moment later two more black sails were lowered, extras that had replaced the ones burned up during the fight with the souls. They snapped and cracked in the gusting wind with the rest of the sails of the *Daemon's Cry*. The other pirate ships followed suit, black sails flapping in the wind as they unfurled.

Hathus moved up to where Caine stood. "You might want to brace yourself," the worldwalker said, looking over as he came up next to him. "Many a man has flown through a portal ahead of his ship because he didn't hold on tightly enough."

Hathus grabbed the railing. "Will it kill you?"

Caine smiled, that grimace of scarred lips and pitted teeth. "As sure as there's an underworld, it will. You'll be so beat up from bouncing around inside the portal that not even your mother would recognize you. A portal this size has enough energy to rip a city apart."

Hathus clutched the railing. "Shouldn't we be below decks, then?" he asked.

"As long as the ships are going as fast, or near enough, as the portal's energy, and as long as you hang on, we'll be fine. If we're not going as fast as the portal's energy, well, then even being belowdecks wouldn't do you any good."

The pirate ships sped toward the portal, which now yawned over them in the sky in a throbbing black circle.

Hathus tried to grab the railing with his left hand as the wind pulled at him. He cursed, looping his leg through the vertical black rods instead. Wind whipped his leather coat out in front of him and pulled his hair away from his face. He could see inside the portal now, where black water met the green and blue water of the Eastern Sea in swirling whorls.

We are going to die.

"Steer the ship toward the middle!" Caine yelled above the noise of the wind screaming along the decks and through the rigging.

Hathus ducked to the side as a barrel not tied down properly burst its ropes and sailed past.

The barrel smashed through the railing by the forecastle deck and flew into the portal in front of them. The portal was growing darker and darker by the moment.

"Why's it getting darker?" Hathus yelled with growing nausea as Sidion, manning the wheel on the poop deck now, pulled sharply on the black spoked wheel with bulging arms. The *Daemon's Cry* lilted hard to the side and raced through the water at an alarmingly fast speed. The other pirate ships followed, moving into a V shape as they sped through the water.

"It's the world on the other side!" Caine yelled back, wind catching his voice and pulling it away. "The closer you get to a portal, the more you can see of the world you're going to."

"What if you don't want to go through?" Hathus yelled, panic rapidly gripping him.

"By this time, you don't have much of a choice. The pull is so strong that even the largest and swiftest of Argdrion's ships couldn't get away from it!"

Hathus felt sick. He didn't know what world Caine was taking them to, but he had a strong feeling that it wasn't a good one.

Gods, I...

"We aren't going fast enough!" Caine yelled as a rope ladder a few feet away broke into two pieces and stretched toward the portal in two flapping lines.

A sail over their heads let out a high-pitched scream, and a tear the size of a sword opened down its middle.

"Shit," Caine wheezed, glancing up at the flapping pieces of cloth as mist and foam sprayed up from either side of the ship and drenched their faces. The worldwalker lurched toward the front of the ship and Hathus followed, grabbing ahold of the railing with his right hand crossed in front of him as his coat painfully whipped around his legs.

"We need to go faster!" Caine shouted up at the forecastle deck as they drew closer to it. "Or the portal will tear us to pieces!"

Bathia, hanging on to the railing on the upper deck with Blackwell, yelled, "What did you sa—" The wind caught the rest of her words and pulled them away.

"We need to go fa—" Caine started.

Another tear started in the night-black, daemon-faced sail above them with a high-pitched ripping sound.

Hathus looked up at it and cursed as his hat flew off his head and flapped away toward the portal.

Boxes and barrels flew over the sides of the ship along with his hat, sailing toward the whirling blackness of the portal in dark streaks.

"How will we get through the portal alive if it can rip a city apart?" Hathus yelled at Caine as the worldwalker wrapped both hands around the railing in front of them for support.

"If we go through at exactly the right spot at exactly the right speed, we will be fine!" Caine yelled in his ear, white hair whipping around his face and stinging Hathus's cheeks.

"But how do we know if we have the right spot or the right speed?" Hathus screamed, feeling like he might pass out.

"When we see the Land of Dragons!" Caine replied.

Hathus cursed at him and hooked one leg around the railing again as the wind ripped so fast across the decks that he heard the masts groaning at the strain. He glanced over at the towering poles, the black wood glistening with mist.

Don't break. Please don't break…

A black-bearded pirate down the deck screamed as the rope he was hanging on to tore in two. He flew over the side of the ship and toward the portal, still screaming.

Hathus paled as the man flipped end over end into the yawning darkness.

A white beam of light split the portal from top to bottom as they neared it, lighting up the sky around him with an echoing sound like cracking ice.

The *Daemon's Cry* lurched forward.

Hathus felt his neck crack as he jerked forward with the ship. Then the light enveloped them in its arms.

For a moment, there was nothing but light—blinding, pulsing, shimmering white light that swirled around them in flashing waves as the *Daemon's Cry* rushed forward. Then blackness appeared amongst the brightness, and a second later the *Daemon's Cry* was in a darkness so thick Hathus thought it might be the underworld.

Is this what death feels like?

"We're here," Caine's voice said somewhere out of the blackness in front of him as the ship slowed and the sound of water lapping at its sides caught Hathus's ear.

Hathus pulled his aching fingers off the railing, hair slowly standing on end, and reached his hand out in front of him to feel for something, anything. He heard Caine turn toward him.

"We're in the Land of Dragons."

CHAPTER 34

Darkmoon

Darkmoon ducked back into the shadow-bound alley where he and the skinchanger hid as a dozen soldiers jogged down the street in front of them, boots slapping loudly on the uneven cobbles and torches throwing fingers of light up the sides of the stone buildings on either side of them.

They really are serious about finding her, Darkmoon mused, watching until the squad had disappeared around the corner before motioning for the skinchanger to follow him.

But then, they always are with magical creatures.

They slipped out into the now-deserted street and kept to the shadows crowding the sides, moving off in the opposite direction than the soldiers had gone.

The Sisters had been almost entirely obliterated by dark rain clouds that had moved in over the city an hour ago, and now most of Crystoln lay in a deep-gray darkness, waiting for the approaching storm.

Darkmoon glanced over his shoulder at the skinchanger as they walked. The brothel madam had found her a black cloak in her whorehouse's assortment of clothing, and in the darkness, he had a hard time finding her creeping along after him.

He ducked down another side alley that sloped steadily downward between tall mortar and stone buildings, feeling in a pocket of his night-black shirt for the usual piece of chocolate that resided there. He was a fool for doing this, helping the skinchanger. But the quietness brought by her presence gave him time to think, and what he was beginning to ponder over was what exactly was the darkness coming to Argdrion, and why did the seer think he could help stop it? He had decided that it couldn't be Torin's movements. The bumbling chief advisor's plans had caused a war, but Argdrion had seen wars, and this one would be nothing new.

Darkmoon led them down an alley that was so narrow that the buildings on either side brushed his shoulders. He knew why the seer had thought he would be able to help stop the coming darkness—his secret that no one knew and no one ever would—but if this coming darkness could be stopped, then why had she been so afraid of it?

"When this darkness comes, nothing will ever be the same again…" the seer's voice croaked in his head. Nothing had been the same after the wars and the Hunting either.

A dog barked several times as Darkmoon slipped between two stone and mortar homes and started down a series of uneven, dirty steps, then fell silent. He glanced back at the skinchanger again. She was still following, but not too closely. She acted like he was the plague for how she avoided him. But then, no magical creatures liked humans, and he doubted they ever would.

They reached the end of the stairs, and Darkmoon stepped off them and down onto a narrow, cobbled walkway running along the edge of a wide sewer. He cocked his head, listening. The night was quiet but for a late-spring breeze that hinted at summer and carried with it the mingled scents of the city—food, sweat, musk, stale wine, and cheap perfume—and the soft slapping of the dark water against the canal's sides.

Darkmoon glanced up and down the sewers, scanning the shadows for movement.

The skinchanger stepped off the stairs and stopped beside him, looking down into the sewers. "Humans are disgusting," she said, deep voice breaking the silence of the night.

Darkmoon glanced at her. She was beautiful, the skinchanger. There weren't many women who he thought were beautiful. After being with and seeing so many, they all began to look alike, but the skinchanger was definitely one of them. Her beauty was different than the others, and not a beauty that all men would notice. It was a fierce beauty, a beauty that came from within her. He motioned with his head for her to follow and moved off down the walk, his soft suede boots making no noise on the cement underfoot.

The seer hadn't said when the darkness was coming, a typical aspect of prophetic warnings. They'd let you know what horror was going to come upon you but were not clear as to when so that you spent your life worrying over it.

Darkmoon heard a door close in the distance, the sound echoing past the deserted factories lining the sewers and down the wide canal that the dark water flowed down. He had been given a warning when he was a boy. Of darkness coming. That warning had been vague as to when, too, but terrifying and dark, and so, so true.

A low stone arch with a rusty iron gate set into its middle loomed out of the darkness ahead. Darkmoon moved toward it, scanning the surrounding shadows for signs of N'san. He put a half-gloved hand to the rusty gate and pushed it open on creaking hinges, then stepped under the arch and into the courtyard. The skinchanger followed.

A flock of pigeons taking rest for the night in the eaves of a closed-up warehouse cooed softly and jostled each other around.

Darkmoon moved farther into the courtyard, glancing up at the birds. How many animals would be killed in the following days as Eromor soldiers combed the city for the skinchanger? And how many humans too, for that matter.

Light footfalls, barely audible over the noise of the sewer as it disappeared into a stone tunnel leading off under the city, caught his ear. He pivoted on the heel of one dark boot.

"You are late, N'san," he said quietly. He hated tardiness. Tardiness was for fine ladies and rich nobles. It was not a luxury that an assassin could afford.

The darkness hovering around a bird-poop streaked warehouse wall several yards away rippled, and N'san, hands folded in front of his large stomach, stepped into the middle of the courtyard. The heavy ruby necklace around his neck glinted dully in the semidarkness.

"My friend." The underworld lord smiled, silver teeth flashing. "I'm so pleased to see you again." He wore a red silk turban, dark-gray tunic, and long-sleeved robe.

Darkmoon glanced at the shadows behind N'san. "I'm sure." N'san was not alone.

"You know, I'm surprised that you're not in the pits tonight, Darkmoon," N'san went on, moving farther into the courtyard. "Earning a little extra money. I could have handled this situation alone if you'd asked, escorted the woman to the sewers myself."

Darkmoon scanned the broken windows of the surrounding warehouses, the dark alleys on either side of the canal. "I wanted to make sure you did what I asked," he said. He glanced back at N'san. "And I thought I should give you time to find more fighters to restock your supply."

N'san threw his head back and laughed.

A few pigeons lunged out of the eaves of the stone factory making up the back wall of the courtyard and winged off over the rooftops.

"Ah, my friend," N'san said, "you know that you can trust me."

Darkmoon didn't reply.

"Is this the woman?" N'san asked, turning toward the skinchanger with his dark brows raised.

The skinchanger, standing beside and behind him a little, looked up sharply. Darkmoon put a hand on her arm to steady her. "Yes," he said, making his voice sad. "The whore who killed a soldier. Poor girl. It was an accident, and now she's being hunted like an animal."

N'san's eyes moved back to him. "Mm, such a pity," the underworld lord murmured. "And an interesting choice of words. Animal."

Darkmoon's eyes narrowed.

He's betrayed me…

"I trust you brought what I told you to?" he asked, scanning the shadows once more, this time for escape routes.

N'san, staring at the skinchanger again, glanced back at him and smiled widely. "I brought what you asked, yes." The underworld lord snapped two ringed fingers, and three men in dark tunics stepped out of the warehouse behind him. "And a few things of my own that I think will not be to your liking."

The skinchanger inhaled sharply and took a step backward.

Darkmoon reached a hand toward her again. What he did not need was her panicking and changing. A scared skinchanger bashing up the sewers of Crystoln would attract the soldiers' attention like wolves to blood. Skinchangers were an intelligent race, but their first reaction to most things was to fight their way out, and in this case, that was not the best plan.

Darkmoon shook his head at N'san, clucking his tongue against the roof of his mouth. "N'san, N'san. Did you really think I hadn't noticed your friends lurking in the shadows? You should know better than to try and trick me. And only three men?" Darkmoon shook his head again. "That's low. Could wound my pride."

N'san laughed again. "You always were quick with words, Darkmoon." He smiled, teeth flashing. "It's such a pity that I'm going have to watch you die. I'll miss your humor, friend."

Darkmoon smiled back humorlessly, his blue and green eyes darting around the courtyard. He curled the fingers of his left hand up toward the knife hidden in his vambrace. He could easily take N'san and his henchmen down, but the skinchanger would probably start fighting if he did and attract the soldiers. If he could just keep her from changing and making noise, everything would be fine, but how to do that was another matter.

"Oh, and by the way," N'san said with another smile, "I didn't think just three men could defeat you and your skinchanger, Darkmoon. That's why I brought more."

Darkmoon looked up as torch light lit up the buildings around them and boots clapping on stones echoed from the street behind.

Soldiers. Clever. He let the knife fall into his hand and threw it at the nearest henchman's neck.

Blood spurted out of the man's throat in a bright-red arc, and he fell backward with a thud on the cobbles of the courtyard, gurgling blood.

Darkmoon threw two more knives at the other henchmen before grabbing the skinchanger around the waist in one quick series of movements.

"What are you doing?" she snarled, the smell of rose oil filling his nose as he half carried, half dragged her toward the rushing sewers. She kicked him in the knee hard. Darkmoon cursed and threw her into the water.

"Swim!" he yelled, looking up as soldiers, torches hissing in the night, jogged down the stairwell and up the sewers. He glanced back down at the skinchanger again, watching until she disappeared into the tunnel before wheeling away from the dark water as soldiers came piling into the courtyard.

His breathing slowed, the feeling of calmness and awareness that overcame him when he was ready to kill slowly coming over him.

N'san caught his eye, still standing where he'd left him, with his hands folded calmly in front of him and a placid expression on his dark face. Darkmoon bent his wrist, and a knife slid into his palm, the blackened blade cool against his skin. He would relish killing N'san. No one had ever betrayed Argdrion's best assassin before and lived to tell of it, and there wouldn't be a first.

"My child…" his mother whispered, appearing out of the mist drifting through the courtyard. Fire crackled around her, melting her skin, burning her hair. She screamed, head flying backward.

Darkmoon staggered back, the knife falling from his fingertips.

Not now!

An arrow whistled by his head, nicking the tightly woven fabric of his cloak.

His mother disappeared as a dozen more arrows flew toward him from opposing rooftops. He jumped into the air, dodging each one as it whistled by.

Shouting echoed through the night from his left.

Darkmoon looked up to see flatboats filled to overflowing with black dragon-helmed soldiers coming down the canal. He let a half dozen stars and daggers fly as the first wave of soldiers on land started toward him, then flipped over backward and landed in the sewers with a splash.

Water engulfed him, soaking his clothes and pulling him downward as it roared in his ears and swept him toward the tunnel.

For a few moments, there was only water as he vainly tried to find where it ended, and a strange, cold feeling slowly began to creep through his veins. Fear. And memories.

Darkmoon saw a dark room flash before his eyes, a large brown barrel of black water sitting in its middle. Screams echoed through the catacombs around the room; iron hooks swung from the stone ceiling above.

His fingers scraped painfully on rough mortar, and he grabbed at the sides of the tunnel. Something solid met the heels of his boots. He shoved away from the floor of the canal and erupted from the surface of the water, spitting water and gasping for air.

Stones came into view above him as Darkmoon's eyes came accustomed to the darkness. He reached out a hand to touch them as they swept past his head.

N'san is going to pay for this.

Something soft brushed by his leg.

Darkmoon tried not to think about what it probably was as the current pulled him back under again. He cursed as water filled his mouth and the image of the room came back. Pushing to the surface once more, he swam forward with strong, sure strokes.

A maintenance ledge ran along one side of the tunnel.

Darkmoon spotted the skinchanger sitting on it, not too far from where he was, and swam toward her, fighting against the increasing current as he went.

"Did you know about this?" she snarled, grabbing his arm with a grip like iron as he hauled himself, water running off his clothes in rivulets, up onto the wet mortar beside her.

Darkmoon spat a piece of debris into the water below. The voices stopped.

"If I did," he said, spitting again, "do you think I'd have come along with you just to take a swim in the sewers?" He wiped a wet sleeve across his mouth, the room with the water barrel still fresh in his mind.

The skinchanger narrowed her golden eyes, like balls of fire in the darkness, and let go of his arm. The cold tunnel air cooled the warmth of her touch.

He would rip N'san's throat out for this. Darkmoon spat another mysterious piece of debris into the dark water rushing past.

No, first he'd torture him until he begged for death, then he'd rip his throat out. He squeezed water out of his shirt with a squish. He did have to admit, though, he was impressed that the underworld lord had had it in him to betray him. It took guts, something he had never thought N'san had.

Darkmoon undid the interlocking blade clasp on his cloak and pulled the wet cloth off his back, wringing it out over the water flowing by beneath them. A small part of him was glad to be with the skinchanger, even if it was for just a little longer. Glad to be free of the voices and memories.

"So, what now?" the skinchanger asked, watching him.

Darkmoon glanced up at her, raising his scar-cut brow. "What now?"

"What do we do now?" she elaborated.

He held one arm up to dump water out of his vambrace. "Well, personally I don't really care what you do, but I'm going to get out of the sewers and kill N'san." He stood.

The skinchanger did the same.

"You said you'd get me out of the city."

"Swim that way." Darkmoon waved an arm down the tunnel. "You'll get out eventually." If she didn't go down the wrong tunnel, that was, and end up back in the heart of the city. He wanted her to stay with him. He hated himself for it, but he did.

The skinchanger stepped closer to him. "You gave me your word," she hissed.

Darkmoon eyed her. She was afraid. Afraid that she couldn't get out of the city on her own.

He looked out at the passing water, the smell of waste and rotting bodies and food tickling his nose. He would get his revenge on N'san, but if he stayed in Crystoln, he wouldn't be able to live like he had before, not with the army now after him for helping a magical creature escape. It would be best to go to Rothborn and his closest mansion and make a plan as he waited for the immediate hunt for him to pass over. The skinchanger would go with him, he knew, until she had repaid her debt to him. Half of him wanted to stop her, the other did not.

"Okay," Darkmoon said, tying his cloak around his waist, "but be prepared to get wet again." He turned toward the water, running three fingers over his belts to see how many knives he'd lost. There were seven vacant sheaths. He scowled. The knives were hard to get. Specially made for him by a blacksmith in Eoithbyn, an ancient mining city in the frozen wastes of Nilfinhèim. The knives were crafted from yuyrin steel, a lightweight but sturdy metal first found in the Second Age and rare enough now that each knife sold for over fifteen thousand aray.

"Well, shouldn't we get going?" the skinchanger said behind him.

Darkmoon watched a turd float by. It angered him that he wanted to be with her. Angered him that he was relying on her presence to drive the voices and memories away and not driving them away himself.

"Try to keep up," he said. He slipped over the edge of the walkway and back into the water.

They floated past two round stone pillars marking the end of the tunnel and into a massive stone room with six dark tunnels leading away from it like the spokes of a wagon wheel.

Darkmoon headed for the tunnel straight across from them, his boots slowly filling with water as he swam, making it harder to stay up. He fought the familiar fear that crept through him as the room with its water-filled barrel flashed through his head again. Using his hands like cups, he pulled himself back up as he slowly started sinking.

"The only creatures who drown are those too afraid to look for a way out..." Arayn J'altayr's voice murmured in his ear. He had been afraid of water and drowning when he had come to Arayn J'altayr. The assassin lord had broken him of that fear by locking him in a massive barrel full of water with only three inches of breathing space at the top. For four days and four nights.

Darkmoon skirted around a mass that looked like a three-day-old half-eaten dog carcass. He glanced back at the skinchanger, who was still following him resolutely. "The current will take you along with it," he said as she came up next to him. "Don't try to swim too much. It will wear you out, and you'll need your strength for the falls."

"Falls?" she asked, glancing up at him.

Darkmoon spat a piece of debris out of his mouth. "You'll see." He swam ahead of her a ways, water tickling his spine.

They floated with just the hiss of the water against the cement sides of the tunnel for over an hour, until a bone-numbing roar began resonating from the darkness ahead, growing steadily.

Darkmoon backpedaled against the now faster-moving current and came to a stop, holding a hand out for the skinchanger to do the same as she came even with him.

She inhaled sharply as his fingers brushed against her shoulder and swam sideways a little so that he wasn't touching her anymore.

"The falls are around the next curve," Darkmoon said, noting the movement. He paddled in place, keeping himself from moving forward too fast. "Whatever you do, don't reach out to try and stop yourself, and don't let your legs flop around. You'll have your limbs ripped off before you know what's happening. Not that it matters to me if you do," he added, looking down the tunnel, "but don't say I didn't give you fair warning."

"Consider me warned," the skinchanger replied. She swam past him, her partially tattooed face glistening with water.

Darkmoon watched her swim away. She had spirit. He'd forgotten how much skinchangers did. He followed her, the roaring so loud now that his ears rang.

They rounded a sharp curve in the tunnel, and the first fall was before them, plunging down hundreds of feet into the darkness, where it would meet the next fall and the next, until the last deposited them into the man-made lake that ran under the city walls and carried the sewers of Crystoln to the River Sar below.

"Remember what I said!" Darkmoon shouted over the noise of the water as they sped toward the white-capped, misting fall. He clamped his legs and arms to his body and sucked in a breath.

And sailed over the edge.

CHAPTER 35

Azkanysh

Shayr Jahayan was dead, murdered. Azkanysh glanced down at the Guardian Council standing below the dais. They had murdered him. She knew by the satisfied looks on their faces, the bold glints in their eyes. They were warning her, warning her of what happened to those who allied with her.

"A sad day," Nupar Abayn'uni said in a voice that could not sound any sadder than if he'd just heard the news that his camel had died. "A very sad day indeed."

Azkanysh curled her slender fingers into the golden armrests of the throne. They thought to scare her by this murder, intimidate her so that she would stop pushing for women's freedom. They would be disappointed.

"Yes," she said, her voice echoing through the crowded, stuffy throne room, "it is a sad day. And the mourners will fill the air of Sussār with their weeping, and black lotuses will be tossed into the River Akhuran, but at the moment, we must address the other side to this death, the murder side."

Voices murmuring rang through the arched throne room. Nupar dipped his head. "It is as you say, Queen of Queens."

"The facts," Azkanysh said, addressing Vyzir Dsamihur.

The vyzir stepped forward. "Shayr Shashun Jahayan was found dead in his home this morning, at the hour of ten," Vyzir Dsamihur called loudly. "His body was discovered by a slave, lying in an alley that leads between the stables of his estate and his house, a knife wound in his back. The weapon used to commit the crime was not found."

The throne room buzzed with hushed voices.

"Are there any suspects?" Azkanysh asked, watching Shayr Nupar to see his reaction. If the Guardian Council had murdered Shayr Jahayan, then Shayr Nupar had led them. He was the loudest in voicing his opinions against women being in the army, and several times over the last week, she had caught him watching Shayr Jahayan and her as they talked, a dark expression on his long face.

"One, Queen of Queens," Vyzir Dsamihur said. "Shayr Jahayan's man-slave, a man called Manuil."

Azkanysh glanced at Vyzir Dsamihur, then back at the council. So, they had a cover story. She should have known that they would not have murdered Shayr Jahayan without someone to place the blame on, someone to point the finger at.

"And why is this man suspected?" she asked, tearing her eyes away from the council to scan the watching faces of the throne room. There were women in the crowd now, shayras and concubines and wives of Vosbarhan who had started attending court sessions after her ruling that women were to be allowed in the throne room.

Paruhi caught her eye by a pillar, and Azkanysh met her daughter's nervous gaze for a moment before looking back to the Guardian Council. The palace did not know yet of Tamar's "sickness." She planned on announcing it at the end of the court, after they had decided on a course of action about Shayr Jahayan's murder. She prayed that they would believe her.

"A stable slave saw the man leaving the alley around nine thirty this morning, Queen of Queens," Vyzir Dsamihur said. "In a hurry, as if running from something."

Azkanysh glanced at Nupar again. The council no doubt thought that without Shayr Jahayan to back her, she would not rule for women working. But she did not need Shayr Jahayan to give her confidence to do what was right. She did not need anyone. "Let the slave be brought in," she said loudly.

Vyzir Dsamihur clapped his long hands together, and a purple-cloaked guard leading a slave boy stepped through the gathered crowd. The guard, hand clamped on the nervous-looking boy's shoulder, stopped with him in front of the parted Guardian Council members.

"What is your name, child?" Azkanysh asked. She caught a whiff of warm horse manure and hay; a few council members wrinkled their noses up in distaste.

"Njdāh, Queen of Queens," the boy squeaked.

"Bow when you address the Queen of Queens," the guard growled. A flat-nosed, ebony-skinned man from the northern deserts, he shoved the slave boy onto his knees on the gold-and-white-tiled floor.

"There is no need for harshness, guard," Azkanysh said evenly. "Come, Njdāh," she said, glancing at the slave boy, "tell us what you saw that day."

The dark-eyed boy glanced up at the guard and whipped a dirty black sleeve across his running nose. "I was doing my job," he began, staring at the floor beneath him, "cleaning out Shayr Jahayan's stalls with the other stable boys. There's two of them—Khot and Hēyros are their names. Then one of the older slaves came in, saying that Shayr Jahayan wanted his horse brought out to him, the big black one with the white socks, his name is Hyrosas, Shayr Jahayan got him in northern Araysann last year from a—"

"Cut the details, boy," the guard growled, slapping the kneeling slave on the side of the head, "and tell the Queen of Queens what you saw."

"Guard!" Azkanysh barked. "That is enough. Next time you do anything other than help the boy up, I'll have your cloak." She hated physical abuse, even to slaves. It reminded her of Vosbarhan's beatings, and she never wanted to remember those again.

The guard bowed stiffly.

"Continue, Njdāh," Azkanysh said as the slave boy rubbed at his reddening ear and glared at the stone-faced guard. "What happened after that?"

"I brought Shayr Jahayan his horse," Njdāh replied, going back to staring at the floor. "Only Shayr Jahayan wasn't in the courtyard like the slave said. No one was."

Someone coughed in the crowd.

Azkanysh watched a fly buzz around Njdāh's head. He didn't seem to notice it. "What did you do then, Njdāh?" she asked.

"I waited, and then Manuil, Shayr Jahayan's man-slave, came out of an alley, quickly like, and he said that Shayr Jahayan wouldn't be needing his horse and that I should go back to the stables."

"And did you go?" Azkanysh asked.

"Yes," Njdāh said, "and then later we heard that Shayr Jahayan had been found dead."

Azkanysh leaned back in the throne as murmurs echoed through the throne room. What she couldn't understand was why the Guardian Council would want Shayr Jahayan's body to be found. It would have been simpler to dump the body in the Akhuran for the crocodiles to eat and claim that the older man had gone for a walk and accidentally fallen in the river. Why did they want people to know that Shayr Jahayan had been murdered?

Azkanysh glanced at the council, standing in a group and murmuring among themselves. Or was it a warning to those who might think of allying with her?

"Where is this slave Manuil?" she asked.

The throne room looked up at her.

Vyzir Dsamihur stepped forward. "We do not know, Queen of Queens," he said evenly. "He disappeared after the slave boy saw him. We have soldiers searching the city for him even now."

Azkanysh nodded. That the slave had run made it look like even more like he had been the one to murder Shayr Jahayan. How would she convince the court otherwise?

"This case, Queen of Queens," Shayr Nupar spoke up, "seems to be a fairly simple one. We know who Shayr Jahayan's murderer was, and when we find him, the man will be executed for his crime."

"But are you sure that the slave killed Shayr Jahayan?" Azkanysh asked sharply.

Nupar, turning back toward the rest of the council, glanced up at her. "Queen of Queens?"

"Just because a slave saw the man coming out of the alley that Shayr Jahayan was found dead in does not mean that the man committed the murder," Azkanysh elaborated. "Perhaps he found the body and grew scared and ran, or maybe he saw the real murderer and, fearing for his life, fled."

"We have a direct witness seeing the man flee from the scene minutes before the body was found," Shayr Tukayr said. "Slaves are notoriously treacherous, as well all know, Queen of Queens. The man probably wanted some trinket that Shayr Jahayan wore, or maybe he simply thought that by killing the shayr, he could get his freedom."

Azkanysh stared at the council. If the stable slave had seen anyone but a slave coming from the direction of Shayr Jahayan's body, then two witnesses would be needed to convict said person. A slave accused of a crime only needed one witness. She wondered if the council had thought of that and if that was why they had accused a slave. Two witnesses would be harder to fabricate, harder to keep their stories matching.

"The Guardian Council advises," Shayr Tukayr spoke up as the council broke apart, "that the man-slave Manuil is guilty of murdering Shayr Jahayan and that he shall be found and executed for his crime."

Heads nodded in the throne room. Azkanysh tapped her fingers on the armrest of the throne. She would not rule for something that was not true, no matter what the kingdom or the council thought.

"I do not share the council's views that Shayr Jahayan's man-slave murdered him," she called. "I feel that some other person may be responsible for his death, and I do not wish for the wrong man to be brought to trial and have Shayr Jahayan's true murderer run free."

"Forgive me, Queen of Queens," Shayr Nupar said, "but feelings should not decide a ruling. There is ample evidence that Shayr Jahayan's man-slave murdered him. I advise that you rule as such."

"And you forget, Shayr Nupar," Azkanysh snapped, looking at him, "that I am Queen of Queens, and I will rule as I see best. I rule that an investigation shall be made into Shayr Jahayan's murder, starting with those closest to him, those having reasons to kill him."

The throne room was silent for a long while. The council's faces were murderous.

Azkanysh ignored them. She was tired of playing games with them, tired of trying to get their favor. She glanced at Vyzir Dsamihur and nodded. He stepped forward.

"A formal announcement from the crown," the vyzir called loudly over the quiet throne room. "Princess Tamar has taken ill with summer fever and will be bedridden for an unknown length of time."

Voices started buzzing again, like flies launching into the air after a short rest.

Azkanysh stood, ending court. Vyzir Dsamihur had found out that morning that Tamar had snuck onto a ship bound for Warulan. She had arrangements to make to bring her daughter back and Shayr Jahayan's relatives to visit to offer her condolences. The old shayr had never married nor spawned any children, but he had a younger brother. Perhaps he knew something about Shayr Jahayan's death, had seen something in the last few days that would help her prove the council guilty.

"There is one more thing that needs to be discussed, Queen of Queens," Nupar said in a voice that bore barely concealed hatred.

The court crier, mouth open to end the court session, glanced at her. Azkanysh looked down at the council. "And what is that?"

"A new Guardian Council member must be elected, Queen of Queens, to replace Shayr Jahayan," Tukayr spoke up, stepping forward.

"And who could be the new member of the council when we all know Shayr Jahayan has no heirs?" Azkanysh asked.

"The Guardian Council," Shayr Nupar said, "has permission, according to law, to appoint a new member upon the event that a deceased member has no heir."

How convenient.

"And do I have a say in the matter?" Azkanysh asked, wondering if she should try and get someone on her side back on the council. If she could find someone who was on her side.

"No, Queen of Queens," Nupar replied, a little smugly, Azkanysh noted. "The council alone decides who is to be their new member. It is the law, if you wish to see it." He said the last words with a slightly mocking air, assuming she could not read.

Azkanysh did not challenge him. True, she could read now, but not the long words found in the laws. Until she could, she would not let the kingdom know of her education. It would avoid embarrassing herself, avoid mocking.

"Then pick your new member," she said coldly, sitting back down. She should have a say on who the new member was, but right now she was restless to be away, arranging for a ship and guards to sail after Tamar before the kingdom found out what had really happened to her, and she did not feel like arguing with the council.

Nupar moved over to Zarmeyr, who was standing a few feet behind the council, and placed a hand on his shoulder. "We already have, Queen of Queens." Nupar turned to the throne room. "The Guardian Council chooses Prince Zarmeyr as its twelfth member!"

Murmurs of consent ran through the throne room. Azkanysh stared at Nupar, horror spreading through her. To have Zarmeyr on the council, and in a position to advise opposite her in court sessions... The kingdom was fond of her son, with many loudly voicing their anticipation of his becoming King of Kings at the end of the year. If she continued to go over the council's heads on rulings with Zarmeyr as one of them, the kingdom would be even more angry than they would be with her just going over the council's heads. They would begin murmuring, saying that she did not care what even the crown prince thought. Azkanysh swallowed, throat dry. This would slow her down.

"Well, then," she said after a moment, voice tight, controlled, "I guess we have our new Guardian Council member."

Shayr Nupar bowed.

She stood again.

"The Queen of Queens is now leaving the throne room!" the court crier yelled loudly to those gathered. "All praise Azkanysh, Queen of Queens..."

Azkanysh moved down the marble stairs leading from the dais, hands folded tightly in front of her to keep them from shaking with anger. Her main course of action now would be to prove that the council had murdered Shayr Jahayan. If she could do that, she could have them executed and dissolve the council before their heirs could take on the white robes, ending hindrance from them for good.

"Tell me, Queen of Queens," Nupar said, approaching her as she reached the floor of the throne room, "should we be worried about Princess Tamar?"

Azkanysh glanced up at the shayr, noting Zarmeyr watching her from where the rest of the council stood. "I do not think so," she said casually, meeting Nupar's gaze. "But I am afraid that she will be in bed for a long while yet."

Nupar dipped his head. "Sad. I would like to pay my respects to her."

Azkanysh held his gaze, pulse quickening. "Her physicians are not allowing her to see any visitors. It would cause too much strain on her health, and there is fear of the sickness spreading."

"Ah." Nupar glanced up at the emptying throne room. "Well, as soon as she is feeling up to visitors and her physicians allow it, let me know, will you?" He looked back at her, gaze unreadable. "Queen of Queens." He bowed and backed away.

Azkanysh stared after him, fear gripping at her heart. He knew. She didn't know how, but he knew. She felt suddenly cold despite the heat of the day. If the kingdom discovered that Tamar had run away and that she had lied to them about it on top of her ruling over the council's heads on Shayr Jahayan's death… There was no legal way that anyone could remove her from the throne yet that she knew of, but she wouldn't be surprised if Nupar and the council were working on it.

The council moved off down the throne room after the last of the shayrs and shayras. Azkanysh watched them. She did not want Zarmeyr to become King of Kings, did not want to give up the golden lyon crown. There was so much she had planned, so little time to do it in between now and the end of the year…

What if Zarmeyr never reached his eighteenth birthday? It was a dark thought. Azkanysh pushed it away. She would not fall to the council's level.

Vyzir Dsamihur stepped up behind her. Azkanysh turned and made for the door in the back wall of the throne room. She needed to make another move to counter the Guardian Council's voting in Zarmeyr, something to prove to them that she was not defeated, and would not be.

A sudden thought occurred to her, like a gift from the Family of gods and goddesses. There was no law that stated women could not learn to read and write, only old tradition and passed-down beliefs. If she were to hire tutors for Paruhi and Kayani and let the kingdom know it, it might encourage others to let their daughters learn as well. She could even have a dinner for all the leading shayrs and shayras of the city, discussing her new idea and encouraging them to do the same for their daughters.

Azkanysh sped up her steps as she moved into the hall outside the throne room, a million ideas blossoming in her mind. She would have to word her idea to the shayrs and shayras carefully, but if she succeeded in winning even just a few of them over, it would be a step toward more change in the kingdom. A step that wouldn't involve going over the council's heads and angering tradition.

"Vyzir Dsamihur," Azkanysh said, glancing at the vyzir as they walked.

"Yes, Queen of Queens?" Vyzir Dsamihur asked, stepping forward.

"I want tutors hired for my daughters," Azkanysh said, looking back at the sunlit hall in front of them. "And a banquet planned for tomorrow night. I have something to tell the city of Sussār."

CHAPTER 36

Tamar

The noise of a hundred thousand horse hooves, hundreds of supply wagons and camp slaves and followers, and three thousand elephants' slow, steady walking was like sitting in the middle of a thunderstorm, earthquake, and sand flurry all at once.

Tamar put a hand to her ear against the noise, eardrums ringing. She had never heard so much racket in all her life. And the dust... There was a pillar of it trailing into the sky as high as a mountain over the ten-mile-long train of soldiers. She coughed, her hijab only filtering out half of the dust that she rode through, and turned in her saddle to look at the dust cloud trailing behind them. If they wanted Eromor to know that they were coming, she couldn't conceive a better way to do it.

She voiced this aloud to Aghasi and Maigar, who rode on either side of her.

"It doesn't matter," Aghasi replied, half yelling to be heard above the clatter of the marching army. "Eromor has known our exact location since we landed on their coast." He pointed a dark finger at the cloud-streaked sky above them, and Tamar followed it to a black speck circling their position.

"A raven?" she asked, glancing back down at Aghasi.

"A raven," Maigar said from her other side.

Tamar glanced at him.

"Eromor's been sending them out ever since we reached Warulan,"

Aghasi said. "We couldn't fart without Eromor knowing it. There's a spy around here somewhere probably." He scanned the waving grasslands around them. "The raven is to send a message back to Eromor's army."

Tamar looked back up at the black shape as it circled once more and then flapped off into the distance. They'd packed up camp and begun marching into the Opherian Plains before the Brothers had risen the night that Paramiz and his men found her, and for the past three days had done nothing but march, lightly camp for the night, and march again. She guessed they'd covered over thirty miles since she'd joined the army. Her backside definitely knew that they had.

But it wasn't unbearable, even with the dust and the long riding and poor-tasting food, and she was getting better at fighting. She had begun training with the rest of the army the morning after the gond had found her, practicing standing and marching and jumping and striking with thousands of other women and men. Her hands were getting callouses, her muscles starting to burn.

Aghasi said that she had a natural-born talent for fighting. Maigar said that he was glad they had her in their gond for when the fighting came.

Tamar turned her gaze to the waving golden grass around them. She was used to men who talked down to her and ignored her and insulted her, but Aghasi and Maigar... they were different. They talked her like an equal, joked and laughed with her like an equal, treated her like an equal. She liked it.

"Why don't we find the spy and kill him?" she asked Aghasi as the horse he'd found for her in the army's extras plodded steadily along after those of the 34th Gond members in front of them.

Aghasi glanced sideways at her, squinting against the Brothers' late-morning rays. "No point. I mean, good luck out here."

Maigar snorted. "It'd be like trying to find a needle in a haystack." He laughed.

Tamar glanced around them again, the waving grasslands stretching off for as far as her eyes could see. Aghasi had a point. But the thought that someone was spying on them angered her. It reminded her of the palace, of Mistress Lorrig watching her from the shadows and pouncing on her when she did something that wasn't proper according to her station as a woman.

They climbed a rolling hill, and Tamar coughed again as fresh dust sifted through the close-knit cloth of her hijab.

Maigar grinned next to her.

"You'll get used to it, Yeva," Aghasi assured her, patting his palomino mare's neck. "Just be glad you're in the 34th Gond of horsemen and not the 107th. You'd have so much dust in your face you couldn't see more than a few feet in front of you."

Maigar laughed. "I almost feel sorry for the poor bastards. But not that sorry," he added with another laugh.

Tamar didn't say anything. She was just happy to be in a gond, in the army, at all, and part of something so big and epic as a battle that it didn't matter to her what gond she was in.

They crested the hill, and the breathtaking view of the plains and distant dark line of the Astarion Mountains that marked the border between Eromor and Dyridura became theirs.

"Of course," said Aghasi, "if you were in the Immortals, then you could ride at the head of the army with the Erāyn Khan and miss the dust altogether, but I guess you're just unlucky that you ran into a gond instead of them."

The Immortals! Tamar leaned forward eagerly in her bay's saddle to try and catch a glimpse of the King of Kings's—or Queen of Queens's, in her mother's case—elite soldiers' golden armor at the distant head of the column. It was impossible to see anything through the dust ahead of her, though, so she eased back down in her saddle. She would love to ride with the Immortals, but the legendary warriors were not conscripted soldiers, and it took years and years of training to become one of them. Many had died trying to meet the Immortals' standards, and some had even gone insane from the brutal tortures that they underwent to make them Zarcayra's best fighters.

"How long have you both been in the army?" Tamar asked Aghasi and Maigar as their horses started down the other side of the hill.

A fly buzzed around her mare's nose, and the horse shook its head, mane flicking against its neck.

"Five years," Aghasi replied first. He patted his mare's neck. "Dshukhiy and I have been through a lot in our years of fighting, haven't we, old girl?" The horse snorted.

"You named your horse after the ancient Heroine of Syrca?" Tamar asked, incredulous.

Aghasi glanced sideways at her, squinting against the sun. "You don't like her?"

"No, I love her! She was fantastic, even if most people try to act like she never truly existed."

"By most people, you mean men, I suppose?" Maigar interjected.

"I do," Tamar replied, glancing at him defiantly.

He grinned.

"I take it you're for the new freedom that the Queen of Queens wants for the women of Zarcayra?" Aghasi said from her other side.

Tamar looked back at him. "More than anything," she said fiercely.

Aghasi patted Dshukhiy's neck again. "Well, I can't say that I think it's such a bad notion."

"Especially if they all turn out to be like the Heroine of Syrca," Maigar added.

Tamar glanced sideways at him. "The Heroine of Syrca" was an old story that had existed before Zarcayra had become a kingdom, when Araysann had had thirteen kingdoms. Syrca had been the capital of one of the thirteen kingdoms, the small kingdom of Heyrostis, and during the latter half of the Fourth Age it had come under siege from two neighboring kingdoms that wanted Heyrostis's lands and wealth.

For seven years, the two kingdoms besieged Syrca, slowly killing off her warriors and starving her people. In the eighth year of the extensive siege, the two kingdoms were sure that they had won, for hardly a soldier was to be seen on the walls of the city or a voice to be heard issuing from her streets. The two kingdoms advanced on Syrca, preparing to overrun the city and take control of it, when a lone figure appeared on the wall, a girl of sixteen with long brown hair billowing in the wind.

The armies of the two kingdoms laughed as the girl mounted the wall and stood there, for she was dressed in dented armor and carried a sword twice her size.

"Sieging kingdoms!" she called, her voice echoing through the valley around Syrca and ringing clearly in every soldier's ear. "You shall not take Syrca. Not today, nor tomorrow, nor any other day!"

The armies of the two kingdoms slowed as the girl spoke, calling out with derision and mockery as she raised her sword up high. She did not seem to hear them, and she called out again as they neared Syrca's walls. "You shall not take Syrca. Not today, nor tomorrow, nor any other day!"

The armies of the two kingdoms reached the walls, and while a battering ram began its ugly work on the gates of the great city, ladders were leaned against her walls and soldiers began scrambling up.

The girl atop the wall called out for the third and final time. "Sieging kingdoms! You shall not take Syrca. Not today, nor tomorrow, nor any other day!"

The battering ram broke through the gates, and the soldiers reached the top of the walls. What happened next was not clearly known, but later men alternated between saying that the girl had the strength of a daemon or the blessing of the Family. Syrca did not fall that day, nor the next, nor any other day. The girl slaughtered the invading kingdoms' armies, and from that day forth the Heroine of Syrca became a legend.

Tamar looked from Maigar to Aghasi, trying to decide if they were mocking her. "If I were like the Heroine of Syrca," she said, "then I would show the men of Zarcayra that women are equal to them and that they have been wrong in how they treat us and subjugate us."

She raised her head fiercely, daring them to argue with her. She was ready if they did, ready with a thousand answers that she had thought of over the years.

Maigar looked at his saddle.

"We do not wish to subjugate you, Yeva," Aghasi said solemnly. "And we are glad that you are in our gond. Even if you aren't the Heroine of Syrca."

Maigar laughed.

Tamar's face slowly slid into a smile. "I'm glad to be in the gond," she said, glancing sideways at Aghasi and this time not shoving down the fluttering that began in her stomach.

They rode until Zen and Yar sat directly above them in the cloud-dotted sky, and then rode more.

Maigar, Tamar learned, was Aghasi's childhood friend, and younger than his twenty by two years.

"Aghasi was like my protector," Maigar said as their horses walked. "Beating up the boys that would try and pick on me. That was how we met, when he was coming home from school one day and heard several boys slapping me around in an alley."

"Where were your parents?" Tamar asked, looking at Maigar. "Didn't they protect you from the boys?"

Maigar grinned. "My parents died from summer fever when I was six. I lived on my own in the streets until I was eleven, when Aghasi found me and let me come live with him."

"And when my mother died in childbirth and my father lost his mind and our business and estate," Aghasi spoke up, "Maigar let me live with him in the streets and taught me how to survive."

Tamar glanced back at Aghasi. "I forgot, you were the son of a shayr."

"Still am," Aghasi said, smiling. "Just one that left me no lands and no money."

"That is why we were so eager to be conscripted when we heard the news of a war being started," Maigar explained. "So that we'd have some chance of furthering ourselves in our lives other than working alongside commoners until we died of summer fever."

"Technically," Aghasi said with a grin, "you are a commoner."

"And you are too, you just have a fancy name to go along with it." Maigar laughed.

Tamar laughed with them, looking at the waving grasslands on either side of them again. What was it like to grow up a commoner? And what was it like to have to work for every meal, knowing that if you didn't, you'd not eat at all? Father had died, yes, but she had not been thrown out into the streets to live as a commoner. How had Aghasi survived such a change? She glanced at him. And why did it make her like him more than she already did?

A horn blared from the front of the army, filling the air with its deep and resonating blare. *Whoooh, whoooh, whoooh.*

"What is it?" Tamar asked as Aghasi stood in his stirrups with a creak of oiled leather and shaded his eyes against the Brothers' afternoon rays.

"Whitegate," he replied, glancing down at her and Maigar with a grin. "We've reached Whitegate."

#

One of Tamar's favorite pastimes as a girl had been to sit and listen to Mistress Ahani's stories. Sometimes the stories would be about the thirteen kingdoms of Araysann before they had become one. Or the nomadic tribes that had roamed Araysann from one end to the other.

Other times the stories would be about magic and what it had been like before the Great Wars, or about heroines and heroes who had done great deeds. But occasionally the stories would be about the other continents of Argdrion and the extraordinary things there, like Whitegate.

"Whitegate is more than just a passage through the White Mountains," Mistress Ahani would say in a soft voice. "Whitegate is where legends begin…"

Tamar had heard the story so often that she could recite it by heart now.

In the Second Great War, the allied armies of wiar and skinchangers had marched into the Opherian Plains to meet the armies of the humans. It was a drive toward Crystoln, Eromor's capital city and a site of human strength.

The skinchangers and wiar were expecting an easy victory, for although the humans had found their weakness to silver by that time, they had not yet begun mining it, and they were weak from long months of losses. There were even rumors that Crystoln had been attacked by summer fever and that her walls were somewhat defenseless.

But the humans, although weak, were not stupid, and the kingdoms of Argdrion had pooled their resources and used the money to hire witches and warlocks to help them fight. It was the first time that humans turned to magic to help defeat magic, and it would not be the last.

The wiar and skinchangers marched toward Crystoln, traveling west through the Opherian Plains and then north, heading toward the smallest neck of the plains where the Scyrn Mountains, making a natural barrier across the plains' narrowest section, opened in a small pass.

The humans were waiting for them there. They knew that if the wiar and skinchangers reached Crystoln, it would mean that great city's fall, for the rumors were true, and a summer fever had ravaged her inhabitants.

The battle raged for days, with both sides losing thousands and neither breaching the pass. Then on the fifth day, something changed—the wiar and skinchangers did not attack. When the humans sent scouts through the pass to find out why, they learned that they had gone, vanishing into the grasslands. Many were overjoyed that the enemy was gone, but some were skeptical that they were indeed truly gone. The skeptical were wise.

The skinchangers and wiar had left the pass through the Scyrn Mountains and traveled thirty miles east to make their own pass.

The humans' first clue that something was wrong was when a great explosion shook the ground on the afternoon of the fifth day. Rocks fell from the mountains into the pass in front of them, and horses screamed in fright as the earth rolled beneath them.

A half hour later, they heard the thunder of approaching masses. Horses began screaming again as dark shapes filled the sky, and the humans and their warlock and witch allies realized too late that the wiar and skinchangers had broken through the Scyrn Mountains and were coming for them.

The wiar and skinchangers won that day and later marched on Crystoln to unsuccessfully siege her. Their numbers during the battle at the Scyrn Mountains had been too diminished to allow them to take the Great White City, but the pass that the wiar had blasted through the towering mountains remained, taking on the name of Whitegate for the stark white rock of the mountains, now exposed to the Brothers' warmth.

A breeze from the distant Astarion Mountains blew the cloud of dust looming over the army away for a moment, and the Scyrn Mountains and stark white pass of Whitegate appeared as if by magic out of the grasslands ahead of them.

Tamar sucked in a breath at the sight. "They're magnificent," she whispered, her bay's black mane stinging her hands as the wind whistled past.

Dark shapes that could only be birds circled around the tall grassy peaks of the towering mountains while the white cliffs of Whitegate shone like freshly fallen snow that a merchant had brought to the palace once from Nilfinhèim.

And there's Eromor's army…

Tamar strained to make out the dark mass sprawling in front of the pass, but it was too far away to see more than a sword or helmet glinting in the Brothers' rays. Her heartbeat sped up. The wiar and skinchangers were an evil that was best gone from Argdrion, but the realization of what they had accomplished in blasting through the Scyrn Mountains was still awesome to behold.

She strained higher in her saddle. Mistress Ahani had said that the wiar had used their magic to break through the mountains, and that if one looked closely, they could see the scars on the sides of the pass from the wiar's fire and wind and ice and a dozen other powers.

A horn blew from the front of the army again, and Tamar shivered with excitement. She was going to be in a battle. At Whitegate. The realization made her want to shout. This was the adventure that she had longed for, not the boring days of sitting at the palace, listening to Mistress Lorrig drone on about the finer points of needlework and how to sew a handkerchief.

The army gradually slowed to a halt, purple flags snapping in the wind.

Tamar sat back down in her saddle. "What do we do now?" she asked Aghasi and Maigar breathlessly as they pulled their horses to a stop behind the horses of those in front of them.

Aghasi and Maigar grinned together. "We fight."

CHAPTER 37

The Unknown Voice

The skinchangers were going to make an attempt to turn the war back in their favor. We learned the news through watchers, men and women who crept close to the enemy camp and spied on their movements.

It was five years after my marriage to Alvyna. She was pregnant with our first child, and King Edomur was dying.

I paid him a visit before that battle, the firing of the trebuchets and catapults shaking the castle as I walked down the long hallway to his room. He was asleep when I went in, but when I stopped beside his bed, he awoke.

"Lord Sythorn," King Edomur whispered. He reached a frail hand for mine, and I took it. His skin was cold like snow. "I am told that the enemy are making an attack on the city."

I nodded. "Yes, Your Majesty, the war machines have begun firing." The room shook as I spoke, dust sprinkling down from the heavy stone beams above our heads.

"Lord Sythorn," King Edomur rasped. His blue eyes, still sharp and piercing as ever, met mine. "Win this war."

I squeezed his hand. I had never considered myself close to anyone in my life. When I was young, I respected my parents as the young are taught to do, maybe even felt a small touch of affection for my mother at one time. But I had never loved anyone in my life, and I never expected to. I had a bond with King Edomur, though, a bond that I can only call the recognition of one survivor toward another.

"I will, Your Majesty," I said.

Later, standing out in the chill night air, I looked down from the wall of the city as thousands of enemies ran and flew toward us and wondered what the point of it all was. King Edomur had fought his whole life for Argdrion, to save her from the magical races. And now he lay dying, an old, forgotten man.

I watched a flaming leather ball full of shrapnel explode among the advancing enemy ranks. Skinchangers screamed, bodies flew through the night air. Most lived their lives trying to make a mark in the world, for something that people would remember them for. Why did no one look for longer life instead? If the wars had never been fought and we had put the energy that had gone into them into finding eternal life on Argdrion, wouldn't that be a greater cause?

"Your Highness?" a knight said, coming up next to me on the wall. He wore the blue and gold of our kingdom's colors, and the golden boar emblazoned on his chest glowed dully in the dimness of the night.

"Yes?" I asked, watching another firebomb explode among the enemy as the first wave reached the base of the wall far below me.

"I have a message for you, Your Highness," the knight said, stepping closer to be heard above the screams of the dying and booms of the trebuchets and catapults. "From King Edomur."

I glanced at the knight, his golden helmet, open at the visor, showing his bearded face. "From King Edomur?"

"Yes, Your Highness, he wrote it just before he died."

I looked back at the skinchangers. A volley of scorpion bolts whizzed through the air, taking down griffons and eagles and other skinchangers in the form of flying animals. King Edomur was dead. I felt a small pang of something, although what, I could not put into words.

"Give me the message," I told the knight without looking at him. He held out a folded paper, and I took it, my eyes scanning through King Edomur's neat, sure writing.

Lord Sythorn,

I feel that the breath the gods and goddesses gave me upon my coming into this world is leaving, and I know that soon I shall be dead.

I did not know how to tell you this to your face. I've long been a foolish old man, but though my four blood sons are dead, I have felt for some years that I had a son ever since you came to be my right-hand man.

When you married Alvyna, you became my son by marriage, but even more than that, I have had a close and trusted friend in you for many years. I know that I shall not see you again. You are taking my place in protecting this kingdom, and I feel that I will be gone before you return. I pray that you are successful in driving the cursed magical creatures from our lands.

Do not forget, when we win this war—as I have faith that you will—do not cease to hunt every last magical creature from Argdrion until they are dead. It was my duty to purge her of magic, and now, as king, it is yours.

King Edomur

I looked up from the paper, moonlight from the Sisters making it glow silver. Purge Argdrion of magic. Why? Why did humans hate magic so much? I did not hate magic, had not since I had read *Spells* for the first time.

Another volley of scorpion bolts hissed over the walls, and more skinchangers fell.

Was it that we feared that which could help us? For the changes it would bring in our lives? Or were we simply so jealous of something that we were not born with, that we could not understand, that we had to stamp it out?

I opened my hand, and King Edomur's message caught on a soft night breeze and drifted over the wall, down toward the enemy.

"Concentrate your firing in the middle of their ranks," I told a nearby lieutenant.

"Yes, Your Highness," the man said. The silver clasp on his cloak that marked him as a lieutenant reflected gold from the fireballs sailing over our heads. He yelled orders to his scorpion crews.

I moved off down the wall, instructing squadrons, watching the trebuchets and catapults fire. When the battle was done, I would officially be made king.

A firebomb exploded in the darkness, far beyond the wall, illuminating thousands upon thousands of skinchangers for a moment before falling dark.

As king, I would have new power, new responsibilities. It would also make it more difficult to perfect the heart spell, because if I wanted to keep my power, I could not change into another body. I paused beside a massive wooden catapult, one that had two heavy arms instead of one.

Sweat-streaked workers loaded leather-wrapped balls the size of four men into the iron buckets on the end of the trebuchets' arms while others waited to pull the levers that released the massive beams. Two shirtless boys ran forward with hissing torches, and the men who had loaded the firebombs stepped back as the children held their torches to the oil-soaked leather. The leather balls roared into life, and the arms of the catapults swung forward as their counterweights fell downward.

I watched the two balls of flaming death roar through the star-filled night sky to join a hundred other firebombs, my body hot from the iron baskets behind me, where children kept fires to light the bombs constantly burning.

The workers who loaded the catapult moved forward again with two more leather balls, and I moved on as the giant machine was readied for firing again. I wanted to be alone. To have no soldiers or enemies or servants or animals around me. No screaming of the dying and wounded, no whistling of arrows, no clash of weapons. I wanted quiet and a long life.

I had never wanted to fight like Father had. I still did not. But there was nowhere in Argdrion where I could go where there was no fighting, nowhere I could go and have peace.

The skinchangers continued their assault against the city walls throughout the night. When morning came, we rode out to meet them.

I led what was left of our kingdom's soldiers and my knights out to the enemy, our horses' hooves pounding the bodies of those slain the night before into the grass beneath us.

The skinchangers fought until there were none left that day. It was one of the bloodiest and highest body-count battles of all of the Great Wars. Over sixty thousand fell, fifty-five thousand skinchangers and seven thousand humans.

My coronation was the next day, Alvyna's two weeks later, for she had gone into labor the day after the battle.

The whole of the city gathered to see me crowned king over them. One of my knights said there were over two million people watching from the city below as I was made king on the balcony of the castle's western tower.

The roar of approval as the aged priest lowered the delicate golden crown on my head was deafening. I stared at my feet as he murmured words over me, wondering if I was truly "blessed" like he said.

King Edomur's body was laid to rest in the royal tomb beneath the castle, the bodies of the dead skinchangers heaped into piles away from the city and burned. It was the last major grouping of the creatures against us until the Last Great Battle.

I received reports of other battles all over Argdrion in the following weeks after that battle. In Zarcayra, where the thirteen kingdoms had been melded into one to save the collapsing countries' infrastructure. In Oridonn, Wyvernos, Ennotar, the BalBayr Islands: everywhere but in Nilfinhèim, where the climate was too cold and the land too barren for either side to bother fighting over. The Third Great War was not over, but it was ending. Finally, it was ending.

Alvyna lost our child during its birth. After she was recovered, she insisted on training and joining me on the battlefield.

Change came about in the countryside, the change of a kingdom rising out of the ashes of war. Farmers slowly moved back to their deserted lands as the skinchangers concentrated their attacks on the larger cities in Warulan, ancient knights left for home as less and less troops were needed. For a king, though, life would never slow down, and I spent the next few years after that battle meeting with foreign rulers and planning with them how to fully crush the skinchangers as well as rebuild my kingdom.

Alvyna became pregnant again five months after I turned forty, and the kingdom rejoiced that they would have an heir. She felt sure it was a boy, but I did not care. I had not had the time or chance to try the heart spell again since my last failure eight years before, and I was beginning to worry again that I never would. I had given up on the idea of taking on a skinchanger's body. I now wanted more than just long life, but power too. The power that came with being king, the power that I would give up if I left my old body.

It occurred to me during this time that to keep my power and yet have longer life, I could change into the body of the child that Alvyna was carrying. Once it was old enough, of course, and when the time was right. The thought was like a spark of life to me, and Alvyna was happy to have me showing sudden interest in her pregnancy.

A few months before she was due, a messenger, shaking and telling stories of how he had been kidnapped, came to the castle. His original message had been from the King of Seyrwyth, King Aolin, son of the late Queen Alistar, but the message that he gave me, through hysterical talking and wild guzzling of wine that I kept coming, was from the creatures that had "kidnapped" him. It was from the wiar.

They wanted to parlay.

#

The wiar looked like humans. My father told me this when I was a boy of four, and when I first went to battle, I had seen that it was true. They stood like humans, walked like humans, ate, slept, and breathed like humans. But they were nothing like us.

The first wiar I saw was when I was fourteen, in the first battle that I fought in after being Father's page for four years. She had been a female wiar, black haired, brown eyed. She was taller than I was, and there had been a power in her bearing, a power that all the wiar held.

Two weeks after the messenger arrived in my kingdom and ten days after the rulers of Warulan responded to my messages to them, the wiar came to my castle.

They walked into the throne room in two rows, led by their king. There were seven of them total.

The wiar did not have many kingdoms and rulers like humans did, but rather one king and one queen who ruled over all wiar throughout Argdrion. Their palace was in the northwestern tip of the Astarion Mountains, and their people, before the wars, had been scattered through every kingdom on every continent of Argdrion. This, in part, had been what had started the unrest before the Great Wars. For the wiar, although they lived in human kingdoms, refused to hold allegiance to any king or queen other than their own.

The wiar stopped in front of the dais of my throne.

Alvyna was not with me. She was not feeling well, as the effects of her pregnancy were wearing on her. The other rulers of Warulan's kingdoms sat on either side of me in wooden chairs that matched my own. King Aolin of Seyrwyth, Queen Dussa of Visguroth —gray since the last time I had seen her—Queen Edrea of Dyridura, King Ronn and Queen Enora of Gyndor, Queen Styrr of Iduiron. There were rulers from the smaller kingdoms of Warulan too, making forty-three of us in total, lined up in two rows on the dais.

The wiar did not bow. Didn't look around them. I had the feeling that they knew of the soldiers in the shadows of the throne room, of the witches and warlocks behind the pillars. I knew that they felt our fear.

"My people are tired of war," the wiar king said. He did not say his name, did not say that they had come to discuss parlay. He knew that we knew his name. King Lysian and the wiar—intelligent beyond any creatures in Argdrion—did not like to say what had already been said before. The messenger had told us they wished to talk, and so it was assumed we'd remember it, or that we could figure it out.

"As are mine," I said. My palms were sweating, so I kept them resting on the cool wooden armrests of my throne. "And I believe that we both wish for a speedy end to this war."

King Lysian dipped his head. He wore a thin silver band on top of his black hair, and his eyes were a striking emerald green. He was muscular, like all his people, but not exceptionally tall. He didn't need to be, though. There was a power and darkness emanating from him that sent shivers down my spine. The same power and darkness that the first wiar I had met had. The same power and darkness that all wiar had. That was what separated the wiar from humans. The feeling that one received from them that they could do anything that they wanted, and there was nothing any could do to stop them. This was not true, of course, after the discovery of silver, but the feeling was still there all the same.

"An agreement between our people would be the best thing, I think," I went on. "An agreement of peace." I chose my words carefully. The wiar were good at twisting one's words to their own advantage.

"A peace," King Lysian said, nodding at my words, "that is satisfactory to both parties."

I watched him, wondering what powers he had. There were rumors of a hundred different things—ice, fire, water, wind—but no one really knew what King Lysian's abilities were. He had rarely appeared in battle. And when he had, they said that thousands had fallen before him.

I glanced at the other wiar, who were standing behind King Lysian with their hands clasped in front of them. It fascinated me, the wiar's magic. The power that they demonstrated in battle as they moved with the speed of wind, shot fire from their hands, made objects turn into water with a single glance. What I would do with such power…

"What is it that you propose to us, King Lysian?" Queen Edrea asked. "You called this meeting. I assume that you have some kind of terms to set before us?"

King Lysian glanced around my throne room at the blue and gold tapestries on the walls, the stone frescoes with their pictures of past rulers. "I could go over the past few hundred years," he said, voice soft and unassuming. "The battles and losses of both our races. The gains of your kind."

He looked back at us, his eyes telling nothing of what was going on in his head. I knew what he was doing. He was saying, in an underhanded way, that his people did not like my people, did not like what had happened in the wars.

"But I will not," he went on, "for that is history, and what we will discuss and agree upon today will be the future. Your people won a great battle against the skinchangers."

No one replied.

"And yet," King Lysian said, "here we are, three years later, and the skinchangers are still not defeated."

My knights, who were standing in a half circle beneath the dais, stiffened. They said that insulting people in underhanded ways was King Lysian's forte. His voice was smooth as he spoke, but his undertone was biting, and I sensed little respect for us in him. The thought of making an agreement with his people was nauseating.

"It is doubtful that the war will end soon," King Lysian went on. "These skirmishes with the skinchangers could last for years, and when they are finally done, you will have lost thousands more of your people."

"What is your point, King Lysian?" Queen Edrea asked sharply.

"That rather than a mere peace, there be an alliance between our people, one that would be beneficial for both," he replied.

I met his eyes as he glanced at each one of us in turn. I felt like I was looking into two cold diamonds.

"My race will help you defeat the skinchangers and end this war sooner than you might be able to do on your own," King Lysian said softly. "And in exchange, your race will leave mine alone and let us live as we will."

Leave them alone. He acted like it had been the humans who had started the Great Wars. But then, everyone thought it was the opposite side's fault. In reality, no one really knew how the wars had begun. The years leading up to them had been filled with disputes and arguments between the skinchangers and wiar and us until finally blood had been spilled, and the wiar and skinchangers had allied against us in war.

Now, I supposed it didn't really matter how the wars had begun. We had been hating and fighting the skinchangers and wiar for so long that it was part of our nature. I saw a chance in King Lysian's proposal, a chance for peace to finally come to Argdrion.

"Let us talk this over amongst ourselves," King Ronn said. "The other rulers of Argdrion will need to be met with and told of your proposal."

King Lysian dipped his head in accession. "Take all the time that you need."

"Give us eight weeks," Queen Styrr said, "and we will give you your answer, King Lysian."

King Lysian dipped his head again. Looking at each of us once more, he turned and strode out of the throne room with the other wiar.

A meeting of all the human rulers in Argdrion was called. We met in Seyrwyth, at King Aolin's castle. The meeting lasted for two weeks. Oppositions were thrown at the wiar's proposal, agreements, hatred. When two months had passed, we called the wiar to meet and hear our answer.

"King Lysian," Queen Styrr said as they stopped in front of the dais of my castle's throne room once more, "we have discussed your proposal of an alliance between us." She paused, the distaste in her next words clear. She had been one of the ones that had said no to the wiar's proposal. "The rulers of our race have agreed to it. You will help us defeat the skinchangers and bring peace to Argdrion, and we will leave your people alone and let you live, as you like, in peace."

Papers were signed, hands shaken, stiff smiles given. There was one thing about our meeting that we did not tell the wiar, though, as the next few weeks rolled past and our armies gathered to sweep Argdrion of the skinchangers.

We would never be at peace with them. And after they had helped us rid Argdrion of the skinchangers, we would rid her of them as well.

CHAPTER 38

Nathaira

Nathaira burst out of the black water with a gasp and followed the killer's strong strokes toward the dim outline of the lake's rocky shore. He had been true to his word and had helped her out of Crystoln. She felt like shouting for joy.

She waded the last few feet out of the lake and climbed up on a moss-covered boulder, water running off her clothes.

She could look for Efamar now.

Thank you, Sisters.

Nathaira scanned the rippling plains below, stretching for as far as she could see in three directions and broken only by the wide, dark line of the River Sar.

No, not yet. Only after she repaid her debt to the killer. The smile on her face faded. Repaying that debt meant staying with him. How would she look for Efamar if she was with a human?

"The Sisters always have a purpose, Nathaira," Moirin's voice whispered in her head.

"I don't know about you," said the killer above the noise of the water rushing out of the lake and to the river below, "but I smell awful."

Nathaira glanced over at him, standing a few feet away, his lean face wet with water.

He spat into the debris-clogged water lapping at their feet.

What would Athrysion say about staying with him? She could only imagine.

"Kill him…" she heard Athrysion's deep voice in her ear.

But then there was Moirin's voice, guiding her softly. "Always repay your debts, Nathaira. The humans may have taken everything else from us, but there is one thing that they will never be able to take, and that is our honor."

"Are you going back into the city?" Nathaira asked.

The killer looked up, black hair plastered down around his face. "Well, that would be rather hard considering that the gates closed an hour ago, and as of yet, I haven't managed to climb over the hundred-foot marble wall. Also"—he pulled a piece of debris out of his hair and threw it into the grass—"I'm now a wanted criminal for helping you escape."

"I didn't ask you to help me," Nathaira said, watching him. She still half expected him to turn her in. That he had helped her seemed too good to be true.

"No. That was my own stupid idea, wasn't it?" the killer replied, spitting again. Nathaira looked back at the River Sar, pulling the water of the lake along with its slow-moving current. The idea of putting off looking for Efamar for one more minute, much less days or maybe weeks, was unbearable. But Moirin was right, and as much as she hated to admit it, she could not forget a debt. Even if it was to a human.

"A word of advice," the killer said after a few minutes, looking at her. "Leave this spot as quickly as possible. The soldiers will figure out where we went before too long, and this time, I won't be around to save you."

"I didn't ask you to help me," Nathaira repeated. The white walls of the city stretched high into the cloud-covered sky above the killer, making his dark figure stand out like a shadow.

"No," he said, eyeing her, "but you didn't refuse either." He started down the hill toward the river below, grass hissing around his lean legs.

Nathaira watched him for a moment, anger and annoyance burning in her. She looked up where she knew the Sisters sat behind the rain-heavy storm clouds. "Moirin said you always have a purpose," she whispered, a cool wind carrying the sweet scent of rain pulling at her damp hair and clothes, "but what is it? Why did you help me out of the city only to put a debt I must pay upon me?" Nathaira paused, staring at the glow of the moons behind the clouds. "I wish that you would give me a sign."

Thunder rumbled in the distance.

Nathaira slipped off the boulder and followed the killer down the hill.

He didn't say anything as she approached him by the edge of the gently flowing river but continued looking out at the water, half-gloved hands by his sides.

"I owe you a debt, human," Nathaira said. The words tasted like rotten meat on her tongue. "And for my honor, I must stay with you until it is repaid."

The killer glanced sideways at her. "We could have sex in the grass. I'd call that payment enough."

Nathaira narrowed her eyes.

"I must repay the debt exactly how it was given. You saved my life, I must save yours."

"Well, that's a shame," the killer said, looking back at the river. He stepped into the shallows of the river, the dark water parting around him in ripples.

"Where are you going?" Nathaira asked, watching him. She prayed that he would go in the direction of Efamar, wherever that was.

"The Ilgerion Forest and my cabin there," the killer called softly over one shoulder. "Well, it's not really my cabin, but since I killed the last owners, I guess you could say it sort of is."

Why did you make me owe a creature like this a debt? Nathaira stepped into the river, wading after him.

The killer glanced at her again. "As much as I like a beautiful woman following me," he said, white teeth flashing in the semidarkness, "you can leave anytime now. I don't like company except in bed."

Nathaira stopped next to him, teeth beginning to chatter as the water brushed past her thighs with icy fingers.

The water was warm near the banks, but farther out where it grew deeper it still held the chill of melting snow.

"I am not following you willingly," Nathaira said in a hard voice, "but my honor demands that I repay you, and until I do, human, I must stay with you."

They stared at each other for a moment.

"Keep up, then," the killer said finally. He turned and sank into the water.

Sucking in a breath, Nathaira did the same.

She followed the killer's dim form down the river for hours, letting the current pull her where it willed as the white walls of Crystoln disappeared into the darkness behind them.

The Opherian Plains rolled past them, waving grass glowing silver when the occasional cloud shifted, and the moons shone through.

The plains faded after a while, and towering goyr trees and thick rorbushes took their place on either side of the river.

Rain began pelting the river as the first massive goyr tree appeared in the semigloom, filling the night with a chorus of splashes.

The Ilgerion Forest. Nathaira coughed as water splashed into her mouth and scanned the thickening trees on either side of the river. The forest looked ancient.

Gray in color, the giant goyr trees that made up the forest stretched for hundreds of feet into the sky and sometimes reached up to a hundred and twenty feet around. Their roots grew above ground, twisting and writhing in tangled masses around their trunks.

The rain turned into a full-fledged spring storm in all its fury as they climbed out of the river a half hour later. They caught the hanging roots of goyr trees that stretched down the sides of the gorge to pull themselves up with. The river whooshed through the deep gash in the ground behind them, and thunder crashed overhead in deafening booms as they scrambled up a leaf-strewn hill.

"Having fun yet?" the killer asked. He stopped under a goyr tree.

"It's better than your stinky city," Nathaira replied, massaging her legs to get some warmth in them again.

The killer smiled dryly and untied his cloak from around his middle. He wrung the soggy piece of material out and slung it over his back. "Don't get too comfortable," he said quietly. "We've got a ways to go yet." He stepped back out into the rain and started off through the trees.

Straightening, Nathaira followed. She pulled her cloak off her waist as she walked and, wringing it out, threw it over her body.

A maidenhair fern brushed against her legs as the killer led her under twisting goyr roots and through a meadow of the lacy green spring plants, and the smell of the forest engulfed them in welcoming arms as they left the swiftly moving river behind them. Nathaira breathed deeply as the soft woodsy smell filled her nose.

Oh, Sisters, how I've missed this...

They walked for over an hour before the forest finally broke, and a small meadow with a squat rock cabin in its flower-filled center appeared out of the drizzling rain.

"Home," the killer said as Nathaira came up next to him. "The roof leaks, and it's colder than Nilfinhèim, but that's what you get with a free house."

Nathaira wrapped her cloak tighter around herself as rain drove into her face, staring at the cabin. She wished it was her home. But her home was gone forever, destroyed by humans.

Like the one next to her.

The killer started out into the meadow.

Nathaira moved after him again, the wet blades of grass tickling her legs with their sharp edges.

Thunder rumbled as the killer pushed the low wooden door of the cabin open on creaky hinges and ducked inside, and Nathaira felt the static energy of lightning in the air as she slipped after him. She shut the door softly behind them, quieting the sounds of the driving rain.

She glanced around the one-room cabin. An ash-filled stone fireplace with a stack of wood leaning against one uneven side sat at the back of the dark room, a dusty table with two chairs crowded around it rested in a cobwebbed corner, and a narrow bed with a folded blanket on it stretched underneath a small lead-paned window by the fireplace.

The killer moved lightly across the room to the fireplace and pulled several pieces of oddly shaped kindling off the stack beside it. "I hate to disappoint you," he said, kneeling in front of the hearth and stacking the wood inside, "but I doubt there'll be much chance for you to repay your debt to me."

He waved a hand over the logs and whispered something unintelligible, and a small wavering gold flame popped into life. "My life's never in danger, and I don't need saving."

"Well, then I will pray to the Sisters that someone will try to kill you so that my debt might be fulfilled," Nathaira replied tonelessly, moving over to the fireplace.

"You are terrifying me," the killer deadpanned, placing another log on the others as the flame crackled into a fire.

Nathaira narrowed her eyes at him. "You believe in the gods?"

"I do not believe in any higher authority," he replied, holding his hands out to the flames. "I am my own master, and I make my own laws."

Nathaira eyed him. Moirin had spoken of such humans, saying they were lost souls. Personally, she thought them fools. "Why do you use magic?" she asked.

The killer pushed his hood back with one hand, black hair tangled, and placed another slender stick on the fire. "I've found it to be quite useful over the years," he replied, standing and undoing the black dagger clasp at his neck that held his cloak together.

"But your kind hates magic," Nathaira challenged.

He glanced up at her, mismatched eyes unreadable. "I don't." He dragged the dripping cloak off his shoulders and hung it on one of the chairs by the table.

He was lying. Or stupid.

"But most of your people do," Nathaira insisted, watching him as he began undoing the clasps on the belts strapped over his chest and around his waist. "And you let those whores see you use it. Are you not afraid that they'll turn you in?"

"Well, I'm already a wanted criminal, more so now that I helped you," the killer said, glancing up at her again. "And I doubt very much 'those whores' will be telling anyone anything ever again. At least not in this life."

Nathaira blinked. He had killed them. She felt a small twinge of guilt. The whores had not wanted to help her, much like she had not wanted to take the killer's help.

She turned and untied the laces on her cloak and laid the large piece of black cloth on the uneven stones in front of the fire.

Rain pelted against the window. Nathaira glanced up at it as lightning flashed outside, followed by the rumbling boom of thunder.

Moirin had loved the rain.

Nathaira stared at the rippling pane, water running down it in streams. *It is the Sisters crying,* her mother would whisper. *Crying over one of their children dying.*

One of the sticks on the fire grew black as flames consumed it and crumbled to the ashes beneath, and Nathaira put another from the stack by the wall in its place as the killer threw his vambraces, belts, and gloves on the chair. It had rained the night Moirin had disappeared, a dark, thick rain that had obscured the very sky itself.

"You're going to freeze to death if you don't take those wet clothes off," the killer said behind her. A clap of thunder followed his words with a boom, rattling the window.

Nathaira glanced up at him as he peeled his wet shirt off over his head.

His well-defined chest glistened with water. Three deep white scars, like the claw marks of some large animal, ran down his left pectoral, white lines against the darker color of his skin. Where did a human get marks like that? Nathaira wondered. He was too young to have fought in the wars, and if he was as dangerous as the woman killer in the arena had said, how would an enemy give him such wounds?

"Find something interesting?" the killer asked.

Nathaira met his eyes. She narrowed her eyes at him. "What is that?" she asked, jerking her chin at a black claw-shaped stone hanging by a thin black cord around his neck.

Naturally shaped, the rock was so black that one felt they could be lost in its depths when they looked at it. A thin band of gold ringed the top of the stone, etched with finely carved runes. She had not seen something so beautifully crafted since the ivory bracelet Zeythra had worn, given to her on their wedding day by her husband, Feirdon.

"It is from the Fourth Age, is it not?" Nathaira murmured, trying to read the etchings on the gold from where she sat. It was not a language she recognized.

The killer hummed in acknowledgment.

"Where did you get it?" Nathaira asked. She glanced up at his face, his ice and pine eyes meeting hers.

Wind whistled underneath the door of the cabin.

The killer turned, pulling a knife out of one boot. He leaned against the mantel of the fireplace. "You really should get out of those clothes." He flipped the knife over the scarred fingers of one hand.

He was good at avoiding questions, Nathaira noted, turning away from him and moving to the bed. She pulled her shirt off over her head, hissing as the wet fabric rubbed against the still-red wound where her collar had been. She put a finger to the mark.

Wind whistled under the door again, howling around the house.

Nathaira closed her eyes as it stroked her bare back. The howling reminded her of running as wolves with the clan on snowy winter nights. A log popped loudly in the fire, and her eyes snapped back open. She picked up the blanket from off the bed and wrapped it around her shivering shoulders before slipping out of her boots and pants and laying them and the shirt on the hearth in front of the fire.

Steam rose from the clothes like mist off a river in the morning.

The cabin was silent for a long while, the hiss of the knife as the killer twirled it filling the room along with the noise of the rain.

"Are you going to kill him, the man who betrayed you?" Nathaira asked after a time, kneeling in front of the fire and glancing up the killer.

He looked at her over the sheen of the knife, mismatched eyes glinting. "How did you know?"

Nathaira looked back at the fire, her heart falling at his words.

"So, you'll be going back to Crystoln, I suppose." If he went back to Crystoln, then she would have to go with him, and that would put her right back where she had started.

How can there be a purpose in that, Sisters?

The killer flicked the knife from one hand to the other, the blade flashing in the light of the flames. "Not right away. I lost most of my weapons fighting the soldiers. I have a mansion in Rothborn. I'll restock there."

Relief washed over Nathaira. "This Rothborn," she said, "how far is it from here?"

"About seventy miles due north," the killer responded, rolling the knife over the back of one hand and pulling it under with his thumb.

Nathaira watched the flames dance. Perhaps she could learn something of Efamar's whereabouts in Rothborn. There were other arenas besides the one in Crystoln, and although she didn't remember ever hearing Zeythra or Moirin or the elders talk about a Rothborn, perhaps there was an arena there, and perhaps Efamar had been taken to it. It was a small hope, but at the moment, the only one she had.

"You know," the killer said, pulling her out of her planning, "I'm used to women wanting to stay with me, but usually it's because they think they love me."

"There must be a lot of stupid human women," Nathaira said without looking at him. Once she got free of her debt to the killer, she would comb every city in Argdrion for Efamar until she found him. And when she did, she'd take him to a place so far away and secluded that no human would ever find them again.

"If you're thinking of a way to try and kill me so that you won't have to repay your debt, I wouldn't bother," the killer said softly behind her.

Nathaira glanced up at him.

He twisted the knife over the back of his hand again. "No one has ever succeeded before, and you won't be the first."

"You are arrogant," Nathaira said, turning back to the fire.

"I have reason to be," the killer said. He threw the knife into the air. Catching it with one hand, he tossed it onto the chair with his clothes. "We should get some sleep. It will be light in four hours, and we'll need all the rest we can get. I plan on keeping up a fast pace in the next few days."

He stretched, muscles flexing. "I'll take the bed. You can have the floor since you've got the only blanket." He lay down on the thin straw mattress on the bed's wood-and-rope frame with a rustle and put one muscular arm over his eyes. A moment later, his even, quiet breathing filled the room.

Nathaira pulled the blanket tighter around herself and lay down on one side on the stones in front of the fire, watching the crackling gold flames leap and dance along the darkening logs. Where was Efamar right now? Was he wondering if she was coming for him?

Sisters, please tell him I am. Send him a sign. She glanced at the killer, his bare chest rising and falling regularly. She didn't think he was asleep. He was probably testing her by leaving the knife on the chair, daring her to try and kill him.

Nathaira looked at the knife, the steel blade glinting sharply in the light of the fire. She was tempted to kill him. But she would not kill without a reason. She would not become like the humans. She rolled over on her back and stared up at the thatched roof of the cabin, listening to the rain beat against it. She would obey the Sisters and repay her debt and uphold her people's honor. And as soon as her debt was repaid, she'd leave.

Nathaira pulled the blanket tighter and rolled back toward the fire, staring into its crackling flames. She just prayed that she had the chance to repay it, and soon, for she didn't know how much more waiting she could handle.

CHAPTER 39

Hathus

What world had Caine taken them to?

A light appeared out of the darkness with a pop and a sizzle, and Hathus winced at the brightness as a pirate a few feet away swung the door of the lantern shut with a creak. He had never seen such darkness in all his life. It was like a living thing, a breathing, moving organism of black, black, black.

"Eerie, isn't it?" Caine's voice asked.

Hathus jumped. He'd almost forgotten that there was anyone else besides him and the pirate with his lantern for a moment. In this darkness, it was easy to.

"Yes," he replied uneasily. He raised his bony hand in front of his face. He couldn't see it. "But why?"

And gods, it smelled awful. Like sulfur, Hathus realized.

"Why is it so dark?" Caine asked.

Hathus nodded, and then remembering that the worldwalker couldn't see him either, grunted.

"The Land of Dragons is not like Argdrion," Caine wheezed, coming into view for a moment as the pirate with the lantern moved past them. "The Land of Dragons has no suns, no moons, no stars, and no vegetation or life other than the dragons and volcanoes. If you can call a volcano life, that is."

"So how does the world survive?" Hathus asked. He may not have graduated from his schools with stellar scores, but he did remember that the suns warmed Argdrion and fed its inhabitants with their heat and light, and without them, nothing could survive.

He put his hand out in front of him, feeling in the blackness. There was nothing there. He had the unshakable feeling that there was something out there, though, watching them, waiting. Or perhaps it was just the blackness that made him think that.

"The volcanoes," Caine rasped. "There are more volcanoes in the Land of Dragons than in all the other worlds put together, and each volcano connects to the other in a series of underground lakes and tunnels full of red-hot lava. There's enough heat here to power five worlds."

Volcanoes? Hathus blanched. "Then why don't I feel them?" he asked, an image of thousands of volcanoes exploding and throwing molten lava over all of the pirate fleet flashing through his head. He waved his hand in front of him again, but although the air felt dead and stagnant, there was no heat, and only a cool staleness brushed his skin.

"We're not in the live volcanic part of the world yet," Caine replied in his gasping voice. "We're still in the sea. Wait until we anchor and go searching underground for your treasure—you'll see how warm it can get then."

"You mean we have to go *inside* the volcanoes?" Hathus asked, incredulous.

"According to legend, that is where we'll find the treasure," Caine wheezed.

Something brushed past him, and Hathus sucked in a breath for a scream and then realized it was a pirate fumbling past. What if Caine had brought them to this otherworld to die? Perhaps they would starve to death drifting on endless seas, or maybe his plan was to stab them to death in the darkness.

"Don't you remember the legends?" Caine asked out of the darkness.

Hathus turned in the direction that the voice came from, hand straying toward his knife. Perhaps he should kill Caine first, before the worldwalker had the chance to kill him...

"You ask me about the Land of Dragons," Caine rasped from in front of him, "but yet you said you believe the legends. They tell you everything you want to know about this world, if you read them."

Hathus mentally kicked himself, remembering that he was supposed to believe in the Land of Dragons and its treasures. "Uh, yes," he said, "but I forgot for a moment. All the excitement and tension, you know."

"Let's move to the front of the ship," Caine said.

Hathus felt his way after the worldwalker and moved toward the glowing lantern that the pirate had taken away, feeling like a blind man on a tightrope as the *Daemon's Cry* slowly creaked forward into the darkness. He heard the other ships around them, muffled whispers and curses as pirates ran into things echoing across the water.

His foot hit something hard, and he cursed, feeling his way up the stairs to the forecastle deck and making his way toward the pirate and his lantern.

"How many miles to shore?" Bathia asked in her lilting voice. Hathus stopped beside the pirate and his lantern, making out Caine, Sidion, Bathia, and Blackwell standing around the man. They stood by the figurehead of the *Daemon's Cry*, looking at the darkness in front of the ship.

"It's hard to say in the Land of Dragons," Caine said. "One cannot judge the distance—we must simply be happy when we reach our destination."

Well, that's encouraging news. Hathus caught Bathia's eye. She looked away.

"We are getting closer, though," Sidion said in his thick accent. He lifted an arm. "The light is getting larger."

Hathus shifted his gaze from Bathia to focus on orange specks in front of them that he had not noticed before. Volcanoes, he reasoned. Maybe that's how Caine would kill them… But then, wouldn't he die with them?

A noise like distant thunder echoed through the darkness, and water lapped at the sides of the *Daemon's Cry* as the sea rocked slightly beneath them.

"What's that?" Hathus whispered, nervous. He wished he could see what was around him. The feeling that something was there was growing, like an itch that wouldn't go away.

"A volcano," Caine replied from his elbow, scarred face visible in the circle of golden light cast by the pirate's lantern. "They erupt constantly."

The sea rocked again, and Hathus glanced to the side as a plume of golden fire exploded in the distant darkness and burst into a weeping orange-and-gold sea of lava flowing out of nothing and into nothing.

"Why are there so many volcanoes?" he asked, debating telling the pirates to turn around and then remembering that two of the men who followed him were still on the ship, listening.

If we all get burned up in a volcano, I hope they go first...

"Who knows?" Caine wheezed. "Why is Argdrion a mixture of hundreds of different topographies? Only the gods who designed the worlds can say."

"You're going to die..."

Hathus jumped and glanced around the circle of pirates around him. "Did someone say something?"

Everyone looked at him.

"No," Caine rasped.

Sidion shook his head, dreadlocks swaying, and looked back at the light in front of them. The rest of the group followed his gaze.

Hathus glanced around at the darkness, the hair on the back of his neck standing on end. Had he imagined it? Like the voices he'd heard in his cell?

The volcano continued to belch red fire and lava into the darkness as they passed by. Hathus watched the glowing light as it faded behind them.

Time was nonexistent. If it was four hours or four days that they drifted across the silent black water, Hathus could not tell. The only thing that let him know they had moved at all was the ever-growing orange light of a volcano in front of them until it dominated his whole view and threw its ghastly red-and-orange light on the black water and the blacker decks of the *Daemon's Cry* like a fiery shadow.

Shapes began appearing out of the darkness ahead.

Hathus made out rocks, gnarled and black, and swirling masses of cooled lava twisting and weaving in a jagged landscape of darkness and ash.

The other pirate ships became visible too, sailing along silently around them in their V formation.

A low, deep groan echoed through the dimness after a while, and the *Daemon's Cry* shuddered as her hull ran against something hard in the black water.

"Cast the anchor!" Blackwell called in the way he had of yelling without sounding like he was doing more than whispering.

Another groan echoed through the air, and the massive anchor chain rattled out the side of the ship. The sharp splash of the anchor hitting the water followed a moment later.

"Lower the boats!" Bathia called as the *Daemon's Cry* slowed to a stop.

Hathus glanced around as pirates moved across the decks, his skin prickling.

They should turn back. There was death waiting for them here, he felt it.

Sidion, Caine, and Blackwell moved past him and toward the rowboats slowly creaking to the water below. Hathus glanced around for the men who followed him but did not see them. He lightly touched Bathia's arm as she stepped past him.

"I think maybe I was wrong to want to come here," he said in a low voice. Wherever here was. "I think maybe we should tur—"

His eyes caught on the men who followed him as they appeared suddenly by the doorway of the hall leading to the cabins. He stopped talking. They were watching him, the men, and although Hathus knew that they could not hear him from across the deck, he had a feeling they knew what he was saying.

"Yes?" Bathia said.

"Um, I just wanted to apologize," Hathus said. "For being such a coward and for betraying your friendship."

If he could get rid of the men following him, then they could turn around, but how could he do that without someone noticing?

"And now what?" Bathia asked.

Hathus looked at her, the orange light cast by the volcano giving her face a reddish glow. "What?"

"Now that you've apologized, Hathus Ryrgorion, what is it that you expect me to do?" Bathia asked, voice tired.

"Uh, forgive me?" Hathus said, his mind not really on the conversation. Was it possible that this was the Land of Dragons, and there were dragons out there, waiting for them to walk into their open jaws? At the moment, in the darkness, he could almost believe that. But no, dragons were just a myth, a story to tell children.

Bathia shook her head and looked away. "And just like that, it's all forgotten, is that it?"

"That's usually how apologies work," Hathus pointed out.

"You told me once, Hathus Ryrgorion," Bathia said, glancing back at him, "that you never had any friends, and you'd always been fine with that. So, if I am not your friend, and you're not mine, then why would you feel sorry for offending me?"

Hathus stared at her, realizing where she was going. "People make mistakes, Bathia," he said.

"Yes," Bathia replied, "people make mistakes, Hathus Ryrgorion. But you killed people. Killed innocent people with your mistake, with your cowardice."

I killed people? What about Caine? He's the one that led us into the souls...

"And you stand here," Bathia said her voice getting a hard, cold edge to it, "apologizing for offending me as if all that is wrong is that I am hurt by what you did. A man like that, Hathus Ryrgorion, is not sorry for what he did. He is sorry because others are avoiding him, and he wants things to go back to the way they were." She brushed past him.

Hathus watched her walk away as the first boat hit the water with a soft splash, annoyance burning through him. Killed people... He hadn't killed anyone, Caine had. And where did she get off being so righteous anyway? She was a pirate, after all, and had probably killed numerous people herself.

A soft, feathery piece of black ash landed on his shoulder, and he glanced up as more drifted over the decks of the *Daemon's Cry* and settled onto the sails, railings, and ropes like fine black snow. He caught a piece floating down in front of him—it disintegrated into black dust in his palm. Volcanic ash. Did that mean one nearby was going to explode soon and incinerate them all?

"Boat's ready!" Sidion called softly from his position by the railing.

Hathus moved toward the second mate.

"Douse the lanterns when we've gone," Blackwell said quietly, swinging a leg over the dark railing. "We don't know what could be out there."

Hathus stopped next to Sidion. He paled. What *could* be out there? What if there was something, perhaps not dragons, but something else? But no, that was stupid. Otherworlds were not inhabited... Were they?

Azaria hopped off Blackwell's shoulder and climbed up into the rigging.
"Ready to find some treasure, Hathus?" Blackwell asked.

Hathus offered him a faint smile. "Always," he said.

But I'm not ready to die... He would never be ready for that.

Blackwell disappeared over the side of the ship, and Hathus moved to follow, swinging one leg over the railing and feeling for the coarse rope ladder below with the toe of his boot.

"Bring back a souvenir," Sidion said in his lilting accent.

Hathus glanced up at him. It wasn't cold by any means, but he found that he was shivering. He gripped the railing to steady himself. "Yeah," he mumbled, "I'll do that."

Sidion grinned, teeth flashing, and Hathus climbed down the ladder to the rowboat below.

It sank gently as he stepped into it and took a seat at the back, and a moment later they were cutting a path through still black water and leaving the softly swaying *Daemon's Cry* behind.

Hathus glanced over his shoulder once at the ships as the pirates manning the oars methodically pulled the rowboat closer and closer to shore. The golden lanterns scattered over the vessels slowly blinked out one by one. A shiver ran up his spine as the last flickered out.

The rowboat slowed to a crawl as they neared the shore, and a moment later ground to a stop roughly against sand the color of night.

Hathus pushed himself to a standing position as pirates silently stood and jumped over the sides of the rowboat and onto the dark beach. He glanced up at the volcano looming above them and the river of glowing orange lava streaming out of its distant black peak.

Gods, will I die here?

"*Yesss,*" the same voice from the ship hissed in his ear. Hathus inhaled sharply and turned again, but as before, no one was there. He pulled his coat tighter around him.

The last of the pirates jumped out of the rowboat. Glancing around again, Hathus followed.

Ash kicked up by his steps floated around his boots as he moved away from the boats and after the pirates, while more falling from the dark sky sprinkled his leather coat and lank hair like the ghastly petals of a shriveled flower. Hathus snorted as a piece went up his nose. There was no way that creatures could survive in a land like this, was there?

"How will we get inside?" a tattooed female captain of one of the other pirate ships asked as Hathus walked over to where Blackwell, Caine, and Bathia stood by the foot of the volcano. A large group of pirates from all seven vessels stood around them.

"Over there," Bathia replied with a nod.

Hathus glanced to where she was looking and saw a natural trail of hardened black lava winding up the side of the volcano.

"There will be tunnels that lead inside farther up," Caine rasped. He and Bathia and Blackwell started up the mountain, the pirates trailing after them.

Hathus glanced around again as the last of the pirates moved up the side of the volcano, shivering more violently now. The men who followed him stood a few feet away, dark cloaks coated in ash. His gaze moved on from them to scan the long beach and other volcanoes, stretching away into the distance.

We shouldn't be here...

"But you are..." the voice whispered again.

Hathus jumped and turned quickly. The beach was empty. He turned all the way around, scanning the darkness. There was no one but the men who followed him. A chill ran up his spine. He wasn't imagining the voice, he was sure of that, but if he wasn't, then where was it coming from?

Dragons... Hathus glanced up the volcano in front of him, scattered with climbing pirates. He laughed nervously at the thought, making the men who followed him glance at him. He shook his head. No, it wasn't dragons; they weren't real. He started climbing, skirting around a waterfall of blackened lava that led to a deep hole.

They climbed for over thirty minutes, the only sound the steady rumbling, hissing, and spluttering of the volcano under them.

A scream split through the air halfway up the volcano.

Hathus looked ahead to see a black-toothed pirate with dirty red dreadlocks lose his footing and tumble over the side of the mountain in a cloud of black ash.

The pirate hit the beach below with a distant thump.

Hathus blanched.

"The gods be damned," cursed a sixty-something pirate in front of him with bushy white whiskers and one eye. The pirate made the sign of peace with a dirty hand.

The line of pirates started moving again.

Hathus crept after them, clinging to the gnarled black rock of the volcano as he went.

He found himself needing to stop several times for want of air and exhaustion as they climbed, and an hour into their upward journey, his stub began throbbing painfully, causing him to rest again, so that after a while, he'd fallen behind the pirates by a good hundred yards or more.

Hathus paused, panting, and wiped sweat from his eyes. The pirate ahead of him disappeared around a gnarled mass of lava.

Why couldn't we have looked for treasure on the beach? He wiped more sweat out of his stinging eyes and moved forward again.

No pirates were anywhere to be seen when he rounded the mass of lava, but the ash was filled with footprints that led to a large hole in the side of the mountain. Hathus eyed the dark opening. A tunnel. He remembered Caine's words from the ship, about going inside the volcanoes to look for treasure. He glanced around him, half expecting to hear the voice again. If he went inside the volcano, would he die? Was there something inside that Caine knew would kill them all?

Like dragons…

Hathus shook his head of the thought and looked back at the tunnel. Why would Caine lead them into a trap if he was with them and might die as well? He had been with them when the souls attacked, Hathus reminded himself, and he could have died than too. The thought wasn't encouraging.

The volcano trembled slightly as he moved into the tunnel, and he stopped for a minute, putting his hand out to steady himself. The walls of the tunnel were hot to the touch, hot enough to make him hiss and pull his hand back. The air was warm too, making sweat drain down his skin.

A faint orange glow from ahead lit the tunnel. Hathus made toward it, the volcano's trembling making his walk unsteady and slow. He heard the Unknown Voice's men following him, always keeping a few paces behind him but always there just the same. He glanced over his shoulder at them.

Maybe he could overpower them and make for the ships…

The tunnel forked thirty yards in, and after staring at the two branches for a moment, Hathus chose the left one. He walked cautiously down a rough incline. Maybe the pirates had taken the other fork. Or maybe whatever was waiting ahead had already killed them and was now waiting for him. Hathus slowed at the thought.

He stepped around a gnarled wall, considering turning back, and came out onto a long black ledge. He stopped.

He was inside the volcano.

A massive churning lake of orange lava lay below the ledge, spreading away toward the distant black walls of the volcano in a bubbling, spitting, hissing sea of fire and heat.

Rocks, some the size of men, others of *small buildings*, fell from the edges of the cone of the volcano's top far above, disappearing into the lake in explosions of fire and steam as glowing bubbles of red and orange lava caved in with dull sucking noises.

Hathus took a step forward. It was hotter than anything he'd ever felt and somewhat terrifying, but it was also beautiful. He listened for the voice from the ship and beach. It was still absent. And there were no monsters or creatures waiting for him, only lava. Relief flooded over him.

He had been letting the darkness get to him. That's why he'd heard the voices.

A drop of orange lava landed on the ledge in front of him with a hiss and pop. Hathus glanced down at it.

"Hey!"

He looked up at the voice.

The pirates and Caine were crowded on another, larger ledge a hundred yards away from him.

So they weren't dead. Hathus raised a hand. Maybe Caine didn't have a scheme to kill them. He looked around at the lake and the black walls of the inside of the volcano. There certainly wasn't anything here that could kill them, unless they fell into the lava, but even Caine, with his spells of magic, couldn't expect to shove forty pirates into the lava without falling in himself.

A black rock the size of a small cottage sheared off the walls of the mountain far above with a loud crack and landed in the lake, causing an eruption of lava.

Hathus hissed and pulled his leather coat up for a shield as hot, molten droplets of lava splattered the ledge.

Gods, it feels like the underworld in here. He hissed again as a piece of lava landed on his right boot and kicked it away with a curse, a small, smoking black hole marring the dark leather above his big toe.

Great, now I'll have to buy new boots…

"I don't see any treasure, Ryrgorion!" Caine yelled across the lake.

Hathus looked back at the pirates and the worldwalker.

Duh. His worries from earlier were unfounded. This wasn't the Land of Dragons. The Land of Dragons didn't exist, as he'd always believed. If it did, and if they were in it, then where were the dragons?

Hathus glanced at the lava lake again, happier than he'd been in days. He would tell the Unknown Voice that there was no Land of Dragons or dragons and, according to their bargain, get his freedom. He felt like dancing.

"No!" he yelled, looking back at the pirates. "I don't either."

He turned, moving back toward the tunnel. It would take three or more weeks to get back to the BalBayr Islands, a week to get to Crystoln, one day to tell the Unknown Voice that there were no dragons in the Land of Dragons and then, freedom was his. He did a little skip dance.

Terrified yells from the other ledge rang through the volcano.

Hathus turned back around, glancing at the pirates. Their faces were ashen, and many were pointing at the lava lake and backing up toward the tunnel that led to their ledge, their hands on their weapons.

Hathus looked at the lake. It remained the same, bubbling and hissing and glowing.

The men who followed him moved up beside him. Hathus glanced at them, but they weren't looking at him—they were looking at the lake. He turned his gaze to the lake again, growing annoyed. "What in the underworld are you all looking at?"

Seven massive, glowing bodies rose from the middle of the lava lake, unanimously pulling back dripping lips from glowing teeth.

"Hello, humans," the dragons hissed.

Hathus fainted.

CHAPTER 40

Esadora

Esadora watched the fat man come into the circle of light that the candle atop the table made.

A few minutes before, she had heard the rattlesnake charm rattle over the door to the shop that she and her clan ran, and she had been standing in the shadows of the bookcases and tables, waiting for her customer.

A feast. Esadora smiled slowly, thin lips pulling up and away from her elongated and pointed black teeth. The fat man would supply her and her sisters with food for at least two days, maybe three if they stretched him. But what did he want in their apothecary shop? He was dressed in a fine silk tunic, robe, and turban that spoke of wealth, and his dark skin said that he was from Araysann. What was an Araysannian doing this far east in Warulan?

Three burly men followed the fat man into the circle of light given off by the candle, their eyes darting around the dark shop.

Esadora moved to the other side of the stone pillar that she hovered behind, her black eyes surveying the men. They were bodyguards of the fat man. She could tell that by the many knives and swords and various other weapons they wore, and from the look of the scars peppering their muscled bodies, they knew how to fight. She moved her head to the right to see around a hanging basket of dried mandrakes. They could not stand against her and her sisters. No humans could stand against a witch and live.

The fat man moved toward the table, ducking a hanging jar full of dead beetles, and Esadora reached out to his mind. A witch was trained from birth in spells and magical substances and by the age of seventy was expected to know all of the basic beginning spells and the names and uses of all the magical plants, body parts, and objects in Argdrion.

Wolfsbane was a poisonous herb that could be used to dip weapons in, mandrakes were for torturing creatures without touching their bodies, unicorn horn was to heal from poison, and royr root allowed the taker to read and talk in others' minds for a few hours at a time. Esadora had taken the root earlier that morning. She took it most every morning to allow her to probe into the minds of the people who passed by her and her clan's shop. There was little else to do in Vingorlon. Little besides snatching stray children off the streets and selling hard-to-find items to needy customers.

The fat man's name was N'san Hor'ayn, and he was an underworld lord from Crystoln. Esadora probed deeper into his thoughts. She raised a white eyebrow. He was here to see her and her clan, here to hire them. She put a long, skeletal hand on the cold stone of the pillar, curious. Maybe she and her clan wouldn't eat him and his men, after all. Not yet, anyway.

Iscara shifted in the shadows behind her, but Esadora whispered in her sister's mind for her to stay where she was. She wanted to find out more about N'san Hor'ayn, wanted to know what the proposition for her and her sisters that he was thinking about was.

She slid out from behind the pillar, three-inch-long black talons where nails should have been on the ends of her fingers scraping against the stone of the pillar.

N'san and his bodyguards looked up at her towering form as she came into the circle of light given off by the candle, and Esadora relished the look of first horror and then fear in their eyes. There had been a time, before the Hunting and during the wars, when all creatures knew to fear witches and warlocks. But that had been before the humans had betrayed them, before they had been hunted and all but exterminated from Argdrion. Now they were just another scary bedtime story that parents told their children.

"You have a question for me and my clan," Esadora rasped, pulling back a chair at the table and sliding her tall frame into it. "Tell your men to wait outside, and then you may ask it." She didn't need the bodyguards to wait outside, but a witch learned early that singling out creatures made them scared, vulnerable, weak. Besides, it made humans nervous to be alone with a witch, and Esadora liked to make creatures nervous.

N'san stared at her, dark eyes small and beady in his heavily bearded and mustached face. He nodded at the guards after a moment, waiting until the sound of the rattlesnake charm above the door rattled again before pulling out the other chair at the table and lowering his bulk into it. The chair groaned as he settled into it, old wood creaking in protest.

Esadora opened a small carved epharia box at her elbow and dumped out a pile of human finger bones onto the scratched wood of the tabletop. She arranged them into three piles, talons scratching on the table in a high-pitched tone. N'san was afraid; she could smell it radiating off him. But she couldn't read his mind again, not about what it was that he wanted; he had blocked it off from her.

"You have dealt with mind readers before," she rasped, glancing up at him.

The underworld lord folded his fat hands in front of his massive stomach, the rings crammed onto his fingers glittering in the candlelight. "No, but I remember the lessons that we were taught during the Third War to guard our minds against such threats."

His teeth were solid silver, Esadora saw, and they flashed every time he opened his mouth. "The twins of King Lysian and Ieren," she said, glancing back at the bones and arranging them according to size. "Yes, I remember the scare that went through the kingdoms."

Ruler of the wiar, King Lysian and his lover Ieren had borne twins during the latter half of the Third Great War, twin sons with the power of reading minds, talking in them and controlling them. The information had been closely guarded by the wiar for the first few years of the twins' lives, but a spy had found it out when the twins were reaching their fifth year, and panic had spread throughout the human kingdoms of Argdrion.

The power of the mind was a rare power among the wiar, and it was considered the deadliest of powers that any creature could have in Argdrion. Before the twin sons of King Lysian and Ieren, only two wiar had had the power of the mind. One of these two had used it to control the minds of the mass population in an attempt to take over the world.

"You must have practiced a lot," Esadora said, looking back up at N'san. "I cannot penetrate your mind at all."

"I was terrified of being controlled," he replied, watching her. "No one likes to think that a creature hundreds of miles away from them can be in their mind, telling them what to do and ordering their movements and actions."

Esadora smiled. "No." She heard her sisters shift in the shadows of the shop behind her, felt their hunger in her mind. It had been three days since they had last eaten. The people of Vingorlon were guarding their children more closely lately, and after residing in the city for over nine years, her clan was running out of drunks and homeless to eat.

Situated deep in the Moaning Mountains, which sat north of the Warulan kingdom of Iduiron, Vingorlon meant "City of Giants" in the old language of Warulan and was a place of thieves, murderers, whores, rent boys, slavers, assassins, and the few magical beings who had escaped from the slayings in the Hunting. Esadora and her sisters had fled to the mountain city shortly after the Hunting began, and they had been lurking in its murky depths ever since.

N'san shifted in his chair, the old wood groaning under his considerable weight.

Esadora went back to arranging the finger bones. She wanted as badly as her sisters did to eat the overweight underworld lord and his bodyguards, but her curiosity was more prominent at the moment. "What is it that you want, human?" she asked.

N'san shifted again, grunting as he tried to comfortably arrange his weight on the chair. "I want to hire you and your clan," he said. "To find and kill a man."

Esadora probed his mind again, caught a small glimpse of his thoughts. He had not come of his own accord to hire her and her clan, but on orders from Torin Ravynston, the chief advisor of Eromor.

Interesting. "And what made you think of us?" she asked the fat man, looking up at him again from the finger bones. "There are hundreds of assassins in Argdrion. Why hire magical creatures when associating with us can get you executed?"

There was darkness in her voice with those last words, and anger. The humans only ever came to witches and warlocks when they wanted dirty deeds done or help in defeating an enemy. They had come to them at the beginning of the Second Great War, asking for them to help fight against the wiar and skinchangers. And when the war had turned in the humans' favor, and the witches and warlocks were no longer needed, the humans had turned on them and slaughtered them like animals.

"Because the man that I want killed is not easily killed," N'san replied. "And this is a job, I think, that only witches can complete."

Esadora eyed him. "How much money are you offering for killing this man?" she asked, "And what guarantee do we have that you do not have a company of soldiers outside Vingorlon, waiting to slaughter me and my clan if we exit the city?"

"I am prepared to pay you fifty thousand aray," N'san said. "And my business is the underworld of Crystoln, not hunting magical creatures."

Esadora looked back at the bones. Fifty thousand aray was enough to put her and her clan up for years, enough so that they wouldn't have to run their apothecary shop unless they wanted to, enough to ensure that they could buy fresh humans to eat instead of scrounging for days on end in the back streets of Vingorlon, looking for warm bodies.

But what if it was a trap to lure her and her sisters out of Vingorlon so that they could be slaughtered? The Hunting was over now these three years, but magical creatures were still hunted by a few, and many considered it their duty to turn them in or kill them on sight.

"This man must have done something horrible to you to make you want to pay fifty thousand aray for his head," Esadora said, pushing the bones into a triangle pattern. "Or you fear him greatly."

The underworld lord's guard slipped suddenly, fear skittering through him at her words, and Esadora probed into his mind.

Esadora saw an image in N'san's head of a candlelit stone room in the chief advisor's office in the palace of Crystoln.

"So, you are the one who reported Darkmoon and the skinchanger escaping the city through the sewers to my soldiers," the chief advisor said. He was a thin man with a pointed black beard and mustache and eyes that bespoke of a keen intelligence.

N'san, seated on the opposite side of the epharia desk, nodded. "Yes,

Your Lordship. Darkmoon came to me," he said, putting a fat hand to his chest, "asking for my help in getting that creature out of the city. Naturally when he asked, I thought of my duty to the crown, and once he had left, I immediately sent word to the city soldiers to alert them of what was happening."

"Naturally," Torin said, steepling his long hands in front of him on the desk. "And why is it, N'san Hor'ayn, that you are here in my office now?"

N'san smiled, silver teeth flashing. "I had hoped that your lordship would look on a poor, simple man who has done his duty for his crown and reward him for his services."

Torin leaned back in his chair and crossed one leg over the other. "You're an underworld lord, am I correct?"

N'san smiled again. "I am a small business owner, my lord."

"And you would like to keep those businesses, would you not?" Torin asked.

N'san didn't stop smiling. "To be certain, Your Lordship. I have done nothing wrong."

"No," Torin said, "but I am sure that I could have things found out about you, things that would allow me to arrest you and turn your business upside down."

The smile left N'san's face.

"How about this," Torin said, leaning forward again and pulling open a drawer on the desk. "The 'reward' that I give you for telling my soldiers the information about Darkmoon and the skinchanger will be me not throwing you in prison to rot." The chief advisor pulled out a paper and scanned it. "Now, I think that will be all, don't you?" He didn't look up.

N'san stood, pulling his green tunic around him. He jerked his head at his bodyguards and started toward the door.

"Oh, and one more thing," Torin said, looking up from the paper. "There is a favor that I would ask of you…"

Esadora hissed and backed up, her talons digging deep grooves into the table. The favor that Torin Ravynston had wanted of N'san Hor'ayn was for him to hire her and her clan to kill Darkmoon and the skinchanger who, even with N'san turning them in, had managed to escape Crystoln. She didn't care about the skinchanger, but Darkmoon…

Esadora heard her sisters move again in the shadows behind her when she put the assassin's name into their minds. They shared her anger, her pain. Darkmoon had killed their sister Yrnayr three years before, when she had become tired of the bad human flesh in Vingorlon and had gone west to look for better food.

"You know Darkmoon?" N'san asked, blocking off his mind again.

Esadora snarled. "*Know* him?" she rasped. "I think of nothing else but finding him and cutting his heart out and *eating* it."

"Then why haven't you?" N'san asked, watching her with the eyes of a man who knew how to read people.

Esadora stood, pushing her chair back from the table and stalking around the small clearing in the shadowed shop. "He moves over all of Argdrion," she hissed. "And to look for him would mean my clan and I would have to leave Vingorlon."

Cobwebs dangled from the ceiling above Esadora's head. Shelves around the empty spot of floor that the table sat on stretched off into the darkness above.

"Well, now he's running, hunted, in Eromor," N'san said as she moved around behind him, "it should be easy for you and your sisters to find him while he's in one kingdom."

Esadora paused behind the underworld lord's chair. "You fear him," she said, looking down at him. She watched a bead of perspiration run out from under N'san's purple turban and trail down the back of his neck. He feared her too.

"I turned him in to the authorities," N'san said, voice uneasy. "And he knows it. Anyone who has betrayed Argdrion's best assassin would fear him."

Esadora leaned down over N'san's shoulder, waist-length white hair brushing against him. The underworld lord smelled like octopus and perfume and sweat but also blood and warm flesh. It was intoxicating.

"I haven't eaten in three days, human," she whispered in N'san's ear. "Nor have my sisters." Esadora dug the black talons of one hand into the back of the chair that the underworld lord sat in, the black veins running under her pale skin popping. "As you can guess, we are very hungry. Now tell me, human, why we shouldn't just eat you and your bodyguards and not take your offer?"

"Because you won't get your money or revenge," N'san said, fear rolling off him now. His posture was stiff, tense.

Esadora probed his thoughts again. He was thinking about how much witches and warlocks loved money and hoping that she and her sisters would take the job.

"We do love money, human," Esadora said. She pulled her talons out of the chair and rested them on N'san's shoulder, curling them into the underworld lord's fat flesh. He gasped and cringed underneath her. "But we also love warm flesh." She let go of N'san as suddenly as she had grabbed him and straightened, moving back to her chair. She could feel her sisters' eyes on her, watching, listening, waiting.

Esadora slid back into her chair. She wanted to eat the fat underworld lord and his bodyguards, but there was something else she wanted more, and that was Darkmoon's beating heart in her hand.

Esadora looked back up at N'san, meeting his dark eyes with her own. She showed her pointed teeth. "We will do what you ask, human."

CHAPTER 41

Darkmoon

Darkmoon's lip twitched as one of the soldiers marching along the road in front of him slipped and dropped her spear with a dull squelch in the ankle-deep mud.

The rainy season was lasting unusually long this year, and even though it was almost summer, the roads were still deep with mud and puddles. An unpleasant fact for travelers.

A northerly breeze blew through the thick entanglement of goyr trees towering over Darkmoon's head, and the night-black leaves of the massive trees sent a shower of raindrops down onto the fern and rorbush covering the forest floor around him.

The misting rain falling from the slate-gray sky slanted at an angle into the faces of the large company of soldiers.

The soldier who'd dropped her spear scrambled to pick it out of the mud and only succeeded in tripping one of her fellows, causing her to drop her spear as well.

It's like a traveling troop of fools…

The second woman cursed loudly, and the captain of the company, a short, broad-shouldered man, bellowed for order from atop his large white gelding as a small fight broke out.

Darkmoon tapped the skinchanger, who was lying on her stomach on the leaf-strewn ground next to him, and slid backward out from beneath the massive rorbush he'd chosen as their hiding spot, carefully so as not to run into any of the five-inch black thorns protruding at all angles from the twisting black branches of the bush.

The soldiers began marching again, kicking mud onto their stained black trousers as they went.

The patrol was the third they had seen since setting out from the cabin in the meadow that morning, and Darkmoon knew that they wouldn't be the last that they ran across before they reached Rothborn. When the humans wanted something, they got it, even if it meant sending out half their army in the process. They were a determined race.

Darkmoon stood, slowly so as not to attract the attention of the soldiers, and they slipped off through the dim forest, the scent of the rorbush, like rosemary and lemon, lingering on their cloaks.

He skirted around a young goyr that twisted its way upward through the dense canopy of its matured counterpart's thick black leaves for hope of the Brothers' rays and glided through a fern-filled meadow, his boots leaving dark imprints in the light-green leaves behind him. They were close to Rothborn now. He expected that they'd reach the ancient mining city sometime in the next two days.

Darkmoon stepped onto a well-trodden game trail that was slick with water and mud and started off down the trail as it wound along the edge of a deep gorge. Once in Rothborn, he would restock his weapons and plot revenge on N'san. There was no need to hurry it, though—the best kind of revenge was not quick but agonizingly slow. The kind that took weeks, months, years even, before it brought satisfaction. The kind that made the one the revenge was aimed at wait, with the knowledge that revenge was coming. A wait that was so long that they eventually begged to die rather than live in dreaded anticipation any longer.

"How many houses do you have?" the skinchanger's deep voice broke into his thoughts.

Darkmoon looked back at her, picking her way through the drizzling rain along the trail behind him. It was always twilight in the Ilgerion Forest, and with the black cloak that the madam from the brothel had given her, she blended in with the shadows of the forest like one of them.

"Nine," he said, glancing back at the trail in front of him. He jumped up on a goyr root arching over the narrow path and hopped nimbly back down onto the other side, boots squelching in the mud. "Why?"

"You said they are safehouses, what do you mean by that?"

She's got a good memory. Darkmoon didn't know why he was continuing to let her come with him. He should have slit her throat outside of Crystoln when she'd insisted on following him. But although it angered him still that the voices and memories stopped around her, he did have to admit that the last few restful nights and peaceful days were nice. Very nice.

"I make a lot of powerful enemies in my business," he replied, stopping at a rain-slick goyr that had fallen across the gorge to create a natural bridge. "And the houses are places where I can rest without the fear of being attacked. Where I can disappear." That and he had to do something with his money besides buying women and chocolate.

At the thought of the sweet, a pain of craving shot through Darkmoon's stomach. The pieces of chocolate in his cloak pocket had been ruined by his swim in the sewers, and it had been too long now since he'd last had the sweet.

"How did you start?" the skinchanger asked, stopping on the eroding trail next to him.

Darkmoon looked up at her from underneath his soaked cowl, noticing the way the rain made her shirt cling to her small breasts. "Start what?"

"Killing," she said, looking down at the white-foamed stream snaking through the bottom of the gorge below.

"Oh, that," Darkmoon said. He looked back at the goyr bridge and stepped up on its rough gray bark. "I like it." He started across the wide log, rain pulling his cloak down behind him.

At midday, a gurgling stream appeared out of the gloom of the forest, and they stopped for a moment to drink from the clear water and replenish the small silver flask that Darkmoon carried in his pocket.

It was too bad that they didn't have another water carrier, he mused, holding the glistening flask under the rippling water and letting it fill. The rain was good for little else besides watering the trees and soaking their clothes and wasn't heavy enough for him to refill the cask by it.

Darkmoon glanced up at the skinchanger as bubbles broke around the flask's narrow mouth. She crouched a few feet away from him, raising a palm full of water to her mouth as her eyes searched the dark shadows between the trees.

Slit her throat.

Darkmoon screwed the cap back on the flask and stood. He would. Not yet… Soon, but not yet.

He stashed the flask back in the folds of his cloak and stood, then jumped nimbly across the stream on the twisting roots of a goyr tree, the winding and intertwining wood spreading out under the water beneath him like veins.

The light faded through the trees a few hours later and with it the rain. Darkness rose and nighttime came.

Darkmoon stepped out onto the King's Highway as a soft wind rustled through the water-heavy trees behind them and scanned the dark road for sign of any travelers. When he saw none, he started off up it. He was tired of navigating through the forest, and it was so late that he doubted whether any soldiers would be out looking for them. He heard the skinchanger's light footfalls behind him, always following.

"How much farther is this Rothborn?" she asked, pushing her hood off her head as she came up next to him.

The clouds drifted apart overhead, and the Sisters glowed down on the road in front of them, bringing clarity to the hundreds of horse and human prints marring the mud.

Darkmoon glanced sideways at the skinchanger, the moonlight dancing over her inky black hair and curling tattoos. "Why, tired?" he asked.

"No," she replied, glancing at him. "Skinchangers have twice the stamina that humans do."

Darkmoon smiled softly and looked back at the trail in front of them. Mist drifted across it in silvery wisps. "Not more than twenty-five miles," he said. "We'll be there in the morning."

The skinchanger nodded, a soft breeze lifting tendrils of her long hair and pulling them along with it.

Darkmoon scanned the dark trees to his left, a prickling feeling running through him. It felt like someone was nearby, not watching them necessarily, but coming.

The skinchanger stopped next to him, and Darkmoon glanced back down at her as she shed her clothing in a heap on the road.

She shifted into a silver timber wolf and turned, running off into the forest.

Darkmoon looked back at the forest around them, listening for noise of approaching soldiers. That was the second time she'd done that since they'd started out. The last time she had brought back a black forest hen.

The skinchanger reappeared a half hour later, slipping out of the forest as silent as a wraith. She carried a dead rabbit, blood still dripping from the wound in its throat as it hung limply from her jaws.

Darkmoon smiled slowly, his stomach growling at the sight. "If I didn't know better, skinchanger," he murmured, "I would think that you were starting to like me, feeding me two nights in a row."

#

Darkmoon wiped rabbit grease off his slender fingers and leaned back against a root of the ancient gray goyr tree they'd made their camp under. He laced his fingers behind his head as a rest. "You catch a good rabbit, skinchanger."

The skinchanger looked up at him from tearing the flesh off a bone on the other side of the crackling fire he had made, the golden flames playing on the tattoos snaking across her face. The light made her look like the beautiful ancient ghost of a creature long dead.

Darkmoon shivered at the thought and crossed his legs in front of him, the warmth of the fire keeping the chill in the air off his outstretched body. It had been two days since he had found the skinchanger and discovered that the voices, dreams, and memories stopped around her, and still he did not understand why. What was it about her that kept them back? Was she one of the ones who would help him "save" Argdrion from the coming darkness like the seer had spoken about? But why would that make his dreams and memories fade?

The skinchanger went back to cleaning her bone.

Darkmoon glanced up at the black goyr leaves far above his head, moving slightly in the fire's trailing smoke. "Where did the slavers find you?" he asked softly after a moment. He felt the skinchanger look up. "Stories had it that your kind were all dead until you showed up in the arena."

"Why do you care?" she said, going back to her bone.

"I don't," Darkmoon replied, rolling his head back down to look at her. "But since you weren't going to start the conversation, I figured I should."

She threw the cleaned bone away into the goyr leaves littering the forest floor, her form wavering with the jumping flames of the fire like she was a mirage.

Darkmoon went back to staring at the leaves above him, pondering what the coming darkness might be.

After a few moments, the skinchanger's deep voice broke the silence. "Ennotar," she said softly. "The slavers found us in Ennotar."

Darkmoon rolled his head back down to look at her. "How?"

The skinchanger glanced up at him, golden eyes meeting his. "I don't know," she said, voice growing hard again. "But they did, and they showed no mercy, as your kind never does." She turned away from him and wrapped her cloak around her, then lay down on her side, back to him.

Darkmoon watched her for a while, mind straying to memories. Humans were good at showing no mercy. He looked back at the leaves above him, glistening softly in the dying light of the fire. Screams echoed through his mind. The room with the iron hooks hanging from the ceiling and the barrel of water in its center appeared. Darkmoon blinked, shoving them away. If one wanted to survive in Argdrion, they could not have mercy.

If they did, it would be their death.

#

Something awoke him a few hours later.

The Sisters had broken through the darkness covering the forest, making the goyr trees glow a dim silver, and the fire had burned down completely, just a few glowing embers marking where it had been.

Darkmoon, lying on his side, blinked and stared into the semidarkness in front of him.

A silvery fern swayed in a soft breeze. A twig cracked somewhere.

What had awoken him? It could have been anything, an owl calling, a snake rustling through the undergrowth...

He watched a rorbush follow suit with the fern and gently sway back and forth in the breeze, its sweet scent stroking his thin nostrils as the wind brushed past and knocked raindrops from the surrounding trees in a shower of sharp pings. Everything was quiet, maybe too quiet.

He rolled over onto his back, slowly in case anyone was watching, and looked over to where the skinchanger lay.

Her golden eyes stared back at him.

She had heard something too. Darkmoon shifted his gaze the other way, scanning the shadowed goyr trunks for any sign of movement. He'd heard rumors that shadows lived in the caves in the northern end of the Ilgerion Forest, and he'd seen footprints of dire wolves more than once on his travels. The Ilgerion Forest was ancient, dense, and dark, and although most of the creatures that had inhabited it before the wars had been killed off long ago, there were still a few that had managed to avoid the traps and weapons of hunters and remained hidden in its murky depths.

The breeze died down. Somewhere in the distance, a raindrop clinging to a leaf fell to the ground with a soft splat.

Darkmoon glanced that way, remembering the feeling of something coming that he'd had on the highway earlier.

They came out of the darkness so fast that he barely saw them, bodies over seven feet tall and white hair streaming from their heads.

A star slid into each of Darkmoon's hands as he lunged to his feet. He heard the skinchanger's clothes shred behind him and saw her jump across the burned-out fire as a snarling wolf before a creature with hair of whitest moonlight slammed into him.

They hit the ground with a thud, the end of a goyr root digging into his neck.

Darkmoon rolled to the side as three-inch black talons slashed toward his face. They ran down the root where his head had been with a shredding screech. He grabbed the black-veined skeletal hand they were attached to and slashed at it with a star.

A piercing scream rang in his ears. Darkmoon writhed sideways as black blood that smelled like rancid flesh sprayed the goyr leaves.

Witches.

Darkmoon kicked the screaming creature off him and threw his legs into the air, using the momentum to lunge to his feet. He'd know the smell and color of their blood anywhere. Only witches had blood the color of writing ink, and only witches—and warlocks, whose blood was as silver as moonlight on water—had blood that would poison whatever living thing it touched. One drop and he would be writhing in the throes of death before three days had passed.

Darkmoon wiped his star off on the bark of a goyr next to him, black lines darting out like spiderwebs from where the poisonous blood touched. What were witches doing this far east? There were only a few remaining in Argdrion since the wars and the Hunting, and those, like all other magical creatures, were very rarely seen. What had made them come out of their hiding place? Or rather, how much money had someone offered them?

The witch snarled at him, white spittle flying out of her mouth, and rushed forward, long white hair streaming out behind her head like a streak of light in the darkness.

Perhaps N'san had hired the witches to find him, but it didn't really seem like the underworld lord's style, and besides, Darkmoon knew that N'san feared witches.

He lunged into the air as the witch neared him, avoiding her dagger-sharp talons. His feet slammed into her leather-armor chestpiece, sending her flying backward into the trunk of the goyr tree with a loud crack.

Torin. Darkmoon narrowed his ice and pine eyes. Torin had hired the witches.

Another witch, taller than the first, flew out of the darkness between the goyr trees, black fangs glistening, eyes pits of darkness, and he bent backward as she swung a massive two-sided broadsword at him. The polished blades whistled shrilly through the air where his middle had been a second before.

The witch charged again, sword blurring with her streaming white hair as she spun it like a baton in front of her, and Darkmoon heard his cloak slice open as one of the sword's blades found its corner. He glanced down at the supple black cloth, a slow smile sliding onto his thin face. It had been years since he'd had an opponent who could cut even so much as his clothing. This fight would require skill.

The witch swung again.

Darkmoon twisted to the side before lunging into the air as she threw the other blade of her sword at his legs.

Movement to his left caught his eye. He glanced sideways to see the witch he'd kicked into the tree rise and run a long, jagged dagger down the palm of her hand. Black blood pooled in her hand, dripping from her fingers, glistening on her veiny white skin.

Darkmoon threw a dagger at the witch with the broadsword.

She dodged it.

Witches' and warlocks' bodies produced blood at an abnormal rate when they lost any, and they were able to lose extraordinary amounts without feeling the effects that other creatures did.

The second witch's blades screamed as they tore through the air.

Darkmoon looked back to her. There were ancient runes engraved on the glimmering steel's edge he noticed as the two blades arced toward his head.

He lunged sideways to avoid the swinging sword and flipped over backward, then ran up the slate-gray trunk of a goyr tree before landing lightly behind the witch with the broadsword. He pulled two other stars from his belts as he hit the ground, the blades hissing, spinning end over end through the air as he threw them at the witch with the broadsword.

One embedded with a thunk into her black shoulder armor, overlapping elaborately carved pieces of boiled leather with tints of red. The other star pinged harmlessly off her massive weapon and sailed into the darkness.

Darkmoon cursed. He was running low.

The witch with the broadsword, a skeletal creature, like all her kind, with a narrow gray scar that cut her face in half, snarled, her elongated, pointed black fangs flashing in a white beam of light from the Sisters.

"You think you can beat us, human?" she hissed, her voice like breaking glass. "We will be licking the remains of your blood and flesh from our fingers by morning."

Darkmoon's eyes darted to where the skinchanger was still holding her own, now as a darting fox, against two other witches. He glanced around the shadowed goyr trees around him. There were five witches in total, two battling the skinchanger and two battling him and another.

Where was the fifth? He scanned the shadows between the towering goyr trees and curving rorbushes. There had been another.

"Are you sure about that?" Darkmoon asked, glancing up at the witch with the double broadsword. "Because the last time I clashed with one of your kind, I killed the bitch with hardly a scratch to myself."

The fury in the witch's black eyes was enough to make the dead quiver. "You'll pay for that, human," she snarled, scarred lips pulling back from her fangs.

Darkmoon smiled humorlessly, sliding his last two knives out of his vambraces and into his slender palms. "Maybe, but you must doubt that if you dragged four of your sisters along to do me in."

"The more to enjoy your blood," the witch hissed. Her black eyes darted to his side for a split second, and Darkmoon heard the soft tread of footfalls on the leaves behind him.

There she is... "You know," he said, meeting the eyes of the witch with the broadsword, "I rather enjoyed killing your sister." He smiled cruelly. "She screamed like a pig when I slit her throat from ear to ear. You should have heard her beg me for mercy."

The witch with the double broadsword let out a scream that shook leaves off the goyr tree over their heads and lunged forward, her white hair streaming like a banner behind her.

Darkmoon moved with her, jumping away from her swinging blow and wheeling around her as she turned for another.

The fifth witch stepped out of shadows in front of him with one bloody, black-veined arm raised above her white head.

Darkmoon let a dagger fly.

The witch gave a cry somewhere between a screech and a gurgle as the dagger embedded itself up to its hilt in her throat. She crumpled sideways to the goyr leaves with black blood shooting out of her white throat.

The witch with the double broadsword screamed. "NO!" she screeched, wheeling. Her blades whistled through the air.

Darkmoon wheeled to the side.

The third witch threw a palmful of black blood.

He cursed and rolled to the leaves, holding his cloak up in front of him as a shield as the dark gore splattered over him.

The witch with the double broadsword stalked toward him, long split skirt swishing around her leather-clad legs. "I told you, assassin," she snarled, "you are no match for us. No mere human can stand against witches and live."

Darkmoon glanced at his cloak. It was peppered with black blood.

He stretched a half-gloved hand out to the remains of the fire and dug underneath the cold ashes on top, grabbed a handful of red-hot embers, and threw them into the face of the witch with the double broadsword.

She screamed and dropped her sword to the goyr leaves, clawing at her face.

Darkmoon lunged to his feet and darted toward the witch he'd slain, dodging another spray of blood from the third witch as he went.

Inky lines appeared on two more goyr trees where the blood splattered, snaking off up the gray bark like black veins.

The witch with the broadsword pulled her hands down from her face, bright-red welts marring the flesh of her face. "Bastard," she spat, bending and seizing her sword from the leaves with one hand.

Darkmoon pulled his dagger from the throat of the slain witch, eyes darting to the third witch who had pulled off one of her vambraces and was slicing open the pale white skin of her forearm. He wiped black blood off his dagger and onto the white hair of the dead witch.

The witch with the double broadsword snarled and rushed across the leaves.

Darkmoon let one of his daggers fly.

It imbedded one of the witch's skeletal white hands. She screamed and slowed to rip it from her hand.

Both witches rushed him next.

Darkmoon moved with them, ducking their blood and dodging their weapons and talons. He was a shadow among ghosts, turning, kicking, twisting, slashing.

Black blood flew around them like gruesome rain, marring the goyr trees surrounding them with a thousand black lines.

He was death, but he was one against two, and they were daemons.

A stinging sensation marred his side. Darkmoon glanced down to see the leather-wrapped hilt of his dagger protruding from his lower stomach.

Damn it.

"You're not the only one who can throw things, assassin," the witch with the double broadsword hissed.

Darkmoon pulled the weapon from his side. Red and black blood dripped off it in shiny drops, blending together as they fell to the forest floor below.

And it's my own weapon too. He staggered backward, the dagger falling from his fingertips.

"Smell the blood, Iscara," the witch with the double broadsword murmured to the other. She ran a glistening black tongue over her pointed black teeth.

How she didn't cut herself, Darkmoon didn't know. He put a gloved hand to his side, it came away soaked with blood.

"Your end has come, witch killer." The witch with the broadsword snarled with an animalistic smile.

Darkmoon took a step backward, a feeling like snakes pushing through his veins, throbbing through him. He fell to his knees on the goyr leaves, needles prickling over his flesh.

He glanced at the skinchanger, who was in the form of a cougar now. She and the other two witches had paused their fight and were looking at him.

The skinchanger's golden eyes met his. Darkmoon thought he saw a flash of fear in them.

"I would say see you in the next life," the witch with the double broadsword rasped, black eyes glistening with hunger as she towered over him, "but I doubt that will be anytime soon." She sneered, fangs glinting. "For me, anyway."

Darkmoon glanced up at her, darkness humming at the edges of his vision as his stomach began to burn like a thousand bees were stinging the inside of it.

"For Argdrion's sake, bitch," he said with a gasp, blackness overwhelming him, "I hope it is."

CHAPTER 42

Azkanysh

A cool breeze from the distant desert blew down the path of the garden, hissing over the sand and whispering through the bushes on either side.

Azkanysh held her face up to the wind, goosebumps rising along her arms beneath the black cotton tunic and robe she wore. The army should be marching toward Crystoln by now. Her military advisors said that they'd probably find the enemy at Whitegate, the last large natural resistance before Crystoln.

Azkanysh fingered a small yellow-and-pink rose on a bush beside the pathway, admiring its delicateness. She'd gone to the temple of Drisahr Aruyn in the heart of the city that evening to pray for victory for the army, after she'd spent the morning hearing case after case during court sessions. Then she'd had lunch with a visiting province king and then wiled away the afternoon hours by poring over her books, trying to learn the larger words so that she could read the laws of Zarcayra.

A wind chime of tarnished brass bells hanging from a sandstone gazebo ahead began ringing as the breeze reached it, and Azkanysh glanced up at the sound, listening to the sweet, melodious notes. Since the Guardian Council had elected Zarmeyr as its newest member following Shayr Jahayan's death, she had been spending every available hour, day and night, practicing her reading and spelling. She wanted to be able to read Zarcayra's laws so that she could be as educated on the kingdom's legal system as the Guardian Council was. So that she would not be surprised again with a law that she knew nothing about.

Azkanysh started walking again, her slippered feet making little noise in the soft sand that marked the pathway. She had held her banquet as planned, and she had announced to the shayrs and shayras of Sussār of her intent to hire a tutor to train Paruhi and Kayani in the art of reading and writing. The reception received by the shayrs and shayras had been better than she had hoped for. Several had said that they, too, would hire tutors. But it felt like a small victory in the face of Zarmeyr on the council, a pointless victory.

Azkanysh walked by a red fountain of a lyon pouring water out of its open mouth into a pool beneath, the sweet music of the water mingling with the distant tinkle of the wind chime.

The path split off into four directions. Azkanysh chose the one on her right, winding past beds of swaying lilum and fragrant lily of the valleys. She had visited Shayr Jahayan's brother the day after the murder, offering her condolences and discreetly fishing for information. She had hoped to learn of something that Shayr Jahayan might have said about someone from the council threatening or scaring him, but his brother had mentioned no such threat, and she still had no proof that the Guardian Council were the true murderers. She doubted that she ever would. And if she didn't find proof, then she would not be able to have them arrested and disbanded.

The breeze died down as quickly as it had come, and the wind chime stopped tinging.

Azkanysh rounded a curve in the pathway. A bench in the shape of an elephant appeared ahead. Exhausted, she made her way toward it, easing down onto the elephants back and listening to the crickets filling the night air with their steady tunes. She glanced up at the star-filled night sky. Ragoyth the dragon winked at her in the west as he blew a streak of stars out of his horned mouth, while in the south the lyon Heyros roared defiance to the world.

Azkanysh eyed the constellations. She was angry at Tamar for disobeying her and running away, angry at being unable to find any evidence to convict the Guardian Council, angry that Zarmeyr was on the council now, angry at the Family that in eight months' time her son would take the golden lyon crown and reverse every ruling that she had made or would make for freedom for Zarcayra's women.

A star streaked across the sky and disappeared into the darkness where the sky met the sand dunes of the desert. Azkanysh followed its trail half-heartedly. She was also worried about Tamar. She assumed that her daughter had hidden her identity well, but if anyone should find out who she truly was, there was the danger of her being kidnapped and held for ransom. The poor of Zarcayra would do anything for money, even kidnap a member of the royal family.

Azkanysh looked back at the constellations, her eye catching on the great bear Jürgain in the north, guarding Nilfinhèim. Vosbarhan had lost a sister to kidnappers when he had been a young man. She remembered hearing the story as it had gone through the kingdom, remembered how angry she had been when she had heard that the reason why the kidnappers had killed the princess was because the royal family had refused to pay as much money as they had wanted for a woman.

A pink-and-white butterfly bush swayed in a new breeze. Azkanysh watched it absently. She prayed every day for Ehurayni to bring her daughter back safely to her, but in her heart she had her doubts that the guards she had sent after Tamar would be able to find her. She could be on any ship sailing for Warulan, and once she reached the eastern continent, it could take the guards months to find her trail. Months that would start to look suspicious if she kept lying to the kingdom about Tamar's "illness."

Sand crunched down the pathway.

Azkanysh glanced up. No one was ever in the gardens this late—it had to be an animal. Perhaps a mouse or one of the palace cats. She pushed off the bench and started up the path again. Tomorrow she had only one court session. She planned on spending the rest of the day practicing her reading and thinking over what she would do if Tamar was not found. She could lie to the kingdom and say that Tamar had died from her sickness, but holding a funeral without the body there to be seen would be difficult, perhaps impossible. Zarcayran tradition held that at funerals the body of the deceased was to be presented for all to see and say goodbye to. What would the people of Zarcayra say when there was no body?

Sand crunched behind her again, louder this time.

Azkanysh paused her walking and turned slightly. She scanned the moonlit sand of the pathway. Perhaps it was one of her guards getting closer to keep an eye on her. She was required to take them with her everywhere she went for safety, but she made them stay out of eyesight during her walks in the gardens. It got tiresome having people around constantly, and sometimes she liked to be alone.

Azkanysh started walking again. And then there was always Zarmeyr, who showed her even more disrespect, if that was possible, now that he was on the Guardian Council. She feared her son, feared what he would do to her when he became King of Kings at the end of the year. She also feared what her son would turn the kingdom into, how he would abuse the women of Zarcayra.

Sand crunched again.

Warning bells tinkled in Azkanysh's head. She had the slowly building feeling that she was being followed, and not by her guards. But who would follow her out in the gardens? Or anywhere, for that matter.

The breeze died down, and the gardens fell still.

Azkanysh stopped and turned again, scanning the garden behind her.

A man appeared out of the semidarkness, dressed completely in black with a cloth over his face and a gleaming dagger in his hand. "It is time you joined your husband, Queen of Queens," he said in a raspy, unnatural voice that sounded strangely familiar. He lunged.

Dull pain wracked her shoulder. Azkanysh stumbled backward, a warm wetness trickling down her arm. She glanced at her shoulder in shock. The man was trying to kill her.

She screamed.

The man uttered a muffled curse and lunged again.

"Guards!" Azkanysh screamed, reeling backward as the man swiped at her with the bloodstained dagger.

She felt a bush against her back.

The man stumbled over a stick in the pathway and crashed into a flower bed, smashing irises and lilies with his boots.

Azkanysh turned and ran, robes fluttering in the wind behind her as she bolted up the path. She heard the man curse again, and a second later, sand crunched behind her. "Guards!" she screamed again.

Ehurayni, help me!

Warm blood slid down her arm as she darted down a path with rosebushes lining it. Azkanysh felt it dripping off her fingers.

Something pulled at her robes.

She jerked to a stop, turning to see them caught on the thorn-laden branch of a rosebush.

No! She yanked on the tightly woven cotton cloth, the man's footsteps drawing closer. The Guardian Council was trying to have her assassinated, murdered like Shayr Jahayan.

Azkanysh yanked harder on her robes. They saw no other way to stop her from ruling opposed to them, no other path to get their way.

The brown branch of the rosebush broke with a loud snap as the man came around a corner in the pathway, and she threw it and her robe in his face and ran again.

Distant shouts echoed through the air.

Azkanysh saw torches bobbing toward her.

A muscled hand grabbed her good arm, and she screamed again and brought her wounded arm toward the man as he wheeled her around. She hit him in the side of the head. He cursed and raised his dagger.

Azkanysh latched her good hand on his upraised arm, muscles screaming as they struggled for control of the dagger.

"Is it worth it to kill me?" She gasped, the knife dripping blood onto her face as they fought over it. "Your life for mine?" She felt her arm weaken under the man's muscles. "If you kill me, you will be executed, you know that!"

The knife drew closer. Azkanysh struggled harder, panic rising in her.

"Stop struggling," the man said, too intent on taking control of the knife to bother concealing his voice again.

Azkanysh glanced to the narrow slits in the cloth over his face, where she knew his eyes were. She inhaled. She knew that voice, knew those eyes. The blood drained from her face.

Her arm gave out under the man's, and she gasped and looked down at her middle as he drove the knife deep into her stomach.

Shouts echoed through the night air, closer now.

Azkanysh had the vague impression of being lifted off the ground before she was flying, and then she landed with a thousand stabs of pain in a rosebush by the side of the path.

The shouts drew closer still, the crunch of sand under many boots echoed through the night air.

Azkanysh glanced through the thorns at the assassin, their eyes meeting. "Why?" she whispered.

The man threw the knife into the gravel and ran off up the path.

The hiss of steel on leather rang through the air. Torchlight glared off the bushes.

Azkanysh was painfully aware of how many thorns were cutting into her flesh as a dozen pairs of feet ran by, of warm blood draining down her stomach and onto her legs.

"Queen of Queens!" Vyzir Dsamihur's black silk slippers appeared on the path. "Over here! I found her!"

Azkanysh drew in a rattling breath, the metallic taste of blood heavy in her mouth.

"Where are you hurt, Queen of Queens?" Vyzir Dsamihur asked, his voice not edged with its usual calmness.

Azkanysh cried out as he lifted her out of the rosebush, thorns pulling out of her flesh and making new wounds.

"I knew his voice," she whispered as several guards with torches surrounded them. Someone shouted for a litter. She met Vyzir Dsamihur's eyes. "I knew his voice."

#

Her son wanted her dead. Azkanysh stared at the painted sandstone ceiling of her bedchamber. She had known that Zarmeyr did not love her, like her, even, but she had never thought that he would try to have her killed.

A slave entered the bedchamber, a wet towel in her hands.

Azkanysh didn't look at the woman as she placed the towel on her forehead. She continued to stare at the ceiling, seeing the eyes of the man who had stabbed her in the gardens the night before, hearing his voice. His eyes had been pink, and his voice was one she recognized, as she heard it often.

He was Zarmeyr's albino bodyguard.

She wondered if the rest of the Guardian Council had been in on the attempted assassination, or only her son.

The golden doors of her chambers ground open. Azkanysh rolled her head to the side to look through the arch leading into the antechamber outside.

Vyzir Dsamihur and the gold-cloaked head of the royal guard stepped inside, faces somber, tired.

"Queen of Queens," said a female slave with a bow as she came into the bedchamber. "Visitors to see you."

Azkanysh nodded.

The slave bowed and backed out of the room again.

"Queen of Queens," Vyzir Dsamihur and the royal-guard leader said in unison, bowing as they stepped into the bedchamber.

Azkanysh raised her good arm slowly, motioning for the slave wiping at her head to leave.

The woman did, backing out of the room with the towel in her hands.

"How are you feeling?" Vyzir Dsamihur queried, stopping a few feet away from the bed.

Azkanysh looked back at the ceiling. "Weak," she whispered.

She sensed Vyzir Dsamihur glance at the guard leader.

"We came here, Queen of Queens," the guard leader spoke up, "to see if you could give us any clue as to who the man was who attacked you."

"Your men did not find him last night?" Azkanysh asked, staring at a painting of a peacock on the ceiling with curling green, blue, and gold tail feathers.

"No, Queen of Queens," the guard leader replied. His voice was deep, husky.

Of course they hadn't. The albino had probably fled back to Zarmeyr's rooms, and who would think to look for an assassin hidden in the bedchambers of the heir to the throne?

"Do you remember anything about the man who attacked you, Queen of Queens?" the royal-guard leader asked after a few heartbeats. "Anything at all that might help us?"

Azkanysh swallowed slowly, the poppy that the physicians had given her for the pain of her wounds making her throat feel thick and swollen. She could not tell anyone that Zarmeyr's man-slave had been the one who had tried to kill her. She could not accuse the heir to the throne of trying to murder her. Zarmeyr was held in high regard by the shayrs of Zarcayra, and if she were to accuse him of trying to kill her, it would mean a scandal that would rock the kingdom. No one would believe a woman's word against the heir to the throne, either, even if that woman was the Queen of Queens. They would say that she was paranoid of losing her crown, that she was being silly, emotional. Female.

"It was dark," Azkanysh said after a few moments. "And I did not see much of the man." She felt Vyzir Dsamihur and the royal-guard leader look at each other again.

"You told me that night, Queen of Queens," Vyzir Dsamihur spoke up, "that you recognized the man's voice. Do you remember?"

Azkanysh felt a loose string in the silken sheet under her good hand. She curled her fingers around it. "No," she lied, "I don't remember. It all happened so fast, and…"

"I understand, Queen of Queens," the royal-guard leader said.

"But I did see his eyes," Azkanysh murmured.

The royal-guard leader and Vyzir Dsamihur looked up at her.

Azkanysh pulled the string out with small pop. If she did not give the guards someone to look for, then they would be forced to search the kingdom and the palace. And if they searched the palace, they would find that Tamar was not lying sick in her bed, like everyone believed.

"What color were they, Queen of Queens?"

Azkanysh turned her head toward the windows lining one wall of her bedchamber. The sky was especially blue this morning, and filled with large white puffy clouds.

A raven flew past the windows, black wings glinting deep purple and dark blue in the Brothers' golden rays.

"Blue," Azkanysh said after a moment. "They were blue."

She felt Vyzir Dsamihur staring at her. "He also had scarred hands," she said, watching another raven follow the first. "And he was missing a finger on his left hand."

"That is excellent, Queen of Queens," the guard leader said, voice growing eager. "Is there anything else you can remember?"

Azkanysh shook her head, eyes focusing on a bloodstained ivory post of her bed. "No," she said quietly, her son's bodyguard's pink eyes flashing through her mind. "There is nothing else."

The guard leader nodded and bowed stiffly, slapping the heels of his leather boots together. "Thank you, Queen of Queens, this will give us something to look for. I'll have my men start searching immediately." He bowed again and backed out of the room, gold cloak swaying around him.

Azkanysh heard the outer doors shut after him. She turned toward Vyzir Dsamihur finally. "Was there something else, Vyzir?" she asked. He knew that she was lying, she could see it in his eyes.

It didn't matter, he couldn't prove it, and she would not have the kingdom find out that Tamar was gone.

Vyzir Dsamihur stared at her for a moment, dark eyes holding an emotion that she could not read. "No, Queen of Queens," he said after a while, "there is nothing else." He bowed low and backed out of the room.

Azkanysh glanced back out the windows. Zarmeyr and the Guardian Council, if they were involved in the attempt on her life, would think that she was scared of them when they found out that she had not pointed the finger at them. But she was not, not anymore. If anything, her son wanting her dead had made her realize something: that she must become like the council in order to beat them. She had to think outside the laws instead of focusing on using them to her advantage. It made her realize that she not only did not want to give up the golden lyon crown, but that she would not.

Azkanysh curled her fingers into the sheet. No matter what it took to hold on to it, no matter who was in the way, or who she had to kill, she would not let Zarmeyr become King of Kings, and she would keep her golden lyon crown.

CHAPTER 43

Tamar

Tamar's ears rang with the cacophony of sound, the rumbling of thousands of horse hooves and the deep blowing of animal-horn trumpets vibrating through her body.

A hundred thousand horses and their riders spread out in lines before the cliffs of Whitegate, lined up according to gond number.

"Do you think we'll win?" Tamar said aloud as the horns blew again and were responded to by the echoing horns of the enemy. Excitement and nervousness trilled through her, and she balled her reins up in her hands to keep her hands from shaking.

"As sure as the Family is on our side, we will," Maigar spoke up from next to her. He glanced up at her as he leaned over the side of his bay horse to check his saddle strap. "Zarcayra outnumbers Eromor two to one now that we allowed women in the army."

"And they do not have the Family on their side," Aghasi said from her other side.

Tamar glanced at him, and he winked at her. Her heartbeat sped up, and she looked at the other gond riders around them. Several women were nearby, members of the 35th Gond, which was made up entirely of women. Aghasi said that the army commanders had set up the gonds that way—one entirely women, the next men, and the next women and so forth. The only reason the 34th Gond had taken her as a member was because they had lost a man, Yurrig, to sickness on the boat ride over, and during war, Gond Saláyrs could fill up their gonds with any soldier they found who was not in a gond. She slept with the other women of the army, of course, but officially, she was a member of the 34th Gond, and as of yet, its only woman.

"And remember that Eromor relies mainly on foot soldiers and archers," Maigar said, straightening. "And that's where we, on horses, will beat them. Horsemen are superior to foot soldiers. Besides"—he grinned—"Zarcayra has never lost a battle, only had dignified retreats."

Aghasi laughed. Tamar smiled and stood up in her stirrups. The battle horns blew again—*whoooh, whoooh, whoooh*—and she strained to see over the heads of the gond members in front of her to try and catch a glimpse of the enemy. She didn't know why, but she had the unshakable feeling that they would win this war, and when they did, she would be a heroine. She grinned.

Yelling echoed through the riders behind them. Tamar turned in her saddle.

"Probably a faint-heart," Aghasi said, twisting in his saddle as well.

Tamar glanced at him. "What is a faint-heart?" she asked.

"A faint-heart is the worst possible kind of soldier there is," Aghasi said, saddle creaking as he turned back to face forward. "They think only of themselves and not their comrades and run away at the first signs of battle or danger."

"What will happen to him?" Tamar asked, turning forward again as well.

Maigar made a slicing noise and ran a finger across his throat.

"Execution?" Tamar asked, skin prickling.

Aghasi nodded. "By beheading. Cowardice cannot be accepted in an army. You should be able to rely on the man, or woman, next to you, not fear that they will betray you and leave you to fight alone." He pulled a curved sword from a sheath on his left hip and inspected it in the Brothers' afternoon glare.

Tamar watched him. He was wise as well as fair toward women. The men at the palace said that any man who thought women were equal to men was an idiot, but Aghasi was living proof to the contrary, a prime example of the perfect man. And the way the light caught in his blue eyes and made them shine and how his lips curved so perfectly upward, and his skin was so chocolaty tan...

Horns blew again, this time from the enemy first, and the lines upon lines of gonds began moving forward again as Zarcayra's horns responded in kind.

"This is it, Yeva," Maigar said, lifting his spear and balancing it on his right knee as the riders in front of them did the same. "Are you scared?" he asked, grinning.

Tamar raised her spear too, noting the riders on either side of them doing the same thing. "No," she said fiercely. Heroines didn't get scared.

Aghasi urged Dshukhiy closer as Maigar turned to look the other way. "It's okay to be scared, Yeva," he said softly. "Everyone is the first time they go to kill a man."

Tamar met his blue eyes, stomach lurching as his leg brushed against hers. "You've killed someone before?" she asked, hoping he would think her breathlessness was from excitement.

Aghasi didn't get a chance to reply, as the horses in front of them broke into a trot.

Their horses followed, moving steadily over the mashed-down golden grass of the plains.

Tamar wound her reins around her hands, the rough leather digging into her palms. The truth was that she was scared. And not because she might die or get hurt, but because by the end of the day she probably would have killed a man or woman. Would it be easy to drive her spear through someone's heart? Or would she lose her nerve at the last minute and become a faint-heart?

No, she would never be a faint-heart. Death would be better than that dishonor.

The horses moved into a half gallop as one, and Tamar leaned down over the neck of her bay and lowered her spear as the trampled grass whizzed by underneath. Ehurayni was with her, and she was going to be in a battle and become a heroine. She grinned. There was nothing to be scared of. She would kill the enemy, and they would win. She let out a yell.

Aghasi and Maigar glanced at her and grinned. Then they started yelling too, screaming for victory, courage, and bravery.

The rider on the other side of Maigar, a thirtysomething man with a bushy brown beard, took up the cry, and soon the air rang with thousands of screams as the call spread throughout the columns of racing horses and riders.

Tamar felt something powerful rising up in her stomach as they raced over the plains toward Whitegate, a feeling that, given the chance, she could defeat any enemy, any foe that was set before her.

A clash like lightning rang through the air, and a new cry rang out over the cheers as the first column of horses and riders reached the enemy: a cry of pain and death.

The noise of steel ringing against steel filled the air, soldiers yelled, and the high-pitched, frantic scream of horses echoed across the plains.

Tamar stopped yelling, her heart hammering loudly in her ears. The battle had begun.

Her mare surged forward after those in front of her, white foam coating its neck in a lather. Tamar adjusted her grip on her spear as sweat trickled down her forehead and into her left eye, knees clamped to her horse's slender sides for support, body still bent low over its neck. Eromor did not stand a chance against them. The Family rode with them; she could feel it.

The soldier in front of her went down so fast that she didn't have time to steer her horse clear of his body as he jerked backward off his horse. A sickening crunch caught her ear as her mare ran over him, trampling him into the grass.

The man in front of Aghasi fell next, screaming, with a black arrow sticking out of his eye.

They were dying, Tamar realized as the metallic smell of blood filled her nose. All around her, men and women were dying. This wasn't one of Mistress Ahani's stories—it was war.

A horse in front of her stumbled to its knees with an arrow in its neck, eyes bulging in terror.

Tamar pulled on her bay's reins to steer it around the thrashing animal, but it was too late, and they went leaping over the wounded horse and landed with a jolt in front of an Eromor soldier on the other side. She drove her spear through the man's chest without thinking, and the weapon was wrenched out of her hand as her horse continued to gallop forward into the fighting, carrying her with it.

Her palm burned where the spear had been.

There were Eromor foot soldiers all around now, red tunics like blood under black chainmail, black dragon-faced helmets glinting in the Brothers' heat.

Tamar heard a man scream to her left. Sweat drained down her back and face and neck. She glanced around for Aghasi and Maigar, but they were nowhere to be seen.

A woman in front of her fell off her horse as she raced past two gond members hacking at several Eromor foot soldiers. An Eromor soldier drove a sword through the woman's eye socket in a spray of blood and fluid.

Tamar's stomach lurched.

A blood-red tunic flashed in the corner of her eye. She pulled on her mare's reins as an Eromor soldier ran screaming at them.

The man swung his hardened steel sword at her left leg, the blade hissing as it cut through the air.

Tamar drew her own sword, parrying the man's strike with the curved weapon. She kicked him in the chest as he swung his sword back and, raising her sword high, brought it down against the man's neck. Bright-red blood sprayed everywhere, sprinkling her leg and the side of her mare like rain.

The Eromor soldier screamed and lurched backward, blood spurting out of his neck in an arcing stream.

Tamar urged her mare past the man, the horse's eyes wide with fright.

Bile filled her mouth, hot and acidic.

This is war, she told herself as a soldier struggling to his feet was trampled by a red-eyed riderless horse.

This is what heroes and heroines do. They kill the enemy and defend their kingdom's honor...

An Eromor woman missing her helmet came at her, and Tamar kicked her in the head as she tried to pull her from her mare's back. She brought the hilt of her sword down onto another man's back.

The scent of blood was overwhelming, filling her nostrils, coating her tongue, swimming before her eyes.

A Zarcayran soldier was dragged from his screaming horse by four

Eromor soldiers and gutted by two as his horse's head was hacked partway off by the others. The thrashing animal pulled back from the soldiers before they could finish their job. Screaming, it galloped off into the fighting with its head half off and flopping around.

Tamar pulled her hijab down and vomited, puke staining her horse's side. This was nothing like the stories Mistress Ahani had told, nothing like she had imagined it would be.

Someone yelled to her right. She turned to see a Zarcayran woman pinned to the ground underneath her horse as the creature was struck with an arrow in the eye and rolled, screaming, to the side.

The woman cried out as she tried in vain to pull herself out from under the horse, which continued to kick and scream, its head thrashing back and hitting the woman in the face.

Tamar turned her mare slowly. The woman's horse would crush her unless someone helped her... She kicked her bay in the side and started toward her.

A black-mailed soldier appeared to her left, driving his sword deep into her mare's neck.

Tamar felt her horse shudder as the weapon cut through tendon and bone and flesh, felt the shock go through it as blood spurted out of its neck and splashed them both.

Her mare stumbled, lurching forward onto its knees in the grass.

Tamar flew forward into nothing.

She landed on the ground on her shoulder, flipping over and over on the trampled, bloody grass in a tangle of chainmail, dirt, and grass. Her sword flew out of her grip on the third roll, pain twisting through her right arm.

Tamar pulled her head off the ground with a gasp as she stopped rolling, hijab half off, dirt filling her mouth along with the acid taste of vomit. She pulled her left arm out from underneath her, something warm and wet draining down it. She looked down at it. A deep gash stretched from the inside of her left elbow to her left shoulder.

A horse ran by, blood and gore covering its white coat.

Tamar dragged her other arm out from underneath her and used it to push herself to a sitting position, glancing around in shock.

A scream rang out behind her.

She twisted to see the Eromor soldier pull his bloody sword from her dying bay's neck.

The man looked up and saw her, started forward.

Tamar wheeled back around, frantically searching the blood-splattered grass for her sword. There were only bodies and glistening pieces of gore.

Ehurayni, help me!

The soldier's footsteps crunched in the grass behind her, chainmail chinking with each step he took.

Tamar grabbed a handful of dirt and grass with her good hand as the steps came closer. Wheeling, she threw it through the slit in the soldier's dragon helmet and into his eyes.

The soldier hissed, clawing at his face with his free hand.

Tamar scrambled to her feet and turned toward him, left arm hanging by her side.

"Bitch!" The soldier laughed, voice metallic and echoing beneath the helmet. "Dirt won't save you, girl!" He swung his sword at her.

Tamar jumped backward.

The soldier yelled, swinging at her again.

Tamar lunged backward again, glancing around for anything she might use as a weapon. Her feet stumbled over a dead Eromor soldier with his head partially hacked off in a congealing pool of blood. She cried out as she landed in the grass on the other side of the body.

Something hard pressed against her foot, and Tamar glanced down to see the silver knob of a dagger lying in the grass by her sandaled foot.

"Zarcayra won't win this war," the soldier said, walking toward her. "And you will die, like all the rest of your army." He raised the sword over his head and with a yell, lunged toward her.

Tamar dove for the dagger. Pulling it out of the grass, she turned as the Eromor soldier ran at her. She came up underneath him, driving the dagger deep into his stomach, just below the dragon sigil on his tunic.

The soldier grunted.

Warm blood stained Tamar's hand and splattered her face.

The soldier glanced down at the knife in his belly, helmet dusty and splattered with blood. "You're just a girl," he croaked.

Tamar drew the dagger out of his stomach with a dull sucking noise and buried it to the hilt again, her arm seeming to move of its own accord. "No," she breathed, "I'm a warrior."

The soldier tried to reply, blood draining out from underneath his helmet. He fell sideways to the grass, blood dripping out of the slits in his visor.

She had done it. Tamar glanced around her at the fighting, which was moving away from her now. She had killed men and women, and she had lived.

A horse with a gaping bloody hole in its stomach and a bloody red flap of flesh hanging from the wound galloped by in a wide-eyed, panicked frenzy. An Eromor soldier several yards off moaned loudly.

The knife... Tamar crawled on her knees and her right hand to the soldier, reaching for the dagger sticking out of his stomach.

A horse's step crunched in the grass behind her.

Tamar's heartbeat sped. She pulled the knife out of the dead soldier's stomach, fingers curling around the leather-wrapped handle.

"You know, I really thought you were scared before the battle, but gods, you fight like a hardened soldier," a playful, breathless voice said.

Tamar let out a cry of joy. "Aghasi!" She turned and pushed herself shakily to her feet. "I thought that you and Maigar had moved on."

"And I thought you were dead," Aghasi replied in a more somber voice, eyes scanning her bare face.

Tamar grinned. "Not yet, although a couple times I thought I was going to be."

Aghasi smiled. "Me too." He offered a hand down to her.

She shoved the dagger into her boot and reached her good hand up to Aghasi.

Aghasi pulled her up behind him on the back of Dshukhiy. Somewhere in the distance, a horn echoed across the trampled and body-littered grass. *Whoooh, whoooh, whoooh.*

"Did we win the war?" Tamar asked, wrapping her right arm around Aghasi's waist and glancing over her shoulder at the fighting soldiers behind them.

Pain shot through her left arm. She sucked in a breath.

"Not hardly," Aghasi replied, urging Dshukhiy into a trot that sent more painful jolts through her arm. "But we did win the battle."

Horsemen chased the last few remnants of Eromor's army back toward the distant cliffs of Whitegate. Tamar tightened her grip on Aghasi as they galloped back across the grasslands and toward the Zarcayran encampment.

Maigar rode toward them across the grass, face splattered with blood. "You found her… Damn, Yeva, that arm looks like shit."

Tamar glanced down at her arm. Blood still oozed out of the gash in it, turning the sleeve of her purple tunic a dark maroon. She would have a scar there, but she was glad for it. Heroines got wounded, and heroines had scars.

"It proves that I fought today," she said, glancing up at Maigar with excitement flushing her cheeks. "And the scar will be something I can show my grandchildren!"

Maigar laughed. "Maybe I should get me one of those, a big one, right here." He drew a line down his cheek. "Do you think it'll make me look any older?"

"Doubtful," Aghasi said with a grin.

Maigar cursed at him, but the horns blowing again drowned him out.

They all looked back at the retreating Eromor army and the following Zarcayrans, dark lines against the towering white cliffs of Whitegate.

"Thank you, Family," Aghasi murmured, bowing his head. "For our victory over our enemies today."

"Amen," Maigar and Tamar said in unison.

"Now, let's go eat," Maigar said, pulling sharply on his gelding's reins and turning it. "I don't know about you both, but I'm starving like I haven't eaten in a month. Something about battle will do that to you." He laughed and kicked his horse into a gallop, riding off toward the Zarcayran camp.

Dshukhiy lurched forward too, and Tamar gripped Aghasi tighter. She looked behind them again as they rode, the noises of fighting growing fainter as the battle died off. Even though it had been terrifying and bloody and horrible and fierce, she had made it through her first battle. She grinned, wind fanning her face and neck. Just like the heroes and heroines in the stories: They had won.

CHAPTER 44

Nathaira

Nathaira saw the killer fall to the tallest witch before a foot connected with her head, and she went sailing backward.

She landed on the leaf-strewn ground with a thud, pain jarring through her body.

Her silver wolf paws slipped back into hands. Where had the witches come from? She had heard stories from Zeythra often while growing up, stories of the witches and warlocks and how they had sided with the humans during the Second Great War and helped kill hundreds of skinchangers before the humans had turned on them. With the help of the wiar, the witches and warlocks had almost annihilated her people in the wars.

"The witches and warlocks were feared by all," Zeythra had told Nathaira once while they tanned a bear hide in the meadow around their tree home. "Well, everyone but the wiar; they never feared anything."

The methodical scraping of their hunting knives on the fleshy white underside of the bear skin rang through the air as they dug away the excess meat and fat and threw it with soft spluts into a wooden bucket. "The only thing that could buy them was money," Zeythra said, wiping the back of one wrinkled and tattooed arm across her glistening forehead. "They cared not for a better world or land; they simply wanted coin. And the humans—controlling the mining in half of Argdrion by the Second Great War—had plenty of it."

Nathaira brushed a fly away as she pushed down on an especially hard glob of fat. They had been scraping at the bear hide for over three hours, and her fingers felt like they were worn to the bone.

"The humans are brutal, it is true," Zeythra went on, silver braids gently swaying around her head as her knife ran down the bear hide, "but their brutality is nothing compared to that of the witches and warlocks. Witches and warlocks enjoy watching suffering. They flourish on pain, live for killing, and at the end of each battle, they would comb the battlefields for those still alive so that they could eat their hearts. They like still-beating hearts the best, although they are not picky as to what part of the body they eat."

Zeythra paused and looked up from scraping the bear hide, a faraway look in her eyes. "We had many dealings with the witches during the better part of the Second War and first part of the Third. We found that once they set their sights on you, they never let up hunting you until either you or they were dead—hence why the humans loved them so much. They used them for scouring the countryside for any survivors after battles and raids."

Nathaira heard the witches she had been fighting move off. She peeked at the tall creatures through the tangle of black hair that had fallen over her face. Zeythra's husband, Feirdon, had been killed by a warlock in the Second Great War. Zeythra had never forgiven the witches and warlocks for it and had hated them with a vehemence closely matched to Athrysion's hatred of the humans.

"Aren't the witches and warlocks children of the Sisters too, like Moirin said the humans are?" Nathaira had asked her once when she was six. Her grandmother had grabbed her arm with a grip of iron, her blue eyes dark and stormy. "The witches and warlocks are not children of the Sisters," she had hissed. "They are spawn of the Brothers, and when they die, they go straight to their fire, where they will burn for all eternity." Humans that had cursed themselves in the beginning of time because they wanted longer life and abilities like the wiar and skinchangers, witches and warlocks were powerful creatures. Over seven feet tall, they could run forty miles an hour, hear sounds from over three miles away, and smell their prey's scent from up to twenty miles away.

Nathaira watched the witches she had battled walk to the body of the witch the killer had slain. Zeythra had explained to her that day what the witches were animalistic, unholy creatures hated equally by every race in Argdrion.

"She's dead, clan leader," the shorter of the two witches called to the witch with the double broadsword who was standing with the fourth by the killer's now prostrate form.

The clan leader hissed in reply, and Nathaira took their moment of distraction to slowly move her hands underneath her.

The goyr leaves littering the ground poked into her palms with sharp edges.

"Bastard," the clan leader hissed. She knelt next to the killer and held one polished steel blade of her double broadsword up to his slender throat. "That's two of my kind you've killed, assassin." The witch snarled, teeth flashing. "I'm going to enjoy watching you die."

Then he isn't dead yet. Nathaira felt a pang of annoyance. She'd hoped the killer might be so that she wouldn't have to repay her debt to him. She knew she shouldn't, but she did.

She curled her fingers into the brittle leaves and soft dirt underneath her, the cool, slightly musty smell of decaying vegetation filling her nose. Her prayers had been answered, and she had her chance now to save his life, but how would she get him away from four witches? She couldn't fight them all on her own, not if she wanted to live.

Sisters, show me what to do...

"Not so great now, are we?" the clan leader sneered. The ends of her white hair lifted on a breeze that rustled the goyr leaves scattered across the ground. "I wonder what humans will think when they hear how the mighty Darkmoon was slain and eaten by witches?" The witch laughed, a hoarse and raspy sound. She brushed the cowl off the killer's face with one tip of her sword.

His skin was the color of freshly fallen snow.

Nathaira eyed him, remembering what Athrysion had told her about witch blood. *One of the deadliest substances in Argdrion, it will kill a full-grown in a few days. Hours if it gets into the blood.*

An ant crawled over Nathaira's bare calf, tiny legs tickling her flesh. If the killer had witch blood in him, then he was as good as dead already, and there was nothing she could do for him. So why waste time repaying her debt? She could just leave now and look for Efamar... only her honor wouldn't let her.

Nathaira ground her teeth together. She couldn't save the killer's life, but perhaps she could repay her debt to him by ensuring that he wasn't eaten alive by the witches. Which meant she'd have to somehow get him away from them, and that brought her back to the problem of how.

"So handsome," the witch with the double broadsword said. She ran a long black talon down the killer's left cheek. "It's too bad you'll be dead soon." The witch smiled, her scarred upper lip curling away from her black fangs. "We could have had some fun with you before we rip the flesh off your bones."

Nathaira's stomach curled.

The witch grabbed a handful of the killer's black hair with one hand and raised her sword high above her head.

Nathaira moved. Changing into a black nighthawk as she lunged to her feet, she sailed over the heads of the two witches she had battled and dove into the clan leader's mane of white hair. She grabbed a beakful of hair and pulled, jerking the witch's head backward.

The clan leader screamed, and the killer's head and her sword fell from her grasp.

Nathaira spat the hair out of her mouth, the strands like sharp needles against her tongue. She dug her talons into the witch's scalp.

The witch screamed again, slashing at her own head with glistening black talons, and the three other witches started forward as one as she sliced a strand of her own hair off with a talon.

It floated like a spiderweb toward the ground.

Nathaira ducked as talons hissed by her head. Pulling one last beakful of hair out of the witch's head, she burst out of her hair, past the outstretched hands of the other witches, and toward the goyr branches above.

She dove into the tree, feathers and leaves exploding around her.

"You think you can stand against us, skinchanger?" the clan leader screamed, black blood draining in rivulets down the sides of her head.

Nathaira glanced out of her hiding spot as the clan leader grabbed her broadsword out of the leaves. The witch looked upward with fire in her black eyes.

Nathaira ducked back down behind the goyr leaves.

"You don't stand a chance against the four of us!" the clan leader yelled.

A night wind rustled through the goyr trees. Nathaira curled her long bird toes tighter around the gray branch of the tree she hid in. No, she did not. She peeked through two leaves at the shadowed forest floor below and the dark shape of the killer.

I wish you had died.

"Where are you, skinchanger?" the leader of the witches hissed.

Nathaira glanced back at the tall skeletal creatures who were standing in a circle below the tree and staring up at her hiding spot.

"Come out, why don't you? If you do, we promise we won't hurt you," the clan leader said. "Just eat the flesh from your bones. But we will be quick, I swear, and you won't feel much pain before you go on to the next life."

Nathaira ignored her, mind racing. The largest creature she could change into would be too slow in the closeness of the forest and too much of a target. And yet anything smaller, although faster, would not be able to stand up against the witches for long. Unless she changed into a black viper and went for their throats…

But it was unlikely that she would be able to kill more than one before the others killed her, and then where would that get her? Nowhere. And she'd join the killer in the taloned creatures' feast and never see the light of day again.

Nathaira peered back down at the witches, dappled moonlight making their hair and skin glow. She would not die for the killer.

"There you are," the witch with the broadsword called.

Nathaira shot into the air as the branch she'd been sitting on was sprayed with black blood and darted to a higher branch on the goyr tree. She dove into the foliage with a rustle.

"You think you can hide from us?"

The leaves hissed around her. Nathaira flapped out of the way as another handful of black blood hit the branch underneath her.

"You'll never get away, skinchanger."

Blood hissed by her head, hitting the tree trunk behind her in an explosion of ebony lines. Nathaira flew sideways.

"We will always find you!"

More blood sprayed the goyr leaves. Nathaira flew to another goyr nearby, pointed leaves grabbing at her feathers and slapping her in the face.

"You may have the power of changing your body, skinchanger," the clan leader of the witches yelled, "but we are witches, and we always find our prey."

Nathaira landed on a branch in the goyr next to the one the witches stood under, heart racing.

Sisters, show me what to do, please. I can't die saving the killer. Efamar needs me, but if I do nothing, then the witches will eat him...

Nathaira looked at the killer again. Black lines were spreading out on his face, visible even at this distance. Either way, he was going to die. Did it matter how? She almost left in that moment, but as she pondered flying away into the forest, the jingle of armor against swords caught her ear, making her look up.

The witches heard it too. They stopped shouting and turned as one in the direction of the noise.

Nathaira peered through the gloom of the forest. Torches flickered in the distance, bobbing through the trees toward them. Soldiers, perhaps? But how had they found them? Or had they been attracted by the noise of their fighting?

She flew to another goyr, this one closer to the killer, and strained to make out the shape of thirty or so men and women in the dragon-crested tunics of Eromor as they came through the forest toward them.

A distraction. Nathaira glanced down at the killer again, directly below her now. Perhaps in the fight that was coming, she could drag his body away. It was the Sisters telling her that they wanted her to uphold her people's honor.

She looked back up as the first of the soldiers appeared over the top of a hill twenty yards away.

The witches snarled and moved into battle formation.

The soldiers saw them and yelled, their captain waving his sword in the air. "Kill them!" the man yelled.

The soldiers charged.

Nathaira looked back at the killer.

#

Nathaira darted through the forest, a hair-raising scream echoing through the shadowed trees behind her. She glanced over one shoulder, golden legs slowing. The witches had discovered they were gone.

She sped up again, a golden blur flashing through the trees. The golden elk was one of the fastest creatures in Argdrion, able to run up to thirty-five miles an hour, but even with that and her head start, she feared that it would not be enough. The witches would catch up, and when they did, the killer would not be the only one they ate.

Nathaira lunged over a moss-covered log, black hooves cutting deep ruts in the dark, leaf-covered soil on the opposite side. After the soldiers had entered the clearing, it had been only a matter of minutes before she had found the chance to pull the killer away into the forest. From there she had used his cloak to tie him onto her back, and while the witches and soldiers filled the forest with their battle cries and weapons clashing, she had changed into a golden elk and fled.

Nathaira splashed through a dirty puddle in the middle of the game trail she followed, water sprinkling her sides. She hated the killer. Hated him because, from what she had overheard of his and the clan leader's conversation, the witches had been hunting him for killing one of their clan, and now, because of him, they were hunting her for taking their victim. How would she find Efamar with witches hunting her? She couldn't lead them to her brother, but how would she get rid of them?

Nathaira jumped over another log, the killer's body flopping against her back. She also hated him because he had not died yet, and until he did, she couldn't leave him. Normal humans would have died by now. Why was he not dead?

Nathaira ran under the roots of a goyr and out into a moonflower-filled meadow that stretched away for acres in all directions.

The smell of rain was heavy in the air, and dark clouds covered the stars and Sisters.

Rain could be to her advantage. It would weaken her scent and make it harder for the witches to hear and see. But it would also make it harder for her to see, and the forest would become treacherously slippery.

Bulbous purple moonflowers knocked against her sides as she ran, releasing their sharp, sweet scent into the cool night air with soft puffs of golden pollen. Nathaira sneezed as pollen caught on her wide nose.

A stream, mist rising from its sparkling silver water, appeared out of the swaying green grass ahead of her, Nathaira slowed her pace to a trot and then a walk as she neared it, desperately craving a drink of the cool liquid to sate her parched throat.

She knelt in the grass next to the warbling water, muscles burning, and slipped back into her natural form. Then she untied the killer's cloak from around her neck and set him down in the grass.

Curling black lines snaked up around his slender neck.

Nathaira turned to the water, a cool breeze heavy with the scent of rain stroking her naked body with soft fingers. It could not be too long before the killer was dead. She dipped a hand into the stream and brought a dripping palmful of water to her mouth, eyes scanning the distant goyr trees surrounding the meadow. Maybe he was stronger than other humans and that was why he was not already dead, but he couldn't last that much longer.

She drained the water out of her palm, some escaping and dribbling down her chin and onto her hair, and dipped her hand back into the stream for more.

Her eyes darted back to the killer. Athrysion had said that creatures poisoned with witch or warlock blood burned, screaming and writhing from the inside out until their bodies could no longer stand the pain, and they finally passed on to the next life.

Nathaira sucked the water out of her palm and reached for another palmful, a stab of pity running through her. The killer was evil, but it didn't seem right that any creature should die in such a ghastly way.

She drank her third handful of water and reached for a fourth, glancing at the killer again. She couldn't stop him from dying, but perhaps she could ease his pain a little and make the transition to the next life bearable. She owed him that much.

Nathaira pushed herself to her feet, muscles feeling like they were on fire. She moved across the mashed grass to the killer's body, knelt by his side, and carefully peeled back his blood-soaked shirt.

A smell like rancid meat and burning blood filled her nose. She hissed and turned her head to the side slightly.

A thick, gooey black crust encircled the hole where the witch had driven her knife into the killer's lower stomach, and glistening pus the color of black ink drained down his side.

Nathaira glanced at the killer's narrow face. Sweat glistened on his scarred forehead.

She stood, remembering seeing poppies amidst the ferns around the goyr roots. They wouldn't take away all his pain, but they might dull it a little.

Nathaira rinsed her hands off in the stream and turned, taking off at a run toward the tree line, her hip-length black hair streaming behind her.

Thunder rumbled as she darted back into the shadows between the goyr trees, and the soft patter of rain landing on the black goyr leaves far above her head caught her ear.

Closed orange poppies glowed softly underneath a goyr's twisting roots. Slipping between two roots the width of her body, Nathaira knelt and pulled the lacy plants from the ground.

An owl hooted as she worked. She glanced up at the noise, the fine hairs on the back of her neck rising. Moirin had said that when an owl hooted, death was coming.

When she came back, the killer had not stirred from the position she had left him in, and Nathaira wondered for a moment if he had died as she hurried through the grass to his dark form. His chest was still rising under his black shirt, although slower and less perceptibly, and when she went to her knees in the bent grass next to him, she heard his shallow breaths above the pattering of the rain.

Nathaira mashed the poppies into a pulp between her hands. Once it was ready, she pried the killer's thin lips apart, pushed the poppies into his mouth, and rubbed his black-webbed throat with the palm of her tattooed hand to make him swallow them. She glanced down at his wound. A black bubble popped over it and drained down the killer's side to the grass below. There was nothing else she could do for him.

Nathaira turned back to the stream and submerged both her hands in it, the gently flowing water washing away the green and orange poppy stains.

Rain pattered on her bare back. The Sisters peeked through a translucent wisp of gray cloud.

"Help him to die quickly," Nathaira whispered, wind rustling through the grass and slanting the misting rain against her cheek. She pulled her hands out of the water and pushed herself to her feet again, turning.

Glowing green eyes met hers from the other side of the killer's silent form.

Nathaira hissed, startled.

A treelike creature stood among the bending grass, watching her.

Nathaira took a step backward, power surging through her. How had she not heard it approach?

The creature had twisting leaf-speckled roots growing out of the top of its head like hair. It glanced at the killer's still form and made a soft rustling noise, like leaves blowing in the wind. Several more creatures stepped out of the rain behind it, glancing at him too.

Nathaira sucked in a breath, uncurling her hands as realization dawned on her. They were Forest Folk, legendary guardians of forests. And they had the magic of healing.

"He was stabbed with a knife covered in witch blood," she said as the bark-covered creatures looked back up at her.

The creatures stared at her, eyes unblinking, and Nathaira stepped forward, hands out in a sign of peace. "Please, can you help us?"

The treelike creatures continued to stare at her for a few moments before the first one nodded slowly and made another rustling noise in the back of its throat.

Three of the others stepped forward and bent toward the killer, gently lifting his body off the ground with long rootlike hands.

"Thank you," Nathaira breathed as they started off through the tall, waving grass with the killer in their arms.

The first Forest Folk nodded and reached a hand toward her, beckoning for her to follow it.

The owl hooted again, the noise echoing eerily across the meadow.

Nathaira glanced back at the forest. Death was coming.

She shivered and turned, hurrying after the Forest Folk.

CHAPTER 45

Esadora

A silver-tipped bolt whistled out of the goyr trees and with a thud, drove through the overlapping black leather armor on Esadora's shoulder and into the flesh beneath. She snarled, her obsidian teeth flashing in the silvery moonlight that streamed in thick beams through the tangled canopy of goyr branches overhead.

Night-black blood drained down her forearm, the inky substance staining the dark-red streaks snaking through her armor.

Esadora pulled the bolt out, throwing her massive double-edged broadsword Slayn up to ward off another volley of the burning bolts as they whistled through the air toward her. It was a day since N'san Hor'ayn had come to her and her sisters at their shop in Vingorlon, a day and two nights. It had been easy to find Darkmoon and the skinchanger for the fat man, but Esadora had never imagined that she would lose a sister in the fight to take him down. And then the soldiers had appeared out of the trees, and now the air was filled with smoke and screams and whistling crossbow bolts.

Iscara screamed behind her.

Esadora wheeled, white hair billowing. She saw her right-hand sister fall to her knees in the overturned black goyr leaves, a crossbow bolt stuck in her pale throat.

No!

Esadora sliced down three soldiers running at her with three vicious swings of Slayn. She jumped over their fallen bodies and ran to Iscara.

"Don't be dead," she said, stabbing Slayn down in the ground next to Iscara with a crunch.

Esadora rolled her prostrate sister's body over.

Two eyes the color of a starless night stared lifelessly up at the goyr trees above. A stream of black blood trickled slowly out of the corner of Iscara's mouth and snaked down her gaunt cheek and onto her white hair.

Esadora cursed and pushed her own hair out of her face. She grabbed the short ash shaft of the bolt that protruded from Iscara's throat and pulled it out with a dull sucking noise, black blood flowing out of the hole left behind.

Iscara didn't move.

Esadora cursed again and leaned down to listen for a heartbeat through her sister witch's armor. A human would die from such a wound, but witches and warlocks were stronger than humans and could take dozens of wounds and still live.

There was no heartbeat under Iscara's armor.

Esadora pulled her sister's body into her lap. A clan of witches or warlocks was like a family. They slept together, shared the catch of the hunt together, lived together, died together.

Esadora ground her fangs together. Darkmoon had killed Thestre, the soldiers Iscara. They should not have come on this hunt; she had known it was too dangerous. She threw her head back and let out a scream.

She looked back down at the clearing, at the soldiers fighting her two remaining sisters, Rargyne and Ayrsah. Darkmoon and the soldiers would pay for her sisters' deaths.

Esadora lowered Iscara's body to the forest floor, her right-hand's blood staining her white hands black. Using Slayn as a balance, she pushed herself to her feet, a cold night breeze blowing her hair out behind her like spiderwebs.

A soldier ran at her from the side, yelling fiercely and brandishing a steel-tipped spear in the air in front of him.

Esadora threw Slayn out without even looking and sliced the man's head off before he'd gone three steps.

Smoke filled the cold night air from the smoldering fire left by

Darkmoon and the skinchanger, kicked out of its pit during the fighting and now burning in the leaves that thickly covered the forest floor. The dense white smoke curled around Esadora as she moved past her two remaining sisters and toward the main body of the soldiers.

Their captain, holding his men and women in a line next to the largest of the goyr trees, yelled out orders as the soldiers loaded and fired their curved crossbows over and over with glinting silver-tipped bolts.

Like the one that killed Iscara... Esadora's long fingers curled around Slayn's bone handle at the thought.

The captain's yells faded off as she stepped from the smoke, white hair streaming behind her, red and black blood covering her, black eyes full of rage.

Esadora raised Slayn in one taloned hand, human blood dripping off the weapon and onto the black leaves below.

The brown-haired captain looked up at her, paled.

That's right, human, you should fear me. You should fear me like a nightmare from which you cannot wake.

Several of the soldiers faltered without their leader's orders, but a few half-heartedly fired bolts.

Esadora easily parried them with Slayn's blades, and they flew off into the darkness with soft hisses. "Which one of you was it that killed my sister?" she snarled. She scanned the row of soldiers. The wound in her hand from the knife that Darkmoon had thrown at her was throbbing, and the burn marks from the coals that he had tossed into her face felt like they were still on fire. She wanted to kill, to bite into a still-beating heart and feel its warmth in her mouth.

A few nervous glances passed among the soldiers. The captain swallowed loudly, the knot in his thick throat bobbing up and down like an apple on a string. "We didn't come here to harm you or your sisters, witch," he said, taking a step backward.

Esadora snarled. The smell of urine caught her nose. "Your kind always means to harm that which is magical." She hissed, noting Ayrsah and Rargyne coming up behind her as a breeze drifted through the looming goyr trees and pulled the scent of blood and death away from them.

"I swear to you," the captain said, holding his hands up in front of him. "We had no idea that you were here before we came into the forest. We simply want the skinchanger and the assassin called Darkmoon." He pointed a shaky hand at the crumpled body of the assassin.

Yes, the skinchanger. Esadora glanced around the smoky clearing. The skinchanger was nowhere in sight. She gripped Slayn harder. "Yet you fought us all the same and killed our sister," she said, turning her gaze back on the soldiers.

The captain swallowed again, the knot in his throat bobbing. "Well, if we didn't, you would have killed us—"

"AND I WILL KILL YOU ALL AS IT IS!" Esadora screamed. She glanced up and down the line of humans, watching her with pale faces and raised weapons. "Unless you tell me who it was that killed my sister."

"It was him!" a woman called, shoving a crossbowman out of the line. "It was him, I saw it! He was the one who killed the witch!"

The man stumbled on a twisting goyr root, dragon-faced helmet falling off his head and landing on the leaf-strewn ground with a dull ping. He took a scrambling step backward as he realized that he was no longer in the safety of his fellows.

Esadora nodded at Ayrsah, and the younger and shorter of her two remaining sisters stepped forward and grabbed the soldier by the collar as he tried to push his way back into line with the others and was shoved further out.

The soldier's crossbow fell uselessly by his feet with his helmet.

"Please," the soldier gasped as Ayrsah dragged him across the leaves by the back of his tunic. "Please, I was just following orders!"

Esadora glanced down at the soldier as Ayrsah dumped him onto the leaves in front of her, ears catching the frantic pumping of his heart.

The soldier raised his hands in front of him in a plea for mercy.

Ayrsah moved back to her place again, knee-length white hair swinging around her legs.

"There," the captain said, taking another step backward toward the rest of his soldiers. "You have the killer. We will be on our way."

Esadora looked up at him. It never ceased to amaze her how fast humans would turn on each other, or others, when circumstances were not in their favor anymore. Or how quickly they would go against their own laws. Normally the soldiers would be trying to take them in for execution, but the captain's group was small, and perhaps he knew the wisdom of retreating when in the minority.

The captain signaled at his soldiers and turned as if to go.

"The man is right," Esadora rasped, flexing her clawlike fingers around Slayn's handle. She was thinking of Iscara and Thestre and Yrnayr, and of Orcyra too, dead now these forty long years.

The captain stopped and turned toward her slowly.

"He was just following orders," Esadora said darkly. She eyed the soldier kneeling in front of her. He was crying now and praying fervently to Edeva, goddess of health, healing, and life. He was handsome, the soldier, and had a complexion like few others. Skin like night bespoke of an Araysannian parent, but his tightly curled hair was as red as a sunset in summer.

Esadora ripped the soldier's throat out with a dull shredding noise.

The line of soldiers gasped. The captain sucked in his breath.

Esadora glanced up at them as the soldier fell over sideways in front of her, warm red blood winding in several streams down her hand and wrist and mixing with the black veins there. She threw the bloody mass of flesh in her hand into her mouth.

The captain looked near to throwing up.

A soldier at the end of the line did, bending over double and hurling into the overturned goyr leaves.

Humans were so weak. Esadora swallowed, red blood draining down her skeletal chin. Her pupils dilated. Fresh blood and flesh tasted so, so good.

"You said that you would not kill us if you got the one who killed your sister," the captain whispered.

Esadora pulled her lips back, blood dripping off her fangs. She met the captain's eyes. "You should know never to believe a witch," she rasped.

The captain turned and ran into the forest.

A middle-aged soldier yelled out the order to fire, and a volley of silver-tipped bolts whizzed through the air.

"The captain's mine," Esadora barked. She dodged the oncoming bolts and tore into the forest after the fleeing captain as Rargyne and Ayrsah attacked the soldiers.

Wind ripped through her white hair, branches tore at her leathers. Esadora caught up to the captain in less than a minute, his face and arms gushing blood where the thorns of rorbushes had slashed him.

She leapt over a fallen goyr log and veered up a hill as she neared the gasping man, cutting bushes out of her way with Slayn's blades and leaping over boulders as she ran. She could cut the captain down from behind, but it was always so much more fun to see the look of terror on a victim's face as she ripped their throat out—more satisfying that way.

Esadora raced around a young goyr tree twisting toward the star-filled sky above, her talons leaving deep gashes in the tree's hard gray bark as she grabbed at it with one hand. She had missed this freedom in Vingorlon, missed having the whole world to run in, hunt in.

The captain burst into a clearing below her, glancing over his shoulder as he stumbled over a moss-covered rock and hastily scrambled to his feet again in a bed of ferns. His heavy breaths echoed up to Esadora's keen ears.

Esadora glanced down at him as she ran along the edge of the ridge, hair whipping behind her.

You think you can outrun me, human? You are a fool. Nothing can outrun a witch, not even a warlock.

She veered to the right sharply at a curving rorbush and skidded down the fern-covered hill at a run, her long white hair and split skirt billowing out behind her as she hurtled over rocks and burst through the branches of a small goyr.

The captain heard her too late and skidded to a halt, sweat and blood trickling down his plain face in rivulets.

Esadora landed in the ferns in front of him with a mighty leap off the hill. "Going somewhere?" she rasped, her breath steady and even after her run, whereas his was so loud and ragged that she was sure Setaron, god of the underworld, could hear it in his fiery black halls.

For a moment, Esadora thought that the captain might fall at her knees, begging for mercy like the other human had done, but he must have remembered what she had done to his soldier and instead turned and bolted off at a run back the way he had come.

Esadora darted in front of him so quickly that he almost ran into her.

"Where do you think it is you'll run to, human?" she hissed, looking down at him.

The captain staggered backward, eyes filled with the terror of one who knew they were going to die, and wheeling, ran the other way.

Esadora moved in front of him again. "There is nowhere you can hide that I won't find you."

The captain's face turned as white as her hair. He turned and ran for the hill, stumbling over his own feet as he went.

Esadora watched him go, slowly walking after him as he tried, and failed, to climb up the steep embankment.

"Don't kill me!" the captain begged, rolling over and holding thorn-torn arms above his head as a shield as she loomed above him. "I'll do anything, but don't kill me!"

Esadora planted a black boot in the middle of the man's shallow chest and held one of Slayn's blades up to his sunburnt throat. "What could you possibly do that I would want, human?" she snarled, pressing the sharp steel of Slayn into the captain's flesh. A small dot of red blood sprouted underneath the blade, trickling down the side of the captain's neck before dripping onto the ferns beneath him.

The captain sucked in a ragged breath, green eyes full of so much fear that Esadora thought he might die of shock. "I have money," he sobbed, sweat rolling off him in fat drops. "Seven thousand aray, saved up these last three years for my wife and child in Ennotar."

Esadora eyed the human over the sheen of Slayn. He had the look of an Ennotarian, dark haired and lean faced. "Who says I want it?" she rasped.

The captain gasped. "I've heard that witches love money!"

"Why is it that you humans never remember that we love blood too?" Esadora rasped, pressing Slayn's blade deeper into his throat.

The captain coughed, and the rank odor of urine drifted up from his black pants. "It's yours if you let me go," he croaked. "All of it."

"And who's to say that you'll actually give it to me, human?" Esadora snarled, the scar cutting her face in half crinkling with the movement.

The captain tried to swallow and coughed again as the knot in his throat caught on Slayn's blade. "I will!" he gasped. "I promise!"

"A human's promise means nothing to me," Esadora hissed, fresh anger rising in her. "Your kind promised mine riches and honor in the wars, and what did we get? Silver knives in our backs like any other magical creature."

She drew Slayn away from the captain's throat, and he coughed loudly and gasped for air. "I am done talking, human."

Slayn flashed as Esadora drove one blade through the captain's neck. The smell of blood, sweet and metallic, filled her nostrils as the captain convulsed underneath her for a few minutes before falling still.

Soft footfalls whispered in the ferns.

Esadora pulled Slayn out of the dead captain's throat as her ears caught the sound.

"The humans are all dead, clan leader," Ayrsah said with a dip of her head as she and Rargyne approached. Tall lacy green ferns still wet with raindrops brushed around their muscled legs with soft hissing noises.

"Good," Esadora said, standing and turning to the other two witches. "We will feast well tonight, my sisters." It was small payment for their losses, but with Darkmoon's heart, this hunt would almost be worth it.

Esadora glanced at Rargyne, twin to Thestre. The scout of their clan was paler than usual and held her left arm with her right hand as black blood drained down her armor through a gaping hole in the boiled leather.

"Your grief is mine, sister," Esadora murmured, dipping her head in respect. "Thestre will be remembered with the others we have lost tonight by feasting on those we have slain."

Rargyne nodded. Esadora breathed deeply of the blood-scented air. "Smell it, my sisters," she whispered, barely suppressing a moan. "When we are done eating the assassin's heart, we shall take our fill of the rest." And for once in over nine years' time, she would be full.

Her sisters were quiet. Esadora opened her eyes to see them glancing at each other nervously. Her black eyes narrowed. "What is it?" she asked. "Rargyne?" she said when they didn't reply.

The quieter witch stared into nothing.

Ayrsah cleared her throat. "The assassin," the younger witch said, glancing up at Esadora with night-black eyes. "He is gone."

Esadora stared at her. Ayrsah was a young, headstrong witch and quite foolish at times, but she didn't think she was foolish enough to joke with her, not at a time like this. "He is what?" Esadora hissed, glancing from one sister witch to the other.

"Gone," Ayrsah repeated, lowering her head as Esadora met her eyes with her own. "We killed the soldiers as you instructed us, and when we had finished, he was gone. The skinchanger must have taken him while we were busy."

A deathly silence rang through the clearing.

Their prey was gone, and with him their money and their revenge. Esadora stared at her two sisters.

They respectfully bowed their heads to her, awaiting her punishment.

"The skinchanger..." she hissed, skeletal fingers curling around Slayn's bone handle so tightly it creaked.

Esadora let out a scream that made her sister witches flinch and embedded Slayn into the trunk of a nearby goyr tree. "Gods damn you, skinchanger!"

CHAPTER 46

Hathus

*D*ragons are real.

Hathus's eyes snapped open. He screamed.

A small piece of rock broke off from the slanting side of the volcano above and fell toward him. He fainted again.

It was the voice that woke him up the second time. The same voice from the deck of the *Daemon's Cry* and from the beach.

"You really are cowardly, aren't you, Hathus?"

Hathus stared at the rock of the volcano far above him, shivering and shaking.

How are you doing that?

"Talking in your mind? I was a wiar once, with powers of the mind, and when I became a dragon, although I lost my wiar body, I retained my powers. It's little recompense for this pit we were cast into, but I am thankful for it."

Oh, my gods, dragons are real. Hathus slowly rolled his shaking head sideways.

He looked through the legs of the men who'd followed him and at the dragons. There were seven of them, like in the legend, each one as different from the other as day was from night and each as terrifying as the last. One was missing the skin over half of its face with black bone, long teeth, and glistening sinew showing underneath, another had only one eye, another a fanned cluster of horns crowning its head, another two large holes in its chest that oozed red lava, and still another a long, wide gash in its neck that had black and gnarled edges.

One of the dragons was watching him, and from what Hathus could tell from the part of their bodies that were above the lava, the largest.

Dragons are real, and they can talk in minds…

"Not all of us, Hathus, only I. My siblings' powers are different than mine and somewhat weaker in ability."

Hathus stared into the largest dragon's eyes. They were yellow with black slit irises, like a lizard's, and filled with intelligence and cunning and wisdom, not at all what he'd imagined a dragon's eyes would look like. Somehow, although he'd never believed the legends, he'd always thought dragons would just be like any other dumb animal.

Hathus screamed again, and the men who followed him turned and moved around behind him, seemingly unperturbed by the fact that seven dragons were staring at them.

"Come now, Hathus," the dragon who had spoken in his mind said aloud. "Surely you have come to grips by now with the fact that we are indeed real."

Hathus stopped screaming, voice hoarse. No, he didn't think that he'd ever come to grips with that fact. The shock was too great. But yet, here he was, looking at seven fire-breathing dragons. Dragons that had once been wiar, according to the legend. Dragons that knew his name.

Hathus shuddered. There had only been four wiar in the history of Argdrion that had held the power of the mind. One in the very beginning of time. Then Erastos, the oldest sibling of the Rahys siblings, and then twins during the end of the Third Great War who had been killed before they could fully come onto their powers and change the course of the war in the wiar's favor.

All wiar were feared, but those who held the power of the mind were feared above anything else in Argdrion. Their powers were unsearchable, and the exploits of the first wiar with mind powers and of Erastos were legendary.

"I'm glad to know that Argdrion has not forgotten me…" Erastos whispered in his mind.

Another of the dragons started talking to the ledge full of pirates. "It has been a long time since we have seen humans," that dragon hissed.

The pirates screamed and drew their weapons, backing toward their tunnel.

Hathus rolled over onto his stomach and slowly pushed himself to his feet. A trail of piss wound down his leg, making his pants stick to his skin.

What do you mean?

"We have been gone so long, I feared that Argdrion had forgotten us."

Well, they kind of have. Everyone thinks you're just a fairy tale...

Erastos snarled, and the other dragon talking stopped and glanced at him with the other five.

"What?" Erastos asked aloud, voice angry.

Hathus took a shaking step backward. He probably shouldn't have thought that.

"What do you mean, Hathus," Erastos hissed, "that Argdrion thinks we are nothing but a fairy tale?"

Hathus swallowed as all seven dragons looked at him. He felt the pirates watching him too. "Well," he started, surprised at the sound of his voice coming out, "no one believes in the Sisters as the makers of Argdrion anymore, so we don't... didn't believe that they had cast you out, hence we didn't... don't believe that you were, or are, real."

"No one believes in the Sisters anymore?" Erastos repeated, voice growing quieter.

"Um, not really," Hathus replied, knees and hand shaking. The thought to back up for the tunnel entered his mind.

He took a small step backward.

"Why not?"

Hathus stared at the dragons. Why not? What should he tell them? That humans had taken over Argdrion, killed off most magical races and realized that the Sisters and Brothers were lies made up by the wiar and skinchangers? He didn't think that would go over very well.

He glanced at the other ledge again, at the pirates who now stood in a defensive position with their weapons raised. Caine was not among them.

Bastard.

Hathus looked back at the dragons. "We just believe that gods and goddesses are the true makers of Argdrion," he murmured, legs shaking so badly he was surprised he was still standing.

"Typical of humans to believe such a lie," said the dragon with the crown of horns. She was a female by the higher-pitched undertone to her hate-filled voice. "Let's just eat them, Erastos. It's been years since I've tasted flesh on my tongue."

Hathus felt more piss drain down his leg. It trickled into his boot and pooled around his foot.

"No, Merav," Erastos said, body a solid black and lined with ridges of horns. "Not yet, anyway," he added when Merav snarled.

"Let us see first why they here," Erastos rumbled.

Hathus blinked, realizing that the dragons were waiting for a reply. "I…" he croaked. Should he tell them he was looking for treasure, like he'd told the pirates? He didn't see any treasure, and if they had any, he doubted that telling them they had come to take it away was the best ploy. He could tell them the truth, that he wanted one of their hearts…

Hathus blanched. That would be worse than telling them about the treasure. "I had heard the legends of dragons…" he began again, voice hoarse and shaky. "And I wanted to see if they were true." Most creatures could be baffled with bullshit. He hoped it held true for dragons as well… Gods, he hoped it did.

"You wanted to see if we were as gruesome as they said," said the dragon with the missing eye, a female also.

"No!" Hathus said hastily, holding his hand out toward her. It shook wildly, and he put it down again. Maybe if he closed his eyes, when he opened them, he would find that this was all a dream and that he was really in the dungeons, hungry but safe.

Hathus tried it. It didn't work.

The dragons were still looking at him when he opened his eyes again.

"Now, Atarah," rumbled another male dragon in a voice that made Hathus's sternum vibrate. "Perhaps the human wanted to see our power."

Hathus nodded. "Yes, I wanted to see that," he said quickly, going over the names of the Seven Siblings of Rahys in his head. Erastos had been the oldest of the septuplets—he remembered that from the legend. Then there was Zelpha, Kyros, Merav, Zadok, Atarah, and Tiras.

The male dragon who had spoken pulled his lips back in what Hathus guessed was supposed to be a smile. Orange lava rolled out of its mouth and drained down over the two holes in its chest and into the lake below. "Don't you have enough wiar in your world to satisfy your curiosity, human?" the dragon said throatily.

Hathus frowned, taken aback for a moment. But of course, he realized. The Seven Siblings of Rahys, according to legend, had been exiled from Argdrion over six thousand years ago. They wouldn't know anything of the Great Wars or the Hunting and the hatred of magic.

Hathus blanched. He didn't want to be the one who told them their race had been exterminated.

"There were wars…" he said slowly, choosing his words carefully. His eyes darted from dragon to dragon. "There were massive wars that lasted hundreds of years and raged over all of Argdrion…"

Merav pulled her lips back in a red lava-filled smile. "And humans died?" she hissed hopefully.

"Uh… um…" Hathus stuttered. "Well, yes, but so did skinchangers and, um, wiar." He took another slow, barely audible step backward.

"How many wiar?" another male dragon asked in a voice that was too soft for a dragon.

"Well," Hathus said, taking another step backward, "the humans emerged the victors in the wars, and they, we, uh, kind of hunted magical creatures and the wiar…" He swallowed. Would the dragons kill him if they knew their fellow wiar were all but dead?

But they're not wiar anymore, are they? "Uh, they're all dead," Hathus finished so softly that he knew the dragons could not hear him.

Erastos drew his head back and to the side like a snake ready to strike. "Dead. The wiar are all dead?"

Hathus nodded, foot warm and wet from the piss in his boot.

"WHAT?" roared Merav.

"Interesting," Erastos said, ignoring her.

Hathus blinked.

Interesting? You just found all your kind is dead, and interesting is all you can come up with?

"And your kind?" hissed the dragon with skin missing from half its face. "Do they rule Argdrion?"

Hathus nodded, throat too dry to allow him to reply. He took another step backward.

All the dragons exhaled loudly, and he froze. More rock broke off from the walls of the volcano and fell into the lava lake.

Hathus hissed as a drop of lava landed on his coat sleeve. He shook it off, skin warm where the molten fire had melted through the leather of his coat.

"Humans are not worthy to rule a dung pit," Merav spat.

Hathus nodded vigorously. "I agree," he croaked.

"Should we kill him, Erastos?" the dragon with the missing skin asked in a snakelike hissing voice.

Hathus began shaking harder. He felt like he might faint again.

"In time, Kyros," Erastos said. "First I want to know more of what has transpired in Argdrion since our exile."

The dragons all turned fiery eyes to him again. Hathus froze halfway to the tunnel. "Well, the cost of living has gone up," he offered.

"Our kind," Erastos said. "You say they are all gone. Since when?"

"Um…" Hathus wracked his brain for a memory of stories of the last of the wiar. "For over thirty years? The last ones to be killed were towards the end of the Third Great War, I think, and that's been ended now for…"—he paused, mentally counting—"thirteen years."

"And how did a kind so weak as yours manage to kill my people?" Erastos asked in Hathus's head.

Silver, Hathus thought, moving toward the tunnel again. "We learned in the Second Great War," he said aloud, feeling weird holding a conversation in his mind, "that silver diminishes the power of magical creatures, and it was mined in force and used to help defeat the skinchangers and wiar." For once, he was glad that he had paid attention in history lessons. Their conversation was giving him time.

"I say we burn his flesh from his limbs," Merav said angrily.

Hathus froze again.

"Not yet, Merav," Erastos said, cocking his head. "I will decide when we kill him."

"Since when?" said the dragon with the holes in its chest, also a male. "I don't remember electing you as leader, Erastos."

"I was born first, Tiras," Erastos said darkly, snapping his head toward the other dragon. "And unless you want to silence the only news of Argdrion we've had in six thousand years, I suggest we listen to the human."

Tiras let out a tongue of fire.

Hathus took another step backward. He glanced at the ledge of pirates—most of them were gone now. His eye caught on Bathia's. She looked scared, genuinely scared. It terrified him. He had never seen her scared before.

Erastos turned. "The Hunting you spoke of, human, what was that?"

Hathus stopped again. "It… it was a hunting of everything magical in Argdrion. Spells, creatures, everything. It was dark." He shivered at the memories that flooded his mind. "Horrible."

Erastos inhaled, seeing what he saw. Hathus cut the memories off. He didn't want the dragon knowing about his life.

"And there is no magic left in Argdrion?" asked the last female dragon, Zelpha.

"We hear rumors of some," Hathus replied, thinking of Caine, "but it's hidden." He slid toward the tunnel again.

"What do you think, Zelpha?" Erastos asked.

"I think we should go back and take our world from the weaklings," the female dragon said in a throaty rumble. She had a black scar marring her neck.

"If only we could," said the dragon with the too-soft voice.

"Zadok is right, why even bring it up, Zelpha, since we can't?" Merav snarled.

"I was simply saying what I think," Zelpha snarled back. "And don't tell me we all don't think of it."

"All we do here is think," Tiras rumbled, the ledge shaking underneath Hathus's feet. "There's nothing else to do besides think and eat lava!"

But of course, Hathus realized, the dragons could never leave the Land of Dragons. Part of their curse was to always be in each other's company. Unless they found a portal big enough for them to all fit through and went through at exactly the same time, they couldn't leave their prison. He took another step backward toward the tunnel entrance. The opening was only an foot away now.

The dragons whipped their heads around as one, three looking at him and four at the pirates on the ledge. "Where do you think you are going, humans?" Merav and Kyros hissed.

Hathus froze again.

A crossbow bolt hissed out of the group of pirates, hitting Zelpha in the left eye and sinking deep.

The female dragon lurched backward in an explosion of lava, a roar shaking the volcano.

Hathus paled.

Oh gods.

"Bastards!" Merav screamed. She turned toward the ledge full of pirates, incinerating half of them in a burst of fire.

Hathus gaped as dozens of pirates melted where they stood or tumbled, screaming, off the ledge into the lava below. He backed up the last foot toward the tunnel.

The dragons turned toward him.

"Leaving already, Hathus?" Erastos rasped.

Hathus turned his head slowly to look at the four dragons watching him. Tiras joined Merav in covering the ledge the pirates had been on with fire.

Zelpha slammed her head into the side of the mountain with a roar of pain. More rocks fell down from above, sending up showers of lava onto the ledge around him.

"You'll never escape from us!" Merav screamed, turning from the blackened ledge where the pirates had been with wide, glowing eyes.

"This is our world, human," Atarah snarled.

"And like us," Erastos breathed, flames swirling in his open mouth, "you will never leave it."

The dragons rose out of the lake, lava cascading off their backs, eyes slowly beginning to glow. They drew their heads back as one.

Hathus turned and ran.

He heard the fire coming down the tunnel behind him, felt the heat that swept before it as it singed the back of his head.

He dove behind a twisted mass of hardened lava.

One of the men who followed him slid behind a shelter of hardened lava opposite, the other ran past, heading for another shelter farther on.

Oh gods, forgive me for all that I have done in my life to offend you. I'm sorry for everything, just let me live. Please let me live!

Fire filled the tunnel, lapping at the walls, scorching the floor.

Hathus watched the man looking for a shelter become enveloped by the flames, heard him scream as the flames swirled around him. He pulled his coat over himself as fire whooshed over the top of the lava rock sheltering him, the heat in the tunnel making his flesh turn red. He had felt fear before, the terrifying knowledge that death was near, but there was something about this that was different. Maybe it was the fact that there were seven monsters that could breathe fire after him, or maybe it was the slowly sinking realization that there was very little chance of them getting out of the Land of Dragons alive.

Hathus crouched lower as fire continued to rage down the tunnel, the fine brown hairs on the back of his hand shriveling and curling in on themselves from the heat.

I promise to give all my money to the poor and never steal again if you get me out of here alive…

As suddenly as it had come, the fire stopped.

Hathus moved his arms away from his face, his skin feeling like it was melting beneath the heated leather of his coat. He glanced at the spot where the man who had not found shelter had been, but there was nothing there. He looked at the other man, still crouching behind the hardened lava across the tunnel.

Hathus pushed away from the rock and ran again.

He heard the man following as he stumbled down the tunnel, felt the soles of his boots grow warm from the heat of the rock beneath him.

Hathus burst out of the tunnel and into the ash-filled air outside, gasping for breath.

He ran into a body, and pain stabbed through his stump.

"Hathus!" Bathia said.

Hathus looked wildly down at the face of the woman in front of him. "Bathia?" he gasped. "I thought you'd been burned up! The dragons burned the pirates up, and they were falling into the lava and screaming—the pirates, not the dragons—and then I ran and one of the men that follows me was incinerated in the tunnel, and I thought I was going to die too, and

I know that this is all my fault that we're here, and we're all going to die, and it's my fault that you've died, and I'm sorry for asking you about magic and killing you and—"

"Hathus!" Bathia slapped him, quieting his rambling.

Hathus blinked, staring at her. For a moment, she had been his mother, and he had been apologizing like he'd always wanted to but never had the chance to.

"Hathus, I'm not dead," Bathia said in a softer voice. "I got away, so did Caine and Blackwell."

Hathus glanced up in a daze to see Caine a few feet away. He blinked again, feeling like he was in a horrible nightmare that would not end.

"He's in shock," Caine's raspy voice said. "Best get him to the ship."

Hathus wanted to tell the worldwalker that he was fine, to yell at him and ask him why he had brought them all here to die, but pirates were yelling and running down the volcano, making too much noise.

"Move carefully," Caine called back as he started down the mountain after the last of the retreating pirates. "The path is steep. We don't need more people dying if we can help it."

But we're all going to die, can't you see that?

The volcano rumbled underneath them. Hathus put his arms out to steady himself as he lurched sideways.

"Come on," Bathia said, taking his arm and pulling him forward.

Hathus grabbed her other arm with his hand, stopping her. "I'm sorry," he whispered when she turned toward him. "I'm sorry for all of this, for the souls... not fighting, everything. It's my fault we came here, and now you're going to die because of my mistake."

"Thank you, Hathus," Bathia said softly as the volcano shook beneath them again. She met his gaze, gray eyes reflecting the orange of the volcano above them. "And as far as the dragons..." She smiled slightly. "You didn't believe that dragons were real, so I can't fault you for bringing us to our deaths. And some of us," she added, face streaked with ash and sweat, "we knew what we were getting into."

Hathus stared at her, not quite understanding what she was talking about.

"I'm a worshipper of the old religion, Hathus," Bathia said quietly.

Oh, gods...

"Why are you telling me this?" Hathus whispered, feeling like he had all those years ago. Betrayed. And very, very scared.

"Because I have a feeling that we aren't going to make it out of this one," Bathia said. "And I can't die knowing that I lied to you, Hathus."

The volcano rocked underneath them again, the ash falling around them grew thicker.

"We need to go," Bathia said. She turned, pulling on his arm again.

Hathus saw the remaining man from the Unknown Voice following them and wondered vaguely if he was going to kill him because he had not gotten a dragon's heart.

Pirates were already rowing toward the pirate fleet when they reached the beach, but one rowboat remained, with Caine, Blackwell, and a half a dozen pirates clambering into it.

Hathus half jumped, half fell into the rowboat as Bathia and several other pirates pushed the boat out into the rocking black water. He sank down at the prow, beside Blackwell, who was watching the volcano with a too-calm expression.

The volcano rumlbed loudly as the rowboat shot out into the sea and bright, golden lines of lava seeped over its top and streamed down its side in rivers.

The sea rocked harder, spraying them with water as pirates pulled, muscles bulging, on the oars. A pirate with a wooden statue of the god Rowan on a leather thong around his neck quietly recited prayers for protection. Several others were crying.

Hathus glanced at the man praying, watching his fingers turn white as he gripped the idol. Bathia was a worshipper of the Sisters... But it didn't really matter, did it? This trip had been doomed from the start, cursed by the presence of magic and magic users.

An explosion rocked the water. Everyone in the rowboat looked up, and several pirates cried out. Fire and lava shot into the darkness as the top of the volcano came off.

Caine cursed, and Hathus turned. He saw the dragons rise out of the caved-in top of the volcano, hovering in the darkness above, seven glowing bodies of fire, power, and death.

Wind from the dragons' wingbeats made his hair lift. His fingers curled around the air where his left hand should have been.

The dragons turned toward the fleeing rowboats.

Hathus closed his eyes, heat tickling his skin.

Screams filled the air.

CHAPTER 47

Darkmoon

He was running, always running.

Darkness enveloped him, and unseen hands—or were they branches?—grabbed at his arms and legs and pulled at his cloak, which flew behind him in an unfelt wind.

They were following him. He didn't know what exactly they were yet; he'd only caught glimpses of them in the darkness behind him—white skin over skeletal frames and obsidian teeth dripping with red blood, but he knew what they wanted with him.

A branch hit him in the face, thorn-weighted wood scratching painfully at his skin, and Darkmoon hissed and pushed it out of the way with one sweaty hand before stumbling down a small hill and into a shallow black pond.

He'd been running for what seemed like days now. In this darkness, a swirling, twisting blackness, who could tell how much time had passed? His muscles were starting to feel like they might pull in half.

Several times he had thought he'd lost them and slowed to a walk to rest his burning legs, but they had always appeared like spirits out of the darkness, and he had to run again, pushing through thorn-laden bushes and ducking under tree roots as he went. He had seen the clearing full of bodies. Bloody, mangled corpses of what used to be humans. He did not want to end his days like that.

His booted foot touched something soft in the black water of the pond, and Darkmoon glanced downward as the water rippled around his legs.

Bodies, the pond was full of bodies. They stared at him with sunken pits of darkness that could only be eyes, as the one he had touched, a man with lanky black hair that floated around his head in a halo, seeped blood into the water from a gaping hole where his throat had been.

"Darkness is coming."

Darkmoon's head snapped upward at the voice. A black raven, blood draining out of its red eyes onto the night-black branch beneath it, caught his eye. He had seen the bird before, in a field, in another dream...

"Blood will follow," the raven squawked, more blood trailing out of its eyes in rivulets. "War is here, death is upon us." The raven cawed loudly and launched off the branch in a flurry of wings, blood, and feathers and disappeared into the darkness, screeching. "Darkness is coming, blood will follow, war is here, death is upon us."

A branch snapped behind him. Darkmoon glanced back and started running again, jumping over the bodies filling the pond as he splashed through the water and scrambled up the hill on the other side.

His foot rolled underneath him as he darted beneath towering trees with black blood oozing out of cracks in their gray bark, and he put his hand against a tree to steady himself as he pitched toward the ground below. His palm came away black with blood.

Something screamed in the darkness behind him, a bone-chilling wail that sent shivers up Darkmoon's spine.

His mother's face flashed before him, blood oozing out of her cheeks in rivulets. "I forgive you, my child," she whispered.

Fire enveloped her. Darkmoon ran harder, breaths like knives cutting into his lungs.

They were in front of him before he could blink, skeletal white hands reaching for him with three-inch black talons, black eyes gleaming with death.

Darkmoon's hands went to the belt around his middle, but his fingers found only air above the leather sheaths on the belt. He cursed, remembering too late that he had used all his knives earlier. He was weaponless.

He fought with the desperation of a man near death, but in a moment two of the creatures were on top of him, pinning him to the ground with grips like iron.

He struggled against them as another stood over him, black blood dripping from her fangs onto his shirt, but their strength was that of ten men, and he was only one.

Obsidian fangs flashed in his face. Black talons hissed in his peripheral vision before slicing into his flesh.

Pain sliced through his body, Darkmoon snarled as three-inch-long claws tore through skin and flesh and tendon. Warm red blood rained over him in droplets, staining his shirt and stinging his eyes.

He thrashed against their hold with a fury, the terror of being at their mercy filling him with a newfound strength.

One of the creatures raised a black-veined white hand above him, talons flashing in the dim light, and Darkmoon screamed as she tore his stomach open in one quick slice and pulled his entrails out in dark-blue coils.

The smell of blood, his blood, metallic and warm, filled his nostrils.

Darkmoon twisted on the leaves. Pain. There was so much pain.

"My son…" his father said, appearing in the mist hovering among the bare tree branches. His face was shadowed, like it always was when he came.

The creature with his entrails in her talons gave an ear-piercing scream that rang in Darkmoon's ears and filled the darkness around him. She glanced back down at him with a gleam in her black eyes and crammed his intestines into her mouth with one hand.

Darkmoon's head flew backward to the blood-soaked leaves, and he screamed like he had never screamed before as pain like nothing he had ever known raked through his body. The creature chewing his entrails leaned over him with a hiss, her breath smelling like rancid blood and maggot-infested flesh.

"Darkness is coming!" the crow cawed loudly from its perch on a branch above his head, bloody eyes watching him. "Darkness is coming…"

The creature leaning over him, swallowed his insides, and with a smile, dove for his throat.

Darkmoon bolted upright, a hand on his stomach.

"My son…" his father's voice whispered in his mind, fading with the dream as the crackling of a fire filled his ears.

Darkmoon glanced down at his abdomen, half expecting to see his intestines curling out in glistening blue coils.

His skin was smooth, a freshly healed pink scar the only thing to mark the spot where the witch had driven his knife into him.

Darkmoon ran a scarred finger over the mark, sweat rolling down his naked torso.

The witch had stabbed him, he remembered that clearly, so how was he still alive?

He glanced up at his surroundings, a crude room underneath the root system of a goyr tree. Twisting, intertwining brown roots filled the gaps between the goyr tree's larger roots, making up the room's walls.

Darkmoon put a hand on the ground to slide up to a sitting position and inhaled as his arm quivered under his weight. He looked at it. It had been a long time since his body had showed weakness. Goyr leaves making up his bed crinkled underneath him. He felt like he had been drained of all energy, like his muscles had been taken from him. It was the witch blood, he knew, which made him wonder again: How was he alive?

"Brother…" Cyron whispered. He stood by one wall of the root room, hands folded in front of him, green eyes watching.

Darkmoon glanced over at him. The skinchanger had left him if the voices were back, but where had she left him?

"Please…" Cyron said.

The fire in the middle of the room crackled merrily, red and gold flames making the shadows that crowded the dirt-crusted underside of the tree far above dance.

A panel of roots opened in the wall across from him with a soft creak. Darkmoon's mismatched eyes darted to it as the skinchanger, dressed in a black dress of goyr leaves, stepped inside. Her long black hair, braided with glowing silver moss, swung softly around her slender hips.

"You're awake, then," she said, pausing as she noticed him sitting up.

"You are astute, aren't you?" Darkmoon replied, pulling one leg underneath him. He watched as Cyron vanished.

The skinchanger shut the root door behind her and padded across the hard-packed dirt toward him. "Here," she said shortly, crouching and holding a purple moonflower out to him.

Darkmoon glanced up at her, noting how her eyes strayed to his naked torso for a moment, although not in an embarrassed or lustful way. "What is it?" he asked, jutting his chin at the bell-shaped flower.

"Water," the skinchanger replied, setting the makeshift cup down on the dirt in front of him.

He slowly reached for it, the glowing purple petals smooth and cool against his lithe fingers, and smelled the shimmering liquid swaying inside. He downed it in one swallow. The water soothed his parched throat like a pool of water on a hot day.

"How am I still alive?" Darkmoon asked, wiping the back of one hand across his mouth as he set the empty moonflower back on the ground.

Weariness made his eyelids droop. He blinked to stop it and glanced up at the skinchanger. And how had she become more beautiful? Bracelets of delicate orange and white flowers adorned her narrow wrists, and a necklace of silver moss and purple moonflower petals hugged her partially tattooed throat.

The skinchanger stood and moved to the fire, leaf dress rustling softly around her. "Forest Folk," she replied softly, voice reverential. She picked up a blackened stick up from the well-trodden dirt next to the crackling flames.

Darkmoon cocked his scarred eyebrow. "You mean wood nymphs?" He'd thought they were all dead.

The skinchanger shrugged with a slight lift of her bare shoulders and went to crouch by the fire, digging the stick into the dancing flames. Glowing orange and gold sparks shot up into the shadows that hugged the underside of the goyr tree, dancing embers of the suns in the darkness. "Your people call them wood nymphs, mine call them Forest Folk. They found us by a stream and healed you with their magic."

Darkmoon glanced down at the jagged pink scar on his side again. He thought that he had felt the presence of magic.

"How long was I out?" he asked, looking back up at the skinchanger.

She glanced over her tattooed shoulder at him, black braids sliding over her opposite shoulder. "Three days," she said.

Darkmoon blinked back sleep.

A lot can happen in three days... "And the witches?" he asked.

The skinchanger turned back to the fire. "As far as I know, they are still looking for us." She put another stick on the fire from a pile next to it. "But the Forest Folk used their magic to hide our scent and tracks. The witches will not find us."

Darkmoon snorted. "Don't bet on it." Witches excelled at tracking. It was rare that magic could fool them or make them lose their trail for very long. He tested his muscles and found them compliant, so he slowly pushed himself to his feet.

His body begged to lie back down and sleep, but he forced it to move over to the fire and sit down beside the skinchanger. "What happened?" Darkmoon murmured, remembering the fight with the witches and passing out.

The skinchanger looked at him. "After the witch stabbed you," she said, going back to poking at the flames, "soldiers found us. A battle ensued, and in the distraction, I managed to drag you away without the witches noticing."

Darkmoon held a hand out to the flames. So, she had saved his life. Her debt was repaid, and she would leave now. He found that he didn't like that idea very much, not when it meant the voices coming back. Only, if her debt was repaid, why was she still here?

She had saved his life, he reasoned, but if she were to leave him now, in his weakened state, he might still die, and then in her eyes, her debt would not be repaid at all. Which meant that she would probably stay with him until he had recovered completely.

The skinchanger reached for another stick to put on the fire, the flames reflecting off the tattoos trailing up the right side of her neck and face.

Darkmoon glanced around the root room, eyes scanning the shadowed nooks in the wall. Shivers ran up his back where the sweat had dried on his skin.

"Are you still going to Rothborn?" the skinchanger asked.

He looked back at her. "Why?"

She prodded at the flames of the fire with the diminishing stick. "I must travel with you," she said, voice tight, annoyed. "Until you are healed completely."

He was right. She was going to stay with him for a while longer.

Darkmoon was secretly relieved. He nodded, eyes trying to close of their own accord again.

The skinchanger stood and moved to a corner where his clothes, neatly folded, sat in a pile.

She returned with the pile and tossed them down to him.

Darkmoon caught them with one hand. He held up his shirt. A neat black stitched hole was all that remained to show that a knife had ever gone through the suede material. He squinted at the stitching binding the hole together.

"Is this your hair?" he asked, glancing up at the skinchanger.

"There was nothing better to sew it together with," she replied with a shrug. "If you don't like it…"

She reached for the shirt, but Darkmoon pulled it back out of her reach. "It's fine," he said, setting the rest of his attire next to the fire. "I'm flattered that you care so much about my clothing."

The skinchanger sat back down beside him, reaching for her stick to prod the fire with again. She didn't reply.

Darkmoon slowly pulled the shirt over his head and down around his chest. He reached for his vambraces from the pile of clothing and slid one etched leather guard over his left arm.

"That witch said that you killed one of their sisters," the skinchanger said.

Darkmoon glanced up at her from lacing the thin leather laces along the bottom of the vambrace. "What of it?"

The skinchanger shrugged. "I wondered when. Witches are hard to kill…"

"Not for me," Darkmoon said, slipping the other vambrace on. "Years ago," he added, tying the last set of black leather laces on the vambrace and reaching for his gloves.

"Why?" the skinchanger asked, glancing at him.

Darkmoon's mouth twitched up in a half smile as he remembered. He hadn't thought about that night in years. "She ruined my sleep," he said. He pulled his gloves on over his lean hands, pushing the metal prongs of the buckles through the holes in the glove straps to secure them. "I was in a small roadside tavern in Gyndor," he went on, feeling generous enough to tell the story. "It's a kingdom two hundred miles north of here."

Darkmoon reached for his belts and began the laborious process of strapping them on. "It was a dingy place, dirty and dark, but I was on the way back from a job in one of the port cities, and it was the only stop between the coast and my closest safe house in Stonrin—that's Gyndor's royal city."

Darkmoon eyed the empty knife and star sheaths on his belts. He'd lost a lot of aray in weapons. "Anyway," he said, "I was sleeping in a bed in the room I'd rented, resting after a hard day's ride and a night with a young tavern girl, when a scream from the alley outside woke me."

Darkmoon stretched one leg out, pulling one of his leather boots on and reaching for the other. "It was the tavern girl. I'd noticed her leaving not long after she thought I went to sleep, and she was coming back from meeting a boy in the stable next door. The witch had ripped her heart out when I came outside and was eating it, blood dribbling down her chin in the alley while everyone else in the tavern cowered inside and prayed to whatever gods and goddesses they worshipped to spare them."

"So you killed the witch for killing your lover?" the skinchanger asked.

Darkmoon glanced up at her, noting again how beautiful she was. "No," he said, pulling his other boot on and reaching for his cloak, "I just don't like witches." He threw the black cloth over his shoulders and fastened the interlocking dagger clasp at his throat. "And the tavern girl was not my lover."

"My people do not mate with every skinchanger that comes along," the skinchanger said.

Darkmoon looked at her. She met his gaze. Her golden eyes were unreadable.

"I know," he said softly. He tucked his necklace down his shirt, feeling dizzy.

The skinchanger turned to the fire again, poking at it with the stick.

Darkmoon watched her. She had lost everything to humans, and yet she was still fighting, going strong. There was a reason behind her strength, but what was it? His had been revenge, but he didn't think that was what she wanted.

"Where are the wood nymphs?" he asked, wanting more than anything to lie down and sleep for a very long time.

The skinchanger didn't look at him. "Around," she said.

The wall of roots next to him came alive at her words, and a wispy pale-brown creature with slithering, twisting roots growing like hair from the top of its head and large soulful green eyes appeared out of the tangle of wood.

Darkmoon eyed it. "Interesting."

The creature blinked at him with its lashless eyes and finished pulling itself from the wall then stepped out into the middle of the room on spindly legs, the roots sprouting from its pointed fingers and toes drawing back into its body with swishing sounds.

Darkmoon had heard stories of wood nymphs as a boy, stories of fantastic treelike creatures who guarded the forests of Argdrion. In the beginning of time, the stories taught, the first wood nymph had been placed in the first forest by the Sisters and tasked with the job of keeping the woods from decay and rot. Every time the wood nymph burned a dead tree, a new nymph was born out of the flames, and hence the creatures spread throughout the forests of the world until all forests had some form of wood nymphs in them.

"I hope that you are feeling better, human they call Darkmoon," the wood nymph said in a voice that sounded like wind whispering through trees.

Darkmoon glanced at the skinchanger, surprised that she'd told the wood nymphs his name instead of just calling him "the killer." She didn't look at him.

"Better," he said, looking back to the wood nymph, who was swaying softly in place as if a wind was blowing against it.

He dipped his head. "Thank you for healing me."

The wood nymph bowed its head in assent, root hair twisting and twining in and out of itself, and turned to the skinchanger. "We would be honored, skinchanger they call Nathaira, to have you and your man stay with us for as long as you wish."

"He's not my man," the skinchanger said quickly, looking up. There was ice in her voice. "We're just traveling together."

The wood nymph glanced at Darkmoon, soulful eyes serene. "My apologies. I did not mean to offend."

"I'm not offended," Darkmoon said.

So, her name is Nathaira. He glanced at the skinchanger, expecting the anger he saw in her golden eyes. Skinchangers held their names in the same high esteem they did their honor and only told them to those they trusted implicitly.

"There is a birthing tonight," the wood nymph said in its windlike voice.

Darkmoon glanced back at it, wishing it would go away so he could sleep.

"As our guests, you are welcome to attend."

"I would be honored," the skinchanger said, standing and turning to the creature.

"Then we will look forward to your presence tonight," the wood nymph replied softly.

"We will not be attending," Darkmoon said.

The wood nymph and Nathaira looked down at him. "I must get to Rothborn, and I will need the skinchanger's help," he said.

"I'm sorry, then," the wood nymph hummed softly. "Until we meet again, Nathaira, Darkmoon." It backed up to its hole in the wall and extended a thousand roots from its body and closed the wall back up again.

Darkmoon eyed the spot where the creature had gone, the interlacing roots giving no clue that they were a creature.

"How could you be so rude?" Nathaira said, turning on him. "An invite to a Forest Folk birthing is an extremely high honor to any creature, and they will be offended that we aren't there."

Darkmoon put a hand on the floor to steady himself as weariness overcame him. He needed to rest. He looked up at Nathaira again. "Your name is Nathaira."

"Do not call me that," she hissed, pointing a finger at him.

He put his other hand on the floor. "Or what?"

"Or I'll finish what the witches started," she snarled.

He glanced at the bed. He needed to get to it. He pushed himself to his feet, muscles screaming in protest. His legs quivered underneath him, threatening to fail.

Nathaira stepped toward him, putting a shoulder underneath his arm to steady him.

Darkmoon glanced at her as she helped him to the bed, holding on to his arm while he eased down onto the pile of black leaves. Her smell of woods and wind and rain filled his nostrils as she leaned over him.

"I know that your people do not like humans to know your names," Darkmoon murmured, causing her to look up at him. "I will not call you by it."

"How do you know so much about my people?" she asked, eyes meeting his.

Darkmoon smiled softly. "If only you knew."

They stared at each other for a minute, and his eyes went to her lips. He wanted to taste her, to feel her against his skin. He moved toward her.

She drew back sharply, standing quickly. "When do you want to leave?" she asked brusquely.

Darkmoon smiled softly and leaned backward, easing down onto his back on the leaves. "In a few hours," he said, closing his eyes and listening to the crackling of the fire. He heard Nathaira move off, the door shutting behind her a second later.

That a skinchanger would kiss him was a ridiculous idea. But he could tell that for a moment Nathaira had thought about it, and she had almost kissed him.

CHAPTER 48

Tamar

Tamar hissed as the camp physician slid a steel needle the length of her smallest finger through the inside skin of her left arm and pulled a coil of tightly woven tan string between the quickly closing gap. She would have a scar there. She gripped the cot underneath her as the phyisican jiggled the needle to push it through the skin on the opposite side of the wound. But she had gone through her first battle, and she had made it out alive.

And killed several of the enemy. Tamar felt a small stab of guilt. Or was it satisfaction?

The physician pushed the needle back through the skin in the opposite direction, and Tamar sucked in another hiss as he unceremoniously cut the strings and stood. "Don't strain your arm," he said in a tired voice. He gathered up his instruments from off the narrow cot she sat on. "And keep the wound clean."

Tamar glanced at her mended arm, ignoring the disdain in the physician's voice. Most of the men in the army made it known that they didn't approve of women among them, making rude gestures as they walked by or leaving piles of feces outside their tent entrances. The day after the 34th Gond had found her, three men had beaten a woman soldier for "talking to them disrespectfully," and she had overheard a gond member say that a gond of men had tried to start a fight with a gond of women the night before they had reached Whitegate. Tension was tight in the camp.

That will change, Tamar thought, eyeing the red flesh around the neatly lined stitches on her arm. The officers were mumbling that women should never have been allowed among them for the disruption it was causing among their soldiers. But when women helped them win the war against Eromor, they would change their minds. All of Zarcayra would.

The physician moved off through the hospital tent, moans and screams and crying following him from the cots of wounded soldiers.

Tamar slipped off her cot, making her way past wounded soldiers and harried physicians and toward the tent flap. Her bed was immediately filled by a screaming woman with part of her left leg jaggedly cut out.

The sky outside was a vibrant shade of reddish-pink as Tamar exited the massive, foul-smelling healing tent, with stars just begging to appear here and there and the Sisters rising in the east.

Tamar breathed deeply of the smell of the camp—trampled grass, horse manure, medicine and blood, leather, steel, and smoke from the campfires that were beginning to crackle into life. A month ago she would have recoiled at the smell, but now, now it smelled like an army, like home.

My home...

"How's the arm?" Aghasi asked, slipping between two gonds moving past and stopping by her elbow.

Tamar glanced up at him, her stomach filling with butterflies. "Sore," she said, moving her left arm slightly and wincing, "but I'll live."

Aghasi grinned. "Hungry?" he asked, starting off through the maze of tents, soldiers, fires, weapons racks, and picketed horses.

"Famished," Tamar replied, sidestepping a sweating soldier supporting a tired, pale-looking comrade and following Aghasi.

"Let's hope the rest of the gond hasn't eaten all the food, then!" Aghasi yelled over the noise of a troop of fresh soldiers jogging past.

"Sentries," he explained as Tamar glanced over her shoulder at the soldiers. "Just in case Eromor tries any moves during the night."

The sentries disappeared into the throng of soldiers, slaves, animals, and camp followers, and Tamar turned back around as they walked past a group of shifting elephants being fed by slaves.

"Do you think they will?" she asked, lifting her booted feet high to step over a fresh pile of horse manure. They split apart to allow a soldier leading a limping gray mare past.

"Perhaps," Aghasi said, hands behind his back. He slid around the back of the horse to rejoin her. "But if they do, we'll give them the same beating they received today."

"Aghasi!" Maigar called as they approached a wavering campfire surrounded by the 34th Gond. "And Yeva! How's the arm?"

They stopped at the edge of the group of men. The fire popped as the wood and grass being burned shifted and settled.

"It's okay," Tamar said, putting her hand to the freshly stitched wound. "Stings a little."

Maigar grinned. "But how you got it! Killing that Eromor soldier by stabbing him in the stomach. You're quiet the fighter, Yeva. I've just been telling the rest of the gond of your exploits."

Tamar blushed. "It wasn't that great," she murmured, secretly pleased.

"Oh, but it was!" Maigar said loudly, making most of the murmuring gond look up. "It was the greatest thing!" He grinned again.

Tamar noticed several angry stares from some of the other gond members. Hazarap was among them, the man who had commented on her missing her hijab the night the gond had found her. She ignored him.

"Say, Aghasi," Maigar said in a conspiratorial whisper, "come and listen to this joke that Samayr was starting. I think it'll be a good one..." He moved over to an older gond member. Aghasi winked at her and followed.

Tamar stared after them. She was slightly bothered that Aghasi left her, although she didn't know why. Maigar had been his friend for years, and it was natural that they should want to spend time together without her.

She glanced around at the rest of the 34th Gond, gathered around the crackling fire with bowls of stew in their hands. None of them were paying her any attention anymore.

She moved to an empty spot on the grass between an aging soldier with silver hair flowing out from under his purple turban and a scar-faced man who gave her a vitriolic look before going back to the slice of bread he was devouring.

Aghasi and Maigar threw their heads back and laughed on the other side of the fire. Samayr smiled wickedly and motioned them closer before starting to murmur again.

Tamar watched them quietly. The first night she had spent around the campfire with the 34th Gond, several of the soldiers had told rude and dirty jokes, glancing at her in the hopes that she would grow uncomfortable. Then she had told them one she had heard from a palace slave, and now most of them ignored her. A few still continued to glare at her and mutter about her place not being with them. Like Hazarap.

Tamar glanced at the fat-nosed soldier. He was still watching her with a hateful expression on his face. She met his gaze again. She wasn't afraid of Hazarap. Men at the palace had watched her all the time. Some with lust in their eyes, others with anger like Hazarap.

She had learned at a young age that men would hate her simply because she was a woman, because they believed that she was an evil spirit sent by Setaron to tempt men and lead them astray from the path that the gods had laid out for them. There were many such men in Zarcayra, men like those of the god Mithrya who swore themselves to celibacy their whole lives and spat at any woman who walked past them on the streets.

Tamar looked back at Aghasi as he laughed again at something Samayr was telling him and Maigar. Aghasi didn't mock her. Perhaps it was part of the reason that she liked him so much. More than she liked Maigar. She wondered suddenly what it would be like to feel Aghasi's lips on hers and quickly looked away, blushing at the thought.

Most of the gond were eating rinds of dark-brown bread and bowls of what could only be, judging from the smell, beef stew from a large black bubbling pot over the fire.

Tamar's stomach growled. She hadn't eaten since morning, and what she had eaten had long ago been turned into energy in the fighting and used up. She eyed the pot.

"That yours, girl?" the scar-faced soldier growled, jabbing a dark finger at the Eromor dagger wedged in her boot.

Tamar glanced at him. "Yes," she said, pride warming her insides. "I took it from an Eromor soldier's dead body and used it to kill another Eromor soldier."

The man ripped a piece of bread off a chunk in his hand and chewed it loudly. "Fine weapon," he said, leaning closer to examine the gleaming blade. "Looks like well-made steel."

Tamar put her hand on the pommel of the dagger as the soldier leaned closer. There was a jealous gleam in his dark eyes.

"You look hungry, girl."

She glanced up at the deep voice, and the scar-faced soldier drew back as Paramiz stopped in front of her with a tarnished copper bowl in one hand and a chunk of bread in the other.

"Here," the graying Salāyr said, holding out the bowl. "Eat."

Tamar blinked. "But, sir," she started, realizing that the bowl was the Gond Salāyr's, "I lost my bowl in the fighting, and—"

Paramiz grunted. "Well, then take mine for the time being." He pushed the bowl into her hand, and Tamar sucked in a breath as the hot metal touched her skin.

"Thank you," she breathed, chancing a glance at the Gond Salāyr as he handed her the jagged piece of bread.

He was watching her with an unreadable expression.

Their fingers rubbed against each other as the bread changed hands, and Tamar noticed how rough Paramiz's were as she shifted the bowl around on her palm so as not to burn her skin.

The gond burst into uproarious laughter again as Samayr continued to tell jokes. A group of infantry marched past noisily.

"I heard you received a wound," Paramiz said, resting one hand on the pommel of his sword.

Tamar pulled her hijab away from her lips, still keeping it in front of her face as a shield, and raised the bowl of steaming stew to her mouth. "Just a small one," she replied, glancing up at Paramiz.

His dark eyes met hers, and she looked back at her bowl as she raised it to her mouth again. The Gond Salāyr's gaze was enough to make an elephant flee in fear. And there was always so much suspicion in them, like he knew that she was lying about who she was.

A sharp stab of pain ran through her arm suddenly as the poppy that the physician had given her wore off, and Tamar sucked in a breath.

"And you lost your horse," Paramiz said.

She glanced back up at him, a prickle of annoyance rising in her at his tone. "Yes, an Eromor soldier killed her. She'll be missed."

"Next time don't lose her, and you won't have anything to miss."

Tamar fancied what she would tell the Salāyr as princess. "Yes, Gond Salāyr," she muttered instead, dipping the bread chunk into the half-empty bowl of stew and cramming it in her mouth. She could feel Paramiz's eyes on her.

"How long was it that you said you were in Northport?" he asked abruptly.

Tamar felt the hair on the back of her neck slowly stand on end.

He knows...

"A couple of years," she said offhandedly, draining the last of the soup and rewrapping her hijab over her face.

"A couple of years?" the Salāyr said. "Don't you remember exactly?"

Tamar glanced over at Aghasi as the gond burst into laughter again, and he gave her a cheerful wink that made her heart beat quicker. How old had she said she was when she became an apprentice? And why did she get the feeling that the Paramiz was trying to catch her at something?

Her arm jolted with pain again, and Tamar bit the inside of her cheek to keep from crying out. She wouldn't show weakness in front of the gond; it would give them another reason to hate her.

"Six years," she said after a moment, hoping that her vague memory of saying she had been ten when she had become an apprentice was right. She held the empty copper bowl up to Paramiz, her heart beating rapidly.

"Keep it," he said, watching her. "And go get yourself some more poppy for that arm. Your face is turning white with pain."

He turned and moved off to wherever it was that he went when the gond was relaxing.

"Good?" Aghasi asked, kneeling next to her and nodding at the empty bowl in her hands.

Tamar felt her stomach start to flutter like it did every time he was near.

"Or maybe good isn't the right word for it," Aghasi said, grinning. "Maybe edible is a better word."

Tamar laughed. He stood and motioned for her to do the same. "I have something that I want to show you."

"What is it?" Tamar asked, setting Paramiz's bowl in the grass and pushing herself to her feet.

"You'll see," Aghasi said with a smile. He led her away from the fire and past other fires, to behind a large tent where the 33rd Gond slept.

Tamar glanced around at the trampled grass and shadows. The 33rd Gond sat around a fire ten feet away, hidden partially by several racks of weapons.

"Grass?" she asked. "Is that what you wanted to show me?"

Aghasi smiled, white teeth flashing in the shadows. "No, silly, I actually wanted to tell you something. Well, not really tell, more like ask, or maybe…" He seemed at a loss for words, the first time that Tamar had seen him like that. He sighed and looked up at the stars glittering above them. "This isn't going how I'd planned."

Tamar realized suddenly that maybe he was going to kiss her. Her heartbeat sped up. "What had you planned?" she whispered, looking up into Aghasi's blue eyes as he glanced down at her.

When she was younger, she had always thought that she would never kiss a man, never fall in love, never marry. But that was before she had met Aghasi, before she had realized that there were men in Zarcayra who thought that she was their equal and treated her accordingly.

Aghasi smiled softly. "What did I plan?" he whispered, leaning closer and pulling her hijab down. "This." He pressed his lips against hers.

Tamar felt like she was racing a horse across the desert.

The noise of the camp faded as Aghasi put a hand on the back of her head and pulled her tighter against him, and there was only his mouth against hers, his smell of horses and campfire smoke and steel, his hands on her body.

Tamar leaned against Aghasi, legs threatening to give out as a quivering lightheadedness overtook her.

Aghasi kissed her harder, week-old whiskers tickling her cheeks. He drew away after a moment, smiling softly. "Was that too forward?"

"No," Tamar whispered, breathless. "It was wonderful." She continued to lean against him, breathing in his scent.

The 33rd Gond stood and started nosily toward their tent.

They both looked up.

"It's late," Aghasi said, making her look back at him. "We should get some sleep. There will be another battle in the morning."

Tamar pulled back from him to look him in the eyes. "Will we take Whitegate tomorrow?" she asked, heart beating faster at the thought.

Aghasi look down at her. "Maybe. Who can tell?" he said, brushing the knuckles of one hand across her cheek. "We can just pray that the Family will help us as they did today." He leaned forward and kissed her again, lingering a little longer than the last time.

They broke apart all too soon for Tamar, moving away from the 33rd Gond's tent and through the camp.

"Good night, Yeva," Aghasi whispered as they moved past weapons racks.

Fires were dying everywhere, sentries moving into place as gonds went to sleep for the night.

"Good night," Tamar whispered, her lips still tingling from his.

Aghasi winked at her. "I'll see you in the morning," he whispered, brushing her cheek again. He turned and slipped off back toward the 34th Gond's tent, leaving her alone.

Tamar made her way to the physicians' tents, waiting in line for more painkiller before heading to the women's tents. She had fought in her first battle, and Aghasi had kissed her. She grinned into the darkness as she slid into a long white tent, moving past softly sleeping women.

She found an empty spot and lay down on her back, staring up at the whiteness of the tent above her. Tomorrow they would fight against Eromor again, and if the Family was with them, they would take Whitegate.

Tamar glanced to the side as the woman next to her grunted in her sleep. She looked back at the ceiling of the tent, suddenly feeling like praying.

Family, thank you for the victory today, and please give us victory again tomorrow.

Tamar remembered Aghasi's kisses and grinned up at the tent ceiling.

And thank you for my first kiss.

She rolled over on her side and tried to sleep, still grinning.

#

The next morning, Paramiz greeted her as she wound through the camp, making her way toward the mounting 34th Gond.

"I found you a new horse and gear, girl," the Gond Salāyr said, clucking his tongue at the buckskin gelding following him.

Tamar stopped, glancing over Paramiz's head at Aghasi as he swung up on Dshukhiy. "He's beautiful," she said, looking back at the horse and running a hand down his slender but sturdy side.

"His name is Oshakin," Paramiz said, offering her the lead.

Tamar took it, glancing into the horse's brown, almost black, eyes as it looked at her. She smiled. "Hello, Oshakin, you and I are to be partners now."

"Just make sure you don't lose this one," Paramiz said next to her, deep voice rumbling through her. "If you do, you'll be walking future battles."

Tamar ignored him, running her hand down the gelding's tan side again.

"We'll be moving out for battle soon," Paramiz said, making her look up at him. "See that you get something to eat before we fall into formation."

"I already did," Tamar said, scratching Oshakin behind one ear. "With the women." She had awoken early after an almost sleepless night of thinking of Aghasi and the coming battle. After finding several of the women eating around a fire, she had joined them.

Paramiz moved around Oshakin, stroking his neck. "And Yeva," he said.

Tamar looked up at him, surprised that he'd called her by her name. Or her fake one, rather.

"Be careful around Aghasi."

Tamar frowned, glancing over Oshakin's back at the Gond Salāyr. "What do you mean?"

"Just be careful," Paramiz repeated, patting Oshakin on the opposite side with a battle-scarred hand. "You're young, and sometimes being friends with certain people is unwise." He gave her a piercing stare and turned, walking over to the rest of the gond, purple cloak swaying around him.

Tamar watched him over Oshakin's back.

Careful... What does he mean careful?

Another gond trotted by on horses, spears raised, and Tamar moved to Oshakin's head, checking his leather bridle. And who did Paramiz think he was, telling her who to be friends with? Aghasi was one of the kindest, smartest men she had ever met. Maybe Paramiz had seen them kissing… Tamar blushed at the thought. But it wasn't illegal, so what could Paramiz have against it?

Horns blew, signaling for the army to fall into formation.

Tamar glanced up at the white cliffs of Whitegate, towering above them in the early-morning sunlight. "We're going to be in another battle, Oshakin." She grinned, pressing her forehead against the horse's muzzle. "I've got a good feeling about this, Oshakin, like we're going to win again and take Whitegate today."

Oshakin nickered softly.

The last of the 34th Gond mounted behind her, so Tamar did the same, glancing at Aghasi again as she settled into Oshakin's saddle.

Aghasi smiled at her.

They lined up before Whitegate as the previous day, rows and rows of spears glinting in the Brothers' light.

Tamar ran the palm of her hand down Oshakin's neck, eyes focused intently on the gaping hole that led through the White Mountains.

Crows circled high up in the gap. Low storm clouds hovered over the peaks of the mountains like smoke over a city.

"We'll break through today," Aghasi said next to her. "I can feel it."

Tamar glanced at him, the fingers of her left hand curling around the smooth wooden shaft of her spear. "Me too," she breathed, growing warm all over as she thought again of his lips against hers.

"And I'll add my vote in on that," Maigar said from her other side, adjusting his reins in his hands. "Where did you two slip off to last night?" he asked, glancing at them. "I looked up and both of you had disappeared."

Tamar reddened and looked at Oshakin's saddle.

"I went to relieve myself, if you must know," Aghasi said opposite her. "And Yeva… I don't know, where did you go off to?"

Tamar glanced up at him. She knew that it wouldn't be wise to tell anyone of their romance, but it still hurt a little when he denied kissing her. "I went to bed early," she lied, looking back at Maigar. "In preparation for today's battle."

Maigar nodded. "Ah, thought maybe you were doing something

together, like, you know, kissing or something." He glanced at them and grinned expectantly.

The horns reverberated out over the battlefield, and the lines of horsemen began moving forward.

Aghasi kissed me. Tamar grinned beneath her dusty purple hijab and looked at the rows and rows of horses and purple-clad riders in front of her, their spears all raised like hers in a thick forest of steel and wood. Mistress Lorrig had said that being in love was like eating too much iced cake and then riding a camel.

She was right, Tamar mused, flicking her fingers out and then curling them back in over her spear handle nervously. She felt as giddy as if she had eaten a hundred iced cakes and as light-headed and nauseous as if she had ridden a camel in a race. If this was what being in love felt like, it was annoying.

She glanced at Aghasi again, following the stubbled line of his jaw as he stood up in Dshukhiy's stirrups and scanned troops ahead of them.

Annoying but delightful at the same time.

"Aghasi!" Paramiz's rough voice called over the nickering and stomping of horses, chinking of chainmail shirts, and jangle of weapons. "Sit down. This is not a damn circus."

Aghasi sat back down in his saddle.

Tamar glanced at him. He winked at her. "He's ornery today," he whispered, leaning closer.

Tamar grinned and glanced over at Paramiz, who sat on his black gelding at the head of the double row of 34th Gond riders. She remembered his warning from earlier to watch out for Aghasi and frowned. Paramiz annoyed her, like Father and Zarmeyr had.

Aghasi leaned closer, his saddle creaking. Tamar felt her pulse quicken. "When this is over and we have won," Aghasi whispered, "we'll finish what we started earlier."

Tamar met Aghasi's gaze. He winked again and straightened back up. The butterflies in her stomach fluttered wildly. She sucked in a small breath through the sweat-scented fabric of her hijab.

"Gond forward!" Paramiz yelled, echoing the order of the other Salāyrs in front of him.

The double line of 34th Gond moved forward, and Tamar tapped her soft-booted heels against Oshakin's side to make him follow.

They trampled over grass turned yellow under the Brothers' summer rays. The stark white cliffs of Whitegate with their mass of red-and-black Eromor soldiers crowded in front drew closer.

Tamar gripped Oshakin's rope reins as the army burst into a gallop, the whistle of arrows from enemy archers slicing through the thundering air. There was confusion in front of Whitegate, yelling and dark shapes moving among the Eromor soldiers.

The Erāyn Khan must have ordered a side attack from the foot soldiers… Tamar kicked her heels against Oshakin's flanks again and started yelling with the others around her.

They were among the Eromor soldiers in minutes, blood-red tunics with dragon sigils mixing harshly with the softer purple and gold hues of Zarcayra colors.

Tamar heard a flag snap in the wind as she drove her spear through an Eromor soldier's chest and glanced upward and in front of her to see a flag with a roaring black dragon on its field of blood flapping in the wind atop a cross-barred wooden pole. She drew her curving sword from the supple leather sheath on her hip, hissing as her mending arm screamed with pain.

Tamar pulled sharply on Oshakin's reins. He screamed and fell back on his withers as she brought him to a stop beside the flag and with a yelling strike, she cut the pole in half just below the vertical crosspiece. The flag fluttered to the trampled grass, and Tamar stabbed it with her sword then raised the flag in a victory yell. She crammed the flag underneath her saddle's pommel and sheathed her sword, urging Oshakin after the horses whizzing past them.

The white cliffs of Whitegate drew closer and closer, looming above them as they pushed the Eromor army back in front of them. Back over the ground they had trampled on the day before.

Tamar followed Dshukhiy's golden flanks, keeping Aghasi and Maigar in her sights as they moved into the Whitegate pass. She did not want to lose them this time, as she might not be so lucky in finding them again so easily after the battle was over.

The white walls of the pass flew past, concealed partly by clouds of dust kicked up by the thousands of horses' hooves.

Tamar put a hand to one ear—the noise echoing off the massive cliffsides was deafening.

An arrow whizzed past her left cheek, cutting her hijab open and tickling her skin. She reeled to the right as another followed close by where her head would have been and cursed as Oshakin's step faltered over a body.

She lurched sideways off Oshakin's back, landing in the grass with a thump.

Damn it, not again! Tamar lunged to her feet, jumping out of the way of an oncoming gond.

The noise of battle was deafening in the pass—sword clashes, screams, moans, horses whinnying and chainmail chinking, all echoing off the towering walls.

Tamar turned as gonds swept past her, searching for Oshakin's tan flanks among the throng of horses and riders.

The gelding was nowhere in sight.

Damn it! She wheeled back the other way.

"Lose something?"

Tamar turned.

Aghasi grinned at her from Dshukhiy's back, Oshakin's reins in one hand.

"Don't tell Paramiz!" Tamar hissed, snatching the reins from Aghasi and climbing onto Oshakin's back. She crammed the Eromor flag down further beneath her saddle as thousands of Zarcayran soldiers thundered around and past them.

Aghasi grinned again, dust billowing through the pass filling their noses. "Souvenir?" He asked, pulling sharply on Dshukhiy's reins to keep her from joining the racing throng around them.

Tamar spat dust out of her mouth and a piece of her hijab that hung loose from the arrow that had cut it.

"You're getting quite the collection," Aghasi yelled, letting Dshukhiy jump forward a few steps.

Tamar grinned. "Something to show my children when I tell them about this!"

Maybe our children. She thought with a thrill.

Aghasi grinned in answer, and they kicked their horses into a gallop and joined the throng swarming past them.

The Eromor army was fleeing before them.

Tamar screamed with exhilaration as the golden grass of the Opherian Plains appeared through the dust ahead of them, the heat of battle in her blood. An old proverb in Zarcayra came to her mind: *The righteous shall win against their enemies and the just shall defeat their foes.*

Tamar screamed louder as dust filled her eyes and the pounding of a hundred thousand horses' hooves jarred through her body. Zarcayra were the righteous in this fight, and they would win against their enemies.

Foam flicked off Oshakin's muzzle. She felt its wet drops splattering on her cheeks. Eromor soldiers' bodies littered the ground underneath and around them, red-and-black uniforms turning brown as thousands of horses mangled the bodies into the dirt beneath.

They burst out of Whitegate like a flood, driving the remains of the Eromor army in front of them and into the swaying grass of the Opherian Plains.

The Eromor army camp was a ruin, smoldering campfires kicked into the grass, tents trampled into shreds and weapons thrown aside.

Red tunics of fleeing Eromor soldiers dotted the plains for hundreds of yards.

Tamar looked at a black metal pointed shield as she galloped past, the eyes on the roaring black dragon engraving on it seeming to meet her eyes. She urged Oshakin faster, jumping over an overturned black kettle.

They had done it.

Tamar grinned, urging Oshakin to run faster as the rest of the Zarcayran army flowed out of Whitegate behind her. She raised her sword in the air and gave a yell that rang in her ears.

They had taken Whitegate.

CHAPTER 49

The Unknown Voice

Alvyna had our child two months after the meeting and following agreement between the wiar and humans. Those two months were busy for me.

One week after the agreement papers between the wiar and humans were made up and signed—we began calling that day the Parlay Between Races—the wiar and human armies united and spread throughout Argdrion, hunting the skinchangers.

Thousands of skinchangers fell in the months following, and the skies of Argdrion were filled with buzzards and ravens and crows waiting for the battlefields to clear so they could feast on the bodies left behind.

We gathered as many of the skinchanger bodies as we could after each battle, and after mutilating them, we placed them on spikes around our cities and along our highways. A warning to all of what happened to magical creatures.

I saw firsthand during this time how powerful the wiar were, and what I saw made me nervous and jealous. Nervous because it was hard to believe that something so simple as silver could weaken and kill such a formidable race, and jealous because I wanted to be able to drown my enemies hundreds of miles away from a body of water and make trees come alive and attack the foe.

I fancied the idea of killing a wiar and changing into its body during this time, for now that they were "allies" with us, it gave me ready access to them, and they, like the skinchangers, lived for over a thousand years. But changing into a magical creature would still take away my power as king, and the wiar would not remain on Argdrion forever.

A skinchanger was captured by my knights not long after the day of the Parlay Between Races, and it was brought back to the castle for questioning as to where more of its kind were. We had found that as we pushed the skinchangers back across Argdrion, that they excelled at hiding in the deep forests and high mountains, and it was making progress slow.

The official word for what we were doing to the captured skinchanger was interrogation, but in reality, it was torture.

"We know that some of your people are hiding in the Ilgerion Forest," one of the interrogators said. "Now tell us where."

There were two of the black-clothed men in the indoor stone pit below me and my knights, as well as the skinchanger, who was chained, naked, in the center of the circular hole.

"If you know they are in the forest," said the skinchanger, a large male with hip-length blond hair and tattoos over all his body, "then find them yourselves."

He was calmer than most of the captured skinchangers I had seen, and I accredited it to his age, which was evident by the white streaks in his tangled hair and the fact that he was covered by tattoos. The skinchangers marked themselves with black ink whenever something important happened in their lives, like a death or battle. The older the creature, the more tattoos they had. It was an interesting practice, one that I someday wanted to study.

The interrogator who had spoken lashed a short, multistranded whip across the skinchanger's face, and my knights who had gathered around me on the edge of the pit chuckled as the skinchanger snarled and lurched backward.

The silver chains stretching from four iron loops in the rock of the sides of the pit rattled, and blood drained down the skinchanger's face to mingle with the swirling black markings of its tattoos.

The first interrogator repeated his question as the second searched among a pile of instruments on a wooden table along one wall of the pit, and the sound of his whip slapping against flesh rang through the stuffy air of the room again as the skinchanger snarled in response.

My knights laughed again, and I watched the skinchanger's eyes. They were brown in color, a deep, rich brown. It was the hate in them that caught my attention, though, the hate directed at the interrogators, at my knights, at me. It was the same hate that I had seen in thousands of my fellow humans' eyes, the same hate that had once filled my own eyes before I had found the heart spell.

All races in Argdrion hated another race. The skinchangers hated us and the wiar, the wiar hated the skinchangers and witches and warlocks, the humans hated the wiar and skinchangers and witches and warlocks. So much hate. What could be done without it?

The whip cracked again, and the skinchanger snarled once more, even more viciously than the last time.

"Do you think it will talk, Your Majesty?" one of my knights asked from next to me.

I drummed the fingers of my right hand against my left behind my back, my eyes riveted on the skinchanger. I hoped it did. I was tired of war, tired of pain, tired of death. But I doubted it—the skinchanger and wiar were strong, stronger than us humans. I voiced this opinion out loud as the second torturer approached the first with an iron bar, the tip heated in an barrel of fire by the table, glowing dark red and swirling orange.

I looked at the skinchanger's eyes again. There was no fear in them. It knew that we were going to kill it eventually, so why did it not show fear? Or did it not have any? The skinchanger and wiar believed in the old religion of Argdrion, the religion that my race had worked so hard to stamp out after we had converted to the new religion in the First Great War. In the old religion, it was believed that the moons had made Argdrion and the otherworlds, and whoever believed in them and worshipped and obeyed them would inherit eternal life in the stars. I did not know which religion I believed in, but I did know that I didn't want eternal life in the stars.

I wanted it on Argdrion.

The first torturer took the heated iron bar from the second and turned, holding it up in front of the skinchanger's face. "There is no need for you to suffer like this," the man murmured quietly, so that we had to strain to hear him. "Tell us where your brothers and sisters are, and we will end your life quickly and painlessly."

"Suffering," the skinchanger said, sweat dripping down his bloody cheeks, "only lasts for a short while, and when I am dead, there is nothing you can do to me, human. I'll have eternal life, and you'll be burning in the Brothers' Fire."

The torturer held the iron up to the skinchanger's cut cheek. The creature's screams vibrated around us.

The sizzle of burning flesh caught my ears. A young knight wrinkled his nose up at the smell.

I had seen torture before. The pit was used daily to "interrogate" humans brought in for questioning about suspected magic users, but there was something about the skinchanger's screams that affected me more than the screams of my fellow kind. Skinchangers, like the wiar, lived to a thousand years of age and sometimes beyond. But even with their longer life, they were still mortal and could be killed easily, like humans.

I had long thought over the fact that, even with changing into other bodies to gain longer life, I could still be killed. There were protection spells that could keep one from being wounded by weapons, yes, but they always wore off in a few hours and were no good against the wiar's powers or more powerful magical spells. Long life was what I wanted, but what good was long life if I could lose it so easily?

It was something that I had never come up with an answer to, something that plagued my mind again as I watched the interrogators work on the skinchanger.

"Tell us where your people are," the torturer with the hot iron said, handing the blackening piece of iron back to the other torturer, who moved to stick it back into the barrel full of fire.

The skinchanger replied with something in its own language and hacked in the back of its throat, using what little strength it had to hock a spitball at the torturer.

One of my knights growled. The torturer wiped the spit off and pulled a pair of specially shaped pliers out of a wide leather belt around his waist.

The skinchanger screamed as the torturer pried a fingernail off with a dull ripping sound. A few of my knights grimaced and absentmindedly hid their hands behind their backs.

"I'll talk!" the skinchanger yelled in the general tongue.

My knights chuckled. "I knew the bastard would," one said.

I glanced at them and then back to the skinchanger. I still doubted it would tell us what we wanted to know.

The torturer drew his pliers back, a fingernail between them as blood began draining down the skinchanger's arm. "Then talk."

"You'll never find all of us," the skinchanger said through gritted teeth. "Not if you search every mountain, river, cave, and hole in Argdrion. We will always be there, at the edges of your vision, waiting to reclaim what is ours."

The knights around me laughed at the threats, the noise sounding hollow as it bounced between the pit and the stone ceiling above us.

"Oh, we'll find you, skinchanger," the torturer with the pliers said. "You think you're unbeatable, but you bleed and die as easy as any human."

"We do not think ourselves unbeatable," the skinchanger hissed, face turning red. With pain or anger, I couldn't tell which.

"Nothing is unbeatable," the skinchanger snarled, "unless it be a sibling of Rahys."

My knights laughed with the torturers. A few of the younger ones bumped each other.

"Now you're talking about fairy tales, skinchanger?" asked the torturer with the pliers, egged on by his audience's amusement. "What next? You think your dead people in the stars are going to come and save you?"

I was not listening as the skinchanger spat back a reply. My mind had stopped on something that the creature had said. I had been a fool, I realized as I watched the skinchanger tortured to death without telling us any information as to where more of its people were. A fool blinded by what I could see, and not what I learned.

"The Seven Siblings of Rahys" was an old story, one that was told to children to make them behave. In the early days of Argdrion, the story went, seven wiar siblings, greedy beyond imagining, thought that they should control all of Argdrion. Spurred by their pride and greed, these siblings formed an army and began attacking their fellow wiar. Their parents, the king and queen of the wiar, were horrified at what their children were doing and after gathering their own army, went to war against the seven siblings. The king was killed in this battle, and the queen, grief-stricken, threw herself from a tower.

The Sisters stepped in then, for they had been watching with growing anger the evil actions of the seven wiar siblings. They cursed the seven siblings and cast them out of Argdrion, sending them to a world of darkness and fire. The Sisters named the seven wiar siblings Rahys, which means, in the old religion, sin.

The interesting part of the story was that the Seven Siblings of Rahys were said to be immortal, so that they could suffer forever in their otherworld prison. They were also said to be monsters of enormous size. Monsters that were nigh invincible.

My mind whirled as the skinchanger died, a new idea taking shape in it. If the old religion was true, and the Sisters real, then the Seven Siblings of Rahys were real and were somewhere in a parallel world to Argdrion, immortal and invincible. If I could get a heart of one of the Seven Siblings, then I could change into its body. And if I could change into its body, I would never need to change again, for I would have a body that would not die, that could not be destroyed.

But how would I get one of the siblings' hearts? The portals to the otherworlds had long ago been destroyed, being magical, and even if there were one left, who would I find to go and fetch a heart for me from an otherworld?

"Your Majesty?"

I blinked, realizing someone had been talking to me for several minutes, and glanced up.

The interrogators kicked disgustedly at the skinchanger's dead body in the pit below. The chains holding it up rattled as it swayed.

An ancient servant stepped into the pit, white hair glowing in the light of torches on either side of the door. "There is an army approaching the city, Your Majesty," the servant quavered. "An army of skinchangers."

My knights cursed and hurried out of the room, jostling the servant between them as they ran out the door.

I followed them slowly, still wondering if the old religion was true, and if it was, how I could get a heart of one of the Seven Siblings of Rahys.

"And Your Majesty," the servant said as I made to pass him. His voice was weak and scratchy, and his breath smelled like rotten garlic.

I turned partway toward the servant, my stomach turning as his breath hit me full in the face.

"The queen is nearing her birthing time, Your Majesty," the man croaked.

I blinked. My new body was coming. But would I need it?

Not if I get one of the siblings' hearts...

"The physicians are sure it is a boy, Your Majesty," the servant said behind me.

I moved through the doorway leading out of the pit and headed down the hallway on the opposite side. I had thought to change into my son's body once he was old enough, but now the thought seemed foolish, small.

"Your Majesty?" the servant quavered behind me, bones cracking and popping as he hurried to keep up with me.

I glanced over my shoulder at the old man.

"The queen wishes to know what you would like to name the boy."

I stopped and stared at the servant for a moment, my mind in an otherworld, envisioning a monstrous creature that would one day hold my soul. "Name him? I don't care what she names him," I said, turning as the heavy beat of the drums that signaled enemies approaching resonated through the castle.

"Yes, Your Majesty," the servant said behind me. And then, a few heartbeats later, "What shall I tell Her Majesty?"

I glanced out a window as the hallway opened up on one side to overlook a courtyard below and beyond the castle wall. "Tell her that I do not have time to think of names for a child," I murmured, eyes straying to the ominous storm clouds rolling toward the city. "Tell her that I have a battle to fight."

The old servant nodded and bowing crookedly, moved off down a side hall.

Warhorses clattered into the courtyard below, led by squires with wild eyes and pale faces. I heard bells begin to toll in the city, echoing the warning of those ringing in the castle. I moved down the hallway again, pulling my gloves on as I went.

No, I did not have time to name my son, for not only did I have a battle to fight and a war to win, I had a dragon's heart to find.

CHAPTER 50

Nathaira

I t's dirty," Nathaira said, staring down at the sprawling smoky city. The killer, leaning on her for support, hummed in agreement.

The sound made Nathaira's body vibrate. He looked pale this morning, and a thin sheen of sweat covered his sharp face.

They stood on the edge of a towering gray cliff face that overlooked a valley surrounded by cliffs, their cloaks lifting in a warm breeze as the distant sound of bells drifted up to them.

"The Valley of Stones, and Rothborn inside, was once home to the largest group of diamond and other precious-stone mines in Argdrion," the killer said. "The wars taxed the mines, and during the end of the Second War, they played out." He pointed at the city below. "Rothborn became a ghost town for some time after that, until the underworld lords took it over and turned it into one of the seediest and wealthiest cities in Argdrion."

There was weariness in the killer's voice as he said that last sentence. Nathaira glanced up at him.

It had been four days since they had left the Forest Folk, four agonizing days of helping the killer down a muddy human road. Each day he grew a little stronger, but it wasn't fast enough.

The killer met her gaze, and Nathaira looked back at the city, glittering windows flashing at her. She had thought of kissing him in the Forest Folks' home, wondered what it would be like. She hated herself for it, but she had.

What would Athrysion think? Moirin? Zeythra?

Nathaira stared at the city, an eagle lazily gliding over the valley catching her eye. Was Efamar down there, waiting for her? Did he even know that she was still alive? Was he still alive?

A shimmering golden stream of fire shot out of the city, startling the eagle as it exploded in a catacomb of sparks. Nathaira inhaled sharply.

The killer smiled next to her. "Fireworks," he said. "With the first day of summer tomorrow, thousands have swarmed to Rothborn for its Summer's Eve festivities. Fireworks, it would appear, are on the menu for tonight's activities. Wait till you see them at night," he added at the look of wonder on Nathaira's face.

Fireworks. Nathaira watched the sparks from the firework fade into the blue sky. Moirin had told her of the powder and chemical explosives the humans used for entertainment purposes. She had said they were wonderful.

"Let's go," the killer said.

Nathaira heard the exhaustion in his voice. She turned, him still leaning on her for support, and they started down the road winding down the cliff face and toward the city below.

It took them two hours to reach the bottom of the Valley of Stones, and when they finally set foot on the valley's rocky floor, their clothes were coated in dry, itchy dust, and their skin was drenched in sweat.

They walked underneath a dark stone arch stretching between two tall stone buildings strung with brightly colored flags and headed into the city beyond.

Tall buildings, crowded streets, thousands of humans... Rothborn looked like Crystoln, if not dirtier.

Nathaira ducked her head as a passing man stared at her. The leaf dress and cloak the Forest Folk had given her were conspicuous, but going naked was her only other option since she had lost her clothes in the fight with the witches, and if she did that, her tattoos would give her away in a flash. Not to mention that most humans didn't walk around naked.

"Is it always this hot here?" she asked the killer as they moved past an open-air sweet stand that smelled of cinnamon. Her voice choked on dust as they pushed their way past a group of men. They were from Oridonn judging by their almond-shaped eyes and long, curling mustaches. They were talking of war.

Nathaira caught a little of what they were saying, how Zarcayra, Araysann's only kingdom, had landed on Warulan's eastern coast in battle formation not two weeks ago. They were there to make war against Eromor, who had killed their king. Nathaira glanced at the Oridonnian men. Another war? Didn't the humans remember how many of all races, including their own, had died in the last wars?

"Pretty much," the killer replied to her question about the heat. He lifted a fat pear of deepest yellow from a fruit seller's stand. A warm breeze carrying the scent of perfume, food, and too many bodies pressed closely together ruffled the brightly colored flags draped from every arch, storefront, and window on the street. "The Valley of Stones is Argdrion's Furnace, they say, and in the summer it gets to well over a hundred and ten degrees." The killer bit into the pear, juice dribbling down his chin.

Nathaira watched an older white-haired woman walk past. Her hair reminded her of the witches.

The Forest Folk had used a cloaking spell to hide their trail from the witches, and when they left, they had assured them that the witches, even with their excellent tracking skills, would not be able to find them.

Nathaira was relieved. The killer seemed to doubt it.

"FRESH BREAD!" bellowed a fat woman from an open-air stand.

Nathaira jumped at the voice, hand sliding into an eagle's foot inside her cloak.

The killer, arm slung over her shoulder, rested his hand against her arm. "Calm down, Nathaira," he said softly. "Jumpiness will only bring attention to you."

"You said you would not say my name," Nathaira hissed, letting her hand slide back into its natural shape.

"I lied," the killer said, biting into the pear again. "And it's such a pretty name that I can't help but use it."

Nathaira resisted the urge to slice him open with an eagle claw.

They moved on down the street, the fat woman's yells of "RYE! WHITE! BARLEY! BAKED TODAY, GET 'EM WHILE THEY'RE HOT!" echoing after them.

Nathaira watched the passing humans, brightly clothed Oridonn traders, turbaned Zarcayrans, and red-haired Wyvernosans all catching her eye. There weren't any soldiers, though. Why weren't there any soldiers?

She voiced this out loud to the killer, and he glanced at her. "Rothborn prides itself on welcoming most everyone," he said. "Thieves, murderers, underworld lords... Most of the inhabitants in this city are wanted for something. The authorities know it's too much trouble to try and bring order to the city, and it brings in quite a lot of money for many of the said authorities, so they leave it alone. The only enforcers of what little law Rothborn has are the underworld lord's goons."

Nathaira watched a young boy slip an envelope out of a woman's pocket.

The killer slowed as they approached a building with a wooden board full of flapping papers, and they stopped in front of the posters, staring at them.

Nathaira's eye caught on one poster in particular.

"WANTED!" the yellowing papers screamed at the top in bold inked letters, and underneath: "Alive, for the sum of twenty thousand aray. Crime: conspiring with a known magic user and killing the king's men." Below the words was a drawing of the killer, his thin face and scar-cut eyebrow caught perfectly.

A red-haired rent boy and laughing woman walked past and into the tavern. The killer bit into his pear again.

"You're hunted now too?" Nathaira said, voice low.

The killer pulled the paper off the wall, a small piece staying behind under the steel nail it had hung from. "It would appear that way," he said. He studied the paper for a while before holding it out to her. "I look cross-eyed."

Nathaira took the paper. Because he had risked his life for her, he was being hunted. And he didn't seem bothered by it. She looked up at the board, at a rough sketch of her on another poster. Her skin crawled. If one human thought she looked suspicious, she could be exposed.

The poster of the killer floated out of her hand on a slow, hot breeze and stuck on the side of a passing carriage, which rolled away into the crowd.

They started moving again, pushing their way through the shoving, talking crowd.

"What are you going to do about it?" Nathaira asked, dusty dress rustling around her as she stepped over a fresh pile of horse manure.

"What?" the killer asked, throwing the pear away into the tramping feet. He seemed revived by the food.

"The poster."

"Oh… nothing. Not right now, anyway."

They walked under another arch shadowing the well-worn cobbles beneath them and into a shadowed overhang.

A teenage girl with flowers in her hair gasped and ran eagerly toward them. "It's beautiful!" she said, reaching for Nathaira's dress.

Nathaira hissed and pulled backward from the girl and away from the killer, panic racing through her as the girl pulled the sleeve of the dress away from her skin and exposed several of her tattoos.

"Where did you get it?" the girl breathed. "Did you make it yourself?"

Nathaira saw the killer move next to her, heard the shing of steel on leather.

The girl crumpled to the cobbles, flowers falling off her heads.

"Why did you kill her?" Nathaira cried out, shocked. She glanced from the girl to the killer. And where had he gotten another knife? When the Forest Folk had healed him, they had found no weapons on him.

"She might have seen your tattoos and turned us in," the killer said, wiping the knife blade off on a flag hanging from a post.

Nathaira glanced back at the girl, a pool of blood slowly spreading out from underneath her. "But you said that there are no authorities…" she exclaimed.

"And you don't like humans, so why care if one dies?" the killer asked, making the knife disappear to wherever he had pulled it from. Nathaira looked up at him. He raised one eyebrow and moved to lean on her shoulders again.

They started forward again.

Nathaira glanced behind them as they walked away. She did not like humans, but it was still murder, and the girl had meant no harm.

The killer, still leaning on her, stopped at a sweet shop a few feet later. They stepped inside, and he nodded at the chocolates kept on ice in a glass display case.

The hawk-nosed shopkeeper moved to put some in a bag.

"Your problem, Nathaira," the killer murmured softly, "is that you really do care about humans, no matter how much you try to deny it."

"Or maybe I just value life," Nathaira replied stiffly as the shopkeeper handed the killer a paper bag full of chocolates. She hated the killer anew. Hated his disrespect for life. His arrogance.

The killer tossed a capus over the low wooden counter and reaching into the bag, popped a piece of milky brown chocolate into his mouth. "Do you?" he queried, looking at her.

A woman with two crying children pushed wearily into the shop, letting her offspring loose to smudge the candy-filled glass display cases scattered around the cool stone room as she eased down on a bench by the door.

The boy of the two children, a fat-nosed child with glistening snot drying on his leather jerkin, shoved past to look at the green and red iced candies in the case in front of him.

Nathaira saw the killer's fingers twitch.

"Where is this mansion of yours?" she asked, hoping to distract him from slicing the children open too.

"That's going to melt outside, you know," the shop owner interrupted in a nasally voice.

Nathaira glanced at him.

The man jutted his beaklike nose at the bag of chocolates in the killer's hand, "Unless you buy some ice to keep it cool."

"If I shoved it up your ass it'd melt too," the killer said, not looking at the man. "Not far," he added to her.

The shop owner blinked. The killer started back outside, Nathaira supporting him.

Zen and Yar were balanced atop the cliffs on the western edge of the valley when they reached the killer's mansion, and the late-afternoon's suns' rays warmed the double iron gates leading to the impending building with a golden-rosy glow.

The killer threw his last piece of chocolate into his mouth and crumpled the bag up in one hand, then tossed it into the narrow cobble street behind them. He pulled on a black cord dangling down in front of one of the ivy-bound stone pillars set in the equally ivy-covered walls bordering the gates.

A small silver bell hanging on one of the gates tinkled sharply.

Footsteps sounded on the gray stone walkway lined with wildly twisting wintergreen bushes and creeping honeysuckle on the other side of the gates, and a moment later a middle-aged man with chin-length braided silver hair and a dark-green coat that lapped at his ankles appeared around a bend on the path.

"You did not say that anyone would be here," Nathaira whispered sharply.

The killer glanced sideways at her, sucking at his teeth. "How else do you think my houses are run?" he said calmly as the silver-haired man approached. "Don't worry, you'll be safe at Windthorn. Aynon, my overseer," he called as the man reached the double iron gates, "how's the weather keeping you?"

"I am well, sir," the overseer replied with a quick, tight-lipped smile. He stopped in front of the gates and produced a key out of his coat's breast pocket. "I have a message for you, sir."

"Oh?" the killer said. "Who from?"

"I do not know, sir, he didn't leave his name. He just said to tell you that if you wanted something of great value and rare existence, to come to the eastern city tonight during the festivities."

"Interesting," the killer said as the overseer pulled the gates open.

The gates swung inward, the twisting, thorn-covered W in their center splitting in two, and the killer and Nathaira stepped through.

Nathaira glanced at the overseer as they walked past, but he didn't give her more than a passing glance.

They climbed the thirteen stairs leading to the double black doors of the mansion.

Glossy green ivy wound up the brick walls on either side of the doors and circled the grooved pillars marking the corners of the patio at the top of the stairs.

"Of course, this means you'll have to come with me tonight," the killer said as they topped the last stair. Nathaira glanced sideways at him. "I fear that I'm not strong enough yet to walk on my own, and I'll need your help getting around in the city."

Nathaira wanted to gut him. She had a feeling that he was toying with her, but she couldn't be certain.

Why won't you heal him so I may leave?

The killer placed a hand on the tarnished brass handles of the carved doors of the mansion, pushing them open. A circular stone room met them on the other side, a tinkling stone fountain in the shape of a faun dominating the center.

Black and white tiles wound away from the fountain in a spiral pattern, and a round iron-latticed window sat in the ceiling high above their heads.

Stairs wound up either side of the room, leading to other levels.

Nathaira saw the killer glance at her out of the corner of her eye. "Welcome to Windthorn," he said.

#

Nathaira listened to the overseer's footsteps fade, eyes scanning the large bedroom he'd escorted her to. The walls were a smooth mossy green offset by dark-gold molding that curved and swirled in leaf and vine patterns. The floor was of polished oak and accented by several gold-tasseled rugs of the same green as the walls, and the furniture was slender and delicate, like the crystal chandelier in the shape of hanging branches that hung from the mossy-green ceiling.

Nathaira stepped away from the narrow oak door, crisscrossed with heavy studded iron bars, and curled her dusty toes into the softness of a green rug with delicate golden vines and flowers swirling over it. She was so close to where Efamar might be, and yet she still had to help the killer until he was healed. Her hands curled. She was trying to uphold her people's honor, but why was it so hard?

Nathaira let her gaze wander over a slender engraved oaken wardrobe and a wing-backed couch of mixed green and gold.

She padded across the rug and past a four-pillared oaken bed draped with green voile to an open iron and glass door that revealed a stone balcony beyond.

A tangled garden stretched away from the stone walls of the mansion below the balcony, winding rose bushes and twisting sloe and crab apple trees fighting for dominance over the overgrown hedged pathways. Fountains speckled with red moss were placed sporadically throughout the garden.

Nathaira curled her hands over the top of the stone railing of the balcony, her gaze traveling over the overgrown gardens and the nearby peaks of another mansion and to the city beyond.

The Brothers had slipped almost completely behind the dark cliffs circling the Valley of Stones, and the vibrant red, orange, and golden hues lighting up the sky from their setting made the roofs and windows of the human city glow like fire.

The killer had said he wanted to rest before they went to the city tonight, get his strength back before he met the man who had left a message for him. Nathaira wished he would get his strength back, wished he would heal quicker.

She stared at the burning city, the heat of the day slowly fading as stars began winking to life.

You thought about kissing him... a soft voice whispered in her head.

A pair of golden eagles lazily soared over the valley, the tips of their wings seeming to brush with the appearing stars for how high they flew.

Nathaira followed the birds' movements, the sweet, wild smell of the garden brushing her sharp nostrils. She had thought about kissing the killer, yes. But the thought had only come from excitement and the fact that the killer was an attractive man, and nothing more.

She would not let it be anything more.

Nathaira turned her gaze back to the glowing city as the eagles faded into the distance, the faraway tinny ringing of bells on a clock tower echoing up as the suns slowly slipped behind the cliffs and the Sisters took their place in the darkening sky.

Her eighteenth nameday was tomorrow.

The sky turned a burning orange. Nathaira stared at it. Normally she would feel excitement at turning another year older, but this year she felt nothing but numbness and the urgent need to find Efamar.

She stared at the city, wondering if Efamar was in it. She itched to be off looking for him.

The suns disappeared behind the cliffs surrounding the Valley of Stones. Nathaira moved back into the bedroom.

Dust fell off her and onto the ornate green carpet under the bed. Nathaira glanced down at the dust-coated leaf dress and cloak the Forest Folk had given her and then up at the wardrobe.

Dozens of dresses filled the carved closet—shades of blue, red, gold, green, and pink, all creating a beautiful rainbow.

Nathaira pulled a green satin dress out, its long sleeves and high neckline catching her eye. She tossed it on the bed and glanced around for something to wipe her body of its dust.

A carved door with a golden handle caught her attention. She moved to it and cautiously pulled it open. A circular stone room sat on the other side of the door, dotted with crystalline windows and filled by a sunken tile pool of blue water.

Candles flickered in niches in the walls of the room, and rose petals floated on the surface of the water.

Nathaira breathed in the smell of the flowers. She hated the humans' cities and homes, but where baths were concerned, she did have to admit that their methods were superior to those of skinchangers.

She slipped out of her cloak and dress and stepped into the warm pool, swimming for the middle.

#

The killer was waiting by the faun fountain when she came down the stairs later, leaning on an ivory-knobbed cane of epharia wood.

"There's something so fascinating about a flower," he said, fingering the white petals of a water lily he'd plucked from the pool at the faun's feet. "One of the most delicate things in existence, it somehow manages to survive the blazing suns and summer rains and still look as beautiful as the day that it was born." The killer crumpled the lily in one hand, scarred fingers curling over the delicate flower like claws.

He had traded in his usual clothes and was garmented in a pair of long, slender-waisted black pants, black shoes, a black cotton high-collared shirt, and a knee-length fitted black coat of velvet that flared at the bottom and hugged his lean shoulders with graceful ease.

Nathaira stepped off the stairs, the green dress hissing around her.

The dress covered most of her tattoos, but her face was still open for anyone to see, making her nervous. There had been nothing in the closet to cover it with, though, and the cloak the Forest Folk had given her had disintegrated as soon as she had taken it off.

The killer let the crumpled petals of the lily fall from his slim fingers and into the water of the fountain and turned. His ice and pine eyes ran boldly up and down her body. He smiled softly, eyes going to hers. "Has anyone ever told you that you are beautiful?"

Nathaira met his gaze. He looked especially handsome too in his new clothes, but she would never say it.

"Your carriage is ready, sir," the overseer said, appearing in the iron arch behind her.

Nathaira turned her head away from him, hiding her tattoos.

The killer stepped toward her, holding up a golden mask lined with flashing diamonds. "Everyone is wearing them," he said, slipping the mask onto her face as the overseer moved further into the room.

Nathaira watched the overseer as the killer slid behind her and tied the laces of the mask over her hair, heartbeat quickening. Had he seen her tattoos? If he had, his face didn't show his reaction.

The killer's finger brushed against her neck, and Nathaira inhaled at the tingling sensation that his flesh sliding over hers made. "I could have tied it myself," she said, turning slightly.

"Shall I have your carriage brought around, sir?" the overseer asked, voice toneless.

"Yes," the killer replied.

The overseer nodded and moved to the entry doors, steps even, unhurried.

"I know," the killer whispered in her ear in reply to her earlier statement, "but it's so much more fun if I do it." His lips brushed softly against her ear, and Nathaira pulled back sharply.

The overseer, appearing back in the doorway, glanced at them.

The killer tied a matching mask onto his face and put his hand out for her to take.

Nathaira looked from him to the overseer. It would be suspicious if she made a scene.

"Shall we go, my lady?" the killer asked, bowing slightly.

Nathaira looked back at the overseer, realizing they were playing a part for the man's benefit.

Did that mean that the killer didn't trust him? She put her hand in the killer's, and he drew her toward him and looped his right arm through hers.

They moved toward the front doors, the overseer watching them with his slate-gray eyes as they passed.

The front steps and courtyard below were bathed in a golden hue from several torches in iron brackets on the pillars at the top of the stairs, and an elegant black carriage glimmered in the light as four gray horses tossed their slender heads and nickered impatiently.

"Your carriage, my lady," the killer said.

They walked to the softly glittering coach, the silver tip on the bottom of the killer's cane tapping on the flagstones of the courtyard.

A short man with skin deeply burned from the suns bowed at the waist as they approached the carriage, and with a flourish of a gloved hand, opened the door of the enclosed vehicle.

Nathaira stared at the dark interior. The last human wagon she had rode in had held chains of burning silver.

"The past will always haunt us," the killer said in her ear, as if reading her mind. His scent of leather and steel whirled around her. "But how we choose to respond to it is ours to decide."

"I don't need your advice," Nathaira replied coldly, breaking out of her trance. She pulled away from him, ignoring his offered hand, and stepped up into the black coach in a hiss of sliding satin.

The interior smelled of leather and perfume.

The killer stepped in behind her, the carriage rocking slightly, and the coachman shut the door with a click behind them as the killer set his cane down and took a seat opposite her.

A moment later they were off, rattling over the gray stones of the courtyard and passing through the open iron gates and down the cobbled street toward the city.

Dark mansions flashed by, occupants out for the night at the city's festivities. Nathaira glanced out her window as they rolled past the last one, a roaring bonfire in the center of a side street with humans in assorted masks twirling and leaping around it catching her eye as they entered the lower section of city. The fire reminded her of the flames that had engulfed the clan's tree home, the dancing people reminded her of the slavers attacking them.

"Nervous?" the killer asked softly.

Nathaira looked over at him.

He was watching her, eyes reflecting the light of the fires outside as the noise of laughter and singing and fire and music echoed into the carriage.

Nathaira glanced back out the window at the humans crowding the streets, slowing their carriage to a crawl. She wasn't nervous, more afraid. Afraid that someone would recognize her, afraid that she would be captured again and killed, but mostly afraid that she would not find Efamar in Rothborn.

"I don't like crowds," she said aloud.

Three men shooting white fire out of their mouths drew the applause of a gathered crowd.

"That makes two of us," the killer replied, looking out his window.

The carriage slowed to a stop, and a moment later the coachman opened the door for them with another deep bow.

Nathaira stepped out onto the cobbled street.

Cool night air stroked her skin through the satin of the dress, making goosebumps rise on her arms and legs.

Sparks from dozens of bonfires hissed toward the stars. A child holding a paper dragon on a stick with orange paper flames crackling out of its mouth ran by, giggling. The smell of roasting apples and sickly sweet beer wafted through the air. Sellers with carts yelled their wares, flags in all colors of the rainbow flapped lazily in an unfelt breeze, and everywhere there was room to stand were humans with elaborate masks, expensive clothes, and gaudy jewelry.

"Would the lovely lady like a rose?"

Nathaira turned at the honeyed voice.

A stick-thin man gave a cross-legged bow, a mask of black metal and gleaming gold carved in the likeness of a goat with curved horns covering his face.

"No," the killer said, appearing at her elbow. "Go find someone else to play with, trickster." He looped his arm through hers and turned, moving off up the street.

"Don't hold me so close," Nathaira hissed as they weaved through a close-knit crowd watching a troupe of half-naked dancers.

The killer didn't look at her. "I need your support," he replied.

He was looking for something, Nathaira noted, his eyes darting around the crowded streets and tall buildings around them. She glanced over her shoulder at the man who'd offered her the rose. He was doing cartwheels for a small crowd now.

"Why didn't you let that man give me the rose?"

"Hmm? Oh... because red is not really your color," the killer said as they walked by shops closed for the night's activities. "And besides," he said, glancing at her finally, "those roses are not all that they seem."

"How so?" Nathaira asked, stepping around a pile of waste. Human or otherwise, she couldn't, and didn't want to, know.

"They're enchanted," the killer replied, following her around a couple kissing passionately. "And whoever smells them will fall madly in love with the person who gave it to them."

Nathaira looked up at him, her dress sliding against her skin as she walked. "What happened to magic being outlawed?"

The killer glanced down a dark alley as they walked by it, the white gems on his mask glinting sharply in the light of the bonfires lining the street. "In Rothborn, as long as your magic isn't too extravagant to attract the attention of the rest of the world, you can pretty much get away with whatever you want."

Nathaira glanced back at the crowd the man had disappeared into.

Hypocrites.

"Now, aren't you glad I stopped you from taking that flower?" the killer asked.

She looked at him again. His eyes sparkled with a hidden smile.

"You'd have been slobbering all over that man the rest of the night."

Nathaira didn't reward him with a reply.

They passed underneath a bobbing chain of lanterns throwing a rainbow of light onto passersby in hues of red, blue, green, yellow, and orange and turned down a side street crammed with masked festivegoers.

A shower of red and gold sparks exploded in the sky above them with a deep boom, making the crowd gasp in wonder.

Nathaira craned her neck back as the killer pushed through the oohing crowd, giving an awed gasp. An eagle lit up the night sky, mouth open in a scream.

"I told you they are better at night," the killer said in her ear.

The killer bought two bowls of tomato soup from a soup stand on a corner, and they watched the fireworks as they ate, the ground shaking under them with every boom.

Nathaira glanced around the street and at a nearby courtyard with a bonfire and dancing humans in it as she sipped at the warm bowl of soup in her hands. Was Efamar nearby, watching the fireworks from a cell? The thought that he might be nearby while she was stuck, unable to look for him, was maddening.

A man in a silver mask moved toward them. Nathaira, now watching a sparkling blue firework of a whale, felt the killer watching him from next to her.

"You came," the man said, stopping beside them. "Who's this?"

"Lover," the killer said.

Nathaira stiffened.

The man didn't seem to notice.

"She can't come, you have to be alone."

"And what exactly is it that I'm seeing alone?" the killer asked.

"Something fabulous," the man replied, glancing around. "You'll like it, trust me."

"I don't," the killer said. "But you've heard enough about me to know that I will kill you if this is some kind of a trap, so I must say that I am intrigued. Dear," he said to her.

Nathaira glanced at him.

"Could you wait for me for a few moments? There's something I must attend to." And just like that, he was gone.

Nathaira stared at the spot where the killer had been. She was alone.

I should leave. She watched the dancers wheel. But the killer wasn't healed completely yet, and until he was, she had to stay, like he had when she had been wounded.

Sisters, please help him to heal quickly.

A man in a striped zebra mask appeared in front of her, his skin a glistening ebony beneath the green velvet jacket he wore.

"You're the one they're looking for," the man said in a deep voice that carried over the noise of the dancers and a street band.

Nathaira's fingers slid into talons.

"You're the skinchanger," the man said.

She turned, ready to run.

"I know where your brother is," the man rumbled behind her.

Nathaira stopped, her heart hammering in her chest.

"Where?" Nathaira asked. She glanced around at the humans watching the fireworks as another explosion, this one a purple flower, shook the air. No one was paying her any attention.

She wheeled and took three quick steps toward the man and grabbed his arm with the talons of an eagle. "Where is my brother?" she hissed breathlessly.

Firelight from the nearby bonfire glinted off the man's mask. The dancers twirled behind them.

"First, answer me one question," the man said, seemingly oblivious to the talons digging into his flesh. "The woman you were caged with on the slaver train. What happened to her?"

Nathaira narrowed her golden eyes. "How do you know about her?" she asked suspiciously. "And how do you know I was on a slaver train?"

"Because I was on the same wagon train," the man said, dark eyes glinting within his mask. "And I saw you and the woman."

"I did not see you," Nathaira replied sharply, tightening her grip on the man's arm. One word out of him and the whole of the city would be down on her, demanding her death.

"Part of the train left when you were still unconscious," the man said. "I was in that part, with your brother."

Nathaira inhaled sharply.

Was it true? Could it be true? "And you saw where he was taken?" she asked. "Tell me!" She stepped closer to the man. She could smell the rich scent of walnuts wafting off him.

"First, tell me what happened to Cordelia," he said.

So that was her name. Nathaira felt a small stab of guilt. "She died," she said. "On the ship over."

The man's eyes glistened with more than the bonfire's light. "How?" It was his turn to step closer.

Nathaira moved backward as his coat brushed against her dress. She let go of his arm but kept her hand in the shape of an eagle's foot. "They put her in a cell with two men to save room," she replied, voice low as dancers whirled maddeningly close to them in their ever-widening dance around the bonfire. "They tried to rape her, and she fought them, and they killed her... I'm sorry," Nathaira added.

The man looked away, the jutting nose of his zebra mask accentuated against the roaring fire behind him. "And the men?" he asked, hands clenching and unclenching at his sides. "What happened to them?"

"I killed them," Nathaira replied, hand slipping back into its normal shape as a trio of dancers whisked inches away from them and fanned her face with their laughter.

The man looked back at her. "Thank you."

"I didn't do it for you," Nathaira replied, not unkindly. Her hair lifted on a gentle night breeze that took the sparks leaping above the fire high into the night sky.

Another firework exploded above them, a peacock with multicolored feathers. The crowd oohed.

"Thank you all the same," the man said. "She was a friend."

"She was kind to me," Nathaira said. "Now what of my brother?" She stepped closer to the man again as the dancers began clapping their hands in time to the music drifting out from the street bands' drums, flutes, and guitars. "Where is he?"

The man stepped sideways as a dancer bumped into him.

Nathaira's hand shot out and wrapped around his arm again, keeping him from leaving.

He glanced down at it. "Nilfinhèim," he said, looking back up at her from under thick black eyelashes shot with specks of silver. "Your brother was taken to Nilfinhèim."

A couple in matching elephant masks trimmed with trails of flashing diamonds danced past, laughing. Shadows of the dancers leapt and twirled over the crowd watching the fireworks.

Nathaira stared at the man. Nilfinhèim was thousands of miles away. Why would the humans take Efamar all the way there? She thought back on what Moirin had told her of the far northern continent, a frozen wasteland of snow, ice caverns, giant trees with icicles for needles, and wind that bit through all clothing. But there was no arena there, so what reason could the humans possibly have for taking Efamar to such a place?

"How do you know this?" Nathaira asked, talons curling into his thick arm.

"We were taken to the city of Ulyotra on Ennotar's northeastern coast, where the ships were bound for Nilfinhèim docks," he said.

"And why did you not go too?"

"My leg was broken when a horse stepped on me," he said. "The slavers sold me cheap in the town to a blacksmith who wanted help, and when I mended, I escaped to Warulan."

"Where in Nilfinhèim was my brother taken?" Nathaira asked, already thinking of how to get there. She would need a ship. Swimming that far would be impossible, even as a fish, and to get a ship she would need to travel to Warulan's northeastern coast. Hundreds of miles in the opposite direction.

"That I do not know," the man murmured, glancing over her head and into the crowd. "But he was taken to Nilfinhèim."

Nathaira let go of his arm again. How would she get there if she was still helping the killer? Or would she still help him now that she knew where her brother was?

"Thank you for telling me thi—" Nathaira started, looking up.

The man was gone.

She scanned the dancers, but he was nowhere to be seen.

She turned, pushing her way through the crowd. She knew where Efamar was now.

Nathaira slowed, glancing behind her. She felt a pull to stay and wait for the killer. But he had left her, and things were different now. She knew where Efamar was.

She moved off down the street again, pushing through the jostling crowd. She stopped at an intersection of four streets, glancing behind her again. Efamar was alive, alone, waiting.

"I am sorry, Sisters," she whispered. She turned and picked the street to the left, then headed down it.

She knew where Efamar, and she was going to save him.

CHAPTER 51

Esadora

ood nymphs. The air reeked of their woodsy, earthy smell, and the ground showed evidence of their rootlike footprints. For those who knew where to look, anyway. A crushed piece of grass, the slight indent of a root mark. Wood nymphs excelled at hiding their trail, but to the trained and extraordinary eye of a witch, the signs were there.

Esadora traced an overturned pebble with two skeletal fingers. The magical creatures had met the skinchanger and Darkmoon by the stream and taken them...

Where? Esadora raised her face to a breeze that rustled through the tall strands of grass crowding the meadow and breathed deeply. Only the scent of wood, water, and distant snow-capped mountains filled her nostrils.

Damn, but they're good. She stood and jumping lightly over the stream, examined the untouched grass on the other side. Her fingers curled and uncurled around Slayn's bone handle. She hated wood nymphs. They were one of the most honorable, caring, and just race of creatures that had ever walked Argdrion. She wished that they had all been destroyed in the Hunting.

Esadora leaned closer to the ground to look at several blades of grass that were broken in half and flapped, bent over, in the breeze. She and her sisters had tracked the skinchanger and Darkmoon for over forty miles after the fight with the soldiers of Eromor, but the skinchanger had had too much of a lead on them, and by the time they had caught up with her fresh scent in the meadow they stood in now, she and Darkmoon had vanished.

Esadora hissed at the memory. The gods must be mad at them, for then it had rained nonstop for two days straight, a heavy downpour that had obscured the trees in front of them, much less any hint of a trail, and they had been forced to wait until it let up to a search the meadow for a clue as to where their prey had gone.

Esadora plucked the broken purple petal of a moonflower from among the grass. She raised it to her nose. It smelled of rain but also faintly of wood nymphs and witch blood.

She crushed the petal in one fist, light-purple juice staining her white skin. Only a handful. That was all that remained of the wood nymphs.

Esadora stood and threw the broken petal away into the field of green blades around her. Only a handful, and they had to be in the Ilgerion Forest to find the skinchanger and Darkmoon.

Gods damn those creatures, and the gods damn the skinchanger.

Esadora ground her black fangs together. When witches and warlocks grew old, their children killed and ate them with the belief that whatever skills and wisdom their parents had would then be passed on to them.

Esadora moved on up the stream, studying the grass and scanning the small round rocks lining the water. Her mother had excelled at catching her prey, and she had never lost a quarry in her life.

Esadora heard her clan's old leader in her head, telling her that she was a failure, a weakling. She had killed that clan leader when she turned 130, and although she knew that the witch had been wrong, she still sometimes wondered if perhaps she was a failure. It had not been uncommon during the wars for clans of witches and warlocks to be wiped out or to lose half their members, but the wars and the Hunting had been over for years now, and yet she had lost two sisters in one night.

Witches and warlocks would say that she was a poor clan leader, that her sisters' deaths were on her head.

Esadora sliced a gently bobbing moonflower off its thick green stalk with Slayn and let out a scream that sent a softly hooting horned owl flapping off its perch in the top of a goyr tree in the nearby forest. She watched the speckled bird disappear into the forest, her voice echoing harmlessly off into the cool night air. Fifty thousand was not enough for two sisters dead.

"Here, clan leader!" Ayrsah called from down the stream.

Esadora glanced up at the younger witch and stepped over a rotting log beside the stream, taking long, quick strides toward her.

"Footprints, or part of them, anyway," Ayrsah said with a nod toward the ground.

Esadora crouched down next to her sister and traced skeletal fingers across the partial outline of a foot with three long, thick roots growing out the front.

Perfect.

"It seems to be the only one," Ayrsah said slowly, glancing up at the waving grass of the meadow around.

"It doesn't matter," Esadora replied shortly, pushing herself to her feet and doing the same. The air rippled a little as she watched, and her black eyes spied a trampled spot of grass that hadn't been there a second before. She smiled, cheeks hurting from the burns she had received during her fight with Darkmoon.

The wood nymphs' magic is starting to wear off.

"It's all we need," Esadora said smugly. She pointed Slayn at the rippling air as another smashed-down spot of grass appeared farther out, as if an invisible creature was walking away from them and leaving its trail behind.

"Amazing," Ayrsah murmured, white hair lifting in another cool breeze.

"No," Esadora replied, "not amazing. Just a cloaking spell, and a good one too." She turned and yelled in the back of her throat for Rargyne, who was scanning the grass down the stream from them.

The quieter witch dropped a rock she'd been examining and started toward them, her long white hair lifting behind her as she ran.

"You're too young to remember these things," Esadora said, turning back to Ayrsah as the breeze rustled their hair and long V-cut skirts around them. "But in the Great Wars, such spells were quite common. A whole army could be hidden for up to three days if needed. It made for many a bloody and dark battle."

Esadora felt the old stab of pain as she remembered those times. And Orcyra.

"Teach me one," Ayrsah said.

Esadora didn't look at her. "You're too young," she said, spotting another mashed spot of grass as it appeared farther out in the meadow. "And it takes years to learn such spells."

Ayrsah didn't say anything, but Esadora could tell that she wasn't happy. It didn't matter. She was not clan leader, and only a clan leader knew when the time was right to teach the younger witches certain spells. Ayrsah, at seventy-five, was the youngest in their clan, and she had much to learn before she would be able to master a cloaking spell like the ones that the wood nymphs had used.

Esadora gripped Slayn. There had been another young witch who had wanted her to teach her advanced spells once, and she had been foolish and taught her even though she had not been ready. It had cost the witch her life, for she had not had the skill to do the spell in the heat and excitement of battle.

Rargyne, pale arm mended by a healing spell where the skinchanger had bitten her, padded up next to them through the tall grass.

Esadora raised her nose to the wind and took a slow, deep breath. There. She could smell them now—the skinchanger, Darkmoon, and the wood nymphs. Just a faint scent, but there nonetheless.

Esadora frowned. Darkmoon's scent should be that of a dead man, but there was life in his scent, life and breath. He should have been dead days ago from the witch blood in his veins. How was he not dead?

"The wood nymphs' magic is wearing off," she said, her raspy voice sounding foreign and strange in the quiet of the softly rustling grass and flowers. "We'll be able to track them now."

Esadora stuck Slayn into the sheath on her back and started forward. Ayrsah and Rargyne fell into place behind her.

More and more tracks appeared in the grass in front of them as they walked. Esadora sped up her pace as the scent became stronger. They were near to their quarry; she could sense it.

They swept into the woods, and Esadora broke into a run as the scent of goyr trees and rorbushes filled her nose. They would find the skinchanger and Darkmoon, she mused as she and her sisters tore through the forest. The suns were coming up in the east, early-morning light just starting to drift through the trees.

Esadora's black eyes flashed with bloodlust.

And when we do, they will die.

#

The city of Rothborn was alive with festivity.

Masked humans swarmed by the thousands through the streets, bonfires raged on every corner, food stands crowded the sides of the streets, fireworks exploded in the night sky above, and bobbing paper lanterns and waving flags decorated every building.

Esadora's mouth filled with saliva. There was enough fresh flesh in Rothborn to last her and her sisters for years, but they could not stay. The city wasn't safe for witches, and they had come for one purpose only: to find Darkmoon and the skinchanger.

A drunk bumped into her as he stumbled, bellowing down the street. Esadora shoved him away with a snarl before quickly pulling her hand back inside of her cloak as a nearby man glanced her way. It made her nervous to be around this many humans. If anyone saw their pointed teeth or their talons and figured out that witches were among them, they would never make it out of the city alive. They might take down a good hundred humans or so, but there were far too many to stand against and live.

Esadora slipped around a brightly attired juggler who had gathered a small crowd and raised her nose to the wind for Darkmoon's leather, steel, and blood scent and the skinchanger's wild, woodsy smell. She and her sisters had split up when they entered the city, keeping just in eyesight of each other but far enough apart that their above-average heights would not attract as much attention singly as together.

Esadora glanced at Rargyne, walking several yards behind her and then at Ayrsah, who moved along the wooden sidewalk that hugged the cobbled street's side. If they walked slowly and didn't attract attention, they would be fine... she hoped. And once they had found Darkmoon and the skinchanger, they would leave and head back to Vingorlon, where the food was scarce but the city was safe.

Darkmoon and the skinchanger's scent led in two different directions at an intersection of three packed streets. Esadora motioned for Rargyne and

Ayrsah to meet with her under the arch of a deserted alley.

"Which way, clan leader?" Ayrsah asked, scanning the busy street in front of them as they melded with the shadows of the alley. "Or should we split up?"

Esadora glanced up as two fireworks in the shape of the Brothers exploded in the night sky. The crowd in the street in front of her oohed, and she looked back down at them. She didn't want to split the clan up; it would make them weaker and more vulnerable. But they couldn't afford to follow the scent one way and have their prey leave the city by another while they hunted.

"Rargyne," Esadora rasped, causing the scout witch to look at her. "You follow the trail left, Ayrsah and I will go right. If you find them, mark the spot and come and find us. Do not try to take them on alone."

Rargyne nodded and moved off. Esadora watched her disappear into the crowd. There was one thing about all this that kept bothering her: the fact that Darkmoon was still alive. A normal human would have died hours after having that much witch blood inside of them, and yet here they were, three days after she had stabbed Darkmoon, and he was still alive.

Esadora motioned for Ayrsah to follow her and moved back out into the street, heading left after the scent. She knew that the wood nymphs had used their magic to heal Darkmoon once they had found him, she had smelled that, but how had he stayed alive those hours in between her stabbing him and the wood nymphs finding him?

Another firework exploded in the sky as they climbed a hill that led away from the night's festivities. Esadora felt the air vibrate around her.

They were heading into a residential area, with gated homes and glowing streetlamps lining either side of the street.

Darkmoon and the skinchanger's scent led them to two heavy iron gates with a twisting W in their center, and beyond, an ivy-covered brick mansion.

Esadora glanced up and down the long street. There was no one in sight. She latched on to the gate and vaulted over.

Ayrsah followed.

Dark evergreen bushes lined the driveway leading to the mansion on the other side of the gates. A lone candle burned in a window to the right of the door.

Esadora mounted the brick steps to the mansion's front doors. The scent of Darkmoon and the skinchanger was strong here, stronger than it had been anywhere else. Excitement and anticipation built in her stomach.

"Should we wait for Rargyne?" Ayrsah asked softly as they stopped in front of the double doors leading into the mansion.

Esadora looked up at an ivy-covered window far above the doors. "No," she said. It would take too long to wait for Rargyne, and she wanted to see Darkmoon and the skinchanger now, to feel their blood on her hands. Darkmoon was alive after she had stabbed him, but he was weak, she could smell it. And if he was weak, he would be easy to take down.

Esadora raised a skeletal hand and rapped twice on the mansion doors, reaching over her back and pulling Slayn off as the sound of her knocks faded off into the mansion. She nodded for Ayrsah to move to the shadows on the right side of the doors and took up a position on the left, waiting, listening, watching.

The sound of footsteps echoed from the other side of the doors a few minutes later.

Esadora glanced at Ayrsah, who held two long, curving daggers in her bony hands.

A man with braided hair opened one door, face long and bored. "I did not expect you back so soon, sir..." he said, trailing off as Esadora stepped from the shadows.

The man eyed her. He looked wary but seemingly unperturbed. "I don't know how you got inside, but if it is my master you're looking for, he's not in," he said. "Now I suggest you get off the property before I have you removed."

Esadora put a hand on the black wood of the open door, pushing it further open. "Would your 'master' be Darkmoon, by any chance?" she rasped, noting the look of surprise in the man's steel-gray eyes as he saw her talons.

"Yes," the man said, eyes darting back to her, "but as I said, he's not home at the moment."

"When will he be?" Esadora rasped.

The man tried to shut the door, but she held it open.

"I don't know," the man said, glaring at her. "He doesn't tell me his schedule."

Darkmoon would come back, Esadora had no doubt of that. And if he was coming back, then Rargyne was no doubt on his trail and would meet up with them. Esadora pushed the door open the rest of the way and stepped inside of the mansion, pushing the man back.

Ayrsah slipped in behind her, shutting the door softly behind them.

Esadora pulled her hood back with one hand, white lips curling up and away from her sharpened teeth at the look of alarm that came into the man's eyes.

"We'll wait," she rasped.

CHAPTER 52

Darkmoon

Lover," Darkmoon said. He felt Nathaira stiffen next to him. The man before them, a silver mask covering his face, didn't seem to notice.

"She can't come, you have to be alone," the man said. He wore a cloak of black velvet, and his hands were fat and marked by a cheap tarnished brass ring.

"And what exactly is it that I'm seeing alone?" Darkmoon asked, watching the man. The nervousness of the man's demeanor said that he had something illegal or stolen to show him, and the red dust on his boots told him that the man had been down in the mines that honeycombed beneath Rothborn. But what could be so important that the man would risk approaching Argdrion's best assassin?

"Something fabulous," the man said, looking back at him. "You'll like it, trust me."

"I don't," Darkmoon replied as a firework of a gray elephant exploded in the night sky above and the crowd around them oohed in wonder. "But you've heard enough about me to know that I will kill you if this is some kind of trap, so I must say that I am intrigued."

It wasn't a trap, Darkmoon could sense that, and although he didn't usually follow his curiosity, tonight he had a feeling that he should. It might help him in getting his revenge on Torin and N'san. "Dear," he said to Nathaira.

She looked up at him, firelight from a bonfire in a nearby courtyard making her golden mask glow. "Could you wait for me for a few moments?" Darkmoon murmured, squeezing her green-sleeved arm softly, "there's something I must attend to."

He nodded for the silver-masked man to lead the way, and the man turned and quickly slipped into the crowd.

As soon as he was away from Nathaira, the voices started.

Darkmoon gasped as they assaulted him, like a rainstorm flooding his senses.

"Brother…"

"My son…"

"…Before you became this creature of darkness…"

"I forgive you, my child…"

"Darkness is coming…"

"…help me, please…"

A nearby group glanced at him as he staggered sideways. Darkmoon used his cane to steady himself. He glanced back in the direction that he had come from, thinking of bringing Nathaira with him, but the silver-masked man was fast disappearing into the crowd, and he knew that he'd lose him if he went back.

"Brother," Cyron whispered, appearing between two jewel-clad women, "why?"

Darkmoon walked through the image, following the silver-masked man's receding cloak.

The voices and memories were growing worse. He sidestepped a bellowing man with a wooden cart piled high with papier-mâché lanterns for sale, his mother's screams ringing in his ears. They were getting worse, and although he did not want to admit it, he would not be able stop them. Not this time.

The silver-masked man stopped at the corner of a side street, waiting for him to catch up before hurrying down the equally crowded street.

Darkmoon followed, snow drifting down on him as the hall of his father's palace slowly grew around him. He pushed back against the memory with all his strength, and it disappeared as the silver-masked man stopped at the heavy oaken door of an aged brick building crowded between two others.

The man knocked twice on the silver-bird knocker emblazoned in the middle of the door, tapping his foot nervously while they waited for an answer.

Darkmoon glanced up and down the street, dozens of fireworks exploding above in a cacophony of pops and booms.

"My son…" his mother whispered in his ear. He felt her breath, heard the tears falling from her cheeks and hitting the stones of the hall below. Darkmoon pushed back against the memory again, but it stayed, snow swirling around him again as the hall slowly took shape in place of the crowded street and masked people around him.

"I forgive you…" his mother whispered, lips brushing his ear. "For murdering us all…"

A red-haired boy with a crackling firework on a stick ran past, laughing, and the hall faded again. Darkmoon leaned on his cane, feeling suddenly tired. He needed Nathaira. And not to lean on as he recovered from the witch's knife, but for the peace she brought from the voices and memories.

The door behind him opened, and candlelight spilled out into the street. Darkmoon turned toward it.

An old shallow-faced man stood in the open doorway, a candle on a pewter plate in one hand.

The old man moved sideways, and the silver-masked man stepped through the doorway. Darkmoon followed, voices humming around him.

A long hallway lay before them. The old man moved down it, his candle throwing a circle of light on the wooden walls on either side of him.

The silver-masked man followed the old man, and Darkmoon started after them, eyeing ropes stained with red dirt piled up against one wall. When Rothborn had survived on her mines, it had not been uncommon for mine holders to build residences on top of their mines with the entrance to said mine inside of their house. For one, it kept their mine more secure, and for another, there was really nowhere else in the Valley of Stones to build houses but on top of the mines.

They walked for a few minutes down the hall, the voices whispering in Darkmoon's head.

The old man stopped at a metal gate that sat in one wall of the hallway and pulled on an iron lever beside the gate, opening it up to reveal a metal pulley-operated elevator on the other side.

The noise of the fireworks exploding in the sky outside shook the hall around them as the old man stepped into the elevator and dust from the roof of the contraption fell down onto the old man's balding head like red snow.

The silver-masked man stepped toward the elevator. Darkmoon grabbed him by the back of the neck and pushed him up against the wall. He held his cane against his throat. "I don't like secretive people," Darkmoon said in a low voice. He pressed the black wood of the cane into the man's throat. "They usually have an ulterior motive that isn't always very pleasant."

The man coughed, choking. Darkmoon used the ivory knob atop the cane to push the man's mask back. His face was fat and ringed with greasy black curls, his skin pale except where red burns marred the right side of his face and ear.

"Now," Darkmoon said, "what is this that you have that I am going to be so interested in, and why is it down in the mines?"

The man gagged.

Darkmoon pulled the cane back a little so that he could talk. The voices whispered in his ears; screams rang through his head. He tried to ignore them.

"Have you heard of explosive powder?" the man croaked.

"Yes," Darkmoon said, "the experimental explosive dust they're using in mines now. I've heard of it."

"Yes, well, now there's another kind of powder," the man said, neck turning red under the cane. "It's called black powder, and it is not just for use in the mines."

"Brother…"

Darkmoon relaxed his grip on the man. "I'm listening."

"This powder," the man said, glancing around like he expected someone to be listening, "is highly explosive, more so than the other powders used in the mines, and it can be used to knock down walls or blow up carriages or really anything that you want it to do. I even heard that they're experimenting, making some kind of weapons with it that shoot lead balls."

Darkmoon felt a bead of sweat drip down his back between his shoulder blades, his mother's voice brushing against his ear. He pressed the cane harder against the man's throat again, wanting more than anything to kill him and stop the voices. Only it wouldn't stop the voices.

"Go on," he whispered, wishing Nathaira was with him.

"I have some," the man gasped, dark eyes bulging, "of this powder. I stole it from an Eromor warship when it wrecked on the western coast of Warulan about a month ago, and I've kept it hidden in the mines since, waiting for the right buyer."

"And I'm the right buyer?" Darkmoon asked, lessening the pressure on the man's throat again as his arm muscles began to weaken.

"One of them," the man said. "I had several people I was going to ask, but I thought of you first."

"How considerate of you," Darkmoon said evenly, another explosion of a firework outside shaking the hall again and causing more dust to rain down on the old man waiting in the elevator.

"Brother, why?" Cyron whispered.

Darkmoon stepped back from the man. "But I never buy what I haven't seen," he said. He motioned for the man to get into the elevator. "Show me."

The elevator took them to an old abandoned mining tunnel far below ground, where the sound of the fireworks exploding did not reach.

Darkmoon stepped out of the rickety metal cage after the fat-faced man, glancing around the red-walled tunnel.

Rusty lanterns and broken pickaxes littered the sides of the tunnels in piles, and footprints marred the dust coating its floor.

"My son, help me…" Darkmoon saw his father's body standing in the shadows of a connecting tunnel as they walked, hands reaching out toward him.

He looked away, eyes catching on a broken rusty birdcage with a few small dusty canary feathers inside.

They walked for a good five minutes before the fat man tapped the old man on the shoulder and they stopped at another adjoining tunnel.

"Here," the fat man said, pointing down the tunnel.

The old man held up his lantern. Darkmoon glanced down the tunnel. It only stretched for ten feet and was full of nine wooden barrels. He stopped beside the fat-faced man, eyeing the barrels. "Open them up."

The man complied, procuring a crowbar from within his cloak and using it to pry the lid off two of the barrels. He motioned for Darkmoon to look at them.

Darkmoon stepped forward, glancing down at the glittering black substance inside the barrels.

He dug a hand into one barrel and raised it, letting the fine, hard grains run between his fingers. If the fat-faced man was right, and the black powder was indeed as flammable as he said…

Darkmoon cocked his head, watching the powder run out of his hand. His revenge on Torin and N'san would reach a whole new level.

"Help me…"

"Show me how it works," he said.

The man scooped a very small amount of black powder out of one of the barrels and took the candle, moving ten feet away. Then he poured the powder onto the dust of the tunnel floor. He glanced up, eyes sparkling, and looked away as he held the candle to the powder.

A small explosion crackled, sparks and fire flying up from the powder as dust puffed into the air.

The fat-faced man stood. "Satisfied?" he asked, moving back over to Darkmoon.

Cyron and his mother and father were silent for the moment. Darkmoon glanced back at the barrels of powder again. He could just imagine what a whole barrel would do, the destruction that it would cause, the death it would bring.

He smiled slowly, his first genuine smile in a long time. "I'll take all of them."

#

Back up on the street twenty minutes later, Darkmoon scanned the crowd of twirling dancers and firework watchers for Nathaira's green dress and dark hair. She was nowhere to be seen.

He felt panic for a moment, the fear that she had left him.

He moved through the crowd, looking for her. Had she realized that he didn't really need her anymore?

He turned slightly, looking at a woman in a green dress. He glanced back the other way as he saw her blonde hair.

"My son," his mother whispered, "I forgive you…"

Darkmoon moved toward the bonfire and the dancing people around it. Although he was still weak from the witch blood that had been in his veins, he was recovered enough now that he could walk on his own and care for himself. Had Nathaira realized this? Or was there something else that had made her leave?

A firework exploded above him, a red rose with unfurling petals.

Darkmoon watched the dancers twirl, shadows playing on the buildings around like dark ghosts.

"Brother…"

He gripped his cane with the fingers of one hand. Maybe he had been wrong earlier. Maybe he could still make the voices go away again with more killing.

He moved down a side alley where a couple kissed in the shadows. He let their blood cover him as he sliced their throats, let it warm his hands and drain down his fingers.

"Darkness is coming…" the seer whispered.

Darkmoon moved away from the bodies of the couple. He needed Nathaira. He moved down the alley and out into another street. He needed her now.

"Brother…" Cyron murmured.

A seer could tell him where she had gone. Another firework exploded in the star-filled sky, this one a peacock with a rainbow of colors in its fanning tail.

Darkmoon ducked down another alley, heading toward Rothborn's poorer districts. There was a seer there, and he could tell him where Nathaira had gone. He knew he was being desperate, looking for her, but he didn't care anymore. He wanted peace, quiet.

No fireworks exploded over the sky of the poorer district, but homemade paper lanterns decked houses, and children with colorful flags ran up and down the crowded streets.

"My son…"

Darkmoon saw his mother standing between two masked men a few feet away, her hand outstretched toward him. The skin on her hand melted, and she threw her head back in a silent scream. He gripped the cane so hard that it creaked.

"You will be burned," the seer whispered again. "Like you should be."

Darkmoon moved with long strides down another alley, stopping in front of a low wooden door. He didn't knock, just pushed it open and stepped into a room of darkest night.

He closed the door behind him softly, the noise of the night festivities fading. "I need answers," he said into the darkness.

"Of where the skinchanger has gone," a soft male voice replied from ahead of him.

"Yes," Darkmoon said, not bothering to look for the seer.

"Son…" his father said.

"Where is she?" Darkmoon demanded, voice strained.

"You are destined to save Argdrion," the seer murmured, "but you will not do it alone. Others will help you."

Darkmoon heard a soft movement behind him. His fingers curled around the cane. "I did not come here to hear prophecies of my future—" he started.

"The skinchanger is one of them," the seer said softly. "You are wise to look for her. Argdrion's saviors will need to be together when the darkness comes."

"I am not looking for the skinchanger to join her in saving Argdrion," Darkmoon hissed, growing angry. Angry at himself for not being able to push the voices away, angry at Nathaira for being the only thing that helped him. Angry at her for leaving him.

"Yes, I know," the seer said from his left now. "You want the voices and memories to stop, but she is the only one who can make them stop anymore."

The seer was quiet for a moment, and Darkmoon heard the voices again, the chains in the room with the water barrel. So he had been right. Killing would not work anymore, nothing would. Nothing but Nathaira…

"Do you know why the skinchanger makes the voices and memories stop?" the seer asked after a minute.

Darkmoon didn't reply.

"It is because you are destined to be together," the seer went on. "Since before you were born, your destinies were intertwined."

"Like lovers?" Darkmoon questioned, catching a glimpse of a cloaked figure to his right.

"I mean as saviors," the seer said. "There are many who will rise up to save Argdrion, Darkmoon, but you and the skinchanger are the two who will lead them. Together, you will be powerful leaders."

"I am not a leader." Darkmoon said. He turned to go. This had been a waste of his time. He would find Nathaira on his own, and this time he would not let her go. Not until he had driven the voices away for good.

"She is on her way to Stonrin," the seer said as Darkmoon's fingers found the handle of the door. "To look for a ship to Nilfinhèim, where her brother is enslaved."

Darkmoon turned back around slowly.

"Your past will burn you…"

"Help me, please…"

He had known that Nathaira had a brother for some time now. So that was why she had left. Darkmoon stared into the darkness. If Cyron was still alive, he would look for him like Nathaira looked for her brother.

"Maybe I won't go after her," he said. "Then what will happen to Argdrion when her saviors do not rise?"

"But you will go after her, Darkmoon," the seer said, voice soft, weak almost. "Or should I call you by your real name? Elon."

Darkmoon snarled.

The seer cried out in pain and fell to the floor with a thud. "You will go after her," the seer gasped, "because your past is slowly taking over your mind."

"I will not let it," Darkmoon spat.

"I know," the seer gasped. "And you will find the skinchanger so that it will stop. Because if you do not, you know as well as I do that your past will make you do things that you would not ordinarily do. Things that will let Argdrion know who and what you are."

Darkmoon stalked forward, the seer coming into view on the floor in front of him. The seer cried out again and fell forward onto his hands.

Darkmoon stood over the man, the voices swirling around his head in an agonizing jumble of sounds.

The seer glanced up at him. "You will find her, Elon," the man choked out, "because you do not want Argdrion to know that you have magic more powerful than any creature to ever walk Argdrion. That you," the seer cried, falling onto his side and curling up into a ball, "are... a..."

The seer inhaled and fell silent. Darkmoon stared down at the dead man, the cane broken into two pieces in his hand. Elon. His given name. It was part of a secret that he had kept hidden for years, a secret that no one but the seer and him knew. And it was a secret that would be exposed if he did not stop the voices and memories from haunting him, tormenting him and driving him to do things that he would not ordinarily do. Darkmoon glanced up at the darkness in front of him and the quiet of the shop.

"I forgive you," his mother screamed, "FOR MURDERING US ALL!"

He turned toward the door, letting the halves of the cane fall from his hand. He would not save Argdrion, but he would find Nathaira, and he would take what she had that kept the voices and memories from haunting him.

For the seer was right. No matter what he had to do, who he had to kill, he would never let Argdrion know his secret.

He would never let the world know that he was a wiar.

THE END

ABOUT THE AUTHOR

Rebecca L. Snowe is an epic fantasy writer.

Her love for fantasy began at age fifteen when she read *The Lord of the Rings*, and her fascination for all things fantasy has not been quenched since.

Rebecca loves the dark and gritty in her writing as well as the books that she reads.

Rebecca lives in California with her family.